DECEIVER'S GAME

✠ ✠ ✠

LEFT BEHIND SERIES

SOUL HARVEST · APOLLYON · ASSASSINS

COLLECTORS EDITION II

DECEIVER'S GAME

TIM LAHAYE

JERRY B. JENKINS

Tyndale House Publishers, Inc., Carol Stream, Illinois

Visit Tyndale's exciting Web site at www.tyndale.com.

For the latest Left Behind news visit the Left Behind Web site at www.leftbehind.com.

TYNDALE, Tyndale's quill logo, and *Left Behind* are registered trademarks of Tyndale House Publishers, Inc.

Deceiver's Game: Left Behind Collectors Edition II

Deceiver's Game: Left Behind Collectors Edition II first published in 2010 by Tyndale House Publishers, Inc.

Cover photography of outer space by NASA/courtesy of nasaimages.org.

Designed by Dean H. Renninger

Published in association with the literary agency of Alive Communications, Inc., 7680 Goddard Street, Suite 200, Colorado Springs, CO 80920, www.alivecommunications.com.

Printed in the United States of America

ISBN: 978-1-61664-296-9

SOUL HARVEST

To our brand-new brothers and sisters

1

RAYFORD STEELE wore the uniform of the enemy of his soul, and he hated himself for it. He strode through Iraqi sand toward Baghdad Airport in his dress blues and was struck by the incongruity of it all.

From across the parched plain he heard the wails and screams of hundreds he wouldn't begin to be able to help. Any prayer of finding his wife alive depended on how quickly he could get to her. But there was no quick here. Only sand. And what about Chloe and Buck in the States? And Tsion?

Desperate, frantic, mad with frustration, he ripped off his natty waistcoat with its yellow braid, heavy epaulettes, and arm patches that identified a senior officer of the Global Community. Rayford did not take the time to unfasten the solid-gold buttons but sent them popping across the desert floor. He let the tailored jacket slide from his shoulders and clutched the collar in his fists. Three, four, five times he raised the garment over his head and slammed it to the ground. Dust billowed and sand kicked up over his patent leather shoes.

Rayford considered abandoning all vestiges of his connection to Nicolae Carpathia's regime, but his attention was drawn again to the luxuriously appointed arm patches. He tore at them, intending to rip them free, as if busting himself from his own rank in the service of the Antichrist. But the craftsmanship allowed not even a fingernail between the stitches, and Rayford slammed the coat to the ground one more time. He stepped and booted it like an extra point, finally aware of what had made it heavier. His phone was in the pocket.

As he knelt to retrieve his coat, Rayford's maddening logic returned—the practicality that made him who he was. Having no idea what he might find in the ruins of his condominium, he couldn't treat as dispensable what might constitute his only remaining set of clothes.

Rayford jammed his arms into the sleeves like a little boy made to wear a jacket on a warm day. He hadn't bothered to shake the grit from it, so as he plunged on toward the skeletal remains of the airport, Rayford's lanky frame was less impressive than usual. He could have been the survivor of a crash, a pilot who'd lost his cap and seen the buttons stripped from his uniform.

Rayford could not remember a chill before sundown in all the months he'd lived in Iraq. Yet something about the earthquake had changed not only the topography, but also the temperature. Rayford had been used to damp shirts and a sticky film on his skin. But now wind, that rare, mysterious draft, chilled him as he speed-dialed Mac McCullum and put the phone to his ear.

At that instant he heard the chug and whir of Mac's chopper behind him. He wondered where they were going.

"Mac here," came McCullum's gravelly voice.

Rayford whirled and watched the copter eclipse the descending sun. "I can't believe this thing works," Rayford said. He had slammed it to the ground and kicked it, but he also assumed the earthquake would have taken out nearby cellular towers.

"Soon as I get out of range, it won't, Ray," Mac said. "Everything's down for as far as I can see. These units act like walkie-talkies when we're close. When you need a cellular boost, you won't find it."

"So any chance of calling the States—"

"Is out of the question," Mac said. "Ray, Potentate Carpathia wants to speak to you, but first—"

"I don't want to talk to him, and you can tell him that."

"But before I give you to him," Mac continued, "I need to remind you that our meeting, yours and mine, is still on for tonight. Right?"

Rayford slowed and stared at the ground, running a hand through his hair. "What? What are you talking about?"

"All right then, very good," Mac said. "We're still meeting tonight then. Now the potentate—"

"I understand you want to talk to me later, Mac, but don't put Carpathia on or I swear I'll—"

"Stand by for the potentate."

Rayford switched the phone to his right hand, ready to smash it on the ground, but he restrained himself. When avenues of communication reopened, he wanted to be able to check on his loved ones.

"Captain Steele," came the emotionless tone of Nicolae Carpathia.

"I'm here," Rayford said, allowing his disgust to come through. He assumed God would forgive anything he said to the Antichrist, but he swallowed what he really wanted to say.

"Though we both know how I *could* respond to your egregious disrespect and insubordination," Carpathia said, "I choose to forgive you."

Rayford continued walking, clenching his teeth to keep from screaming at the man.

"I can tell you are at a loss for how to express your gratitude," Carpathia continued. "Now listen to me. I have a safe place and provisions where my international ambassadors and staff will join me. You and I both know we need each other, so I suggest—"

"You don't need me," Rayford said. "And I don't need your forgiveness. You have a perfectly capable pilot right next to you, so let *me* suggest that you forget me."

"Just be ready when he lands," Carpathia said, the first hint of frustration in his voice.

"The only place I would accept a ride to is the airport," Rayford said. "And I'm almost there. Don't have Mac set down any closer to this mess."

"Captain Steele," Carpathia began again, condescendingly, "I admire your irrational belief that you can somehow find your wife, but we both know that is not going to happen."

Rayford said nothing. He feared Carpathia was right, but he would never give him the satisfaction of admitting it. And he would certainly never quit looking until he proved to himself Amanda had not survived.

"Come with us, Captain Steele. Just reboard, and I will treat your outburst as if it never—"

"I'm not going anywhere until I've found my wife! Let me talk to Mac."

"Officer McCullum is busy. I will pass along a message."

"Mac could fly that thing with no hands. Now let me talk to him."

"If there is no message, then, Captain Steele—"

"All right, you win. Just tell Mac—"

"Now is no time to neglect protocol, Captain Steele. A pardoned subordinate is behooved to address his superior—"

"All right, *Potentate* Carpathia, just tell Mac to come for me if I don't find a way back by 2200 hours."

"And should you find a way back, the shelter is three and a half clicks northeast of the original headquarters. You will need the following password: 'Operation Wrath.'"

"What?" Carpathia knew this was coming?

"You heard me, Captain Steele."

+ + +

Cameron "Buck" Williams stepped gingerly through the rubble near the ventilation shaft where he had heard the clear, healthy voice of Rabbi Tsion Ben-Judah, trapped in the underground shelter. Tsion assured him he was unhurt, just scared and claustrophobic. That place was small enough without the church imploding above it. With no way out unless someone tunneled to him, the rabbi, Buck knew, would soon feel like a caged animal.

Had Tsion been in immediate danger, Buck would have dug with his bare hands to free him. But Buck felt like a doctor in triage, having to determine who most urgently needed his help. Assuring Tsion he would return, he headed toward the safe house to find his wife.

To get through the trash that had been the only church home he ever knew, Buck had to again crawl past the remains of the beloved Loretta. What a friend she had been, first to the late Bruce Barnes and then to the rest of the Tribulation Force. The Force had begun with four: Rayford, Chloe, Bruce, and Buck. Amanda was added. Bruce was lost. Tsion was added.

Was it possible now that they had been reduced to just Buck and Tsion? Buck didn't want to think about it. He found his watch gunked up with mud, asphalt, and a tiny shard of windshield. He wiped the crystal across his pant leg and felt the crusty mixture tear his trousers and bite into his knee. It was nine o'clock in the morning in Mount Prospect, and Buck heard an air raid siren, a tornado warning siren, emergency vehicle sirens—one close, two farther away. Shouts. Screams. Sobbing. Engines.

Could he live without Chloe? Buck had been given a second chance; he was here for a purpose. He wanted the love of his life by his side, and he prayed—selfishly, he realized—that she had not already preceded him to heaven.

In his peripheral vision, Buck noticed the swelling of his own left cheek. He had felt neither pain nor blood and had assumed the wound was minor. Now he wondered. He reached in his breast pocket for his mirror-lensed sunglasses. One lens was in pieces. In the reflection of the other he saw a scarecrow, hair wild, eyes white with fear, mouth open and sucking air. The wound was not bleeding, yet it appeared deep. There would be no time for treatment.

Buck emptied his shirt pocket but kept the frames—a gift from Chloe. He studied the ground as he moved back to the Range Rover, picking his way through glass, nails, and bricks like an old man, assuring himself solid purchase.

Buck passed Loretta's car and what was left of her, determined not to look. Suddenly the earth moved, and he stumbled. Loretta's car, which he had been unable to budge moments before, rocked and disappeared. The ground had given way under the parking lot. Buck stretched out on his stomach and peeked over the edge of a new crevice. The mangled car rested atop a water main twenty feet beneath the earth. The blown tires pointed up like the feet of bloated roadkill. Curled in a frail ball atop the wreckage was the Raggedy Ann–like body of Loretta, a tribulation saint. There would be more shifting of the earth. Reaching Loretta's body would be impossible. If he was also to find Chloe dead, Buck wished God had let him plunge under the earth with Loretta's car.

Buck rose slowly, suddenly aware of what the roller-coaster ride through the earthquake had done to his joints and muscles. He surveyed the damage to his vehicle. Though it had rolled and been hit from all sides, it appeared remarkably roadworthy. The driver's-side door was jammed, the windshield in gummy pieces throughout the interior, and the rear seat had broken away from the floor on one side. One tire had been slashed to the steel belts but looked strong and held air.

Where were Buck's phone and laptop? He had set them on the front seat. He hoped against hope neither had flown out in the mayhem. Buck opened the passenger door and peered onto the floor of the front seat. Nothing. He looked under the rear seats, all the way to the back. In a corner, open and with one screen hinge cracked, was his laptop.

Buck found his phone in a door well. He didn't expect to be able to get through to anyone, with all the damage to cellular towers (and everything else above ground). He switched it on, and it went through a self-test and showed zero range. Still, he had to try. He dialed Loretta's home. He didn't even get a malfunction message from the phone company. The same happened when he dialed the church, then Tsion's shelter. As if playing a cruel joke, the phone made noises as if trying to get through. Then, nothing.

Buck's landmarks were gone. He was grateful the Range Rover had a built-in compass. Even the church seemed twisted from its normal perspective on the corner. Poles and lines and traffic lights were down, buildings flattened, trees uprooted, fences strewn about.

Buck made sure the Range Rover was in four-wheel drive. He could barely travel twenty feet before having to punch the car over some rise. He kept his eyes peeled to avoid anything that might further damage the Rover—it might have to last him through the end of the Tribulation. The best he could figure, that was still more than five years away.

As Buck rolled over chunks of asphalt and concrete where the street once lay, he glanced again at the vestiges of New Hope Village Church. Half the building was underground. But that one section of pews, which had once faced west, now faced north and glistened in the sun. The entire sanctuary floor appeared to have turned ninety degrees.

As he passed the church, he stopped and stared. A shaft of light appeared between each pair of pews in the ten-pew section except in one spot. There something blocked Buck's view. He threw the Rover into reverse and carefully backed up. On the floor in front of one of those pews were the bottoms of a pair of tennis shoes, toes pointing up. Buck wanted, above all, to get to Loretta's and search for Chloe, but he could not leave someone lying in the debris. Was it possible someone had survived?

He set the brake and scrambled over the passenger seat and out the door, recklessly trotting through stuff that could slice through his shoes. He wanted to be practical, but there was no time for that. Buck lost his footing ten feet from those tennis shoes and pitched face forward. He took the brunt of the fall on his palms and chest.

He pulled himself up and knelt next to the tennis shoes, which were attached to a body. Thin legs in dark blue jeans led to narrow hips. From the waist up, the small body was hidden under the pew. The right hand was tucked underneath, the left lay open and limp. Buck found no pulse, but he noticed the hand was broad and bony, the third finger bearing a man's wedding band. Buck slipped it off, assuming a surviving wife might want it.

Buck grabbed the belt buckle and dragged the body from under the bench. When the head slid into view, Buck turned away. He had recognized Donny Moore's blond coloring only from his eyebrows. The rest of his hair, even his sideburns, was encrusted with blood.

Buck didn't know what to do in the face of the dead and dying at a time like this. Where would anyone begin disposing of millions of corpses all over the world? Buck gently pushed the body back under the pew but was stopped by an obstruction. He reached underneath and found Donny's beat-up, hard-sided briefcase. Buck tried the latches, but combination locks had been set. He lugged the briefcase back to the Range Rover and tried again to find his bearings. He was a scant four blocks from Loretta's, but could he even find the street?

\+ \+ \+

Rayford was encouraged to see movement in the distance at Baghdad Airport. He saw more wreckage and carnage on the ground than people scurrying about, but at least not all had been lost.

A small, dark figure with a strange gait appeared on the horizon. Rayford watched, fascinated, as the image materialized into a stocky, middle-aged Asian in a business suit. The man walked directly toward Rayford, who waited expectantly, wondering if he could help. But as the man drew near, Rayford realized he was not aware of his surroundings. He wore a wing-tipped dress shoe on one foot with only a sock sliding down the ankle of the other. His suit coat was buttoned, but his tie hung outside it. His left hand dripped blood. His hair was mussed, yet his glasses appeared to have been untouched by whatever he had endured.

"Are you all right?" Rayford asked. The man ignored him. "Can I help you?"

The man limped past, mumbling in his own tongue. Rayford turned to call him back, and the man became a silhouette in the orange sun. There was nothing in that direction but the Tigris River. "Wait!" Rayford called after him. "Come back! Let me help you!"

The man ignored him, and Rayford dialed Mac again. "Let me talk to Carpathia," he said.

"Sure," Mac said. "We're set on that meeting tonight, right?"

"Right, now let me talk to him."

"I mean our personal meeting, right?"

"Yes! I don't know what you want, but yes, I get the point. Now I need to talk to Carpathia."

"OK, sorry. Here he is."

"Change your mind, Captain Steele?" Carpathia said.

"Hardly. Listen, do you know Asian languages?"

"Some. Why?"

"What does this mean?" he asked, repeating what the man had said.

"That is easy," Carpathia said. "It means, 'You cannot help me. Leave me alone.'"

"Bring Mac back around, would you? This man is going to die of exposure."

"I thought you were looking for your wife."

"I can't leave a man to wander to his death."

"Millions are dead and dying. You cannot save all of them."

"So you're going to let this man die?"

"I do not see him, Captain Steele. If you think you can save him, be my guest. I do not mean to be cold, but I have the whole world at heart just now."

Rayford slapped his phone shut and hurried back to the lurching, mumbling man. As he drew near, Rayford was horrified to see why his gait was so strange and why he trailed a river of blood. He had been impaled by a gleaming white chunk of metal, apparently some piece of a fuselage. Why he was still alive, how he survived or climbed out, Rayford couldn't imagine. The shard was embedded from his hip to the back of his head. It had to have missed vital organs by centimeters.

Rayford touched the man's shoulder, causing him to wrench away. He sat heavily, and with a huge sigh toppled slowly in the sand and breathed his last. Rayford checked for a pulse, not surprised to find none. Overcome, he turned his back and knelt in the dirt. Sobs wracked his body.

Rayford raised his hands to the sky. "Why, God? Why do I have to see this? Why send someone across my path I can't even help? Spare Chloe and Buck!

Please keep Amanda alive for me! I know I don't deserve anything, but I can't go on without her!"

\+ + +

Usually Buck drove two blocks south and two east from the church to Loretta's. But now there were no more blocks. No sidewalks, no streets, no intersections. For as far as Buck could see, every house in every neighborhood had been leveled. Could it have been this bad all over the world? Tsion taught that a quarter of the world's population would fall victim to the wrath of the Lamb. But Buck would be surprised if even a quarter of the population of Mount Prospect was still alive.

He lined up the Range Rover on a southeastern course. A few degrees above the horizon the day was as beautiful as any Buck could remember. The sky, where not interrupted by smoke and dust, was baby blue. No clouds. Bright sun.

Geysers shot skyward where fire hydrants had ruptured. A woman crawled out from the wreckage of her home, a bloody stump at her shoulder where her arm had been. She screamed at Buck, "Kill me! Kill me!"

He shouted, "No!" and leaped from the Rover as she bent and grabbed a chunk of glass from a broken window and dragged it across her neck. Buck continued to yell as he sprinted to her. He only hoped she was too weak to do anything but superficial damage to her neck, and he prayed she would miss her carotid artery.

He was within a few feet of her when she stared, startled. The glass broke and tinkled to the ground. She stepped back and tripped, her head smacking loudly on a chunk of concrete. Immediately the blood stopped pumping from her exposed arteries. Her eyes were lifeless as Buck forced her jaw open and covered her mouth with his. Buck blew air into her throat, making her chest rise and her blood trickle, but it was futile.

Buck looked around, wondering whether to try to cover her. Across the way an elderly man stood at the edge of a crater and seemed to will himself to tumble into it. Buck could take no more. Was God preparing him for the likelihood that Chloe had not survived?

He wearily climbed back into the Range Rover, deciding he absolutely could not stop and help anyone else who did not appear to really want it. Everywhere he looked he saw devastation, fire, water, and blood.

\+ + +

Against his better judgment, Rayford left the dead man in the desert sand. What would he do when he saw others in various states of demise? How could

Carpathia ignore this? Had he not a shred of humanity? Mac would have stayed and helped.

Rayford despaired of seeing Amanda alive again, and though he would search with all that was in him, he already wished he had arranged an earlier rendezvous with Mac. He'd seen awful things in his life, but the carnage at this airport was going to top them all. A shelter, even the Antichrist's, sounded better than this.

2

BUCK HAD COVERED disasters, but as a journalist he had not felt guilty about ignoring the dying. Normally, by the time he arrived on a scene, medical personnel were usually in place. There was nothing he could do but stay out of the way. He had taken pride in not forcing his way into situations that would make things more difficult for emergency workers.

But now it was just him. Sounds of sirens told him others were at work somewhere, but surely there were too few rescuers to go around. He could work twenty-four hours finding barely breathing survivors, but he would not make a dent in the magnitude of this disaster. Someone else might ignore Chloe to get to his own loved one. Those who had somehow escaped with their lives could hope only that they had their own hero, fighting the odds to get to them.

Buck had never believed in extrasensory perception or telepathy, even before he had become a believer in Christ. Yet now he felt such a deep longing for Chloe, such a desperate grief at even the prospect of losing her, that he felt as if his love oozed from every pore. How could she not know he was thinking of her, praying for her, trying to get to her at all cost?

Having kept his eyes straight ahead as despairing, wounded people waved or screamed out to him, Buck bounced to a dusty stop. A couple of blocks east of the main drag was some semblance of recognizable geography. Nothing looked like it had before, but ribbons of road, gouged up by the churning earth, lay sideways in roughly the same configuration they had before. The pavement of Loretta's street now stood vertically, blocking the view of what was left of the homes. Buck scrambled from his car and climbed atop the asphalt wall. He found the upturned street about four feet thick with a bed of gravel and sand on its other side. He reached up and over and dug his fingers into the soft part, hanging there and staring at Loretta's block.

Four stately homes had stood in that section, Loretta's the second from the right. The entire block looked like some child's box of toys that had been shaken and tossed to the ground. The home directly in front of Buck, larger even than Loretta's, had been knocked back off its foundation, flipped onto its front, and collapsed. The roof had toppled off upside down in one piece, apparently when the house hit the ground. Buck could see the rafters, as he would have had he been in the attic. All four walls of the house lay flat, flooring strewn about. In two places, Buck saw lifeless hands at the ends of stiff arms poking through the debris.

A towering tree, more than four feet in diameter, had been uprooted and had crashed into the basement. Two feet of water lay on the cement floor, and the water level was slowly rising. Strangely, what appeared to be a guest room in the northeast corner of the cellar looked unmolested, neat and tidy. It would soon be under water.

Buck forced himself to look at the next house, Loretta's. He and Chloe had not lived there long, but he knew it well. The house, now barely recognizable, seemed to have been lifted off the ground and slammed down in place, causing the roof to split in two and settle over the giant box of sticks. The roofline, all the way around, was now about four feet off the ground. Three massive trees in the front yard had fallen toward the street, angled toward each other, branches intertwined, as if three swordsmen had touched their blades together.

Between the two destroyed houses stood a small metal shed that, while pitched at an angle, had nonsensically escaped serious damage. How could an earthquake shake, rattle, and roll a pair of five-bedroom, two-story homes into oblivion and leave untouched a tiny utility shed? Buck could only surmise that the structure was so flexible it did not snap when the earth rolled beneath it.

Loretta's home had shrunk flat where it sat, leaving her backyard empty and bare. All this, Buck realized, had happened in seconds.

A fire truck with makeshift bullhorns on the back rolled slowly into view behind Buck. As he hung on that vertical stretch of pavement, he heard: "Stay out of your homes! Do not return to your homes! If you need help, get to an open area where we can find you!"

A half-dozen police officers and firefighters rode the giant ladder truck. A uniformed cop leaned out the window. "You all right there, buddy?"

"I'm all right!" Buck hollered.

"That your vehicle?"

"Yes!"

"We could sure use it in the relief effort!"

"I've got people I'm trying to dig out!" Buck said.

The cop nodded. "Don't be trying to get into any of these homes!"

Buck let go and slid to the ground. He walked toward the fire truck as it slowed to a stop. "I heard the announcement, but what are you guys talking about?"

"We're worried about looters. But we're also worried about danger. These places are hardly stable."

"Obviously!" Buck said. "But looters? You are the only healthy people I've seen. There's nothing of value left, and where would somebody take anything if they found it?"

"We're just doing what we're told, sir. Don't try to go in any of the homes, OK?"

"Of course I will! I'm gonna be digging through that house to find out if somebody I know and love is still alive."

"Trust me, pal, you're not going to find survivors on this street. Stay out of there."

"Are you gonna arrest me? Do you have a jail still standing?"

The cop turned to the fireman driving. Buck wanted an answer. Apparently, the cop was more levelheaded than he was, because they slowly rolled away. Buck scaled the wall of pavement and slid down the other side, covering his entire front with mud. He tried wiping it off, but it stuck between his fingers. He slapped at his pants to get the bulk of it off his hands, then hurried between the fallen trees to the front of the fractured house.

+ + +

It seemed to Rayford that the closer he got to the Baghdad airport, the less he could see. Great fissures had swallowed every inch of runway in all directions, pushing mounds of dirt and sand several feet into the air, blocking a view of the terminal. As Rayford made his way through, he could barely breathe. Two jumbo jets—one a 747 and the other a DC-10, apparently fully loaded and in line for takeoff on an east-west runway—appeared to have been in tandem before the earthquake slammed them together and ripped them apart. The result was piles of lifeless bodies. He couldn't imagine the force of a collision that would kill so many without a fire.

From a massive ditch on the far side of the terminal, at least a quarter mile from where Rayford stood, a line of survivors clawed their way to the surface from another swallowed aircraft. Black smoke billowed from deep in the earth, and Rayford knew if he was close enough he could hear the screams of survivors not strong enough to climb out. Of those who emerged, some ran from the scene, while most, like the Asian, staggered trancelike through the desert.

The terminal itself, formerly a structure of steel and wood and glass, had not only been knocked flat, but it had also been shaken as a prospector would sift sand through a screen. The pieces were spread so widely that none of the piles stood higher than two feet. Hundreds of bodies lay in various states of repose. Rayford felt as if he were in hell.

He knew what he was looking for. Amanda's scheduled flight had been on a Pan-Continental 747, the airline and equipment he used to fly. It would not have surprised him if she were on one of the very aircraft he had once piloted. It would have been scheduled to land south to north on the big runway.

If the earthquake occurred with the plane in the air, the pilot would have tried to stay airborne until it was over, then looked for a flat patch of ground to put down. If it occurred at any time after landing, the plane could be anywhere on that strip, which was now fully underground and covered with sand. It was a huge, long runway, but surely if a plane was buried there, Rayford ought to be able to sight it before the sun went down.

Might it be facing the other direction on one of the auxiliary runways, having already begun taxiing back to the terminal? He could only hope it was obvious and pray there was something he could do in the event that Amanda had somehow miraculously survived. The best-case scenario, short of the pilot having had enough foresight to have landed somewhere safely, would have been if the plane had landed and either stopped or was traveling very slowly when the earthquake hit. If it had somehow been fortunate enough to be in the middle of the airstrip when the runway slipped from the surface, there was a chance it would still be upright and intact. If it was covered with sand, who knew how long the air supply would last?

It seemed to Rayford there were at least ten people dead for every one alive near the terminal. Those who had escaped had to have been outside when the quake hit. It didn't appear anyone inside the terminal had survived. Those few Global Community uniformed officers who patrolled the area with their high-powered weapons looked as shell-shocked as anyone. Occasionally one shot Rayford a double take as he moved past, but they backed off and didn't even ask to see identification when they noticed his uniform. With hanging threads where the buttons should have been, he knew he looked like just another lucky survivor from the crew of some ill-fated plane.

To get to the runway in question, Rayford had to cross paths with a zombied and bleeding queue of fortunates who staggered out of a crater. He was grateful none of them pleaded for help. Most appeared not to even see him, following one another as if trusting that someone somewhere near the front of the line had an idea where he might find help. From deep in the hole, Rayford heard the wailing and moaning he knew he would never be able to forget. If there was anything he could do, he would have done it.

Finally he reached the near end of the long runway. There, directly in the middle, lay the sand-blown but easily recognizable humpbacked fuselage of a 747.

There might have been an hour's worth of sunlight left, but it was fading. As he hurried along the edge of the canyon the sinking runway had gorged out of the sand, Rayford shook his head and squinted, shading his eyes as he tried to make sense of what he saw. As he came to within a hundred feet of the back of the monstrous plane, it became clear what had happened. The plane had been near mid-runway when the pavement simply dropped at least fifty feet beneath it. The weight of that pavement pulled the sand in toward the plane, which now rested on both wingtips, its body hanging precariously over the chasm.

Someone had had the presence of mind to get the doors open and the inflatable evacuation chutes deployed, but even the ends of those chutes hung several feet in the air over the collapsed runway.

Had the walls of sand at the sides of the plane been any farther apart, no way could the wings have supported the weight of the cabin. The fuselage squeaked and groaned as the weight of the plane threatened to send it plummeting. The plane might be able to drop another ten feet without seriously injuring anyone, and hundreds could be saved, Rayford believed, if only it could settle gradually.

He prayed desperately that Amanda was safe, that she had been buckled in, that the plane had stopped before the runway gave way. The closer he got, the more obvious it was that the plane must have been moving at the time of the cave-in. The wings were buried several feet in the sand. That may have kept the craft from dropping, but it also would have provided a killing jolt for anyone not fastened in.

Rayford's heart sank when he drew close enough to see that this was not a Pan-Con 747 at all but a British Airways jet. He was struck with such conflicting emotions that he could barely sort them out. What kind of a cold, selfish person is so obsessed with the survival of his own wife that he would be disappointed that hundreds of people might have been saved on this plane? He had to face the ugly truth about himself that he cared mostly for Amanda. Where was her Pan-Con flight?

He spun and scanned the horizon. What a cauldron of death! There was nowhere else to look for the Pan-Con jet. Until he knew for sure, he would not accept that Amanda was gone. With no other recourse and the inability to call Mac for an earlier pickup, he turned his attention back to the British Airways plane. At one of the open doors a flight attendant, staring ghostlike from the cabin, helplessly surveyed their precarious position. Rayford cupped his hands and called out to her, "I am a pilot! I have some ideas!"

"Are we on fire?" she screamed.

"No! And you should be very low on fuel! You don't seem to be in danger!"

"This is very unstable!" she shouted. "Should I move everyone to the back so we don't go nose down?"

"You won't go nose down anyway! Your wings are stuck in the sand! Get everyone toward the middle and see if you can exit onto the wings without breaking up!"

"Can we be sure of that?"

"No! But you can't wait for heavy equipment to tunnel down there and scaffold up to you! The earthquake was worldwide, and it's unlikely anyone will get to you for days!"

"These people want out of here now! How sure are you that this will work?"

"Not very! But you have no choice! An aftershock could drop the plane all the way!"

\+ + +

As far as Buck knew, Chloe had been alone at Loretta's. His only hope of finding her was to guess where she might have been in the house when it collapsed. Their bedroom in the southwest corner upstairs was now at ground level—a mass of brick, siding, drywall, glass, framing, trim, floor, studs, wiring, and furniture—covered by half of the split roof.

Chloe kept her computer in the basement, now buried under the two other floors on that same side of the house. Or she might have been in the kitchen, at the front of the house but also on that same side. That left Buck with no options. He had to get rid of a major section of that roof and start digging. If he didn't find her in the bedroom or the basement, his last hope was the kitchen.

He had no boots, no gloves, no work clothes, no goggles, no helmet. All he had were the filthy, flimsy clothes on his back, normal shoes, and his bare hands. It was too late to worry about tetanus. He leaped onto the shifting roof. He edged up the steep incline, trying to see where it might be weak or could fall apart. It felt solid, though unsteady. He slid to the ground and pushed up under the eaves. No way could he do this by himself. Might there be an ax or chain saw in the metal shed?

He couldn't get it open at first. The door was jammed. It seemed such a frail thing, but having shifted in the earthquake, the shed had bent upon itself and was unwilling to budge. Buck lowered his shoulder and rammed it like a football player. It groaned in protest but snapped back into position. He karate kicked it six times, then lowered his shoulder and barreled into it again. Finally he backed up twenty feet and raced toward it, but his slick shoes slipped in the grass and sent him sprawling. In a rage he trotted back farther, started slower, and gradually picked up speed. This time he smashed into the side of the shed so hard that he tore it from its moorings. It flipped over the tools inside, and he went with it, riding it to the ground before bouncing off. A jagged edge of the roof caught his rib cage as he hurtled down, and flesh gave way. He grabbed his side and felt a trickle, but unless he severed an artery, he wouldn't slow down.

He dragged shovels and axes to the house and propped long-handled garden implements under the eaves. When Buck leaned against them, the edge of the roof lifted and something snapped beneath the few remaining shingles. He attacked that with a shovel, imagining how ridiculous he looked and what his father might say if he saw him using the wrong tool for the wrong job.

But what else could he do? Time was of the essence. He was fighting all odds anyway. Yet stranger things had happened. People had stayed alive under rubble for days. But if water was getting into the foundation of the house next door, what about this one? What if Chloe was trapped in the basement? He prayed that if she had to die, it had already happened quickly and painlessly. He did not want her life to ebb slowly away in a horrifying drowning. He also feared electrocution when water met open electric lines.

With a chunk of the roof gone, Buck shoveled debris away until he hit bigger pieces that had to be removed by hand. He was in decent shape, but this was beyond his routine. His muscles burned as he tossed aside heavy hunks of wall and flooring. He seemed to make little progress, huffing and puffing and sweating.

Buck twisted conduit out of the way and tossed aside ceiling plaster. He finally reached the bed frame, which had been snapped like kindling. He pushed in to where Chloe often sat at a small desk. It took him another half hour to dig through there, calling her name every so often. When he stopped to catch his breath he fought to listen for the faintest noise. Would he be able to hear a moan, a cry, a sigh? If she made the smallest sound, he would find her.

Buck began to despair. This was going too slowly. He hit huge chunks of floor too heavy to move. The distance between the floorboards of the upstairs bedroom and the concrete floor of the basement was simply not that great. Anyone caught between there had surely been smashed flat. But he could not quit. If he couldn't get through this stuff by himself, he would get Tsion to help him.

Buck dragged the tools out to the front and tossed them over the pavement wall. Getting over from this side was a lot harder than from the other because the mud was slippery. He looked up one way and down the other and couldn't see the end of where the road had been flipped vertical. He dug his feet into the mud and finally got to where he could reach the asphalt on the other side at the top. He pulled himself up and slid over, landing painfully on his elbow. He tossed the tools into the back of the Rover and slid his muddy body behind the wheel.

* * *

The sun was dropping in Iraq as several survivors of other crashes joined Rayford to watch the plight of the British Air 747. He stood helpless, hoping. The last thing he wanted was to be responsible for injury or death to anyone. But he was certain that exiting onto the wings was their only hope. He prayed they could then climb the steep banks of sand.

Rayford was encouraged at first when he saw the first passengers crawl onto the wings. Apparently the flight attendant had rallied the people and gotten them to work together. Rayford's encouragement soon turned to alarm when he saw how much motion they generated and how it strained the fragile support. The plane was going to break up. Then what would happen to the fuselage? If one end or the other tipped too quickly, dozens could be killed. Those not strapped in would be hurtled to one end of the plane or the other, landing atop each other.

Rayford wanted to shout, to plead with the people inside to spread out. They needed to go about this with more precision and care. But it was too late, and they would never hear him. The noise inside the plane had to be deafening. The two on the right wing leaped into the sand.

The left wing gave way first but was not totally sheared off. The fuselage rotated left, and it was clear passengers inside fell that way too. The rear of the plane was going down first. Rayford could only hope the right wing would give way in time to even it out. At the last instant, that happened. But though the plane landed nearly perfectly flat on its tires, it had dropped much too far. People had to have been horribly bounced against each other and the plane. When the front tire collapsed, the nose of the plane drove so hard into the pavement that it shook more sand avalanches loose from the sides, which quickly filled the gorge. Rayford stuffed his phone in his pants pocket and tossed his jacket aside. He and others dug with their hands and began burrowing to the plane to allow air and escape passages. Sweat soaked through his clothes. The shine of his shoes would never return, but when might he ever again need dress shoes anyway?

When he and his compatriots finally reached the plane, they met passengers digging their way out. Rescuers behind Rayford cleared the area when they heard helicopter blades. Rayford assumed, as everyone probably did, that it was a relief chopper. Then he remembered. If it was Mac, it must be ten already. Was it because he cared, Rayford wondered, or was he more concerned with their meeting?

Rayford phoned Mac from deep in the gorge and told him he wanted to be sure no one had been killed on board the 747. Mac told him he'd be waiting on the other side of the terminal.

A few minutes later, relieved that all had survived, Rayford climbed back to the surface. He could not, however, find his jacket. That was just as well. He assumed Carpathia would soon fire him anyway.

Rayford picked his way through the flattened terminal and around the back. Mac's helicopter idled a hundred yards away. In the darkness, Rayford assumed a clear path to the small craft and began hurrying. Amanda was not here, and this was a place of death. He wanted out of Iraq altogether, but for now he wanted away from Baghdad. He might have to endure Carpathia's shelter, whatever that was, but as soon as he was able he would put distance between himself and Nicolae.

Rayford picked up speed, still in shape in his early forties. But suddenly he somersaulted into what? Bodies! He had tripped over one and landed atop others. Rayford stood and rubbed a painful knee, fearing he had desecrated these people. He slowed and walked to the chopper.

"Let's go, Mac!" he said as he climbed aboard.

"I don't need to be told *that* twice," Mac said, throttling up. "I need to talk to you in a bad way."

\+ + +

It was afternoon in the Central Standard Time zone when Buck pulled within sight of the wreckage of the church. He was coming out the passenger door when an aftershock rumbled through. It lifted the truck and propelled Buck into the dirt on his rear. He turned to watch the remains of the church sift, shift, and toss about. The pews that had escaped the ravages of the quake now cracked and flipped. Buck could only imagine what had happened to poor Donny Moore's body. Perhaps God himself had handled the burial.

Buck worried about Tsion. What might have broken loose and fallen in his underground shelter? Buck scrambled to the ventilation shaft, which had provided Tsion's only source of air. "Tsion! Are you all right?"

He heard a faint, breathy voice. "Thank God you have returned, Cameron! I was lying here with my nose next to the vent when I heard the rumble and something clattering its way toward me. I rolled out of the way just in time. There are pieces of brick down here. Was it an aftershock?"

"Yes!"

"Forgive me, Cameron, but I have been brave long enough. Get me out of here!"

It took Buck more than an hour of grueling digging to reach the entrance to the underground shelter. As soon as he began the tricky procedure to unlock and open the door, Tsion began pushing it from the inside. Together they forced it open against the weight of cinder blocks and other trash. Tsion squinted against the light and drank in the air. He embraced Buck tightly and asked, "What about Chloe?"

"I need your help."

"Let us go. Any word from the others?"

"It could be days before communication opens to the Middle East. Amanda should be there with Rayford by now, but I have no idea about either of them."

"One thing you can be sure of," Tsion said in his thick Israeli accent, "is that if Rayford was near Nicolae, he is likely safe. The Scriptures are clear that the Antichrist will not meet his demise until a little over a year from now."

"I wouldn't mind having a hand in that," Buck said.

"God will take care of that. But it is not the due time. Repulsive as it must be for Captain Steele to be in proximity to such evil, at least he should be safe."

+ + +

In the air, Mac McCullum radioed back to the safe shelter and told the radio operator, "We're involved in a rescue here, so we're gonna be another hour or two. Over."

"Roger that. I'll inform the potentate. Over."

Rayford wondered what could be so important that Mac would risk lying to Nicolae Carpathia?

Once Rayford's headset was in place, Mac said, "What the blazes is going on? What is Carpathia up to? What's all this about the 'wrath of the Lamb,' and what in the world was I lookin' at earlier when I thought I was lookin' at the moon? I've seen a lot of natural disasters, and I've seen some strange atmospheric phenomena, but I swear on my mother's eyes I've never seen anything make a full moon look like it's turned to blood. Why would an earthquake do that?"

Man, Rayford thought, *this guy is ripe.* But Rayford was also puzzled. "I'll tell you what I think, Mac, but first tell me why you think I would know."

"I can tell, that's all. I wouldn't dare cross Carpathia in a million years, even though I can tell he's up to no good. You don't seem to be intimidated by him at all. I about lost my lunch when I saw that red moon, and you acted like you knew it would be there."

Rayford nodded but didn't expound. "I have a question for you, Mac. You knew why I went to the Baghdad airport. Why didn't you ask me what I found out about my wife or Hattie Durham?"

"None of my business, that's all," Mac said.

"Don't give me that. Unless Carpathia knows more than I do, he would have wanted to know about Hattie's whereabouts as soon as either of us knew anything."

"No, Rayford, it's like this. See, I just knew—I mean, everybody knows—that it wasn't likely either your wife or Miss Durham would have survived a crash at that airport."

"Mac! You saw yourself that hundreds of people were going to get off that 747. Sure, nine out of ten people died in that place, but lots survived, too. Now if you want answers from me, you'd better start giving me some."

Mac nodded toward a clearing he had illuminated with a spotlight. "We'll talk down there."

+ + +

Tsion brought only his phone, his laptop, and a few changes of clothes that had been smuggled in to him. Buck waited until they parked near the torn-up pavement in front of Loretta's house to tell him about Donny Moore.

"That is a tragedy," Tsion said. "And he was—?"

"The one I told you about. The computer whiz who put together our laptops. One of those quiet geniuses. He had gone to this church for years and was still embarrassed that he had this astronomical IQ and yet had been spiritually blind. He said he simply missed the essence of the gospel that whole time. He said he couldn't blame it on the staff or the teaching or anything or anyone but himself. His wife had hardly ever come with him in those days because she didn't see the point. They lost a baby in the Rapture. And once Donny became a believer, his wife soon followed. They became quite devout."

Tsion shook his head. "How sad to die this way. But now they are reunited with their child."

"What do you think I ought to do about the briefcase?" Buck asked.

"Do about it?"

"Donny must have something very important in there. I saw him with it constantly. But I don't know the combinations. Should I leave it alone?"

Tsion seemed in deep thought. Finally he said, "At a time like this you must decide if there is something in there that might further the cause of Christ. The young man would want you to have access to it. Should you break into it and find only personal things, it would be only right to maintain his privacy."

Tsion and Buck clambered out of the Rover. As soon as they had tossed their tools over the wall and climbed over, Tsion said, "Buck! Where is Chloe's car?"

3

RAYFORD COULD NOT SWEAR to the credibility of Mac McCullum. All he knew was that the freckled, twice-divorced man had just turned fifty and had never had kids. He was a careful and able aviator, facile with various types of aircraft, having flown both militarily and commercially.

Mac had proved a friendly, interested listener, earthy in expression. They had not known each other long enough for Rayford to expect him to be more forthcoming. Though he seemed a bright and engaging guy, their limited relationship had involved only surface cordiality. Mac knew Rayford was a believer; Rayford hid that from no one. But Mac had never shown the slightest interest in the matter. Until now.

Paramount in Rayford's mind was what not to say. Mac had finally expressed frustration over Carpathia, going so far as to allow that he was "up to no good." But what if Mac was a subversive, working for Carpathia as more than a pilot? What a way to entrap Rayford. Dare he both share his faith with Mac *and* reveal all that he and the Tribulation Force knew about Carpathia? And what of the bugging device built into the Condor 216? Even if Mac expressed an interest in Christ, Rayford would keep that volatile secret until he was sure Mac was not a fake.

Mac turned off everything on the chopper except auxiliary power that kept the control panel lights and radio on. All Rayford could see across the expanse of inky desert was moon and stars. If he hadn't known better, he might have been persuaded that the little craft was drifting along on an aircraft carrier in the middle of the ocean.

"Mac," Rayford said, "tell me about the shelter. What does it look like? And how did Carpathia know he needed it?"

"I don't know," Mac said. "Maybe it was a security blanket in case one or more of his ambassadors turned on him again. It's deep, it's concrete, and it'll protect him from radiation. And I'll tell you one more thing: It's plenty big enough for the 216."

Rayford was dumbfounded. "The 216? I left that at the end of the long runway in New Babylon."

"And I was assigned to move it early this morning."

"Move it where?"

"Didn't you ask me just the other day about that new utility road Carpathia had built?"

"That single-lane thing that seemed to lead only to the fence at the edge of the airstrip?"

"Yeah. Well, now there's a gate in the fence where that road ends."

"So you open the gate," Rayford said, "and you go where, across desert sand, right?"

"That's what it looks like," Mac said. "But a huge expanse of that sand has been treated with something. Wouldn't you think a craft as big as the 216 would sink in the sand if it ever got that far?"

"You're telling me you taxied the 216 down that little utility road to a gate in the fence? How big must that gate be?"

"Only big enough for the fuselage. The wings are higher than the fence."

"So you ferried the Condor off the airstrip and across the sand to where?"

"Three and a half clicks northeast of headquarters, just like Carpathia said."

"So this shelter isn't in a populated area."

"Nope. I doubt anyone's ever seen it without Carpathia's knowledge. It's huge, Ray. And it must have taken ages to build. I could have fit two aircraft that size in there and only half filled the space. It's about thirty feet below ground with plenty of supplies, plumbing, lodging, cooking areas, you name it."

"How does something underground withstand the shifting of the earth?"

"Part genius, part luck, I guess," Mac said. "The whole thing floats, suspended on some sort of a membrane filled with hydraulic fluid and sitting on a platform of springs that serve as mammoth shock absorbers."

"So the rest of New Babylon is in ruins, but the Condor and Carpathia's little hideout, or I should say big hideout, escaped damage?"

"That's where the ingenious part comes in, Ray. The place was rocked pretty good, but the technology delivered. The one eventuality they couldn't escape, even though they predicted it, was that the main entrance, the huge opening that allowed the plane to easily slip in there, was completely covered over with rock and sand by the quake. They were able to shelter a couple of other smaller openings on the other side to maintain passage, and Carpathia already has earthmovers reopening the original entrance. They're working on it right now."

"So, what, he's looking to go somewhere? Can't stand the heat?"

"No, not at all. He's expecting company."

"His kings are on their way?"

"He calls them ambassadors. He and Fortunato have big plans."

Rayford shook his head. "Fortunato! I saw him in Carpathia's office when the earthquake started. How'd he survive?"

"I was as surprised as you, Ray. Unless I missed him, I didn't see him come out that door on the roof. I figured the only people with a prayer of surviving the collapse of that place were the few who were on the roof when the thing went down. That's more than a sixty-foot drop with concrete crashing all around you, so even that's a long shot. But I've heard stranger. I read about a guy in Korea who was on top of a hotel that collapsed, and he said he felt like he was surfing on a concrete slab until he hit the ground and rolled and wound up with only a broken arm."

"So what's the story? How did Fortunato get out?"

"You're not going to believe it."

"I'd believe anything at this point."

"Here's the story the way I saw it. I take Carpathia back to the shelter, and I put her down near the entrance where I had parked the Condor. It was totally covered over, like I say, so Carpathia directs me around to the side where there's a smaller opening. We go in and find a big staff of people working, almost as if nothing's happened. I mean, there's people cooking, cleaning, setting up, all that."

"Carpathia's secretary?"

Mac shook his head. "I guess she was killed in the building collapse, along with most of the other headquarters staff. But he's got her and all the rest of 'em replaced already."

"Unbelievable. And Fortunato?"

"He wasn't there either. Somebody tells Carpathia there were no survivors at headquarters, and I swear, Ray, it looked to me like Carpathia paled. It was the first time I've ever seen him rattled, except when he pretends to go into a rage about something. I think those are always planned."

"Me too. So what about Leon?"

"Carpathia recovers real quick and says, 'We'll just see about that.' He says he'll be right back, and I ask him can I take him somewhere. He says no and leaves. When was the last time you saw him go anywhere by himself?"

"Never."

"Bingo. He's gone about half an hour, and the next thing you know he's back and he's got Fortunato with him. Fortunato was covered with dust from his head to his feet, and his suit was a mess. But his shirt was tucked in and his coat buttoned up, tie straightened and everything. There wasn't a scratch on him."

"What was his story?"

"It gave me chills, Ray. A bunch of people gathered around, I'd say about a hundred. Fortunato, real emotional, calls for order. Then he claims he went crying and screaming down in the rubble along with everybody else. He said halfway down he was wondering if it was possible to get lucky enough to be wedged in somewhere where he could breathe and stay alive until rescuers might find him. He said he felt himself free-falling and smacking into huge chunks of building; then something caught his feet and flipped him so he was going straight down, headfirst. When he hit, he said, it felt and sounded like he'd cracked his head open. Then it was like the whole weight of the building came down on him. He felt his bones breaking and his lungs bursting and everything went black. He said it was like somebody pulled the plug on his life. He believes he died."

"And yet there he is, wearing a dusty suit and not a scratch on him?"

"I saw him with my own eyes, Ray. He claims he was lying there dead, not conscious of anything, no out-of-body experience or anything like that. Just black nothingness, like the deepest sleep a person could ever have. He says he woke up, came back from the dead, when he heard his name called. At first he thought he was dreaming, he says. He thought he was a little boy again and his mother was softly calling his name, trying to rouse him. But then, he says, he heard Nicolae's loud call, 'Leonardo, come forth!'"

"What?"

"I'm tellin' you, Ray, it gave me the willies. I was never that religious, but I know that story from the Bible, and it sure sounded like Nicolae was pretending to be Jesus or something."

"You think the story's a lie?" Rayford asked. "You know, the Bible also says it's appointed unto man once to die. No second chances."

"I didn't know that, and I didn't know what to think when he told that story. Carpathia bringing somebody back from the dead? You know, at first I loved Carpathia and couldn't wait to work for him. There were times I thought he *was* a godly man, maybe some kind of deity himself. But it didn't add up. Him making me take off from the top of that building while people were hanging onto the struts and screaming for their lives. Him putting you down because you wanted to help that crash survivor in the desert. What kind of a god-man is that?"

"He's no god-man," Rayford said. "He's an anti-god-man."

"You think he's the Antichrist, like some say?"

So there it was. Mac had put the question to him. Rayford knew he had been reckless. Had he now sealed his own fate? Had he revealed himself completely to one of Carpathia's own henchmen, or was Mac sincere? How could he ever know for sure?

\+ + +

Buck spun in a circle. Where *was* Chloe's car? She always parked it in the driveway in front of the garage that contained Loretta's junk. Loretta's own car was usually in the other stall. It wouldn't have made sense for Chloe to move her car into Loretta's stall just because Loretta had driven to the church. "It could have been tossed anywhere, Tsion," Buck said.

"Yes, my friend, but not so far away that we could not see it."

"It could have been swallowed up."

"We should look, Cameron. If her car is here, we can assume she is here."

Buck moved up and down the street, looking between wrecked houses and into great holes in the earth. Nothing resembling Chloe's car turned up anywhere. When he met Tsion back at what used to be Loretta's garage, the rabbi was trembling. Though only in his middle forties, Tsion suddenly looked old to Buck. He moved with a shaky gait and stumbled, dropping to his knees.

"Tsion, are you all right?"

"Have you ever seen anything like it?" Tsion said, his voice just above a whisper. "I have seen devastation and waste, but this is overwhelming. Such widespread death and destruction . . ."

Buck put his hand on the man's shoulder and felt sobs wrack his body. "Tsion, we must not allow the enormity of all this to penetrate our minds. I have to somehow keep it separated from myself. I know it's not a dream. I know exactly what we're going through, but I can't dwell on it. I'm not equipped. If I allow it to overwhelm me, I'll be good to no one. We need each other. Let's be strong." Buck realized his own voice was weak as he pleaded with Tsion to be strong.

"Yes," Tsion said tearfully, trying to collect himself. "The glory of the Lord must be our rear guard. We will rejoice in the Lord always, and he will lift us up."

With that, Tsion rose and grabbed a shovel. Before Buck could catch up, Tsion began digging at the base of the garage.

\+ + +

The helicopter's radio crackled to life, giving Rayford time to search himself, to think and silently pray that God would keep him from saying something stupid. He still didn't know whether Amanda was dead or alive. He didn't know whether Chloe, or Buck, or Tsion were still on earth or in heaven. Finding them, reuniting with them was his top priority. Was he now risking everything?

The dispatcher at the shelter requested Mac's ten-twenty.

Mac glanced ruefully at Rayford. "Better make it sound like we're in the air," he said, cranking the engines. The noise was deafening. "Still workin' rescue at Baghdad," he said. "Be at least another hour."

"Roger that."

Mac shut the chopper down. "Bought us some time," he said.

Rayford covered his eyes briefly. "God," he prayed silently, "all I can do is trust you and follow my instincts. I believe this man is sincere. If he's not, keep me from saying anything I shouldn't. If he is sincere, I don't want to keep from telling him what he needs to know. You've been so overt, so clear with Buck and Tsion. Couldn't you give me a sign? Anything that would assure me I'm doing the right thing?"

Rayford looked uncertainly into Mac's eyes, dimly illuminated by the glow from the control panel. For the moment, God seemed silent. He had not made a habit of speaking directly to Rayford, though Rayford had enjoyed his share of answers to prayer. There was no turning back now. While he sensed no divine green light, neither did he sense a red or even a yellow. Knowing the outcome could be a result of his own foolishness, he realized he had nothing to lose.

"Mac, I'm gonna tell you my whole story and everything I feel about what's happened, about Nicolae, and about what is to come. But before I do, I need you to tell me what Carpathia knows, if you know, about whether Hattie or Amanda were really expected in Baghdad tonight."

Mac sighed and looked away, and Rayford's heart fell. Clearly he was about to hear something he'd rather not hear.

"Well, Ray, the truth is Carpathia knows Hattie is still in the States. She got as far as Boston, but his sources tell him she boarded a nonstop to Denver before the earthquake hit."

"To Denver? I thought that's where she had come from."

"It was. That's where her family is. Nobody knows why she went back."

Rayford's voice caught in his throat. "And Amanda?"

"Carpathia's people tell him she was on a Pan-Con heavy out of Boston that should have been on the ground in Baghdad before the quake hit. It had lost a little time over the Atlantic for some reason, but the last he knew, it was in Iraqi airspace."

Rayford dropped his head and fought for composure. "So, it's underground somewhere," he said. "Why wouldn't I have seen it at the airport?"

"I don't know," Mac said. "Maybe it was completely swallowed by the desert. But all the other planes monitored by Baghdad tower have been accounted for, so that doesn't seem likely."

"There's still hope then," Rayford said. "Maybe that pilot was far enough behind schedule that he was still in the air and just stayed there until everything stopped moving and he could find a spot to put down."

"Maybe," Mac said, but Rayford detected flatness in his voice. Clearly, Mac was dubious.

"I won't stop looking until I know." Mac nodded, and Rayford sensed something more. "Mac, what are you not telling me?" Mac looked down and shook his head. "Listen to me, Mac. I've already hinted what I think of Carpathia. That's a huge risk for me. I don't know where your true loyalties lie, and I'm about to tell you more than I should tell anyone that I wouldn't trust with my life. If you know something about Amanda that I need to know, you've got to tell me."

Mac drew a hesitant breath. "You really don't want to know. Trust me, you don't want to know."

"Is she dead?"

"Probably," he said. "I honestly don't know that, and I don't think Carpathia does either. But this is worse than that, Rayford. This is worse than her being dead."

+ + +

Getting into the garage at the wreckage of Loretta's home seemed impossible even for two grown men. It had been attached to the house and somehow appeared the least damaged. There was no basement under the garage area, thus not far for its cement slab and foundation to go. When the roof had fallen in, the sectioned doors had been so heavily compressed that their panels had overlapped by several inches. One door was angled at least two feet off track, pointing to the right. The other was off track about half that much and pointed in the other direction. There was no budging them. All Buck and Tsion could do was start hacking through them. In their normal state, the wood doors might easily have been cracked through, but now they sat with a huge section of roof and eaves jamming them awkwardly down to concrete, which rested two feet below the surface.

To Buck, every whack at the wood with his ax felt as if he were crashing steel against steel. With both hands at the bottom of the handle and swinging with all his might, the best he could do was chip tiny pieces with each blow. This was a quality door, made only more solid by the crush of nature.

Buck was exhausted. Only nervous energy and grief held in check kept him going. With every swing of the ax, his desire grew to find Chloe. He knew the odds were against him, but he believed he could face her loss if he knew anything for sure. He went from hoping and praying that he would find her alive to that he would simply find her in a state that proved she died relatively painlessly. It wouldn't be long, he feared, before he would be praying that he find her regardless.

Tsion Ben-Judah was in good shape for his age. Up until he had gone into hiding, he had worked out every day. He had told Buck that though he had never been an athlete, he knew that the health of his scholar's mind depended also on the health of his body. Tsion was keeping up his end of the task, whaling away at the door in various spots, testing for any weakness that would allow him to drive through it more quickly. He was panting and sweating, yet still he tried to talk while he worked.

"Cameron, you do not expect to find Chloe's car in here anyway, do you?"

"No."

"And if you do not, from that you will conclude that she somehow escaped?"

"That's my hope."

"So this is a process of elimination?"

"That's right."

"As soon as we have established that her car is not here, Cameron, let us try to salvage whatever we can from the house."

"Like what?"

"Foodstuffs. Your clothes. Did you say you had already cleared your bedroom area?"

"Yes, but I didn't see the closet or its contents. It can't be far."

"And the chest of drawers? Surely you have clothes in there."

"Good idea," Buck said.

Between the two axes and their resounding *thwack*s against the garage door, Buck heard something else. He stopped swinging and held up a hand to stop Tsion. The older man leaned on his ax to catch his breath, and Buck recognized the *thump-thump-thump* of helicopter blades. It grew so loud and close that Buck assumed it was two or three choppers. But when he caught sight of the craft, he was astounded to see it was just one, big as a bus. The only other he'd seen like it was in the Holy Land during an air attack years before.

But this one, setting down just a hundred or so yards away, resembled those old gray-and-black Israeli transport choppers only in size. This was sparkling white and appeared to have just come off the assembly line. It carried the huge insignia of the Global Community.

"Do you believe this?" Buck asked.

"What do you make of it?" Tsion said.

"No idea. I just hope they're not looking for you."

"Frankly, Cameron, I think I have become a very low priority to the GC all of a sudden, don't you?"

"We'll find out soon enough. Come on."

They dropped their axes and crept back to the upturned pavement that had served as Loretta's street not that many hours before. Through a gouge in that fortress they saw the GC copter settle next to a toppled utility pole. A high-tension wire snapped and crackled on the ground while at least a dozen GC emergency workers piled out of the aircraft. The leader communicated on a walkie-talkie, and within seconds power was cut to the area and the sparking line fell dead. The leader directed a wire cutter to snip the other lines that led to the power pole.

Two uniformed officers carried a large circular metal framework from the helicopter, and technicians quickly jury-rigged a connection that fastened it to one end of the now bare pole. Meanwhile, others used a massive earth drill to dig a new hole for the pole. A water tank and fast-setting concrete mixer dumped a solution in the hole, and a portable pulley was anchored on four sides by two officers putting their entire weight on its metal feet at each corner. The rest maneuvered the quickly refashioned pole into position. It was drawn up to a forty-five degree angle, and three officers bent low to slide its bottom end into the hole. The pulley tightened and straightened the pole, which dropped fast and deep, sending the excess concrete solution shooting up the sides of the pole.

Within seconds, everything was reloaded into the helicopter and the GC team lifted off. In fewer than five minutes, a utility pole that had borne both electrical power and telephone lines had been transformed.

Buck turned to Tsion. "Do you realize what we just saw?"

"Unbelievable," Tsion said. "It is now a cellular tower, is it not?"

"It is. It's lower than it should be, but it will do the trick. Somebody believes that keeping the cell areas functioning is more important than electricity or telephone wires."

Buck pulled his phone from his pocket. It showed full power and full range, at least in the shadow of that new tower. "I wonder," he said, "how long it will be before enough towers are up to allow us to call anywhere again."

Tsion had started back toward the garage. Buck caught up with him. "It cannot be long," Tsion said. "Carpathia must have crews like this working around the clock all over the world."

+ + +

"We better get heading back soon," Mac said.

"Oh sure," Rayford said. "I'm going to let you take me back to Carpathia and his safe shelter before you tell me something about my own wife that I'll hate worse than knowing she's dead?"

"Ray, please don't make me say any more. I said too much already. I can't corroborate any of this stuff, and I don't trust Carpathia."

"Just tell me," Rayford said.

"But if you respond the way I would, you won't want to talk about what I want to talk about."

Rayford had nearly forgotten. And Mac was right. The prospect of bad news about his wife had made him obsess over it to the exclusion of anything else important enough to talk about.

"Mac, I give you my word I'll answer any question you have and talk about anything you want. But you must tell me anything you know about Amanda."

Mac still seemed reluctant. "Well, for one thing, I do know that that Pan-Con heavy would not have had enough fuel to go looking for somewhere else to land. If the quake happened before they touched down and it became obvious to the pilot he couldn't land at Baghdad, he wouldn't have had a whole lot farther to go."

"So that's good news, Mac. Since I didn't find the plane at Baghdad, it has to be somewhere relatively close by. I'll keep looking. Meanwhile, tell me what you know."

"All right, Ray. I don't guess we're at any point in history where it makes sense to play games. If this doesn't convince you I'm not one of Carpathia's spies, nothing will. If it gets back that I quoted him to you, I'm a dead man. So regardless of what you think of this or how you react to it or what you might want to say to him about it, you can't ever let on. Understand?"

"Yes, yes! Now what?"

Mac took a breath but, maddeningly, said nothing. Rayford was about to explode. "I gotta get out of this cockpit," Mac said finally, unbuckling himself. "Go on, Ray. Get out. Don't make me climb over you."

Mac was out of his seat and standing between his and Rayford's, bent low to keep from knocking his head on the ceiling of the Plexiglas bubble. Rayford unstrapped himself and popped the door open, jumping down into the sand. He was through begging. He simply determined he would not let Mac back in that chopper until he told him whatever it was he needed to know.

Mac stood there, hands thrust deep into his pants pockets. Light from the full moon highlighted the reddish-blond hair, the craggy features, and the freckles on his weathered face. He looked like a man on his way to the gallows.

Mac suddenly stepped forward and put both palms on the side of the chopper. His head hung low. Finally, he raised it and turned to face Rayford. "All right, here it is. Don't forget you made me tell you. . . . Carpathia talks about Amanda like he knows her."

Rayford grimaced and held his hands out, palms up. He shrugged. "He does know her. So what?"

"No! I mean he talks about her as if he *really* knows her."

"What's that supposed to mean? An affair? I know better than that."

"No, Ray! I'm saying he talks about her as if he's known her since before she knew you."

Rayford nearly dropped in the sand. "You're not saying—"

"I'm telling you that behind closed doors, Carpathia makes comments about Amanda. She's a team player, he says. She's in the right place. She plays her role well. That kind of stuff. What am I supposed to make of that?"

Rayford could not speak. He didn't believe it. No, of course not. But the very idea. The gall of that man to make such an implication about the character of a woman Rayford knew so well.

"I hardly know your wife, Ray. I have no idea if it's possible. I'm just telling you what—"

"It's not possible," Rayford finally managed. "I know you don't know her, but I do."

"I didn't expect you to believe it, Ray. I'm not even saying it makes me suspicious."

"You don't have to be suspicious. The man is a liar. He works for the father of lies. He would say anything about anybody to further his own agenda. I don't know why he needs to besmirch her reputation, but—"

"Ray, I told you I'm not saying I think he's right or anything. But you have to admit he's getting information from somewhere."

"Don't even suggest—"

"I'm not suggesting anything. I'm just saying—"

"Mac, I can't say I've known Amanda long in the larger scheme of things. I can't say she bore me children like my first wife did. I can't say we've been together twenty years like I was with Irene. I *can* say, though, that we are not just husband and wife. We are brother and sister in Christ. If I had shared Irene's faith, she and I would have been true soul mates too, but that was my fault. Amanda and I met after we had both become believers, and so we shared an almost instantaneous bond. It is a bond no one could break. That woman is no more a liar or a betrayer or a subversive or a turncoat than anyone. No one could be that good. No one could share my bed and hold my gaze and pledge her love and loyalty to me that earnestly and be a liar without my suspecting. No way."

"That's good enough for me, Cap," Mac said.

Rayford was furious with Carpathia. If he had not pledged to maintain Mac's confidentiality, it would have been difficult to stop himself from jumping on the radio right then and demanding to talk directly to Nicolae. He wondered how he would face the man. What would he say or do when he saw him later?

"Why should I expect any different from a man like him?" Rayford said.

"Good question," Mac said. "Now we'd better get back, don't you think?"

Rayford wanted to tell Mac he was still willing to talk about the questions he had raised, but he really didn't feel like talking anymore. If Mac raised it again, Rayford would follow through. But if Mac let him off the hook, he'd be grateful to wait for a better time.

"Mac," he said as they strapped themselves into the chopper, "since we're supposed to be on a rescue mission anyway, would you mind doing a twenty-five-mile circle search?"

"It'd sure be a lot easier during daylight," Mac said. "You want me to bring you back tomorrow?"

"Yeah, but let's do a cursory look right now anyway. If that plane went down anywhere near Baghdad, the only hope of finding survivors is to find them quick."

Rayford saw sympathy on Mac's face.

"I know," Rayford said. "I'm dreaming. But I can't run back to Carpathia and take advantage of shelter and supplies if I don't exhaust every effort to find Amanda."

"I was just wondering," Mac said. "If there *was* anything to Carpathia's claims—"

"There's not, Mac, and I mean it. Now get off of that."

"I'm just saying, if there is, do you think there might be a chance that he would have had her on another plane? Kept her safe somehow?"

"Oh, I get it!" Rayford said. "The upside of my wife working for the enemy is that she might still be alive?"

"I wasn't looking at it that way," Mac said.

"What's the point then?"

"No point. We don't have to talk about it anymore."

"We sure don't."

But as Mac took the chopper in wider and wider concentric circles from the Baghdad terminal, all Rayford saw on the ground was shifting and sinking sand. Now he wanted to find Amanda, not just for himself, but also to prove that she was who he knew her to be.

By the time they gave up the search and Mac promised the dispatcher they were finally on their way in, a sliver of doubt had crept into Rayford's mind.

He felt guilty for entertaining it at all, but he could not shake it. He feared the damage that sliver could do to his love and reverence for this woman who had completed his life, and he was determined to eradicate it from his mind.

His problem was that despite how romantic she had made him, and how emotional he had waxed since his conversion (and his exposure to more tragedy than anyone should ever endure), he still possessed the practical, analytical, scientific mind that made him the airman he was. He hated that he couldn't simply dismiss a doubt because it didn't fit what he felt in his heart. He would have to exonerate Amanda by somehow proving her loyalty and the genuineness of her faith—with her help if she was alive, and without it if she was dead.

\+ \+ \+

It was midafternoon when Buck and Tsion finally ripped a big enough hole in one of the garage doors to allow Tsion to crawl through.

Tsion's voice was so hoarse and faint that Buck had to turn his ear toward the opening. "Cameron, Chloe's car is here. I can get the door open just far enough to put the inside light on. It is empty except for her phone and computer."

"I'll meet you at the back of the house!" Buck shouted. "Hurry, Tsion! If her car's still here, she's still here!"

Buck scooped up as many of the tools as he could carry and raced to the back. This was the evidence he had hoped and prayed for. If Chloe was buried in that rubble, and there was one chance in a million she was still alive, he would not rest.

Buck attacked the wreckage with all his might, having to remind himself to breathe. Tsion appeared and picked up a shovel and an ax. "Should I start in at some other location?" he asked.

"No! We have to work together if we have any hope!"

4

"SO WHAT HAPPENED to the dusty clothes?" Rayford whispered as he and Mac were escorted into the auxiliary entrance of Carpathia's huge underground shelter. Far across the structure, past the Condor 216 and amongst many subordinates and assistants, Fortunato looked chipper in a fresh suit.

"Nicolae's got him cleaned up already," Mac muttered.

Rayford had eaten nothing for more than twelve hours but had not thought about hunger until now. The milling crowd of surprisingly upbeat Carpathia lackeys had been through a buffet line and sat balancing plates and cups on their knees.

Suddenly ravenous, Rayford noticed ham, chicken, and beef, as well as all sorts of Middle Eastern delicacies. Fortunato greeted him with a smile and a handshake. Rayford did not smile and barely gripped the man's hand.

"Potentate Carpathia would like us to join him in his office in a few moments. But please, eat first."

"Don't mind if I do," Rayford said. Though an employee, he felt as if he was eating in the enemy's camp. Yet it would be foolish to go hungry just to make a point. He needed strength.

As he and Mac made their way around the buffet, Mac whispered, "Maybe we shouldn't look too buddy-buddy."

"Yeah," Rayford said. "Carpathia knows where I stand, but I assume he sees you as a loyalist."

"I'm not, but there's no future for those who admit that."

"Like me?" Rayford said.

"A future for you? Not a long one. But what can I say? He likes you. Maybe he feels secure knowing you don't hide anything from him."

Rayford ate even as he ladled choices onto his plate. *It might be the enemy's food,* he thought, *but it does the job.*

He felt well fed and suddenly logy when he and Mac were ushered into Carpathia's office. Mac's presence surprised Rayford. He had never before been in on a meeting with Carpathia.

As was often true during times of international crisis and terror, it seemed Nicolae could barely contain a grin. He too had changed into fresh clothes and appeared well rested. Rayford knew he himself looked terrible.

"Please," Carpathia said expansively, "Captain Steele and Officer McCullum. Sit."

"I prefer to stand, if you don't mind," Rayford said.

"There is no need. You look weary, and we have important items on the agenda."

Rayford reluctantly settled into a chair. He did not understand these people. Here was a beautifully decorated office that rivaled Carpathia's main digs, now in a pile less than half a mile away. How was it this man was prepared for every eventuality?

Leon Fortunato stood at a corner of Carpathia's desk. Carpathia sat on the front edge, staring down at Rayford, who decided to beat him to the punch. "Sir, my wife. I—"

"Captain Steele, I have some bad news for you."

"Oh, no." Rayford's mind immediately went on the defensive. It didn't feel as if Amanda was dead, and so she wasn't. He didn't care what this liar said—the same man who dared call her his compatriot. If Carpathia said Amanda was dead, Rayford didn't know if he could keep Mac's confidence and refrain from attacking him and making him retract the slander.

"Your wife, God rest her soul, was—"

Rayford gripped the chair so tight he thought his fingertips might burst. He clenched his teeth. The Antichrist himself bestowing a God-rest-her-soul on his wife? Rayford trembled with rage. He prayed desperately that if it was true, if he had lost Amanda, that God would use him in the death of Nicolae Carpathia. That was not to come until three and a half years into the Tribulation, and the Bible foretold that Antichrist would then be resurrected and indwelt by Satan anyway. Still, Rayford pleaded with God for the privilege of killing this man. What satisfaction, what revenge he might exact from it, he did not know. It was all he could do to keep from executing the deed right then.

"As you know, she was aboard a Pan-Continental 747 flight from Boston to Baghdad today. The earthquake hit moments before the plane was to touch down. The best our sources can tell is that the pilot apparently saw the chaos, realized he could not land near the airport, pulled up, and turned the plane around."

Rayford knew what was coming, if the story was true. The pilot would not have had power to regain altitude if he both pulled up and turned around that quickly.

"Pan-Con officials tell me," Carpathia continued, "that the plane was simply not airworthy at that speed. Eyewitnesses say it cleared the banks of the Tigris, hit first nearly halfway across the river, flipped tail up, then plunged out of sight."

Rayford's whole body pulsed with every heartbeat. He lowered his chin to his chest and fought for composure. He looked up at Carpathia, wanting details, but could not open his mouth, let alone utter a sound.

"The current is swift there, Captain Steele. But Pan-Con tells me a plane like that would drop like a stone. Nothing has surfaced downriver. No bodies have been discovered. It will be days before we get equipment for a salvage operation. I am sorry."

Rayford no more believed Carpathia was sorry than that Amanda was dead. He believed even less that she had ever acted in concert with Nicolae Carpathia.

\+ + +

Buck worked like a madman, his fingers nicked and blistered. Chloe had to be in there somewhere. He didn't want to talk. He just wanted to dig. But Tsion enjoyed hashing things over. "I do not understand, Cameron," he said, "why Chloe's car would have been in the garage where Loretta's car usually sits."

"I don't know," Buck said dismissively. "But it's there, and that means she's here somewhere."

"Perhaps the earthquake plunged the car right into the garage," Tsion suggested.

"Unlikely," Buck said. "I don't really care. I'm still kicking myself for not noticing her car missing when I got here."

"What would you have surmised?"

"That she had driven away! Escaped."

"Is that not still possible?"

Buck straightened up and pressed his knuckles into his back, trying to stretch sore muscles. "She wouldn't have gotten anywhere on foot. This thing hit so suddenly. There was no warning."

"Oh, but there was."

Buck stared at the rabbi. "You were underground, Tsion. How would you know?"

"I heard rumblings, a couple of minutes before the shaking began."

Buck had been in his Range Rover. He had seen roadkill, dogs barking and running, and other animals not usually seen in the daytime. Before the sky turned black he had noticed not a leaf moving, yet stoplights and traffic signs swayed. That was when he knew the earthquake was coming. There had been at least a brief warning. Was it possible Chloe had had an inkling? What would she have done? Where would she have gone?

Buck went back to digging. "What did you say was in her car, Tsion?"

"Just her computer and her phone."

Buck stopped digging. "Could she be in the garage?"

"I am afraid not, Cameron. I looked carefully. If she was there when it all came down," Tsion said, "you would not want to find her anyway."

I might not like it, Buck thought, but I have to know.

* * *

Rayford's body went rigid when Carpathia touched his shoulder. He envisioned leaping from the chair and choking the life out of Carpathia. He sat seething, eyes closed, feeling as if he were about to explode.

"I can sympathize with your grief," Nicolae said. "Perhaps you can understand my own feeling of loss over the many lives this calamity has cost. It was worldwide, every continent suffering severe damage. The only region spared was Israel."

Rayford wrenched away from Carpathia's touch and regained his voice. "And you don't believe this was the wrath of the Lamb?"

"Rayford, Rayford," Carpathia said. "Surely you do not lay at the feet of some Supreme Being an act so spiteful and capricious and deadly as this."

Rayford shook his head. What had he been thinking? Was he actually trying to persuade the Antichrist he was wrong?

Carpathia moved behind his desk to a high-backed leather chair. "Let me tell you what I am going to tell the rest of the staff, so you can skip the meeting and find your quarters and get some rest."

"I don't mind hearing it along with the rest."

"Magnanimous, Captain Steele. However, there are as well things I need to say only to you. I hesitate to raise this while your loss is so fresh, but you do understand that I could have you imprisoned."

"I'm sure you could," Rayford said.

"But I choose not to do that."

Should he feel grateful or disappointed? A stretch in prison didn't sound bad. If he knew his daughter and son-in-law and Tsion were all right, he could endure that.

Carpathia continued, "I understand you better than you know. We will put behind us our encounter, and you will continue to serve me in the manner you have up to now."

"And if I resign?"

"That is not an option. You will come through this nobly, as you have other crises. Otherwise, I will charge you with insubordination and have you imprisoned."

"That's putting the encounter behind us? You *want* someone working for you who would rather not?"

"In time I will win you over," Carpathia said. "You are aware that your living quarters were destroyed?"

"I can't say I'm surprised."

"Teams will try to salvage anything of use. Meanwhile, we have uniforms and necessities for you. You will find your quarters adequate, though not luxurious. Top priority for my administration is to rebuild New Babylon. It will become the new capital of the world. All banking, commerce, religion, and government will start and end right here. The greatest rebuilding challenge in the rest of the world is in communications. We have already begun rebuilding an international network that—"

"Communications is more important than people? More than cleaning up areas that might otherwise become diseased? Clearing away bodies? Reuniting families?"

"In due time, Captain Steele. Such efforts depend on communications too. Fortunately, the timing of my most ambitious project could not have been more propitious. The Global Community recently secured sole ownership of all international satellite and cellular communications companies. We will have in place in a few months the first truly global communications network. It is cellular, and it is solar powered. I call it Cellular-Solar. Once the cellular towers have been re-erected and satellites are maneuvered to geosynchronous orbit, anyone will be able to communicate with anyone else anywhere at any time."

Carpathia appeared to have lost the ability to hide his glee. If this technology worked, it solidified Carpathia's grip on the earth. His takeover was complete. He owned and controlled everything and everybody.

"As soon as you are up to it, you and Officer McCullum are to fly my ambassadors here. A handful of major airports around the world are operational, but with the use of smaller aircraft, we should be able to get my key men to where you can collect them in the Condor 216 and deliver them to me."

Rayford could not concentrate. "I have a couple of requests," he said.

"I love when you ask," Carpathia said.

"I would like information about my family."

"I will put someone on that right away. And?"

"I need a day or two to be trained by Mac in helicopters. I may be called upon to ferry someone from somewhere only a chopper can go."

"Whatever you need, Captain, you know that."

Rayford glanced at Mac, who looked puzzled. He shouldn't have been surprised. Unless Mac was a closet Carpathia sympathizer, they had serious things to discuss. They wouldn't be able to do that inside, where every room was likely wiretapped. Rayford wanted Mac for the kingdom. He would be a wonderful addition to the Tribulation Force, especially as long as they kept his true loyalties from Carpathia.

\+ \+ \+

"I am weak from hunger, Cameron," Tsion said. They had dug halfway through the rubble, Buck despairing more with every shovelful. There was plenty of evidence Chloe lived in this place, but none that she was still there, dead or alive.

"I can dig to the basement within the hour, Tsion. Start on the kitchen. You might find food there. I'm hungry too."

Even with Tsion just around the side of the house, Buck felt overwhelmed with loneliness. His eyes stung with tears as he dug and grabbed and lifted and tossed in what was a likely futile effort to find his wife.

Early in the evening Buck climbed wearily out of the basement at the back corner. He dragged his shovel to the front, willing to help Tsion, but hoping the rabbi had found something to eat.

Tsion lifted a split and crushed secretary desk and flung it at Buck's feet. "Oh, Cameron! I did not see you there."

"Trying to get to the refrigerator?"

"Exactly. The power has been out for hours, but there must be something edible still in there."

Two large beams were lodged in front of the refrigerator door. As Buck tried to help move them, his foot caught the edge of the broken desk, and papers and phone books flopped out onto the ground. One was the membership directory at New Hope Village Church. *That might come in handy,* he thought. He rolled it up and stuck it in his pants pocket.

A few minutes later Buck and Tsion sat back against the refrigerator, munching. That took the edge off his hunger, but Buck felt he could sleep for a week. The last thing he wanted was to finish digging. He dreaded evidence that Chloe had died. He was grateful Tsion finally didn't need to converse. Buck needed to think. Where would they spend the night? What would they eat tomorrow? But for now, Buck wanted to just sit, eat, and let memories of Chloe wash over him.

How he loved her! Was it possible he had known her less than two years? She had seemed much older than twenty when they had met, and she had the bearing of someone ten or fifteen years older now. She had been a gift from God, more precious than anything he had ever received except salvation. What would his life have been worth following the Rapture, had it not been for Chloe? He would have been grateful and would have enjoyed that deep satisfaction of knowing he was right with God, but he would have also been lonely and alone.

Even now, Buck was grateful for his father-in-law and Amanda. Grateful for his friendship with Chaim Rosenzweig. Grateful for his friendship with Tsion. He and Tsion would have to work on Chaim. The old Israeli was still enamored of Carpathia. That had to change. Chaim needed Christ. So did Ken Ritz, the pilot Buck had used so many times. He would have to check on Ken, make sure he was all right, see if he had planes that still flew. He pushed his food aside and hung his head, nearly asleep.

"I need to go back to Israel," Tsion said.

"Hm?" Buck mumbled.

"I need to go back to my homeland."

Buck raised his head and stared at Tsion. "We're homeless," he said. "We can barely drive to the next block. We don't know we'll survive tomorrow. You are a hunted criminal in Israel. You think they'll forget about you, now that they have earthquake relief to do?"

"On the contrary. But I have to assume the bulk of the 144,000 witnesses, of whom I am one, must come from Israel. Not all of them will. Many will come from tribes all over the globe. But the greatest source of Jews is Israel. These will be zealous as Paul but new to the faith and untrained. I feel a call to meet them and greet them and teach them. They must be mobilized and sent out. They are already empowered."

"Let's assume I get you to Israel. How do I keep you alive?"

"What, you think *you* kept me alive on our flight across the Sinai?"

"I helped."

"You helped? You amuse me, Cameron. In many ways, yes, I owe you my life. But you were as much in the way as I was. That was God's work, and we both know it."

Buck stood. "Fair enough. Still, taking you back to where you are a fugitive seems lunacy."

He helped Tsion stand. "Send word ahead that I was killed in the earthquake," the rabbi said. "Then I can go in disguise under one of those phony names you come up with."

"Not without plastic surgery you won't," Buck said. "You're a recognizable guy, even in Israel where everybody your age looks like you."

The sunlight softened and faded as they finished picking through the kitchen. Tsion found plastic bags and wrapped food he would store in the car. Buck wrenched a few clothes out of the mess that had been his and Chloe's bedroom while Tsion collected Chloe's computer and phone from the garage.

Neither had the strength to climb over the pavement barrier, so they took the long way around. When they reached the Range Rover, both had to get in the passenger side.

"And so what do you think now?" Tsion said. "If Chloe were alive somewhere in there, she would have heard us and called out to us, would she not?"

Buck nodded miserably. "I'm trying to resign myself to the fact that she's at the bottom. I was wrong, that's all. She wasn't in the bedroom or the kitchen or the basement. Maybe she ran to another part of the house. It would take heavy equipment to pull all the trash out of that place and find her. I can't imagine leaving her there, but neither can I think about more digging tonight."

Buck drove toward the church. "Should we stay in the shelter tonight?"

"I worry it is unstable," Tsion said. "Another shift and it could come down on us."

Buck drove on. He was a mile south of the church when he came to a neighborhood twisted and shaken but not broken. Many structures were damaged, but most still stood. A filling station, illuminated by butane torches, serviced a small line of cars.

"We're not the only civilians who survived," Tsion said.

Buck pulled into line. The man running the station had a shotgun propped up against the pumps. He shouted over a gasoline generator, "Cash only! Twenty-gallon limit! When it's gone, it's gone."

Buck topped off his tank and said, "I'll give you a thousand cash for—"

"The generator, yeah, I know. Take a number. I could get ten thousand for it by tomorrow."

"Know where I could get another one?"

"I don't know anything," the man said wearily. "My house is gone. I'll be sleeping here tonight."

"Need some company?"

"Not especially. If you get desperate, come back. I wouldn't turn you away."

Buck couldn't blame him. Where would you start and end taking in strangers at a time like this?

"Cameron," Tsion began when Buck got back in the car, "I have been thinking. Do we know whether the computer technician's wife knows about her husband?"

Buck shook his head. "I met his wife only one time. I don't remember her name. Wait a minute." He dug into his pocket and pulled out the church directory. "Here it is," he said. "Sandy. Let me call her." He punched in the numbers, and while he was not surprised the call did not go through, he was encouraged to get as far as a recorded message that all circuits were busy. That was progress, at least.

"Where do they live?" Tsion said. "It's not likely standing, but we could check."

Buck read the street address. "I don't know where that is." He saw a squad car ahead, lights flashing. "Let's ask him." The cop was leaning against his car, having a cigarette. "You on duty?" Buck asked.

"Takin' a break," the cop said. "I've seen more in one day than I cared to see in a lifetime, if you know what I mean." Buck showed him the address. "I don't know what I'll tell you as far as landmarks, but, ah, just follow me."

"You sure?"

"There's nothin' more I can do for anybody tonight. In fact, I didn't do anybody any good today. Follow me, and I'll point out the street you want. Then I'm gone."

A few minutes later Buck flashed his lights in thanks and pulled in front of a duplex. Tsion opened the passenger door, but Buck put a hand on his arm.

"Let me see Chloe's phone."

Tsion crawled back and fished it from a pile he had wrapped in a blanket. Buck flipped it open and found it had been left on. He rummaged in the glove box and produced a cigarette lighter adapter that fit the phone and made it come to life. He touched a button that brought up the last dialed number. He sighed. It was his own.

Tsion nodded, and they got out. Buck pulled a flashlight from his emergency toolbox. The left side of the duplex had broken windows all around and a foundational brick wall that had crumbled and left the front of the place sagging. Buck got into position where he could shine his light through the windows.

"Empty," he said. "No furniture."

"Look," Tsion said. A For Rent sign lay in the grass.

Buck looked again at the directory. "Donny and Sandy lived on the other side."

The place looked remarkably intact. The drapes were open. Buck gripped the wrought iron railing on the steps and leaned over to flash his light into the living room. It looked lived-in. Buck tried the front door and found it unlocked. As he and Tsion tiptoed through the house, it became obvious something was amiss in the tiny breakfast nook at the back. Buck gaped, and Tsion turned away and bent at the waist.

Sandy Moore had been at the table with her newspaper and coffee when a huge oak tree crashed through the roof with such force that it flattened her and the heavy wood table. The dead girl's finger was still curled around the cup handle, and her cheek rested on the Tempo section of the *Chicago Tribune*. Had not the rest of her body been compressed to inches, she might have appeared to be dozing.

"She and her husband must have died within seconds of each other," Tsion said quietly. "Miles apart."

Buck nodded in the faint light. "We should bury this girl."

"We will never get her out from under that tree," Tsion said.

"We have to try."

In the alley Buck found planks, which they forced under the tree as levers, but a trunk with enough mass to destroy roof, wall, window, woman, and table would not be budged.

"We need heavy equipment," Tsion said.

"What's the use?" Buck said. "No one will ever be able to bury all of the dead."

"I confess I am thinking less of respect for her body than for the possibility that we have found a place to live." Buck shot him a double take. "What?" Tsion said. "Is it not ideal? There's actually a bit of pavement out front. This room, open to the elements, can be easily closed off. I don't know how long it would take to get power, but—"

"Say no more," Buck said. "We have no other prospects."

Buck threaded the Rover between the duplex and the burned-out shell of whatever had been next door. He parked out of sight in the back, and he and Tsion unloaded the car. Coming through the back door Buck noticed they might be able to extricate Mrs. Moore's body from underneath. Branches were lodged against a huge cabinet in the corner. That would keep the tree from dropping further if they could somehow cut under the floor.

"I am so tired I can barely stand, Cameron," Tsion said as they descended narrow stairs to the cellar.

"I'm about to collapse myself," Buck said. He shined his light toward the underside of the first floor and saw that Sandy's elbow had been driven through and hung exposed. They found mostly discarded computer parts until they came upon Donny's stash of tools. *A hammer, chisels, a crowbar, and a handsaw should do it,* Buck thought. He dragged a stepladder under the spot, and Tsion held it as Buck wrapped his legs around the top step to brace himself. Then began the arduous task of driving the crowbar up through the floorboards with a hammer. His arms ached, but he stayed at it until he had punched out a few holes large enough to get the saw wedged in. He and Tsion traded off sawing the hardwood, which seemed to take forever with the dull blade.

They were careful not to touch Sandy Moore's body with the saw. Buck was struck that the shape of the cut looked like the pine boxes in which cowboys were buried in the old west. When they had sawn to about her waist, the weight of her upper body made the boards beneath her give way, and she slowly dropped into Buck's arms. He gasped and held his breath, fighting to keep his balance. His shirt was covered with her sticky blood, and she felt light and fragile as a child.

Tsion guided him down. All Buck could think of as he carried her broken body out the back door was that this was what he had expected to do with Chloe at Loretta's. He lay her body gently in the dewy grass, and he and Tsion quickly dug a shallow grave. The work was easy because the quake had loosened the topsoil. Before they lowered her into the hole, Buck pulled Donny's wedding ring from deep in his pocket. He put it in her palm and closed her fingers around it. They covered her with the dirt. Tsion knelt, and Buck followed suit.

Tsion had not known Donny or his wife. He pronounced no eulogy. He merely quoted an old hymn, which made Buck cry so loudly he knew he could be heard down the block. But no one was around, and he could not stop the sobs.

"I will love Thee in life, I will love Thee in death,
And praise Thee as long as Thou lendest me breath;
And say, when the death-dew lies cold on my brow;
If ever I loved Thee, my Jesus, 'tis now."

Buck and Tsion found two tiny bedrooms upstairs, one with a double bed, the other with a single. "Take the bigger bed," Tsion insisted. "I pray Chloe will join you soon." Buck took him up on it.

Buck went into the bathroom and shed his mud- and blood-caked clothes. With only his flashlight for illumination, he hand dipped enough water out of the toilet tank for a sponge bath. He found a big towel to dry off with, then collapsed onto Donny and Sandy Moore's bed.

Buck slept the sleep of the mourning, praying he would never have to wake up.

+ + +

Half a world away, Rayford Steele was awakened by a phone call from his first officer. It was nine o'clock Tuesday morning in New Babylon, and he had to face another day whether he wanted to or not. At the very least, he hoped he would get a chance to tell Mac about God.

5

RAYFORD ATE with the stragglers at a bountiful breakfast. Across the way, dozens of aides hunched over maps and charts and crowded phone and radio banks. He ate lethargically, Mac next to him drumming his fingers and bouncing a foot. Carpathia sat with Fortunato and other senior staffers at a table not far from his office. Now he pressed a cell phone to his ear and talked earnestly in a corner, his back to the room.

Rayford eyed him with disinterest. He wondered about himself now, about his resolve. If it was true Amanda had gone down with the 747, Chloe and Buck and Tsion were all he cared about. Could he be the only Tribulation Force member left standing?

Rayford could muster not a whit of interest in whom Carpathia might be talking to or what about. If a gadget allowed him to listen in, he wouldn't even flip the switch. He had prayed before he ate, a prayer ambivalent about sustenance provided by the Antichrist. Still, he had eaten. And it was good that he had. His spirits began to lift. No way could he cogently share his faith with Mac if he stayed in a funk.

Mac's fidgeting made him nervous. "Eager to get flying?" Rayford said.

"Eager to get talking. But not here. Too many ears. But are you up for this, Rayford? With what you're going through?"

Mac seemed as ready to hear about God as anyone he had ever talked to. Why did it happen this way? When he had been most eager to share, he had tried to get through to his old senior pilot, Earl Halliday, who had had no interest and was now dead. He had tried without success to reach Hattie Durham, and now he could only pray there was still time for her. Here was Mac, in essence begging him for the truth, and Rayford would rather be back in bed.

He crossed his legs and folded his arms. He would will himself to move today. In the corner Carpathia wheeled around and stared at him, the phone still at his ear. Nicolae waved enthusiastically, then seemed to think better of showing such enthusiasm to a man who had just lost his wife. His face grew somber and his wave stiffened. Rayford did not respond, though he held Carpathia's gaze. Nicolae beckoned with a finger.

"Oh, no," Mac said. "Let's go, let's go."

But they couldn't walk out on Nicolae Carpathia.

Rayford was in a testy mood. He didn't want to talk to Carpathia; Carpathia wanted to talk to him. He could come Rayford's way. *What have I become?* Rayford wondered. He was playing games with the potentate of the world. Petty. Silly. Immature. *But I don't care.*

Carpathia snapped his phone shut and slipped it into his pocket. He waved at Rayford, who pretended not to notice and turned his back. Rayford leaned toward Mac. "So, what are you going to teach me today?"

"Don't look now, but Carpathia wants you."

"He knows where I am."

"Ray! He could still toss you in jail."

"I wish he would. So anyway, what *are* you going to teach me today?"

"Teach you! You've flown whirlybirds."

"A long time ago," Rayford said. "More than twenty years."

"Chopper jockeying is like riding a bike," Mac said. "You'll be as good as me in an hour."

Mac looked over Rayford's shoulder, stood, and thrust out his hand. "Potentate Carpathia, sir!"

"Excuse Captain Steele and me for a moment, would you, Officer McCullum?"

"I'll meet you in the hangar," Rayford said.

Carpathia slid McCullum's chair close to Rayford's and sat. He unbuttoned his suit coat and leaned forward, forearms on his knees. Rayford still had legs crossed and arms folded.

Carpathia spoke earnestly. "Rayford, I hope you do not mind my calling you by your first name, but I know you are in pain."

Rayford tasted bile. "Lord, please," he prayed silently, "keep my mouth shut." It only made sense that the embodiment of evil himself was the slimiest of liars. To imply that Amanda had been his plant, a mole in the Tribulation Force for the Global Community, and then to feign sorrow over her death? A lethal wound to the head was too good for him. Rayford imagined torturing the man who led the forces of evil against the God of the universe.

"I wish you had been here earlier, Rayford. Well, actually I am glad you were able to get the rest you needed. But those of us here for the first breakfast were treated to Leon Fortunato's account of last night."

"Mac said something about it."

"Yes, Officer McCullum has heard it twice. You should ask him to share it with you again. Better yet, schedule some time with Mr. Fortunato."

It was all Rayford could do to feign civility. "I'm aware of Leon's devotion to you."

"As am I. However, even I was moved and flattered at how his view has been elevated."

Rayford knew the story but couldn't resist baiting Carpathia. "It doesn't surprise me that Leon is grateful for your rescuing him."

Carpathia sat back and looked amused. "McCullum has heard the story twice, and that is his assessment? Have you not heard? I did not rescue Mr. Fortunato at all! I did not even save his life! According to *his* testimony, I brought him back from the dead."

"Indeed."

"I do not claim this for myself, Rayford. I am telling you only what Mr. Fortunato says."

"You were there. What's *your* account?"

"Well, when I heard that my most trusted aide and personal confidant had been lost in the ruins of our headquarters, something came over me. I simply refused to believe it. I willed it to be untrue. Every fiber of my being told me to simply go, by myself, to the site and bring him back."

"Too bad you didn't take witnesses."

"You do not believe me?"

"It's quite a tale."

"You must talk with Mr. Fortunato."

"I'm really not interested."

"Rayford, that fifty-foot pile of bricks, mortar, and debris had been a two-hundred-foot tall building. Leon Fortunato had been with me on the top floor when that building gave way. Despite the earthquake precautions designed into it, everyone in there should have been killed. And they were. You know there were no survivors."

"So you're saying it's Leon's contention, and yours, that even he was killed in the fall."

"I called him out of the middle of that wreckage. No one could have survived that."

"And yet he did."

"He did not. He was dead. He had to be."

"And how did you extricate him?"

"I commanded him to come forth, and he did."

Rayford leaned forward. "That had to make you believe the story of Lazarus. Too bad it's from a book of fairy tales, huh?"

"Now, Rayford, I have been most tolerant and have never disparaged your beliefs. Neither have I hidden that I believe you are, at best, misguided. But, yes, it gave me pause that this incident mirrored an account I believe was allegorical."

"Is it true you used the same words Jesus used with Lazarus?"

"So Mr. Fortunato says. I was unaware of precisely what I said. I left here with full confidence that I would come back with him, and my resolve never wavered, not even when I saw that mountain of ruins and knew that rescuers had found no one alive."

Rayford wanted to vomit. "So now you're some sort of deity?"

"That is not for me to say, though clearly, raising a dead man is a divine act. Mr. Fortunato believes I could be the Messiah."

Rayford raised his eyebrows. "If I were you, I'd be quick to deny that, unless I knew it to be true."

Carpathia softened. "It does not seem the time for me to make such a claim, but I am not so sure it is untrue."

Rayford squinted. "You think you might be the Messiah."

"Let me just say, especially after what happened last night, I have not ruled out the possibility."

Rayford thrust his hands in his pockets and looked away.

"Come now, Rayford. Do not assume I do not see the irony. I am not blind. I know a faction out there, including many of your so-called tribulation saints, labels me an antichrist, or even *the* Antichrist. I would delight in proving the opposite."

Rayford leaned forward, pulled his hands from his pockets, and entwined his fingers. "Let me get this straight. There's a possibility you are the Messiah, but you don't know for sure?"

Carpathia nodded solemnly.

"That makes no sense," Rayford said.

"Matters of faith are mysteries," Carpathia intoned. "I urge you to spend time with Mr. Fortunato. See what you think after that."

Rayford made no promises. He looked toward the exit.

"I know you need to go, Captain Steele. I just wanted to share with you the tremendous progress already made in my rebuilding initiative. As early as tomorrow we expect to be able to communicate with half the world. At that time I will address anyone who can listen." He pulled a sheet from his coat pocket. "Meanwhile, I would like you and Mr. McCullum to load whatever equipment you need onto the 216 and chart a course to bring these international ambassadors to join those who are already here."

Rayford scanned the list. It appeared he would fly more than twenty thousand miles. "Where are you on rebuilding runways?"

"Global Community forces are working around the clock in every country. Cellular-Solar will network the entire world within weeks. Virtually anyone not on that project is rebuilding airstrips, roads, and centers of commerce."

"I have my assignment," Rayford said flatly.

"I would like to know your itinerary as soon as it is set. Did you notice the name on the back?"

Rayford turned the sheet over. "Pontifex Maximus Peter Mathews, Enigma Babylon One World Faith. So we bring him, too?"

"Though he is in Rome, pick him up first. I would like him on the plane when each of the other ambassadors boards."

Rayford shrugged. He wasn't sure why God had put him in this position, but until he felt led to leave it, he would hang in.

"One more thing," Carpathia said. "Mr. Fortunato will go with you and serve as host."

Rayford shrugged again. "Now may I ask you something?" Carpathia nodded, standing. "Could you let me know when the dredging operation commences?"

"The what?"

"When they pull the Pan-Con 747 out of the Tigris," Rayford said evenly.

"Oh, yes, that. Now, Rayford, I have been advised it would be futile."

"There's a chance you won't do it?"

"Most likely we will not. The airline informed us who was aboard, and we know there are no survivors. We are already at a loss for what to do with the bodies of so many victims of this disaster. I have been advised to consider the aircraft a sacred burial vault."

Rayford felt his face flush, and he slumped. "You're not going to prove to me my wife is dead, are you?"

"Oh, Rayford, is there any doubt?"

"As a matter of fact, there is. It doesn't feel like she's dead, if you know what I—well, of course you don't know what I mean."

"I know it is difficult for loved ones to let go unless they see the body. But you are an intelligent man. Time heals—"

"I want that plane dredged up. I want to know whether my wife is dead or alive."

Carpathia stepped behind Rayford and placed a hand on each shoulder. Rayford closed his eyes, wishing he could melt away. Carpathia spoke soothingly. "Next you will be asking me to resurrect her."

Rayford spoke through clenched teeth. "If you are who you think you are, you ought to be able to pull that off for one of your most trusted employees."

+ + +

Buck had fallen asleep atop the bedspread. Now, well after midnight, he couldn't imagine he had slept more than two hours. Sitting up, gathering the covers around him, he didn't want to move. But what had awakened him? Had he seen lights flicker in the hallway?

It had to have been a dream. Surely electricity would not be reconnected in Mount Prospect for days, maybe weeks. Buck held his breath. Now he *did* hear something from the other room, the low, whispering cadence of Tsion Ben-Judah. Had something awakened him too? Tsion was praying in his own tongue. Buck wished he understood Hebrew. The prayer grew fainter, and Buck lay back down and rolled onto his side. As he lost consciousness he reminded himself that in the morning he needed one last look around Loretta's neighborhood—one more desperate attempt to find Chloe.

+ + +

Rayford found Mac in the cockpit of the idle helicopter. He was reading.

"Finally let you go, did he?" Mac said. Rayford always ignored obvious questions. He just shook his head. "I don't know how he does it," Mac said.

"What's that?"

Mac rattled his magazine. "The latest *Modern Avionics.* Where would Carpathia get this? And how would he know to stock it in the shelter?"

"Who knows?" Rayford said. "Maybe he's the god he thinks he is."

"I told you about Leon's diatribe last night."

"Carpathia told me again."

"What, that he agrees with Leon about his own divinity?"

"He's not going that far yet," Rayford said. "But he will. The Bible says he will."

"Whoa!" Mac said. "You're gonna have to start from the beginning."

"Fair enough," Rayford said, unfolding Carpathia's passenger list. "First let me show you this. After my training, I want you to plot our course to these countries. First we pick up Mathews in Rome. Then let's go to the States and pick up all the other ambassadors on the way back."

Mac studied the sheet. "Should be easy. Take me a half hour or so to plot it. Are there spots to land in all these places?"

"We'll get close enough. We'll put the chopper and a fixed-wing in the cargo hold, just in case."

"So when do we get to talk?"

"Our training session should take until about five, don't you think?"

"Nah! I told you, you'll be up to speed in no time."

"We'll need to break for a late lunch somewhere," Rayford said. "And then we'll still have several hours to train, right?"

"You're not following me, Ray. You don't need a whole day playing with this toy. You know what you're doing, and these things fly themselves."

Rayford leaned close. "Who's not following whom?" he said. "You and I are away from the shelter today, training until 1700 hours. Is that understood?"

Mac smiled sheepishly. "Oh. You learn the whirlybird by late lunch at around one, and we're still on leave until five."

"You catch on quick."

Rayford took notes as Mac walked him through every button, every switch, every key. With the blades at top speed, Mac feathered the controls until the bird lifted off. He went through a series of maneuvers, turning this way and that, dipping and climbing. "It'll come back to you quick, Ray."

"Let me ask you something first, Mac. You were stationed in this area, weren't you?"

"For many years," Mac said, slowly flying south.

"You know people, then."

"Locals, you mean? Yeah. I couldn't tell you if any of them survived the earthquake. What are you looking for?"

"Scuba equipment."

Mac glanced at Rayford, who did not return his gaze. "There's a new one for the middle of the desert. Where do you want to go diving? In the Tigris?" Mac grinned, but Rayford shot him a serious look and he paled. "Oh, sure, forgive me, Rayford. Man, you don't really want to do that, do you?"

"I've never wanted anything more, Mac. Now do you know somebody or not?"

"Let 'em dredge the thing, Ray."

"Carpathia says they're gonna leave it alone."

Mac shook his head. "I don't know, Ray. You ever scuba dive in a river?"

"I'm a good diver. But no, never in a river."

"Well, I have, and it's not the same, believe me. The current isn't much calmer at the bottom than the top. You'll spend half your time keeping from getting sucked downstream. You could wind up three hundred miles southeast in the Persian Gulf."

Rayford was not amused. "What's the story, Mac? You got a source for me?"

"Yeah, I know a guy. He was always able to get anything I wanted from just about anywhere. I've never seen scuba stuff around here, but if it's available and he's still alive, he can get it."

"Who and where?"

"He's a national. He runs the tower at the airstrip down at Al Basrah. That's northwest of Abadan where the Tigris becomes the Shatt al Arab. I wouldn't begin to try to pronounce his real name. To all of his, ahem, clients, he goes by Al B. I call him Albie."

"What's his arrangement?"

"He takes all the risks. Charges you double retail, no questions asked. You get caught with contraband stuff, he's never heard of you."

"Try to reach him for me?"

"Just say the word."

"That's what I'm saying, Mac."

"Quite a risk."

"Being honest with you is a risk, Mac."

"How do you know you can trust me?"

"I don't. I have no choice."

"Thanks a lot."

"You'd feel the same way if the shoe was on the other foot."

"True enough," Mac said. "Only time will prove I'm not a rat."

"Yeah," Rayford said, feeling as reckless as he had ever been. "If you're not a friend, there's nothing I can do about it now."

"Uh-huh, but would a fink make a dangerous dive with you?"

Rayford stared at him. "I couldn't let you do that."

"You can't stop me. If my guy can get a suit and a tank for you, he can get them for me, too."

"Why would you do that?"

"Well, not just to prove myself. I'd like to keep you around awhile. You deserve to know if your wife's in the drink. But that dive's gonna be dangerous enough for two, let alone solo."

"I'll have to think about that."

"For once, quit thinking so much. I'm goin' with you and that's that. I gotta figure some way to keep you alive long enough to tell me what the devil has been going on since the disappearances."

"Put her down," Rayford said, "and I'll tell you."

"Right here? Right now?"

"Right now."

Mac had flown a few miles to where Rayford could see the city of Al Hillah. He banked left and headed for the desert, landing in the middle of nowhere. He shut the engine down quickly to avoid sand damage. Still, Rayford saw grains on the back of his hands and tasted them on his lips.

"Let me get behind the controls," Rayford said, unstrapping himself.

"Not on your life," Mac said. "Next you're gonna try startin' her up and liftin' off. I know you can do it and it's not that dangerous, but Lord knows nobody else around here can explain things to me. Now out with it, let's go."

Rayford hopped out and landed in the sand. Mac followed. They strolled half an hour in the sun, Rayford sweating through his clothes. Finally Rayford led the way back to the helicopter, where they leaned against the struts on the shade side.

He told Mac his life story, starting with the kind of family he was raised in—decent, hardworking, but uneducated people. He had shown a proclivity for math and science and was fascinated by aviation. He did well in school, but his father could not afford to send him to college. A high school counselor told him he should be able to get scholarships, but that he needed something extra on his résumé.

"Like what?" Rayford had asked her.

"Extracurricular activities, student government, things like that."

"What about flying solo before I graduate?"

"Now *that* would be impressive," she admitted.

"I've done it."

That helped him earn a college education that led to military training and commercial flying. All the while, he said, "I was a pretty good guy. Good citizen—you know the drill. Drank a little, chased a little. Never anything illegal. Never saw myself as a rascal. Patriotic, the whole bit. I was even a churchgoer."

He told Mac he had been smitten with Irene from the beginning. "She was a little too goody-goody for me," he admitted, "but she was pretty and loving and selfless. She amazed me. I asked, she accepted, and though it turned out she was a lot more into church than I was, I wasn't about to let her go."

Rayford told of how he broke his promise to be a regular churchgoer. They'd had fights and Irene had shed tears, but he sensed she had resigned herself to the fact that "at least in this one area, I was a creep who couldn't be trusted. I was faithful, a good provider, respected in the community. I thought she was living with the rest of it. Anyway, she left me alone about it. She couldn't have been happy about it, but I told myself she didn't care. I sure didn't.

"When we had Chloe, I turned over a new leaf. I believed I was a new man. Seeing her born convinced me of miracles, forced me to acknowledge God, and made me want to be the best father and husband in history. I made no promises. I just started going back to church with Irene."

Rayford explained how he realized that "church wasn't that bad. Some of the same people we saw at the country club we saw at church. We showed up, gave our money, sang the songs, closed our eyes during the prayers, and listened to the homilies. Every once in a while a sermon or part of one offended me. But I let it slide. Nobody was checking up on me. The same things offended most of our friends. We called it getting our toes stepped on, but it never happened twice in a row."

Rayford said he had never stopped to think about heaven or hell. "They didn't talk much about that. Well, never about hell. Any mention of heaven was that everybody winds up there eventually. I didn't want to be embarrassed in heaven by having done too many bad things. I compared myself with other guys and figured if they were going to make it, I was too.

"The thing is, Mac, I was happy. I know people say they feel some void in their lives, but I didn't. To me, this was life. Funny thing was, Irene talked about feeling empty. I argued with her. Sometimes a lot. I reminded her I was back in church and she hadn't even had to badger me about it. What more did she want?"

What Irene wanted, Rayford said, was something more. Something deeper. She had friends who talked about a personal relationship with God, and it intrigued her. "Scared *me* to death," Rayford said. "I repeated the phrase so she could hear how wacky it sounded, 'personal relationship with God?' She said, of all things, 'Yes. Through his Son, Jesus Christ.'" Rayford shook his head. "Well, I mean, you can imagine how that went down with me."

Mac nodded. "I know what I would have thought."

Rayford said, "I had just enough religion to make me feel all right. Saying words like *God* or *Jesus Christ* out loud, in front of people? That was for pastors and priests and theologians. I resonated with people who said religion was private. Anybody who tried to convince you of something from the Bible or 'shared his faith' with you, well, those guys were right-wingers or zealots or fundamentalists or something. I stayed as far away from them as I could."

"I know what you mean," Mac said. "There was always somebody around trying to 'win souls for Jesus.'"

Rayford nodded. "Well, fast forward a whole bunch of years. Now we've got Rayford Junior. I had the same feeling when he was born as I had with Chloe. And I admit I had always wanted a son. I figured God must be pretty pleased with me to bless me that way. And let me tell you something I've told precious few other people, Mac. I was almost unfaithful to Irene while she was pregnant with Raymie. I was drunk, it was at a company Christmas party, and it was stupid. I felt so guilty, not because of God I don't think, but because of Irene. She didn't deserve that. But she never suspected, and that made it worse. I knew she loved me. I convinced myself I was the scum of the earth and I made all kinds of bargains with God. Somewhere I had this idea he might punish me. I told him if I could just put this behind me and never do it again, would he please not let our unborn baby die. If anything had been wrong with our baby, I don't know what I would have done."

But the baby had been perfect, Rayford explained. He soon got a promotion and a raise, they moved to a beautiful home in the suburbs, he kept going to church, and he was soon satisfied with his life again.

"But . . ."

"But?" Mac said. "What happened then?"

"Irene switched churches on me," Rayford said. "You getting hungry?"

"I'm sorry?"

"Are you hungry? It's coming up on one o'clock."

"That's the storyteller you are? Leave me hanging so you can eat? You ran that all together like Irene's changing churches should make me hungry."

"Point me to a place to eat," Rayford said. "I'll get us there."

"You'd better."

6

RAYFORD SPENT TWENTY MINUTES scaring the life out of himself and Mac. The skill of piloting a chopper may never leave, but with the advance of technology, this took some getting used to. He remembered bulky, sluggish, heavy copters. This one darted like a dragonfly. The control was as responsive as a joystick, and he found himself overcompensating. He banked one way—too hard and too fast—then the other, straightening himself quickly but then rolling the other way.

"I'm about to barf!" Mac shouted.

"Not in my chopper, you're not!" Rayford said.

He put the helicopter down four times, the second time much too hard. "That won't happen again," he promised. As he took off for the last time, he said, "I've got it now. This should be easy to keep straight and steady."

"It is for me," Mac said. "You want to go all the way to Albie's?"

"You mean put down at an airport, in front of people?"

"A baptism of fire." Mac plotted their bearings. "Keep her set right there, and we could snooze till we see the tower at Al Basrah. Line her up, let her go, and tell me about Irene's new church."

Rayford spent the trip finishing his story. He told how Irene's frustration with finding nothing deep or meaty or personal at their church gave him an excuse to start going only sporadically himself. When she called him on it, he reminded her that she wasn't happy there either. "When I pretty much stopped going altogether, she started church shopping. She met a couple of women she really liked at a church she didn't care so much for, but they invited her to a women's Bible study. That's where she heard something about God she had never known was in the Bible. She found out where the speaker went to church, started going there, and eventually dragged me along."

"What was it she heard?"

"I'm getting to it."

"Don't stall."

Rayford checked his instruments to make sure the engines were still operating in the green arcs.

"I mean don't stall your story," Mac said.

"Well, I didn't understand the new message myself," Rayford said. "In fact, I never really got it until after she was gone. The church was different all right. It made me uncomfortable. When people didn't see me around, they had to figure I was working. When I did show up, people asked me about work, and I just kept smiling and telling them how wonderful life was. But even when I *was* home I went only about half the time. My daughter, Chloe, was a teenager by then, and she picked up on that. If Dad didn't have to go, she didn't have to go."

"Irene, however, really loved the new church. She made me nervous when she started talking about sin and salvation and forgiveness and the blood of Christ and winning souls. She said she had received Christ and been born again. She was pushing me, but I would have none of that. It sounded weird. Like a cult. The people seemed all right, but I was sure I was going to get pushed into knocking on doors and handing out literature or something. I found more reasons to not be in church.

"One day Irene was going off about how Pastor Billings was preaching on the end times and the return of Christ. He called it the Rapture. She said something like, 'Wouldn't it be great to not die but to meet Jesus in the air?' I came back with something like, 'Yeah, that would kill me.' I offended her. She told me I shouldn't be so flippant if I didn't know where I was going. That made me mad. I told her I was glad she was sure. I told her I figured she'd fly to heaven and I'd go straight to hell. She didn't like that a bit."

"I can imagine," Mac said.

"The whole issue of church became so volatile that we just avoided it. Eventually I started to get those old stirrings again, and I had my eye on my senior flight attendant."

"Uh-oh," Mac said.

"Tell me about it. We had a few drinks, shared a few meals, but it never went past that. Not that I didn't want it to. One night I decided to ask her out when we got to London. Then I thought, hey, I'll ask her in advance. I'm way out over the Atlantic in the middle of the night with a fully loaded seven-four-seven, so I put it on autopilot and go looking for her."

Rayford paused, disgusted with himself even now for how low he had sunk.

Mac looked at him. "Yeah?"

"Everybody remembers where they were when the disappearances happened."

"You're not saying . . ." Mac said.

"I was looking for a date when all those people disappeared."

"Man!"

Rayford snorted. "She wanted to know what was going on. Were we gonna die? I told her I was pretty sure we weren't going to die but that I had no more idea than she did what had happened. The truth was, I knew. Irene had been right. Christ had come to rapture his church, and we had all been left behind."

There was a lot more to Rayford's story, of course, but he just wanted that to sink in. Mac sat staring straight ahead. He would turn, take a breath, and then turn back and watch the scenery as they continued toward Al Basrah.

Mac checked his clipboard and stared at the dials. "We're close enough," he said. "I'm gonna see what I can find out." He set the frequency and depressed the mike button. "Golf Charlie Niner Niner to Al Basrah tower. Do you read?"

Static.

"Al Basrah tower, this is Golf Charlie Niner Niner. I'm switching to channel eleven, over." Mac made the switch and repeated the call.

"Al Basrah tower," came the reply. "Go ahead, Niner Niner."

"Albie around?"

"Stand by, niner."

Mac turned to Rayford. "Here's hoping," he said.

"Golf Charlie, this is Albie, over."

"Albie, you old son of a gun! Mac here! You're OK then?"

"Not totally, my friend. We just raised our temporary tower. Lost two hangars. I'm on crutches. Please, not to be bringing a fixed-wing plane. Not for two, three days."

"We're in a bird," Mac said.

"Welcome then," Albie said. "We need help. We need company."

"We can't stay long, Albie. Our ETA is thirty minutes."

"Roger that, Mac. We watch for you."

Rayford saw Mac bite his lip. "That's a relief," he whispered, his voice shaky. He monitored the controls, stashed his clipboard, and turned to Rayford. "Back to your story."

Rayford was intrigued that Mac cared so much for his friend. Had Rayford had a friend like that before he was a believer? Had he ever cared about another man enough to become emotional over his well-being?

Rayford looked at the devastation below. Tents had been erected where homes had disappeared in the quake. Bodies dotted the landscape, and expeditions of cheap trailers came to cart them off. Here and there bands of people with shovels and pickaxes worked on a paved road. If they saw what Rayford could see, they would know that even if they spent days on their tiny stretch of twisted pavement, the road for miles ahead would take months to fix, even with heavy equipment.

Rayford told Mac how he had landed at O'Hare after the disappearances, walked to the terminal, saw the devastating reports from around the world, lost his copilot to suicide, paid heavily for a ride home, and had his worst fears confirmed. "Irene and Raymie were gone. Chloe, a skeptic like me, was trying to get home from Stanford. It was my fault. She followed my example. And we had both been left behind."

Rayford remembered as if it were yesterday. He didn't mind telling the story because it came to a good end, but he hated this part. Not just the horror, not just the loneliness, but the blame. If Chloe had never come to Christ, he wasn't sure he could have forgiven himself.

He wondered about Mac. He would tell Mac what was going on, exactly who Nicolae Carpathia was, the whole package. He would tell him of the prophecies in Revelation, walk him through the judgments that had already come, show him how they had been foretold and could not be disputed. But if Mac was phony, if Mac worked for Carpathia, he would have already been brainwashed. He could fake this emotion, this interest. He could even insist he wanted to make a dangerous scuba dive with Rayford, just to stay on his good side.

But Rayford was already beyond the point of no return. Again he prayed silently that God might give him a sign whether Mac was sincere. If he wasn't, he was one of the better actors Rayford had seen. It was hard to trust anyone anymore.

When they finally came in sight of the airfield at Al Basrah, Mac coached Ray to a gentle, if lengthy, touchdown. As Ray shut down the engine, Mac said, "That's him. Coming down the ladder."

They scrambled out of the chopper as a tiny, dark-faced, long-nosed, turbaned man in bare feet gingerly made his way down from a tower that looked more like a guard station at a prison. He had tossed his crutches down, and when he reached the ground, he hopped to them and deftly used them to rush to Mac. They embraced.

"What happened to you?" Mac asked.

"I was in the mess hall," Albie said. "When the rumbles began, I knew immediately what it was. Foolishly, I raced for the tower. No one was there. We were not expecting traffic for a couple of hours. What I would do up there, I had no idea. The tower began falling before I even reached it. I was able to elude it, but a fuel truck was thrown into my path. I saw it at the last instant and tried to leap over the cab, which lay on its side. I almost reached the other side but twisted my ankle on the tire and scraped my shin on the lug nuts. But that is not the worst of it. I have broken bones in my foot. But there are no supplies to set it, and I am low on the priority list. It will grow strong. Allah will bless me."

Mac introduced Rayford. "I want to hear your stories," Albie said. "Where were you when it hit? Everything. I want to know everything. But first, if you have time, we could use help."

Heavy machinery was already grading a huge area, preparing it for asphalt. "Your boss, the potentate himself, has expressed pleasure at our cooperation. We are trying to get underway as soon as possible to help the global peacekeeping effort. What a tragedy to have thrown in our way after all he has accomplished."

Rayford said nothing.

Mac said, "Albie, we might be able to help later, but we need to eat."

"The mess hall is gone," Albie said. "As for your favorite place in town, I have not heard. Shall we check?"

"Do you have a vehicle?"

"That old pickup," Albie said. They followed as he crutched his way to it. "Clutching will be difficult," he said. "Do you mind?"

Mac slid behind the wheel. Albie sat in the middle, knees spread to keep from blocking the gearshift. The pickup rattled and lurched over unpaved roads until it arrived at the outskirts of the city. Rayford was sickened by the smell. He still found it hard to accept that this was part of God's ultimate plan. Did this many people have to suffer to make some eternal point? He took comfort in that this was not God's desired result. Rayford believed God was true to his word, that he had given people enough chances that he could now justify allowing this to get their attention.

Wailing men and women carried bodies over their shoulders or pushed them in wheelbarrows through the crowded streets. It seemed every other block had been left in pieces by the earthquake. Mac's favorite eatery was missing a concrete block wall, but the management had draped something over it and was open for business. One of few eating establishments still open, it was wall to wall with customers who ate while standing. Mac and Rayford shouldered their way in, drawing angry stares until the townspeople saw Albie. Then they made room, as much as they could, still pressed shoulder to shoulder.

Rayford had little faith in the sanitation of this food, but still he was grateful for it. After two bites of a rolled-up pastry stuffed with ground lamb and seasonings, he whispered to Mac, "I can see and I can smell and yet somehow, even here, hunger is the best seasoning."

On the way back, Mac pulled to the side of a dusty field and turned off the engine. "I wanted to know you were all right, Albie," he said. "But this is also a business mission."

"Splendid," Albie said. "How can I help?"

"Scuba gear," Mac said.

Albie furrowed his brow and pursed his lips. "Scuba," he said simply. "You need everything? Wet suit, mask, snorkel, tanks, fins?"

"All that, yes."

"Weights? Ballast? Lights?"

"I suppose."

"Cash?"

"Of course."

"I'll have to check," Albie said. "I have a source. I have not heard from him since the disaster. If the stuff is to be had, I can get it. Let's leave it this way: If you do not hear from me, return in one month and it will be here."

"I can't wait that long," Rayford said quickly.

"I cannot guarantee any sooner. Even that long seems very fast to me at a time like this." Rayford couldn't argue with that. "I thought this was for you, Mac," Albie added.

"We need two sets."

"Are you going to make a career of diving?"

"Hardly," Mac said. "Why? You think we should rent instead?"

"Could we?" Rayford said.

Albie and Mac looked at Rayford and burst into laughter. "No rental on the black market," Albie said.

Rayford had to grin at his own naiveté, but laughing seemed a distant pleasure.

Back at the airport Rayford and Mac each manned a shovel while a dump truck brought in a gravel base for the runway. Before they knew it, several hours had passed. They sent someone for Albie.

"Can you get a message to New Babylon?" Mac said.

"It will require a relay, but both Qar and Wasit have been on the air since this morning, so yes, is possible."

Mac wrote the instructions, asking that a dispatch go to Global Community radio base informing them that Steele and McCullum were engaged in a cooperative volunteer airport rebuilding project and would return by nightfall.

✢ ✢ ✢

It was nearly nine-thirty Tuesday morning, Central Standard Time, when Buck was jolted awake. The day was bright and sunny, yet he had slept soundly since that brief dream in the middle of the night. A constant sound had played at the edges of his consciousness. But for how long? As his eyes grew accustomed to the light, he realized the noise had been with him for some time.

It seemed to come from the backyard, from beyond the Range Rover. He padded to the window and opened it, pressing his cheek against the screen and looking as far that way as he could. Maybe it was emergency workers, and he and Tsion would have power sooner than they thought.

What was that smell? Had a catering truck pulled up for the workmen? He threw on some clothes. The light was on in the hallway. Had it not been a dream after all? He skipped down the stairs in his bare feet. "Tsion! We have power! What's happening?"

Tsion came from the kitchen with a skillet full of food and began scooping it onto a plate at the table. "Sit down, sit down, my friend. Are you not proud of me?"

"You found food!"

"I did more than that, Buck! I discovered a generator, and a big one!"

Buck bowed his head and said a brief prayer. "Did you eat, Tsion?"

"Yes, go ahead. I could not wait. I could not sleep in the middle of the night, so I tiptoed in and took your flashlight. I did not rouse you, did I?"

"No," Buck said, his mouth full. "But later I thought I dreamed I saw lights in the hallway."

"It was not a dream, Buck! I lugged that generator out of the cellar and into the backyard myself. It took me forever to fill it with gas and clean the spark plug and get it fired up. But as soon as I hooked it to the cable in the basement, lights came on, the refrigerator came on, everything started happening. I am sorry to have disturbed you. I tiptoed into my bedroom and knelt by my bed, just praising the Lord for our good fortune."

"I heard you."

"Forgive me."

"It was like music," Buck said. "And this food is like nectar."

"You need sustenance. You are going back to Loretta's. I will stay here and see if I can get on the Internet. If I cannot, I have much studying to do and messages to write so they will be ready to go to the faithful when I can get hooked up. Before you leave, however, you will help me get into Donny's briefcase, no?"

"You've decided that's OK, then?"

"Under other circumstances, no. But we have so few tools for survival now, Cameron. We must take advantage of anything that might be there."

Fortunately, Donny's well remained intact, and somehow, under a steaming shower a few minutes later, Buck's spirits were raised. What was it about creature comforts that made the day look brighter, despite the crisis? Buck knew he was in denial. Whenever he felt his realistic, practical, journalist side take over, he fought it. He wanted to think Chloe had somehow escaped death, but her car was still at the house. On the other hand, he hadn't found her body. Tons of debris still covered the place, and he had not been able to dig through much of it. Was he up to displacing every piece of trash from the foundation to prove to himself she was or wasn't there? He was willing. He simply hoped there was a better way.

On his way out of the house, Buck was intrigued that Tsion had not waited for him to get Donny's briefcase from the Rover. The rabbi had it on the table. He wore a shy, impish look. They were about to break into someone's personal belongings, and both had convinced themselves it was what Donny would have wanted. They were also prepared to close it back up and discard it if what they found was personal.

"There are all kinds of tools in the basement," Tsion said. "I could use some care and do this in such a way that it would not threaten the integrity of the structure."

"What!?" Buck said. "Threaten the integrity of the structure? You mean not hurt this cheap briefcase? How 'bout I just save you the time and effort?"

Buck turned the five-inch-deep plastic briefcase vertically and held it between his knees as he sat in a kitchen chair. He angled both knees left and drove the heel of his hand into the case, forcing it to fall between his ankles and land on one corner. That caused the latches to separate and the case to spring out of shape and fly open. His legs kept it from opening wide and spilling. With a feeling of accomplishment, he plopped it on the table and spun it around so Tsion could open it.

"This is what this young man has been lugging with him everywhere he goes?" Tsion said.

Buck leaned over to peek in. There, in neatly stacked rows, were dozens of small spiral notebooks, each not quite as large as a stenographer's notebook. They were labeled on the front with dates in block hand printing. Tsion grabbed a few and Buck took more. He fanned them in his hands and noticed that each contained approximately two months' worth of entries.

"This may be his personal diary," Buck said.

"Yes," Tsion said. "If so, we must not violate his confidence."

They looked at each other. Buck wondered which of them was going to look, to determine whether these were private notes that should be discarded or technical notes that might be of assistance to the Tribulation Force. Tsion raised his eyebrows and nodded to Buck. Buck opened one notebook to the middle. It read: "Talked to Bruce B. about underground necessities. He still seems reluctant about suggesting location. I don't need to know. I outlined specifications, electric, water, phone, ventilation, etc."

"That is not personal," Tsion said. "Let me study these today and see if there is anything we can use. I am amazed how he stacked them. I do not believe he could have fit another one in, and he used every bit of space."

"What's this?" Buck said, leafing to the back. "Look at these. He hand drew these schematics."

"That is my shelter!" Tsion exalted. "That is where I have been staying. So, *he* designed it."

"But it looks like Bruce never told him where he was building it."

Tsion pointed to a passage on the next page: "Putting a duplicate shelter in my backyard has proven more labor intensive than I expected. Sandy is getting a kick out of it. Bagging the dirt and storing it in her van takes her mind off our loss. She enjoys the clandestine nature of it. We take turns dumping it in various locations. Today we loaded so much that the back tires looked as if they might explode. It was the first time I had seen her smile in months."

Buck and Tsion looked at each other. "Is it possible?" Tsion said. "A shelter in his backyard?"

"How did we miss it?" Buck said. "We were digging out there last night."

They moved to the back door and gazed out on the lawn. A fence between Donny's home and the rubble next door had been ripped up and moved by the quake. "Maybe I parked over the entrance," Buck said.

He backed the Rover out of the way. "I see nothing here," Tsion said. "But the journal indicates this was more than a dream. They were moving dirt."

"I'll find some metal rods today," Buck said. "We can poke them through the grass and see if we can find this thing."

"Yes, you go. Finish up at Loretta's. I have much work today on the computer."

\+ \+ \+

The sun was setting in Iraq. "We'd better head back," Rayford said, breathing hard.

"What are they gonna do?" Mac said. "Fire us?"

"As long as he's got you around, Mac, he could follow through on his threat to put me in jail."

"That would be just like him, to think one man can fly that Condor halfway around the world and back. By the way, you ever wonder why he calls that thing the 216? The number on his office was 216 too, even though it was on the top floor of an eighteen-story building."

"Never thought about it," Rayford said. "I can't see a reason to care. Maybe he's got a fetish for that number."

As he and Mac trudged back toward the new tower with shovels over their shoulders, Albie hurried to them on his crutches. "I can't thank you enough for your help, gentlemen. You are true friends of Allah and Iraq. True friends of the Global Community."

"The Global Community might not appreciate hearing you honor Allah," Rayford said. "You are a loyalist, and yet you have not joined Enigma Babylon Faith?"

"On my mother's grave, I should never mock Allah with such blasphemy."

So, Rayford thought, *Christians and Jews are not the only holdouts against the new Pope Peter.*

Albie led them back to where they turned in their shovels. He spoke in hushed tones. "I am happy to inform you that I have already made some initial inquiries. I should have no trouble procuring your equipment."

"All of it?" Mac said.

"All of it."

"How much?" Mac said.

"I have taken the liberty of writing that down," Albie said.

He pulled a scrap of paper from his pocket and leaned on his crutches as he opened it in the fading light.

"Ho! Man!" Rayford said. "That's four times what I would pay for two scuba outfits."

Albie stuffed the paper back into his pocket. "It is exactly double retail. Not a penny more. If you do not want the merchandise, tell me now."

"That does look high," Mac said. "But you have never done me wrong. We will trust you."

"Need a deposit?" Rayford said, hoping to assuage the man's feelings.

"No," he said, eyes darting to Mac but not at Rayford. "You trust me, I'll trust you."

Rayford nodded.

Albie thrust out his bony hand and gripped Rayford's fiercely. "I will see you in thirty days then, unless you hear from me otherwise."

Mac took the controls for the flight back. "Got enough energy to finish your story, Ray?"

+ + +

Buck stopped at the ruins of New Hope Village Church on his way to Loretta's and strolled past the crater where the old woman's car rested twenty feet below.

Her body was there too, but he could not bring himself to look. If animals had gotten to her, he didn't want to know. He also avoided the spot where he had found Donny Moore. More movement of the earth had further entombed him.

He carefully climbed to where the underground shelter lay. Clearly, more debris had shifted. He slipped and nearly fell down the concrete stairs that led to the door. He wondered if anything salvageable could be dragged out. He could always come back. Buck headed for the Range Rover and brushed his fingers across his still swollen cheek. Why was it flesh wounds looked worse and felt more tender the second day?

Traffic dotted the area today. Any front-end loader, bulldozer, or dragline that had not sunk out of sight appeared to have been called into service. Buck couldn't park where he had the day before. Road crews rammed the uptwisted pavement in front of Loretta's house. Dump trucks were loaded with the huge chunks. Where they would take it and what they would do with it, Buck had no idea. All he knew was that there was nothing else for anyone to do but start rebuilding. He couldn't imagine this area ever looking like its old self again, but he knew it wouldn't be long before it was rebuilt.

Buck drove over a small pile of trash and parked next to one of the felled trees in Loretta's front yard. Workers ignored him as he slowly circled the house, wondering whether to continue picking through what was left of it.

A man with a clipboard studied the residue of the house next door. He shot pictures and took notes.

"Didn't think insurance would cover an act of God like this," Buck said.

"It wouldn't," the man said. "I'm not with an insurance company." He turned so Buck could see the ID tag clipped to his collar. It read, "Sunny Kuntz, Senior Field Supervisor, Global Community Relief."

Buck nodded. "What happens next?"

"We fax pictures and stats to headquarters. They send money. We rebuild."

"GC headquarters is still standing?"

"Nope. They're rebuilding too. Whoever's left there is in an underground shelter with pretty sophisticated technology."

"You can communicate with New Babylon?"

"Since this morning."

"My father-in-law works over there. You think I could get through?"

"You ought to be able to." Kuntz glanced at his watch. "It's not 9:00 p.m. there yet. I talked to somebody there about four hours ago. I wanted them to know we found at least one survivor from this area."

"You did? Who?"

"I'm not at liberty to share that information, Mr. —"

"Oh, sorry." Buck reached for his own ID, identifying himself as also a GC employee.

"Ah, press," Kuntz said. He peeled up two pages from his clipboard. "Name's Cavenaugh. Helen. Age seventy."

"She lived here?"

"That's right. Said she ran to the basement when she felt the place rattling. Never heard of an earthquake in this area before, so she thought it was a tornado. She was just flat lucky. Last place you want to be in an earthquake is where everything can fall on you."

"She survived though, huh?"

Kuntz pointed to the foundation about twenty feet east of Loretta's house. "See those two openings, one up here and the other in back?" Buck nodded. "That's one long room in the basement. First she ran to the front. When the whole house shifted and the glass blew in from that window, she ran to the other end. The glass was already out of that window, so she just planted herself in the corner and waited it out. If she had stayed up front, she'd have never made it. Wound up in the only corner of the house where she wouldn't have been killed."

"She told you this?"

"Yep."

"She didn't say whether she saw anybody next door, did she?"

"Matter of fact, she did."

Buck nearly lost his breath. "What'd she say?"

"Just that she saw a young woman running out of the house. Just before the window gave way on this end, the woman jumped in her car, but when the road started rising on her, she drove into the garage."

Buck trembled, desperate to stay calm until he got the whole story. "Then what?"

"Mrs. Cavenaugh said she had to move to the back because of that window, and when that house started to give way, she thought she saw the woman come out the side door of the garage and run through the backyard."

Buck lost all objectivity. "Sir, that was my wife. Any more details?"

"None I can remember."

"Where is this Mrs. Cavenaugh?"

"In a shelter about six miles due east. A furniture store somehow suffered very little damage. There's probably two hundred survivors in there, the least injured. It's more of a holding station than a hospital."

"Tell me exactly where this place is. I need to talk to her."

"OK, Mr. Williams, but I need to caution you not to get your hopes up about your wife."

"What are you talking about? I didn't have my hopes up until I found out she ran from this. My hopes were nowhere when I tried to dig through the mess. Don't tell me to not get my hopes up now."

"I'm sorry. I'm just trying to be realistic. I worked disaster relief for more than fifteen years before joining the GC task force. This is the worst I've ever seen, and I need to ask you if you've seen the escape route your wife might have taken, if Mrs. Cavenaugh was right and she ran through that backyard."

Buck followed Kuntz to the back. Kuntz swept the horizon with his arm. "Where would you go?" he asked. "Where would anybody go?"

Buck nodded somberly. He got the message. As far as he could see was nothing but piles, crevices, craters, fallen trees, and downed utility poles. There had certainly been no place to run.

7

"SO," MAC SAID, "your daughter was your real reason for finding out what happened to your wife and son."

"Right."

"Did you wonder about your motive?"

"You mean guilt? Maybe partly. But I *was* guilty, Mac. I had let down my daughter. I wasn't going to let that happen again."

"You couldn't force her to believe."

"No. And for a while I thought she wouldn't. She was tough, analytical, the way I had been."

"Well, Ray, we flyboys are all alike. We get off the ground because of aerodynamics. No magic, no miracles, nothing you can't see, feel, or hear."

"That was me all the way."

"So what happened? What made the difference?"

The sun dipped below the horizon, and from the helicopter, Rayford and Mac saw the yellow ball flatten and melt in the distance. Rayford was into his story, earnestly trying to persuade Mac of the truth. He was suddenly warm. Though the Iraqi desert cooled quickly after sundown, he had to shed his jacket.

"No closets here, Ray. I just lay mine behind the seat."

Once situated, Rayford continued. "Ironically, everything that convinced me of the truth I should have known in time to go with Irene when Christ came back. I had gone to church for years, and I had even heard the terms *Virgin Birth* and *atonement* and all that. But I never stopped to figure what they meant. I understood that one of the legends said Jesus was born to a woman who had never been with a man. I couldn't have told you whether I believed that or even thought it was important. It seemed like just a religious story and, I thought, explained why a lot of people thought sex was dirty."

Rayford told Mac of finding Irene's Bible, digging out the phone number of the church she loved so much, reaching Bruce Barnes, and seeing Pastor Billings's videotape prepared for those left behind.

"He had this whole thing figured out?" Mac said.

"Oh, yes. Just about anybody who was raptured knew it was coming. They didn't know when, but they looked forward to it. That tape really did it for me, Mac."

"I'd like a look at that."

"I might be able to track down a copy for you, if the church is still standing."

✣ ✣ ✣

Buck got directions to the makeshift shelter from Kuntz and hurried to the Range Rover. He tried calling Tsion and was frustrated to get a busy signal. But that was encouraging, too. It wasn't the normal buzz of a malfunctioning phone. It sounded like a true busy signal, as if Tsion's phone was engaged. Buck dialed Rayford's private number. If this worked, through cellular technology and solar power, they should have been able to connect with each other anywhere on Earth.

✣ ✣ ✣

The problem was, Rayford was not on Earth. The roar of the engine, the *thwock-thwock-thwock* of the blades, and the static in his headset made a cacophony of chaos. He and Mac heard the phone at the same time. Mac slapped his pocket and yanked out his phone. "Not mine," he said.

Rayford turned to fish his out of his folded jacket, but by the time he whipped off his headphones, flipped open the phone, and pressed it to his ear, he heard only that empty echo of an open connection. He couldn't imagine cellular towers close enough to relay a signal. He had to have gotten that ring off a satellite. He turned in his seat, angling the phone and its antenna to try to pick up a stronger signal.

"Hello? Rayford Steele here. Can you hear me? If you can, call me back! I'm in the air and can hear nothing. If you're family, call me within twenty seconds to make this phone ring again right away, even if we can't communicate. Otherwise, call me in about—" He looked to Mac.

"Ninety minutes."

"Ninety minutes from now. We should be on the ground and reachable. Hello?"

Nothing.

✣ ✣ ✣

Buck had heard Rayford's phone ringing. Then nothing but static. At least he had not gotten an unanswered ring. Another busy signal would have been encouraging. But what was this? A click, static, nothing understandable. He slapped his phone shut.

Buck knew the furniture store. It was on the way to the Edens Expressway. The drive normally took no more than ten minutes, but the terrain had changed. He had to drive miles out of the way to go around mountains of destruction. His landmarks were gone or flat. His favorite restaurant was identifiable only by its massive neon sign on the ground. About forty feet away, the roof peeked from a hole that swallowed the rest of the place. Rescue crews filed in and out of the hole, but they weren't hurrying. Apparently anyone they brought out of there was in a bag.

Buck dialed the Chicago bureau office of *Global Community Weekly*. No answer. He called headquarters in New York City. What had been a lavish area covering three floors of a skyscraper had been rebuilt in an abandoned warehouse following the bombing of New York. That attack had cost Buck the life of every friend he had ever made at the magazine.

After several rings, a harried voice answered. "We're closed. Unless this is an emergency, please let us leave the lines open."

"Buck Williams from Chicago," he said.

"Yes, Mr. Williams. You've gotten the word then?"

"I'm sorry?"

"You've not been in touch with anyone in the Chicago office?"

"Our phones just came back up. I got no answer."

"You won't. The building is gone. Almost every staff member is confirmed dead."

"Oh no."

"I'm sorry. A secretary and an intern survived and checked on the staff. They never reached you?"

"I was not reachable."

"It's a relief you're OK. You *are* OK?"

"I'm looking for my wife, but I'm all right, yes."

"The two survivors are cooperating with the *Tribune* and have a Web page already. Punch in any name, and whatever is known is flashed: dead, alive, being treated, or no known whereabouts. I'm the only one on the phones here. We've been decimated, Mr. Williams. You know we're printed on, what, ten or twelve different presses around the world—"

"Fourteen."

"Yes, well, as far as we know, one in Tennessee still has some printing capability and one in southeast Asia. Who knows how long it will be before we can go back to press?"

"How about the North American staff?"

"I'm online right now," she said. "We're about 50 percent confirmed dead and 40 percent unaccounted for. It's over, isn't it?"

"For the *Weekly*, you mean?"

"What else would I mean?"

"Mankind, I thought you were saying."

"It's pretty much over for mankind, too, wouldn't you say, Mr. Williams?"

"It looks bleak," Buck said. "But it's far from over. Maybe we can talk about that sometime." Buck heard phones ringing in the background.

"Maybe," she said. "I've got to get these."

After more than forty minutes of driving, Buck had to stop for a procession of emergency vehicles. A grader built a dirt mound over a fissure in a road that had otherwise escaped damage. No one could drive through until that mound was leveled off. Buck grabbed his laptop and plugged it into the cigarette lighter. He searched the Web for the *Global Community Weekly* information page. It was not working. He called up the *Tribune* page. He ran a people search and found the listing the secretary had told him about. A warning stipulated that no one could vouch for the authenticity of the information, given that many reports of the dead could not be corroborated for days.

Buck entered Chloe's name and was not surprised to find her in the "no known whereabouts" category. He found himself, Loretta, and even Donny Moore and his wife in the same category. He updated each entry, but he chose not to include his private phone number. Anyone needing that already had it. He entered Tsion's name. No one seemed to know where he was either.

Buck tapped in "Rayford Steele, Captain, Global Community Senior Administration." He held his breath until he saw: "Confirmed alive; Global Community temporary headquarters, New Babylon, Iraq."

Buck let his head fall back and breathed a quivering sigh. "Thank you, God," he whispered.

He straightened and checked the rearview mirror. Several cars were behind him, and he was fourth in line. It would be several more minutes. He entered "Amanda White Steele."

The computer ground on for a while and then noted with an asterisk, "Check domestic airlines, Pan-Continental, international."

He entered that. "Subject confirmed on Boston to New Babylon nonstop, reported crashed and submerged in Tigris River, no survivors."

Poor Rayford! Buck thought. Buck had never gotten to know Amanda as well as he'd wanted to, but he knew her to be a sweet person and a true gift to Rayford. Now he wanted all the more to reach his father-in-law.

Buck checked on Chaim Rosenzweig, who was confirmed alive and en route from Israel to New Babylon. *Good,* he thought. He listed his own father and brother, and they came up unaccounted for. No news, he decided, was good news for now.

He entered Hattie Durham's name. The name was not recognized. *Hattie can't be her real name. What is Hattie short for? Hilda? Hildegard? What else starts with an* H*? Harriet? That sounds as old as Hattie.* It worked.

He was again directed to the airlines, this time for a domestic flight. He found Hattie confirmed on a nonstop flight from Boston to Denver. "No report of arrival."

So, Buck thought, *if Amanda made her flight, she's gone. If Hattie made her flight, she* could *be gone. If Mrs. Cavenaugh was right, and she saw Chloe run from Loretta's house, Chloe might still be alive.*

Buck could not get his mind around the possibility that Chloe could be dead. He wouldn't allow himself to consider it until he had no other alternatives.

+ + +

"I have to admit, Mac, a lot of it was just plain logic," Rayford said. "Pastor Billings had been raptured. But he'd made that video first, and on it he talked about everything that had just happened, what we were going through, and what we were probably thinking about. He had me pegged. He knew I'd be scared, he knew I'd be grieving, he knew I'd be desperate and searching. And he showed from the Bible the prophecies that told of this. He reminded me I'd probably heard about it somewhere along the line. He even told of things to watch out for. Best of all, he answered my biggest question: Did I still have a chance?

"I didn't know a lot of people had questions about that very thing. Was the Rapture the end? If you missed out because you didn't believe, were you lost forever? I had never thought about it, but supposedly lots of preachers believed you couldn't become a believer after the Rapture. They used that to scare people into making their decisions in advance. I wish I'd heard that before because I might have believed."

Mac looked sharply at Rayford. "No you wouldn't. If you were going to believe before, you would have believed your wife."

"Probably. But I sure couldn't argue now. What other explanation was there? I was ready. I wanted to tell God that if there was one more chance, if the Rapture had been his last attempt to get my attention, it had worked."

"So then, what? You had to do something? Say something? Talk to a pastor, what?"

"On the tape, Billings walked through what he called the Bible's plan of salvation. That was a strange term to me. I'd heard it at some time or another, but not in our first church. And at New Hope I wasn't listening. I was sure listening now."

"So, what's the plan?"

"It's simple and straightforward, Mac." Rayford outlined from memory the basics about man's sin separating him from God and God's desire to welcome him back. "Everybody's a sinner," Rayford said. "I wasn't open to that before. But with everything my wife said coming true, I saw myself for what I was. There were worse people. A lot of people would say I was better than most, but next to God I felt worthless."

"That's one thing I don't have any problem with, Ray. You won't find me claiming to be anything but a scoundrel."

"And yet, see? Most people think you're a nice guy."

"I'm OK, I guess. But I know the real me."

"Pastor Billings pointed out that the Bible says, 'There is none righteous, no, not one' and that 'all we like sheep have gone astray,' and that 'all our righteousnesses are like filthy rags.' It didn't make me feel better to know I wasn't unique. I was just grateful there was some plan to reconnect me with God. When he explained how a holy God had to punish sin but didn't want any of the people he created to die, I finally started to see it. Jesus, the Son of God, the only man who ever lived without sin, died for everybody's sin. All we had to do was believe that, repent of our sins, receive the gift of salvation. We would be forgiven and what Billings referred to as 'reconciled' to God."

"So if I believe that, I'm in?" Mac said.

"You also have to believe that God raised Jesus from the dead. That provided the victory over sin and death, and it also proved Jesus was divine."

"I believe all that, Ray, so is that it? Am I in?"

Rayford's blood ran cold. What was troubling him? Whatever made him sure Amanda was alive was also making him wonder whether Mac was sincere. This was too easy. Mac had seen the turmoil of almost two years of the Tribulation already. But was that enough to persuade him?

He seemed sincere. But Rayford didn't really know him, didn't know his background. Mac could be a loyalist, a Carpathia plant. Rayford had already exposed himself to mortal danger if Mac was merely entrapping him. Silently he prayed again, "God, how will I know for sure?"

"Bruce Barnes, my first pastor, encouraged us to memorize Scripture. I don't know if I'll find my Bible again, but I remember lots of passages. One of the first I learned was Romans 10:9-10. It says, 'If you confess with your mouth the Lord Jesus and believe in your heart that God has raised Him from the dead, you will be saved. For with the heart one believes unto righteousness, and with the mouth confession is made unto salvation.'"

Mac stared ahead, as if concentrating on flying. He was suddenly less animated. He spoke more deliberately. Rayford didn't know what to make of it. "What does it mean to confess with your mouth?" Mac said.

"Just what it sounds like. You've got to say it. You've got to tell somebody. In fact, you're supposed to tell lots of people."

"You think Nicolae Carpathia is the Antichrist. Is there anything in the Bible about telling him?"

Rayford shook his head. "Not that I know of. Not too many people have to make that choice. Carpathia knows where I stand because he has ears everywhere. He knows my son-in-law is a believer, but Buck never told him. He thought it best to keep that to himself so he could be more effective." Rayford was either persuading Mac or burying himself, he wasn't sure which.

Mac was silent several minutes. Finally he sighed. "So how does it work? How did you know when you'd done whatever it was God wanted you to do?"

"Pastor Billings walked the viewers of that tape through a prayer. We were to tell God we knew we were sinners and that we needed his forgiveness. We were to tell him we believed Jesus died for our sins and God raised him from the dead. Then we were to accept his gift of salvation and thank him for it."

"Seems too easy."

"Believe me, it might have been easier if I had done it before. But this isn't what I call easy."

For another long stretch, Mac said nothing. Every time that happened, Rayford felt gloomier. Was he handing himself to the enemy? "Mac, this is something you can do on your own, or I could pray with you, or—"

"No. This is definitely something a person should do on his own. *You* were alone, weren't you?"

"I was," Rayford said.

Mac seemed nervous. Distracted. He didn't look at Rayford. Rayford didn't want to push, and yet he hadn't decided yet whether Mac was a live prospect or just playing him. If the former was true, he didn't want to let Mac off the hook by being too polite.

"So what do you think, Mac? What are you gonna do about this?"

Rayford's heart sank when Mac not only did not respond, but also looked the other way. Rayford wished he was clairvoyant. He would have liked to know whether he had come on too strong or had exposed Mac for the phony he was.

Mac took a deep breath and held it. Finally he exhaled and shook his head.

"Ray, I appreciate your telling me this. It's quite a story. Very impressive. I'm moved. I can see why you believe, and no doubt it works for you."

So that was it, Rayford thought. *Mac was going to blow it off by using the glad-it-works-for-you routine.*

"But it's personal and private, isn't it?" Mac continued. "I want to be careful not to pretend or rush into it in an emotional moment."

"I understand," Rayford said, desperately wishing he knew Mac's heart.

"So you won't take it personally if I sleep on this?"

"Not at all," Rayford said. "I hope there's no aftershock or attack that might get you killed before you are assured of heaven, but—"

"I have to think God knows how close I am and wouldn't allow that."

"I don't claim to know the mind of God," Rayford said. "Just let me say I wouldn't push my luck."

"Are you pressuring me?"

"Sorry. You're right. No one can be badgered into it."

Rayford feared he had offended Mac. That or Mac's attitude was a stalling technique. On the other hand, if Mac *was* a subversive, he wouldn't be above faking a salvation experience to ingratiate himself to Rayford. He wondered when he would ever be sure of Mac's credibility.

+ + +

When Buck finally reached the furniture store, he found jerry-built construction. No semblance of streets or roads existed, so emergency vehicles staked out their spots with no thought to conserving space or leaving paths open to the doors. Global Community peacekeeping emergency forces traipsed in and out with supplies as well as new patients.

Buck got in only because of the security clearance level on his Global Community identification tag. He asked for Mrs. Cavenaugh and was pointed to a row of a dozen wood-and-canvas cots lining a wall in one corner. They were so close no one could walk between them.

Buck smelled freshly cut wood and was surprised to see new two-by-fours nailed together for railings throughout. The rear of the building had sunk about three feet, causing the concrete floor to split in the middle. When he got to the crack, he had to hang on to the two-by-fours because the pitch was so steep. Wood blocks anchored to the floor kept the cots from sliding. Emergency personnel took tiny steps, shoulders back, to keep from tumbling forward.

Each cot had a strip of paper stapled to the foot end, with either a hand-printed or computer-generated name. When Buck walked through, most of the conscious patients rolled up on their elbows, as if to see if he was their loved one. They reclined again when they didn't recognize him.

The paper on the third cot from the wall read "Cavenaugh, Helen."

She was asleep. Men were on either side of her. One, who appeared homeless, sat with his back to the wall. He seemed to protect a paper bag full of clothes. He eyed Buck warily and pulled out a department store catalog, which he pretended to read with great interest.

On Helen Cavenaugh's other side was a thin young man who appeared in his early twenties. His eyes darted and he ran his hands through his hair. "I need a smoke," he said. "You got any cigarettes?"

Buck shook his head. The man rolled onto his side, pulled his knees up to his chest, and lay rocking. Buck would not have been surprised to find the man's thumb in his mouth.

Time was of the essence, but who knew what trauma Mrs. Cavenaugh was sleeping off? She had very nearly been killed, and she had no doubt seen the remains of her house when she was carted away. Buck grabbed a plastic chair and sat at the foot of her cot. He wouldn't wake her, but he would talk to her at the first sign of consciousness.

+ + +

Rayford wondered when he had become such a pessimist. And why hadn't it affected his bedrock belief that his wife was still alive? He didn't believe Carpathia's implication that she had been working for the Global Community. Or was that, too, just a story from Mac?

Since he had become a believer, Rayford had begun to look on the brighter side, in spite of the chaos. But now, a deep, dark sense of foreboding came over him as Mac landed, still silent. They secured the helicopter and completed postflight procedures. Before they passed security to enter the shelter, Mac said, "This is all complicated too, Captain, because you are my boss."

That had not seemed to affect anything else that day. They had flown more as buddies than as boss and subordinate. Rayford would have no trouble maintaining decorum, but it sounded as if Mac might.

Rayford wanted to leave their conversation concrete, but he didn't want to give Mac an ultimatum or tell him to report back. "I'll see you tomorrow," he said.

Mac nodded, but as they headed for their own quarters, a uniformed orderly approached. "Captain Steele and Officer McCullum? You are requested in the central command area." He handed each a card.

Rayford read silently, "My office, ASAP. Leonardo Fortunato." Since when had Leon begun using his entire first name?

"Wonder what Leon wants at this time of the night?"

Mac peeked at Rayford's card. "Leon? I've got a meeting with Carpathia." He showed Rayford his card.

Was that really a surprise to Mac, or was this all one big setup? He and Mac had not gotten into why Rayford and the rest of the Tribulation Force believed Carpathia fit the bill of the Antichrist. Still, Mac had enough information on Rayford to bury him. And, apparently, he had the right audience.

+ + +

Buck was fidgety. Mrs. Cavenaugh looked healthy, but she lay so still he was hardly able to detect the rise and fall of her chest. He was tempted to cross his legs and kick her cot in the process, but who knew how an old woman would respond to that? It might push her over the edge. Antsy, Buck dialed Tsion. He finally got through, and Buck gushed that he had reason to believe Chloe was alive.

"Wonderful, Cameron! I am doing well here, too. I have been able to get on the Net, and I have more reason than ever to get back to Israel."

"We'll have to talk about that," Buck said. "I still think it's too dangerous, and I don't know how we would get you there."

"Cameron, there is news all over the Internet that one of Carpathia's top priorities is rebuilding transportation networks."

Buck spoke louder than he needed to, hoping to rouse Mrs. Cavenaugh. "I'll be back as soon as I can, and I plan to have Chloe with me."

"I will pray," Tsion said.

Buck hit the speed dial for Rayford's phone.

+ + +

Rayford was amazed that Leon's office was only slightly smaller and every bit as exquisitely appointed as Nicolae's. Everything in the shelter was state-of-the-art, but the opulence began and ended in those two offices.

Fortunato had a glow. He shook Rayford's hand, bowed at the waist, motioned to a chair, then sat behind his desk. Rayford had always found him curious, a dark, swarthy man, short and stocky with black hair and dark eyes. He didn't unbutton his suit jacket when he sat, so it bowed comically at the chest, spoiling whatever formality he was trying to engender.

"Captain Steele," Fortunato began, but before he could say anything, Rayford's phone chirped. Fortunato raised a hand and let it fall, as if he couldn't believe Rayford would take a call at a time like this.

"Excuse me, Leon, but this could be family."

"You can't take calls in here," Leon said.

"Well, I'm going to," Rayford said. "I have no information about my daughter and son-in-law."

"I mean you're technically not able to receive phone calls in here," Leon said. All Rayford heard was static. "We're way underground and surrounded by concrete. Think, man."

Rayford knew the trunk lines from the center led to solar panels and satellite dishes on the surface. Of course his cell phone would not work here. Still, he was hopeful. Few people knew his number, and the ones who did he cared about most in the world.

"You have my full attention, Leon."

"Not willingly, I surmise." Rayford shrugged. "I have more than one reason for asking to see you," Leon said. Rayford wondered when these people slept. "We have information on your family, at least part of it."

"You do?" Rayford said, leaning forward. "What? Who? My daughter?"

"No, I'm sorry. Your daughter is unaccounted for. However, your son-in-law has been spotted in a Chicago suburb."

"Unharmed?"

"To the best of our knowledge."

"And what is the state of communications between here and there?"

Fortunato smiled condescendingly. "I believe those lines are open," he said, "but of course not from down here, unless you use our equipment."

Chalk one up for Fortunato, Rayford thought. "I'd like to call him as soon as possible to check on my daughter."

"Of course. Just a few more items. Salvage teams are working around the clock in the compound where you lived. In the unlikely event they are able to find anything of value, you should submit a detailed inventory. Anything of value not preidentified will be confiscated."

"That makes no sense," Rayford said.

"Nevertheless . . . ," Fortunato said dismissively.

"Anything else?" Rayford said, as if he wanted to leave.

"Yes," Fortunato said slowly. Rayford had the idea Fortunato was stalling to make him squirm before calling Buck. "One of His Excellency's most trusted international advisers has arrived from Israel. I'm sure you know of Dr. Chaim Rosenzweig."

"Of course," Rayford said. "But *His Excellency*? At first I thought you were referring to Mathews."

"Captain Steele, I have been meaning to talk to you about protocol. You inappropriately refer to me by my first name. Sometimes you even refer to the potentate by his first name. We are aware that you do not sympathize with the beliefs of Pontifex Maximus Peter; however, it is most disrespectful for you to refer to him by only his last name."

"And yet you are using a title that has for generations been limited to religious leaders and royalty for Carpath—uh, Nicolae Carpath—, Potentate Carpathia."

"Yes, and I believe the time has come to refer to him in that manner. The potentate has contributed more to world unity than anyone who ever lived. He is beloved by citizens of every kingdom. And now that he has demonstrated supernatural power, *Excellency* is hardly too lofty a title."

"Demonstrated these powers to whom?"

"He has asked me to share with you my own story."

"I have heard the story."

"From me?"

"From others."

"Then I won't bore you with the details, Captain Steele. Let me just say that regardless of the differences you and I have had, because of my experience I am eager to reconcile. When a man is literally brought back from death, his perspectives change. You will feel a new sense of respect from me, whether you deserve it or not. And it will be genuine."

"I can't wait. Now what was it about Rosen—?"

"Now, Captain Steele! That was sarcastic, and I was being sincere. And there you go again. It's *Dr.* Rosenzweig to you. The man is one of the leading botanists in history."

"OK, fine, Leon. I mean, Dr. Fortunato—"

"I am not a doctor! You should refer to me as Commander Fortunato."

"I'm not sure I'm going to be able to do that," Rayford said with a sigh. "When did you get that title?"

"Truth be known, my title has recently changed to Supreme Commander. It was bestowed upon me by His Excellency."

"This is all getting a little crazy," Rayford said. "Wasn't it more fun when you and I were just Rayford and Leon?"

Fortunato grimaced. "Apparently you are unable to take anything seriously."

"Well, I'm serious about whatever it is you have to tell me about Rosenzweig. Um, *Dr.* Rosenzweig."

8

WHILE HE WAITED for Mrs. Cavenaugh, Buck thought about heading to the Range Rover so he could look up Ken Ritz's number on his computer. If Ken could get him and Tsion to Israel, he was taking Chloe. He never wanted her out of his sight again.

He was about to step out when Mrs. Cavenaugh finally stirred. He didn't want to startle her. He just watched her. When her eyes opened, he smiled. She looked puzzled, then sat up and pointed at him.

"You were gone, young man. Weren't you?"

"Gone?"

"You and your wife. You lived with Loretta, didn't you?"

"Yes, ma'am."

"But you weren't there yesterday morning."

"No."

"And your wife. I saw her! Is she all right?"

"That's what I want to talk about, Mrs. Cavenaugh. Are you up to it?"

"Oh, I'm all right! I just have nowhere to stay. I got the dickens scared out of me, and I don't care to see the remains of my house, but I'm all right."

"Want to take a walk?"

"There's nothing I'd like more, but I'm not going anywhere with a man unless I know his name."

Buck apologized and introduced himself.

"I knew that," she said. "I never met you, but I saw you around and Loretta told me about you. I met your wife. Corky?"

"Chloe."

"Of course! I should remember because I liked that name so much. Well, come on, help me up."

Thumbsucker hadn't budged except to keep rocking. Homeless looked wary and held his bag tighter. Buck considered yanking one of their cots so he could get in and help Mrs. Cavenaugh off of hers. But he didn't want a scene. He just stood at the end of her cot and reached for her. As she stepped off the end of the flimsy thing, the other end went straight up. Buck saw it coming at him over her head. He blocked it with his hand and it slammed back down with such a thunderous resound that Homeless cried out and Thumbsucker jumped two feet. He split the canvas cot when he came back down. It slowly separated, and he dropped out of sight. Homeless lowered his face into his sack, and Buck couldn't tell if he was laughing or crying. Thumbsucker reappeared looking as if he thought Buck might have done that on purpose. Mrs. Cavenaugh, who missed it all, slipped her hand through Buck's elbow, and they walked to where they could talk with more privacy.

"I already told this to one young man with disaster relief or some such, but anyway I thought all the racket was a tornado. Who ever heard of an earthquake in the Midwest? You hear about a little rattling and shaking downstate once in a while, but an honest to goodness earthquake that knocks over buildings and kills people? I thought I was smart, but I was a fool. I ran to the basement. Of course, *ran* is relative. It just means I didn't go a step at a time, as usual. I went down those stairs like a little girl. The only pain now is in my knees.

"I went to the window to see if there was a funnel. It was bright and sunny, but the noise was getting louder and the house banged all around me, so I still figured I knew what it was. That's when I saw your wife."

"Where, exactly?"

"That window is too high for me to see out. All I could see was the sky and the trees. They were really moving. My late husband kept a stepladder down there. I climbed just high enough so I could see the ground. That's when your wife, Chloe, came running out. She was carrying something. Whatever it was was more important than putting something on her feet. She was barefoot."

"And she ran where?"

"To your car. It's stupid, but I hollered at her. She was holding her stuff in one arm and trying to unlock the car with the other, and I was yelling, 'You don't want to be outside, girl!' I was hoping she'd put that stuff down and get in the car quick enough to outrun the funnel, but she wasn't even looking up. She finally got it open and started the car, and that's when everything broke loose. I swear one of my basement walls actually moved. I've never seen anything like that in my life. That car started to move, and the biggest tree in Loretta's yard tore itself right from the ground, roots and all. It took half Loretta's yard with it and sounded like a bomb dropping in the street, right in front of her car.

"She backed up, and the tree on the other side of Loretta's yard started to give way. I was still yellin' at that girl like she could hear me inside the car. I was sure that second tree would land right on her. She jerked left, and the whole road twisted up right in front of her. If she had pulled onto that pavement a split second earlier, that street flipping up would have tipped her over. She must have been scared to death, one tree lying in front of her, one threatening to fall on her, and the street sticking straight up. She whipped around that first tree and raced right up the driveway into the garage. I was cheering for her. I hoped she'd have enough sense to get to the basement. I couldn't believe a tornado could do that much damage without me seeing it. When I heard everything crash to the floor like the whole house was coming apart—well, of course, it was—I finally got it into my thick head that this wasn't a tornado. When the other two trees in Loretta's yard came down, that window blew out, so I climbed down and ran to the other end of the basement.

"When my front room furniture crashed into where I'd just been, I stepped over the sump pump and pulled myself up on the concrete cutout to the window. I don't know what I was thinking. I was just hoping Chloe was where she could hear me. I screamed bloody murder out that window. She came out the side door white as a sheet, still barefooted and now empty-handed, and she went runnin' to the back as fast as she could go. That was the last I saw of her. The rest of my house fell in, and somehow the pipes deflected everything a little and left me a tiny space to wait until somebody found me."

"I'm glad you're all right."

"It was pretty exciting. I hope you find Chloe."

"Do you remember what she was wearing?"

"Sure. That off-white dress, a shift."

"Thank you, Mrs. Cavenaugh."

The old woman stared into the distance and shook her head slowly.

Chloe's still alive, Buck thought.

+ + +

"The first thing Dr. Rosenzweig asked about was your well-being, Captain Steele."

"I hardly know the man, Supreme Commander Fortunato," Rayford said, carefully enunciating.

"*Commander* is sufficient, Captain."

"You can call me Ray."

Now Fortunato was angry. "I could call you *Private*," he said.

"Oh, good one, Commander."

"You're not going to bait me, Captain. As I told you, I'm a new man."

"Brand-new," Rayford said, "if you really were dead yesterday and alive today."

"The truth is, Dr. Rosenzweig next asked after your son-in-law, daughter, and Tsion Ben-Judah."

Rayford froze. Rosenzweig couldn't have been that stupid. On the other hand, Buck always said Rosenzweig was enamored of Carpathia. He didn't know Carpathia was as much an enemy of Ben-Judah as the State of Israel was. Rayford maintained eye contact with the glaring Fortunato, who seemed to know he had Rayford on the ropes. Rayford prayed silently.

"I brought him up-to-date and told him your daughter was unaccounted for," Leon said. He let that hang in the air. Rayford did not respond. "And what did you wish us to tell him of Tsion Ben-Judah?"

"What did *I* wish?" Rayford said. "I have no knowledge of his whereabouts."

"Then why did Dr. Rosenzweig ask about him in the same breath with your daughter and son-in-law?"

"Why don't you ask him?"

"Because I'm asking you, Captain! You think we weren't aware that Cameron Williams aided and abetted his escape from the State of Israel?"

"Do you believe everything you hear?"

"We know that to be fact," Fortunato said.

"Then why do you need my input?"

"We want to know where Tsion Ben-Judah is. It is important to Dr. Rosenzweig that His Excellency come to Dr. Ben-Judah's aid."

Rayford had listened in when that request was brought to Carpathia. Nicolae had laughed it off, suggesting his people make it appear he tried to help while actually informing Ben-Judah's enemies where they could find him.

"If I knew the whereabouts of Tsion Ben-Judah," Rayford said, "I would not tell you. I would ask him if he wanted you to know."

Fortunato stood. Apparently the meeting was over. He walked Rayford to the door. "Captain Steele, your disloyalty has no future. I say again, you will find me most conciliatory. I would consider it a favor if you would not intimate to Dr. Rosenzweig that His Excellency is as eager to know the whereabouts of Dr. Ben-Judah as he is."

"Why would I do you a favor?"

Fortunato spread his hands and shook his head. "I rest my case," he said. "Nicolae, er, the poten—His Excellency has more patience than I. You would not be my pilot."

"That's correct, Supreme Commander. I will, however, be piloting this week when you pick up the rest of the Global Community boys."

"I assume you're referring to the other world leaders."

"And Peter Mathews."

"Pontifex Maximus, yes. But he's not actually GC."

"He has a lot of power," Rayford said.

"Yes, but more popular than diplomatic. He has no political authority."

"Whatever you say."

+ + +

Buck walked Mrs. Cavenaugh back to her bunk, but before helping her settle, he approached the woman in charge of that area. "Does she have to be between these wackos?"

"You can put her in any open cot," the woman said. "Just make sure her name sticker goes with her."

Buck guided Mrs. Cavenaugh to a cot near other people her age. On his way out he approached the supervisor again. "What is anyone doing about missing persons?"

"Ask Ernie," she said, pointing to a small, middle-aged man plotting something on a map on the wall. "He's with GC, and he's in charge of the transfer of patients between shelters."

Ernie proved formal and distracted. "Missing persons?" he repeated, not looking at Buck but still working on his map. "First off, most of them are going to wind up dead. There are so many, we don't know where to start."

Buck pulled a photo of Chloe from his wallet. "Start here," he said.

He finally had Ernie's attention. He studied the picture, turning it toward the battery-powered lights. "Wow," he said. "Your daughter?"

"She's twenty-two. To be her dad I'd have to be at least forty."

"So?"

"I'm thirty-two," he said, astounded at his vanity at a time like this. "This is my wife, and I was told she escaped from our house before the quake leveled it."

"Show me," Ernie said, turning toward his map. Buck pointed to Loretta's block. "Hmm. Not good. This was a worldwide quake, but GC has pinpointed several epicenters. That part of Mount Prospect was close to the epicenter for northern Illinois."

"So it's worse here?"

"It's not much better anywhere else, but this is pretty much the worst of it in this state." Ernie pointed to a mile stretch from behind Loretta's block in direct line with where they were. "Major devastation. She would not have been able to get through there."

"Where might she have gone?"

"Can't help you there. Tell you what I can do, though. I can blow her picture up and fax it to the other shelters. That's about it."

"I'd be grateful."

Ernie did the clerical work himself. Buck was impressed at how sharp the enlarged copy was. "We only got this machine working about an hour ago," Ernie said. "Obviously, it's cellular. You hear about the potentate's communications company?"

"No," Buck said, sighing. "But it wouldn't surprise me to know he's cornered the market."

"That's fair," Ernie said. "It's called Cellular-Solar, and the whole world will be linked again before you know it. GC headquarters calls it Cell-Sol for short."

Ernie wrote on the enlargement, "Missing Person: Chloe Irene Steele Williams. Age 22. 5' 7", 125. Blonde hair. Green eyes. No distinguishing marks or characteristics." He added his name and phone number.

"Tell me where I can reach you, Mr. Williams. You know not to get your hopes up."

"Too late, Ernie," Buck said, jotting his number. He thanked him again and turned to leave, then returned. "You say they call the potentate's communications network Cell-Sol?"

"Yeah. Short for—"

"Cellular-Solar, yeah." Buck left, shaking his head.

As he climbed into the Range Rover, he felt helpless. But he couldn't shake the feeling that Chloe was out there somewhere. He decided to drive back to Loretta's another way. No sense being out without looking for her. Always.

+ + +

It was late, and Rayford was tired. Carpathia's office door was shut, but light streamed beneath the door. He assumed Mac was still there. Curious as he was, Rayford wasn't confident Mac would honestly debrief him. For all he knew, Mac was spilling his guts about everything Rayford had said that day.

His top priority before sleep was to try to get through to Buck. At the communications command post he was told he had to have permission from a superior to use a secure outside line. Rayford was surprised. "Look up my level of clearance," he said.

"Sorry, sir. Those are my orders."

"How long will you be here?" Rayford asked.

"Another twenty minutes, sir."

Rayford was tempted to interrupt Carpathia's meeting with Mac. He knew Nicolae would give him permission to use the phone, and by barging in, he would show he was not afraid of His Excellency the Potentate meeting with his own subordinate. But he thought better of it when he saw Fortunato had turned the light off in his office and was locking his door.

Rayford walked briskly to him. Without a trace of sarcasm, he said, "Commander Fortunato, sir, a request."

"Certainly, Captain Steele."

"I need permission from a superior to use an outside line."

"And you're calling—?"

"My son-in-law in the States."

Fortunato backed up against the wall, spread his feet, and crossed his arms. "This is interesting, Captain Steele. Let me ask you, would the Leonardo Fortunato of last week have acceded to this request?"

"I don't know. Probably not."

"Would my permitting it, despite how cavalierly you treated me this evening, prove to you I have changed?"

"Well, it would show me something."

"Feel free to use the phone, Captain. Take all the time you need, and best wishes on finding everything OK at home."

"Thank you," Rayford said.

+ + +

Buck prayed for Chloe as he drove, imagining Chloe had found her way to safety and simply needed to hear from him. He called to give Tsion an update but didn't stay on the phone long. Tsion seemed down, distracted. Something was on his mind, but Buck didn't want to pursue it while trying to keep the phone open.

Buck flipped open his laptop and looked up Ken Ritz's number. A minute later Ritz's answering machine said, "I'm either flyin', eatin', sleepin', or on the other line. Leave a message."

Short beeps indicating messages Ritz already had waiting seemed to go forever. Buck grew impatient, not wanting to tie up his phone. Finally he heard the long beep. "Ken," he said. "Buck Williams. The two of us you flew out of Israel might need a return trip soon. Call me."

+ + +

Rayford couldn't believe Buck's phone was busy. He slammed the phone down and waited a few minutes before redialing. *Busy again!* Rayford smacked his hand on the table.

The young communications supervisor said, "We've got a gadget that will keep dialing that number and leave a message."

"I can tell him to call me here, and you'll wake me?"

"Unfortunately, no, sir. But you could ask that he call you at 0700 hours, when we open."

* * *

Buck wondered about Ritz's answering machine. How would anyone know if he had been killed in the earthquake? He lived alone, and that machine would just run until it filled.

Buck was about half an hour from Donny and Sandy Moore's house when his phone rang. "God, let it be Ernie," he pleaded.

"This is Buck."

"Buck, this is a recorded message from Rayford. I'm sorry I couldn't reach you. Please call me at the following number at seven o'clock in the morning my time. That's going to be 10:00 p.m., if you're in the Central Standard Time zone. Praying Chloe's all right. You and our friend, too, of course. I want to hear everything. I'm still looking for Amanda. I feel in my soul she's still alive. Call me."

Buck looked at his watch. Why couldn't he call Rayford right then? Buck was tempted to call Ernie, but he didn't want to bug him. He wended his way back to Tsion. As soon as he came into the house, Buck knew something was wrong. Tsion would not look him in the eye.

Buck said, "I didn't find any rods to poke in the backyard. Did you find the shelter?"

"Yes," Tsion said flatly. "It is a duplicate of where I lived at the church. You want to see it?"

"What's wrong, Tsion?"

"We need to talk. Did you want to see the shelter?"

"That can wait. I just want to know how you get to it."

"You will not believe how close we were last night when we were doing our unpleasant business. The door that appears to lead to a storage area actually opens into a larger door. Through that door is the shelter. Let us pray we never have to use it."

"Here's thanking God it's there if we *do* need it," Buck said. "Now, what's up? We've been through too much for you to keep anything from me."

"I am not keeping it from you for my sake," Tsion said. "I would not want to hear if I were you."

Buck slumped in a chair. "Tsion! Tell me you didn't get word about Chloe!"

"No, no. I am sorry, Cameron. It is not that. I am still praying for the best there. It is just that for all the treasures in Donny's briefcase, the journals also led me where I wish I had not gone."

Tsion sat too, and he looked as bad as he had when his family had been massacred. Buck laid a hand on the rabbi's forearm. "Tsion, what is it?"

Tsion stood and looked out the window over the sink, then turned to face Buck. With his hands deep in his pockets, he moved to the doors that separated the kitchen from the breakfast nook. Buck hoped he wouldn't open them. He didn't need to be reminded of cutting Sandy Moore's body from under the tree. Tsion opened the door and walked to the edge of the cutout.

Buck was struck by the weirdness of where he was and what he was looking at. How had it come to this? He had been Ivy League educated, New York headquartered, at the top of his profession. Now here he sat in a tiny duplex in a Chicago suburb, having moved into the home of a dead couple he barely knew. In less than two years he had seen millions disappear from all over the globe, become a believer in Christ, met and worked for the Antichrist, fallen in love and married, befriended a great biblical scholar, and survived an earthquake.

Tsion slid the door shut and trudged back. He sat wearily, elbows on the table, his troubled face in his hands. Finally, he spoke. "It should come as no surprise, Cameron, that Donny Moore was a genius. I was intrigued by his journals. I have not had time to get through all of them, but after discovering his shelter, I went in to see it. Impressive. I spent a couple of hours putting the finishing touches on one of Bruce Barnes's studies that was quite ingenious. I added some linguistics that I humbly believe added some insight, and then I tried to connect to the Internet. You will be happy to know I was successful."

"You kept your own e-mail address invisible, I hope."

"You have taught me well. I posted the teaching on a central bulletin board. My hope and prayer is that many of the 144,000 witnesses will see it and benefit from it and respond to it. I'll check tomorrow. Much bad teaching is going out on the Net, Cameron. I am jealous that believers not be swayed."

Buck nodded.

"But I digress," Tsion said. "Finished with my work, I went back to Donny's journals and started from the beginning. I am only about a quarter of the way through. I want to finish, but I am heartsick."

"Why?"

"First let me say that Donny was a true believer. He wrote eloquently of his remorse over missing his first chance to receive Christ. He told of the loss of their baby and how his wife eventually also found God. It is a very sad, poignant account of how they found some joy in anticipation of being reunited with their child. Praise the Lord that has now been realized." Tsion's voice began to quaver. "But, Cameron, I came upon some information I wish I had not discovered. Maybe I should have known it was to be avoided. Donny taught Bruce to encrypt personal messages to make anything he wished inaccessible without his own password. As you recall, no one knew that password. Not Loretta; not even Donny."

"That's right," Buck said. "I asked him."

"Donny must have been protecting Bruce's privacy when he told you that."

"Donny knew Bruce's password? We could have used that. There was a whole gigabyte or so of information we were never able to access off Bruce's computer."

"It was not that Donny knew the password," Tsion said, "but he developed his own code-breaking software. He loaded it onto all the computers he sold you. As you know, during my time in the shelter, I downloaded to my computer—which has astounding storage capacity—everything that had been on Bruce's. We also had those thousands and thousands of pages of printouts, helpful for when my eyes grew tired of peering at the screen. However, it simply seemed to make sense to also make an electronic backup for that material."

"You weren't the only one who did that," Buck said. "I think that stuff is on Chloe's computer and maybe Amanda's."

"We did not, however, leave anything out. Even encrypted files were copied because we didn't want to slow the process by being selective. But we never had access to those."

Buck stared at the ceiling. "Until now, right? That's what you're telling me?"

"Sadly, yes," Tsion said.

Buck stood. "If you're about to tell me something that will affect my esteem for Bruce and his memory, be careful. He is the man who led me to Christ and who helped me grow and—"

"Put your mind at ease, Cameron. My esteem for Pastor Barnes was only elevated by what I found. I found the encryption-solving files on my own computer. I applied these to Bruce's files, and within a few minutes, everything encrypted glowed from my screen.

"The files were not locked. I confess I took a peek and noticed many that were merely personal. Mostly memories of his wife and family. He wrote of his remorse over losing them, not being with them, that sort of thing. I felt guilty and did not read everything there. It must have been my old nature that attracted me to other private files.

"Cameron, I confess this excited me to no end. I believed I had found more riches from his personal study, but what I found I thought better to not risk printing. It is on my computer in my bedroom. Painful as it will be, you must see it."

Nothing would have kept Buck from it. But he mounted the stairs with the same reluctance he had felt digging through the rubble at Loretta's. Tsion followed Buck into the bedroom and sat on the edge of the high, squeaky bed. A plastic folding chair sat in front of the dresser, on which Tsion's laptop rested. The screen saver bore the message "I Know That My Redeemer Liveth."

Buck sat and brushed the touchpad with his finger. The date of the file indicated it had been in Bruce's computer since two weeks after he had officiated the double wedding of Buck and Chloe and Rayford and Amanda.

Buck spoke into the computer's microphone. "Open document."

The screen read:

Personal prayer journal. 6:35 a.m.: My question this morning, Father, is what would you have me do with this information? I don't know it to be true, but I cannot ignore it. I feel heavily my responsibility as shepherd and mentor to the Tribulation Force. If an interloper has compromised us, I must confront the issue.

Is it possible? Could it be true? I don't claim special powers of discernment; however, I loved this woman and trusted her and believed in her from the day I met her. I thought her perfect for Rayford, and she seemed so spiritually attuned.

Buck stood, his seat hitting the back of the chair and knocking it to the floor. He bent over the laptop, palms on the dresser. *Not Amanda!* he thought. *Please! What damage might she have done?*

Bruce's journal continued: "They are planning a visit soon. Buck and Chloe will come from New York and Rayford and Amanda from Washington. I will be returning from an international trip. I will have to get Rayford alone and show him what has come to me. In the meantime, I feel impotent, given their proximity to NC. Lord, I need wisdom."

Buck's heart raced and he panted. "So where's the file in question?" he said. "What did he receive and from whom?"

"It's attached to the previous day's journal entry," Tsion said.

"Whatever it is, I'm not going to believe it."

"I feel the same, Cameron. I feel it deep in my heart. And yet, here we are, despairing."

Buck said, "Previous entry. Open document."

That day's entry: "God, I feel like David when you refused to respond to him. He pleaded with you not to turn away from him. That is my plea today. I feel so desolate. What am I to make of this?"

"Open attached," Buck said.

The message had been sent from Europe. It was to Bruce, but his last name had been misspelled *Barns*. The sender was "an interested friend."

"Scroll down," Buck said, sick to his stomach. As the computer responded, the phone rang in his pocket.

9

HE FLIPPED HIS PHONE OPEN. "This is Buck."

"I'm trying to reach Cameron Williams of *Global Weekly Magazine*."

"Speaking."

"Lieutenant Ernest Kivisto here. Met you earlier today."

"Yes, Ernie! What have you got?"

"First off, headquarters is looking for you."

"Headquarters?"

"The big man. Or at least somebody close to him. I thought I'd widen the search for your wife, so I faxed that sheet to surrounding states. You never know. If she was hurt or got evacuated, she could be anywhere. Anyway, somebody recognized the name. Then a guy named Kuntz said he'd seen you earlier too. Somehow your whereabouts gets into the database and we get word headquarters is looking for you."

"Thanks. I'll check in."

"I know you don't report to me, and I have no jurisdiction, but since I'm the last one who saw you, I'm gonna have to answer for it if you don't check in."

"I said I would check in."

"I'm not naggin' ya or anything. I'm just saying—"

Buck was tired of military types covering their own tails. But this was a man he wanted to get back to him as soon as possible if Chloe turned up. "Ernie, I appreciate all you're doing for me, and you may rest assured that I will not only check in with headquarters, but I will also mention that I got the word from you. You want to spell that last name for me?"

Kivisto did. "Now for the good news, sir. One of the Cell-Sol guys got the fax in his truck. He wasn't happy about me broadcasting it everywhere. He said I shouldn't be tying up the whole GC network for a missing person's bulletin. Anyway, he said they saw a young woman who might fit that description being lifted into one of those Ambu-Vans late yesterday."

"Where?"

"I'm not sure exactly where, but for sure it was between that block you pointed out to me and where I am now."

"That's a pretty big area, Ernie. Can we narrow that at all?"

"Sorry, I wish I could."

"Can I talk to this guy?"

"I doubt it. He said something about having been awake since the earthquake. I think he's bedding down in one of the shelters."

"I didn't see any Ambu-Vans at your shelter."

"We're taking in only the ambulatory."

"This woman wasn't?"

"Apparently not. If she had serious ailments, she would have been taken to, just a minute here . . . Kenosha. A couple of hotels right next to each other just inside the city limits have been turned into hospitals."

Ernie gave Buck the number for the medical center in Kenosha. Buck thanked him and asked, "In case I have trouble getting through, what are the odds I can drive to Kenosha?"

"Got a four-wheel drive?"

"Yeah."

"You're gonna need it. I-94 lost every overpass between here and Madison. There's a couple places you can get on, but then before you get to the next overpass you have to go through single-lane roads, little towns, or just open fields and hope for the best. Thousands are trying it. It's a mess."

"I don't have a helicopter, so I have no choice."

"Call first. No sense trying a trip like that for nothing."

Buck couldn't help feeling as if Chloe were within reach. It bothered him that she might be hurt, but at least she was alive. What would she think about Amanda?

Buck scrolled back down through Bruce's journal entry and found the e-mail Bruce had received. The message, from the "interested friend" read: "Suspect the root beer lady. Investigate her maiden name and beware the eyes and ears of New Babylon. Special forces are only as strong as their weakest links. Insurrection begins in the home. Battles are lost in the field, but wars are lost from within."

Buck turned to face Tsion. "What did you deduce from that?"

"Someone was warning Bruce about somebody within the Tribulation Force. We have only two women. The one with a maiden name Bruce might not know would have been Amanda. I still do not know why he or she referred to her as the root beer lady."

"Her initials."

"A. W.," Tsion said, as if to himself as he righted Buck's chair. "I do not follow."

"A&W is an old brand of root beer in this country," Buck said. "How is she supposed to be the ears and eyes of, what, Carpathia? Is that what we're supposed to get out of New Babylon?"

"It is all in the maiden name," Tsion said. "I was going to look it up, but you will see Bruce has already done the work. Amanda's maiden name was Recus, which meant nothing to Bruce and stalled him for a while."

"It means nothing to me either," Buck said.

"Bruce dug deeper. Apparently, Amanda's mother's maiden name, before she married Recus, was Fortunato."

Buck blanched and dropped into the chair again.

"Bruce must have had the same reaction," Tsion said. "He writes in there, 'Please God, don't let it be true.' What is the significance of that name?"

Buck sighed. "Nicolae Carpathia's right-hand man, a total sycophant, is named Leonardo Fortunato."

Buck turned back to Tsion's computer. "Close files. Re-encrypt. Open search engine. Find *Chicago Tribune*. Open name search. Ken or Kenneth Ritz, Illinois, U.S.A."

"Our pilot!" Tsion said. "You are going to get me home after all!"

"I only want to see if the guy's still alive, just in case."

Ritz was listed "among patients in stable condition, Arthur Young Memorial Hospital, Palatine, Illinois."

"How come all the good news is about someone else?"

Buck dialed the number Ernie had given him for Kenosha. It was busy. Again and again for fifteen minutes. "We can keep trying while we're on the road."

"The road?" Tsion said.

"In a manner of speaking," Buck said. He looked at his watch. It was after seven in the evening, Tuesday.

Two hours later, he and Tsion were still in Illinois. The Rover bounced slowly along with hundreds of other cars snaking their way north. Just as many were coming the other way, fifty to a hundred feet from where I-94 once propelled cars at eighty-plus miles an hour in both directions.

While Buck looked for alternate routes or some way to pass poky vehicles, Tsion manned the phone. They powered it from the cigarette lighter to save the battery, and every minute or so Tsion hit the redial button. Either the phone in Kenosha was hopelessly overloaded or it was not working.

+ + +

For the second day in a row, his first officer, Mac McCullum, awakened Rayford. A tick past 6:30 Wednesday morning in New Babylon, Rayford heard soft but insistent knocking. He sat up, tangled in sheet and blankets. "Gimme a minute," he slurred, realizing this might be news of his call from Buck. He opened the door, saw it was Mac, and collapsed back into bed. "I'm not ready to wake up yet. What's up?"

Mac flipped the light on, making Rayford hide his face in the pillow. "I did it, Cap. I did it!"

"Did what?" Rayford said, his voice muffled.

"I prayed. I did it."

Rayford turned over, covering his left eye and peeking at Mac through a slit in his right. "Really?"

"I'm a believer, man. Can you believe it?"

Keeping his eyes shielded, Rayford reached with his free hand to shake Mac's. Mac sat on the edge of Rayford's bed. "Man, this feels great!" he said. "Just a while ago I woke up and decided to quit thinking about it and do it."

Rayford sat up with his back to Mac and rubbed his eyes. He ran his hands through his hair and felt his bangs brush his eyebrows. Few people ever saw him that way.

What was he to make of this? He hadn't even debriefed Mac on his meeting with Carpathia from the night before. How he wished it were true. What if it was all a big act, a plot to reel him in and incapacitate him? Surely that had to be Carpathia's long-range plan—to take at least one member of the opposition out of action.

All he could do until he knew for sure was to take this at face value. If Mac could fake a conversion and the emotion that went along with it, Rayford could fake being thrilled. His eyes finally adjusted to the light, and he turned to face Mac. The usually dapper first officer was wearing his uniform as usual. Rayford had never seen him casual. But what was that? "Did you shower this morning, Mac?"

"Always. What do you mean?"

"You've got a smudge on your forehead."

Mac swiped with his fingers just below the hairline.

"Still there," Rayford said. "Looks like what Catholics used to get on Ash Wednesday."

Mac stood and moved to the mirror attached to Rayford's wall. He leaned close, turning this way and that. "What the heck are you talking about, Ray? I don't see a thing."

"Maybe it was a shadow," Rayford said.

"I've got freckles, you know."

When Mac turned around, Rayford saw it again, plain as day. He felt foolish, making such a big deal of it, but he knew Mac was fastidious about his appearance. "You don't see that?" Rayford said, standing, grabbing Mac by the shoulders, and turning him back to face the mirror.

Mac looked again and shook his head.

Rayford pushed him closer and leaned in so their faces were side by side. "Right there!" he said, pointing at the mirror. Mac still had a blank stare. Rayford turned Mac's face toward him, put a finger directly on his forehead, and turned him back toward the mirror. "Right there. That charcoal-looking smudge about the size of a thumbprint."

Mac's shoulders slumped and he shook his head. "Either you're seeing things, or I'm blind," he said.

"Wait just a doggone minute," Rayford said slowly. Chills ran up his spine. "Let me look at that again."

Mac looked uncomfortable with Rayford staring at him, their noses inches apart. "What are you looking for?"

"Shh!"

Rayford held Mac by the shoulders. "Mac?" he said solemnly. "You know those 3-D images that look like a complicated pattern until you stare at it—"

"Yeah, and you can make out some sort of a picture."

"Yes! There it is! I can see it!"

"What?!"

"It's a cross! Oh, my word! It's a cross, Mac!"

Mac wrenched away and looked in the mirror again. He leaned to within inches of the glass and held his hair back from his forehead. "Why can't I see it?"

Rayford leaned into the mirror and held his own hair away from his forehead. "Wait! Do I have one too? Nope, I don't see one."

Mac paled. "You do!" he said. "Let me look at that."

Rayford could barely breathe as Mac stared. "Unbelievable!" Mac said. "It *is* a cross. I can see yours and you can see mine, but we can't see our own."

\+ + +

Buck's neck and shoulders were stiff and sore. "I don't suppose you've driven a vehicle like this one, Tsion," he said.

"No, brother, but I am willing."

"No, I'm all right." He glanced at his watch. "Less than a half hour before I'm supposed to call Rayford."

The caravan to nowhere finally crossed into Wisconsin, and the traffic weaved west of the expressway. Thousands began to blaze new trails. Thirty to thirty-five miles an hour was top speed, but there were always nuts in all-terrain vehicles who took advantage of the fact that there were no rules anymore. When Buck got inside the city limits of Kenosha, he asked a member of the Global Community Peacekeeping Force for directions.

"You're gonna go east about five miles," the young woman said. "And it's not gonna look like a hospital. It's two—"

"Hotels, yeah, I heard."

Traffic into Kenosha was lighter than that heading north, but that soon changed too. Buck could not get within a mile of the hospital. GC forces detoured vehicles until it became obvious that anyone getting to those hotels had to do it on foot. Buck parked the Range Rover, and they set off toward the east.

By the time their destination came into view, it was time to call Rayford.

\+ + +

"Mac," Rayford said, fighting tears, "I can hardly believe this. I prayed for a sign, and God answered. I needed a sign. How can I know who to trust these days?"

"I wondered," Mac said. "I was hungry for God and knew you had what I needed, but I was afraid you would be suspicious."

"I was, but I had already said way too much if you were working against me for Carpathia."

Mac was gazing into the mirror and Rayford was dressing when he heard a brief knock and the door flew open. A young assistant from the communications center said, "Excuse me, sirs, but whichever one of you is Captain Steele has a phone call."

"Be right there," Rayford said. "By the way, have I got a smudge on my forehead right here?"

The young man looked. "No sir. Don't think so."

Rayford caught Mac's eye. Then he tucked in his undershirt and slid off down the hall in his stocking feet. Somebody like Fortunato—or worse, Carpathia—could court-martial him for appearing in front of subordinates half dressed. He knew he couldn't be in the employ of the Antichrist much longer anyway.

\+ + +

Buck stood silently in the Wisconsin wasteland with the phone pressed to his ear. When Rayford finally came on, he said quickly, "Buck, just answer yes or no. Are you there?"

"Yes."

"This is not a secure phone, so tell me how everyone is without using names, please."

"I'm fine," Buck said. "Mentor is safe and OK. She escaped, we believe. Close to reconnecting now."

"Others?"

"Secretary is gone. Computer techie and wife are gone."

"That hurts."

"I know. You?"

"They tell me Amanda went down with a Pan-Con flight into the Tigris," Rayford said.

"She's listed on the manifest, if you can believe what's on the Internet, but you're not buying it?"

"Not until I see her with my own eyes."

"I understand. Boy, it's good to hear your voice."

"Yours too. Your own family?"

"Unaccounted for, but that's true of most everyone."

"How are the buildings?"

"Both gone."

"You have accommodations?" Rayford asked.

"I'm fine. Keeping a low profile."

They agreed to e-mail each other and disconnected. Buck turned to Tsion. "She couldn't be a double-crosser. He's too perceptive, too aware."

"He could have been blinded by love," Tsion said. Buck looked sharply at him. "Cameron, I no more want to believe this than you do. But it appears Bruce strongly suspected."

Buck shook his head. "You'd better stay out here in the shadows, Tsion."

"Why? I'm the least of anyone's worries here, now."

"Maybe, but GC communications makes this a small world. They know I'm bound to show up sooner or later if Chloe is here. If they're still looking for you and Verna Zee broke our agreement and ratted on me to Carpathia, they might expect to find you with me."

"You have a creative mind, Buck. Paranoid too."

"Maybe. But let's not take chances. If I'm being followed when I come out, hopefully with Chloe, keep your distance. I'll pick you up about two hundred yards west of where I'm parked."

Buck walked into chaos. Not only was the place a madhouse of equipment and patients and officials competing to prove who had authority, but there was also a lot of yelling. Things had to happen fast, and no one had time for cordiality.

It took Buck a long time to get the attention of a woman at the front desk. She appeared to be doing the work of reception and admittance and also a bit of triage. After getting out of the way of two stretchers, each bearing a bloody body Buck bet was dead, he pushed up to the counter. "Excuse me, ma'am, I'm looking for this woman." He held up a copy of the fax Ernie had broadcast.

"If she looks like that, she wouldn't be here," the woman barked. "Does she have a name?"

"The name's on the picture," Buck said. "You need me to read it to you?"

"What I don't need is your sarcasm, pal. As a matter of fact, I *do* need you to read it to me."

Buck did.

"I don't recognize the name, but I've processed hundreds today."

"How many without names?"

"About a quarter. We found most of these people in or under their homes, so we cross-checked addresses. Anybody away from home mostly carried ID."

"Let's say she was away from home but had no ID, and she's not in a position to tell you who she is?"

"Then your guess is as good as mine. We don't have a special ward for unidentifieds."

"Mind if I look around?"

"What are you gonna do, check every patient?"

"If I have to."

"Not unless you're a GC employee and—"

"I am," Buck said, flashing his ID.

"—make sure you stay out of the way."

Buck traipsed through the first hotel, pausing at any bed that had a patient with no name card. He ignored several huge bodies and didn't waste time on people with gray or white hair. If anyone looked small or thin or feminine enough to be Chloe, he took a good look.

He was on his way to the second hotel when a tall black man backed out of a room, locking the door. Buck nodded and kept moving, but the man apparently noticed his fax. "Looking for someone?"

"My wife." Buck held up the page.

"Haven't seen her, but you might want to check in here."

"More patients?"

"This is our morgue, sir. You don't have to if you don't want to, but I've got the key."

Buck pursed his lips. "Guess I'd better."

Buck stepped behind the man as he unlocked the door. When he pushed, however, the door stuck a bit and Buck bumped into him. Buck apologized, and the man turned and said, "No prob—"

He stopped and stared at Buck's face. "Are you all right, sir? I'm a doctor."

"Oh, the cheek's all right. I just fell. It looks OK, doesn't it?"

The doctor cocked his head to look more closely. "Oh, that looks superficial. I thought I noticed a bruise on your forehead, just under the hairline."

"Nope. Didn't get banged there, far as I know."

"Bumps there can cause subcutaneous bleeding. It's not dangerous, but you could look like a raccoon in a day or two. Mind if I take a peek?"

Buck shrugged. "I'm in kind of a hurry. But go ahead."

The doctor grabbed a fresh pair of rubber gloves from a box in his pocket and pulled them on.

"Oh, please don't make a big production of it," Buck said. "I don't have any diseases or anything."

"That may be," the doctor said, pushing Buck's hair out of the way. "I can't claim the same for all the bodies I deal with." They were in a huge room, nearly every foot of the floor covered with sheeted corpses.

"You *do* have a mark there," the doctor said. He pushed on it and around it. "No pain?"

"No."

"You know," Buck said, "you've got something on your forehead too. Looks like a smudge."

The doctor swiped his forehead with his sleeve. "May have picked up some newsprint."

The doctor showed Buck how to pull back the shroud at the head of each body. He would have a clear view of the face and could simply let the material drop again. "Ignore this row. It's all men."

Buck jumped when the first body proved that of an elderly woman with bared teeth, eyes open and scared.

"I'm sorry, sir," the doctor said. "I have not manipulated the bodies. Some appear asleep. Others look like that. Sorry to startle you."

Buck grew more cautious and breathed a prayer of desperation before each unveiling. He was horrified at the parade of death but grateful each time he did not find Chloe. When he finished, Buck thanked the doctor and headed for the door. The doctor looked at him curiously and apologetically reached for Buck's "smudge" once more, rubbing it lightly with his thumb, as if he could wash it away. He shrugged. "Sorry."

Buck opened the door. "Yours is still there too, Doc."

In the first room of the other hotel, Buck saw two middle-aged women who looked as if they'd been through a war. On his way out he caught a glimpse of himself in a mirror. He held his hair away from his forehead. He saw nothing.

Buck waited so long for an elevator that he almost gave up and took the stairs. But when a car finally had room for him, he stood there with the picture of Chloe dangling from his fingers. A heavyset, older doctor stepped on at the third floor and stared. Buck raised the picture to eye level. "May I?" the doctor asked, reaching for it. "She belong to you?"

"My wife."

"I saw her."

Buck felt a lump in his throat. "Where is she?"

"Don't you mean *how* is she?"

"Is she all right?"

"When last I saw her, she was alive. Step off on four so we can talk."

Buck tried to withhold his excitement. She was alive, that was all that mattered. He followed the doctor off the elevator, and the big man motioned him to a corner. "I advised she needed surgery, but we're not operating here. If they followed my advice, they scheduled her for Milwaukee or Madison or Minneapolis."

"What was wrong with her?"

"At first I thought she had been run over. Her right side was pretty banged up from her ankle to her head. She had what appeared to be chunks of asphalt embedded into that side of her body, and she had broken bones and possibly a fractured skull, totally on that side. But for her to be run over on asphalt, she would have had to have damage on her other side. And there was nothing there but a slight abrasion on her hip."

"Is she going to live?"

"I don't know. We couldn't do X-rays or MRIs here. I have no idea about the extent of damage to bones or to internal organs. I did, however, finally come to some hypothesis of what might have happened to her. I believe she was struck by a section of roofing. It probably knocked her to the ground, causing that abrasion. She was brought here by Ambu-Van. I understand she was unconscious, and they had no idea how long she'd been lying there."

"Did she regain consciousness?"

"Yes, but she was unable to communicate."

"She couldn't speak?"

"No. And she did not squeeze my hand or blink or nod or shake her head."

"You're sure she's not here?"

"I'd be disappointed if she was still here, sir. We're sending all the acute cases to one of the three *M*s, as I told you."

"Who would know where she was sent?"

The doctor pointed down the hall. "Ask that man right there for the disposition of *Mother* Doe."

"Thanks so much," Buck said. He hurried down the hall, then stopped and turned around. "Mother Doe?"

"We have been through the alphabet several times with all the unidentified Does. By the time your wife arrived, we were into descriptive terms."

"But she's not."

"Not what?"

"A mother."

"Well, if she and the baby survive this, she *will* be, in about seven months."

The doctor strode away; Buck nearly fainted.

\+ + +

Rayford and Mac sat at breakfast that morning planning the lengthy tour in the Condor 216 that would commence Friday. "So, what did His Excellency want last night?"

"His Excellency?"

"Haven't you been informed that that's what we're to call him from now on?"

"Oh brother!"

"I got that straight from Leon, or should I say 'Supreme Commander Leonardo Fortunato.'"

"That's his new moniker?" Rayford nodded. Mac shook his head. "These guys get more like Keystone Kops all the time. All Carpathia wanted to know was how long I thought you'd be staying with him. I told him I thought that was up to him and he said no, that he sensed you were getting restless. I told him he ought to let up on you over that little incident near the airport, and he said he already had. He said he could have really come down hard on you for that, and he hoped you'd stay with him longer since he hadn't."

"Who knows?" Rayford said. "Anything else?"

"He wanted to know if I knew your son-in-law. I told him I knew who he was but that I had never met him."

"Why do you think he asked that?"

"I don't know. He was trying to get in good with me for some reason. Maybe he's gonna be checking up on you. He told me he thought it strange that he'd gotten an intelligence report that Mr. Williams, as he likes to call him, had survived but not checked in. He told me Mr. Williams was publisher of *Global Community Weekly*, as if I wouldn't know that."

"Buck called this morning. I'm sure they have that logged, probably even recorded. If they wanted to talk to him so bad, why didn't they break in and do it then?"

"Maybe they're trying to let him hang himself. How long do you think Carpathia will trust a believer in a position like that?"

"That honeymoon is already over. You have to do what you have to do, Mac, but if I were you, I wouldn't be quick to declare myself as a new believer. Obviously, nobody but fellow believers can see these marks."

"Yeah, but what about that verse about confessing with your mouth?"

"I have no idea. Do the rules still stand at a time like this? Are you supposed to confess your faith to the Antichrist? I just don't know."

"Well, I already confessed it to you. I don't know whether that counts, but meanwhile, you're right. I'll be more help to you this way. What they don't know won't hurt them, and it can only help us."

+ + +

With a lump in his throat, Buck prayed silently as he approached the doctor at the other end of the hall. "Lord, keep her alive. I don't care where she is, as long as you take care of her and our baby."

A moment later he was saying, "Minneapolis! That's got to be over three hundred miles from here."

"I drove it last week in six hours," the doctor said. "But I understand the foothills that make that western edge of Wisconsin so beautiful around Tomah were turned into mini mountains in the quake."

10

RAYFORD AND MAC were on their way to board the Condor 216 and confirm she was flightworthy. Rayford threw an arm around Mac's shoulder and drew him close. "There's also something I need to show you on board," he whispered. "Installed just for me by an old friend no longer with us."

Rayford heard footsteps behind him. It was a uniformed young woman with a message. It read, "Captain Steele: Please meet briefly with Dr. Chaim Rosenzweig of Israel and me in my office immediately. I shall not keep you long. Signed, Supreme Commander Leonardo Fortunato."

"Thank you, Officer," Rayford said. "Tell them I'm on my way." He turned back to Mac and shrugged.

+ + +

"Any chance I can drive to Minnesota?" Buck said.

"Sure, but it'll take you forever," the doctor said.

"What would be the chance of my catching a ride with one of the Medivac planes?"

"Out of the question."

Buck showed him his ID. "I work for the Global Community."

"Doesn't just about everybody?"

"How do I find out if she made it up there?"

"We'd know if she didn't. She's there."

"And if she took a turn for the worse, or if she, you know . . ."

"We're informed of that, too, sir. It'll be on the computer so everyone is up-to-date."

Buck ran down four flights of stairs and emerged at the far end of the second hotel. He looked across the parking lot and saw Ben-Judah where he had left him. Two uniformed GC officers were talking with him. Buck held his breath. Somehow, the conversation did not look like a confrontation. It appeared friendly banter.

Tsion turned and began walking away, turning again after a few steps to proffer a shy wave. They both waved, and he kept walking. Buck wondered where he was going. Would he go straight to the Range Rover or to the prearranged meeting spot?

Buck stayed in the shadows as Ben-Judah steadily made his way past the front of the hotels and into a rocky area gouged by the earthquake. When he was nearly out of sight, the GC men began following. Buck sighed. He prayed Tsion would have the wisdom to not lead them to the Range Rover. *Just go to the spot, friend,* he thought, *and stay a couple of hundred yards ahead of these yokels.*

Buck did a couple of jumping jacks to loosen up and get the blood pumping. He jogged around the back of the second hotel, continued around the back of the first hotel, and emerged into the parking lot. He made a wide arc fifty yards to the left of the GC pair and maintained a leisurely pace as he jogged into the night. If the GC men noticed him, they didn't let on. They concentrated on the smaller, older man. Buck hoped that if Tsion noticed him, he wouldn't call out or follow.

It had been a long time since Buck had jogged more than a mile, especially scared to death. He huffed and puffed as he reached the area where he had left the Range Rover. A new section of cars had parked beyond his, so he had to search to find it.

Tsion plodded along, making his own trail over a difficult course. The GC men were still 100 to 150 yards behind him. Buck guessed Tsion knew he was being followed. He was not heading for the Rover but toward their spot. When Buck started the engine and turned on the headlights, Tsion touched a hand to his nose and increased his tempo. Buck raced over the open spaces, bouncing and banging but on pace to intersect with Tsion. The rabbi began trotting, and the GC men now sprinted. Buck was doing about thirty miles an hour, much too fast for the uneven ground. As he flopped in the seat, corralled only by his seat belt, he leaned over and lifted the handle on the passenger door. When he slid to a stop in front of Tsion, the door flew open, Tsion grabbed the inside handle, and Buck floored the accelerator. The door swung back and smacked Tsion in the rear, sending him across the seat and nearly into Buck's lap. Tsion laughed hysterically.

Buck looked at him, bemused, and jerked the wheel left. He put such distance between himself and the GC men that they would not have been able to see even the color of the vehicle, let alone the license number.

"What is so funny?" he asked Tsion, who cackled through his tears.

"I am Joe Baker," Tsion said in a ridiculously labored American accent. "I run a bakery shop and bake the rolls for you, because I am Joe Baker!" He laughed and laughed, covering his face and letting the tears come.

"Have you lost your mind?" Buck asked. "What is this about?"

"Those officers!" Tsion said, pointing over his shoulder. "Those brilliant, highly trained bloodhounds!" He laughed so hard he could hardly breathe.

Buck had to laugh himself. He had wondered if he would ever smile again.

Tsion kept one hand over his eyes and raised the other as if to inform Buck that if he could just calm himself he would be able to tell the story. Finally, he managed. "They greeted me in a friendly way. I was wary. I camouflaged my Hebrew accent and did not say much, hoping they would get bored and walk away. But they continued to study me in the dim light. Finally they asked who I was." He began to giggle again and had to collect himself. "That is when I told them. I said, 'My name is Joe Baker, and I am a baker. I have a bakery.'"

"You didn't!" Buck roared.

"They asked me where was I from, and I asked them to guess. One said Lithuania, and so I pointed at him and smiled and said, 'Yes! Yes, I am Joe the Baker from Lithuania!'"

"You're crazy!"

"Yes," he said. "But am I not a good soldier?"

"You are."

"They asked me if I had papers. I told them I had them at the bakery. I had just come out for a stroll to see the damage. My bakery survived, you know."

"I had heard that," Buck said.

"I told them to come by sometime for free donuts. They said they just might do that and asked where Joe's Bakery was located. I told them to head west to the only establishment on Route 50 still standing. I said God must like donuts, and they laughed. When I left, I waved at them, but soon enough they began to follow. I knew you would know where to look for me if I was not where I was supposed to be. But I worried that if you stayed in the hotels much longer, they would overtake me. God was watching over us, as usual."

+ + +

"You are acquainted with Dr. Rosenzweig, I'm sure," Fortunato said.

"I am indeed, Commander," Rayford said, shaking Chaim's hand.

Rosenzweig was his usual enthusiastic self, an elflike septuagenarian with broad features, a deeply lined face, and wisps of curly white hair independent of his control.

"Captain Steele!" he said, "It is such an honor to see you again. I came to ask after your son-in-law, Cameron."

"I spoke with him this morning, and he's fine." Rayford looked directly into

Rosenzweig's eyes, hoping to communicate the importance of confidentiality. "*Everyone* is fine, Doctor," he said.

"And Dr. Ben-Judah?" Rosenzweig said.

Rayford felt Fortunato's eyes all over him. "Doctor Ben-Judah?" he said.

"Surely you know him. An old protégé of mine. Cameron helped him escape zealots in Israel, with the help of Poten—, I mean Excellency Carpathia."

Leon appeared pleased that Rosenzweig had used the proper title. He said, "You know how much His Excellency thinks of you, Doctor. We promised to do all we could."

"And so where did Cameron take him?" Rosenzweig asked. "And why has he not reported to the Global Community?"

Rayford fought for composure. "If what you say is true, Dr. Rosenzweig, it was done independent of my involvement. I followed the news of the rabbi's misfortune and escape, but I was here."

"Surely your own son-in-law would tell you—"

"As I say, Doctor, I have no firsthand knowledge of the operation. I was unaware the Global Community was involved."

"So he didn't bring Tsion back to the States?"

"I am unaware of the rabbi's whereabouts. My son-in-law is in the States, but whether he is with Dr. Ben-Judah, I could not say."

Rosenzweig slumped and crossed his arms. "Oh, this is awful! I had so hoped to learn that he is safe. The Global Community could offer tremendous assistance in protecting him. Cameron was not sure of Excellency Carpathia's concern for Tsion, but surely he proved himself by helping to find Tsion and get him out of the country!"

What had Fortunato and Carpathia fed Dr. Rosenzweig?

Fortunato spoke up. "As I told you, Doctor, we provided manpower and equipment that escorted Mr. Williams and Rabbi Ben-Judah as far as the Israeli-Egyptian border. Past that, they fled, apparently by plane, out of Al Arish on the Mediterranean. Naturally we hoped to be brought up to speed, if for no other reason than that we expected some modicum of gratitude. If Mr. Williams feels Dr. Ben-Judah is safe, wherever he has hidden him, that's fine with us. We simply want to be of assistance until you feel it is no longer necessary."

Rosenzweig leaned forward and gestured broadly. "That is the point! I hate to leave it in Cameron's hands. He is a busy man, important to the Global Community. I know that when His Excellency pledges support, he follows through. And with the personal story you just told me, Commander Fortunato, well, there is clearly much, much more to my young friend Nicolae—pardon the familiar reference—than meets the eye!"

+ + +

It was after midnight in the Midwest. Buck had brought Tsion up to speed on Chloe. Now he was on the phone to the Arthur Young Memorial Hospital in Palatine. "I understand that," Buck said. "Tell him it's his old friend, Buck."

"Sir, the patient is stable but sleeping. I will not be telling him anything tonight."

"It's urgent that I talk to him."

"You've said that, sir. Please try again tomorrow."

"Just listen—"

Click.

Buck hardly noticed road construction ahead. He skidded to a stop. A traffic director approached. "Sorry, sir, but I'm gonna hold you here for a minute. We're filling in a fissure."

Buck put the Rover in park and rested his head against the back of the seat. "So, what do you think, Joe the Baker? Should we let Ritz test his wings to Minneapolis before we let him take us back to Israel?"

Tsion smiled at the mention of Joe the Baker, but he suddenly sobered.

"What is it?" Buck said.

"Just a minute," Tsion said.

Up ahead a bulldozer turned, its lights shining through the Range Rover. "I did not notice you had injured your forehead, too," Tsion said.

Buck sat up quickly and looked in the rearview mirror. "I don't see anything. You're the second person tonight who said he saw something on my forehead." He spread his hair. "Now where? What?"

"Look at me," Tsion said. He pointed to Buck's forehead.

Buck said, "Well, look at yourself! There's something on yours, too."

Tsion pulled down the visor mirror. "Nothing," he muttered. "Now you are teasing me."

"All right," Buck said, frustrated. "Let me look again. OK, yours is still there. Is mine still there?"

Tsion nodded.

"Yours looks like some kind of a 3-D thing. What does mine look like?"

"The same. Like a shadow or a bruise, or a, what do you call it? A relief?"

"Yes," Buck said. "Hey! This is like one of those puzzles that looks like a bunch of sticks until you sort of reverse it in your mind and see the background as the foreground and vice versa. That's a cross on your forehead."

Tsion seemed to stare desperately at Buck. Suddenly he said, "Yes! Cameron! We have the seal, visible to only other believers."

"What are you talking about?"

"The seventh chapter of Revelation tells of 'the servants of our God' being sealed on their foreheads. That has to be what this is!"

Buck didn't notice the flagman waving him through. The man approached the car. "What's up with you two? Let's go!"

Buck and Tsion looked at each other, grinning stupidly. They laughed, and Buck drove on. Suddenly, he slammed on the brakes.

"What?" Tsion said.

"I met another believer back there!"

"Where?"

"At the hospital! A black doctor in charge of the morgue had the same sign. He saw mine and I saw his, but neither of us knew what we were looking at. I've got to call him."

Tsion dug out the number. "He will be most encouraged, Cameron."

"If I can get through. I may have to drive back and find him."

"No! What if those GC men figured out who I was? Even if they think I am Joe the Baker, they are going to want to know why I ran away."

"It's ringing!"

"GC Hospital, Kenosha."

"Hello, yes. I need the doctor in charge of the morgue."

"He has his own cell phone, sir. Here's that number."

Buck wrote it down and punched it in.

"Morgue. This is Floyd Charles."

"Doctor Charles! Are you the one who let me into the morgue to look for my wife tonight?"

"Yes, any luck?"

"Yes, I think I know where she is, but—"

"Wonderful. I'm happy for—"

"But that's not why I'm calling. Remember that mark on my forehead?"

"Yes," Doctor Charles said slowly.

"That's the sign of the sealed servants of God! You have one too, so I know you're a believer. Right?"

"Praise God!" the doctor said. "I am, but I don't think I have the mark."

"We can't see our own! Only others'."

"Wow! Oh, hey, listen! Your wife isn't Mother Doe, is she?"

Buck recoiled. "Yes, why?"

"Then I know who you are, too. And so do they. You're driving to Minneapolis. That gives them time to get your wife out of there."

"Why do they want to do that?"

"Because you've got something or somebody they want. . . . Are you still there, sir?"

"I'm here. Listen, brother to brother, tell me what you know. When will they move her and where would they take her?"

"I don't know. But I heard something about flying someone out of Glenview Naval Air Station—you know, the old shut-down base that—"

"I know."

"Late tomorrow."

"Are you sure?"

"That's what I heard."

"Let me give you my private number, Doctor. If you hear any more, please let me know. And if you ever, and I mean ever, need anything, you let me know."

"Thank you, Mr. Doe."

+ + +

Rayford showed Mac McCullum the bugging device that connected the pilot's headphone to the cabin. McCullum whistled through his teeth. "Ray, when they discover this and put you away for the rest of your life, I'm gonna deny any knowledge."

"It's a deal. But in case anything happens to me before they find out, you know where it is."

"No I don't," Mac said, smiling.

"Invent something to get us outside. I need to talk to Buck on my own phone."

"I could use some help with the skyhooks on that chopper," Mac said.

"With the what?"

"The skyhooks. The ones I attach to the sky that let me pull the helicopter off the ground and work underneath it."

"Oh, *those* skyhooks! Yes, let's check on those."

+ + +

It was well after midnight when Buck and Tsion dragged themselves into the house. "I don't know what I'm going to run into in Minneapolis," Buck said, "but I have to go there in better shape than I'm in right now. Pray that Ken Ritz is up to this. I don't know if I should even hope for that."

"We don't hope," Tsion said. "We pray."

"Then pray for this: One, that Ritz is healthy enough. Two, that he's got a plane that works. Three, that it's at an airport he can take off from."

Buck was at the top of the stairs when his phone rang. "Rayford!"

Rayford quickly filled Buck in on the fiasco with Rosenzweig.

"I love that old buzzard," Buck said, "but he sure is naive. I told him and told him not to trust Carpathia. He loves the guy."

"He more than loves him, Buck. He believes he's divine."

"Oh, no."

Rayford and Buck debriefed each other on everything that had happened that day. "I can't wait to meet Mac," Buck said.

"If you're in as much trouble as it appears, Buck, you may never meet him."

"Well, maybe not this side of heaven."

Rayford brought up Amanda. "Would you believe Carpathia tried to make Mac think she was working for him?"

Buck didn't know what to say. "Working for Carpathia?" he said lamely.

"Think of it! I know her like I know myself, and I'll tell you something else. I'm convinced she's alive. I'm praying you can get to Chloe before the GC does. You pray I find Amanda."

"She wasn't on the plane that went down?"

"That's all I can believe," Rayford said. "If she was on it, she's gone. But I'm gonna check that out too."

"How?"

"I'll tell you later. I don't want to know where Tsion is, but just tell me, you're not taking him to Minnesota, are you? If something goes wrong, there's no way you want to be forced to trade him for Chloe."

"Of course not. He thinks he's going, but he'll understand. I don't think anybody knows where we are, and there is that shelter I told you about."

"Perfect."

\+ + +

Wednesday morning Buck had to talk Tsion out of coming with him even to Palatine. The rabbi understood the danger of going to Minnesota, but he insisted he could help Buck get Ken Ritz out of the hospital. "If you need a distraction, I could be Joe the Baker again."

"Much as I would enjoy seeing that, Tsion, we just don't know who's onto us. I don't even know whether anyone ever found out it was Ken who flew me to Israel and you and me back. Who knows whether they've got that hospital staked out? Ken might not even be there. It could all be a setup."

"Cameron! Don't we have enough real worries without you inventing more?"

Tsion reluctantly stayed. Buck urged him to prepare the shelter in the event things went haywire in Minneapolis and Global Community forces began to track him in earnest. Tsion would be broadcasting his teachings and encouragement to the 144,000 witnesses and any other clandestine believers all over the world via the Internet. That would irritate Carpathia, not to mention Peter Mathews, and no one knew when the technology might be advanced enough to trace such messages.

The normally short jaunt from Mount Prospect to Palatine was now an arduous two-hour journey. Arthur Young Memorial Hospital had somehow escaped serious damage, though with only a few exceptions, the rest of Palatine had been wasted. It looked nearly as bad as Mount Prospect. Buck parked near fallen trees about fifty yards from the entrance. Seeing nothing suspicious, he walked straight in. The hospital was full and busy, and with auxiliary power and the fact that the place was not just a retrofitted hotel like the ones the night before, it seemed to run much more efficiently.

"I'm here to see Ken Ritz," he said.

"And you are?" a candy striper said.

Buck hesitated. "Herb Katz," he said, using an alias Ken Ritz would recognize.

"May I see some identification?"

"No, you may not."

"I'm sorry?"

"My identification was lost with my house in Mount Prospect, which is now earthquake residue, OK?"

"Mount Prospect? I lost a sister and brother-in-law there. I understand it was the hardest hit."

"Palatine doesn't look much better."

"We're short-staffed, but several of us were lucky, knock on wood."

"So, how 'bout it? Can I see Ken?"

"I'll try. But my supervisor is tougher than me. She hasn't let anyone in without ID. But I'll tell her your situation."

The girl left the desk and poked her head through a door behind her. Buck was tempted to just head into the main hospital and find Ritz, especially when he overheard the conversation.

"Absolutely not. You know the rules."

"But he lost his home and his ID and—"

"If you can't tell him no, I'll have to."

The candy striper turned and shrugged apologetically. She sat as her supervisor, a striking, dark-haired woman in her late twenties, stepped into view. Buck saw the mark on her forehead and smiled, wondering if she was aware of it yet.

She smiled shyly, quickly growing serious when the girl turned to look. "Who was it you wanted to see, sir?"

"Ken Ritz."

"Tiffany, please show this gentleman to Ken Ritz's room." She held Buck's gaze, then turned and went back into her office.

Tiffany shook her head. "She's always had a thing for blonds." She walked Buck to the ward.

"I have to make sure the patient wants visitors," she said.

Buck waited in the hall as Tiffany knocked and entered Ken's room. "Mr. Ritz, are you up to a visitor?"

"Not really," came the gravelly but weak voice Buck recognized. "Who is it?"

"A Herb Katz."

"Herb Katz, Herb Katz." Ritz seemed to turn the name over in his mind. "Herb Katz! Send him in, and shut the door."

When they were alone, Ken winced as he sat up. He thrust out an entubed hand and shook Buck's weakly. "Herb Katz, how in the world are ya?"

"That's what I was gonna ask you. You look terrible."

"Thanks for nothing. I got hurt in the stupidest possible way, but please tell me you've got a job for me. I need to get out of this place and get busy. I'm going stir-crazy. I wanted to call you, but I lost all my phone numbers. Nobody knows how to get ahold of you."

"I've got a couple of jobs for you, Ken, but are you up to them?"

"I'll be good as new by tomorrow," he said. "I just got banged on the head with one of my own little fixed-wingers."

"What?"

"The danged earthquake hit while I was in the air. I circled and circled waitin' for the thing to stop, almost crashed when the sun went out, and finally put down over here at Palwaukee. I didn't see the crater. In fact, I don't think it was there until after I hit the ground. Anyway, I was almost stopped, just rolling a couple miles an hour, and the plane fell right down into that thing. Worst of it is I was OK, but the plane wasn't anchored like I thought it was. I jumped out, worrying about fuel and everything and wanting to see how my other aircraft were and how everybody else was, so I hopped up top and ran down the wing to jump out of the hole.

"Just before I took my last step, my weight flipped that little Piper right over and the other wing conked me on the back of the head. I was hanging there on the edge of the hole, trying to get all the way up, and I knew I'd been sliced pretty deep. I reach back there with one hand and feel this big flap of scalp hanging down, and then I start getting dizzy. I lost my grip and slid down underneath that plane. I was scared I was gonna make it fall on me again, so I just stayed put till somebody pulled me out. Dang near bled to death."

"You look a little pale."

"Aren't you full of encouragement today."

"Sorry."

"You want to see it?"

"See it?"

"My wound!"

"Sure, I guess."

Ritz turned so Buck could see the back of his head. Buck grimaced. It was as ugly an injury as he had seen. The huge flap that had been stitched into place had been shaved, along with an extra one-inch border around the area.

"No brain damage, they tell me, so I still got no excuse for bein' crazy."

Buck filled him in on his dilemma and that he needed to get to Minneapolis before the GC did something stupid with Chloe. "I'm gonna need you to recommend somebody, Ken. I can't wait till tomorrow."

"The heck I'll recommend somebody else," Ken said. He unhooked the IV and yanked the tape off.

"Slow down, Ken. I can't let you do this. You've got to get a clean bill of health before—"

"Forget me, will ya? I may have to go slow, but we both know if there's no brain trauma, there's little danger I'm gonna hurt myself worse. I'll be a little uncomfortable, that's all. Now come on, help me get dressed and get out of here."

"I appreciate this, but really—"

"Williams, if you don't let me do this, I'm gonna hate you for the rest of my life."

"I sure wouldn't want to be responsible for that."

There was no way to sneak out. Buck put his arm around Ken and tucked his hand in Ken's armpit. They moved as quickly as possible, but a male nurse came running. "Whoa! He's not allowed out of bed! Help! Someone! Get his doctor!"

"This ain't prison," Ken called out. "I signed in, and I'm checkin' out!"

They were headed through the lobby when a doctor hurried toward them. The girl at the desk summoned her supervisor. Buck pleaded with his eyes. The supervisor glared at him but stepped directly in front of the doctor, and he stumbled trying to avoid her. "I'll handle this," she said.

The doctor left with a suspicious look, and the candy striper was sent to the pharmacy to get Ken's prescriptions. The supervisor whispered, "Being a believer doesn't guarantee you're not stupid. I'm making this happen, but it had better be necessary."

Buck nodded his thanks.

Once in the Rover, Ken sat still, gently cradling his head in his fingers. "You OK?" Buck asked.

Ritz nodded. "Run me by Palwaukee. I got a bag of stuff they're keepin' for me. And we've got to get to Waukegan."

"Waukegan?"

"Yeah. My Learjet got blown around over there, but it's OK. Only problem is, the hangars are gone. Their fuel tanks are fine, they tell me. One problem, though."

"I'll bite."

"Runways."

"What about 'em?"

"Apparently they don't exist anymore."

Buck was cruising as quickly as he could manage. One advantage of no roads was that he could drive from one place to another as the crow flies. "Can you take off in a Learjet without pavement beneath you?"

"Never had to worry about it before. We'll find out though, won't we?"

"Ritz, you're crazier than I am."

"That'll be the day. Every time I'm with you I'm sure you're gonna get me killed." Ritz fell silent for a moment. Then, "Speakin' of getting killed, you know I wasn't just calling you because I needed work."

"No?"

"I read your article. That 'wrath of the Lamb' thing in your magazine."

"What did you think?"

"Wrong question. It isn't what I thought when I read it, which frankly wasn't much. I mean, I've always been impressed with your writing."

"I didn't know that."

"So sue me, I didn't want you to get the big head. Anyway, I didn't like any of the theories you came up with. And no, I didn't believe we were going to suffer the wrath of the Lamb. But what you ought to be asking is what do I think about it now?"

"All right. Shoot."

"Well, a guy would have to be a fool to think the first worldwide earthquake in the history of mankind was a coincidence, after you predicted it in your article."

"Hey, I didn't predict it. I was totally objective."

"I know. But you and I talked about this stuff before, so I knew where you were comin' from. You made it look like all those Bible scholar guys were just giving more opinions to stack up against the space aliens and the conspiracy nuts. Then, wham, bang, my head's split open, and all of a sudden the only guy I know crazier than me is the one that had the thing figured out."

"So you wanted to get hold of me. Here I am."

"Good. 'Cause I figure if what the globe just went through *was* the wrath of the Lamb, I better make friends with that Lamb."

Buck always thought Ritz was too smart to miss all the signs. "I can help you there," he said.

"I kind of thought you might."

It was close to noon by the time Buck came out of the ditch where Green Bay Road used to be and drove slowly over the flattened fence and around the crumpled landing lights at the Waukegan Airport. The runways had not just sunk or twisted. They lay in huge chunks from end to end.

There, in one of the few open spaces, was Ken Ritz's Learjet, apparently none the worse for wear.

Ritz moved slowly, but he was able to gingerly taxi the thing between hazards to the fuel pump. "She'll take us to Minneapolis and back more than once with a full tank," he said.

"The question is how fast?" Buck said.

"Less than an hour."

Buck looked at his watch. "Where are you gonna take off from?"

"It's sloped, but from the cockpit I saw one patch across Wadsworth on the golf course that looks like our best bet."

"How are you gonna get across the road and through those thickets?"

"Oh, we'll do it. But it's gonna take longer than flying to Minneapolis. You're gonna be doing most of the work. I'll steer the jet, and you'll clear the way. It's not gonna be easy."

"I'll hack my way to Minneapolis if I have to," Buck said.

11

RAYFORD WAS LEARNING joy in the midst of sorrow. His heart told him Amanda was alive. His mind told him she was dead. As for her betrayal of him, of the Tribulation Force, and ultimately of God himself, neither Rayford's head nor heart accepted that.

Yet with his conflicting emotions and turmoil of spirit, Rayford was as grateful for Mac's conversion as he had been for his own, for Chloe's, and for Buck's. And the timing of God's choosing to put his mark on his own! Rayford would be eager to get Tsion Ben-Judah's input on that.

It was late Wednesday evening in New Babylon. Rayford and Mac had been working side by side all day. Rayford had told him the whole story of the Tribulation Force and each of their accounts of their own conversions. Mac seemed especially intrigued that God had provided them a pastor/teacher/mentor from the beginning in Bruce Barnes. And then, following Bruce's death, God sent a new spiritual leader with even more biblical expertise.

"God has proven personal to us, Mac," Rayford said. "He doesn't always answer our prayers the way we think he will, but we've learned he knows best. And we have to be careful not to think that everything we feel deeply is necessarily true."

"I don't follow," Mac said.

"For instance, I can't shake the feeling that Amanda is still alive. But I can't swear that is from God." Rayford hesitated, suddenly overcome. "I want to be sure that if it turns out I'm wrong, I don't hold it against God."

Mac nodded. "I can't imagine holding anything against God, but I see what you mean."

Rayford was thrilled by Mac's hunger to learn. Rayford showed him where to search on the Internet for Tsion's teachings, his sermons, his commentaries on Bruce Barnes's messages, and especially his end-times chart that plotted where he believed the church was in the sequence of the seven-year tribulation.

Mac was fascinated by evidence that pointed to Nicolae Carpathia as the

Antichrist. "But this wrath of the Lamb and the moon turning to blood, man, if nothing else convinced me, that sure did."

Once their route plans were finished, Rayford e-mailed Buck his itinerary. After picking up Peter Mathews in Rome, he and Mac were to fly him and Leon to Dallas to pick up a former Texas senator. He was the newly installed ambassador to the Global Community from the United States of North America. "You have to wonder, Mac, whether this guy ever dreamed when he got into politics that he would one day be one of the ten kings foretold of in the Bible."

A little more than half the Dallas/Ft. Worth airport was still operational, and the rest was quickly being rebuilt. To Rayford, reconstruction around the world already clipped along at a staggering pace. It was as if Carpathia had been a student of prophecy, and though he insisted that events were not as they seemed, he seemed to have been prepared to begin rebuilding immediately.

Rayford knew Carpathia was mortal. Still, he wondered if the man ever slept. He saw Nicolae around the compound at all hours, always in suit and tie, shoes polished, face shaved, hair trimmed. He was amazing. Despite the hours he kept, he was short-tempered only when it served his purpose. Normally he was gregarious, smiling, confident. When appropriate, he feigned grief and empathy. Handsome and charming, it was easy to see how he could deceive so many.

Earlier that evening, Carpathia had broadcast a live global television and radio address. He told the masses: "Brothers and sisters in the Global Community, I address you from New Babylon. Like you, I lost many loved ones, dear friends, and loyal associates in the tragedy. Please accept my deepest and most sincere sympathy for your losses on behalf of the administration of the Global Community.

"No one could have predicted this random act of nature, the worst in history to strike the globe. We were in the final stages of our rebuilding effort following the war against a resistant minority. Now, as I trust you are able to witness wherever you are, rebuilding has already begun again.

"New Babylon will, within a very short time, become the most magnificent city the world has ever known. Your new international capitol will be the center of banking and commerce, the headquarters for all Global Community governing agencies, and eventually the new Holy City, where Enigma Babylon One World Faith will relocate.

"It will be my joy to welcome you to this beautiful place. Give us a few months to finish, and then plan your pilgrimage. Every citizen should make it his or her life's goal to experience this new utopia and see the prototype for every city."

With a couple of hundred other GC employees, Rayford and Mac had watched on a television high in the corner of the mess hall. Nicolae, in a small studio down the hall, played a virtual reality disk that took the viewer through the new city, gleaming as if already completed. It was dizzying and impressive.

Carpathia pointed out every high-tech, state-of-the-art convenience known to man, each blended into the beautiful new metropolis. Mac whispered, "With those gold spires, it looks like old Sunday school pictures of heaven."

Rayford nodded. "Both Bruce and Tsion say Antichrist just counterfeits what God does."

Carpathia finished with a stirring pep talk. "Because you are survivors, I have unwavering confidence in your drive and determination and commitment to work together, to never give up, to stand shoulder to shoulder and rebuild our world.

"I am humbled to serve you and pledge that I will give my all for as long as you allow me the privilege. Now let me just add that I am aware that, due to speculative reporting in one of our own Global Community publications, many have been confused by recent events. While it may appear that the global earthquake coincided with the so-called wrath of the Lamb, let me clarify. Those who believe this disaster was God's doing are also those who believe that the disappearances nearly two years ago were people being swept away to heaven.

"Of course, every citizen of the Global Community is free to believe as he or she wants and to exercise that faith in any way that does not infringe upon the same freedom for others. The point of Enigma Babylon One World Faith is religious freedom and tolerance.

"For that reason, I am loath to criticize the beliefs of others. However, I plead for common sense. I do not begrudge anyone the right to believe in a personal god. However, I do not understand how a god they describe as just and loving would capriciously decide who is or is not worthy of heaven and effect that decision in what they refer to as 'the twinkling of an eye.'

"Has this same loving god come back two years later to rub it in? He expresses his anger to those unfortunates he left behind by laying waste their world and killing off a huge percentage of them?" Carpathia smiled condescendingly. "I humbly ask devout believers in such a Supreme Being to forgive me if I have mischaracterized your god. But any thinking citizen realizes that this picture simply does not add up.

"So, my brothers and sisters, do not blame God for what we are enduring. See it simply as one of life's crucibles, a test of our spirit and will, an opportunity to look within ourselves and draw on that deep wellspring of goodness we were born with. Let us work together to make our world a global phoenix, rising from the ashes of tragedy to become the greatest society ever known. I bid you good-bye and goodwill until next I speak with you."

When the Global Community employees in the mess hall leaped to their feet, cheering and clapping, Rayford and Mac stood only to keep from appearing conspicuous. Rayford noticed Mac staring off to the left.

"What?" Rayford said.

"Just a minute," Mac said. Rayford was about to leave when everyone sat back down, still glued to the TV. "I noticed someone else slow to stand," Mac whispered. "A young guy. Works in communications, I think."

Everyone had sat back down because a message on the screen read, "Please stand by for Supreme Commander Leonardo Fortunato."

Fortunato did not cut as impressive a figure as Carpathia, but he had a dynamic television visage. He came across friendly and approachable, humble yet direct, seeming to look the viewer in the eye. He told the story of his death in the earthquake and subsequent resurrection by Nicolae. "My only regret," he added, "was that there were no witnesses. But I know what I experienced and believe with all my heart that this gift our Supreme Potentate possesses will be used in public in the future. A man bestowed with this power is worthy of a new title. I am suggesting that he hereafter be referred to as His Excellency Nicolae Carpathia. I have already instituted this policy within the Global Community government and urge all citizens who respect and love our leader to follow suit.

"As you may know, His Excellency would never require or even request such a title. Though reluctantly thrust into leadership, he has expressed a willingness to give his life for his fellow citizens. Though he will never insist upon appropriate deference, I urge it on your part.

"I have not consulted His Excellency on what I am about to tell you, and I only hope he accepts it in the spirit in which I offer it and is not embarrassed. Most of you could not know that he is going through intense personal pain."

"I do not believe where this is going," Rayford muttered.

"Our leader and his fiancée, the love of his life, joyfully anticipate the birth of their child within the next several months. But the soon-to-be Mrs. Carpathia is currently unaccounted for. She was about to return from the United States of North America after a visit to her family when the earthquake made international travel impossible. If anyone knows the whereabouts of Miss Hattie Durham, please forward that information to your local Global Community representative as soon as possible. Thank you."

Mac made a beeline to the young man he had been watching. Rayford headed back toward the Condor 216 and was near the steps when Mac caught up with him. "Rayford, that kid had the mark on his forehead. When I said I knew he was a believer, he turned white. I showed him my mark, told him about you and me, and he almost cried. His name is David Hassid. He's a Jew from Eastern Europe who joined GC because he was impressed with Carpathia. He's been surfing the Net for six months, and get this, he considers Tsion Ben-Judah his spiritual mentor."

"When did he become a believer?"

"Just a few weeks ago, but he's not ready to make it known. He was convinced he was the only one here. He says Tsion put something on the Net called the 'Romans Road' to salvation. I guess all the verses come from Romans. Anyway, he wants to meet you. He can't believe you know Ben-Judah personally."

"Shoot, I can probably get the kid an autograph."

+ + +

Getting Ken Ritz's Learjet across the ravaged Waukegan Airport to the mess formerly known as Wadsworth Road was easy. Buck rode next to Ken as he slowly taxied until a pile of rubbish or chunk of concrete or gouge in the earth had to be moved, broken up, or filled in. The tools Buck had found were not intended for what he was doing, but his aching muscles and calloused hands told him he was making progress.

The tricky part was getting across Wadsworth Road to the golf course. First there was the ditch. "It's not the best thing to do to a Lear," Ken said, "but I think I can roll in there and up and out. It's going to take just the right momentum, and I have to stop within a few feet."

The pavement had been bowed at least eight feet, so steep that a car would not have the right angle to get over it. "Where do we go from there?" Buck asked.

"Every action has a reaction, right?" Ritz said cryptically. "Where there's a bow, there's gotta be a dip somewhere. How far east do we have to go till we can cross?"

Buck jogged about two hundred yards before seeing a huge split in the pavement. If Ritz could get the plane that far, keeping his left wing from touching the bowed pavement and his right wheel from the ditch, he could turn left across the road. After guiding Ken in and out of the ditch on that side, Buck would have to clear a fence and shrubbery that blocked the golf course.

Ritz negotiated the first ditch easily, but being careful to stop before the upcropping of pavement, he rolled back down. At the nadir of the ditch, he couldn't back out and had a trickier time going forward. He finally made it but jumped out to find he had bent the front landing gear. "Shouldn't affect anything, but I wouldn't want to land on it too many times," he said.

Buck was not reassured. He walked ahead as Ritz taxied east down the shoulder. Ken kept an eye on the left wing, keeping it inches from the bulge of the road, while Buck watched the right tire and made sure it didn't slip into the ditch.

Once across the road, it was down into and up out of the other ditch, Ken jamming the brakes again to miss the fence. He began helping Buck move stuff out of the way, but when they started yanking shrubbery, he had to sit down. "Save your strength," Buck said. "I can do this."

Ritz looked at his watch. "You'd better hurry. What time did you want to be in Minneapolis?"

"Not much after three. My source says GC guys are coming from Glenview late this afternoon."

+ + +

When Rayford and Mac finished in the Condor, Rayford said, "Let me leave first. You and I shouldn't constantly be seen together. You need credibility with the brass."

Rayford was tired but eager to get the long trip behind him and get back for his scuba expedition. He prayed his hunch would be right and he would not find Amanda in that submerged plane. Then he would demand to know what Carpathia had done with her. As long as she was alive and he could get to her, he didn't worry about the ridiculous claims of her being a plant.

An officer greeted Rayford as he got to his quarters. "His Excellency would like to see you, sir."

Rayford thanked him and masked his disgust. He had enjoyed a day without Carpathia. His disappointment was doubled when he discovered Fortunato in Carpathia's office as well. They apparently didn't feel the need for their usual smarmy cordiality. Neither rose to greet him or shake his hand. Carpathia pointed to a chair and referred to a copy of Rayford's itinerary.

"I see you have scheduled a twenty-four-hour layover in North America."

"We need the downtime for the plane and the pilots."

"Will you be seeing your daughter and son-in-law?"

"Why?"

"I am not implying your personal time is my business," Carpathia said. "But I need a favor."

"I'm listening."

"It is the same matter we discussed before the earthquake."

"Hattie."

"Yes."

"You know where she is, then?" Rayford said.

"No, but I assume you do."

"How would I, if you don't?"

Carpathia stood. "Is it time for the gloves to come off, Captain Steele? Do you really think I could run the international government and not have eyes and ears everywhere? I have sources you could not even imagine. You do not think I know that the last time you and Miss Durham flew to North America, you were on the same flight?"

"I have not seen her since, sir."

"But she interacted with your people. Who knows what they might have filled her head with? She was supposed to have come back much earlier. You had your assignment. Whatever she was doing over there, she missed her original flight, and we know she was then traveling with your wife."

"That was my understanding too."

"She did not board that plane, Captain Steele. If she had, as you know, she would no longer be a problem."

"She's a problem again?" Carpathia did not respond. Rayford continued. "I saw your broadcast. I was under the impression you were despairing over your fiancée."

"I did not say that."

"I did," Fortunato said. "I was on my own there."

"Oh," Rayford said. "That's right. His Excellency had no idea you were going to confer divinity upon him and then overstate his turmoil over the missing fiancée."

"Do not be naive, Captain Steele," Carpathia said. "All I want to know is that you will have the talk with Miss Durham."

"The talk in which I tell her she can keep the ring, live in New Babylon, and then, what was it about the baby?"

"I'm going to assume she's already made the right decision there, and you may assure her that I will cover all expenses."

"For the child throughout its life?"

"That is not the decision I was referring to," Carpathia said.

"Just so I'm clear, then, you will pay for the murder of the child?"

"Do not be maudlin, Rayford. It is a safe, simple procedure. Just pass along my message. She will understand."

"Believe it or not, I don't know where she is. But if I do pass along your message, I can't guarantee she'll make the choice you want. What if she chooses to bear the child?"

Carpathia shook his head. "I must end this relationship, but it will not go over well if there is a child."

"I understand," Rayford said.

"We agree then."

"I didn't say that. I said I understood."

"You will talk to her then?"

"I have no idea of her whereabouts or well-being."

"Could she have been lost in the earthquake?" Carpathia said, his eyes brightening.

"Wouldn't that be the best solution?" Rayford suggested with disgust.

"Actually, yes," Carpathia said. "But my contacts believe she is hiding."

"And you think I know where."

"She is not the only person in exile with whom you have a connection, Captain Steele. Such leverage is keeping you out of prison."

Rayford was amused. Carpathia had overestimated him. If Rayford had thought harboring Hattie and Tsion would give him the upper hand, he might have done it on purpose. But Hattie was on her own. And Tsion was Buck's doing.

Nonetheless, he left Carpathia's office that night with a temporary advantage, according to the enemy himself.

+ + +

Buck was sweaty and exhausted when he finally strapped himself in next to Ken Ritz. The plane sat at the south end of the golf course, which itself had been snapped and rolled by the earthquake. Before them lay a long stretch of rolling, grassy turf. "We really ought to walk that and see if it's as solid as it looks," Ken said. "But we don't have time."

Against his better judgment, Buck did not protest. Still, Ken sat there staring. "I don't like it," he said finally. "It looks long enough, and we'll know right away if it's solid. The question is, can I gain enough speed to get airborne?"

"Can you abort if you don't?"

"I can try."

Ken Ritz trying was better than anyone else promising. Buck said, "Let's do it."

Ritz throttled up and gradually increased the speed. Buck felt his pulse race as they roller-coastered the hills of the fairway, engines screaming. Ken hit the flat stretch and throttled up all the way. The force pressed Buck to his seat, but as he braced for liftoff, Ritz throttled back.

Ritz shook his head. "We've got to be at top speed by the flats. I was only at about three-quarters." He turned around and took the plane back. "Just have to start faster," he said. "It's like popping the clutch. If you spin, you don't accelerate fast. If you feather it for the right purchase, you've got a chance."

The rolling start was slow again, but this time Ken throttled up as quickly as possible. They nearly left the ground as they skimmed dips and skipped mounds. They reached the flat area at what seemed twice the speed as before. Ken shouted over the din, "Now we're talkin', baby!"

The Learjet took off like a shot, and Ken maneuvered it so it felt as if they were going straight up. Buck was plastered against the back of his seat, unable to move. He could barely catch his breath, but when he did he let out a yelp and Ritz laughed. "If I don't die of this headache, I'm gonna get you to the church on time!"

Buck's phone was chirping. He had to will his hand to pull it out, so strong were the g-forces. "This is Buck!" he hollered.

It was Tsion. "You are still on the plane?" he said.

"Just took off. But we're going to make good time."

Buck told Tsion about Ken's injury and getting him out of the hospital.

"He is amazing," Tsion said. "Listen, Cameron, I just received an e-mail from Rayford. He and his copilot have discovered that one of the Jewish witnesses works right there at the shelter. A young man. I will be e-mailing him personally. I have just put out onto a central bulletin board the result of several days of study and writing. Check it when you get a chance. I call it 'The Coming Soul Harvest,' and it concerns the 144,000 witnesses, their winning many millions to Christ, the visible seal, and what we can expect in the way of judgments over the next year or so."

"What *can* we expect?"

"Read it on the Net when you get back. And please talk to Ken about getting us to Israel."

"That seems impossible now," Buck said. "Didn't Rayford tell you Carpathia's people are claiming to have helped you escape so they can be reunited with you?"

"Cameron! God will not let anything happen to me for a while. I feel a huge responsibility to the rest of the witnesses. Get me to Israel and leave my safety in the Lord's hands!"

"You have more faith than I do, Tsion," Buck said.

"Then start working on yours, my brother!"

"Pray for Chloe!" Buck said.

"Constantly," Tsion said. "For all of you."

Less than an hour later, Ritz radioed Minneapolis for landing instructions and asked to be put through to a rental car agency. With the shortage of staff and vehicles, prices had been doubled. However, cars were available, and he was given directions to the Global Community hospital.

Buck had no idea what he might encounter there. He couldn't imagine easy access or the ability to get Chloe out. GC officials weren't expected to take custody of her until late that afternoon, but surely she was already under guard. He wished he had some clue to her health. Was it wise to move her? Should he kidnap her even if he could?

"Ken, if you're up to it, I might use you and your crazy head wound as a distraction. They might be looking for me, hopefully not this soon, but I don't think anyone's ever put you together with us anyway."

"I hope you're serious, Buck," Ken said, "because I love to act. Plus, you're one of the good guys. Somebody's watching out for you and your friends."

Just outside Minneapolis, Ritz was informed that air traffic was heavier than expected and he would be in a landing pattern for another ten minutes. "Roger that," he said. "I do have a bit of an emergency here. It's not life or death, but one passenger on this plane has a serious head wound."

"Roger, Lear. We'll see if we can move you up a couple of slots. Let us know if your situation changes."

"Pretty crafty," Buck said.

When Ritz was finally cleared to bring in the Learjet, he banked and swooped over the terminal, apparently the target of major quake damage. Rebuilding had begun, but the entire operation, from ticket counters to rental car agencies, was now housed in mobile units. Buck was stunned at the amount of activity at an airport where only two runways functioned.

The harried ground control manager apologized for having nowhere to hangar the Learjet. He accepted Ken's pledge that he would not leave the plane longer than twenty-four hours. "I hope not," Buck whispered.

Ritz taxied near one of the old runways where heavy equipment was moving massive amounts of earth. He parked the Lear in line with everything from single engine Piper Cubs to Boeing 727s. They couldn't have stopped farther from the car rental agencies and still been on airport property.

Ken, wincing, gasping, and moving slowly, urged Buck to hurry ahead, but Buck was afraid Ken might collapse.

"Don't go into your wounded old coot act yet," Buck teased. "At least wait until we get to the hospital."

"If you know me," Ritz said, "you know this is no act."

"I don't believe this," Buck said, when they finally reached the car rental area and found themselves at the end of a long line. "Looks like they're sending people to the other side of the parking lot for cars."

Ken, several inches taller than Buck, stood on tiptoes and peered into the distance. "You're right," he said. "And you may have to get the car and come get me. I'm not up to walking any more now."

As they neared the head of the line, Buck told Ritz to rent the car on his credit card and Buck would reimburse him. "I don't want my name all over the state, in case the GC thinks to check around."

Ritz slapped his card on the counter. A young woman studied it. "We're down to subcompacts. Will that be acceptable?"

"What if I say no, honey?" he said.

She made a face. "That's all we have."

"Then what difference does it make whether it's acceptable?"

"You want it then?"

"I don't have any choice. Just how subcompact is this rig?"

She slid a glossy card across the counter and pointed to the smallest car pictured. "My word," Ritz said, "there's barely room in there for me, let alone my son here."

Buck fought a smile. The young woman, already clearly weary of Ritz and his banter, began filling out the paperwork.

"That thing even have a backseat?"

"Not really. There's a little space behind the seats, though. You put your luggage there."

Ritz looked at Buck, and Buck knew what he was thinking. The two of them were going to get to know each other better than they cared to in that car. Adding a grown woman in fragile condition took more imagination than Buck possessed.

"Do you have a color preference?" the girl asked.

"I get to choose?" Ritz said. "You've got only one model left, but it comes in different colors?"

"Usually," she said. "We're down to just the red ones now."

"But I get to choose?"

"If you choose red."

"OK, then. Give me a second. You know what I think I'd like? You got any red ones?"

"Yes."

"I'll take a red one. Wait a minute. Son, red OK with you?"

Buck just closed his eyes and shook his head. As soon as he had the keys he ran for the car. He tossed his and Ritz's bags behind the seats, pushed both seats back as far as they would go, jammed himself behind the wheel, and raced back to the exit road where Ritz waited. Buck had been gone only a few minutes, but apparently standing there had become too much for Ken. He sat with his knees pulled up, hands clasped in front of him.

Ritz struggled to his feet and appeared woozy, covering his eyes. Buck whipped open his door, but Ken said, "Stay there. I'm all right."

He squeezed himself in, knees pushing against the dashboard and his head pressing against the roof. He chuckled. "Buddy boy, I have to duck to see out."

"There's not much to see," Buck said. "Try to relax."

Ritz snorted. "You must've never been hit in the back of the head with an airplane."

"Can't say I have," Buck said, pulling onto the shoulder and passing several cars.

"Relaxing isn't the point. Surviving is. Why did you let me out of that hospital anyway? I needed another day or two of shut-eye."

"Don't put that on me. I tried to talk you out of leaving."

"I know. Just help me find my dope, would ya? Where's my bag?"

The Twin Cities' expressways were in relatively decent shape, compared to the Chicago area. By snaking between lane closures and detours, Buck moved at a steady pace. With his eyes on the road and one hand on the wheel, he reached behind Ken and grabbed his big leather bag. He strained, pulling it over the back of Ken's seat, and in the process dragged it hard across the back of Ken's head, causing him to screech.

"Oh, Ken! I'm so sorry! Are you all right?"

Ken sat with the bag in his lap. Tears streamed, and he grimaced so hard his teeth showed. "If I thought you did that on purpose," he rasped, "I'd kill you."

12

RAYFORD STEELE enjoyed a hunger for the Word of God from the day he had received Christ. He found, however, that as the world slowly began to get back to speed following the disappearances, he became busier than ever. It became increasingly difficult to spend the time he wanted to in the Bible.

His first pastor, the late Bruce Barnes, had impressed upon the Tribulation Force how important it was that they "search the Scriptures daily." Rayford tried to get himself in that groove, but for weeks he was frustrated. He tried getting up earlier but found himself involved in so many late-night discussions and activities that it wasn't practical. He tried reading his Bible during breaks on his flights, but that caused tension between him and his various copilots and first officers.

Finally he hit upon a solution. No matter where he was in the world, regardless of what he had done during the day or evening, sometime he would be going to bed. Regardless of the location or situation, before he turned out the light, he would get his daily Bible study in.

Bruce had at first been skeptical, urging him to give God the first few minutes of the day rather than the last. "You have to get up in the morning too," Bruce had said. "Wouldn't you rather give God your freshest and most energetic moments?"

Rayford saw the wisdom of that, but when it didn't seem to work, he went back to his own plan. Yes, he had at times fallen asleep while reading or praying, but usually he was able to stay alert, and God always showed him something.

Since losing his Bible in the earthquake, Rayford had been frustrated. Now, in the wee hours, he wanted to get onto the Internet, download a Bible, and see if Tsion Ben-Judah had posted anything. Rayford was grateful he had kept his laptop in his flight bag. If only he had kept his Bible there, he would still have that too.

In his undershirt, trousers, and socks, Rayford lugged his laptop to the communications center. Answering machines were engaged, but no personnel were around. He found an open phone jack, attached the cord, and sat where he could see his own door down the hall.

As information began appearing on his screen, he was distracted by footsteps. He lowered the screen and stared down the hall. A young, dark-haired man stopped at Rayford's door and knocked quietly. When there was no answer, he tried the knob. Rayford wondered if someone had been assigned to rob him or look for clues to the whereabouts of Hattie Durham or Tsion Ben-Judah.

The young man knocked again, his shoulders slumped, and he turned away. Then it hit Rayford. Could it be Hassid? He gave a loud "Psst!"

The young man stopped and looked toward the sound. Rayford was in the dark, so he raised his computer screen. The young man paused, clearly wondering if the figure at the computer was whom he wanted to see. Rayford imagined his concocting a story in case he encountered a superior officer.

Rayford signaled him, and the young man approached. His nameplate read David Hassid.

"May I see your mark?" Hassid whispered. Rayford put his face near the screen and pulled his hair back. "Like the young Americans say, that is so cool."

Rayford said, "You were looking for me?"

"I just wanted to meet you," Hassid said. "By the way, I work here in communications." Rayford nodded. "Though we don't have phones in our rooms, we do have phone jacks."

"I don't. I looked."

"They are covered with stainless steel plates."

"I did see that," Rayford said.

"So you don't need to risk getting caught out here, Captain Steele."

"That's good to know. It wouldn't surprise me if they could tell where I've been on the Web through here."

"They could. They can trace it through the lines in your room, too, but what will they find?"

"I'm just trying to find out what my friend, Tsion Ben-Judah, is saying these days."

"I could tell you by heart," Hassid said. "He is my spiritual father."

"Mine too."

"He led you to Christ?"

"Well, no," Rayford admitted. "That was his predecessor. But I still see the rabbi as my pastor and mentor."

"Let me write down for you the address of the central bulletin board where I found his message for today. It's a long one, but it's so good. He and a brother of his discovered their marks yesterday too. It's so exciting. Do you know that I am probably one of the 144,000 witnesses?"

"Well, that would be right, wouldn't it?" Rayford said.

"I can't wait to find out my assignment. I feel so new to this, so ignorant of the truth. I know the gospel, but it seems I need to know so much more if I'm going to be a bold evangelist, preaching like the apostle Paul."

"We're all new at this, David, if you think about it."

"But I'm newer than most. Wait till you see all the messages on the bulletin board. Thousands and thousands of believers have already responded. I don't know how Dr. Ben-Judah will have time to read them all. They're pleading with him to come to their countries and to teach them and train them face-to-face. I would give everything I owned for that privilege."

"You know, of course, that Dr. Ben-Judah is a fugitive."

"Yes, but he believes he is one of the 144,000 as well. He's teaching that we are sealed, at least for a time, and that the forces of evil cannot come against us."

"Really?"

"Yes. That protection is not for everyone who has the mark, apparently. But it is for the converted Jewish evangelists."

"In other words, I could be in danger, but you couldn't, at least for a while."

"That seems to be what he's teaching. I'll be eager to hear your response."

"I can't wait to plug in."

Rayford unplugged his machine and the two strolled down the corridor, whispering. Rayford discovered Hassid was just twenty-two years old, a college graduate who had aspired to military service in Poland. "But I was so enamored of Carpathia, I immediately applied for service to the Global Community. It wasn't long before I discovered the truth on the Internet. Now I am enlisted behind enemy lines, but I didn't plan it that way."

Rayford advised the young man that he was wise in not declaring himself until the time was right. "It will be dangerous enough for you to be a believer, but you'll be of greater help to the cause right now if you remain silent about it, as Officer McCullum is doing."

At Rayford's door, Hassid gripped his hand fiercely and squeezed hard. "It is so good to know I am not alone," he said. "Did you want to see my mark?"

Rayford smiled. "Sure."

Still shaking Rayford's hand, Hassid reached with his free hand and pulled his hair out of the way.

"Sure enough," Rayford said. "Welcome to the family."

\+ \+ \+

Buck found parking at the hospital similar to what it had been at the airport. The original pavement had sunk, and a turnaround had been scraped from the dirt at the front. But people had created their own parking places, and the only spot Buck could find was several hundred yards from the entrance. He dropped Ken off in front with his bag and told him to wait.

"If you promise not to smack me in the head again," Ken said. "Man, gettin' out of this car is like being born."

Buck parked in a haphazard line of other vehicles and grabbed a few toiletries from his own bag. As he headed toward the hospital, he tucked in his shirt, brushed himself down, combed his hair, and applied a few sprays of deodorant. When he got near the entrance he saw Ken on the ground, using his bag as a pillow. He wondered if pressing him into service had been a good idea. A few people stared at him. Ken appeared comatose. *Oh no!* Buck thought.

He knelt by Ken. "Are you all right?" he whispered. "Let me get you up."

Ken spoke without opening his eyes. "Oh, man! Buck, I did something royally stupid."

"What?"

"'Member when you got me my medicine?" Ken's words were slurred. "I popped 'em in my mouth without water, right?"

"I offered to get you something to drink."

"That's not the point. I was s'posed to take one from one bottle and three from the other, every four hours. I missed my last dose, so I took two of one and six of the other."

"Yeah?"

"But I mixed up the bottles."

"What are they?"

Ritz shrugged and his breathing became deep and regular.

"Don't fall asleep on me, Ken. I've got to get you inside."

Buck pawed through Ken's bag and found the bottles. The larger recommended dose was for local pain. The smaller appeared to be a combination of morphine, Demerol, and Prozac. "You took six of *these*?"

"Mm-hmm."

"Come on, Ken. Get up. Right now."

"Oh, Buck. Let me sleep."

"No way. Right now, we have to go."

Buck didn't think Ken was in danger or had to have his stomach pumped, but if he didn't get him inside, he'd be a dead weight and worthless. Worse, he would probably be hauled away.

Buck lifted one of Ken's hands and stuck his own head under Ken's arm. When he tried to straighten, Ken was no help and too heavy. "Come on, man. You've got to help me."

Ken just mumbled.

Buck held Ken's head gently and pulled the bag out from under him. "Let's go, let's go!"

"You mm-hmm."

Buck feared Ken's head was the only place still sensitive, and that might be dulled soon too. Rather than risk contaminating the wound, Buck looked for inflammation other than at the opening. Below where Ken had been gouged the hairline was fiery red. Buck spread his feet and braced himself, then pressed directly on the spot. Ritz leaped to his feet as if he'd been shot from a gun. He swung at Buck, who ducked, wrapped one arm around Ken's back, scooped up the bag with the other, and marched him to the entrance.

Ken looked and sounded like the deliriously injured man that he was. People moved out of the way.

Inside the hospital, things were worse. It was all Buck could do to hold Ken up. The lines at the front desk were five deep. Buck dragged Ken to the waiting area, where every chair was filled and several people were standing. Buck looked for someone who might give up his seat, and finally a stocky middle-aged woman stood. Buck thanked her and lowered Ken into the chair. Ken curled sideways, lifted his knees, drew his hands to his cheek, and rested on the shoulder of an old man next to him. The man caught sight of the wound, recoiled, then apparently resigned himself to serving as Ken's pillow.

Buck stuffed Ken's bag under his chair, apologized to the old man, and promised to be back as soon as he could. When he tried to move to the front at the receptionist's desk, people in two lines rebuffed him. He called out, "I'm sorry, but I have an emergency here!"

"We all do!" one shouted back.

He stood in line for several minutes, worrying more about Chloe than Ken. Ken would sleep this off. The only problem was, Buck was still stuck. Unless . . .

Buck stepped out of line and hurried into a public washroom. He washed his face; watered down and slicked back his hair, and made sure his clothes were as neat as possible. He pulled his identification card from his pocket and clipped it to his shirt, turning it around so his picture and name were hidden.

He popped the remaining lens out of his broken sunglasses, but the frames looked so phony that he pulled them up into his hair. He looked in the mirror and affected a grim expression, telling himself, "You are a doctor. A no-nonsense, big ego, all-action doctor."

He burst from the bathroom as if he knew where he was going. He needed a pigeon. The first two doctors he passed looked too old and mature for his ruse.

But here came a thin, young doctor looking wide-eyed and out of place. Buck stepped in front of him.

"Doctor, did I not tell you to check on that trauma in emergency two?"

The young physician was speechless.

"Well?" Buck demanded.

"No! No, Doctor. That must have been someone else."

"All right, then! Listen! I need a stethoscope—a sterile one this time!—a large, freshly laundered smock, and the chart on Mother Doe. You got that?"

The intern closed his eyes and repeated, "Stethoscope, smock, chart."

Buck continued barking. "Sterile, big, Mother Doe."

"Right away, Doctor."

"I'll be at the elevators."

"Yes, sir."

The intern turned and walked away. Buck called after him, "Sometime today, Doctor!" The intern ran.

Now Buck had to find the elevators. He slipped back into the reception area to find Ken still snoozing in the same position, the old man next to him looking as intimidated as ever. He asked a Hispanic woman if she knew where the elevators were. She pointed down the hall. As he hurried that way, he saw his intern behind the counter, hassling the receptionists. "Just do it!" he was saying.

A few minutes later the young doctor rushed to him with everything he had asked for. He held the smock open and Buck hastily slipped into it, draped the stethoscope around his neck, and grabbed the chart.

"Thank you, Doctor. Where are you from?"

"Right here!" the intern said. "This hospital."

"Oh, well then, good. Very good. I'm from . . ." Buck hesitated a second. "Young Memorial. Thanks for your help."

The intern looked puzzled, as if trying to think where Young Memorial was. "Any time," he said.

Buck left the elevators and hurried to the washroom. He locked himself in a stall and flipped open Chloe's chart. The photographs made him burst into tears. Buck set the clipboard on the floor and doubled over. "God," he prayed silently, "how could you have let this happen?"

He clenched his teeth and shuddered, willing himself to calm down. He didn't want to be heard. After about a minute, he opened the chart again. Staring at him from the photographs was the almost unrecognizable face of his young wife. Had she looked that swollen when she was brought to Kenosha, no doctor would have recognized her from Buck's picture.

As the doctor in Kenosha had told him, the right side of her body had apparently been slammed full force by a section of roofing. Her normally smooth, pale skin was now blotched red and yellow and invaded by pitch, tar, and bits of shingling. Worse, her right foot looked as if someone had tried to fold it. A bone protruded from her shin. Bruising began on the outside of her knee and ran to the kneecap, which looked severely damaged. From the position of her body, it appeared her right hip had been knocked out of joint. Bruises and bumps in her midsection evidenced broken ribs. Her elbow had been laid open, and her right shoulder appeared dislocated. Her right collarbone pressed against the skin. The right side of her face appeared flatter, and there was damage to her jaw, teeth, cheekbone, and eye. Her face was so misshapen that Buck could hardly bear to look. The eye was swollen huge and shut. The only abrasion on her left side was a raspberry near her hip, so the doctor had probably correctly deduced that she had been knocked off her feet by a blow to her right side.

Buck determined he would not recoil when he saw her in person. Of course, he wanted her to survive. But was that best for her? Could she communicate? Would she recognize him? He flipped through the rest of the chart, trying to interpret the notations. It appeared she had escaped injury to her internal organs. She suffered several fractures, including three in her foot, one in her ankle, her kneecap, her elbow, and two ribs. She had dislocated both hip and shoulder. She had also sustained fractures of the jaw, cheekbone, and cranium.

Buck scanned the rest quickly, looking for a key word. There it was. Fetal heartbeat detected. *Oh, God! Save them both!*

Buck didn't know medicine, but her vital signs looked good for someone who had suffered such a trauma. Though she had not regained consciousness at the time of the report, her pulse, respiration, blood pressure, and even brain waves were normal.

Buck looked at his watch. The GC contingent should arrive soon. He needed time to think and to collect himself. He would be no good to Chloe if he went off half-cocked. He memorized as much of the chart as he could, noted that she was in room 335A, and tucked the clipboard under his arm. He left the restroom with rubbery knees, but he affected a purposeful stride once he was in the corridor. While he pondered his options, he moved back into the reception area. The old man was gone. Ken Ritz no longer leaned on anyone, but his gigantic frame was curled in a fetal position like an overgrown child, the healthy part of his head resting on the back of the chair. He looked as if he could sleep for a week.

Buck took the elevator to the third floor to get the lay of the land. As the doors opened, however, something struck him. He whipped open the chart.

"335A." She was in a double room. What if he was the doctor for the other patient? Even if he wasn't on a security list, they'd have to let him in, wouldn't they? He might have to bluster, but he would get in.

Two uniformed GC guards stood on either side of the 335 doorway. One was a young man, the other a slightly older woman. Two strips of white adhesive tape were attached to the door, both written on in black marker. The top said, "A: Mother Doe, No Visitors." The other read, "B: A. Ashton."

Buck was weak with longing to check on Chloe. With the clock working against him, he wanted to get in there before GC officials did. He passed the room, and at the end of the hall turned and walked directly back to 335.

* * *

Rayford had not been prepared for what he found on the Internet. Tsion had outdone himself. As David Hassid had said, thousands upon thousands had already responded. Many put messages on the bulletin board identifying themselves as members of the 144,000. Rayford scrolled through the messages for more than an hour, still not coming to the end. Hundreds testified that they had received Christ after reading Tsion's message and the verses from Romans that showed their need of God.

It was late, and Rayford was bleary-eyed. He had intended to spend not more than an hour on the Net, but he had spent that and more merely working through Tsion's message. "The Coming Soul Harvest" was a fascinating study of biblical prophecy. Tsion made himself so understandable and personable that it did not surprise Rayford that thousands considered themselves his protégés, though they had never met him. From the looks of the bulletin board, however, that would have to change. They clamored for him to come where they could meet him and sit under his tutelage.

Tsion responded to the requests by telling his own story, how as a biblical scholar he had been commissioned by the State of Israel to study the claims of the coming Messiah. He explained that by the time of the rapture of the church, he had come to the conclusion that Jesus of Nazareth fulfilled every qualification of the Messiah prophesied in the Old Testament. But he did not receive Christ as his own savior until the Rapture convinced him.

He kept his belief to himself until he was asked to go on international television to reveal the results of his lengthy study. He was astounded that the Jews still refused to believe that Jesus was who the Bible claimed he was. Tsion revealed his finding at the very end of the program, causing tremendous outcry, especially among the orthodox. His wife and two teenage children were later slaughtered, and he barely escaped. He told his Internet audience he was now in hiding but that he would "continue to teach and to proclaim that Jesus Christ is the only name under heaven given among men through whom one can be saved."

Rayford forced himself to stay awake, poring over Tsion's teachings. A meter on his screen showed the number of responses as they were added to the central bulletin board. He believed the meter was malfunctioning. It raced so fast he could not even see the individual numerals. He sampled a few of the responses. Not only were many converted Jews claiming to be among the 144,000 witnesses, but Jews and Gentiles were also trusting Christ. Thousands more encouraged each other to petition the Global Community for protection and asylum for this great scholar.

Rayford felt a tingle behind his knees that shot to his head. One bit of leverage with Nicolae Carpathia was the court of public opinion. It wasn't beyond him to have Tsion Ben-Judah assassinated or "accidentally" killed and make it appear other forces were at work. But with thousands all over the globe appealing to Nicolae on Tsion's behalf, he would be forced to prove he could deliver. Rayford wished there was some way to make him do the right thing by Hattie Durham as well.

Tsion's main message for the day was based on Revelation 8 and 9. Those chapters supported his contention that the earthquake, the foretold wrath of the Lamb, ushered in the second twenty-one months of the Tribulation.

There are seven years, or eighty-four months, in all. So, my dear friends, you can see that we are now one quarter of the way through. Unfortunately, as bad as things have been, they get progressively worse as we race headlong toward the end, the glorious appearing of Christ.

What is next? In Revelation 8:5 an angel takes a censer, fills it with fire from the altar of God, and throws it to the earth. That results in noise, thunder, lightning, and an earthquake.

That same chapter goes on to say that seven angels with seven trumpets prepared themselves to sound. That is where we are now. Sometime over the next twenty-one months, the first angel will sound, and hail and fire will follow, mingled with blood, thrown down to the earth. This will burn a third of the trees and all the green grass.

Later a second angel will sound the second trumpet, and the Bible says a great mountain burning with fire will be thrown into the sea. This will turn a third of the water to blood, kill a third of the living creatures in the sea, and sink a third of the ships.

The third angel's trumpet sound will result in a great star falling from heaven, burning like a torch. It will somehow fall over a wide area and land in a third of the rivers and springs. This star is even named in Scripture. The book of Revelation calls it Wormwood. Where it falls, the water becomes bitter and people die from drinking it.

How can a thinking person see all that has happened and not fear what is to come? If there are still unbelievers after the third Trumpet Judgment, the fourth should convince everyone. Anyone who resists the warnings of God at that time will likely have already decided to serve the enemy. The fourth Trumpet Judgment is a striking of the sun, the moon, and the stars so that a third of the sun, a third of the moon, and a third of the stars are darkened. We will never again see sunshine as bright as we have before. The brightest summer day with the sun high in the sky will be only two-thirds as bright as it ever was. How will this be explained away?

In the middle of this, the writer of the Revelation says he looked and heard an angel "flying through the midst of heaven." It was saying with a loud voice, "Woe, woe, woe to the inhabitants of the earth, because of the remaining blasts of the trumpet of the three angels who are about to sound!"

In my next lesson, I will cover those last three Trumpet Judgments of the second twenty-one months of the Tribulation. But, my beloved brothers and sisters in Christ, victory is also coming. Let me remind you with a few choice passages of Scripture that the outcome has already been determined. We win! But we must share the truth and expose the darkness and bring as many as possible to Christ in these last days.

I want to show you why I believe there is a great soul harvest coming. But first, consider these statements and promises:

In the Old Testament book of Joel 2:28-32, God is speaking. He says, "And it shall come to pass afterward that I will pour out My Spirit on all flesh; your sons and your daughters shall prophesy, your old men shall dream dreams, your young men shall see visions. And also on My menservants and on My maidservants I will pour out My Spirit in those days.

"And I will show wonders in the heavens and in the earth: blood and fire and pillars of smoke. The sun shall be turned into darkness, and the moon into blood, before the coming of the great and awesome day of the Lord.

"And it shall come to pass that whoever calls on the name of the Lord shall be saved. For in Mount Zion and in Jerusalem there shall be deliverance, as the Lord has said, among the remnant whom the Lord calls."

Is that not a wonderful and most blessed promise? Revelation 7 indicates that the Trumpet Judgments I just mentioned will not come until the servants of God have been sealed on their foreheads. There will no longer be any question who the true believers are. Those first four angels, to whom it was granted to carry out the first four Trumpet Judgments, were instructed, "Do not harm the earth, the sea, or the trees till we have sealed the servants of our God on their foreheads." Thus it is clear that this sealing comes first. Just within the last several hours, it has become clear to me and to other brothers and sisters in Christ that the seal on the forehead of the true believer is already visible, but apparently only to other believers. This was a thrilling discovery, and I look forward to hearing from many of you who detect it on each other.

The word servants, *from the Greek word* doulos, *is the same word the apostles Paul and James used when they referred to themselves as the bond slaves of Jesus Christ. The chief function of a servant of Christ is to communicate the gospel of the grace of God. We will be inspired by the fact that we can understand the book of Revelation, which was given by God, according to the first verse of the first chapter "to show His servants things which must shortly take place." The third verse says, "Blessed is he who reads and those who hear the words of this prophecy, and keep those things which are written in it, for the time is near."*

Although we will go through great persecution, we can comfort ourselves that during the Tribulation we look forward to astounding events outlined in Revelation, the last book in God's revealed plan for man.

Now indulge me for one more verse from Revelation 7, and I will conclude with why I anticipate this great harvest of souls.

Revelation 7:9 quotes John the revelator, "After these things I looked, and behold, a great multitude which no one could number *[emphasis mine], of all nations, tribes, peoples, and tongues, standing before the throne and before the Lamb, clothed with white robes, with palm branches in their hands. . . ."*

These are the tribulation saints. Now follow me carefully. In a later verse, Revelation 9:16, the writer numbers the army of horsemen in a battle at two hundred million. If such a vast army can *be numbered, what might the Scriptures mean when they refer to the tribulation saints, those who come to Christ during this period, as "a great multitude* which no one could number*" [emphasis mine]?*

Do you see why I believe we are justified in trusting God for more than a billion souls during this period? Let us pray for that great harvest. All who name Christ as their Redeemer can have a part in this, the greatest task ever assigned to mankind. I look forward to interacting with you again soon.

With love, in the matchless name of the Lord Jesus Christ, our Savior, Tsion Ben-Judah.

Rayford could barely keep his eyes open, but he was thrilled with Tsion's boundless enthusiasm and insightful teaching. He returned to the bulletin board and blinked. The number at the top of the screen was in the tens of thousands and rising. Rayford wanted to add to the avalanche, but he was exhausted.

Nicolae Carpathia had addressed the globe on radio and television. No doubt the response would be monumental. But would it rival the reaction to this converted rabbi, communicating from exile to a new, growing family?

+ + +

Buck reminded himself that, for the moment, he was not just a doctor, but also an egomaniac. He strode to room 335 without so much as a nod to the two Global Community guards. As he pushed open the door, they stepped into his path.

"Excuse me!" he said with disgust. "Miss Ashton's alarm rang, so unless you want to be responsible for the death of my patient, you will let me pass."

The guards looked at each other, appearing uncertain. The woman reached for Buck's ID tag. He pushed her hand away and entered the room, locking the door. He hesitated before turning around, prepared to respond if they began banging. They didn't.

Draperies hid both patients. Buck pulled back the first to reveal his wife. He held his breath as his eyes traveled over the sheet from feet to neck. It felt as if his heart was literally breaking. Poor sweet Chloe had no idea what she was getting into when she agreed to marry him. He bit his lip hard. There was no time to emote. He was grateful she seemed to be sleeping peacefully. Her right arm was in a cast from wrist to shoulder. Her left arm lay motionless at her side, an IV needle in the back of her hand.

Buck set the clipboard on the bed and slipped his hand under hers. The baby-soft skin he cherished made him long to gather her in his arms, to soothe her, to take her pain. He bent and brushed her fingers with his lips, his tears falling between them. He jumped when he felt a weak grip and looked at her. She stared at him. "I'm here!" he whispered desperately. He moved to where he could caress her cheek. "Chloe, sweetheart, it's Buck."

He leaned close. Her gaze followed him. He forced himself not to look at her shattered right side. She was his sweet, innocent wife on one side and a monster on the other. He took her hand again.

"Can you hear me? Chloe, squeeze my hand again."

No response.

Buck hurried to the other side and pulled back the drape to peek through to the other bed. A. Ashton was in her late fifties and appeared to be in a coma.

Buck returned, grabbed his clipboard, and studied Chloe's face. Her look still followed him. Could she hear? Was she conscious?

He unlocked the door and stepped quickly into the hall. "She's out of danger for the moment," he said, "but we've got a problem. Who told you Miss Ashton was in bed B?"

"Excuse me, doctor," the woman guard said, "but we have nothing to do with the patients. Our responsibility is the door."

"So, you're not responsible for this screwup?"

"Absolutely not," the woman said.

Buck pulled the adhesive strips from the door and reversed them. "Ma'am, can you handle this post yourself while this young man finds me a marker?"

"Certainly, sir. Craig, get him a marker."

13

BUCK SLIPPED BACK into Chloe's room, desperate to let her know he was there and she was safe.

He could hardly bear to look at her black and purple face with the eye so swollen. He gently took her hand and leaned close. "Chloe, I'm here, and I won't let anything happen to you. But I need your help. Squeeze my hand. Blink. Let me know you're with me."

No response. Buck laid his cheek on her pillow, his lips inches from her ear. "Oh, God," he prayed, "why couldn't you have let this happen to me? Why her? Help me get her out of here, God, please!"

Her hand felt like a feather, and she seemed fragile as a newborn. What a contrast to the strong woman he had loved and come to know. She was not only fearless, but she was also smart. How he wished she was up to being his ally in this.

Chloe's breathing accelerated, and Buck opened his eyes as a tear slid past her ear. He looked her in the face. She blinked furiously, and he wondered if she was trying to communicate. "I'm here," he said over and over. "Chloe, it's Buck."

The GC guard had been gone too long. Buck prayed he was out there waiting with the marker but too intimidated to knock. Otherwise, who knew whom he might bring with him and what might squash any chance Buck had to protect Chloe.

He spoke quickly. "Sweetheart, I don't know if you can hear me, but try to concentrate. I'm switching your name with the woman's in the other bed. Her name is Ashton. And I'm pretending to be your doctor. OK? Can you grasp that?"

Buck waited, hoping. Finally, a flicker.

"I got you those," she whispered.

"What? Chloe, what? It's me, Buck. You got me what?"

She licked her lips and swallowed. "I got you those, and you broke them."

He concluded she was delirious. This was gibberish. He shook his head and smiled at her. "Stick with me, kid, and we'll pull something off."

"Doctor Buck," she rasped, attempting a lopsided smile.

"Yes! Chloe! You know me."

She squinted and blinked slowly now as if staying awake was an effort. "You should take better care of gifts."

"I don't know what you're saying, sweetness, and I'm not sure you do either. But whatever I did, I'm sorry."

For the first time, she turned to face him. "You broke your glasses, Doctor Buck."

Buck reflexively touched the frames on his head. "Yes! Chloe, listen to me. I'm trying to protect you. I switched the names on the door. You're—"

"Ashton," she managed.

"Yes! And your first initial is *A*. What's a good *A* name?"

"Annie," she said. "I'm Annie Ashton."

"Perfect. And who am I?"

She pressed her lips together and started to form a *B*, then changed. "My doctor," she said.

Buck turned to go see if Craig, the guard, had brought the marker. "Doctor," Chloe called out. "Wristbands."

She was thinking! How could he forget that someone could easily check their hospital ID bracelets?

He yanked hers apart, careful not to dislodge the IV. He slipped behind A. Ashton's curtain. She still appeared sound asleep. He carefully removed her bracelet, noticing she did not appear even to be breathing. He put his ear close to her nose but heard and felt nothing. He could find no pulse. He switched the wristbands.

Buck knew this only bought him time. It wouldn't be long before someone discovered that this postmenopausal dead woman was not a pregnant twenty-two-year-old. But for the time being, she was Mother Doe.

When Buck emerged, the guards were talking to an older doctor. Craig, black marker in hand, was saying, ". . . we weren't sure what to do."

The doctor, tall, bespectacled, and gray, carried three charts. He scowled at Buck.

Buck sneaked a peek at the name sewn on his breast pocket. "Dr. Lloyd!" he exulted, thrusting out his hand.

The doctor reluctantly shook it, "Do I—?"

"Why, I haven't seen you since that, uh, that—"

"The symposium?"

"Right! The one at, um—"

"Bemidji?"

"Yeah, you were brilliant."

The doctor looked flustered, as if trying to remember Buck, yet the praise had not been lost on him. "Well, I—"

"And one of your kids was up to something. What was it?"

"Oh, I may have mentioned my son, who just got his internship."

"Right! How's he doing anyway?"

"Wonderfully. We're very proud of him. Now, Doctor—"

Buck interrupted. "I'll bet you are. Listen," he said, pulling Ken Ritz's pill bottles from his pocket, "I wonder if you could advise me. . . ."

"I'll certainly try."

"Thank you, Doctor Lloyd." He held up the tranquilizer bottle. "I prescribed this to a patient with a severe head wound, and he inadvertently exceeded the dosage. What's the best antidote?"

Dr. Lloyd studied the bottle. "It's not that serious. He'll be very sleepy for a few hours, but it'll wear off. Head trauma, you say?"

"Yes, that's why I'd rather he not sleep."

"Of course. You'll most safely counteract this with an injection of Benzedrine."

"Not being on staff here," Buck said, "I can't get anything from the pharmacy. . . ."

Dr. Lloyd scribbled him a prescription. "If you'll excuse me, Doctor—?"

"Cameron," Buck said before thinking.

"Of course, Dr. Cameron. Great to see you again."

"You too, Dr. Lloyd, and thanks."

Buck accepted the marker from the chagrined Craig and changed the strips on the door from *B* and *A* to *A* and *B*. "I'll be back soon, Craig," he said, slapping the marker into the guard's palm.

Buck hurried off, pretending to know where he was going but scanning directories and following signs as he went. Dr. Lloyd's prescription was like gold at the pharmacy, and he was soon on his way back to the lobby for Ken Ritz. On the way he appropriated a wheelchair.

He found Ken leaning forward, elbows on his knees, chin in his hands, snoring. Grateful for his training taking his turn giving his mother insulin injections, Buck deftly opened the package, raised Ken's sleeve without toppling him, swabbed the area, and pulled the cap off the hypodermic needle with his teeth. As he drove the point into Ken's biceps, the cap popped from his mouth and rattled to the floor. Someone muttered, "Shouldn't he be wearing gloves?"

Buck found the cap, replaced it, and put everything in his pocket. Facing Ken, he thrust his wrists into the big man's armpits and pulled him from the chair. He turned him 45 degrees and lowered him into the wheelchair, having forgotten to set the brake. When Ken hit the chair, it began rolling backwards, and Buck had no leverage to remove his hands. Straddling Ritz's long legs, his face in Ken's chest, Buck stumbled across the waiting room as onlookers dived out of the way. As the chair picked up speed, Buck's only option was to drag his feet. He wound up sprawled across the lanky pilot, who roused briefly and called out, "Charlie Bravo Alpha to base!"

Buck extracted himself, lowered the footrests, and lifted Ritz's knees to set his feet in place. Then they were off to find a gurney. His hope was that Ritz would respond quickly enough to the Benzedrine to be able to help him take Miss Ashton's body, with Mother Doe's wristband, to the morgue. If he could temporarily convince the Global Community delegation that their potential hostage had expired, he could buy time.

As Buck wheeled him toward the elevators, Ken's arms kept flopping out of the chair and acting as brakes on the wheels. Buck would grab them and tuck them back in, only to find himself veering into traffic. Buck finally secured Ken's arms by the time they backed onto an elevator, but Ritz chose that moment to let his chin drop to his chest, exposing his scalp wound to everyone aboard.

When Ritz seemed to begin coming out of his fog, Buck was able to get him out of the chair and onto a gurney he had absconded with. The sudden rise, however, had made Ken dizzy. He flopped onto his back, and his head wound brushed the sheet. "OK!" he hollered like a drunk. "All right!"

He rolled to his side, and Buck covered him to the neck, then wheeled him next to the wall, where he waited for him to fully awaken. Twice, as lots of traffic walked by, Ken spontaneously sat up, looked around, and lay back down.

When he finally came to and was able to sit and then stand without dizziness, he was still disoriented. "Man, that was some good sleep. I could use more of that."

Buck explained that he wanted to find Ken a smock and have him play an orderly, helping Dr. Cameron. Buck went over it several times until Ken convinced him he was awake and understood. "Wait right here," Buck said.

Near a surgical unit he saw a doctor hang a smock on a hook before heading the other way. It looked clean, so Buck took it back to Ken. But Ken was gone.

Buck found him at the elevator. "What are you doing?"

"I've gotta get my bag," Ken said. "We left it outside."

"It's under a chair in the waiting room. We'll get it later. Now put this on." The sleeves were four inches short. Ken looked like the last renter in a costume shop.

Pushing the gurney, they hurried to 335 as fast as Ken could go. The woman guard said, "Doctor, we just got a call from our superiors that a delegation is on its way from the airport, and—"

"I'm sorry, ma'am," Buck said, "but the patient you're guarding has died."

"Died?" she said. "Well, it certainly wasn't our fault. We—"

"No one is saying it's your fault. Now I need to take the body to the morgue. You can tell your delegation or whomever where to find her."

"Then we don't need to stay here, do we?"

"Of course not. Thanks for your service."

As Buck and Ken entered the room, Craig caught sight of Ritz's head. "Man, are you an orderly or a patient?"

Ken whirled around. "Are you discriminating against the handicapped?"

"No, sir, I'm sorry. It's just—"

"Everybody needs a job!" Ken said.

Chloe tried to smile when she saw Ken, whom she had met at Palwaukee after Buck and Tsion's flight from Egypt. Buck looked pointedly at Ritz. "Meet Annie Ashton," he said. "I'm her doctor."

"Dr. Buck," Chloe said quietly. "He broke his glasses."

Ritz smiled. "Sounds like we're on the same medication."

Buck pulled the sheet over the dead woman's head, rolled her bed out, and replaced it with the gurney. He wheeled the bed to the door and asked Ken to stay with Chloe, "just in case."

"In case what?"

"In case those GC guys show up."

"I get to play doctor?"

"In a manner of speaking. If we can convince them the woman they want is in the morgue, we might have time to hide Chloe."

"You don't want to strap her to the top of our rental car?"

Buck pushed the bed down the corridor to the elevators. Getting off were four people, three of them men, dressed in dark business suits. Tags on their jackets identified them as Global Community operatives. One said, "What are we looking for again?"

Another said, "335."

Buck averted his face, not knowing whether his picture had been circulated. As soon as he rolled the bed onto the elevator, a doctor hit the emergency stop button. A half dozen people were in the car with Buck and the body. "I'm sorry, ladies and gentlemen," the doctor said. "Just a moment, please."

He whispered in Buck's ear, "You're not a resident here, are you?"

"No."

"There are strict rules about transporting corpses on other than the service elevators."

"I didn't know."

The doctor turned to the others. "I'm sorry, but you're going to need to take another elevator."

"Gladly," somebody said.

The doctor turned the elevator back on, and everyone else got off. He hit the button for the subbasement. "First time in this hospital?"

"Yes."

"Left and all the way to the end."

At the morgue, Buck thought about leaving the body outside the door and hoping it would be misidentified temporarily as Mother Doe. But he was seen by a man behind the desk who said, "You're not supposed to bring beds in here. We can't be responsible for that. You'll have to take it back with you."

"I'm on a tight schedule."

"That's your problem. We're not answering for a room bed being down here."

Two orderlies lifted the body to a gurney, and the man said, "Papers?"

"I'm sorry?"

"Papers! Death certificate. Doctor's sign-off."

Buck said, "Wristband says Mother Doe. I was told to bring her down here. That's all I know."

"Who's her doctor?"

"I have no idea."

"What room?"

"335."

"We'll look it up. Now get this bed out of here."

Buck hurried back to the elevator, praying the ruse had worked and that the GC contingent was on its way to the morgue to make sure about Mother Doe. He did not cross paths with them, however, on the way back.

He was almost at room 335 when they emerged. He looked the other way and kept walking.

One said, "Where's Charles, anyway?"

The woman said, "We should have waited. He was parking the car. How's he supposed to find us now?"

"He can't be far. When he gets here, we'll get to the bottom of this."

When they were out of sight, Buck pushed the bed back into 335. "It's just me," he said as he passed Chloe's curtain. He found Chloe even paler and now trembling. Ken sat next to the bed, hands resting lightly atop his head.

"Are you cold, hon?" Buck asked. Chloe shook her head. Her discoloration had spread. The ugly streaks caused by bleeding under the skin nearly reached her temple.

"She's a little shook, that's all," Ritz said. "Me too, though I deserve an Oscar."

"Doctor Airplane," Chloe said, and Ritz laughed.

"That's what she said. That's all they could get out of her, except her name."

"Annie Ashton," she whispered.

"Screwed up those guys' heads something awful. They come in complaining, especially the woman, about having no guards assigned like they asked. 'We didn't ask,' Ken said, mimicking her voice. 'It was a directive.'"

Chloe nodded.

Ken continued. "They shuffle past, snagging the end of our drape, talking about how she's in bed B, all proud of themselves because they can read an adhesive strip on the door. I call out, 'Two visitors at a time, please, and I'd appreciate you keeping it down. I have a toxic patient here.' I meant infectious, but it means the same, doesn't it?

"'Course they saw right away there was just an empty gurney over there. One of the guys pokes his head in here and I raise way up on my tiptoes, doctorlike, and say, 'If you don't want typhoid fever, you'd better pull your face outta here.'"

"Typhoid fever?"

"It sounded good to me. And it did the trick."

"That scared them off?"

"Well, almost. He shut the curtain and said from behind it, 'Doctor, may we speak to you in private, please?' I said, 'I can't leave my patient. And I'd have to scrub before I talk to anybody. I'm immune, but I can carry the disease.'"

Buck raised his eyebrows. "They bought this?"

Chloe shook her head, appearing amused.

Ken said, "Hey, I was good. They asked who my patient was. I could have told them Annie Ashton, but I thought it was more realistic if I acted insulted by the question. I said, 'Her name's not as important as her prognosis. Anyway, her name's on the door.' I heard them *tsk-tsk*ing and one said, 'Is she conscious?' I said, 'If you're not a doctor, it's none of your business.' The woman said something about their having a doctor who hadn't caught up to them yet, and I said, 'You can ask me whatever you need to know.'

"One of them says, 'We know what it says on the door, but we were told Mother Doe was in that bed.' I said, 'I'm not going to stand here and argue. My patient is not Mother Doe.'

"One of the guys says, 'You mind if we ask her what *her* name is?' I say, 'As a matter of fact, I do mind. She needs to concentrate on getting better.' The guy says, 'Ma'am, if you can hear me, tell me your name.'

"I nod to Chloe so she'll tell 'em, but I'm stomping toward the curtain like I'm mad. She hesitates, not sure what I'm up to, but finally she says, acting real weak like, 'Annie Ashton.'"

Chloe raised her hand. "Not acting," she said. "Why'd they name me Mother Doe?"

"You don't know?" Buck said, reaching for her hand.

She shook her head.

"Let me finish my story," Ritz said. "I think they're coming back. I whipped that curtain open and stared them down. I don't guess they expected me to be so big. I said, 'There! Satisfied? Now you've upset her and me too.' The woman says, 'Excuse us, Doctor, ah—' and Chloe says, 'Doctor Airplane.' I had to bite my tongue. I said, 'The medication's getting to her,' which it was. I said, 'I'm Doctor Lalaine, but we'd better not shake hands, all things considered.'

"The rest of 'em are all crowded around the door, and the woman peeks through the curtain and says, 'Do you have any idea what happened to Mother Doe?' I tell her, 'One patient from this room was taken to the morgue.'

"She says, 'Oh, really?' in a tone that tells me she doesn't believe that one bit. She says, 'What caused *this* young lady's injuries? Typhoid?' Real sarcastic. I wasn't ready for that one, and while I'm trying to think up a smart, doctory answer, she says, 'I'm going to have our physician examine her.'

"I tell her, 'I don't know how they do it where you're from, but in this hospital only the attending physician or the patient can ask for a second opinion.' Well, even though she's a good foot shorter than me, she somehow looks down her nose at me. She says, 'We are from the Global Community, here under orders from His Excellency himself. So be prepared to give ground.'

"I say, 'Who the heck is His Excellency?' She says, 'Where have you been, under a rock?' Well, I couldn't tell her that was just about right and that because I had OD'd on tranqs I wasn't too sure where I was now, so I said, 'Servin' mankind, trying to save lives, ma'am.' She huffed out, and a couple minutes later, you walked in. You're up-to-date."

"And they're bringing in a doctor," Buck said. "Terrific. We'd better hide her someplace and see if we can get her lost in the system."

"Answer me," Chloe whispered.

"What?"

"Buck, am I pregnant?"

"Yes."

"Is the baby OK?"

"So far."

"How 'bout me?"

"You're pretty banged up, but you're not in danger."

"Your typhoid fever is almost gone," Ritz said.

Chloe frowned. "Dr. Airplane," she scolded. "Buck, I have to get better fast. What do these people want?"

"It's a long story. Basically, they want to trade you for either Tsion or Hattie or both."

"No," she said, her voice stronger.

"Don't worry," Buck said. "But we'd better get going. We're not going to fool a real doctor for long, despite Joe Thespian here."

"That's Dr. Airplane to you," Ken said.

Buck heard people at the door. He dropped to the floor and crawled under two curtains, squatting in the area already crowded with both bed and gurney.

"Dr. Lalaine," one of the men said, "this is our physician from Kenosha. We would appreciate it if you would let him examine this patient."

"I don't understand," Ritz said.

"Of course you don't," the doctor said, "but I helped treat an unidentified patient yesterday who matched this description. That's why I was invited."

Buck shut his eyes. The voice sounded familiar. If it was the last doctor he had talked to in Kenosha, the one who'd taken pictures of Chloe, all hope was gone. Even if Buck surprised them and came out swinging, there was no way he could get Chloe out of that place.

Ritz said, "I've already told these people who this patient is."

"And we've already proven your story false, Doctor," the woman said. "We asked for Mother Doe in the morgue. It didn't take long to determine that that was the real Ms. Ashton."

Buck heard an envelope being opened, something being pulled out. "Look at these pictures," the woman said. "She may not be a dead ringer, but she's close. I think that's her."

"There's one way to be sure," the doctor said. "My patient had three small scars on her left knee from arthroscopic surgery when she was a teenager, and also an appendectomy scar."

Buck was reeling. Neither was true of Chloe. What was going on?

Buck heard the rustle of blanket, sheet, and gown. "You know, this doesn't really surprise me," the doctor said. "I thought the face was a little too round and the bruising more extensive on this girl."

"Well," the woman said, "even if this isn't who we're looking for, it isn't Annie Ashton, and she certainly doesn't have typhoid fever."

"Nobody in this hospital has typhoid fever," Ken said. "I say that to keep people's noses out of my patients' business."

"I want this man brought up on charges," the woman said. "Why wouldn't he know the name of his own patient?"

"There are too many patients right now," Ken said. "Anyway, I was told this was Annie Ashton. That's what it says on the door."

"I'll talk to the chief of staff here about Dr. Lalaine," the doctor said. "I suggest the rest of you check admissions again for Mother Doe."

"Doctor?" Chloe said in a tiny voice. "You have something on your forehead."

"I do?" he said.

"I don't see anything," the woman said. "This girl is doped up."

"No, I'm not," Chloe said. "You do have something there, Doctor."

"Well," he said, pleasantly but dismissively, "you're probably going to have something on your forehead too, once you recover."

"Let's get going," one of the men said.

"I'll find you after I've talked to the chief of staff," the doctor said.

The others left. As soon as the door shut, the doctor said, "I know who *she* is. Who are *you*?"

"I'm Dr. —"

"We both know you're no doctor."

"Yes he is," Chloe slurred. "He's Dr. Airplane."

Buck emerged from behind the curtain. "Dr. Charles, meet my pilot, Ken Ritz. Have you ever been an answer to prayer before?"

"It wasn't easy getting assigned to this," Floyd Charles said. "But I thought I might come in handy."

"I don't know how I can ever thank you," Buck said.

"Keep in touch," the doctor said. "I may need you someday. I suggest we transfer your wife out of here. They'll come look more closely when they don't find Mother Doe."

"Can you arrange transportation to the airport and everything we'll need to take care of her?" Buck asked.

"Sure. As soon as I get Dr. Airplane's medical license suspended."

Ken whipped off his smock. "I've had enough of doctorin' anyway," he said. "I'm going back to sky jockeying."

"Will I be able to take care of her at home?" Buck asked.

"She'll be in a lot of pain for a long time and may never feel like she used to, but there's nothing life-threatening here. The baby's fine too, as far as we know."

"I didn't know until today," Chloe said. "I suspected, but I didn't know."

"You almost gave me away with that forehead remark," Dr. Charles said.

"Yeah," Ken said. "What was that all about?"

"I'll tell you both on the plane," Buck said.

* * *

Early Thursday morning in New Babylon, Nicolae Carpathia and Leon Fortunato met with Rayford. "We have communicated your itinerary to the dignitaries," Carpathia said. "They have arranged for appropriate accommodations for the Supreme Commander, but you and your first officer should make your own arrangements."

Rayford nodded. This meeting, as with so many, was unnecessary.

"Now on a personal note," Carpathia added, "while I understand your position, it has been decided not to dredge the wreckage of the Pan-Con flight from the Tigris. I am sorry, but it has been confirmed your wife was on board. We should consider that her final resting place, along with the other passengers."

Rayford believed in his gut Carpathia was lying. Amanda was alive, and she was certainly no traitor to the cause of Christ. He and Mac had scuba gear coming, and while he had no idea where Amanda *was*, he would start by proving she was *not* on board that submerged 747.

Two hours before flight time Friday, Mac told Rayford he had replaced the fixed-wing aircraft in the cargo hold. "We're already takin' the chopper," he said. "That little two-engine job is redundant. I replaced it with the Challenger 3."

"Where'd you find that?" The Challenger was about the size of a Learjet but nearly twice as fast. It had been developed during the last six months.

"I thought we lost everything but the chopper, the fixed-wing, and the Condor. But beyond the rise in the middle of the airstrip, I found the Challenger. I had to install a new antenna and a new tail rudder system, but she's good as new."

"I wish I knew how to fly it," Rayford said. "Maybe I could see my family while Fortunato's laying over in Texas."

"They found your daughter?"

"Just got the word. She's banged up, but she's fine. And I'm going to be a grandpa."

"That's great, Ray!" Mac said, patting Rayford on the shoulder. "I'll teach you the Challenger. You'll know how to drive it in no time."

"I've got to finish packing and get an e-mail to Buck," Rayford said.

"You're not sending or receiving through the system here, are you?"

"No. I got a coded e-mail from Buck informing me when my private phone would be ringing. I made sure I was outside at that time."

"We've got to talk to Hassid about how secure the Internet is in here. You and he and I have all been on the Net, keeping track of your friend Tsion. I'm worried that the brass can tell who's been on. Carpathia's got to be furious about Tsion. We could all be in trouble."

"David told me that if we stay with the bulletin boards, we're not traceable."

"He'd like to be going with us, you know," Mac said.

"David? I know. But we need him right where he is."

14

THE FLIGHT TO WAUKEGAN had been difficult for Chloe. The drive from Waukegan to Wheeling to drop off Ken Ritz, and then on to Mount Prospect, was worse. She had slept in Buck's arms during virtually the entire flight, but the Range Rover had been torture.

The best Buck could do was let her lie across the backseat, but one of the fasteners connecting the seat to the floor had broken loose during the earthquake, so he had to drive even slower than normal. Still, Chloe seemed to bounce the whole way. Finally Ken knelt, facing the back, and tried to brace the seat with his hands.

When they got to Palwaukee Airport, Buck walked Ken to the Quonset hut where he had been given a corner to move into. "Always an adventure," Ken said wearily. "One of these days you're gonna get me killed."

"It was stupid to ask you to fly so soon after surgery, Ken, but you were a lifesaver. I'll send you a check."

"You always do. But I also want to know more about where all you guys are, you know, with your beliefs and everything."

"Ken, we've been through this before. It's becoming pretty clear now, wouldn't you say? This whole period of history, this is it. Just a little more than five more years, and it's all over. I can see why people might not have understood what was happening before the Rapture. I was one of them. But it's come to one giant countdown. The whole deal now is which side you're on. You're either serving God or you're serving the Antichrist. You've been a supplier for the good guys. It's time you joined our team."

"I know, Buck. I've never seen anything like how you people take care of each other. It'd be good for me if I could see it all one more time in black and white, you know, like on one sheet of paper, pros and cons. That's how I am. I figure it out, and I make my decision."

"I can get you a Bible."

"I've got a Bible somewhere. Are there like one or two pages that have the whole deal spelled out?"

"Read John. And then Romans. You'll see the stuff we've talked about. We're sinners. We're separated from God. He wants us back. He's provided the way."

Ken looked uncomfortable. Buck knew he was light-headed and in pain. "Have you got a computer?"

"Yeah, even an e-mail address."

"Let me have it, and I'll write down a newsgroup for you. The guy you brought back from Egypt with me is the hottest thing on the Internet. Talk about putting everything on one page for you, he does it."

"So once I join up I get the secret mark on my forehead?"

"You sure do."

Buck reclined the front passenger seat and moved Chloe there. But it wasn't flat enough, and she soon retreated again to the back. When Buck finally pulled into the backyard at Donny's, Tsion rushed out to greet Chloe. As soon as he saw her he burst into tears. "Oh, you poor child. Welcome to your new home. You are safe."

Tsion helped Buck remove her from the backseat and opened the door so Buck could carry her inside. Buck headed for the stairs, but Tsion stopped him. "Right here, Cameron. See?" Tsion had brought down his bed for her. "She cannot use the stairs yet."

Buck shook his head. "I suppose next comes the chicken soup."

Tsion smiled and pushed a button on the microwave. "Give me sixty seconds."

But Chloe did not eat. She slept through the night and off and on the next day.

"You need a goal," Tsion told her. "Where would you like to go on your first day out?"

"I want to see the church. And Loretta's house."

"Will not that be—"

"It will be painful. But Buck says if I hadn't run, I never would have survived. I need to see why. And I want to see where Loretta and Donny died."

When she hobbled to the kitchen table and sat by herself, she asked only for her computer. It pained Buck to watch her peck away with one hand. When he tried to help, she rebuffed him. He must have looked hurt.

"Honey, I know you want to help," she said. "You searched for me until you found me, and nobody can ask for more than that. But, please, don't do anything for me unless I ask."

"You never ask."

"I'm not a dependent person, Buck. I don't want to be waited on. This is war, and there aren't enough days left to waste. As soon as I get this hand working, I'm gonna take some of the load off Tsion. He's on the computer day and night."

Buck got his own laptop and wrote to Ken Ritz about the possibility of going to Israel. He couldn't imagine it ever being safe for Tsion there, but Tsion was so determined to go, Buck was afraid there would be no choice. His ulterior motive with Ken, of course, was to see if he had come to a spiritual decision. As he was transmitting the message, Chloe called out from the kitchen.

"Oh, my word! Buck! You've got to see this!"

He hurried to peer over her shoulder. The message on the screen was several days old. It was from Hattie Durham.

+ + +

Rayford was afraid Leon Fortunato would be bored on the trip to Rome and might pester him and Mac in the cockpit. But every time Rayford clicked on the secret intercom to monitor the cabin, Leon was whistling, humming, singing, talking on the phone, or noisily moving about.

Once Rayford had Mac take over while he found an excuse to wander into the cabin. Leon was arranging the mahogany table where he and Pontifex Maximus Peter Mathews and the ten kings would meet prior to seeing Carpathia.

Leon looked excited enough to burst. "You will remain in the cockpit as soon as our guests join us, will you not?"

"Sure," Rayford said. It was clear Leon needed no company.

Rayford didn't expect any secrets listening in on Leon and Mathews, but he loved the entertainment possibilities. Fortunato was such a Carpathia groupie and Mathews so condescending and independent that the two were like oil and water. Mathews was used to being treated like royalty. Fortunato treated Carpathia like the king of the world that he was but was slow to serve anyone else and often curt with those who served him.

When Mathews boarded in Rome he immediately treated Fortunato as one of his valets. And he already had two. A young man and woman carried his things aboard and stood chatting with him. As Rayford listened in, he was exposed again to Mathews's gall. Every time Fortunato suggested it was time to get under way, Mathews interrupted.

"Could I get a cold drink, Leon?" Mathews said.

There was a long pause. "Certainly," Fortunato said flatly. Then, with sarcasm, "And your staff?"

"Yes, something for them as well."

"Fine, Pontiff Mathews. And then I think we should really be—"

"And something to munch. Thank you, Leon."

After two such encounters, Fortunato's silence was deafening. Finally Leon said, "Pontiff Mathews, I really think it's time—"

"How long are we going to sit here, Leon? What do you say we get this show on the road?"

"We cannot move with unauthorized personnel on the plane."

"Who's not authorized?"

"Your people."

"I introduced you, Leon. These are my personal assistants."

"You were under the impression they were invited?"

"I go nowhere without them."

"I'm going to have to check with His Excellency."

"I'm sorry?"

"I'll have to check with Nicolae Carpathia."

"You said 'His Excellency.'"

"I planned to talk that over with you en route."

"Talk to me now, Leon."

"Pontiff, I would appreciate your addressing me by my title. Is that too much to ask?"

"Titles are what we're talking about. Where does Carpathia get off using *Excellency*?"

"It was not his choice. I—"

"Yes, and I suppose *Potentate* wasn't his choice either. *Secretary-general* just never did it for him, did it?"

"As I said, I want to discuss the new title with you during the trip."

"Then let's get going!"

"I'm not authorized to transport uninvited guests."

"Mr. Fortunato, these are *invited* guests. I invited them."

"My title is not *mister*."

"Oh, so the Potentate is now His Excellency and you're what, Potentate? No, let me guess. You're Supreme Something-or-Other. Am I right?"

"I need to check this with His Excellency."

"Well, hurry. And tell 'His Excellency' that Pontifex Maximus thinks it's nervy to switch from a royal title—already an overstatement—to a sacred one."

Rayford heard only Fortunato's end of the conversation with Nicolae, of course, but Leon had to eat crow.

"Pontiff," he said finally, "His Excellency has asked me to express his welcome and his assurance that anyone you feel necessary to make your flight comfortable is an honor for him to have on board."

"Really?" Mathews said. "Then I insist on a cabin crew." Fortunato laughed. "I'm serious, Leon—or, I mean, what *is* your title, man?"

"I serve at the rank of Commander."

"Commander? Tell the truth now, Commander, is it actually *Supreme* Commander?" Fortunato did not respond, but Mathews must have detected something in his face. "It is, isn't it? Well, even if it isn't, I insist. If I am to call you Commander, it shall be Supreme Commander. Is that acceptable?"

Fortunato sighed loudly. "The actual title is Supreme Commander, yes. You may call me either."

"Oh, no I may not. Supreme Commander it is. Now, Supreme Commander Fortunato, I am deadly serious about cabin service on a long flight like this, and I'm shocked at your lack of foresight in not providing it."

"We have all the amenities, Pontiff. We felt it more necessary to have a full complement of service personnel when the regional ambassadors begin to join us."

"You were wrong. I wish not to leave the ground until this plane is properly staffed. If you have to check that with His Excellency, feel free."

There was a long silence, and Rayford assumed the two were staring each other down. "You're serious about this?" Fortunato said.

"Serious as an earthquake."

The call button sounded in the cockpit. "Flight deck," Mac said. "Go ahead."

"Gentlemen, I have decided to employ a cabin crew between here and Dallas. I shall be contracting with one of the airlines here. Please communicate with the tower that we could be delayed for as long as two or three hours. Thank you."

"Begging your pardon, sir," Mac said, "but our delay here has already cost us four places in line for takeoff. They're being flexible because of who we are, but—"

"Did you misunderstand something?" Leon said.

"Not at all, sir. Roger that delay."

+ + +

Hattie's e-mail message read:

> *Dear CW, I didn't know who else to turn to. Well, actually I did. But I got no response from AS at the private number she gave me. She said she carries her phone all the time, so I'm worried what happened to her.*
>
> *I need your help. I lied to my former boss and told him my people were from Denver. When I changed my flight from Boston to go west instead of east, I was hoping he would think I was going to see my family. Actually, they live in Santa Monica. I'm in Denver for a whole other reason.*

I'm at a reproductive clinic here. Now, don't overreact. Yes, they do abortions, and they're pushing me that direction. In fact, that's mostly what they do. But they do also ask every mother if she's considered her options, and every once in a while a baby is carried to term. Some are put up for adoption; some are raised by the mother. Others are raised by the clinic.

This place also serves as a safe house, and I am here anonymously. I cut my hair short and dyed it black, and I wear colored contact lenses. I'm sure no one recognizes me.

They give us access to these computers a few hours every week. At other times we write things and draw pictures and exercise. They also encourage us to write to friends and loved ones and make amends. Sometimes they urge us to write to the fathers of our children.

I couldn't do that. But I do need to talk to you. I have a private cell phone. Do you have a number like AS does? I'm scared. I'm confused. Some days abortion seems the easiest solution.

But I'm already growing attached to this child. I might be able to give it up, but I don't think I could end its life. I told a counselor I felt guilty about becoming pregnant when I wasn't married. She had never heard anything like that in her life. She said I ought to stop obsessing about right and wrong and start thinking about what was best for me.

I feel more guilty about considering abortion than I do about what you would call immorality. I don't want to make a mistake. And I don't want to keep living like this. I envy you and your close friends. I sure hope you all survived the earthquake. I suppose your dad and your husband believe it was the wrath of the Lamb. Maybe it was. I wouldn't be surprised.

If I don't hear from you, I'm going to assume the worst, so please get back to me if you can. Say hi to everybody. My love to L. Love, H.

"Now, Buck," Chloe said, "I don't mind if you help me. Just reply as fast as you can that I was hurt and away from my e-mail, that I'm going to be fine, and here's my phone number. OK?"

Buck was already typing.

\+ \+ \+

Rayford slipped his laptop out of his flight bag and left the plane. On the way he passed the two bored young people, a red-faced and sweating Leon on the phone, and Mathews. The Supreme Pontiff of Enigma Babylon glanced at Rayford and looked away. *So much for pastoral interest,* Rayford thought. Pilots were just props on this guy's stage.

Rayford sat near a window in the terminal. With his amazing computer, powered by the sun and connected by cellular zones, he could communicate from anywhere. He checked the bulletin board where Tsion kept in touch with his growing church. In just a few days, hundreds of thousands of people had responded to his messages. Open messages to Nicolae Carpathia pleaded for amnesty for Tsion Ben-Judah. One poignantly summarized the consensus: "Surely a lover of peace like yourself, Potentate Carpathia, who aided in Rabbi Ben-Judah's escape from orthodox zealots in his homeland, has the power to return him safely to Israel, where he can communicate with so many of us who love him. We're counting on you."

Rayford smiled. Many were so new in the faith that they did not know Carpathia's true identity. When, he wondered, might Tsion himself have to blatantly expose Carpathia?

When he downloaded his mail, Rayford was dumbfounded to learn of the contact from Hattie. He had strangely mixed emotions. He was glad she and her baby were safe, but he so badly wanted a message from Amanda that he found himself jealous. He resented that Chloe had heard from Hattie before he heard from Amanda. "God, forgive me," he prayed silently.

Several hours later, the Condor 216 finally took off from Rome with a full cabin crew, compliments of Alitalia Airlines.

When Rayford wasn't planning the Tigris River dive, he eavesdropped on the cabin.

"Now this is more like it, Supreme Commander Fortunato," Mathews was saying. "Isn't this better than the buffet line you had planned? Admit it."

"Everyone appreciates being served," Fortunato allowed. "Now there are some issues His Excellency has asked me to brief you on."

"Quit calling him that! It drives me nuts. I was going to save this news, but I might as well tell you now. Response to my leadership has been so overwhelming that my staff has planned a weeklong festival next month to celebrate my installation. Though I no longer serve the Catholic church, which has been blended into our much bigger faith, it seemed appropriate to some that my title change as well. I believe it will have more immediate impact and be more easily understood by the masses if I simply go by Peter the Second."

"That sounds like a pope's title," Fortunato said.

"Of course it is. Though some would call my position a papacy, I frankly see it as much larger."

"You prefer Peter the Second over Supreme Pontiff or even Pontifex Maximus?"

"Less is more. It has a ring to it, doesn't it?"

"We'll have to see how His—ah, Potentate Carpathia feels about it."

"What does the Global Community potentate have to do with the One World Faith?"

"Oh, he feels responsible for the idea and for your elevation to this post."

"He needs to remember that democracy wasn't all bad. At least they had separation between church and state."

"Pontiff, you asked what His Excellency has to do with you. I must ask, where would Enigma Babylon be without financing from the Global Community?"

"I could ask the reverse. People need something to believe in. They need faith. They need tolerance. We need to stand together and rid the world of the hatemongers. The vanishings took care of narrow-minded fundamentalists and intolerant zealots. Have you seen what's happening on the Internet? That rabbi who blasphemed his own religion in his own country is now developing a huge following. It falls to me to compete with that. I have a request here—" Rayford heard rustling papers—"for increased financial support from the Global Community."

"His Excellency was afraid of that."

"Bull! I've never known Carpathia to be afraid of anything. He knows we have tremendous expenses. We are living up to our name. We're a one-world faith. We influence every continent for peace and unity and tolerance. Every ambassador ought to be mandated to increase his share of contributions to Enigma Babylon."

"Pontiff, no one has ever faced the fiscal problems His Excellency faces now. The balance of power has shifted to the Middle East. New Babylon is the capital of the world. Everything will be centralized. The rebuilding of that city alone has caused the potentate to propose significant tax increases across the board. But he's also rebuilding the whole world. Global Community forces are at work on every continent, reestablishing communications and transportation and engaging in cleanup, rescue, relief, sanitation, you name it. Every region leader will be asked to call his subjects to sacrifice."

"And you get that dirty work, don't you, Supreme Commander?"

"I do not consider it dirty work, Pontiff. It is my honor to facilitate His Excellency's vision."

"There you go again with that *excellency* business."

"Allow me to tell you a personal story I will share with each ambassador during this trip. Indulge me, and you'll see that the potentate is a deeply spiritual man with a spark of the divine."

"This I have to hear," Mathews said, chuckling. "Carpathia as clergy. Now there's a picture."

"I pledge that every word is true. It will change forever the way you see our potentate."

Rayford turned off the surveillance switch. "Leon's telling Mathews his Lazarus story," he muttered.

"Oh boy," Mac said.

The Condor was over the Atlantic in the middle of the night, and Rayford was dozing. The intercom roused him. "When convenient, Captain Steele," Fortunato said, "I would appreciate a moment."

"I hate to cater," Rayford told Mac. "But I'd just as soon get it out of the way." He depressed the button. "Is now OK?"

Fortunato met him midplane and beckoned him to the rear, far from where Mathews and his two young charges were sleeping. "His Excellency has asked me to approach you on a delicate matter. It is becoming increasingly embarrassing to not be able to produce Rabbi Tsion Ben-Judah of Israel for his followers."

"Oh?"

"His Excellency knows you to be a man of your word. When you tell us you do not know where Ben-Judah is, we take this at face value. The question then becomes, do you have access to someone who does know where he is?"

"Why?"

"His Excellency is prepared to personally ensure the rabbi's safety. He will make any threat to the safety of Ben-Judah simply not worth the consequences."

"So why not put that word out, and see if Ben-Judah comes to you?"

"Too risky. You may think you know how His Excellency views you. However, as the one who knows him best, I know he trusts you. He admires your integrity."

"And he's convinced I have access to Ben-Judah."

"Let's not play games, Captain Steele. The Global Community is far-reaching now. We know from more sources than just the talkative Dr. Rosenzweig that your son-in-law helped the rabbi escape."

"Rosenzweig is one of Carpathia's greatest admirers, more loyal than Nicolae deserves. Didn't Chaim seek Carpathia's help in the Ben-Judah matter back when Nicolae first became prominent?"

"We did all we could—"

"That is not true. If you expect me to be a man of my word, don't insult my intelligence. If my own son-in-law aided in Ben-Judah's flight from Israel, wouldn't I have an idea whether he had assistance from the Global Community?"

Fortunato did not respond.

Rayford was careful not to reveal anything he had heard solely through the bugging device. He would never forget when Fortunato had passed on Rosenzweig's plea for help for his beleaguered friend. Ben-Judah's family had been massacred and he was in hiding, yet Carpathia had laughed it off and said in so many words that he might turn Ben-Judah over to the zealots.

"Those close to the situation know the truth, Leon. Carpathia's claim to credit for the well-being of Tsion Ben-Judah is bogus. I have no doubt he could protect the rabbi, and he would have been able to then, but he did not."

"You may be right, Captain Steele. I do not have personal knowledge of that situation."

"Leon, you know every detail of everything that goes on."

It appeared Leon enjoyed hearing that. He didn't argue it. "Regardless, it would be counterproductive from a public relations standpoint for us to adjust our position now. We are believed to have helped him escape, and we would lose credibility to admit we had nothing to do with that."

"But since I know," Rayford said, "am I not allowed some skepticism?"

Leon sat back and steepled his fingers. He exhaled. "All right," he said. "His Excellency has authorized me to ask what you require in order to grant him this favor."

"And the favor is?"

"The delivery of Tsion Ben-Judah."

"To?"

"Israel."

What Rayford wanted was his wife's name cleared, but he could not betray Mac's confidence. "So I'm asked my price now, rather than being required to trade my own daughter?"

It didn't seem to surprise Fortunato that Rayford had heard about the fiasco in Minneapolis. "That was a mistake in communications," he said. "You have His Excellency's personal word that he intended that the wife of one of his employees be reunited with her husband and given the best care."

Rayford wanted to laugh aloud or spit in Fortunato's face; he couldn't decide which. "Let me think about it," he said.

"How long do you need? There is pressure on His Excellency to do something about Ben-Judah. We will be in the States tomorrow. Can we not make some arrangement?"

"You want me to ferry him back on the Condor with all the ambassadors?"

"Of course not. But as long as we are going to be in that region, it only makes sense that we take care of it now."

"Assuming Tsion Ben-Judah is there."

"We believe that if we can locate Cameron Williams, we will have located Tsion Ben-Judah."

"Then you know more than I do."

Rayford began to stand, but Fortunato held up a hand. "There is one more thing."

"Let me guess. Are her initials H. D.?"

"Yes. It is important to His Excellency that the relationship be gracefully severed."

"Despite what he said to the world?"

"Actually, I said it. He did not sanction it."

"I don't believe that."

"Believe what you wish. You are aware of the exigencies of public perception. His Excellency is determined not to be embarrassed by Miss Durham. You'll recall they were introduced by your son-in-law."

"Whom I had not even met yet," Rayford said.

"Granted. Her disappearance was a nuisance. It made His Excellency appear incapable of controlling his own household. The earthquake provided a logical explanation for their separation. It is crucial that while out on her own, Miss Durham not do or say anything embarrassing."

"And so you want me to do what? Tell her to behave?"

"Frankly, Captain, you would not be overstating it to inform her that accidents happen. She cannot remain invisible long. If it becomes necessary to eliminate the risk, we have the ability to effect this with expediency, and in a manner that would not reflect on His Excellency but would allow him to gain sympathy."

"May I tell you what I just heard you say, so we're clear?"

"Certainly."

"You want me to tell Hattie Durham to keep her mouth shut or you'll kill her and deny it."

Fortunato appeared stricken. Then he softened and stared at the ceiling. "We are communicating," he said.

"Rest assured that if I make contact with Miss Durham, I will pass along your threat."

"I assume you will remind her that repeating that message would constitute cause."

"Oh, I got it. It's a blanket threat."

"You'll handle both assignments then?"

"You don't see the irony? I'm to pass along a death threat to Miss Durham yet trust you with protecting Tsion Ben-Judah."

"Right."

"Well, it may be correct, but it's not right."

Rayford trudged to the cockpit, where he was met with Mac's knowing look. "You hear that?"

"I heard," Mac said. "I wish I had taped it."

"Who would you play it for?"

"Fellow believers."

"You'd be preaching to the choir. In the old days, you could take a tape like that to the authorities. But these *are* the authorities."

"What's your price gonna be, Ray?"

"What do you mean?"

"Ben-Judah belongs in Israel. And Carpathia has to ensure his safety, doesn't he?"

"You heard Fortunato. They can cause an accident and wind up with sympathy."

"But if he pledges a personal guarantee, Ray, he'll keep Tsion safe."

"Don't forget what Tsion wants to do in Israel. He's not just going to chat with the two witnesses or look up old friends. He'll be training as many of the 144,000 evangelists as can get there. He'll be Nicolae's worst nightmare."

"Like I said, what's your price?"

"What's the difference? You expect the Antichrist to stand by a deal? I wouldn't give a nickel for Hattie Durham's future, whether she toes the line or not. Maybe if I string this out long enough I can learn something from Fortunato about Amanda. I'm telling you, Mac, she's alive somewhere."

"If she's alive, Ray, why no contact? I don't want to offend you, but is it possible she's what they say she is?"

15

BUCK WAS AWAKENED a little after midnight by the chirping of Chloe's phone downstairs. Though she kept it within arm's length, it kept ringing. Buck sat up, wondering. He decided her medication must have kicked in, so he hurried down.

Only people most crucial to the Tribulation Force knew the members' private cell phone numbers. Every incoming call was potentially momentous. Buck couldn't see the phone in the darkness, and he didn't want to turn on the light. He followed the sound to the ledge above Chloe. He put a knee carefully on the mattress, trying not to wake her, grabbed the phone, and settled in a chair next to her bed.

"Chloe's phone," he whispered.

All he heard was crying. "Hattie?" he tried.

"Buck!" she said.

"Chloe slept through the ring, Hattie. I hate to wake her."

"Please don't," she said through sobs. "I'm sorry to call so late."

"She really wanted to talk to you, Hattie. Is there anything I can do?"

"Oh, Buck!" she said, and lost control again.

"Hattie, I know you don't know where we are, but it's not close enough to help if you're in danger. Do you need me to call someone?"

"No!"

"Don't rush, then. I can wait. I'm not going anywhere."

"Thank you," she managed.

As Buck waited, his eyes grew accustomed to the darkness. For the first time since she had been home, Chloe was not on her left side, keeping weight off the myriad breaks, bruises, strains, sprains, and scrapes of her other side. Every morning she spent half an hour massaging sleeping body parts. He prayed that someday soon she would enjoy a restful night's sleep. Maybe she was doing that now. But could one really enjoy a sleep so deep that a ringing phone a few feet away would not penetrate? He hoped her body would benefit, and her spirit as well. Chloe lay still, flat on her back, her left arm by her side, her mangled right foot pigeon-toed to the left, her casted arm resting on her stomach.

"Bear with me," Hattie managed.

"No rush," Buck said, scratching his head and stretching. He was struck by Chloe in repose. What a gift of God she was, and how grateful he was that she had survived. Her top sheet and blanket were bunched. She often fell asleep uncovered and curled under blankets later.

Buck pressed the back of his hand to her cheek. She felt cool. Still listening for Hattie, Buck pulled the sheet and blanket up to Chloe's neck, worrying that he might have dragged it across her foot, her most sensitive injury. But she did not move.

"Hattie, are you there?"

"Buck, I got word tonight that I lost my mother and my sisters in the earthquake."

"Oh, Hattie, I'm so sorry."

"It's such a waste," she said. "When L.A. and San Francisco were bombed, Nicolae and I were still close. He warned me they should leave the area and swore me to secrecy. His intelligence people feared a militia attack, and he was right."

Buck said nothing. Rayford had told him he had heard Carpathia himself, through the Condor 216's bugging device, give the order for the bombing of San Francisco and Los Angeles.

"Hattie, where are you calling from?"

"I told you in the e-mail," she said.

"I know, but you're not using their phones, are you?"

"No! That's why I'm calling so late. I had to wait until I could sneak outside."

"And the news about your family. How did that get to you?"

"I had to let the authorities in Santa Monica know where they could reach me. I gave them my private number and the number of the clinic here."

"I'm sorry to say this at such a difficult time for you, Hattie, but that was not a good idea."

"I didn't have a choice. It took a long time to get through to Santa Monica, and when I finally did, my family was unaccounted for. I had to leave numbers. I've been worried sick."

"You've probably led the GC right to you."

"I don't care anymore."

"Don't say that."

"I don't want to go back to Nicolae, but I want him to take responsibility for our child. I have no job, no income, and now no family."

"We care about you and love you, Hattie. Don't forget that."

She broke down again.

"Hattie, have you considered that the news about your family may be untrue?"

"What?"

"I wouldn't put it past the GC. Once they knew where you were, they may have just wanted to give you a reason to stay there. If you think your family is gone, there's no reason for you to go to California."

"But I told Nicolae my family had moved here after the bombings out there."

"It wouldn't have taken him long to discover that was untrue."

"Why would he want me to stay here?"

"Maybe he assumes that the longer you're there, the more likely you are to have an abortion."

"That's true."

"Don't say that."

"I don't see any options, Buck. I can't raise a child in a world like this with my prospects."

"I don't want to make you feel worse, Hattie, but I don't think you're safe there."

"What are you saying?"

Buck wished Chloe would rouse and help him talk to Hattie. He had an idea, but he'd rather consult her first.

"Hattie, I know these people. They would much rather have you out of the picture than deal with you."

"I'm nobody from nowhere. I can't hurt him."

"Something happening to you could engender tremendous sympathy for him. More than anything, he wants attention, and he doesn't care whether that comes as fear, respect, admiration, or pity."

"I'll tell you one thing, I'll have an abortion before I'll let him hurt me or my child."

"You're not making sense. You would kill your child so he can't?"

"You sound like Rayford now."

"We happen to agree on this," Buck said. "Please don't do that. At the very least get somewhere where you're not in danger and can think this through."

"I have nowhere to go!"

"If I came and got you, would you come here with us?"

Silence.

"Chloe needs you. We could use help with her. And she could be good for you during your pregnancy. She's pregnant too."

"Really? Oh, Buck, I couldn't burden you. I'd feel so obliged, so in the way."

"Hey, this was my idea."

"I don't see how it would work."

"Hattie, tell me where you are. I'll come and get you by noon tomorrow."

"You mean noon today?"

Buck looked at the clock. "I guess I do."

"Shouldn't you run this by Chloe?"

"I don't dare bother her. If there's a problem, I'll get back to you. Otherwise, be ready to go."

No response.

"Hattie?"

"I'm still here, Buck. I was just thinking. Remember when we met?"

"Of course. It was a rather momentous day."

"On Rayford's 747 the night of the disappearances."

"The Rapture," Buck said.

"If you say so. Look what we've been through since then."

"I'll call you when we're within an hour of you," Buck said.

"I'll never be able to repay you."

"Who said anything about that?"

Buck put the phone away, straightened Chloe's covers, and knelt to kiss her. She still seemed cold. He went to get her a blanket but stopped midstride. Was she too still? Was she breathing? He rushed back and put his ear to her nose. He couldn't tell. He ran his thumb and forefinger under her jaw to check her pulse. Before he could detect anything, she pulled away. She was alive. He slipped to his knees. "Thank you, God!"

Chloe mumbled something. He took her hand in both of his. "What, sweetie? What do you need?"

She appeared to be trying to open her eyes. "Buck?" she said.

"It's me."

"What's wrong?"

"I just got off the phone with Hattie. Go back to sleep."

"I'm cold."

"I'll get you a blanket."

"I wanted to talk to Hattie. What did she say?"

"I'll tell you tomorrow."

"Mm-hm."

Buck found a coverlet and spread it over her. "OK?" he said.

She did not respond. When he began to tiptoe away, she said something. He turned back. "What, hon?"

"Hattie."

"In the morning," he said.

"Hattie has my bunny."

Buck smiled. "Your bunny?"

"My blanket."

"OK."

"Thanks for my blanket."

Buck wondered if she would remember any of this.

* * *

Mac was in the cockpit and Rayford asleep in his quarters when his personal phone rang. It was Buck.

Rayford sat up. "What time is it where you are?"

"If I tell you that, anyone listening will know what time zone I'm in."

"Donny assured us these phones were secure."

"That was last month," Buck said. "These phones are almost obsolete already."

They filled in each other on the latest. "You're right about getting Hattie away from there. After what I told you Leon said, don't you agree she's in danger?"

"No question," Buck said.

"And is Tsion willing to go to Israel?"

"Willing? I have to sit on him to keep him from starting to walk there now. He's going to be suspicious, though, if the big man wants to take credit for getting him there."

"I don't see how he could go otherwise, Buck. His life would be worthless."

"He takes comfort in the prophecies that he and the rest of the 144,000 witnesses are sealed and protected, at least for now. He feels he could walk into the enemy's lair and come out unharmed."

"He's the expert."

"I want to go with him. Being in the same country as the two witnesses at the Wailing Wall would make this soul harvest he's been predicting just explode."

"Buck, have you checked in with headquarters? All I hear from the top is that you're on dangerous ground. You have no secrets anymore."

"Funny you should ask. I just transmitted a long message to the big boss."

"Is it going to do you any good?"

"You seem to have survived by being straightforward, Rayford. I'm doing the same. I told them I've been too busy rescuing friends and burying others to worry about my publication. Besides, 90 percent of the staff is gone and virtually all the production capabilities. I'm proposing continuing the magazine on the Net until Carpathia decides whether to rebuild printing plants and all that."

"Ingenious."

"Yeah, well, the fact is there might be two simultaneous magazines coming out on the Internet at the same time, if you know what I mean."

"There are already dozens."

"I mean there might be two coming out simultaneously, edited by the same guy."

"But only one of them financed and sanctioned by the king of the world?"

"Right. The other wouldn't be funded at all. It would tell the truth. And no one would know where it's coming from."

"I like your mind, Buck. I'm glad you're part of my family."

"It hasn't been dull, I can say that."

"So what should I tell Leon I'll do about Hattie and Tsion?"

"Tell him you'll get the message to the lady. As for Tsion, negotiate whatever you want and we'll get him to Israel inside a month."

"You think there's that kind of patience in the East?"

"It's important to stretch it out. Make it a huge event. Keep control of the timing. That'll drive Tsion crazy too, but it will give us time to rally everyone on the Internet so they can show up."

"Like I said, I like your mind. You ought to be a magazine publisher."

"Before long we'll all be just fugitives."

+ + +

Buck was right. In the morning Chloe recalled nothing from the night before. "I woke up toasty and knew somebody had brought me a blanket," she said. "It doesn't surprise me it was one of the guys upstairs."

She grabbed her phone and used a cane to get to the table. She punched the buttons with her bloated right hand. "I'm going to call her right now," she said. "I'm going to tell her I can't wait to have some female companionship around here."

Chloe sat with the phone to her ear for several moments.

"No answer?" Buck said. "You'd better hang up, hon. If she's where she can't talk, she probably turned it off at the first ring. You can try her later, but don't jeopardize her."

A chortle came from Tsion upstairs. "You two are not going to believe this!" he hollered, and Buck heard his footsteps overhead. Chloe closed her phone and looked up expectantly.

"He's so easily entertained," she said. "What a joy! I learn something from him every day."

Buck nodded, and Tsion emerged from the stairs. He sat at the table, eagerness on his face. "I am reading through some of the thousands of messages left for me on the bulletin board. I do not know how many I miss for every few I read. I am guessing I have seen only about ten percent of the total, because the total keeps growing. I feel bad I cannot answer them individually, but you see the impossibility. Anyway, I got an anonymous message this morning from 'One Who Knows.' Of course, I cannot be sure he actually *is* one who knows, but he may be. Who can know? It is an interesting conundrum, is it not? Anonymous correspondence could be phony. Someone could claim to be me and engage in false teaching. I must come up with something that proves my authenticity, no?"

"Tsion!" Chloe said. "What did One Who Knows write that amused you so?"

"Oh, yes. That is why I came down here, right? Forgive me. I printed it out." He looked at the table, then patted his shirt pocket. "Oh," he said, checking his pants pockets. "It is still in my printer. Do not go away."

"Tsion?" Chloe called after him. "I just wanted to tell you I'll be here when you get back."

He looked puzzled. "Oh, well, yes. Of course."

"He's going to be thrilled he's going home," Buck said.

"And you're going with him?"

"Wouldn't miss it," Buck said. "Big story."

"I'm going with you."

"Oh, no you're not!" Buck said, but Tsion was back.

He spread the sheet on the table and read, "'Rabbi, it is only fair to tell you that one person who has been assigned to carefully monitor all your transmissions is the top military adviser for the Global Community. That may not mean much to you, but he is particularly interested in your interpretation of the prophecies about things falling to the earth and causing great damage in the upcoming months. The fact that you take these prophecies literally has him working on nuclear defenses against such catastrophes. Signed, One Who Knows.'"

Tsion looked up, bright-eyed. "It is so funny because it must be true! Carpathia, who continually tries to explain as natural phenomenon anything that supports biblical prophecy, has his senior military adviser planning to, what? Shoot a burning mountain from the sky? This is like a gnat shaking his tiny fist in the elephant's eye. Anyway, is this not a private admission on his part that there may be something to these prophecies?"

Buck wondered if One Who Knows was Rayford's and Mac's new brother inside GC headquarters. "Intriguing," Buck said. "Now are you ready for some good news?"

Tsion put a hand on Chloe's shoulder. "The daily improvement in this precious little one is good news enough for me. Unless you are talking about Israel."

Chloe said, "I'll forgive that condescending remark, Tsion, because I'm sure no insult was intended."

Tsion looked puzzled.

"Forgive her," Buck said. "She's going through a twenty-two-year-old's bout with political correctness."

Chloe leveled her eyes at Buck. "Excuse me for saying this in front of Tsion, Cameron, but that truly offended me."

"OK," Buck said quickly, "guilty. I'm sorry. But I'm about to tell Tsion he's going to get his wish—"

"Yes!" Tsion exulted.

"And, Chloe, I don't have the energy to fight over whether you're going."

"Then let's not fight. I'm going."

"Oh, no!" Tsion said. "You must not! You are not nearly up to it."

"Tsion! It's not for another month. By then I'll—"

"Another month?" Tsion said. "Why so long? I am ready now. I must go soon. The people are clamoring for it, and I believe God wants me there."

"We're concerned about security, Tsion," Buck said. "A month will also allow us to get as many of the witnesses there as possible from around the world."

"But a month!"

"Works for me," Chloe said. "I'll be walking on my own by then."

Buck shook his head.

Tsion was already in his own world. "You do not need to worry about security, Cameron. God will protect me. He will protect the witnesses. I do not know about other believers. I know they are sealed, but I do not know yet if they are also supernaturally protected during this time of harvest."

"If God can protect you," Chloe said, "he can protect me."

Buck said, "Chloe, you know I have your best interest at heart. I'd love for you to go. I never miss you more than when I'm away from you in Jerusalem."

"Then tell me why I can't go."

"I would never forgive myself if something happened to you. I can't risk it."

"I'm just as vulnerable here, Buck. Every day is a risk. Why are we allowed to risk your life and not mine?"

Buck had no answer. He scrambled for one. "Hattie will be that much closer to her delivery date. She'll need you. And what about our child?"

"I won't even be showing by then, Buck. I'll be three months along. You're going to need me. Who's going to handle logistics? I'll be communicating with thousands of people on the Internet, arranging these meetings. It only makes sense that I show up."

"You haven't answered the Hattie question."

"Hattie's more independent than I am. She would want me to go. She can take care of herself."

Buck was losing, and he knew it. He looked away, unwilling to give in so soon. Yes, he was being protective. "It's just that I so recently nearly lost you."

"Listen to yourself, Buck. I knew enough to get out of that house before it crushed me. You can't blame that flying roof on me."

"We'll see how healthy you are in a few weeks."

"I'll start packing."

"Don't jump to conclusions."

"Don't parent me, Buck. Seriously, I don't have a problem submitting to you because I know how much you love me. I'm willing to obey you even when you're wrong. But don't be unreasonable. And don't be wrong if you don't have to be. You know I'm going to do what you say, and I'll even get over it if you make me miss out on one of the greatest events in history. But don't do it out of some old-fashioned, macho sense of protecting the little woman. I'll take this pity and help for just so long, and then I want back in the game full-time. I thought that was one of the things you liked about me."

It was. Pride kept him from agreeing right then. He'd give it a day or two and then tell her he'd come to a decision. Her eyes were boring into his. It was clear she was eager to win this one. He tried to stare her down and lost. He glanced at Tsion.

"Listen to her," Tsion said.

"You keep out of it," Buck said, smiling. "I don't need to be ganged up on. I thought you were on *my* side. I thought you would agree that this was no place for—"

"For what?" Chloe said. "A girl? The 'little woman'? An injured, pregnant woman? Am I still a member of the Tribulation Force, or have I been demoted to mascot now?"

Buck had interviewed heads of state easier than this.

"You can't defend this one, Buck," she added.

"You want to just pin me while I'm down," Buck said.

"I won't say another word," she said.

Buck chuckled. "That'll be the day."

"If you two chauvinists will excuse me, I want to try Hattie again. We're going to have a telephone meeting of the weak sister club."

Buck flinched. "Hey! You weren't going to say another word."

"Well then get out of here so you don't have to listen."

"I need to call Ritz anyway. When you reach Hattie, be sure and find out what name she was admitted under there."

Buck went to follow Tsion up the stairs, but Chloe called out to him.

"C'mere a minute, big guy." He turned to face her. She beckoned him closer. "C'mon," she said. She lifted her arm, the one with the cast from shoulder to wrist, and hooked him with it behind the neck. She pulled his face to hers and kissed him long and hard. He pulled back and smiled shyly. "You're so easy," she whispered.

"Who loves ya, baby?" he said, heading for the stairs again.

"Hey," she said, "if you see my husband up there, tell him I'm tired of sleeping alone."

+ + +

Rayford listened through the bugging device as Peter Mathews and Leon Fortunato spent the last hour and a half of the flight arguing over protocol for their arrival in Dallas. Mathews, of course, prevailed on nearly every point.

The regional ambassador, the former U.S. senator from Texas, had arranged for limousines, a red carpet, an official welcome and greeting, and even a marching band. Fortunato spent half an hour on the phone with the ambassador's people, slowly reading the official announcement and presentation of honored guests that was to be read as he and Mathews disembarked. Though Rayford could hear only Fortunato's end of the conversation, it was clear the ambassador's people were barely tolerating this presumption.

After Fortunato and Mathews had showered and changed for the occasion, Leon buzzed the cockpit.

"I would like you gentlemen to assist the ground crew with the exit stairs as soon as we have come to a stop."

"Before postflight checks?" Mac said, giving Rayford a look as if this was one of the dumbest things he had ever heard. Rayford shrugged.

"Yes, before postflight checks," Fortunato said. "Be sure everything is in order, tell the cabin crew to wait until after the welcoming ceremony to deplane, and you two should be last off."

Mac switched off the intercom. "If we're putting off postflight checks, we'll be the last off all right. Wouldn't you think priority would be making sure this rig is airworthy for the return trip?"

"He figures we've got thirty-six hours, we can do it anytime."

"I was trained to check the important stuff while it's hot."

"Me too," Rayford said. "But we'll do what we're told when we're told, and you know why?"

"Tell me, O Supreme Excellent Pilot."

"Because the red carpet ain't for us."

"Doesn't that just break your heart?" Mac said.

Rayford updated ground control as Mac followed the signalman's directions to the tarmac and a small grandstand area where the public, the band, and dignitaries waited. Rayford peered out at the ragtag musicians. "Wonder where they got this bunch?" he said. "And how many they had with them before the quake."

The signalman directed Mac to the edge of the carpet and crossed his coned flashlights to signify a slow stop. "Watch this," Mac said.

"Careful, you rascal," Rayford said.

At the last instant, Mac rolled over the end of the red carpet.

"Did I do that?" he asked.

"You're bad."

Once the stairs were in place, the band was finished, and the dignitaries were situated, the Global Community ambassador stepped to the microphone. "Ladies and gentlemen," he announced with great solemnity, "representing His Excellency, Global Community Potentate Nicolae Carpathia, Supreme Commander Leonardo Fortunato!"

The crowd broke into cheering and applause as Leon waved and made his way down the steps.

"Ladies and gentlemen, the personal attendants from the office of the Supreme Pontiff of Enigma Babylon One World Faith!"

The reaction was subdued as the crowd seemed to wonder if these two young people had names, and if so, why they were not mentioned.

After a pause long enough to make people wonder if anyone else was aboard, Mathews stepped near the door but stayed out of sight. Rayford stood by the cockpit, waiting to start the postflight check when the folderol was over. "I'm waiting," Mathews sing-songed to himself. "I'm not stepping out until I'm announced."

Rayford was tempted to poke his head out and say, "Announce Pete!" He restrained himself. Finally Fortunato trotted back up the steps. He didn't come far enough to see Mathews just beyond the edge of the door. He stopped when he saw Rayford and mouthed, "Is he ready?" Rayford nodded. Leon skipped back down the steps and whispered to the ambassador.

"Ladies and gentlemen, from Enigma Babylon One World Faith, Pontifex Maximus Peter the Second!"

The band struck up, the crowd erupted, and Mathews stepped to the doorway, waiting for several beats and looking humbled at the generous response. He solemnly descended, waving a blessing as he went.

As the welcoming speeches droned, Rayford grabbed his clipboard and settled into the cockpit. Mac said, "Ladies and gentlemen! First officer of the Condor 216, with a lifetime batting average of—"

Rayford smacked him on the shoulder with his clipboard. "Knock it off, you idiot."

* * *

"How are you feeling, Ken?" Buck asked over the phone.

"I've been better. There are days that hospital looks pretty good. But I'm a far sight better than I was last time I saw you. I'm supposed to get the stitches out Monday."

"I've got another job for you, if you're up to it."

"I'm always game. Where we goin'?"

"Denver."

"Hmm. The old airport's open there, they tell me. The new one will probably never be open again."

"We pick up an hour going, and I told my client I'd pick her up by noon."

"Another damsel in distress?"

"As a matter of fact, yes. You got wheels?"

"Yep."

"I need you to pick me up on the way this time. Need to leave a vehicle here."

"I'd like to check in on Chloe anyway," Ken said. "How's she doing?"

"Come see for yourself."

"I better get goin' if you're gonna keep your commitment. You never schedule a lot of play time, do ya?"

"Sorry. Hey, Ken, did you check out that Web site I told you about?"

"Yeah. I've spent a good bit of time there."

"Come to any conclusions?"

"I need to talk to you about that."

"We'll have time in the air."

* * *

"I appreciate your giving me so much flying time on this trip," Mac said as he and Rayford left the plane.

"I had an ulterior motive. I know the FAA rules are out the window now that Carpathia is a law unto himself, but I still follow the maximum flying hours rules."

"So do I. You going somewhere?"

"As soon as you teach me how to get around in the Challenger. I'd like to drop in on my daughter and surprise her. Buck gave me directions."

"Good for you."

"What are you gonna do, Mac?"

"Hole up here awhile. I got some buddies I might look up a couple hundred miles west. If I can track them down, I'll use the chopper."

* * *

Ken Ritz's Suburban came rumbling around the back of the house just before nine.

"Somebody wants to see you when you're halfway conscious," Buck said.

"Find out if he wants to arm wrestle," Chloe said.

"Aren't *you* getting frisky?"

Tsion was on his way down the stairs when Buck met Ken at the back door. Ken wore cowboy boots, blue jeans, a long-sleeve khaki shirt, and a cowboy hat. "I know we're in a hurry," he said, "but where's the patient?"

"Right here, Dr. Airplane," Chloe said. She hobbled to the kitchen door. Ken tipped his hat.

"You can do better than that, cowboy," she said, extending her good arm for a hug. He hurried to her.

"You sure look a lot better than the last time I saw you," he said.

"Thanks. So do you."

He laughed. "I *am* a lot better. Notice anything different about me?"

"A little better color, I think," Buck said. "And you might have gained a pound in the last day or two."

"Never shows on this frame," Ritz said.

"It has been a long time, Mr. Ritz," Tsion said.

Ritz shook the rabbi's hand. "Hey, we all look healthier than last time, don't we?"

"We really need to get going," Buck said.

"So nobody notices anything different about me, huh?" Ken said. "You can't see it in my face? It doesn't show?"

"What?" Chloe said. "Are you pregnant too?"

As the others laughed, Ken took off his hat and ran a hand through his hair. "First day I've been able to get a hat on this sore head."

"So that's what's different?" Buck said.

"That, and this." Ken ran his hand through his hair again, and this time left it atop his head with his hair pulled out of the way. "Maybe it shows on my forehead. I can see yours. Can you see mine?"

16

RAYFORD MADE THE APPROACH for yet another landing in the Challenger 3. "They're getting tired of me hogging this runway. If I can't get it right, you may have to fly me to Illinois."

"Dallas Tower to Charlie Tango, over."

Rayford raised an eyebrow. "See what I mean?"

"I'll get it," Mac said. "This is Charlie Tango, over."

"Tango X-ray message for Condor 216 captain, over."

"Go ahead with TX message, tower, over."

"Subject is to call Supreme Commander at the following number. . . ."

Mac wrote it down.

"What now?" Rayford wondered aloud. He put the screaming jet down for his smoothest landing of the morning.

"Why don't you take her back up," Mac said, "then I'll take over while you call Captain Kangaroo."

"That's Supreme Commander Kangaroo to you, pal," Rayford said. He lined up the Challenger and hurtled down the runway at three hundred miles an hour. Once he was in the air and leveled off, Mac took the controls.

Rayford reached Fortunato at the ambassador's residence. "I expected an immediate call," Leon said.

"I'm in the middle of a training maneuver."

"I have an assignment for you."

"I have plans today, sir. Do I have a choice?"

"This is straight from the top."

"My question remains."

"No, you have no choice. If this delays our return, we will inform the respective ambassadors. His Excellency requests that you fly to Denver today."

Denver?

"I'm not ready to fly this thing solo yet," Rayford said. "Is this something my first officer can handle?"

"Intelligence sources have located the subject we asked you to communicate with. Follow?"

"I follow."

"His Excellency would appreciate his message being delivered as soon as possible, in person."

"What's the rush?"

"The subject is at a Global Community facility that can assist in determining the consequences of the response."

"She's at an abortion clinic?"

"Captain Steele! This is an unsecured transmission!"

"I may have to fly commercial."

"Just get there today. GC personnel are stalling the subject."

+ + +

"Before you go, Cameron," Tsion said, "we must thank the Lord for our new brother."

Buck, Chloe, Tsion, and Ken huddled in the kitchen. Tsion put a hand on Ken's back and looked up. "Lord God Almighty, your Word tells us the angels rejoice with us over Ken Ritz. We believe the prophecy of a great soul harvest, and we thank you that Ken is merely one of the first of many millions who will be swept into your kingdom over the next few years. We know many will suffer and die at the hands of Antichrist, but their eternal fate is sealed. We pray especially that our new brother develops a hunger for your Word, that he possesses the boldness of Christ in the face of persecution, and that he be used to bring others into the family. And now may the God of peace himself sanctify us completely, and may our spirits, souls, and bodies be preserved blameless at the coming of our Lord Jesus Christ. We believe that he who called us is faithful, who will also do it. We pray in the matchless name of Jesus, the Messiah and our Redeemer."

Ken brushed tears from his cheeks, put his hat on, and pulled it down over his eyes. "Hoo boy! That's what I call some prayin'!"

Tsion trotted upstairs and returned with a dog-eared paperback book called *How to Begin the Christian Life*.

He handed it to Ken, who looked thrilled. "Will you sign it?"

"Oh, no," Tsion said. "I did not write it. It was smuggled to me from Pastor Bruce Barnes's library at the church. I know he would want you to have it. I must clarify that the Scriptures do not refer to us who become believers after the Rapture as Christians. We are referred to as tribulation saints. But the truths of this book still apply."

Ken held it in both hands as if it were a treasure.

Tsion, nearly a foot shorter than Ken, put an arm around his waist. "As the new elder of this little band, allow me to welcome you to the Tribulation Force. We now number six, and one-third of us are pilots."

Ritz went out to start the Suburban. Tsion wished Buck God's speed and headed back upstairs. Buck drew Chloe to him and enveloped her like a fragile china doll. "Did you ever get hold of Hattie? Do we know her alias?"

"No. I'll keep trying."

"Keep following Dr. Tsion's orders too, you hear?"

She nodded. "I know you're coming right back, Buck, but I don't like saying good-bye. Last time you left me I woke up in Minnesota."

"Next week we'll sneak Dr. Charles over here and get your stitches out."

"I'm waiting for the day I have no more stitches, cast, cane, or limp. I don't know how you can stand to look at me."

Buck cupped her face in his hands. Her right eye was still black and purple, her forehead crimson. Her right cheek was sunken where teeth were missing, and her cheekbone was broken.

"Chloe," he whispered, "when I look at you I see the love of my life." She started to protest and he shushed her. "When I thought I had lost you, I would have given anything to have you back for just one minute. I could look at you until Jesus comes and still want to share eternity with you."

He helped her to a chair. Buck bent and kissed her between her eyes. Then their mouths met. "I wish you were going with me," he whispered.

"When I get healthy, you're going to wish I'd stay home once in a while."

+ + +

Rayford stalled as long as possible to get more comfortable with the Challenger 3 and also to make sure Buck and Ken Ritz got to Hattie before he did. He wanted to be able to tell Fortunato she was gone when he got there. Soon he would call Buck to warn him that the GC would try to keep her from bolting.

Rayford didn't like his instructions. Fortunato would not commit to a specific destination. He said local GC forces would give Rayford that information. Rayford didn't care where they wanted him to take Hattie. If this worked the way he hoped, she would be jetting back to the Chicago area with Buck and Ken, and his orders would be moot.

Buck would have to fly over a thousand miles to Denver, Rayford fewer than eight hundred. He throttled back, reaching nowhere near the potential of the powerful jet. An hour later, Rayford was on the phone with Buck. While they talked, a couple of calls came over his radio, but not hearing his call letters or name, he ignored them.

"Our ETA is noon at Stapleton," Buck said. "Ken tells me I was too ambitious, promising we'd see her that early. She still has to tell us how to get there, and we haven't been able to reach her. I don't even know her alias."

Rayford told him his own predicament.

"I don't like it," Buck said. "I don't trust any of them with her."

"The whole thing's squirrelly."

"Albie to Scuba, over," the radio crackled. Rayford ignored it.

"I'm way behind you, Buck. I'll make sure I don't get there until around two."

"Albie to Scuba, over," the radio repeated.

"That'll make it logical for Leon," Rayford continued. "He can't expect me to get there faster than that."

"Albie to Scuba, do you read me, over?"

It finally sank in. "Hold on a minute, Buck."

Rayford felt gooseflesh on his arms as he grabbed the mike. "This is Scuba. Go ahead, Albie."

"Need your ten-twenty, Scuba, over."

"Stand by."

"Buck, I'm gonna have to call you back. Something's up with Mac."

Rayford checked his instruments. "Wichita Falls, Albie, over."

"Put down at Liberal. Over and out."

"Albie, wait. I—"

"Stay put and I'll find you. Albie over and out."

Why had Mac had to use code names? He set a course for Liberal, Kansas, and radioed the tower there for landing coordinates. Surely Mac wasn't flying to Liberal on the Condor. But the chopper would take hours.

He got back on the radio. "Scuba to Albie, over."

"Standing by, Scuba."

"Just wondering if I could head back and meet you on your way, over."

"Negative, Scuba. Over and out."

Rayford phoned Buck and updated him.

"Strange," Buck said. "Keep me posted."

"Roger."

"Want some good news?"

"Gladly."

"Ken Ritz is the newest member of the Tribulation Force."

\+ + +

Just before noon, Mountain Time, Ritz landed the Learjet at Stapleton Airport, Denver. Buck had still not heard from Chloe. He called her.

"Nothing, Buck. Sorry. I'll keep trying. I called several reproductive centers there, but the ones I reached said they did only same-day surgery, no residents. I asked if they also delivered babies. They said no. I don't know where to go from here, Buck."

"You and me both. Keep trying her number."

\+ \+ \+

Rayford pacified suspicious tower personnel at the tiny Liberal airport by topping off his fuel tank. The base operator was surprised how little he needed.

He set his laptop near the cockpit window and sat on the tarmac surfing the Internet. He found Tsion's bulletin board, which had become the talk of the globe. Hundreds of thousands of responses were added every day. Tsion continued to direct the attention of his growing flock to God himself. He added to his personal daily message a fairly deep Bible study aimed at the 144,000 witnesses. It warmed Rayford's heart to read it, and he was impressed that a scholar was so sensitive to his audience. Besides the witnesses, his readers were the curious, the scared, the seekers, and the new believers. Tsion had something for everyone, but most impressive was his ability, as Bruce Barnes used to say, to "put the cookies on the lower shelf."

Tsion's writing read the way he sounded to Rayford in person when the Tribulation Force sat with him and discussed what Tsion called "the unsearchable riches of Christ Jesus."

Tsion's ability with the Scriptures, Rayford knew, had to do with more than just his facility with the languages and texts. He was anointed of God, gifted to teach and evangelize. That morning he had put the following call-to-arms on the Internet:

> *Good day to you, my dear brother or sister in the Lord. I come to you with a heart both heavy with sorrow and yet full of joy. I sorrow personally over the loss of my precious wife and teenagers. I mourn for so many who have died since the coming of Christ to rapture his church. I mourn for mothers all over the globe who lost their children. And I weep for a world that has lost an entire generation.*
>
> *How strange to not see the smiling faces or hear the laughter of children. As much as we enjoyed them, we could not have known how much they taught us and how much they added to our lives until they were gone.*
>
> *I am also melancholy this morning because of the results of the wrath of the Lamb. It should be clear to any thinking person, even the nonbeliever, that prophecy was fulfilled. The great earthquake appears to have snuffed out 25 percent of the remaining population. For generations people have called*

natural disasters "acts of God." This has been a misnomer. Eons ago, God the Father conceded control of Earth's weather to Satan himself, the prince and power of the air. God allowed destruction and death by natural phenomena, yes, because of the fall of man. And no doubt God at times intervened against such actions by the evil one because of the fervent prayers of his people.

But this recent earthquake was indeed an act of God. It was sadly necessary, and I choose to discuss this today because of one thing that happened where I am hiding in exile. A most bizarre and impressive occurrence that can be credited to the incredible organizational, motivational, and industrial abilities of the Global Community. I have never hidden that I believe the very idea of a one-world government, or currency, or especially faith (or I should say nonfaith) is from the pit of hell. That is not to say that everything resulting from these unholy alliances will be obviously evil.

Today, in my secret part of the world, I learned via radio that the astounding Cellular-Solar network had made it possible already for television to be returned to certain areas. A friend and I, curious, turned on the television set. We were astounded. I expected an all-news network or perhaps also a local emergency station. But as I am sure you know by now, where television has returned, it is back full force.

Our television accesses hundreds of channels from all over the world, beamed to it by satellite. Every picture on every channel representing every station and network available is transmitted into our home in images so crisp and clear you feel you could reach inside the screen and touch them. What a marvel of technology!

But this does not thrill me. I admit I was never an avid TV watcher. I bored others with my insistence on watching educational or news programs and otherwise criticizing what was offered. I expressed fresh shock every month or so at how much worse television had become.

I shall no longer apologize for my horror at what has become of this entertainment medium. Today, as my friend and I sampled the hundreds of stations, I was unable to even pause at most offerings, they were so overtly evil. Stopping even to criticize them would have subjected my brain to poison. I concede that approximately 5 percent was something as inoffensive as the news. (Of course, even the news is owned and controlled by the Global Community and carries its unique spin. But at least I was not subjected to vile language or lascivious images.) On virtually every other channel, however, I saw—in that split second before the signal changed—final proof that society has reached rock bottom.

I am neither naive nor prudish. But I saw things today I never thought

I would see. All restraint, all boundaries, all limits have been eradicated. It was a microcosm of the reason for the wrath of the Lamb. Sexuality and sensuality and nudity have been part of the industry for many years. But even those who used to justify these on the basis of freedom of expression or a stand against censorship at the very least made them available only to people who knew what they were choosing.

Perhaps it is the very loss of the children that has caused us not to forget God but to acknowledge him in the worst possible way, by sticking out our tongues, raising our fists, and spitting in his face. To see not just simulated perversion but actual portrayals of every deadly sin listed in the Scriptures left us feeling unclean.

My friend left the room. I wept. It is no surprise to me that many have turned against God. But to be exposed to the depths of the result of this abandonment of the Creator is a depressing and sorrowful thing. Real violence, actual tortures and murders, are proudly advertised as available twenty-four hours a day on some channels. Sorcery, black magic, clairvoyance, fortune-telling, witchcraft, séances, and spell casting are offered as simple alternatives to anything normal, let alone positive.

Is this balanced? Is there one station that carries stories, comedies, variety shows, musical entertainment, education, anything religious other than Enigma Babylon One World Faith? For all the trumpeting by the Global Community that freedom of expression has arrived, the same has been denied those of us who know and believe the truth of God.

Ask yourself if the message I write today would be allowed on even one of the hundreds of stations broadcast to every TV around the world? Of course not. I fear the day that technology will allow the Global Community to silence even this form of expression, which no doubt soon will be considered a crime against the state. Our message flies in the face of a one-world faith that denies belief in the one true God, a God of justice and judgment.

And so I am a dissenter, as are you if you count yourself part of this kingdom family. Belief in Jesus Christ as the only begotten Son of God the Father, Maker of heaven and earth, trust in the one who offered his life as a sacrifice for the sin of the world, is ultimately antithetical to everything taught by Enigma Babylon. Those who pride themselves on tolerance and call us exclusivists, judgmental, unloving, and shrill are illogical to the point of absurdity. Enigma Babylon welcomes every organized religion into its ranks, with the proviso that all are acceptable and none are discriminated against. And yet the very tenets of many of those same religions make this impossible. When everything is tolerated, nothing is limited.

There are those who ask, why not cooperate? Why not be loving and accepting? Loving we are. Accepting we cannot be. It is as if Enigma Babylon is an organization of "one-and-only true" religions. It may be that many of these belief systems eagerly gave up their claims of exclusivity because they never made sense.

Belief in Christ, however, is unique and, yes, exclusive on the face of it. Those who pride themselves on "accepting" Jesus Christ as a great man, perhaps a god, a great teacher, or one of the prophets, expose themselves as fools. I have been gratified to read many kind comments about my teaching. I thank God for the privilege and pray I will always seek his guidance and expound his truth with care. But imagine if I announced to you that not only am I a believer, but that I am also God himself. Would that not negate every positive thing I have ever taught? It may be true that we should love everyone and live in peace. Be kind to our neighbors. Do unto others as we would have them do unto us. The principles are sound, but is the teacher still admirable and acceptable if he also claims to be God?

Jesus was a man who was also God. Well, you say, that is where we differ. You consider him simply a man. If that is all he was, he was an egomaniac or he was deranged or he was a liar. Can you say aloud without hearing the vapidness of it that Jesus was a great teacher except for that business about claiming to be the Son of God, the only way to the Father?

One argument against a deep, sincere commitment to faith used to be that various religious beliefs were so similar that it did not seem to make much difference which somebody chose. Living a moral, spiritual life was assumed to entail doing the best you could, treating other people nicely, and hoping your good deeds outweighed your bad.

Indeed, those tenets are common to many of the religions that came together to form the One World Faith. As cooperating members they have cast aside all other distinctions and enjoy the harmony of tolerance.

Frankly, this clarifies the matter. I no longer must compare faith in Christ to every other belief system. They are all one now, and the difference between Enigma Babylon and the Way, the Truth, and the Life, is so clear that the choosing, if not the choice, has become easy.

Enigma Babylon, sanctioned by the Global Community itself, does not believe in the one true God. It believes in any god, or no god, or god as a concept. There is no right or wrong; there is only relativism. The self is the center of this man-made religion, and devoting one's life to the glory of God stands in stark relief.

My challenge to you today is to choose up sides. Join a team. If one side is right, the other is wrong. We cannot both be right. Go to the page that walks you through those Scriptures that clarify man's condition. Discover that you are a sinner, separated from God, but that you can be reconciled to him by accepting the gift of salvation he offers. As I have pointed out before, the Bible foretells of an army of horsemen that numbers 200 million, but a crowd of tribulation saints—those who become believers during this period—that cannot be numbered.

Though that clearly indicates there will be hundreds of millions of us, I call you not to a life of ease. During the next five years before the glorious return of Christ to set up his kingdom on earth, three-fourths of the population that was left after the Rapture will die. In the meantime, we should invest our lives in the cause. A great missionary martyr of the twentieth century named Jim Elliot is credited with one of the most poignant summaries of commitment to Christ ever penned: "He is no fool who gives up what he cannot keep [this temporal life] to gain what he cannot lose [eternal life with Christ]."

And now a word to my fellow converted Jews from each of the twelve tribes: Plan on rallying in Jerusalem a month from today for fellowship and teaching and unction to evangelize with the fervor of the apostle Paul and reap the great soul harvest that is ours to gather.

And now unto him who is able to keep you from falling, to Christ, that great shepherd of the sheep, be power and dominion and glory now and forevermore, world without end, Amen. Your servant, Tsion Ben-Judah.

Rayford and Amanda had loved reading such missives from Bruce Barnes and then Tsion. Was it possible she was in hiding somewhere, able to access this very thing? Could it be they were reading it at the same time? Would a message from Amanda someday appear on Rayford's screen? Each day with no news made it harder for him to believe she was still alive, and yet he could not accept that she was gone. He would not stop looking. He couldn't wait to get back to the equipment that would allow him to dive and prove Amanda was not on that plane.

"Albie to Scuba, over."

"This is Scuba, go," Rayford said.

"ETA three minutes. Sit tight. Over and out."

\+ \+ \+

Buck and Chloe agreed that he would keep trying Hattie's number while she continued to call medical facilities in Denver. Buck got a taste of Chloe's frustration when he began hitting the redial button for Hattie's phone every minute or so. Even a busy signal would have been encouraging. "I can't stand just sitting here," Buck said. "I feel like heading off on foot and searching for her."

"Got your laptop with you?" Ritz said.

"Always," Buck said. Ken had been riveted to his for some time.

"Tsion's on the Net, rallying the troops. He's gotta be gettin' under Carpathia's skin. I know there's a lot more people who still love Carpathia than there are like us who finally saw the light, but look at this."

Ritz turned his computer so Buck could watch the numbers whiz by, indicating how many responses hit the bulletin board every minute. With a fresh message out there, the total was multiplying again.

Ritz was right, of course, Buck thought. Carpathia had to be enraged by the response to Tsion. No wonder he wanted credit for Tsion's escape and also for eventually bringing him back to the public. But how long would that satisfy Carpathia? How long before his jealousy got the best of him?

"If it's true, Buck, that the Global Community would like to sponsor Tsion's return to Israel, they ought to look at what he's saying about Enigma Babylon."

"Carpathia's got Mathews in charge of Enigma Babylon right now," Buck said, "and he regrets it. Mathews sees himself and the faith as bigger and more important than even the GC. Tsion says the Bible teaches that Mathews will only last so long."

The phone rang. It was Chloe.

"Buck, where are you?"

"Still sitting here on the runway."

"You and Ken head for a rental car. I'll talk as you walk."

"What's up?" Buck said, climbing out and signaling Ken to follow.

"I got through to a small, private hospital. A woman told me they were being shut down in three weeks because they're better off to sell to the Global Community than pay the ridiculous taxes."

Buck jogged toward the terminal but soon slowed when he realized Ken was lagging. "Is that where Hattie is?" he asked Chloe.

"No, but this woman told me there's a big GC testing laboratory in Littleton. It's housed in a huge church Enigma Babylon took over and then sold to Carpathia when attendance dwindled. A reproductive clinic in the old educational wing of that church takes in longer-term patients. She wasn't fond of it. The clinic and the lab work hand in hand, and apparently there's a lot of cloning and fetal tissue research going on."

"So you reached Hattie there?"

"I think I did. I described Hattie, and the receptionist got suspicious when

I didn't know what name she might be using. She told me that if someone was using a phony name, that meant they didn't want to be contacted. I told her it was important, but she didn't buy it. I asked if she would just tell every patient that one of them had a message to call CW, but I'm sure she ignored it. I called a little later and disguised my voice. I said my uncle was the janitor and could somebody get him to come to the phone. Pretty soon this guy came on and I told him I had a friend in there who forgot to give me her alias. I told him my husband was on the way there with a gift, but he would have to know whom to ask for to be able to get in. He wasn't sure he ought to help until I told him my husband would give him a hundred dollars. He was so excited he gave me his name before he gave me the names of the four women staying there right now."

Buck reached the rental car desk and Ken, knowing the drill, slapped his driver's license and credit card on the counter. "You're gonna owe me a ton," he said. "Let's hope they've got a decent-sized car."

"Give me the names, hon," Buck said, pulling out a pen.

"I'll give you all four just in case," Chloe said, "but you're gonna know right away which is hers."

"Don't tell me she called herself something like Derby Bull."

"Nothing so creative. It's just that with the makeup of the women represented, we got lucky. Conchita Fernandez, Suzie Ng, Mary Johnson, and Li Yamamoto."

"Give me the address, and have Uncle Janitor tell Mary we're on our way."

\+ \+ \+

Mac set the chopper down close to the Challenger and jumped aboard with Rayford.

"I don't know what all's going down, Ray, but I wouldn't stall you like that without a reason. It gives me chills to think I almost missed this, but after you dropped me off, I taxied the Condor into that south hangar, like you said. I'm coming out of there and heading to the cab line when Fortunato pages me from the ambassador's house. He asks me will I let him back on the Condor because he's got a classified call he's gotta make and the only secure phone is on board. I tell him sure, but that I'm gonna have to unlock it for him and get some power on for his call and then lock up after him. He tells me that's OK as long as I stay in the pilot's quarters or in the cockpit and give him privacy. I told him I had stuff to do in the cockpit. Check this out, Ray."

Mac pulled a dictation machine from his pocket. "Do I think ahead, or what? I slipped in there, jammed on those headphones, and flipped the switch. I tucked the machine inside one of the phones and turned it on. Listen."

Rayford heard dialing, then Fortunato saying, "OK, Your Excellency, I'm on the Condor, so this is secure. . . . Yes, I'm alone. . . . Officer McCullum let me in. . . . In the cockpit. No problem. . . . On his way to Denver. . . . They're gonna do it right there? . . . It's as good a place as any. It's going to change our trip back, though. . . . One pilot simply can't physically do this whole trip. I wouldn't feel safe. . . . Yes, start telling the ambassadors we'll need more time to get back. Did you want me to try to hire a pilot from here in Dallas? . . . I see. I'll check in with you later."

"What do you make of that, Mac?"

"It's pretty clear, Ray. They want to take you both out at once. What got to me is when he rushed to the cockpit and knocked quickly. He looked flushed and shaken. He asked if I would come back and join him and to please sit down. He looks nervous, wiping his mouth and looking away, totally unlike him, you know. He says, 'I just heard from Captain Steele, and there's a chance he'll be delayed. I would like you to plot our return and work in enough rest time for yourself in case you have to do all the flying.'

"I say, '*All* the flying? The whole way back and all the stops en route?'

"He says I should make the schedule easy on myself and that with enough rest, they have full confidence I can do it. He adds, 'You will find His Excellency much in your debt.'"

Rayford was not amused. "So he recruited you to be the new captain."

"Just about."

"And I'm going to be delayed. Well, isn't that a nice way to say I'm going to be toast."

17

BY THE TIME Buck and Ken got their car—with more room than they needed—and were informed of shortcuts around destruction, it took nearly forty-five minutes to get to Littleton. Finding a church that had been retrofitted into a testing laboratory and reproductive clinic was easy. It was on the only navigable street in a fifteen-mile radius. Every vehicle they saw was dusty and mud-caked.

Buck went in alone to see if he could sneak Hattie from the place. Ken waited out front with the engine idling and monitored Buck's phone.

Buck approached the receptionist. "Hi!" he said breezily. "I'm here to see Mary."

"Mary?"

"Johnson. She's expecting me."

"And who may I say is asking for her?"

"Just tell her it's B."

"Are you related?"

"We soon will be, I think. I hope."

"One moment."

Buck sat and found a magazine as if he had all the time in the world. The receptionist picked up the phone. "Ms. Johnson, were you expecting a visitor? . . . No? . . . A young man who calls himself B. . . . I'll check."

The receptionist motioned to Buck. "She would like to ask where you know her from."

Buck smiled as if exasperated. "Remind her we met on an airplane."

"He says you met on an airplane. . . . Very well."

The receptionist hung up. "I'm sorry, sir, but she believes you may have her confused with someone else."

"Can you tell me if she's alone?"

"Why?"

"That may be the reason she's not admitting she knows me. She may need some assistance and doesn't know how to tell me."

"Sir, she is recovering from a medical procedure. I'm quite sure she's alone and well taken care of. Without her permission, I am not at liberty to share anything more with you."

In his peripheral vision, Buck saw a small, dark figure shuffle past in a long robe. The tiny, long-haired, severe-looking Asian woman peered curiously at Buck, then quickly looked away and disappeared down the hallway.

The receptionist's phone rang. She whispered, "Yes, Mary? . . . You don't recognize him at all? Thank you."

+ + +

"So, Mac, am I paranoid, or does it sound like they're using Hattie as bait to get the two of us together?"

"Sounds that way to me," Mac said. "And neither of you are going to walk away."

Rayford grabbed his phone. "I'd better let Buck know what he's getting into before I decide what to do about it."

+ + +

It sounded to Buck as if the receptionist was calling security. It would do no good to be ushered out by security, or worse, detained by them. His first thought was to bolt. But still there was a chance to bluff his way past the receptionist. Maybe Ken could distract her. Or maybe Buck could convince her he didn't know what name his friend used and had been only guessing.

The receptionist stunned him, however, when she suddenly hung up and said, "You don't happen to work for the Global Community, do you?"

How she knew that was as puzzling as Hattie using an ethnic alias while an Asian girl was either named Mary Johnson or had selected that as *her* pseudonym. If Buck denied working for the Global Community, he might never find out why she asked. "Uh, yeah, as a matter of fact I do," he said.

The front door swung open behind him. Ken was on the run, Buck's phone in hand.

The receptionist said, "And does your name happen to be Rayford Steele?"

"Uh . . ."

Ken shouted, "Sir? Is that your car out there with the lights on?"

Buck could tell he should not hesitate. He spun, calling over his shoulder, "I'll be back."

"But, sir! Captain Steele!"

Buck and Ken bounded down the steps to the car. "They thought I was Rayford! I was almost in!"

"You don't want in there, Buck. Rayford's been set up. He's sure he would have walked into an ambush."

Ken tried to shift into Drive, but it wouldn't budge. "I thought I left this thing running." The keys were gone.

A uniformed GC security officer materialized at his window. "Here, sir," he said, handing Ken the keys. "Which of you is Captain Steele?"

Buck could tell Ken was tempted to race off. He leaned across Ken's lap and said, "That would be me. Were you expecting me?"

"Yes, we were. When your driver left the car, I thought I'd shut it off and bring him the keys. Captain Steele, we have your cargo inside, if you'll join us." Turning to Ken, he said, "Are you also with the GC?"

"Me? Nope. I work for the rental company. The captain here wasn't sure he'd be bringing the car back, so I drove him. He still pays for a round trip, of course."

"Of course. And if there's nothing you need from the car then, Captain, you may follow me." To Ken, "And we will provide transportation, so you may take the car."

"Let me settle up with him," Buck said. "And I'll be right with you."

Ken closed his window. "Say the word, Buck, and they'll never catch us. You go in there as Rayford Steele and neither you or Hattie will come out."

Buck made a show of taking out a few bills for Ken. "I have to go in," he said. "If they think I'm Rayford and that I smelled a rat and slipped away, Hattie's life is worthless. She's carrying a child, and she's not a believer yet. I'm not about to hand her over to the GC." Buck glanced at the guard on the sidewalk. "I gotta go."

"I'll stay close," Ritz said. "If you aren't out of there soon, I'm comin' in."

+ + +

"I'm tempted to fly straight to Baghdad and prove to myself Amanda isn't buried in the Tigris. What's Carpathia going to do when I show up? Take credit for my resurrection?"

"You know where your daughter is, right? If they've found a place to hide, that's the place to go. By the time it gets back to Carpathia that you didn't show in Denver, you'll be hidden."

"It's not like me to hide, Mac. I knew this gig with Carpathia was temporary, but it's strange to be a target. None of us are likely to make it to the Glorious Appearing, but that's been my goal since day one. What are the odds now?"

Mac shook his head.

Rayford's phone rang. Ritz told him what was going on.

"Oh, no!" Rayford said. "You shouldn't have let him go back in there. They may not figure out he's not me until after they've killed him. Get him out of there!"

"There was no stopping him, Rayford. He thinks if we do something suspicious, Hattie is history. Trust me, if he's not out in a few minutes, I'm going in."

"These people have unlimited weapons," Rayford said. "Are you armed?"

"Yes, but they're not going to risk shooting inside, are they?"

"Why not? They care for no one but themselves. What are you carrying?"

"Buck doesn't know, and I've never had to use it, but I carry a Beretta anytime I fly for him."

\+ + +

Buck and the GC guard were met inside by an unhappy receptionist. "Had you simply told me who you were, Captain Steele, and used the proper name for the person you were seeking, I could have easily accommodated you."

Buck smiled and shrugged. A younger guard emerged. "She will see you now," he said. "Then we'll all fill out a little paperwork, and we'll run you both out to Stapleton."

"Oh," Buck said, "you know, we didn't put down at Stapleton after all."

The guards caught each other's eyes. "You didn't?"

"We were told the terrain between here and Stapleton was worse than between here and Denver International, so we—"

"I thought DIA was closed."

"Closed to commercial, yes," Buck said, scrambling. "If you can get us out there, we'll be heading back."

"Back where? We haven't given you your orders yet."

"Oh, yeah. I know. I just assumed New Babylon."

"Hey," the younger guard said. "If DIA is closed to commercial, where'd you get the car?"

"One outfit was still open," Buck said. "Guess they're serving the GC military."

The older guard glanced at the receptionist. "Tell her we're on our way."

As the receptionist reached for the phone, the guards asked Buck to follow them down the hall. They entered a room labeled "Yamamoto." Buck was afraid Hattie would say his name as soon as she saw him. She lay facing the wall. He couldn't tell whether she was awake.

"She's going to be surprised to see her old captain," Buck said. "She used to call me Buck for short. But in front of the crew and passengers, it was always Captain Steele. Yeah, she was my senior flight attendant at Pan-Con for many years. Always did a good job."

The older guard put a hand on her shoulder. "Time to go, dear."

Hattie rolled over, appearing puzzled, squinting against the light. "Where are we going?" she said.

"Captain Steele is here for you, ma'am. He'll take you to an intermediate site and then back to New Babylon."

"Oh, hi, Captain Steele," she said groggily. "I don't want to go to New Babylon."

"Just following orders, Ms. Durham," Buck said. "You know all about that."

"I just don't want to go that far," she said.

"We'll take it in stages. You'll make it."

"But I—"

"Let's get started, ma'am," the older guard said. "We're on a schedule."

Hattie sat up. Her pregnancy was beginning to show. "I would appreciate it if you gentlemen would excuse me while I dress."

Buck followed the guards into the hall. The younger said, "So, what did you fly up here?"

"Oh, one of the little jets that survived the quake."

The other asked, "How was the flight from Baghdad?"

Buck thought Rayford had told him Baghdad Airport was unusable. Relieved they hadn't asked more about the plane, he wondered if he was being tested. "We flew out of New Babylon," he said. "You wouldn't believe how fast the rebuilding is going."

"Long flight?"

"Very. But of course we stopped every so many hours to pick up another dignitary." Buck had no idea how many, when, or where, and he hoped they wouldn't ask.

"What's that like? All those muckety-mucks on the same plane?"

"Another day, another dollar," Buck said. "Pilots stay in the cockpit or in our quarters anyway. We don't get involved in the pageantry."

Buck knew he had already been inside long enough to worry Ken Ritz. No way these guys were taking him or Hattie to either airport, regardless of how he misled them. He was surprised they hadn't already offered them a poisoned drink. Apparently they had orders to make it neat and clean and quiet. There could be no witnesses.

When the older guard knocked on Hattie's door, Buck caught sight of Ken with a janitor down the hall, both carrying brooms. Buck engaged the guards in conversation, hoping Ken could get out of sight quickly. Though Ken was wearing a clinic cap like the janitor, there was no hiding his features.

"So what kind of a vehicle did you guys get issued?" Buck said. "Anything that'll get us through this terrain faster than a rented sedan?"

"Not really. A minivan. Rear-wheel drive, unfortunately. But we can get you to DIA with no trouble."

"Where are they sending us, anyway?" Buck said.

The younger guard pulled a sheet from his pocket. "I'll give you this in a few minutes in the other room, but it says Washington Dulles."

Buck eyed the man. He knew one thing for sure: There weren't even plans to rebuild Dulles. It had been obliterated in the war, and the earthquake had wiped out Reagan National. Reagan had an operable runway or two, Rayford had told him, but Dulles was a pile of debris.

"I'll be another second," Hattie called out. The guard sighed.

"What's in the other room?" Buck said.

"A debriefing. We give you your orders, make sure you've got everything you need; then we head to the airport."

Buck didn't like the idea of the other room. He wished he could talk to Ritz. Buck couldn't tell if the GC men were carrying sidearms, but they were purported to have Uzis in holsters strapped at their ribs in the back. He wondered if he was going to die trying to save Hattie Durham.

\+ + +

Rayford didn't want Fortunato to know he was not yet in Denver, in case GC forces there had already reported his arrival. If Denver was tipped off that the real Rayford was still in the air, Buck would be exposed, and neither he nor Hattie would have a chance. Rayford sat on the runway in Kansas as helpless as he had ever felt.

"You'd better get heading back, Mac. Fortunato thinks you were visiting friends, right?"

"I am, aren't I?"

"How does he contact you?"

"Has the tower call me, and then we switch to frequency 11 to talk privately."

Rayford nodded. "Safe trip."

\+ + +

"All right, ma'am," the guard said through Hattie's door. "Time's up. Now let's go."

Buck heard nothing from Hattie's room. The guards looked at each other. The older turned the doorknob. It was locked. He swore. Both yanked weapons from their jackets and banged loudly on the door, commanding Hattie to come out. Other women peeked from their rooms, including one from each end of the hall. The younger guard waved his Uzi at them and they ducked back in. The older burped four shots at Hattie's door, blowing the latch and lock housing to the floor and causing screams down the hall. The receptionist came running, but when she appeared in the corridor, the younger guard sprayed a fusillade that ripped from her waist to her face. She dropped loudly onto the marble floor.

The older guard rushed into Hattie's room as the younger spun to follow him. Buck was between them. He wished he'd had some defense or assault training. There must be some strategic response to a man in your face carrying an Uzi.

With nothing in his repertoire, he planted his right foot, stepped quickly with his left, and drove his fist square into the young guard's nose with all he could muster. He felt the crush of cartilage, the cracking of teeth, and the ripping of flesh. The guard must have been in midstride when Buck hit him, because the back of his head hit the floor first.

The Uzi rattled on the marble, but the strap wound up tucked under him. Buck turned and ran toward the last room to his left, where he'd seen a panicky face peek out a moment before. Swimming in his mind in slow motion were the curtains blowing from the open window in Hattie's room, the riddled body of the receptionist, and the whites of the eyes of the guard when Buck drove his nose so deep into his head that it was flush with his face.

Blood dripped from Buck's hand as he ran. He glanced back as he raced into the room at the end. No sign of the older guard yet. A pregnant Hispanic woman shrieked as he flashed into her room. He knew he looked awful, the sore on his cheek still fiery, his hand and shirt covered with the blood from the young guard's face. The woman covered her eyes and trembled.

"Lock that door and stay under the bed!" Buck said. She didn't move at first. "Now or you'll die!"

Buck opened the window and saw he would have to turn sideways to get out. The screen wouldn't budge. He backed up and lifted his leg, driving it through. The momentum carried him out and down into some bushes. As he regained his footing, bullets ripped through the door behind him, and he saw the woman cower under her bed. He raced along the side of the building past Hattie's open window. In the distance, Ken Ritz was helping her into the back of the car. The Global Community minivan sat between Buck and the sedan.

Buck felt as if he were in a dream, unable to move faster. He made the mistake of holding his breath as he ran and soon had to gasp for air, his heart cracking against his ribs. As he neared the van he shot a look back as the guard leaped from the window he had escaped through. Buck ducked around the other side of the van as bullets drilled the chassis. A block ahead, Ritz waited behind the wheel. Buck could stay put and be massacred or held hostage, or he could take his chances and run to the car.

He ran. With every step he feared the next sound would be a bullet crashing into his head. Hattie was out of sight on the seat or the floor, and Ken leaned right and disappeared as well. The passenger door flew open and beckoned like a spring in the desert. The more Buck ran, the more vulnerable he felt, but he dared not look back.

He heard a sound, but not gunfire. Duller. The van door. The guard had jumped into the van. Buck was within fifty yards of the car.

\+ + +

Rayford dialed Buck's phone. It rang several times, but Rayford did not want to hang up. If a GC man answered, Rayford would bluff him until he found out what he wanted to know. If Buck answered, Rayford would allow him to talk in code in case he was in front of people who shouldn't know who was on the other end. The phone kept ringing.

Rayford hated helplessness and immobility more than anything. He was tired of games with Nicolae Carpathia and the Global Community. Their sanctimony and sympathy drove him wild. "God," he prayed silently, "let me be Carpathia's out-and-out enemy, please."

A petrified female voice answered the phone. "What!" she shouted.

"Hattie? Don't let on, but this is Rayford."

"Rayford! Buck's pilot scared me to death outside my window but then helped me get out! We're waiting for Buck! We're scared he's going to be killed!"

"Give me that phone!" Rayford heard. It was Ritz. "Ray, he looks fine, but he's got a guy shootin' at him. As soon as he gets to the car, I'm gone. I may have to hang up on you."

"Just take care of them!" Rayford said.

\+ + +

A few steps from the car, expecting to be leveled, Buck had heard nothing more. No shots, no van. He stole one last look as the GC man clambered out of the van. He dropped into a crouch and began firing. Buck heard a huge blast next to him as the right rear tire was blown. He dove for the open door, grabbing the handle and trying to get a foot inside. The back windshield blew through the car in pieces.

Buck tried to keep his balance. His left foot was on the floorboard, his right on the pavement. His left hand gripped the chassis and his right the door handle. Ken had leaned over onto the passenger's seat again to escape the bullets, and before Buck could pull himself in, Ken blindly floored the accelerator. The door swung open, and to keep from flying out Buck swiveled and sat on Ritz's head. Ken screamed as the car spun, flat tire flapping and good tires peeling rubber. Buck tried to keep out of the firing line too, but he had to get off Ken's painful head.

Ken let go of the wheel and used both hands to fight his way out from under Buck. He sat up to get his bearings and wrenched the wheel left, not in time to miss the corner of a building. The right corner panel tore and crumpled high. Ken straightened the car and tried to put some distance between them and the shooter.

The car was not cooperating. More bullets narrowly missed Ritz, and Buck saw his demeanor change. Ken went from scared to mad in a flash.

"That's it!" Ritz hollered. "I've been shot at for the last time!"

To Buck's horror, Ritz swung the car around and raced toward the guard. Buck peeked over the dashboard as Ritz pulled his 9mm automatic from an ankle holster, braced his left wrist between the outside mirror and the chassis, and fired.

The guard scrambled to the other side of the van. Buck hollered for Ken to head for the airport.

"No way!" Ken said. "This guy's mine!"

He skidded to a stop about fifty feet from the van and leaped from the car. He squatted, the Beretta in two hands, squeezing shots off just above ground level.

Buck screamed for Ritz to get back in the car as the GC man turned and ran toward the building. Ritz fired off three more shots and one hit the guard in the foot, sending his leg shooting up in front of him and flipping him backwards. "I'll kill you, you—"

Buck ran from the car and grabbed Ritz, dragging him back. "No way he's alone!" Buck said. "We've got to go!"

They jumped into the car, and Ken spun the wheel with the accelerator on the floor. A huge cloud of dust boiled up behind them as they bounced and shimmied across the earthquake-ravaged terrain toward Stapleton.

"If we can get out of sight," Buck said, "they think we're headed toward DEN. Why couldn't he get that van started?"

Ritz reached under his seat and pulled out a distributor cap, wires dangling. "This might have somethin' to do with it," he said.

The car protested noisily. Buck put a hand on the ceiling to keep from hitting his head as they bounced along. With his other he reached across Ritz and buckled him in. Then he buckled himself in and saw his phone slide by his feet. He grabbed it and saw it was in use. "Hello?" he said.

"Buck! It's Ray! Are you safe?"

"We're on the way to the airport! We've got a blown rear tire, but all we can do is go till we stop."

"We've also got a gas leak!" Ritz said. "The gauge is dropping fast!"

"How's Hattie?" Rayford asked.

"Hanging on for dear life!" Buck said. He wanted to buckle her in but knew it would be impossible in her condition, especially with the bouncing. She lay in the backseat, feet pressed against the door, one hand holding her stomach, the other pushing against the back of the seat. She was pale.

"Hold on!" Ritz hollered.

Buck looked up in time to see a tall dirt mound they would not be able to avoid. Ritz neither slowed nor tried to stop. He kept the pedal to the floor and steered for the center of the dirt. Buck braced himself with his feet and reached back to try to keep Hattie from flying forward upon impact. When the car dived into the dirt pile, Hattie slammed into the back of the front seat and nearly pushed Buck's shoulder from the socket. The phone flew from his hand, cracked into the windshield, and skidded to the floor.

+ + +

"Call me when you can!" Rayford shouted, hanging up. He taxied the Challenger 3 to the end of the runway.

"Scuba to Albie," he said. "Albie, do you copy?"

"Go ahead, Scuba."

"Get back to base and find out what they know. The cargo is safe temporarily, but I'm going to need some kind of a story when I show up."

"Roger that, Scuba. Consider a Minot."

Rayford paused. "Good call, Albie. Will do. Need everything you can give me ASAP."

"Roger."

Brilliant, Rayford thought. He had long ago told Mac of an experience while he was stationed in Minot, North Dakota. His jet fighter malfunctioned, and he had to abort a training mission. He would tell Fortunato that's what had happened to the Challenger, and Leon wouldn't know the difference. Mac would vouch for whatever Rayford said. The biggest problem was that by the time he got back, Leon would know of the fiasco in Denver and would suspect Rayford's involvement.

What he needed was leverage to keep himself alive. Was Hattie important enough to Carpathia that he would keep Rayford around until he knew where she was? Rayford had to get back to Baghdad to know what had become of Amanda. There was no guarantee Carpathia wouldn't have him killed as an example to the rest of the Tribulation Force.

+ + +

"She's overheating!" Ritz said.

"I'm overheating too!" Hattie wailed. She sat up and braced herself with a hand on each of the front headrests. Her face was flushed, her forehead sweaty.

"We have no choice but to keep going," Buck said. He and Ken tried to brace themselves against the violent shuddering of the wounded vehicle. The temperature needle was buried in the red, steam billowed from under the hood, the gas gauge was perilously low, and Buck saw flames coming from the flat rear tire. "If you stop, the gas will hit those flames. Even if we get to the airport, make sure we're empty before we stop!"

Hattie shouted, "What if the tire burns up the car anyway?"

"Hope you're right with God!" Ritz shouted.

"You took the words right out of my mouth!" Buck said.

+ + +

Rocketing toward Dallas at several hundred miles an hour, Rayford was afraid he would overtake Mac in the chopper. He had to time his arrival appropriately. Several minutes later he heard Fortunato contact Mac.

"Dallas tower to Golf Charlie Niner Niner, over."

"This is Golf Charlie. Go ahead, tower."

"Switch to alternate frequency for your superior, over."

"Roger that."

Rayford switched to frequency 11 to listen in.

"Mac, this is the Supreme Commander."

"Go ahead, sir."

"What's your location?"

"Two hours west of you, sir. Returning from a visit."

"Were you coming straight back?"

"No, sir. But I can."

"Please do. There was a major foul-up north of us, do you follow?"

"What happened?"

"We're not sure yet. We need to find our operative and then we need to get back on schedule as soon as possible."

"I'm on my way, sir."

\+ + +

Buck prayed the car would run out of gas soon, but he didn't know how they would get Hattie across the torn-up ground. The flames licked the back right side of the car, and only Ken's keeping the thing rolling kept them from exploding.

The fire was closest to Hattie, and even with the car jerking this way and that, she managed to crawl into the front seat, jamming between the men.

"The engine will blow before I run out of gas!" Ken shouted. "We may have to jump!"

"Easier said than done!" Hattie said.

Buck had an idea. He found his phone and punched in an emergency code. "Warn Stapleton tower!" he yelled. "Small craft approaching on fire!"

The dispatcher tried to ask something, but Buck hung up. The engine rattled and banged, the back of the car was a torch, and Ken nursed it over one last rise to the far end of the runway. A foam truck moved into position.

"Keep her rolling, Ken!" Buck said.

The engine finally quit. Ken shifted into neutral and both men grabbed their door handles. Hattie latched onto Buck's arm with both hands. The car was barely rolling when the foam truck reached it and unloaded, smothering the vehicle and snuffing the fire. Ken burst out one side and Buck the other, Hattie in tow. Lurching blindly through the foam, Buck lifted Hattie into his arms, stunned at her added weight. Weak from the ordeal, he fell in behind Ken and followed him to the Learjet. Ken lowered the steps, told Buck to hand Hattie to him and get aboard, then carried her to where Buck helped her into a seat. Ken had the door shut, the engines screaming, and the Learjet rolling within a minute.

As they jetted into the sky, the foam crew finished with the car and stared at the fleeing plane.

Buck spread his knees and let his hands dangle. His knuckles were raw. He couldn't wipe from his mind the images of the receptionist—dead before she hit the ground—the guard he rocked off his feet, and the woman trembling as she locked her door.

"Ken, if they find out who we are, you and I are fugitives."

"What happened to noon?" Hattie said, her voice thin.

"What happened to your phone?" Buck asked. "Chloe and I tried to reach you all morning."

"They took it," she said. "Said they had to run diagnostics on it or something."

"Are you healthy?" Buck said. "I mean, other than your condition?"

"I've felt better," she said. "I'm still pregnant, if you're curious."

"I gathered that while carrying you."

"Sorry."

"We're going to be in hiding," Buck said. "Are you up to it?"

"Who else is there?"

Buck told her.

"What about medical care?"

"I have an idea there, too," Buck said. "No promises, but we'll see what we can do."

Ken seemed to still be wired. "I couldn't believe my luck when I paid off that janitor and he took me outside where I could look right through the window."

"When you said you were with Buck," Hattie said, "I had to trust you."

"How in the world did you get out of there, Buck?" Ken said.

"I wonder that myself. That guard murdered the receptionist."

Hattie looked stricken. "Claire?" she said. "Claire Blackburn's dead?"

"I didn't know her name," Buck said, "but she's dead all right."

"That's what they wanted to do to me," Hattie said.

"You got that right," Ken said.

"I'll stay with you guys for as long as you'll have me," she said.

Buck got on his phone, updated Rayford and Chloe, then punched in the number of Dr. Floyd Charles in Kenosha.

✢ ✢ ✢

Rayford concocted a story he believed would be convincing. The only problem, he knew, was that it might not be long before Buck was identified as his impostor.

18

BEFORE RETURNING to Dallas, Rayford hoped to find out what Leon knew or believed had happened in Denver. But he was unable to reach Mac. Was it possible Buck had been recognized? No one would believe Rayford had not had a part in Hattie's escape if it was known his son-in-law was there. Rayford would accept the consequences of his actions in what he considered a holy war. He did, however, want to stay out of prison long enough to find Amanda and clear her name.

If Tsion was right, the 144,000 witnesses were sealed by God and protected from harm for a certain period. Though he was not one of the witnesses, Rayford was a believer; he had the mark of God on his forehead, and he trusted God to protect him. If God did not, then, as the apostle Paul put it, to die would be "gain."

Rayford had not heard from Mac and couldn't raise him. Either Mac could not get away from Leon long enough to get in touch with him, or something was wrong on the ground. Rayford had to do something. If he was to say he had aborted his mission, it only made sense to radio Leon before showing up again in Dallas.

+ + +

Buck was rocked to think he might have killed someone. When Dr. Charles met them at Waukegan Airport before following them to Mount Prospect, Buck whispered his fear. "I have to know how bad I hurt that guard."

"I know a guy at the GC emergency facility outside Littleton," Dr. Charles said. "I can find out."

Dr. Charles stayed in his car on the phone after Ken wheeled the Suburban into the backyard. Chloe and Tsion demanded every detail. Chloe navigated the stairs with her cane, insisting that Hattie take the downstairs bed. Hattie looked exhausted. Ken and Tsion helped her up the stairs and urged her to call for them after her shower so they could help her back down.

Buck and Chloe spoke in private. "You could have been killed," she said.

"I'm surprised I wasn't. I just know I killed that guard. I can't believe it. But he had just murdered the receptionist, and I knew he would do the same to us. I reacted instinctively. If I'd thought about it, I might have frozen."

"There was nothing else you could do, Buck. But you can't kill a man with a punch, can you?"

"I hope not. But he had spun around and was moving right toward me when I hit him. I'm not exaggerating, hon. I don't think I could have hit him harder if I had been running at him. It felt as if my fist was inside his head. Everything crumbled beneath it, and he landed flush on the back of his head. It sounded like a bomb."

"It was self-defense, Buck."

"I don't know what I'll do if I find out he's dead."

"What will the Global Community do if they find out it was you?"

Buck wondered how long that might take. The young guard had gotten a good look at him, but he was likely dead. The other guard assumed he was Rayford Steele. Until someone showed him a picture of Rayford, he might still believe it. But could he describe Buck?

Buck moved to a mirror in the hallway. His face was grimy, his cheek red and purple almost to his nose. His hair was wild and dark with sweat. He needed a shower. But what had he looked like at that clinic? What might the surviving guard say about him?

\+ \+ \+

"Charlie Tango to Dallas tower, over."

"Tower, go ahead, Charlie Tango."

"Relay urgent message to Global Community Supreme Commander. Mission aborted due to mechanical failure. Checking equipment before return to base. ETA two hours, over."

"Roger that, Charlie Tango."

Rayford put down at an unattended and seemingly abandoned airstrip east of Amarillo and waited for Leon Fortunato's call.

\+ \+ \+

Buck worried when Dr. Charles finally came into the house and would not make eye contact. The doctor agreed to check Chloe, Ken, and Hattie before heading back to Kenosha. He appeared most concerned about Hattie and her baby. She was to remain at rest for other than nature calls. He told the others how to care for her and what symptoms to monitor.

The doctor removed Ken's stitches and advised him also to take it easy for several days.

"What, no more shoot-outs? Guess I can't work for Buck for a while."

The doctor told Chloe again that time was her ally. Her arm and foot casts were not ready to be removed, but he prescribed therapy that would help her snap back more quickly.

Buck waited, watching. If Dr. Charles ignored him altogether, that meant Buck had killed a man and the doctor didn't know how to tell him. "Could you check my cheek?" Buck asked.

Without a word, Dr. Charles approached. He held Buck's face in his hands and turned him this way and that in the light. "I need to clean that," he said. "You risk infection unless we get some alcohol in there."

The others left them while the doctor worked on Buck. "You'll feel better after a shower, too," he said.

"I'll feel better when you tell me what you found out. You were on that phone a long time."

"The man is dead," Dr. Charles said.

Buck stared.

"I don't see that you had any choice, Buck."

"They'll come looking for me. They had cameras throughout that place."

"If you looked like you look now, even people who know you might not have recognized you."

"I have to turn myself in."

Dr. Charles stepped back. "If you shot an enemy soldier during a battle, would you turn yourself in?"

"I didn't mean to kill him."

"But if you had not, he would have killed you. He killed someone right in front of you. You know his assignment was to take out both you and Hattie."

"How did a punch kill him?"

The doctor applied a butterfly bandage and sat on the table. "My colleague in Littleton tells me that either of the two blows—to the face or to the back of the head—could have done it. But the combination made it unavoidable. The guard suffered severe facial trauma, a shattering of cartilage and bone around the nose, some of it driven into his skull. Both optic nerves were destroyed. Several teeth were shattered, and the upper jaw cracked. That damage alone might have killed him."

"*Might* have?"

"My associate leans toward the posterior cranial damage as the cause of death. The back of his head hitting flush on the floor caused his skull to shatter like an eggshell. Several shards of cranial tissue were embedded in the brain. He died instantly."

Buck hung his head. What kind of a soldier was he? How could he be expected to fight in this cosmic battle of good versus evil if he couldn't handle killing the enemy?

The doctor began putting his things away. "I've never met anyone who caused another person's death and didn't feel awful for a while," he said. "I've talked with parents who killed someone while protecting their own child, but still they were haunted and sobered. Ask yourself where Hattie would be if not for what you did. Where would *you* be?"

"I'd be in heaven. Hattie would be in hell."

"Then you bought her some time."

\+ \+ \+

Rayford finally received a call from the Dallas tower, asking that he inform them when he was half an hour from touchdown. "The Supreme Commander awaits your arrival."

He told them he was about to get underway. Half an hour out of Dallas, he radioed in, and forty minutes later he taxied to the hangar that also housed the Condor 216. He alighted to face a glowering Leon Fortunato, Mac McCullum behind him with a knowing look. Rayford couldn't wait to talk to Mac privately.

"What happened, Captain Steele?"

"It was sluggish, Commander, and only prudent to check it out. I was able to make an adjustment, but I was so far behind schedule I thought I'd better check in."

"You don't know what happened, then?"

"To the plane? Not entirely, but it was unstable and—"

"I mean what happened in Denver!"

Rayford glanced at Mac, who almost imperceptibly shook his head.

"In Denver?"

"I told you, Commander," Mac said, "I was unable to reach him."

"Follow me," Fortunato said. He led Rayford and Mac to an office, where he punched up on a computer a video and text e-mail from the Global Community office in Denver. The three bent over the monitor and watched as Fortunato narrated. "We knew Miss Durham was unwilling to return to New Babylon, but His Excellency believed it was in her best interest and in the best interest of global security. To protect his fiancée and their child, we assigned two security officers to meet with you and her and to give you your orders. Their top priority was the transfer of Miss Durham to you for her transport to the Middle East. They were to ensure she was still in Denver when you arrived.

"While the laboratory and clinic there were largely undamaged by the earthquake, we thought the surveillance system had been knocked out. However, the surviving security officer double-checked the system, just in case, and found a view of the impostor."

"The impostor?" Rayford said.

"The man claiming to be you."

Rayford raised his eyebrows.

"These were professionals, Captain Steele."

"These?"

"At least two. Maybe more. The cameras in front of the building and in the reception area were not operating. There are cameras at either end of the main corridor and one in the middle. The action you'll see here took place in the middle, but the only camera working was the one at the north end of the corridor. Nearly every view of the impostor is blocked by one of the security men, or the impostor has his back to the camera. The tape begins here with the security guards and the perpetrator stepping outside Miss Durham's door while she dressed for the trip."

It was clear Buck was the man between the two guards, but his face was indistinct. His hair was out of place, and he had an ugly cheek wound.

"Now watch, gentlemen. When the senior guard knocks on Miss Durham's door, the other also turns toward the door, but the perp glances down the hall. That's the clearest view we get of his face."

Again, Rayford was relieved that the image was not clear.

"The senior guard believes the perp was distracted by two janitors who appear earlier on the tape. He will interview them later today. Now here, a few moments later, he has lost patience with Miss Durham. He calls to her and both guards bang on the door. Here the junior guard orders curious patients back into their rooms. The perp backs up a couple of steps when the senior guard blows open the door. That brings the receptionist. While the junior guard is distracted, the perp somehow disarms him, and see? See the gunfire? He murders the receptionist where she stands. When the junior guard attempts to disarm him, he drives the butt end of the Uzi so hard into his face that the guard is dead before he hits the floor.

Mac and Rayford caught each other's eyes and leaned closer to study the video. Rayford wondered if Fortunato thought he had the power Carpathia possessed, to convince people they had seen something they had not. He couldn't let it pass.

"That's not what I see there, Leon."

Leon looked sharply at him. "What are you saying?"

"The junior guard did the firing." Fortunato backed up the tape. "See?" Rayford said. "There! He's firing. The perp is stepping back. The guard wheels back around, and the perp steps forward as the guard appears to slip on his own expelled shell casings. See? He has no footing, so the blow drives his head to the floor."

Fortunato looked angry. He reran the video a couple more times.

Mac said, "The perp didn't even attempt to grab the gun."

"Say what you will, gentlemen, but that impostor murdered the receptionist and the guard."

"The guard?" Rayford said. "He might have fallen on his head even if he hadn't been punched."

"Anyway," Fortunato continued, "the accomplice pulled Miss Durham through the window and sent her to the getaway car. As soon as the senior guard opened the door, the accomplice fired at him."

That was not, of course, the way Rayford had heard it. "How did he escape being killed?"

"He nearly *was*. He has a severe wound to his heel."

"I thought you said he was coming *into* the room when he was fired upon?"

"Correct."

"He was running *out* of the room if he got shot in the heel."

The computer beeped, and Fortunato asked an aide for help. "Another message is coming in," he said. "Bring it up for me."

The aide hit a few buttons, and a new message flashed from the senior guard. It read, "Foot being treated. Surgery required. Accomplice was second janitor in first scene on tape. Real janitor found with wad of cash. Says accomplice forced on him to appear like bribe. Says accomplice held knife to throat until he got information."

Fortunato's aide backed the video all the way to where the two janitors entered the hallway and walked toward the camera. Rayford, who had never met Ritz, guessed which one he was only by his incomplete janitorial outfit. The only thing resembling a uniform was the cap he had apparently borrowed from the janitor. He carried a broom, but his clothing was western.

"He could be from that area," Fortunato said.

"Good call," Rayford said.

"Well, it doesn't take a trained eye to identify regional clothing."

"Still, Commander, that's an insightful catch."

"I don't see a knife," Mac said, as the figures neared the camera. Ritz's cap was pulled low over his eyes. Rayford held his breath as he reached for the bill of his cap. He lifted it and reset it on his head, showing his face more clearly. Rayford and Mac looked at each other behind Fortunato.

"After they passed that camera," Fortunato said, "the accomplice got the information he needed and ran the janitor off. He absconded with Miss Durham and opened fire on our guard. And those guards were there only to protect Miss Durham."

The guard had conveniently left out details that would have made him appear an idiot. Until someone could thoroughly investigate the scene, the Global Community had not a shred of evidence implicating Rayford.

"She will contact you," Fortunato said. "She always does. You had better not have had anything to do with this. His Excellency would consider that high treason and punishable by death."

"You suspect *me*?"

"I have come to no conclusions."

"Am I returning to New Babylon as a suspect or as a pilot?"

"A pilot, of course."

"You want me at the controls of the Condor 216?"

"Of course. You can't kill us without killing yourself, and I don't gauge you suicidal. Yet."

\+ + +

Buck spent more than three weeks working on the Internet version of *Global Community Weekly*. He was in touch with Carpathia nearly every day. Nothing was said about Hattie Durham, but Carpathia often reminded Buck that their mutual "friend," Rabbi Tsion Ben-Judah, would be protected by the Global Community anytime he chose to return to the Holy Land. Buck did not tell Tsion. He merely kept alive his promise that the rabbi could return to Israel within the month.

Donny Moore's duplex proved more ideal every day. Nothing else in the neighborhood had survived. Virtually no traffic came by.

Ken Ritz, now fully on the mend, moved out of the tiny sliver of the Quonset hut he had been allotted at Palwaukee and commuted between Wheeling and Waukegan from his new digs in the basement of the safe house. Dr. Charles visited every few days, and every chance they got, the Tribulation Force met together and sat under Tsion's teaching.

It was no accident that they met around the kitchen table with Hattie not eight feet away on her sickbed. Often she rolled onto her side with her back to them, pretending to sleep, but Buck was convinced she heard every word.

They were careful not to say anything that might incriminate them with

Carpathia, having no idea what the future held for Nicolae and Hattie. But they cried together, prayed together, laughed, sang, studied, and shared their stories. Dr. Charles was often present.

Tsion rehearsed the entire plan of salvation in nearly every meeting. It might come in the form of one of their stories or his simply expositing a Scripture passage. Hattie had lots of questions, but she asked them only of Chloe later.

The Tribulation Force wanted Dr. Charles to become a full-fledged member, but he declined, fearful that more frequent daily trips to the house might lead the wrong people there. Ritz spent many days tinkering in the underground shelter, getting it into shape in case any or all of them needed complete seclusion. They hoped it would not come to that.

\+ \+ \+

The flight from Dallas to New Babylon, with several stops to pick up Carpathia's regional ambassadors, had been a harrowing one for Rayford. He and Mac both worried that Fortunato might enlist Mac to eliminate him. Rayford felt vulnerable, assuming Fortunato believed he was involved in the rescue of Hattie Durham.

The device that allowed Rayford to hear what was going on in the main cabin yielded fascinating listening throughout the trip. One of the strategically placed transmitters was near the seat usually occupied by Nicolae Carpathia himself. Of course, Leon had appropriated that one, which was propitious for Rayford. He found Leon an incredible master of deceit, second only to Nicolae.

Each ambassador came aboard with attendant fanfare, and Fortunato immediately ingratiated himself. He ordered the cabin crew to wait on them, whispered to them, flattered them, took them into his confidence. Each heard Fortunato's tale of having been raised from the dead by Carpathia. It sounded to Rayford as if each was either truly impressed or put on a good front. "I assume you know that you're among His Excellency's favorite two regional potentates," Fortunato privately told each king.

Their responses were variations of "I didn't know for sure, but I can't say it surprises me. I am most supportive of His Excellency's regime."

"That has not gone unnoticed," Fortunato would say. "He appreciates very much your suggesting the ocean harvesting operation. His Excellency believes this will result in huge profits to the entire world. He's asking that your region split the income equally with his Global Community administration, and he will then redistribute the GC share to the less fortunate regions."

If that made a king blanch, Fortunato went into overdrive. "Of course, His Excellency realizes the burden this puts on you. But, you know the old saying:

'To whom much is given, much is required.' The potentate believes you have governed with such brilliance and vigor that you can be counted on as one of the globe's great benefactors. In exchange, he has given me the liberty to show you this list and these plans for your personal encouragement and comfort." As Fortunato would unroll papers—which Rayford assumed were elaborate architectural drawings and lists of perquisites—he would say, "His Excellency himself pleaded with me to assure you that he does not in any way believe this is anything but appropriate for a person of your stature and station. While it may appear opulent to the point of ostentation, he asked that I personally convey that he believes you are worthy of such accommodations. While your new domicile, which will be constructed and equipped within the next six months, may appear to elevate you even beyond where he is, he insists that you not reject his plans."

Whatever Fortunato showed them seemed to impress. "Well," they would say, "I would never ask this for myself, but if His Excellency insists . . ."

Fortunato saved his slimiest approach. Just before his official conversation with each king was finished, he added: "Now, sir, His Excellency asked that I broach with you a delicate matter that must remain confidential. May I count on you?"

"Certainly!"

"Thank you. He is gathering sensitive data on the workings of the Enigma Babylon One World Faith. Being careful not to prejudice you, but also not wanting to act without your insight, he is curious. How do you feel about Pontifex Maximus Peter Mathews's self-serving—no, that is pejorative—let me state it another way. Again, being careful not to sway you, do you share His Excellency's, shall we say, hesitation over the pontiff's independence from the rest of the Global Community administration?"

To a man, every king expressed outrage over Mathews's machinations. Each considered him a threat. One said, "We do our share. We pay the taxes. We are loyal to His Excellency. With Mathews, it's just take, take, take. It's never enough. I, for one, and you may express this to His Excellency, would love to see Mathews out of office."

"Then let me broach a yet more sensitive issue, if I may."

"Absolutely."

"If it came to taking an extreme course of action against the very person of the pontiff, would you be one upon whom His Excellency could depend?"

"You mean . . . ?"

"You understand."

"You may count on me."

The day before the Condor 216 was to deliver the dignitaries to New Babylon, Mac received word from Albie. "Your delivery is early and ready for pickup."

Rayford spent nearly an hour scheduling his and Mac's time in the cockpit and in the sleeping quarters so both would feel as fresh as possible at the end of the trip. Rayford penciled himself in for the last block of piloting. Mac would sleep and then be available to make the chopper run to make the pickup and pay off Albie. Meanwhile, Rayford would sleep in his quarters at the shelter. Come nightfall, Rayford and Mac would slip away and helicopter to the Tigris.

It worked almost as planned. Rayford had not anticipated David Hassid's eagerness to debrief him on everything that had happened in his absence. "Carpathia actually has missiles pointing into outer space, anticipating judgmental meteors."

Rayford flinched. "He believes the prophecies that God will pour out more judgments?"

"He would never admit that," David said. "But it sure sounds like he's afraid of it."

Rayford thanked David and finally told him he needed rest. On his way out, Hassid shared one more bit of news, and it was all Rayford could do to stay off the Internet. "Carpathia has been manic the last several days," David said. "He discovered that Web site where you can tap into a live camera shot of the Wailing Wall. He spent days carrying his laptop everywhere he went, watching and listening to the two preachers at the Wall. He's convinced they're speaking directly to him, and of course they are. Oh, he's mad. Twice I heard him scream, 'I want them dead! And soon!'"

"That won't happen before the due time," Rayford said.

"You don't have to tell me," David said. "I'm reading Tsion Ben-Judah's messages every chance I get."

Rayford posted coded notes on bulletin boards all over the Net, trying to locate Amanda. He may have been too obscure, but he didn't dare make it more obvious. He believed she was alive, and so unless it was proven otherwise, to him she was. All he knew was that if she could communicate with him, she would. As for the charges that she was working for Carpathia, there were moments he actually wished that were true. That would mean she was alive for sure. But if she had been a traitor—no, he would not allow himself to run with that logic. He believed the only reason he had not heard from her was that she did not have the means to contact him.

Rayford was so eager to prove Amanda was not entombed in the Tigris that he wasn't sure he could sleep. He was fitful, peeking at the clock every half hour or so. Finally, about twenty minutes before Mac was due, Rayford showered and dressed and accessed the Internet.

The camera at the Wailing Wall carried live audio as well. The preachers Rayford knew to be the two witnesses prophesied in Revelation were holding forth. He could almost smell their smoky burlap robes. Their dark, bony bare feet and knuckled hands made them appear thousands of years old. They had long, coarse beards, dark, piercing eyes, and long, wild hair. Eli and Moishe they called each other, and they preached with power and authority. And volume. The video identified the one on the left as Eli, and subtitles carried his message in English. He was saying, "Beware, men of Jerusalem! You have now been without the waters of heaven since the signing of the evil pact. Continue to blaspheme the name of Jesus Christ, the Lord and Savior, and you will continue to see your land parched and your throats dry. To reject Jesus as Messiah is to spit in the face of almighty God. He will not be mocked.

"Woe unto him who sits on the throne of this earth. Should he dare stand in the way of God's sealed and anointed witnesses, twelve thousand from each of the twelve tribes making a pilgrimage here for the purpose of preparation, he shall surely suffer for it."

Here Moishe took over. "Yea, any attempt to impede the moving of God among the sealed will cause your plants to wither and die, rain to remain in the clouds, and your water—all of it—to turn to blood! The Lord of hosts hath sworn, saying, 'Surely, as I have thought, so it shall come to pass, and as I have purposed, so it shall stand!'"

Rayford wanted to shout. He hoped Buck and Tsion were watching this. The two witnesses warned Carpathia to stay away from those among the 144,000 coming to Israel for inspiration. No wonder Nicolae had been seething. Surely he saw himself as the one who sits on the throne of the earth.

Rayford appreciated that Mac did not try to dissuade him from his mission. He had never been more determined to finish a task. He and Mac latched their gear to the struts for the short hop from New Babylon to the Tigris. Rayford strapped himself in and pointed toward Baghdad. By the time they landed, the sky was dark.

"You don't have to do this with me, you know," Rayford said. "No hard feelings if you just want to keep an eye out for me."

"Not a chance, brother. I'll be right there with you."

They unloaded at a steep bank. Rayford stripped down, pulled on his wet suit and booties, and stretched the rubber cap over his head. Had the suit been any smaller, it would not have worked. "Did I get yours?" he asked.

"Albie says one size fits all."

"Terrific."

When they were completely outfitted with eighty-cubic-foot tanks, buoyancy control devices (BCDs), weight belts, and fins, they fog-proofed their masks with spit and pulled them on.

"I believe in my heart she's not down there," Rayford said.

"I know," Mac said.

They inspected each other's gear, inflated their BCDs, stuffed in their mouthpieces, then slid down the sandy bank into the cold, rushing water, and slipped beneath the surface.

Rayford had only guessed where the 747 dropped into the river. While he agreed with Pan-Con officials who told Carpathia the plane was too heavy to have been affected much by the current, he believed it could have gone dozens of feet downstream before embedding itself in the bottom. Because no vestige of the plane had ever surfaced, Rayford was convinced the fuselage had holes front and back. That would have resulted in the plane hitting the bottom rather than being held aloft by air pockets.

The water was murky. Rayford was a good diver, but he was still claustrophobic when unable to see more than a few feet, even with the powerful light strapped to his wrist. It seemed to shine no more than ten feet in front of him. Mac's was even dimmer and suddenly disappeared.

Did Mac have bad equipment, or had he turned his off for some reason? It made no sense. The last thing Rayford wanted was to lose sight of his partner. They could spend too much time searching for the wreckage and have little time to investigate it.

Rayford watched clouds of sand shoot past and realized what had happened. Mac had been pulled downstream. He was far enough ahead that neither could see the other's light.

Rayford tried to steer himself. It only made sense that the lower he went, the less the current would pull him. He let more air out of his BCD and kicked harder to dive, peeling his eyes to see past the end of his beam. Ahead a dim, blinking light appeared stationary. How could Mac have stopped?

As the blinking beam grew larger and stronger, Rayford kicked hard, laboring to align himself with Mac's light. He was coming fast when the top of his head smacked violently into Mac's tank. Mac hooked Rayford's elbow in the crook of his own arm and held firm. Mac had snagged a tree root. His mask was half off and his regulator mouthpiece was out. With one arm holding Rayford and the other gripping the root, he wasn't free to help himself.

Rayford grabbed the root, allowing Mac to let go of him. Mac reinserted his regulator and cleared his mask. Dangling in the current, each with a hand on the root, they were unable to communicate. Rayford felt the spot on his head where he had banged into Mac's tank. A flap of rubber rose from his cap; a matching patch of skin and hair had been gouged from his scalp.

Mac pointed his light toward Rayford's head and motioned him to lean over. Rayford didn't know what Mac saw, but Mac signaled to the surface. Rayford shook his head, which made his wound throb.

Mac pushed away from the root, inflated his BCD, and rose to the top. Rayford reluctantly followed. In that current, he could do nothing without Mac. Rayford popped out of the water in time to see Mac reach an outcropping on the bank. Rayford labored to join him. When they had raised their masks and snorkels, Mac spoke quickly.

"I'm not trying to talk you out of your mission, Ray. But I am telling you we have to work together. See how far we've come from the chopper already?" Rayford was stunned to see the dim outline of the helicopter way upriver.

"If we don't find the plane soon, that means we're probably already past it. The lights don't help much. We're going to have to be lucky."

"We're going to have to pray," Rayford said.

"And you're gonna have to get that head treated. You're bleeding."

Rayford felt his head again and shined the light on his fingers. "It's not serious, Mac. Now let's get back to it."

"We've got one shot. We need to stay close to the bank until we're ready to search in the middle. Once we get out there, we'll be going fast. If the plane is there, we could run right into it. If it's not, we've got to get back to the bank. I'm going to wait for your lead, Ray. You follow me while I'm navigating the edge of the river. I'll follow you when you signal me it's time to venture out."

"How will *I* know?"

"You're the one doing the praying."

19

IT WAS JUST BEFORE one o'clock in the afternoon in Mount Prospect. Tsion had spent the morning logging another long message to the faithful and to the seekers on the Internet. The number of messages back to him continued to spiral. He called out to Buck, who trotted upstairs and looked over his shoulder at the quantity meter.

"So," Buck said, "it's finally slowed?"

"I knew you would say that, Cameron," Tsion said, smiling. "A message came across at four this morning explaining that the server would now flash a new number not for every response but for every thousand."

Buck shook his head and stared as the number changed every one to two seconds. "Tsion, this is astounding."

"It is a miracle, Cameron. I am humbled and yet energized. God fills me with love for every person who stands with us, and especially for all who have questions. I remind them that almost anywhere you click on our bulletin board, you find the plan of salvation. The only problem is, because it is not our own Web site, all this has to be refreshed and posted new every week."

Buck put a hand on the rabbi's shoulder. "It won't be long before the mass meetings in Israel. I pray God's protection for you."

"I feel such boldness—not based on my own strength, but on the promises of God—that I believe I could walk alone to the Temple Mount without being harmed."

"I'm not going to let you try that, Tsion, but you're probably right."

"Here, look, Cameron." Tsion clicked onto the icon allowing him to see the two witnesses at the Wailing Wall. "I long to talk with them again in person. I feel a kinship even though they are supernatural beings, come from heaven. We will spend eternity with them, hearing the stories of God's miracles from people who were there."

Buck was fascinated. The two preached when they wanted to and fell silent when they chose. Crowds knew to keep their distance. Anyone trying to harm them had dropped dead or had been incinerated by fire from the witnesses' mouths. And yet Buck and Tsion had stood within a few feet of them, only a fence separating them. It seemed they spoke in riddles, yet God always gave Buck understanding. As he watched now, Eli sat in Jerusalem's gathering darkness with his back to an abandoned room made of stone. It looked as if guards may have once used it. Two heavy iron doors were sealed, and a small barred opening served as a window. Moishe stood, facing the fence that separated him from spectators. None was within thirty feet. His feet were spread, his arms straight at his sides. He did not move. It appeared Moishe was not blinking. He looked like something carved from stone, save for the occasional wisp of hair ruffling in the breeze.

Eli shifted his weight occasionally. He massaged his forehead, making him appear to be thinking or praying.

Tsion glanced at Buck. "You are doing what I do. When I need a break, I go to this site and watch my brothers. I love to catch them preaching. They are so bold, so forthright. They do not use Antichrist's name, but they warn enemies of the Messiah of what is to come. They will be so inspiring to those of the 144,000 who can make it to Israel. We will join hands. We will sing. We will pray. We will study. We will be motivated to go forth with boldness to preach the gospel of Christ around the world. The fields are ripe and white unto harvest. We missed the opportunity to join Christ in the air, but what an unspeakable privilege to be alive during this time! Many of us will give our lives for our Savior, but what higher calling could a man have?"

"You should say that to your cyberspace congregation."

"As a matter of fact, I was reciting the conclusion of today's message. Now you do not have to read it."

"I never miss."

"Today I am warning believers and nonbelievers alike to stay away from trees and grass until the first Trumpet Judgment is passed."

Buck looked at him quizzically. "And how will we know it has passed?"

"It will be the biggest news since the earthquake. We need to ask Ken and Floyd to help us clear several feet of grass from around the house and maybe trim some trees."

"You take the predictions literally then?" Buck said.

"My dear brother, when the Bible is figurative, it sounds figurative. When it says all the grass and one-third of all trees will be scorched, I cannot imagine what that might be symbolic for. In the event our trees are part of the one-third, I want to be out of the way. Do you not?"

"Where are Donny's garden tools?"

\+ + +

The Tigris was not frigid, but it was uncomfortable. Rayford used muscles he hadn't used in years. His wet suit was too tight, his head throbbed, and keeping from being dragged downriver made navigating a chore. His pulse was higher than it should have been, and he worked hard to regulate his breathing. He worried about running out of air.

He disagreed with Mac. They may have only one shot, but if they didn't find the plane that night, Rayford would come back again and again. He wouldn't ask Mac to do the same, though he knew Mac would never abandon him.

Rayford prayed as he felt his way along behind Mac. Mac eased himself lower by releasing air from his BCD, and Rayford followed. When either Rayford or Mac went more than ten feet without something to grip on the side, the current threatened to pull them away from the bank.

Rayford worked hard to stay with Mac. "Please, God, help me finish this. Show me she isn't there, and then direct me to her. If she's in danger, let me save her." Rayford fought to keep from his mind the possibility that Carpathia had been telling the truth about Amanda's true loyalties. He didn't want to believe it, not for a second, but the thought nagged him nonetheless.

While the souls of bodies in the Tigris were either in heaven or in hell, Rayford sensed he was to leave every one in the plane. *If* he found any. Was that feeling a signal from God that they were near the wreck? Rayford considered tapping Mac's trailing fin, but he waited.

The plane had to have hit with enough force to immediately kill everyone on board. Otherwise, passengers would have been able to unstrap and get out through holes in the fuselage or doors and windows that had burst open. But no corpses had surfaced.

Rayford knew the wings would have been sheared off, and perhaps the tail. These planes were marvels of aerodynamics, but they were not indestructible. He dreaded seeing the result of such an impact.

Rayford was surprised to see Mac two or three feet from the bank now, not holding onto anything. Apparently they were low enough that the powerful current was diminished. Mac stopped and checked his pressure gauge. Rayford did the same and gave a thumbs-up. Mac pointed to his head. Rayford gave the OK sign, though his head was only so-so. He moved ahead, leading the way. They were within six feet of the bottom now. Rayford sensed he would soon find what he was looking for. He prayed he would not find what he did not wish to find.

Away from the sidewall of the river, less muck was stirred with their movements, and their lights had more range. Rayford's picked up something, and he put up a hand to stop Mac. Despite the relative calm, they angled toward the side to keep from drifting. Both shined lights where Rayford indicated. There, bigger than life, was the huge, wholly intact right wing of a 747. Rayford fought for composure.

Rayford scanned the area. Not far ahead they found the left wing, also intact except for a huge tear from the flaps to where it had connected to the plane. Rayford guessed they'd find the tail section next. Witnesses said the plane went in nose first, which would have brought the back of the plane down with such force that the tail should have been ripped apart or broken off.

Rayford stayed low and moved approximately midway between where they had found the wings. Mac grabbed Rayford's ankle just before Rayford collided with the gigantic tail of the plane. It had been severed. The plane itself had to be dead ahead. Rayford moved twenty feet ahead of the tail and turned upright so he was almost standing on the bottom. When one of his fins touched he realized how mushy it was and how dangerous it would be to get stuck.

+ + +

It was Buck's turn to feed Hattie, who had become so weak she could barely move. Dr. Charles was on his way.

Buck spoke softly as he spooned soup to her lips. "Hattie, we all love you and your baby. We want only the best for you. You've heard Dr. Ben-Judah's teaching. You know what's been foretold and what's already happened. There's no way you can deny that the prophecies of the Word of God have been fulfilled from the day of the disappearances until now. What will it take to convince you? How much more proof do you need? Bad as these times are, God is making clear that there is only one choice. You're either on his side or you're on the side of evil. Don't let it get to where you or your baby are killed in one of the judgments to come."

Hattie pressed her lips together and refused the next offering of soup. "I don't need any more convincing, Buck," she whispered.

Chloe hobbled over. "Should I get Tsion?"

Buck shook his head, keeping his eyes on Hattie. He leaned close to hear her. "I know this all has to be true," she managed. "If I needed more convincing, I'd have to be the biggest skeptic in history."

Chloe brushed Hattie's hair away from her forehead and tucked the bangs up. "She's really hot, Buck."

"Crumble some Tylenol in this soup."

Hattie seemed to be sleeping, but Buck was worried. What a waste if they somehow lost her when she was this close to a decision for Christ. "Hattie, if you know it's true, if you believe, all you have to do is receive God's gift. Just agree with him that you're a sinner like everyone else and that you need his forgiveness. Do it, Hattie. Make sure of it."

She appeared to be struggling to open her eyes. Her lips parted and then closed. She held a breath, as if to speak, but she did not. Finally, she whispered again. "I want that, Buck. I really do. But you don't know what I've done."

"It doesn't make any difference, Hattie. Even people who were raptured with Christ were just sinners saved by grace. No one is perfect. We've all done awful things."

"Not like me," she said.

"God wants to forgive you."

Chloe returned with a spoonful of crushed Tylenol and stirred it into the soup. Buck waited, praying silently. "Hattie," he said gently, "you need more of this soup. We put medicine in it for you."

Tears slid down Hattie's cheeks, and her eyes closed. "Just let me die," she said.

"No!" Chloe said. "You promised to be my baby's godmother."

"You don't want somebody like me for that," Hattie said.

"You're not going to die," Chloe said. "You're my friend, and I want you for a sister."

"I'm too old to be your sister," she said.

"Too late. You can't back out now."

Buck got some soup down her. "You want Jesus, don't you?" he whispered, his lips near her ear.

He waited a long time for her response. "I want him, but he couldn't want me."

"He does," Chloe said. "Hattie, please. You know we're telling you the truth. The same God that fulfills prophecies centuries old loves you and wants you. Don't say no to him."

"I'm not saying no to him. He's saying no to me."

Chloe tugged at Hattie's wrist. Buck looked at her in surprise. "Help me sit her up, Buck."

"Chloe! She can't."

"She has to be able to think and listen, Buck. We can't let her go."

Buck took Hattie's other wrist, and they pulled until she sat up. She pressed her fingers against her temples and sat moaning.

"Listen to me," Chloe said. "The Bible says God is not willing that *any* should perish. Are you the one person in history who did something so bad that not even the God of the universe can forgive you? If God forgives only minor sins, there's no hope for any of us. Whatever you've done, God is like the father of the Prodigal Son, scanning the horizon. He stands with his arms wide open, waiting for you."

Hattie rocked and shook her head. "I've done bad things," she said.

Buck looked at Chloe, helpless, wondering.

+ + +

It was worse than Rayford could have imagined. He came upon the colossal fuselage, its nose and a quarter of its length buried in the muck of the Tigris at a forty-five-degree angle. The wheel housings were gone. Rayford could only dread what he and Mac were about to see. Everything in that plane, from equipment to carry-on luggage, seats and seat backs, tray tables, phones, and even passengers, would be in one massive heap at the front. An impact violent enough to snap landing gear from a plane would immediately break the neck of any passenger. The seats would have ripped from the floor and accordioned atop each other, passengers stacked upon each other like cordwood. Everything attached would have broken loose and been forced to the front.

Rayford wished he at least knew what seat Amanda was supposed to have been in, so he could save the time of digging through the entire wreckage to rule her out as a victim. Where to start? Rayford pointed up to the protruding tail end, and Mac followed him as they ascended.

Rayford grabbed the edge of an open window to keep from being pulled by the current. He shined his light into the cabin, and his worst fears were confirmed. All Rayford could make out in that back section was bare floor, walls, and ceiling. Everything had been driven to the other end.

He and Mac used the windows as grips to pull themselves down at least fifty feet to the top of the debris. The rear lavatories, storage compartments, walls, and overhead bins lay atop everything else.

+ + +

Hattie hung her head. Buck worried they were pushing her too far. Yet he would have a hard time forgiving himself if he didn't give her every opportunity and something happened to her.

"Do I have to tell him everything I've done?" Hattie breathed.

"He already knows," Chloe said. "If it makes you feel better to tell him, then tell him."

"I don't want to say it out loud," Hattie said. "It's more than affairs with men. It's even more than wanting an abortion!"

"But you didn't go through with it," Chloe said.

"Nothing is beyond God's power to forgive," Buck said. "Believe me, I know."

Hattie sat shaking her head. Buck was relieved to hear the doctor drive in. Floyd examined Hattie quickly and helped her lie down. He asked about medication, and they told him of the Tylenol. "She needs more," he said. "Her temperature is higher than you reported just a few hours ago. She'll be delirious soon. I need to find whatever is causing the fever."

"How bad is it?"

"I'm not optimistic."

Hattie was moaning, trying to talk. Dr. Charles held up a finger to keep Buck and Chloe away. "You and Tsion might want to pray for her right now," the doctor said.

+ + +

Rayford wondered about the wisdom of swimming through hundreds of corpses, especially with an open wound. Well, he figured, whatever might contaminate him had already done so. He worked feverishly with Mac to start removing the debris. They kicked wider a gash in the hull between two windows, through which they painstakingly pushed chunks of the interior.

When they reached an unusually heavy panel, Rayford got beneath it and pushed. He quickly realized what added the weight. It had been the rear seat for the flight attendant. She was still strapped in, hands balled into fists, eyes open, long hair floating free. The men gently set the panel aside. Rayford noticed Mac's light was dimmer.

That panel had protected the bodies from fish. Rayford wondered what they were subjecting these corpses to now. He shined his light through the mass of tangled seats and trash. Everyone had been strapped in. Every seat appeared occupied. No one could have suffered long.

Mac smacked his light and the beam grew brighter. He shined it into the carnage, touched Rayford's shoulder, and shook his head as if to say they should not go farther. Rayford couldn't blame him, but he couldn't quit. He knew beyond doubt that the search would put him at ease about Amanda. He had to go through this grisly ordeal for his own peace of mind.

Rayford pointed to Mac and then to the surface. Then he pointed to the bodies and smacked himself on the chest as if to say, you go and I'll stay.

Mac shook his head slowly as if disgusted. But he didn't go anywhere. They began lifting bodies, belted into seats.

+ + +

Buck helped Chloe up the stairs, where they met with Tsion to pray for Hattie. When they finished, Tsion showed them that Carpathia had become his computer competition. "He must be jealous of the response," Tsion said sadly. "Look at this."

Carpathia communicated to the masses in a series of short messages. Each sang the praises of the rebuilding forces. They encouraged people to show their devotion to the Enigma Babylon faith. Some reiterated the Global Community's pledge to protect Rabbi Ben-Judah from zealots, should he choose to return to his homeland.

"Look what I put in response to that," Ben-Judah said.

Buck peered at the screen. Tsion had written, "Potentate Carpathia: I gratefully accept your offer of personal protection and congratulate you that this makes you an instrument of the one true, living God. He has promised to seal and protect his own during this season when we are commissioned to preach his gospel to the world. We are grateful that he has apparently chosen you as our protector and wonder how you feel about it. In the name of Jesus Christ, the Messiah and our Lord and Savior, Rabbi Tsion Ben-Judah, in exile."

"It won't be long now, Tsion," Buck said.

"I just hope I can go," Chloe said.

"I didn't think there was an option," Buck said.

"I'm thinking of Hattie," she said. "I can't leave her unless she's healthy."

They made their way back downstairs. Hattie was asleep, but her breathing was labored, her face flushed, her forehead damp. Chloe dabbed at her face with a cool washcloth. Dr. Charles stood at the back door, gazing through the screen.

"Can you stay with us tonight?" Buck asked.

"I wish I could. Actually, I wish I could take Hattie for care. But she's so recognizable, we wouldn't get far. After that caper in Minneapolis, I'm being looked upon with suspicion myself. I'm being watched more and more."

"If you have to go, you have to go."

"Take a look at the sky," the doctor said.

Buck stepped closer and looked out. The sun still rode high, but dark clouds formed on the horizon.

"Great," Buck said. "What will rain do to the ruts we call roads?"

"I'd better check on Hattie and get going."

"How did you get her to sleep?"

"That fever knocked her out. I gave her enough Tylenol to dent it, but watch for dehydration."

Buck didn't respond. He was studying the sky.

"Buck?"

He turned. "Yeah."

"She was moaning and mumbling about something she feels guilty about."

"I know."

"You do?"

"We were urging her to receive Christ, and she said she wasn't worthy. She's done some things, she says, and she can't accept that God would still love her."

"Did she tell you what those things were?"

"No."

"Then I shouldn't say."

"If it's something you think I should know, let's have it."

"It's crazy."

"Nothing would surprise me anymore."

"She's carrying a tremendous load of guilt about Amanda and Bruce Barnes. Amanda is Chloe's father's wife?"

"Yeah, and I told you all about Bruce. What about them?"

"She cried, telling me that she and Amanda were going to fly together from Boston to Baghdad. When Hattie told Amanda she was changing plans and flying to Denver, Amanda insisted on going with her. Hattie kept telling me, 'Amanda knew I had no relatives in Denver. She thought she knew what I was up to. And she was right.' She told me Amanda actually canceled her reservation for Baghdad and was on her way to the counter to buy a ticket to Denver on Hattie's plane. Hattie pleaded with her not to do this. The only way she could keep Amanda from going was to swear that she herself would not go if Amanda tried to accompany her. Amanda made her promise she would not do anything stupid in Denver. Hattie knew she meant not having an abortion. She promised Amanda she would not."

"What's she feeling so bad about?"

"She says Amanda went back to get on the original flight to Baghdad but that it was now sold out. She told Hattie she wasn't interested in waiting on a standby list and that she would still be more than happy to accompany her on her flight west. Hattie refused, and she believes Amanda boarded that plane to Baghdad. She said over and over that she should have been on it too, and she wishes she had been. I told her she shouldn't say things like that and she said, 'Then why couldn't I have let Amanda come with me? She'd still be alive.'"

"You haven't met my father-in-law or Amanda yet, Floyd, but Rayford doesn't believe Amanda got on that plane. We don't know that she did."

"But if she wasn't on that plane and didn't go with Hattie, where is she? Hundreds of thousands died in the earthquake. Realistically, don't you think you would have heard from her by now if she had survived?"

Buck watched the gathering clouds. "I don't know," he said. "It's likely that if she's not dead, she's hurt. Maybe, like Chloe, she can't contact us."

"Maybe. Uh, Buck, there were a couple of other issues."

"Don't hold back."

"Hattie said something about what she knew about Amanda."

Buck froze. Was it possible? He tried to maintain composure. "What was it she supposedly knew?"

"Some secret she should have told but now can't tell."

Buck was afraid he knew what it was. "You said there was something else?"

Now the doctor appeared nervous. "I'd like to attribute this to delirium," he said.

"Shoot."

"I took a blood sample. I'm going to check it for food poisoning. I'm worried that my colleagues in Denver might have poisoned her in advance of the projected hit. I asked her what she had eaten out there, and she caught on to what I suspected. She shuddered and appeared petrified. I helped her lie down. She grabbed my shirt and pulled me close. She said, 'If Nicolae had me poisoned, I'll be his second victim.' I asked what she meant. She said, 'Bruce Barnes. Nicolae had him poisoned overseas. He made it all the way back to the States before he was hospitalized. Everyone thinks he died in the bombing, and maybe he did. But if he wasn't dead already, he would have died even if the hospital had never been bombed. And I knew all about it. I've never told anyone.'"

Buck was shaken. "I only wish you could have met Bruce," he mumbled.

"It would have been an honor. You can know for sure about his death, you know. It's not too late for an autopsy."

"It wouldn't bring him back," Buck said. "But just knowing gives me a reason. . . ."

"A reason?"

"An excuse, anyway. To murder Nicolae Carpathia."

20

THOUGH WATER PROVIDED nearly the same weightlessness as outer space, pushing debris up and out and displacing rows of seats with bodies attached was grueling. Rayford's light was dim and his air supply low. His scalp wound throbbed, and he felt light-headed. He assumed Mac was in the same shape, but neither signaled any intention of quitting.

Rayford expected to feel awful searching corpses, but deep foreboding overwhelmed him. What a macabre business! Victims were bloated, horribly disfigured, hands in fists, arms floating. Their hair waved with the motion of the water. Most eyes and mouths were open, faces black, red, or purple.

Rayford felt a sense of urgency. Mac tapped him, pointed to his gauge, and held up ten fingers. Rayford tried to work faster, but having checked only sixty or seventy bodies, there was no way he could finish without another air tank. He could work only five more minutes.

Directly below was an intact middle section row. It faced the front of the plane, as did all the others, but had rotated a little farther. All he saw in his fading light were the backs of five heads and the heels of ten feet. Seven shoes had come loose. He had never understood the phenomenon of the contraction of human feet in the face of violent collision. He estimated this row had been driven forward as many as twenty-five feet. He motioned to Mac to grab the armrest at one end while he took the other. Mac held up one finger, as if this needed to be the last effort before they surfaced. Rayford nodded.

As they tried to pull the row upright, it caught something and they had to reposition it and yank again. Mac's end came up slightly ahead of Rayford's, but when Rayford jostled his it finally rotated. The five bodies now rested on their backs. Rayford shined his flickering light into the panic-stricken face of an elderly man in a three-piece suit. The man's bloated hands floated before Rayford's face. He gently nudged them aside and directed his beam to the next passenger. She was salt-and-pepper-haired. Her eyes were open, her expression blank. The neck and face were discolored and swollen, but her arms did not rise as the others. She had apparently grabbed her laptop computer case and hooked its strap in the crook of her arm. Entwining her fingers, she had died with her hands pressed between her knees, the computer bag secure at her side.

Rayford recognized the earrings, the necklace, the jacket. He wanted to die. He could not take his eyes from hers. The irises had lost all color, and her image was one he would fight to forget. Mac hurried to him and gripped a bicep in each hand. Rayford felt his gentle tug. Dazed, he turned to Mac.

Mac tapped urgently on Rayford's tank. Rayford was drifting, having lost sense of what he was doing. He didn't want to move. He suddenly became aware his heart was thudding and he would soon be out of oxygen. He didn't want Mac to know. He was tempted to suck in enough water to flood his lungs and reunite him with his beloved.

It was too much to hope for. He should have known Mac would not have used up his own air supply as quickly. Mac pried apart Amanda's fingers and pulled the case strap over his head so the laptop hung behind his tanks.

Rayford felt Mac behind him, his forearms under his armpits. Rayford wanted to fight him off, but Mac had apparently thought ahead. At Rayford's first hint of resistance, Mac yanked both hands out and pinned Rayford's arms back. Mac kicked mightily and steered them out of the carcass of the 747 and into the rushing current. He made a controlled ascent.

Rayford had lost the will to live. When they broke the surface, he spit out his regulator and with it the sobs gushed out. He cried a fierce, primal wail that pierced the night and reflected the agonizing loneliness of his soul. Mac talked to him, but Rayford was not listening. Mac manhandled him, kicking, staying afloat, dragging him toward the bank. While Rayford's system greedily took in the life-giving air, the rest of him was numb. He wondered if he could swim if he wanted to. But he didn't want to. He felt sorry for Mac, working so hard to push a bigger man up the muddy slope onto the sand.

Rayford continued to bawl, the sound of his despair frightening even himself. But he could not stop. Mac yanked off his own mask and popped out his mouthpiece, then reached for Rayford's. He unstrapped Rayford's tanks and set them aside. Rayford rolled over and lay motionless on his back.

Mac peeled back Rayford's torn headliner to reveal blood inside his suit. With his head and face bare, Rayford's cries turned to moans. Mac sat on his haunches and breathed deeply. Rayford watched like a cat, waiting for him to relax, to step back, to believe this was over.

But it was not over. Rayford had truly believed, truly felt Amanda had survived and that he would be reunited with her. He had been through so much in the last two years, but there had always been grace in just enough measure to keep him sane. Not now. He didn't even want it. Ask God to carry him through? He could not face five more years without Amanda.

Mac stood and began unzipping his own wet suit. Rayford slowly lifted his knees and dug his heels deep into the sand. He pushed so hard he felt the strain deep in both hamstrings as the thrust carried him over the edge. As if in slow motion, Rayford felt cool air on his face as he dropped headfirst into the water. He heard Mac swear and shout, "Oh, no you don't!"

Mac would have to slip off his own tanks before jumping in. Rayford only hoped he could elude him in the dark or be lucky enough to have Mac land on him and knock him unconscious. His body plummeted through the water, then turned and began to rise. He moved not a finger, hoping the Tigris would envelop him forever. But somehow he could not will himself to gulp in the water that would kill him.

He felt the shock and heard Mac splash past him. Mac's hands brushed him as he slid past feet first. Rayford couldn't muster the energy to resist. From deep in his heart came sympathy for Mac, who didn't deserve this. It wasn't fair to make him work so hard. Rayford carried his own weight enough on the way back to the bank to show Mac he was finally cooperating. As he hauled himself up onto the sand again, he fell to his knees and pressed his cheek to the ground.

"I have no answers for you right now, Ray. Just hear me. To die in this river tonight, you're going to have to take me with you. You got that?"

Rayford nodded miserably.

Without another word, Mac pulled Rayford to his feet. He examined Rayford's wound with his fingers in the darkness. He removed Rayford's fins, stacked them with the mask on top of his tanks, and handed the set to Rayford. Mac picked up his own gear and led the way back to the chopper. There he stored the gear, helped Rayford out of his wet suit like a little boy getting ready for bed, and tossed him a huge towel. They changed into dry clothes.

Without warning, Rayford's punctured scalp felt as if it were being pelted by rocks. He covered his head and bent at the waist but now felt the same sharp stings on his arms, his neck, his back. Had he pushed too far? Had he been foolish to continue a dive with an open wound? He peeked as Mac lurched toward the chopper.

"Get in, Ray! It's hailing!"

\+ + +

Buck had always enjoyed storms. At least before he lived through the wrath of the Lamb. As a boy he had sat before the picture window in his Tucson home and watched the rare thunderstorm. Something about the weather since the Rapture, however, spooked him.

Dr. Charles left instructions on how to care for Hattie, then departed for Kenosha. As the afternoon steadily grew darker, Chloe found extra blankets for the dozing Hattie while Tsion and Buck closed windows.

"I am taking only half a risk," Tsion said. "I am going to run my computer on batteries until the storm passes, but I will remain connected to the phone lines."

Buck laughed. "For once I am able to correct the brilliant scholar," he said. "You forget we are running the electricity on a gas-powered generator, unlikely to be affected by the storm. Your phone line is connected to the dish on the roof, the highest point here. If you are worried about lightning, you'd be better to disconnect the phone and connect the power."

"I will never be mistaken for an electrician," Tsion said, shaking his head. "The truth is, I need not be connected to the Internet for a few hours either." He went upstairs.

Buck and Chloe sat next to each other at the foot of Hattie's bed. "She sleeps too much," Chloe said. "And she's so pale."

Buck was lost in his thoughts of the dark secrets that burdened Hattie. What would Rayford think of the possibility that Bruce had been poisoned? Rayford always said it was strange how peaceful Bruce looked compared to the other victims of the bombing. Doctors had come to no conclusions about the illness he had brought back from the Third World. Who would have dreamed Carpathia might be behind that?

Buck also still struggled with his killing of the Global Community guard. The videotape had been shown over and over on television news channels. He couldn't bear to see it again, though Chloe insisted it was clear from the tape he had had no choice. "More people would have died, Buck," she said. "And one of them would have been you."

It was true. He could come to no other conclusion. Why couldn't he feel a sense of satisfaction or even accomplishment from it? He was not a battle-minded man. And yet here he was on the front lines.

Buck took Chloe's hand and pulled her close. She laid her cheek on his chest, and he brushed the hair from her wounded face. Her eye, still swollen shut and morbidly discolored, seemed to be improving. He touched her forehead with his lips and whispered, "I love you with my whole heart."

Buck glanced at Hattie. She had not moved for an hour.

And the hail came.

Buck and Chloe stood and watched out the window as the tiny balls of ice bounced in the yard. Tsion hurried downstairs. "Oh, my! Look at this!"

The sky grew black, and the hailstones got bigger. Only slightly smaller than golf balls now, they rattled against the roof, clanged off the downspouts, thundered on the Range Rover, and the power failed. A chirp of protest burst from Tsion, but Buck assured him, "The hail has just knocked the cord out, that's all. Easily fixed."

But as they watched, the sky lit up. But it wasn't lightning. The hailstones, at least half of them, were in flames!

"Oh, dear ones!" Tsion said. "You know what this is, do you not? Let us pull Hattie's bed away from the window just in case! The angel of the first Trumpet Judgment is throwing hail and fire to the earth."

+ + +

Rayford and Mac had left their scuba equipment on the ground near the chopper. Now protected by the Plexiglas bubble of the tiny cockpit, Rayford felt as if he were inside a popcorn popper. As the hailstones grew, they pinged off the oxygen tanks and drilled the helicopter. Mac started the engine and set the blades turning, but he was going nowhere. He would not leave the scuba equipment, and helicopters and hailstorms did not mix.

"I know you don't want to hear this, Ray," he shouted over the din, "but you need to leave that wreckage and your wife's body right where they lie. I don't like it or understand it any more than you do, but I believe God is going to get you through this. Don't shake your head. I know she was everything to you. But God left you here for a purpose. I need you. Your daughter and son-in-law need you. The rabbi you've told me so much about, he needs you too. All I'm saying is, don't make any decisions when your emotions are raw. We'll get through this together."

Rayford was disgusted with himself, but everything Mac—the brand-new believer—said sounded like so many hollow platitudes. True or not, it wasn't what he wanted to hear. "Tell me the truth, Mac. Did you check her forehead for the sign?"

Mac pursed his lips and did not respond.

"You did, didn't you?" Rayford pressed.

"Yes, I did."

"And it wasn't there, was it?"

"No, it was not."

"What am I supposed to think of that?"

"How should I know, Ray? I wasn't a believer before the earthquake. I don't know that you had a mark on your forehead before that either."

"I probably did!"

"Maybe you did, but didn't Dr. Ben-Judah write later about how believers were starting to notice the sign on each other? That came after the earthquake. If they had died in the quake, they wouldn't have had the mark either. And even if they had it before, how do we know it's still there when we die?"

"If Amanda wasn't a believer, she probably *was* working for Carpathia," Rayford spat. "Mac, I don't think I could handle that."

"Think of David," Mac said. "He'll be looking to us for leadership and guidance, and I'm newer at this than *he* is."

When plummeting tongues of fire joined the hailstones, Rayford just stared. Mac said, "Wow!" over and over. "This is like the ultimate fireworks!"

Huge hailstones plopped into the river and floated downstream. They accumulated on the bank and turned the sand white like snow. Snow in the desert. Flaming darts sizzled and hissed as they hit the water. They made the same sound when they settled atop the hailstones on shore, and they did not burn out right away.

The chopper lights illuminated an area of twenty feet in front of the craft. Mac suddenly unclipped his belt and leaned forward. "What is that, Ray? It's raining, but it's red! Look at that! All over the snow!"

"It's blood," Rayford said, a peace flooding his soul. It did not assuage his grief or take away his dread over the truth about Amanda. But this show, this shower of fire and ice and blood, reminded him yet again that God is faithful. He keeps his promises. While our ways are not his ways and we can never understand him this side of heaven, Rayford was assured again that he was on the side of the army that had already won this war.

\+ \+ \+

Tsion hurried to the back of the house and watched the flames melt the hail and set the grass afire. It burned a few moments, and then more hail put the fire out. The entire yard was black. Balls of fire dropped into the trees that bordered the backyard. They burst into flames as one, their branches sending a giant orange mushroom into the air. The trees cooled as quickly as they had ignited.

"Here comes the blood," Tsion said, and suddenly Hattie sat straight up. She stared out the window as blood poured from the skies. She struggled to kneel on the bed so she could see farther. The parched yard was wet with melted hail and now red with blood.

Lightning cracked and thunder rolled. Softball-size hailstones drummed the roof, rolling and filling the yard. Tsion shouted, "Praise the Lord God Almighty, maker of heaven and earth! What you see before you is a picture of Isaiah 1:18:

'Though your sins are like scarlet, they shall be as white as snow; though they are red like crimson, they shall be as wool.'"

"Did you see it, Hattie?" Chloe asked.

Hattie turned and Buck saw her tears. She nodded but looked woozy. Buck helped her lie back down, and she was soon asleep.

As the clouds faded and the sun returned, the results of the light show became obvious. The bark on the trees had been blackened, the foliage all burned off. As the hail melted and blood seeped into the ground, the charred grass showed through.

"The Scriptures told us that one-third of the trees and all of the green grass in the world would be burned," Tsion said. "I cannot wait until we have power so we can see what Carpathia's newsmen make of this."

Yet another clear movement of God's hand had moved Buck. He longed for Hattie to stay healthy so she could pursue the truth. Whether Bruce Barnes had been poisoned by Nicolae Carpathia or had lost his life in the first volley of bombs in World War III made little difference in the larger scheme of things. But if Hattie Durham had information about Amanda that could confirm or deny what Tsion had stumbled onto in Bruce's computer files, Buck wanted to hear it.

+ + +

Mac left the chopper running, but Rayford was cold. With nothing green to scorch in that part of the world, the fire and blood had been overcome by the hail. The result was the chilliest night in the history of the Iraqi desert.

"Stay put," Mac said. "I'll get the stuff."

Rayford reached for the door handle. "That's all right, I'll do my share."

"No! Now I mean it. Just let me do this."

Rayford wouldn't admit it, but he was grateful. He stayed inside as Mac sloshed in the melting hail. He stored the scuba equipment behind the seats. When he reboarded he had Amanda's waterlogged laptop computer.

"What's the point, Mac? Those things aren't waterproof."

"True," Mac said. "Your screen is shot, your solar panels are ruined, your keyboard won't function, the motherboard is gone. You name it, that much water had to kill it. Except for the hard drive. It is encased and waterproof. Experts can run a diagnostic and copy any files you want."

"I don't expect any surprises."

"I'm sorry to be blunt, Rayford," Mac said, "but you didn't expect to see her in the Tigris. If I were you, I'd look for evidence to prove Amanda was everything you thought she was."

Rayford wasn't sure. "I'd have to use someone I know, like David Hassid or someone else I can trust."

"That narrows it to David and me, yes."

"If it's bad news, I couldn't let a stranger discover it before I do. Why don't you handle it, Mac? In the meantime, I don't even want to think about it. If I do, I'm going to break your confidence and go straight to Carpathia and demand he clear Amanda's name with anybody he ever talked to about her."

"You can't do that, Ray."

"I might not be able to help myself if I have exclusive access to that computer. Just do it for me and give me the results."

"I'm not an expert, Ray. How about if I supervise David, or let him run me through it? We won't look at one file. We'll just find whatever is available."

* * *

Nicolae Carpathia announced a postponement of travel due to "the strange natural phenomenon" and its effect on airport reconstruction. Over the next few weeks, as the expanded Chicago contingent of the Tribulation Force grew closer to their departure date for Israel, Buck was dumbfounded at the improvement in Chloe. Floyd Charles took her casts off, and within a few days, atrophied muscles began to come back. It appeared she might always have a limp, residual pain, and a slightly cockeyed face and frame. But to Buck, she had never looked better. All she talked about was going to Israel to see the incredible mass rally of the witnesses.

The first twenty-five thousand to arrive would meet with Tsion in Teddy Kollek Stadium. The rest would gather at sites all over the Holy Land, watching on closed-circuit television. Tsion told Buck he planned to invite Moishe and Eli to join him in the stadium.

Following God's shower of hail, fire, and blood, remaining skeptics were few. There was no longer any ambiguity about the war. The world was taking sides.

* * *

Rayford's head healed quickly, but he still had an aching heart. He spent his days mourning, praying, studying, following Tsion's teaching carefully on the Internet, and e-mailing Buck and Chloe every day.

He also kept his mind occupied with route plans, mentoring David Hassid, and discipling Mac. For the first few days, of course, their roles had been reversed as Mac helped Rayford through the worst period of grief. Rayford had to admit God gave him just enough strength for each day. No extra, none to invest for the future, but sufficient for each day.

Nearly a month from the night Rayford had discovered Amanda's body, David Hassid presented him with a high-tech disk with all of Amanda's computer files listed. "They're all encrypted and therefore inaccessible without decoding," David told him.

Rayford was so quiet around Carpathia and Fortunato, even when pressed into flying them here and there, that he believed they had become bored with him. Perfect. Until God released him from this assignment, he would simply endure it.

He was astonished at the progress of rebuilding around the world. Carpathia had troops humming, opening roads, airstrips, cities, trade routes, everything. The balance of travel, commerce, and government had shifted to the Middle East, Iraq, New Babylon, the capital of the world.

^ ^ ^

People around the world begged to know God. Their requests flooded the Internet, and Tsion, Chloe, and Buck worked day and night corresponding with new converts and planning the huge Holy Land event.

Hattie did not improve. Dr. Charles looked into a secret medical facility but finally told Buck he would take care of her where she was while Buck and the others were in Israel. It would be risky for them both, and she might have to occasionally be alone longer than he was comfortable with, but it was the best he could come up with.

Buck and Chloe prayed for Hattie every day. Chloe confided in Buck, "The only thing that will keep me from going is if Hattie has not received Christ first. I can't leave her in that state."

Buck had his own reasons for wishing she would revive. Her salvation was paramount, of course, but he needed to know things only she could tell him.

^ ^ ^

Through his own observation and the input of David Hassid, Rayford saw how enraged Carpathia was with Tsion Ben-Judah, the two witnesses, the upcoming conference, and especially the massive groundswell of interest in Christ.

Carpathia had always been motivated and disciplined, but now it was clear he was on a mission. His eyes were wild, his face taut. He rose early every day and worked late every night. Rayford hoped he would work himself into a frenzy. *Your day is coming,* Rayford thought, *and I hope God lets me pull the trigger.*

^ ^ ^

Two days before their scheduled departure for the Holy Land, the beeping of his computer awakened Buck. A message from Rayford said, "It's happening! Turn on the TV. This is going to be some ride!"

Buck tiptoed downstairs and flipped on the television, finding an all-news station. As soon as he saw what was going on, he woke up everyone in the house except Hattie. He told Chloe, Tsion, and Ken, "It's almost noon in New Babylon, and I've just heard from Rayford. Follow me."

Newscasters told the story of what astronomers had discovered just two hours before—a brand-new comet on a collision course with Earth. Global Community scientists analyzed data transmitted from hastily launched probes that circled the object. They said *meteor* was the wrong term for the hurtling rock formation, which was the consistency of chalk or perhaps sandstone.

Pictures from the probes showed an irregularly shaped projectile, light in color. The anchorman reported, "Ladies and gentlemen, I urge you to put this in perspective. This object is about to enter Earth's atmosphere. Scientists have not determined its makeup, but if—as it appears—it *is* less dense than granite, the friction resulting from entry will make it burst into flames.

"Once subject to Earth's gravitational pull, it will accelerate at thirty-two feet per second squared. As you can see from these pictures, it is immense. But until you realize its size, you cannot fathom the potential destruction on the way. GC astronomers estimate it at no less than the mass of the entire Appalachian Mountain range. It has the potential to split the earth or to knock it from its orbit.

"The Global Community Aeronautics and Space Administration projects the collision at approximately 9:00 a.m., Central Standard Time. They anticipate the best possible scenario, that it will take place in the middle of the Atlantic Ocean.

"Tidal waves are expected to engulf coasts on both sides of the Atlantic for up to fifty miles inland. Coastal areas are being evacuated as we speak. Crews of oceangoing vessels are being plucked from their ships by helicopters, though it is unknown how many can be moved to safety in time. Experts agree the impact on marine life will be inestimable.

"His Excellency Potentate Nicolae Carpathia has issued a statement verifying that his personnel could not have known earlier about this phenomenon. While Potentate Carpathia says he is confident he has the firepower to destroy the object, he has been advised that the unpredictability of fragments is too great a risk, especially considering that the falling mountain is on course to land in the ocean."

The Tribulation Force went to their computers to spread the word that this was the second Trumpet Judgment foretold in Revelation 8:8-9. "Will we look like expert prognosticators when the results are in?" Tsion wrote. "Will it shock the powers that be to discover that, just as the Bible says, one-third of the fish will die and one-third of the ships at sea will sink, and tidal waves will wreak havoc on the entire world? Or will officials reinterpret the event to make it appear the Bible was wrong? Do not be fooled! Do not delay! Now is the accepted time. Now is the day of salvation. Come to Christ before it is too late. Things will only get worse. We were all left behind the first time. Do not be left wanting when you breathe your last."

The Global Community military positioned camera-toting aircraft strategically to film the most spectacular splash in history. The more than thousand-mile-square mountain, finally determined to consist largely of sulfur, burst into flames upon entry to the atmosphere. It eclipsed the sun, blew clouds out of its path, and created hurricane-force winds between itself and the surface of the sea for the last hour it dropped from the heavens. When it finally resounded on the surface of the deep, geysers, waterspouts, and typhoons miles high were displaced, rocketing from the ocean and downing several of the GC planes. Those able to film the result produced such incredible images that they would air around the clock on TV for weeks.

Damage inland was so extensive that nearly all modes of travel were interrupted. The Israel rally of the Jewish witnesses was postponed ten weeks.

The two witnesses at the Wailing Wall went on the offensive, threatening to continue the Holy Land drought they had maintained since the day of the signing of the covenant between the Antichrist and Israel. They promised rivers of blood in retaliation for any threat to God's sealed evangelists. Then, in a comical display of power, they called upon God to let it rain only on the Temple Mount for seven minutes. From a cloudless sky came a warm downpour that turned the dust to mud and brought Israelis running from their homes. They lifted hands and faces and stuck out their tongues. They laughed and sang and danced over what this miracle would mean to their crops. But seven minutes later it stopped and evaporated, and the mud turned to dust and blew away.

"Woe unto you, mockers of the one true God!" Eli and Moishe shouted. "Until the due time, when God allows us to be felled and later returns us to his side, you shall have no power over us or over those God has called to proclaim his name throughout the earth!"

* * *

Rayford had at first been warmed by the commiseration of Chloe and Buck and Tsion in his grief over Amanda. But as he extolled her virtues in e-mailed memories, their responses were tepid. Was it possible they had been exposed to Carpathia's innuendoes? Surely they knew and loved Amanda enough to believe she was innocent.

The day finally came when Rayford received from Buck a long, tentative message. It concluded, "Our patient has rallied enough to be able to share troubling secrets of the past that have kept said patient from taking a vital step with the Creator. This information is most alarming and revealing. Only face-to-face can we discuss it, and so we urge you to coordinate a personal meeting as soon as feasible."

Rayford felt as low as he had in ages. What could that message mean other than that Hattie had shed light on the charges about Amanda? Unless Hattie could prove those charges bogus, Rayford was in no hurry to meet face-to-face.

+ + +

Just days before the rescheduled departure of the Tribulation Force for Israel, the GCASA again detected a threat in the heavens. This object was similar in size to the previous burning mountain but had the consistency of rotting wood. Carpathia, eager to turn the attention from Christ and Tsion Ben-Judah to himself again, pledged to blast it from the skies.

With great fanfare, the press showed the launch of a colossal ground-to-air nuclear missile designed to vaporize the new threat. As the whole world watched, the flaming meteor the Bible called Wormwood split itself into billions of pieces before the missile arrived. The residue wafted down for hours and landed in one-third of the fountains, springs, and rivers of the earth, turning the water a bitter poison. Thousands would die from drinking it.

Carpathia once again announced his decision to delay the Israel conference. But Tsion Ben-Judah would not hear of it. He posted on the Internet bulletin board his response and urged as many of the 144,000 witnesses as possible to converge on Israel the following week.

"Mr. Carpathia," he wrote, purposely not using any other titles, "we will be in Jerusalem as scheduled, with or without your approval, permission, or promised protection. The glory of the Lord will be our rear guard."

+ + +

The list of encrypted files from Amanda's hard drive evidenced extensive correspondence between her and Nicolae Carpathia. Much as Rayford dreaded it, his desire grew to decode those files. Tsion had told him of Donny's program that unveiled material from Bruce's files. If Rayford could get to Israel when the rest of the Tribulation Force was there, he might finally get to the bottom of the ugly mystery.

Wouldn't his own daughter and son-in-law put his mind at ease? Every day he felt worse, convinced that regardless of the truth or anything he could say to dissuade them, his own loved ones had been swayed. He had not come right out and asked their opinions. He didn't have to. If they were still standing with him—and with the memory of his wife—he would know.

Rayford believed the only way to exonerate Amanda was to decode her files, but he also knew the risk. He would have to face whatever they revealed. Did he want the truth, regardless? The more he prayed about that, the more convinced he became that he must not fear the truth.

What he learned would affect how he functioned for the rest of the Tribulation. If the woman who had shared his life had fooled him, whom could he trust? If he was that bad a judge of character, what good was he to the cause? Maddening doubts filled him, but he became obsessed with knowing. Either way, lover or liar, wife or witch, he had to know.

The morning before the start of the most talked-about mass meeting in the world, Rayford approached Carpathia in his office.

"Your Excellency," he began, swallowing any vestige of pride, "I'm assuming you'll need Mac and me to get you to Israel tomorrow."

"Talk to me about this, Captain Steele. They are meeting against my wishes, so I had planned not to sanction it with my presence."

"But your promise of protection—"

"Ah, that resonated with you, did it not?"

"You know well where I stand."

"And you also know that I tell you where to fly, not vice versa. Do you not think that if I wanted to be in Israel tomorrow I would have told you before this?"

"So, those who wonder if you are afraid of the scholar who—"

"Afraid!"

"—showed you up on the Internet and called your bluff before an international audience—"

"You are trying to bait me, Captain Steele," Carpathia said, smiling.

"Frankly, I believe you know you will be upstaged in Israel by the two witnesses and by Dr. Ben-Judah."

"The two witnesses? If they do not stop their black magic, the drought, and the blood, they will answer to me."

"They say you can't harm them until the due time."

"I will decide the due time."

"And yet Israel was protected from the earthquake and the meteors—"

"You believe the witnesses are responsible for that?"

"I believe God is."

"Tell me, Captain Steele. Do you still believe that a man who has been known to raise the dead could actually be the Antichrist?"

Rayford hesitated, wishing Tsion was in the room. "The enemy has been known to imitate miracles," he said. "Imagine the audience in Israel if you were to do something like that. Here are people of faith coming together for inspiration. If you are God, if you could be the Messiah, wouldn't they be thrilled to meet you?"

Carpathia stared at Rayford, seeming to study his eyes. Rayford believed God. He had faith that regardless of his power, regardless of his intentions, Nicolae would be impotent in the face of any of the 144,000 witnesses who carried the seal of almighty God on their foreheads.

"If you are suggesting," Carpathia said carefully, "that it only makes sense that the Global Community Potentate bestow upon those guests a regal welcome second to none, you may have a point."

Rayford had said nothing of the sort, but Carpathia heard what he wanted to hear. "Thank you," Rayford said.

"Captain Steele, schedule that flight."

APOLLYON

To Norman B. Rohrer,
friend and mentor

1

RAYFORD STEELE worried about Mac McCullum's silence in the cockpit of *Global Community One* during the short flight from New Babylon to Tel Aviv. "Do we need to talk later?" Rayford said quietly. Mac put a finger to his lips and nodded.

Rayford finished communicating with New Babylon ground and air traffic control, then reached beneath his seat for the hidden reverse intercom button. It would allow him to listen in on conversations in the Condor 216's cabin between Global Community Potentate Nicolae Carpathia, Supreme Commander Leon Fortunato, and Pontifex Maximus Peter Mathews, head of Enigma Babylon One World Faith. But just before Rayford depressed the button, he felt Mac's hand on his arm. Mac shook his head.

Rayford shuddered. "They know?" he mouthed.

Mac whispered, "Don't risk it until we talk."

Rayford received the treatment he had come to expect on initial descent into Tel Aviv. The tower at Ben Gurion cleared other planes from the area, even those that had begun landing sequences. Rayford heard anger in the voices of other pilots as they were directed into holding patterns miles from the Condor. Per protocol, no other aircraft were to be in proximity to the Condor, despite the extraordinary air traffic expected in Israel for the Meeting of the Witnesses.

"Take the landing, Mac," Rayford said. Mac gave a puzzled glance but complied. Rayford was impressed at how the Holy Land had been spared damage from the wrath of the Lamb earthquake. Other calamities had befallen the land and the people, but to Rayford, Israel was the one place that looked normal from the air since the earthquake and the subsequent judgments.

Ben Gurion Airport was alive with traffic. The big planes had to land there, while smaller craft could put down near Jerusalem. Worried about Mac's misgivings, still Rayford couldn't suppress a smile. Carpathia had been forced not only to allow this meeting of believers, but also to pledge his personal protection of them. Of course, he was the opposite of a man of his word, but having gone public with his assurances, he was stuck. He would have to protect even Rabbi Tsion Ben-Judah, spiritual head of the Tribulation Force.

Not long before, Dr. Ben-Judah had been forced to flee his homeland under cover of night, a universal bounty on his head. Now he was back as Carpathia's avowed enemy, leader of the 144,000 witnesses and their converts. Carpathia had used the results of the most recent Trumpet Judgments to twice postpone the Israel conference, but there was no stopping it again.

Just before touchdown, when everyone aboard should have been tightly strapped in, Rayford was surprised by a knock at the cockpit door. "Leon," he said, turning. "We're about to land."

"Protocol, Captain!" Fortunato barked.

"What do you want?"

"Besides that you refer to me as Supreme Commander, His Excellency asks that you remain in the cockpit after landing for orders."

"We're not going to Jerusalem?" Rayford said. Mac stared straight ahead.

"Precisely," Fortunato said. "Much as we all know you want to be there."

Rayford had been certain Carpathia's people would try to follow him to the rest of the Tribulation Force.

Fortunato left and shut the door, and Rayford said, "I'll take it, Mac."

Mac shifted control of the craft, and Rayford immediately exaggerated the angle of descent while depressing the reverse intercom button. He heard Carpathia and Mathews asking after Fortunato, who had clearly taken a tumble. Once the plane was parked, Fortunato burst into the cockpit.

"What was that, Officer McCullum?"

"My apologies, Commander," Mac said. "It was out of my hands. All due respect, sir, but you should not have been out of your seat during landing."

"Listen up, gentlemen," Fortunato said, kneeling between them. "His Excellency asks that you remain in Tel Aviv, as we are not certain when he might need to return to New Babylon. We have rented you rooms near the airport. GC personnel will transport you."

+ + +

Buck Williams sat in the bowels of Teddy Kollek Stadium in Jerusalem with his pregnant wife, Chloe. He knew she was in no way healed enough from injuries she had suffered in the great earthquake to have justified the flight from the States, but she would not be dissuaded. Now she appeared weary. Her bruises and scars were fading, but Chloe still had a severe limp, and her beauty had been turned into a strange cuteness by the unique reshaping of her cheekbone and eye socket.

"You need to help the others, Buck," she said. "Now go on. I'll be fine."

"I wish you'd go back to the compound," he said.

"I'm fine," she insisted. "I just need to sit awhile. I'm worried about Hattie. I said I wouldn't leave her unless she improved or became a believer, and she has done neither." Pregnant, Hattie Durham had been left home fighting for her life against poison in her system. Dr. Floyd Charles attended her while the rest of the Tribulation Force—including new member Ken Ritz, another pilot—had made the pilgrimage to Israel.

"Floyd will take good care of her."

"I know. Now leave me alone awhile."

\+ + +

Rayford and Mac were instructed to wait on the plane as Carpathia, Fortunato, and Mathews were received with enthusiasm on the tarmac. Fortunato stood dutifully in the background as Mathews declined to make a public statement but introduced Carpathia.

"I cannot tell you what a pleasure it is to be back in Israel," Carpathia said with a broad smile. "I am eager to welcome the devotees of Dr. Ben-Judah and to display the openness of the Global Community to diverse opinion and belief. I am pleased to reaffirm my guarantee of safety to the rabbi and the thousands of visitors from all over the world. I will withhold further comment, assuming I will be welcome to address the honored assemblage within the next few days."

The dignitaries were ushered to a helicopter for the hop to Jerusalem, while their respective entourages boarded an opulent motor coach.

When Rayford and Mac finished postflight checks and finally disembarked, a Global Community Jeep delivered them to their hotel. Mac signaled Rayford not to say anything in the car or either of their rooms. In the coffee shop, Rayford finally demanded to know what was going on.

\+ + +

Buck wished Chloe had been able to sleep on the flight from the States. Ken Ritz had procured a Gulfstream jet, so it was the most comfortable international flight Buck had ever enjoyed. But the four of them—Ken, Buck, Chloe, and Tsion—had been too excited to rest. Tsion spent half the time on his laptop, which Ken transmitted to a satellite, keeping the rabbi in touch with his worldwide flock of millions.

A vast network of house churches had sprung up—seemingly spontaneously—with converted Jews, clearly part of the 144,000 witnesses, taking leadership positions. They taught their charges daily based on the cyberspace sermons and lessons from the prolific Ben-Judah. Tens of thousands of such clandestine local house churches, their very existence flying in the face of the all-inclusive Enigma Babylon One World Faith, saw courageous converts added to the church every day.

Tsion had been urging the local congregations to send their leaders to the great Meeting of the Witnesses, despite warnings from the Global Community. Nicolae Carpathia had again tried to cancel the gathering at the last minute, citing thousands of deaths from contaminated water in over a third of the world. Thrilling the faithful by calling Carpathia's bluff, Tsion responded publicly on the Internet.

"Mr. Carpathia," he had written, "we will be in Jerusalem as scheduled, with or without your approval, permission, or promised protection. The glory of the Lord will be our rear guard."

Buck would need the protection almost as much as Tsion. By choosing to show up and appear in public with Ben-Judah, Buck was sacrificing his position as Carpathia's publishing chief and his exorbitant salary. Showing his face in proximity to the rabbi's would confirm Carpathia's contention that Buck had become an active enemy of the Global Community.

Rabbi Ben-Judah himself had come up with the strategy of simply trusting God. "Stand right beside me when we get off the plane," he said. "No disguises, no misdirection, no hiding. If God can protect me, he can protect you. Let us stop playing Carpathia's games."

Buck had long been anonymously broadcasting his own cyberspace magazine, *The Truth,* which would now be his sole writing outlet. Ironically, it attracted ten times the largest reading audience he had ever enjoyed. He worried for his safety, of course, but more for Chloe's.

Tsion seemed supernaturally protected. But after this conference, the entire Tribulation Force, not to mention the 144,000 witnesses and their millions of converts, would become open archenemies of the Antichrist. Their lives would consist of half ministry, half survival. For all they had been through, it was as if the seven-year tribulation had just begun. They still had nearly five years until the glorious appearing of Christ to set up his thousand-year reign on earth.

What Tsion's Internet missives and Buck's underground electronic magazine had wrought in Israel was stunning. The whole of Israel crawled with tens of thousands of converted Jewish witnesses from the twelve tribes all over the world.

Rather than asking Ken Ritz to find an out-of-the-way airstrip where the Tribulation Force could slip into the country unnoticed, Tsion informed his audience—and also, of course, Carpathia & Co.—of their itinerary.

Ken had landed at the tiny Jerusalem Airport north of the city, and well-wishers immediately besieged the plane. A small cadre of Global Community armed guards, apparently Carpathia's idea of protection for Tsion, would have had to open fire to get near him. The international witnesses cheered and sang and reached out to touch Tsion as the Tribulation Force made its way to a van. The Israeli driver carefully picked his way through the crowd and south down the main drag toward the Holy City and the King David Hotel.

There they had discovered that Supreme Commander Leon Fortunato had summarily bounced their reservations and several others' by supremely commandeering the top floor for Nicolae Carpathia and his people. "I assume you have made provisions for our alternative," Tsion told the desk clerk after half an hour in line.

"I apologize," the young man said, slipping Tsion an envelope. The rabbi glanced at Buck and pulled him away from the crowd, where they opened the note. Buck looked back at Ken, who nodded to assure him he had the fragile Chloe in tow.

The note was in Hebrew. "It is from Chaim," Tsion said. "He writes, 'Forgive my trusted friend Nicolae for this shameful insensitivity. I have room for you and your colleagues and insist you stay with me. Page Jacov, and you will be taken care of.'"

Jacov was Chaim Rosenzweig's driver and valet. He loaded their stuff into a Mercedes van and soon had the Tribulation Force installed in guest rooms at Chaim's walled and gated estate within walking distance of the Old City. Buck tried to get Chloe to stay and rest while he and Ken and Tsion went to the stadium.

"I didn't come here to be on the sidelines," she said. "I know you're concerned about me, but let me decide what I'm up to."

At Kollek Stadium, Buck had been as stunned as the others at what had been arranged. Tsion was right. It had to have been God who used the rabbi's cyber pleas to pull together Israeli witnesses to handle the logistics of this most unlikely conference.

In spite of and in the midst of global chaos, ad hoc committees had arranged transportation, lodging, food, sound, interpretation, and programming. Buck could tell that Tsion was nearly overcome with the streamlined efficiency and no-frills program. "All you need worry about, Dr. Ben-Judah," he had been told, "is being prepared to inspire and inform us when you are due at the microphone."

Tsion smiled sadly. "That and praying that we all remain under the care of our heavenly Father."

* * *

"They're onto you, Rayford," Mac said over pita bread and sauce.

Rayford shook his head. "I haven't been a mystery to Carpathia for months. What are you talking about?"

"You've been assigned to me."

"I'm listening."

"I don't rate direct contact with the big man anymore. But last night I was called to a meeting with Leon. The good news is they're not onto me."

"That *is* good. But they know about the device on the plane?"

"He didn't say, but he couldn't have been clearer that you're history. If the device still works—"

"It does."

"—then I'll use it and keep you posted."

"Where will I be?"

"Anywhere but here, Ray. I'm convinced the driver was listening, the car may have been bugged, the cockpit, no question about our rooms."

"They hope I'll lead them to the others, but they'll be in plain sight in Jerusalem."

"They want to *keep* you from the others, Ray. Why do you think we've been assigned to Tel Aviv?"

"And if I leave?"

"I'm to let them know immediately. It'll be the end of you, Ray."

"But I've got to see my family, the rest of the Force."

"Not here. Carpathia's pledge is to protect Tsion and the others. Not you."

"They really think I won't go to Jerusalem?"

"They hope you will. You must not."

Rayford sat back and pursed his lips. He would not miss the job, close as it had brought him to what was going on in the camp of the enemy. He had long wondered how the end would come to this bizarre season of his life. "You're taking over?"

Mac nodded. "So they tell me. There's more good news. They like and trust David."

"Hassid? Good!"

"He's been put in charge of purchasing. Beyond all the computer stuff he's been doing, he contracts for all major purchases. Even in avionics."

Rayford squinted. Mac pulled a yellow sheet from his jacket and slid it across the table. "Don't tell me he's bought me a plane," Rayford said.

Mac snorted. "Should have thought of that. You know those little handheld electronic organizers? David ordered a half dozen specially built. He doesn't even know yet that he won't be seeing you around anymore."

"I can't steal these, not even from Carpathia."

"You don't have to steal them, Ray. These are just the specs and where to get 'em. They're not cheap, but wait till you see what these babies can do. No more laptops for you guys. Well, maybe the rabbi still needs a keyboard, but these things are solar powered, satellite connected, and contain geographic positioning chips. You can access the Internet, send and receive, use them as phones, you name it."

Rayford shook his head. "I suppose he thought of tracer blocks."

"Of course."

Rayford stuffed the sheet into a pocket. "What am I going to do, Mac?"

"You're going to get your tail out of this hemisphere, what else?"

"But I have to know about Amanda. Buck will tell me only face-to-face, and he's in Jerusalem."

Mac looked down. "You know how that's going to go, Ray. I'd be the last one to try to tell a man about his own wife, but you know as well as I do that everything points to what you don't want to hear."

"I haven't accepted it yet, but I have to know."

"Buck found out for sure?"

"Sounds like it."

"How can *he* be sure?"

"I told you about Hattie."

"Uh-huh."

"She knows."

"So ask her yourself, Ray. Go home."

"Like I wouldn't be noticed trying to slip out of here tomorrow morning."

"The GC can't keep track of everything. Use your people's pilot—Ritz, is it? What's he got to do the next few days?"

Rayford looked at Mac with admiration. "You're not as dumb as you look, old-timer."

Mac pulled a phone from his pocket. "Know his number?"

"Your phone scrambled? If I get detected talking to Ken Ritz on either of our phones—"

"You *are* dumber than *you* look if you think I'd risk that. I know the purchasing guy, remember?" Mac showed Rayford the phone, a generic model that had been doctored by David Hassid.

Rayford dialed Chloe's phone. "Daddy!" she exulted. "Are you here?"

\+ \+ \+

Buck considered it a privilege to pray with the Israeli committee before he and Ken and Tsion headed back to find Chloe. He threw his arm around Tsion. "Are you as tired as I am?"

"Exhausted. I only hope the Lord will allow me to sleep tonight. I am ready to share his message with these dear members of the family, and all that is left before that is to talk with Eli and Moishe. You will go with me, will you not?"

"I wouldn't miss it."

"Me either," Ken said.

But the news from Chloe changed Ken's plans. "Daddy called," she whispered. "He needs a ride home tomorrow."

After she explained Rayford's situation, Ken decided to get the Gulfstream out of the Jerusalem Airport and into Ben Gurion that night. Buck was nearly despondent, wanting to talk to Rayford personally. "At least he can hear the truth about Amanda from the horse's mouth," he said.

An hour later Jacov drove as they delivered Ken to the airport. "We will see you back here Friday," Tsion said, embracing him.

Chloe fell asleep on Buck's shoulder during the after-dark ride to the Temple Mount. As they left the car, the spectacular new temple gleamed on the horizon. "I do not even want to see the new structure," Tsion said. "It is an abomination."

"I can't wait to meet the witnesses," Chloe said.

"You may not actually meet them," Tsion cautioned. "These are heavenly beings with their own agenda. They may communicate with us; they may not. We approach them with great caution."

Buck felt the usual tingle to the soles of his feet. "You know the stories, hon."

Chloe nodded. "I'm not saying I'm not scared."

The three slowed as they approached the typical crowd that gathered thirty feet from the wrought-iron fence, behind which the witnesses stood, sat, or spoke. Usually they spoke. No one had seen them sleep, and none dared get closer. Threats on the lives of the two witnesses had ended in the ugly deaths of would-be assassins.

Buck's excitement masked his fatigue. He worried about Chloe but would not deny her this privilege. At the edge of the crowd of about forty, Buck was able to see past the fence to where Eli sat, Indian style, his back to the stone wall of a small building beyond the fence. His long hair and beard wafted softly in the breeze, but he was unmoving, unblinking, his leathery skin and burlap-like garb appearing to meld.

Moishe stood two feet from the fence, silent, unmoving, staring at the crowd. Occasionally someone shouted. "Speak! Say something!" But that made others back away, obviously fearing the violent reactions they had heard of. Moishe's feet were spread, his arms loose at his sides. Earlier in the day Buck had monitored on his computer a long monologue from Moishe. Sometimes the two traded off speaking, but this day must have been all Moishe's responsibility.

"Watch them carefully," Buck whispered to Chloe. "Sometimes they communicate without opening their mouths. I love how everyone understands them in his own language."

Commotion near the front caused several people to back away, opening a gap in the crowd. Someone said, "Carpathia! It's the potentate!"

Tsion held up a hand. "Let us stay right here," he whispered.

Buck was riveted as Leon Fortunato smoothly supervised GC guards who kept gawkers from Carpathia. The potentate appeared bemused, boldly moving to within ten feet of the fence. "Hail, Potentate!" someone shouted. Carpathia half turned, holding a finger to his lips, and Fortunato nodded to a guard, who stepped toward the crowd. They backed away farther.

"Stay here," Buck said, slipping away.

"Honey, wait!" Chloe called, but Buck moved around behind the crowd and into the shadows.

He knew he would appear to the guards as simply someone leaving. But when he was far enough away to be ignored, he doubled back through shrubbery to where he could see Carpathia's face as he stared at Moishe.

Carpathia appeared startled when Moishe suddenly spoke in a loud voice. "Woe unto the enemy of the Most High God!"

Nicolae seemed to quickly collect himself. He smiled and spoke softly. "I am hardly the enemy of God," he said. "Many say I *am* the Most High God."

Moishe moved for the first time, crossing his arms over his chest. Carpathia, his chin in his hand, cocked his head and studied Moishe. The ancient witness spoke softly, and Buck knew only he and Carpathia could hear him.

"A sword shall pierce your head," Moishe said in a haunting monotone. "And you shall surely die."

Buck shivered, but it was clear that Carpathia was unmoved. "Let me tell you and your companion something," he said through clenched teeth. "You have persecuted Israel long enough with the drought and the water turned to blood. You will lift your hocus-pocus or live to regret it."

Eli rose and traded places with Moishe, beckoning Carpathia closer. The potentate hesitated and looked back to his guards, who tentatively raised their weapons. Eli spoke with such volume that the crowd dispersed and ran, and even Tsion and Chloe recoiled.

"Until the due time, you have no authority over the lampstands of God Almighty!"

The guards lowered their weapons, and Fortunato seemed to hide behind them. Carpathia's smirk remained, but Buck was convinced he was seething. "We shall see," he said, "who will win in the end."

Eli seemed to look through Carpathia. "Who will win in the end was determined before the beginning of time. Lo, the poison you inflict on the earth shall rot you from within for eternity."

Carpathia stepped back, still grinning. "I warn you to stay away from the charade of the so-called saints. I have guaranteed their safety, not yours."

Eli and Moishe spoke in unison. "He and she who have ears, let them hear. We are bound neither by time nor space, and those who shall benefit by our presence and testimony stand within the sound of our proclamation."

Buck thrilled at the message and looked beyond the square to where Tsion stood with Chloe. The rabbi thrust his fists in the air as if he had gotten the message, and he walked Chloe back toward the car. Buck ducked out of the shrubs and headed around the other way, arriving in the parking lot seconds later.

"Did you hear that?" Tsion said.

Buck nodded. "Incredible!"

"I didn't get it," Chloe said. "What were they saying?"

"Did it sound like Hebrew to you?" Tsion said. "They spoke in Hebrew."

"I heard it in English," she said.

"Me too," Buck said. "They said that he *or she* who had ears to hear—"

"I heard," Chloe said. "I just don't understand."

"That is the first time I ever heard them add 'or she,'" Tsion said. "That was for you, Chloe. They knew we were here. We did not have to approach them, did not have to identify ourselves, did not have to face Carpathia before we were ready. We did not even have to discuss with Eli and Moishe plans for their appearance at the stadium. They said that those who would benefit by their presence and testimony stood within the sound of their proclamation."

"They're coming?" Chloe said.

"That is what I gather," Tsion said.

"When?"

"At just the right time."

2

RAYFORD HAD a lot in common with Ken Ritz and found him fascinating. Distraught over his own future—and income—and fearful of what he might learn about his late wife, Rayford nonetheless enjoyed Ken's company. More than ten years his senior, Ken was former military, gruff, to the point, and aglow in what Tsion Ben-Judah called his "first love" of Christ.

Rayford and Ken spent hours in the air on the way home bringing each other up to date on their pasts, and Rayford silently thanked God for a new friend. His relationship with Tsion was as student to mentor. To Buck he was the father-in-law. How he missed Bruce Barnes, his first friend and spiritual guide after the Rapture! Ken seemed a gift from God.

Ritz assured Rayford he could learn the Gulfstream in no time. "You guys who drive the heavies can handle these skiffs like a bike racer goin' back to a trike."

"I wish it were that easy," Rayford said, "but I'll count on you for driver's training."

"Roger. And, man, with your replacement there for Carpathia—what's his name again?"

"Mac. Mac McCullum."

"Yeah. He gives us three pilots in the Trib Force. Now we gotta talk Sawbones into gettin' out of that GC hospital before they catch onto him. That'll give us a doctor. So, three pilots, a doc, and a rabbi—sounds like the start of a joke. The only member without a specialty is your daughter, and she's what I call the voice of reason. Nobody's more reasonable than Tsion, of course, but Chloe's the voice of reason for guys like me who don't understand everything the scholar says."

Rayford told Ritz about David Hassid. "I have no idea how long he'll be safe, but he gives us another pair of eyes and ears inside. Someday both he and Mac will have to run. Then look at the lineup we'll have."

"Hot dog!" Ritz said, clapping. "I don't like bein' on the defensive, man! Let's take on that rascal!"

Rayford had never heard Nicolae referred to as a rascal, but he liked Ritz's attitude. Weary and wary after so long in Carpathia's orbit, he too longed to quit playing and get to war.

Ritz seemed to grow uncomfortable when Rayford told him about Amanda. "I'm sorry for your loss," he said, when Rayford's story came full circle to the plane crash into the Tigris that had killed her.

"So you've heard the rest, too?" Rayford asked, having left out the charges of her duplicity.

"Yes, sir. I didn't come to any conclusions, but I can imagine how it all makes you feel."

"But you didn't hear from Buck what he found out from Hattie?"

"I didn't even know she was talking. Tell you the truth, I'll be surprised if she's still kickin' when we get back."

"That wasn't what I wanted to hear."

\+ + +

Buck hoped staying up late would make sleep come easily in the new time zone. But his brain was on Chicago time, and he lay staring at the ceiling. Chloe slept soundly beside him, and for that he was grateful.

By dawn in Israel, when he felt Chloe stir, Buck was so exhausted he could neither move nor open his eyes. He felt the brush of her lips on his cheek but couldn't even emit a groan.

"Stay still, big guy," she whispered. "Huge day ahead."

She got up, and Buck soon smelled breakfast, but he fell asleep and didn't rouse until early afternoon.

\+ + +

Rayford was impressed with Ken Ritz's facility on the radio and on the ground at Palwaukee Airport at dawn in the Chicago suburbs. "You push this thing around like you own it," he said.

"It'd be a good staff plane for the Trib Force, don't you think?"

Buck's Range Rover sat gleaming behind a damaged hangar. As they approached, a young man angled toward them. "Rover cleans up pretty good, doesn't she?" he said, a shock of red hair in his face.

"Yeah," Ritz said. "You been playin' under the hood too?"

"Lucky for you. Timing was all screwed up."

"I told you that, Ernie."

"You also told me you wouldn't be back for another week. I only got into that engine 'cause I was bored."

Ritz introduced Ernie to Rayford, who remained guarded until Ritz pulled the young man close and said, "Notice anything?"

Ernie stepped toward Rayford and peered at his forehead. Ernie smiled and held his hair away from his face with both hands. Rayford embraced him. "Brother."

"There's more of us around here, including the boss man," Ritz said, "but not too many, so we're careful. Ernie here's a Ben-Judah groupie."

"You got that right," Ernie said. "I can't wait for the big meeting. It's gonna be on the Net at noon tomorrow."

"We'll be watching," Rayford said, eager to get going. Half an hour later, he and Ken pulled behind the safe house in Mount Prospect in the amazingly smooth-running Rover. "We've got to stay close to Ernie," he said. "This vehicle needs to be as travel worthy as whatever plane we wind up with."

"Did you see the front curtain move when we came by, Ray? Until he saw it was us, Floyd was probably wondering how he was gonna get Hattie underground."

"You get a lot of snoops?"

"Hardly any. The block is deserted; the roads, as you saw, nearly impassable. So far, this has been a perfect spot. You wanna see Donny's wife's grave?"

Rayford had heard how Buck and Tsion had found the place. He nodded as Dr. Floyd Charles came out, the obvious question on his face. "We tried to call you," Ritz said.

"I've been on the phone to my guy at the hospital."

"This here's Rayford Steele. I was about to show him the grave."

"Of the woman neither of us ever met, but I suppose you did, Captain."

Rayford shook his head. "Knew who she was is all. Hey, we're brothers, Doctor. Call me Ray."

"Thanks. Call me anything you want except Floyd."

"How's Hattie?"

"Not well. Sleeping."

"She going to make it?"

Dr. Charles shook his head. "I'm not optimistic. The backup at CDC in Atlanta is ridiculous. She and I both have a hunch that what's in her system was put there by the GC. If they ever get to the sample I sent, they'll disavow it or steer me wrong."

They walked back to the primitive grave and stood in silence. "Wish we could put up some kind of marker," Rayford said, "but it would be only for us anyway, and we know who she was and where she is. We don't need to draw attention to this place."

Rayford felt deep gratitude that the Tribulation Force was headquartered in what was once this woman's home. He couldn't help cataloguing in his mind the deaths in his own circle. The list grew long and ultimately led to Amanda. He had grieved so much already, and he feared he would suffer many more losses before his own number came up.

Floyd Charles gave Rayford a quick tour of the place while they brought each other up to date on their respective situations. Rayford was impressed with the house, especially the underground shelter Donny had fashioned before his own demise. The day would surely come when they would all have to live under, rather than in, the house. How soon he could not guess. Nothing was predictable anymore, save for the judgments from heaven meticulously outlined on Tsion's scriptural charts. Who would survive and for how long was all in God's control and timing.

Rayford had heard death-rattle breathing before, but the emaciated frame of his former coworker, friend, and object of flirtation strangely moved him. Rayford stood over Hattie, pitying her, hoping for her, praying for her. He wanted to know what she knew about Amanda, of course, but he was not so selfish as to wish she would stay alive only long enough to communicate that. He gently pushed her bangs off her forehead. In the dim light he couldn't tell whether a mark was there. Dr. Charles shook his head. "She's been talking a lot lately, but she hasn't come to any decision yet. At least she hasn't decided the way we'd like."

"Chloe thought she was close," Rayford said. "Lord knows she has enough information. I don't know what it'll take."

"I plead with her all the time," the doctor said. "She's stubborn. Waiting for something. I don't know. I'm at a loss."

"Pray she survives another day," Rayford said. "And wake me if she comes to."

"You want something to help you sleep?"

Rayford raised his eyebrows. "I didn't figure you for a pill pusher."

"I'm careful. Don't use 'em myself, but I'm sympathetic to globe-trotters like you."

"I've never had trouble sleeping."

"Good for you."

Rayford turned to head upstairs and stopped. "How about you, Doc? Having trouble sleeping?"

"I told you, I don't use sleeping pills."

"That's not what I asked."

Dr. Charles looked down and shook his head. "How'd you guess?"

"You look wasted, sorry to say."

Floyd nodded without expression.

"You want to talk?" Rayford said.

"You're tired."

"Hey, Doc, the way I understand it, when you leave the hospital, you're going to join us. We're like family. I make time for family."

"It's just that I didn't expect to tell anybody about this until everyone got back."

Rayford pulled out a kitchen chair. "About what?"

"I'm in your boat, Rayford."

"Free of the GC, you mean? You've been fired?"

"I've got a believer friend at the hospital. I was on the phone to him in the middle of the night, apparently when Ken was trying to reach me. He told me he didn't know where I was and didn't want to know, but he said, friend to friend, disappear."

Rayford reached to shake his hand. "Welcome to the club. You think anybody followed you here?"

"No. I made sure of that. But I've been gone from the hospital so much and was apparently suspicious enough."

"If they don't know where you are, you're safe and so are we."

Dr. Charles leaned back against the refrigerator. "Thing is, I don't want to be a burden. The GC paid well, and I never compromised my principles. I worked hard to save lives and get people well."

"In other words, you're allowed to have less of a conscience problem than I about making a living working for the enemy?"

"I wasn't implying anything."

"I know. You're worried about joining us without being able to carry your weight."

"Exactly."

"Look at me, Doc. I'm one of the charter members, and here I am without income."

"I wish that made me feel better."

"I think we can provide room and board in exchange for medical services. That puts you way ahead of me. I'm just an extra pilot now, and I've got no plane." Rayford saw the hint of a smile. But then Floyd's knees buckled. "You all right?"

"Just tired."

"When did you sleep last?"

"It's been awhile, but don't worry about—"

"How long since you've slept?"

"Too long, but I'm all right."

"Ken?" Rayford called. Ritz came up from the basement. "You feel up to sitting with Hattie awhile?"

"I'm good. I got so much caffeine in me I'll be up all day anyway."

The doctor looked deeply thankful. "I'm going to take you gentlemen up on this. Thank you." He gave Ken a few instructions, then trudged upstairs.

Ken sat next to Hattie's bed with his Bible on one knee and a laptop on the other. Rayford was amused at Ken's peeking over the top of his half-glasses to be sure Hattie was all right. He was one long-legged babysitter.

A few minutes later, as Rayford stretched out on the bed upstairs, he could hear Floyd snoring already in the next room.

+ + +

Twenty-four hours before the opening evening session of the Meeting of the Witnesses, Buck, Chloe, and Tsion joined the local committee at the stadium for a final walk-through of the program. They returned to the van to find a message from Chaim via Jacov. The driver read from a scrap of paper: "Dr. Rosenzweig was summoned to the quarters of the potentate and has come back with a personal request from the Supreme Commander."

"I can't wait," Buck said.

"I beg your pardon, sir?"

"Just an expression. Can you tell us what the req—"

"Oh, no sir. I was merely asked to get you back to Dr. Rosenzweig as quickly as possible."

Buck leaned closer to Tsion. "What do you make of it? What would Fortunato want?"

"I should expect Carpathia would like to meet me. Probably for public relations or political reasons."

"Why wouldn't Carpathia have talked to Rosenzweig himself?"

"Protocol. You know that, Cameron."

"But they're old friends," Chloe said. "They go way back. Didn't Dr. Rosenzweig introduce you to Carpathia in the first place, Buck?"

Buck nodded. "No doubt Nicolae enjoys keeping him in his place."

They arrived back at Chaim's complex to find him bubbling with enthusiasm. "I am not a fool, Tsion," the old man said. "I am aware that you have pitted yourself against my friend and argued with him publicly via the Internet. But I am telling you, you have him wrong. He is a wonderful man, a godly man, if I may say. The fact that he is humbly asking for a place on the program shows his goodwill and—"

"A place on the program!" Chloe said. "Impossible! The stadium will be full of Jewish converts who are convinced Nicolae is Antichrist himself."

"Oh, sweetheart," Chaim said, smiling at her. "Nicolae Carpathia? He seeks world peace, disarmament, global unity."

"My point exactly."

Chaim turned to his protégé. "Tsion, surely you can see that the only expedient thing to do is to cordially welcome him to the stage."

"You spoke with Carpathia yourself, Chaim?"

The older man cocked his head and shrugged. "Of course not. He is a very busy man. Supreme Commander Fortunato is his most trusted—"

"Too busy for you?" Tsion said. "You are a national hero, an icon, the man who helped make Israel what she is today! Your formula was the key to Carpathia's power. How can he forget that and refuse to see an old friend like—"

"He did not refuse me, Tsion! If I had merely asked, he would have granted me an audience."

"Regardless," Tsion said, "Chloe is right. Much as I would love to humiliate him, it would be just too awkward. What kind of reception do you think he will get from the twenty-five thousand witnesses we will cram into the stadium and nearly a hundred thousand more at other sites around the city?"

"Surely, out of Christian charity, they would be cordial to the world ruler."

Tsion shook his head and leaned forward, resting his hand on his former mentor's knee. "Dr. Rosenzweig, you have been like a father to me. I love you. I would welcome you to the stadium with open arms. But Nic—"

"I am not a believer, Tsion. So why not welcome another with the same openness?"

"Because he is more than simply not a believer. He is the enemy of God, of everything we stand for. Though you are not yet a believer, we do not consider you an en—"

"Not *yet* a believer!" Chaim rocked back and laughed. "You say that with such confidence."

"I pray for you every day."

"And I appreciate that more than I can say, my friend. But I am Jewish born and bred. Though I am not religious, I do believe Messiah is yet to come. Do not hold out hope that I shall become one of your witnesses. I—"

"Chaim, Chaim! Did you not hear my evidence the night I shared it with the world?"

"Yes! It was fascinating, and no one can argue it was not persuasive. Look at what has come of it. But surely you do not claim it is for everyone!"

Buck could feel Tsion's incredulity. "Dr. Rosenzweig," the rabbi said, "I would be so grateful if you would allow me to plead my case to you. If I could personally show you my texts, my arguments, I believe I could prove to you that Jesus Christ is the Messiah and that Nicolae Carpathia is his archenemy. I would love to just—"

"I will give you that privilege one day, my friend," Rosenzweig said. "But not the night before one of the biggest days of your life. And I must tell you, I would sooner believe Jesus was the Messiah than that Nicolae is his enemy. That is simply not the man I know."

"I have the energy and the enthusiasm tonight, Doctor. Please."

"Well," Chaim said, smiling, "I do not. I will make a deal with you, however. You grant Nicolae a place on the program during your opening night, and I will give you my full attention on these matters at a later date."

Rosenzweig sat back, appearing pleased with his suggestion. Tsion, clearly frustrated, looked at Buck, then at Chloe. He shrugged. "I do not know," he said. "I just do not know. Frankly, Doctor, I could wish that a dear, old friend like you would listen to the heart of an admirer without condition."

Rosenzweig stood and stepped to the window, where he peered through a sliver between the curtains. "Nicolae has provided the armed guards that ensure you will not suffer the way your family did and that you will not again be chased from your homeland. All I ask is that you treat the most powerful man in the world with the deference he deserves. If you choose not to, I will be disappointed. But I will not make this a condition of eventually letting you try to persuade me of your position."

Tsion stood and thrust his hands deep into his pockets. He turned his back to Buck and the others. "Well, thank you for that," he said, barely above a whisper. "I shall have to pray about what to do about Carpathia's request."

Buck couldn't imagine how Carpathia could show his face at such a meeting or what response he might get from the assembled. Why would Carpathia subject himself to it?

"Tsion," Chaim said, "I must get back to the potentate with a response tonight. I said I would."

"Chaim, I will not have an answer until I have prayed about it. If Mr. Fortunato insists—"

"It is not his insistence, Tsion. I gave my word."

"I do not have an answer."

"All I can tell him is that you are praying about it?"

"Exactly."

"Tsion, who do you think secured Kollek Stadium for you?"

"I do not know."

"Nicolae! Do you think my countrymen would have offered it? You have aligned yourself with the two at the Wailing Wall who have cursed our country, *your* country! They have boasted of causing the drought that has crippled us. They turn water into blood, bring plagues upon us. It is rumored they will appear at the stadium themselves!"

"I can only hope," Tsion said.

The men turned to face each other, both with hands spread. "My dear Tsion," Chaim said, "you see what we have come to? If Nicolae is bold enough to address a stadium full of his enemies, he must be admired."

"I will pray," Tsion said. "That is all I can say."

As they went off to bed, Buck heard Chaim on the phone with Fortunato. "Leon, I am sorry. . . ."

+ + +

Late in the afternoon in Illinois, Rayford was awakened by footsteps on the stairs. The door opened. "You awake, Ray?" Rayford sat up, staring, squinting against the light. "Should I get the doc? Hattie's wakin' up."

"Does she need anything?"

"I don't think so."

"Then let him sleep. She seems OK?"

"She's trying to talk."

"Tell her I'm coming down."

Rayford staggered to the bathroom and splashed cold water on his face. His heart raced. He hurried stiff-legged down the stairs to find Ken gently giving Hattie a drink of water.

"Captain Steele!" she rasped, eyes wide. She beckoned him close. "Could you excuse us?" she asked Ken. As he stepped away she reached for Rayford. "Nicolae wants me dead. He poisoned me. He can reach anywhere."

"How do you know, Hattie? How do you know he poisoned you?"

"I knew he would." Her voice was weak and thin. She gasped for air as she spoke. "He poisoned your friend Bruce Barnes."

Rayford sat back. "You *know* this?"

"He bragged about it. Told me it was a timed-release thing. Bruce would get sicker and sicker, and if all went according to plan, he would die after he returned to the States."

"Are you strong enough to tell me more?" Hattie nodded. "I don't want to cause you to get worse."

"I can talk."

"Do you know about Amanda?"

Her lips trembled, and she turned her face away.

"Do you?" he repeated. She nodded, looking miserable. "Tell me."

"I'm so sorry, Rayford. I knew from the beginning and could have told you."

He gritted his teeth, his temples pounding painfully. "Told me what?"

"I was involved," she said. "It wasn't my idea, but I could have stopped it."

3

RAYFORD'S MIND REELED. The farthest he had allowed his imagination to take him was that Amanda might have been a plant at the beginning. Hattie could have told Carpathia enough about Rayford and his first wife to give Amanda a believable story about having met Irene. But even if that was true, Amanda surely could not have faked her conversion. He would not accept that.

"Did Carpathia have her killed because she became a believer?"

Hattie stared at him. "What?"

"Hattie, please. I have to know."

"You'll hate me."

"No. I care about you. I can tell you feel bad about your part in this. Tell me."

Hattie lay panting. "It was phony, Rayford. All of it."

"Amanda?"

She nodded and tried to sit up but needed Rayford's help. "The e-mails were bogus, Rayford. I was trained to do it. I saw it all."

"The e-mails?"

"The anonymous ones to Bruce. We knew someone would find them eventually. And the ones between Nicolae and Amanda, both ways. She didn't even know they were on her hard drive. They were encrypted and encoded; she would have had to have been an expert to even find them."

Rayford hardly knew what to ask. "But they sounded like her, read the way she expressed herself. They scared me to death."

"Nicolae has experts trained in that. They intercepted all your e-mails and used her style against her."

Rayford was drained. Tears welled up from so deep inside that he felt as if his heart and lungs would burst. "She was all I believed she was?" he said.

Hattie nodded. "She was more, Rayford. She loved you deeply, was totally devoted to you. I felt so despicable the last time I saw her, it was all I could do to keep from telling her. I knew I should. I wanted to. But what I had done was so awful, so evil. She had shown me nothing but love from the first. She knew about you and me. We disagreed about everything important in life, yet she loved me. I couldn't let her know I had helped make her look like a traitor."

Rayford sat shaking his head, trying to take it all in. "Thank you, Hattie," he said. So the reason he had not seen the seal of God on Amanda's forehead, besides her grotesque and discolored death mask, was that the plane had gone down before the mark appeared on any believers.

Rayford's faith in Amanda had been restored, and he had never doubted her salvation. Even when he had been forced to wonder about how she had come to him in the first place, he never questioned the genuineness of her devotion to God.

Rayford helped Hattie lie back down. "I'll get you something to eat," he said. "And then we're going to talk about you."

"Spare me that, Rayford. You and your friends have been doing that for two years. There's nothing you can tell me that I don't know. But I just told you what I have done, and there's even more that's worse than that."

"You know God will forgive you."

She nodded. "But should he? I don't believe that in my heart."

"Of course he shouldn't. None of us deserves forgiveness."

"But you accepted it anyway," she said. "I can't do that. I know as well as God does that I'm not worthy."

"So you're going to decide for him."

"If it's up to me—"

"And it is."

"I've decided I'm unworthy and can't live with that much, um, what do you call it?"

"Grace?"

"Well, I guess, but I mean there's too much of a gap between what may be true and what should be true."

"Inequity."

"That's it. God saving me when he and I both know who I am and what I've done—that's too much of an inequity."

+ + +

At quarter to five in the afternoon at Chaim Rosenzweig's estate, Tsion asked Buck and Chloe to join him in his room. Buck smiled, noticing the ever-present laptop on a small table. The three knelt by the bed. "We will pray with the committee at the stadium," Tsion said. "But in case the rush of the details gets in the way, I do not want to start the meeting without seeking the Lord."

"May I ask," Chloe said, "what message you sent back to Mr. Fortunato?"

"I merely told Chaim that I would neither acknowledge nor recognize

Nicolae. Neither will I introduce him or ask anyone else to. If he comes to the platform, I will not stand in his way." Tsion smiled wearily. "As you might expect, Chaim argued earnestly, warning me not to commit such an affront to the potentate. But how can I do otherwise? I will not say what I would like to say, will not rally the believers to express their distaste for him, will not expose him for who I know him to be. That is the best I can do."

Chloe nodded. "When do you expect the witnesses?"

"I should think they are beginning to arrive even now."

"I mean Eli and Moishe."

"Oh! I have left that with the Lord. They said they would be there, and the conference extends to two more whole days and nights. You can be sure I will gladly welcome *them* to the platform whenever they choose to appear."

Buck never failed to be moved by the heartfelt prayers of Dr. Ben-Judah. He had seen the rabbi at the lowest point of grief a man could bear, reeling from the slaughter of his wife and two teenagers. He had heard him pray in the midst of terror, certain he would be apprehended on a midnight flight from Israel. Now, as Tsion looked forward to uniting with tens of thousands of new brothers and sisters in Christ from all twelve tribes of Israel and from all over the world, he was on his knees in humility.

"God, our Father," he began, "thank you for the privilege we are about to enjoy. On the front lines of battle we advance with your boldness, under your power and protection. These precious saints will be hungry to learn more of your Word. Give the other teachers and me the words. May we say what you would have us say, and may they hear what you want them to hear."

Buck was deep in his own prayer when a tap at the door interrupted them. "Forgive me, Tsion," Chaim said. "A GC escort is here."

"But I thought Jacov would drive us—"

"He will. But they tell us you have to leave immediately if you hope to reach the stadium in time."

"But it is so close!"

"Nevertheless. Traffic is already so thick that only the GC escort can ensure you will get there on time."

"Have you decided to come with us, Chaim?"

"I will be watching on television. I have asked Jacov to load a case of bottled water for you. Those two preachers at the Wall have taken credit for blood in the drinking water again. Though it supposedly has cleared since the visitors began arriving, you never know. Westerners should not risk our tap water anyway."

The GC escort proved to be two Jeeps with flashing yellow lights, each vehicle carrying four armed guards who merely stared at the Tribulation Force as they climbed into the Mercedes van. "Another bit of one-upmanship from Carpathia," Chloe said.

"If he was smart," Tsion said, "he would have left us to our own devices and let us be late."

"You would not have been late," Jacov said in his thick accent. "I would have gotten you there on time anyway."

Buck had never seen—even in New York—traffic like this. Every artery to the stadium was jammed with cars and pedestrians. Neither had he seen so many happy faces since before the Rapture. Carrying satchels and notebooks and water bottles, the pedestrians hurried along with earnest and determined looks. Many made better time than the cars and vans and buses.

Because of the conspicuous escort, the crowds recognized that the Mercedes carried Tsion Ben-Judah. They waved and shouted and gleefully pounded on doors and windows. The trailing GC vehicle shooed them away with warnings over a loudspeaker and by brandishing their automatic weapons.

"I hate to appear to be here under the aegis of the Global Community," Tsion said.

"They don't know the shortcuts anyway," Jacov said. "All three of these vehicles are equipped to go off-road."

"You know a faster way?" Tsion said. "Take it!"

"May I?"

"They won't open fire. They'll have to scramble just to keep up."

Jacov whipped the wheel to the left, flew down and up a ditch in the median, picked his way through crawling cars on the other side, and headed toward open fields. The GC Jeeps blew their sirens and bounced crazily behind him. The lead car finally caught up and pulled ahead, the driver pointing out the window and shouting at Jacov in Hebrew.

"He says to never do that again," Tsion said. "But I rather enjoyed it."

Jacov slammed on the brakes, and the trailing Jeep tore up grass stopping short of him. Jacov opened his door and stood with his head high above the roofline. The lead driver finally noticed he was leaving Jacov and slid to a stop. He waited at first, then backed up as Jacov shouted, "Unless you want trouble for making us late, you will follow me!"

Tsion looked gleefully at Chloe. "What is it your father is so fond of saying?"

"Lead, follow, or get out of the way."

As Jacov led the angry GC drivers to the stadium, it quickly became obvious that many more than twenty-five thousand hoped to get in. "Do we have monitors outside?" Tsion said.

Buck nodded. "The overflow was supposed to go to several off-site locations, but it appears they all want to stay here."

Having been shown up by Jacov, the GC soldiers leaped from their vehicles and insisted on escorting the little entourage inside the stadium. They scowled at Jacov, who told Buck he would be waiting in the van where he had dropped them off.

"Can you see a monitor?" Buck asked, looking around.

Jacov pointed to one about twenty feet away. "And I can listen on the radio."

"Does this interest you?"

"Very much. I find it confusing, but I have long been suspicious of the potentate, even though Dr. Rosenzweig admires him. And your teacher is such a wise and gentle man."

"Did you see him on television when he—"

"Everyone did, sir."

"Then this isn't totally new to you. We'll talk later."

Inside, the local committee was ecstatic. Buck loved hearing group prayer in English, Hebrew, and a few other languages he couldn't identify. All over the room he heard "Jesus the Messiah" and *"Jesu Cristo"* and *"Yeshua Hamashiach."*

On his knees next to Chloe, Buck felt her strong grip. She laid her head on his shoulder. "Oh, Buck," she said, "this is like heaven."

He whispered, "And we haven't even started."

As the stadium filled, shouts and chants resounded. "What are they saying?" Buck said.

"'Hallelujah,' and 'Praise the Lord,'" someone said. "And they're spelling out the name of Jesus."

The master of ceremonies, Daniel, addressed the group as the clock sped toward seven. "As you know, the program is simple. I will give a brief welcome and then open in prayer. I will lead in the singing of 'Amazing Grace,' and I will then introduce Dr. Ben-Judah. He will preach and teach for as long as he feels led. You twelve translators should have your copy of Dr. Ben-Judah's notes and know which of the microphones at the base of the stage is yours."

"And remember," Tsion said quietly, "I cannot guarantee I will follow the script. I will try not to get ahead of you."

People in the room nodded solemnly, and many looked at their watches. Buck heard the rumble of chants and singing above and was as excited as he had ever been. "All these people are our brothers and sisters," he told Chloe.

Three minutes before seven, as Tsion stood apart from the others, head bowed, a young man rushed in. "The other venues are empty!" he said. "Everyone is here. Everyone had the same idea!"

"How many?" someone asked.

"More than fifty thousand surrounding the stadium," he said, "at least twice as many outside as in. And they are not all witnesses. They are not even all Jewish. People are just curious."

Daniel raised his hands, and the room fell silent. "Follow me down this corridor, up the ramp, then up the stairs to the stage. You can watch from the wings, but translators go first and get into position at ground level in front of the platform. No one on the stage but Dr. Ben-Judah and me. Quiet please. Dear God in heaven, we are yours."

With one hand still raised, he and Tsion led the group toward the back of the stage. Buck peeked out to see every seat filled and people in the aisles and the infield. Many held hands. Others wrapped their arms around each other's shoulders and sang and swayed.

The interpreters slipped out and down the steps to get into position, and the crowd quieted. At seven, Daniel strode to a simple, wood lectern and said, "Welcome my brothers and sisters in the name of the Lord God Almighty, . . ."

He paused for the interpreters, but before they could translate, the stadium erupted in cheering and applause. Daniel was taken aback and smiled apologetically at the translators. "I'll wait for you," he mouthed, as the thousands continued to cheer.

When the applause finally died, he nodded to the interpreters, and they repeated his phrase. "No! No!" came the response from the crowd. *"Nein!" "Nyet!"*

Daniel continued, ". . . maker of heaven and earth, . . ." And again the crowd erupted. He waited for the translation, but they shouted it down again.

". . . and his Son, Jesus Christ, the Messiah!"

The crowd went wild, and an aide hurried to the stage. "Please!" Daniel scolded him. "No one on the stage except—"

"No translation is necessary!" the aide shouted. "Don't use the interpreters! The crowd understands you in their own languages, and they want you to just keep going!"

As the crowd continued to exult, Daniel stepped to the front of the stage and beckoned the translators to gather before him. "You're not needed!" he said, smiling. As they dispersed, looking surprised but pleased, he went back to the microphone. "Shall we express our appreciation to these who were willing—"

Thunderous ovations rolled out of the stands.

Finally Daniel held up his hands to quiet the crowd. Every phrase from then on was greeted with resounding cheers. "You don't need to be told why you're here!" he said. "We've long been known as God's chosen people, but how about this? Would you pray with me?"

Silence descended quickly. Many knelt. "Father, we are grateful for having been spared by your grace and love. You are indeed the God of new beginnings and second chances. We are about to hear from our beloved rabbi, and our prayer is that you would supernaturally quicken our hearts and minds to absorb every jot and tittle of what you have given him to say. We pray this in the matchless name of the King of kings and Lord of lords. Amen."

A huge "Amen!" echoed from the crowd. Daniel directed the massive congregation as he began to sing quietly, "Amazing grace! how sweet the sound that saved a wretch like me! I once was lost, but now am found, was blind but now I see."

Buck could not sing. "Amazing Grace" had become his favorite hymn, a poignant picture of his faith. But twenty-five thousand believers singing it from their hearts nearly knocked him over. The mass outside added their voices. Buck and Chloe stood weeping at the beauty of it.

"When we've been there ten thousand years, bright shining as the sun, we've no less days to sing God's praise than when we'd first begun."

As the final strains trailed off, Daniel asked the crowd to sit. "The vast majority of us know our speaker tonight only as a name on our computer screens," he began. "It is my honor—"

But the assembled had come to their feet en masse, cheering, clapping, shouting, whistling. Daniel tried to quiet them, but finally shrugged and walked away as Tsion, embarrassed, hesitated. He was nudged from the wings, and the cacophony deafened Buck. He and Chloe clapped too, honoring their personal pastor and mentor. Never had Buck felt so privileged to be part of the Tribulation Force and to know this man.

Tsion stood meekly at the lectern, spreading his Bible and his notes before him. The noisy welcome continued until he finally looked up with a shy smile and mouthed his thanks, holding up both hands to request silence. At long last, the crowd settled into their seats.

"My beloved brothers and sisters, I accept your warm greeting in the name that is above all names. All glory and honor is due the triune God." As the crowd began to respond again, Tsion quickly held up a hand. "Dear ones, we are in the midst of a mountaintop experience in which anything and everything said about our God could justifiably be celebrated. But we are guests here. There is a curfew. And I trust you will forgive me if I request that we withhold expressions of praise from now until the end of the teaching."

The crowd fell deathly silent so quickly that Tsion raised his brows and looked around. "I have not offended you, have I?" A smattering of applause urged him to continue.

"Later it will be wholly appropriate if our master of ceremonies gives you an opportunity to raise your voices again in praise of our God. The Bible says, 'Let them praise the name of the Lord, for His name alone is exalted; His glory is above the earth and heaven.'

"Ladies and gentlemen," Tsion continued, spreading his feet and hunching his shoulders as he gazed at his notes, "never in my life have I been more eager to share a message from the Word of God. I stand before you with the unique privilege, I believe, of addressing many of the 144,000 witnesses prophesied in the Scriptures. I count myself one of you, and God has burdened me to help you learn to evangelize. Most of you already know how, of course, and have been winning converts to the Savior every day. Millions around the world have come to faith already.

"But let me review for you again the basics of God's plan of salvation so we may soon leave this place and get back to the work to which he has called us. You have each been assigned a location for all-day training tomorrow and the next day. On both nights we will meet back here for encouragement and fellowship and teaching."

Tsion then outlined the same evidence he had used on the controversial television broadcast that had made him a fugitive, proving from the Old Testament that Jesus was the Messiah. He recited the many names of God and finished with the powerful passage from Isaiah 9:6, "For unto us a Child is born, unto us a Son is given; and the government will be upon His shoulder. And His name will be called Wonderful, Counselor, Mighty God, Everlasting Father, Prince of Peace."

The crowd could not contain itself, leaping to its feet. Tsion smiled and nodded and waved encouragement, pointing to the heavens. "Yes, yes," he said finally. "Even I would not stifle your praise to the Most High God. Jesus himself said that if we do not glorify God, the very stones would have to cry out."

Tsion walked through God's plan of redemption from the beginning of time, showing that Jesus was sent as the spotless lamb, a sacrifice to take away the sins of the world. He explained the truths that had so recently become clear to these initiates, that man is born in sin and that nothing he can do for himself can reconcile him to God. Only by believing and trusting in the work Christ did for him on the cross can he be born again spiritually into eternal life. "In John 14:6," Tsion said, his voice rising for the first time, "Jesus himself said he was the way, the truth, and the life, and that no man can come to the Father except through him. This is our message to the nations. This is our message to the desperate, the sick, the terrified, the bound. By now there should be no doubt in anyone's mind—even those who have chosen to live in opposition to God—that he is real and that a person is either for him or against him. We of all people should have the boldness of Christ to aggressively tell the world of its only hope in him.

"The bottom line, my brothers and sisters, is that we have been called as his divine witnesses—144,000 strong—through whom he has begun a great soul harvest. This will result in what John the Revelator calls 'a great multitude which no one could number.' Before you fall asleep tonight, read Revelation 7 and thrill with me to the description of the harvest you and I have been called to reap. John says it is made up of souls from all nations, kindreds, peoples, tribes, and tongues. One day they will stand before his throne and before the Lamb, clothed with white robes and carrying palms in their hands!"

Spontaneously, the crowd at Teddy Kollek Stadium stood as Tsion's voice rose and fell. Buck held Chloe tight and wanted to shout amen as Tsion thundered on. "They will cry with a loud voice, saying, 'Salvation belongs to our God who sits on the throne, and to the Lamb!'

"The angels around the throne will fall on their faces and worship God, saying, 'Amen! Blessing and glory and wisdom, thanksgiving and honor and power and might, be to our God forever and ever. Amen.'"

The crowd began to roar again, and Tsion did not quiet them. He merely stepped back and gazed at the floor, and Buck had the impression he was overcome and welcomed the pause to collect himself. When he moved back to the microphone, the standing thousands quieted again, as if desperate to catch every word. "John was asked by one of the elders at the throne, 'Who are these arrayed in white robes, and where did they come from?' And John said, 'Sir, you know.' And the elder said, 'These are the ones who come out of the great tribulation, and washed their robes and made them white in the blood of the Lamb.'"

Tsion waited through another reverberating response, then continued: "'They shall neither hunger anymore nor thirst anymore.' The Lamb himself shall feed them and lead them to fountains of living water. And, best of all, my dear family, God shall wipe away all tears from their eyes."

This time when the crowd began to respond, Tsion stayed in the lectern and raised a hand, and they listened. "We shall be here in Israel two more full days and nights, preparing for battle. Put aside fear! Put on boldness! Were you surprised that all of us, each and every one, were spared the last few judgments I wrote about? When the rain and hail and fire came from the sky and the meteors scorched a third of the plant life and poisoned a third of the waters of the world, how was it that we escaped? Luck? Chance?"

The crowd shouted, "No!"

"No!" Tsion echoed. "The Scriptures say that an angel ascending from the east, having the seal of the living God, cried with a loud voice to the four angels to whom it was granted to harm the earth and the sea. And what did he tell them? He said, 'Do not harm the earth, the sea, or the trees till we have sealed the servants of our God on their foreheads.' And John writes, 'I heard the number of those who were sealed. One hundred and forty-four thousand of all the tribes of the children of Israel were sealed.'

"And now let me close by reminding you that the bedrock of our faith remains the verse our Gentile brothers and sisters have so cherished from the beginning. John 3:16 says," and here Tsion spoke so softly, so tenderly that he had to be right on the microphone, and people edged forward to hear, "'For God so loved the world that He gave His only—'"

A faint rumble in the sky became a persistent *thwock-thwock-thwock* that drowned out Tsion as a gleaming white helicopter drew every eye. The crowd stared as the chopper, with GC emblazoned on the side, slowly descended, its massive blades whipping Tsion's hair and clothes until he was forced to back away from the lectern.

The engine shuddered and stopped, and the crowd murmured when Leon Fortunato bounded from the craft to the lectern. He nodded to Tsion, who did not respond, then adjusted the microphone to his own height. "Dr. Ben-Judah, local and international organizing committee, and assembled guests," he began with great enthusiasm, but immediately thousands looked puzzled, looked at each other, shrugged, and began jabbering.

"Translators!" someone shouted. "We need interpreters!"

Fortunato looked expectantly at Tsion, who continued staring straight ahead. "Dr. Ben-Judah," Fortunato implored, "is there someone who can translate? Whom are you using?"

Tsion did not look at him.

"Excuse me," Fortunato said into the microphone, "but interpreters have been assigned. If you would come forward quickly, His Excellency, your potentate, would be grateful for your service."

Buck stepped out and peered into an area near the front row in the infield where the interpreters sat. As one they looked to Tsion, but Fortunato didn't even know whom he was addressing. "Please," he said. "It isn't fair that only those who understand English may enjoy the remarks of your next two hosts."

Hosts? Buck thought. That got even Tsion's attention, and his head jerked as he glanced at Leon. "Please," Leon mouthed, as the crowd grew louder. Tsion glanced at the translators, who eyed him, waiting. He raised his head slightly, as if to give the OK. They hurried to their microphones.

"Thank you kindly, Dr. Ben-Judah," Fortunato said. "You're most helpful, and His Excellency thanks you as well." Tsion ignored him.

With the singsong cadence necessary to keep the interpreters on pace, Fortunato addressed the crowd anew. "As supreme commander of the Global Community and as one who has personally benefited from his supernatural ability to perform miracles, it shall be my pleasure in a moment to introduce you to His Excellency, Global Community potentate Nicolae Carpathia!"

Fortunato had ended with a flourish, as if expecting cheering and applause. He stood smiling and—to Buck's mind—embarrassed and perturbed when no one responded. No one even moved. Every eye was on Fortunato except Tsion's.

Leon quickly gathered himself. "His Excellency will personally welcome you, but first I would like to introduce the revered head of the new Enigma Babylon One World Faith, the supreme pontiff, Pontifex Maximus, Peter the Second!"

Fortunato swept grandly back, beckoning to the helicopter, from which emerged the comical figure of the man Buck knew as Peter Mathews, former archbishop of Cincinnati. He had become pope briefly after the disappearance of the previous pontiff but was now the amalgamator of nearly every religion on the globe save Judaism and Christianity.

Mathews had somehow emerged from the helicopter with style, despite being decked out in the most elaborate clerical garb Buck had ever seen. "What in the world is that?" Chloe said.

Buck watched agape as Peter the Second lifted his hands to the crowd and turned slowly in a circle as if to include everyone in his pompous and pious greeting. He wore a high, peaked cap with an infinity symbol on the front and a floor-length, iridescent yellow robe with a long train and billowy sleeves. His vestments were bedecked with huge, inlaid, brightly colored stones and appointed with tassels, woven cords, and bright blue, crushed velvet stripes, six on each sleeve, as if he had earned some sort of a double doctorate from Black Light Discotheque University. Buck covered his mouth to stifle a laugh. When Mathews turned around, he revealed astrological signs on the train of his robe.

His hands moved in circles as if to bless everyone, and Buck wondered how he felt about hearing nothing from the audience. Would Carpathia dare face this indifference, this hostility?

Peter pulled the mike up to his mouth and spoke with arms outstretched. "My blessed brothers and sisters in the pursuit of higher consciousness, it warms my heart to see all of you here, studying under the well-intentioned scholarship of my colleague and respected litterateur, Dr. Tsion Ben-Judah!" Mathews clearly expected that announcing their hero as if introducing a heavyweight boxer would elicit a roar, but the crowd remained silent and unmoving.

"I confer upon this gathering the blessings of the universal father and mother and animal deities who lovingly guide us on our path to true spirituality. In the spirit of harmony and ecumenism, I appeal to Dr. Ben-Judah and others in your leadership to add your rich heritage and history and scholarship to our coat of many colors. To the patchwork quilt that so beautifully encompasses and includes and affirms and accepts the major tenets of all the world's great religions, I urge you to include your own. Until the day comes that you agree to plant your flag under the umbrella of Enigma Babylon One World Faith, rest assured that I will defend your right to disagree and to oppose and to seek our multilayered plural godhead in your own fashion."

Mathews turned regally and traded places with Fortunato, both clearly pretending to be unfazed by the apathy of the crowd. Fortunato announced, "And now it gives me pleasure to introduce to you the man who has united the world into one global community, His Excellency and your potentate, Nicolae Carpathia! Would you rise as he comes with a word of greeting."

No one stood.

Carpathia, a frozen smile etched on his face, had never—in Buck's experience—failed to captivate a crowd. He was the most dynamic, engaging, charming speaker Buck had ever heard. Buck himself was, of course, far past being impressed with Nicolae, but he wondered if the seal of God on the foreheads of the witnesses and their converts also protected their minds against his evil manipulation.

"Fellow citizens of the Global Community," Carpathia began, waiting for the interpreters and appearing to Buck to work hard at connecting with the crowd. "As your potentate, I welcome you to Israel and to this great arena, named after a man of the past, a man of peace and harmony and statesmanship."

Buck was impressed. Nicolae had immediately tried to align himself with a former mayor of the Holy City, one a huge percentage of this crowd would have heard of. Buck began to worry that Nicolae's power of persuasion might sway someone like Jacov. He put a hand on Chloe's shoulder and whispered, "I'll be right back."

"How can you walk out on this?" she said. "I wouldn't miss this show for the world. Don't you think Peter's getup would work on me, maybe as an evening kind of a thing?"

"I'll be with Jacov for a minute."

"Good idea."

As Buck stepped away, his cell phone vibrated in his pocket. "Buck here," he said.

"Where you goin'?"

"Who's this?"

"That was you at stage right with the blonde, right?"

Buck stopped. "I have to know who this is."

"Mac McCullum. Nice to meet ya."

"Mac! What's up? Where are you?"

"On the chopper, man! This is the best theater I've seen in ages. All this friendly folderol! You should have heard these guys on board! Swearing, cursing Ben-Judah and the whole crowd. Carpathia spit all over me, railing about the two witnesses."

"Doesn't surprise me. Hey, you sure this connection is secure?"

"Only my life depends on it, son."

"Guess that's true." Buck told Mac where he was going and why.

"Nick's a piece of work, ain't he?" Mac said.

"Chloe's particularly fond of Mathews's sartorial resplendence."

"Hey, me too! Gotta go. Don't want to have to tell 'em who I was talkin' to."

"Keep in touch, Mac."

"Don't worry. But listen, make yourselves scarce too. I wouldn't put anything past these guys."

"Wait," Buck said, a smile in his voice. "You mean we can't take Carpathia at his word? He's not a trustworthy guy?"

"All right, just watch yourselves."

4

KNOWING THE GC BRASS was away from New Babylon, Rayford e-mailed David Hassid at the underground shelter. "Be where you can receive TX at six your time, brother."

At nine in the morning Chicago time, an hour before the Meeting of the Witnesses was to be broadcast live internationally via the Internet, Rayford reached David by phone. "Where are you?" he said.

"Outside," David said. "Things are pretty quiet with Abbott and Costello away."

Rayford chuckled. "I would have guessed you way too young for them."

"They're my favorites," David said. "Especially now that they're ruling the world. What's up? I was about to watch the festivities. They've got it on the wall-sized screen in the compound."

Rayford filled him in on the latest. "Sad to say, the next time I see you may be because you need to hide out with us."

"I can't imagine escaping here, but Mac's right that it's good you slipped away. Your days were numbered."

"I'm shocked Nicolae didn't do me in months ago."

"Your son-in-law better lay low, too. His name pops up all the time. They've assigned me to locate where his webzine originates. But you know, Rayford, as hard as I work on that and as much time as I put into it, I just can't seem to break through the scramble and find it."

"No kidding."

"I'm doing my best. Honest I am. Boy it's frustrating when you can't deliver information to your boss that would cost the life of a brother. Know what I mean?"

"Well, you keep working on it, David, and I'm sure you'll at least find a misdirection that can waste more of their time."

"Great idea."

"Listen, can you walk me through hooking my laptop to a TV so we can see this meeting easier?"

David laughed. "Next you'll tell me your minidisc player is blinking twelve o'clock all day and night."

"How'd you know?"

"Just a lucky guess."

"You know we consider you a member of the Tribulation Force," Rayford said, "though the others have not met you. You and Mac are our guys inside now, and we know well how dangerous that is."

David grew serious. "Thanks. I'd love to meet everybody and be with you all, but like you say, when that happens, it'll be because I'm running . . . and from the most technologically advanced regime in history. I may not see you until heaven. Until then, you need a plane or anything?"

"We're going to have to talk about that here. If all's fair in love and war, it might make sense for us to appropriate enemy equipment."

"You could abscond with millions' worth and not cripple the GC. You wouldn't even scratch them."

"How much longer will you be underground?"

"Not long. The new palace—yeah, it's a palace this time—is almost done. Spectacular. Wish I were proud to work here. It'd be a pretty good deal."

After David got him set up, Rayford set the TV where he, Dr. Charles, Ken Ritz, and Hattie would be able to see it. Hattie lay rocking and groaning. She refused food or medication, so Rayford merely covered her. A few minutes before ten, he asked Ken to rouse Floyd, who wanted to watch with them.

The doctor expressed alarm when he saw Hattie. "How long has she been this way?"

"About an hour," Ken said. "Should we have woken you?"

The doctor shrugged. "I'm shooting in the dark, experimenting with antidotes for a poison that hasn't been identified. She rallies and I get encouraged, and then she reverts to this." He medicated her and fed her, and she slept quietly.

Rayford was moved to tears by the broadcast from Israel, but the men laughing at Peter Mathews's apparel awoke Hattie. She slowly and apparently painfully pushed herself up onto her elbows to watch. "Nicolae hates Mathews with a passion," she said. "You watch, he'll have him murdered someday."

Rayford shot her a double take. She was right, of course, but how did she know? Had it been in the plans as early as when Hattie worked for Carpathia? "You watch," she repeated.

When Nicolae emerged from the helicopter and joined Fortunato and Mathews onstage, Rayford's phone rang. "First chance I've had to call you, Ray," Mac said. "First off, nobody knows you're gone yet. Good job. 'Course, I can play dumb only so long. Now listen, your son-in-law and daughter—is he a good-looking kid, early thirties, and she a cute blonde?"

"That's them. Where are they? I can see the copter, but I don't see them."

"They're off camera, in the wings."

"Mac, let me tell you what Hattie told me about—"

"I've only got a second here, Ray. Let me call Buck. Will he have his phone on him, the one with the number you gave me?"

"He should, but Mac—"

"I'll check back with you, Ray."

+ + +

As Buck emerged from the stadium, Carpathia's eloquence reverberated. When Buck reached the van, he saw Jacov facing front, hands on the wheel. He seemed to be peering over the crowd at the monitor while listening to the radio. Buck reached for the door handle, but Jacov had locked himself inside and recoiled at the sound, looking terrified.

"Oh, it's you," he said, unlocking the door.

"Who were you expecting?" Buck said, climbing in.

"I just didn't notice you. I apologize."

"So, what do you make of all this?"

Jacov held his hand out, palm down, to show Buck that he was trembling.

Buck offered Jacov his bottle of water. "What are you afraid of?"

"God," Jacov said, smiling self-consciously and declining the bottle.

"You don't need to be. He loves you."

"Don't need to be? Rabbi Ben-Judah teaches that all these things we have endured are the judgments of God. It seems I should have feared him long ago. But pardon me, I wish to hear the potentate."

"You know Dr. Ben-Judah is not a friend of his."

"That is clear. He has been received most coldly."

"Appropriately so, Jacov. He is an enemy of God."

"But I owe it to him to listen."

Buck was tempted to keep talking anyway, to nullify any deleterious effect Carpathia might have on Jacov. But he didn't want to be rude, and he wanted to trust God to work in the man's heart and mind. He fell silent as Carpathia's liquid tones filled the air.

"And so, my beloved friends, it is not a requirement that your sect align itself with the One World Faith for you to remain citizens of the Global Community. Within reasonable limits, there is room for dissent and alternative approaches. But consider with me for a moment the advantages and privileges and benefits that have resulted from the uniting of every nation into one global village."

Nicolae recited his litany of achievements. It ranged from the rebuilding of cities and roads and airports to the nearly miraculous reconstruction of New Babylon into the most magnificent city ever built. "It is a masterpiece I hope you will visit as soon as you can." He mentioned his cellular/solar satellite system (Cell-Sol) that allowed everyone access to each other by phone and Internet regardless of time or location. Buck shook his head. All this merely ushered in the superstructure necessary for Nicolae to rule the world until the time came to declare himself God.

Buck could see that Nicolae was succeeding in changing Jacov's mind. "This is hard to argue with," the driver said. "He has worked wonders."

"But Jacov," Buck said, "you have been exposed to the teaching of Dr. Ben-Judah. Surely you must be convinced that the Scriptures are true, that Jesus is the Messiah, that the disappearances were the rapture of Christ's church."

Jacov stared ahead, gripping the wheel tightly, his arms shaking. He nodded, but he looked conflicted. Buck no longer cared about rudeness. He would talk over Nicolae; he would not allow the enemy to steal this soul through slick talking.

"What did you think of the teaching tonight?"

"Most impressive," Jacov admitted. "I cried. I felt myself drawn to him, but mostly drawn to God. I love and respect Dr. Rosenzweig, and he would never understand if I became a believer in Jesus. But if it is true, what else can I do?"

Buck prayed silently, desperately.

"But, Mr. Williams, I had never before heard the verse that Dr. Ben-Judah said was the reason for this meeting. And he was interrupted, was he not? He did not finish the verse."

"You're right, he didn't. It was John 3:16, and it goes, 'For God so loved the world that He gave His only—'"

But Buck got no further than Tsion had when Jacov held up a hand to silence him. "The potentate is finishing," he said.

Carpathia seemed to be wrapping up his remarks, but something was strange about his voice. Buck had never heard him struggle to speak, but he had grown hoarse. Carpathia turned away from the mike, covered his mouth, and attempted to clear his throat. "Pardon me," he said, his voice still raspy. "But I wish you and the rabbi here all the best and welcome you, *ahem, ahem,* once again, excuse me—"

Nicolae turned pleadingly to Tsion, who was still ignoring him. "Would someone have some water?"

Someone passed a fresh bottle to the stage, where Nicolae nodded his thanks. When he opened it, the release of the pressure was magnified over the loudspeaker. But when he drank, he gagged and spit the water out. His lips and chin were covered in blood, and he held the bottle at arm's length, staring at it in horror. Jacov jumped from the car and moved closer to the monitor. Buck knew why. Even at that distance, it was obvious the bottle contained blood.

Buck followed as they heard Carpathia swearing, cursing Tsion and his "evil gaggle of enemies of the Global Community! You would humiliate me like this for your own gain? I should pull from you my pledge of protection and allow my men to shoot you dead where you stand!"

From the middle of the stunned crowd came the shouted, unison voices of Eli and Moishe. Without need of amplification, everyone within a block of the place could hear them. The crowd fell back from around them, and the two stood in the eerie light of the stadium, shoulder to shoulder, barefoot and in sackcloth.

"Woe unto you who would threaten the chosen vessel of the Most High God!"

Carpathia threw the water bottle onto the floor of the stage, and clear, clean water splashed everywhere. Buck knew the witnesses had turned only Nicolae's water to blood and that they had likely caused him to need the drink in the first place. Nicolae pointed at Eli and Moishe and screamed, "Your time is nigh! I swear I will kill you or have you killed before—"

But the witnesses were louder, and Carpathia had to fall silent. "Woe!" they said again. "Woe to the impostor who would dare threaten the chosen ones before the due time! Sealed followers of the Messiah, drink deeply and be refreshed!"

The bottle in Buck's pocket suddenly felt cold. He pulled it out and felt the sting of frigidity in his palm. He twisted off the top and drank deeply. Icy, smooth, rich, thirst-quenching nectar cascaded down his throat. He moaned, not wanting to pull the bottle from his lips but needing to catch his breath. All around he heard the sighs of satisfied believers, sharing cold, refreshing bottles.

"Taste this, Jacov!" Buck said, wiping off the top and handing it to him. "It's *very* cold."

Jacov reached for the water. "It doesn't feel cold to me," he said.

"How can you say that? Feel my hand." Buck put his hand on Jacov's arm, and Jacov flinched.

"Your hand is freezing," he said, "but the bottle feels warm to me." He held it up to the light. "Agh! Blood!" And he dropped it. The bottle bounced at Buck's feet, and he snatched it up before it emptied. It was again cold in his hands, and he couldn't resist guzzling from it.

"Don't!" Jacov said. But as he watched Buck enjoy the clean water, he fell to his hands and knees. "Oh, God, I am no better than Carpathia! I want to be a child of God! I want to be a sealed one!"

Buck squatted next to him and put an arm around his shoulder. "God wants you as part of his family," he said.

Jacov wept bitterly, then looked up at the whir of chopper blades. He and Buck stared at the TV monitor, where Tsion stood alone again on the stage. His hair and clothes flapped in the wind from the helicopter, and his notes were whipped into a funnel before scattering. Translators leapt onto the stage to retrieve them and set them back on the lectern. Tsion remained motionless, staring, having ignored the entire episode with Nicolae and the two witnesses.

The camera panned to where the witnesses had appeared, but they had left as quickly as they had come. The crowd stood, mouths open, many still drinking and passing around water bottles. When they noticed Tsion back at the lectern, they quieted and sat. As if nothing had happened since he began quoting John 3:16, Tsion continued:

"'—begotten Son, that whoever believes in Him should not perish but have everlasting life.'"

Jacov, still on his knees, hands on his thighs, seemed glued to the TV image. "What?" he cried out. "What?"

And as if he had heard Jacov, Tsion repeated the verse: "'For God so loved the world that He gave His only begotten Son, that whoever believes in Him should not perish but have everlasting life.'"

Jacov lowered his face to the pavement, sobbing. "I believe! I believe! God save me! Don't let me perish! Give me everlasting life!"

"He hears you," Buck said. "He will not turn away a true seeker."

But Jacov continued to wail. Others in the crowd had fallen to their knees. Tsion said, "There may be some here, inside or outside, who want to receive Christ. I urge you to pray after me, 'Dear God, I know I am a sinner. Forgive me and pardon me for waiting so long. I receive your love and salvation and ask you to live your life through me. I accept you as my Savior and resolve to live for you until you come again.'"

Jacov repeated the prayer through tears, then rose to embrace Buck. He squeezed him so tight Buck could hardly breathe. Buck pulled away and thrust the water bottle into Jacov's hand again.

"Cold!" Jacov exulted.

"Drink!" Buck said.

Jacov held the bottle to the light again, smiling. It was clear. "And it's full!"

Buck stared. It was! Jacov put it to his lips and tilted his head back so far that he staggered and Buck had to hold him up. He gulped, but not fast enough, and the cool clear water gushed over his face and down his neck. Jacov laughed and cried and shouted, "Praise God! Praise God! Praise God!"

"Let me look at you," Buck said, laughing.

"Do I look different?"

"You'd better." He took Jacov's head in his hands and turned him toward the light. "You have the mark," he said. "On your forehead."

Jacov pulled away and ran back toward the van. "I want to see it in the mirror."

"You won't," Buck said, following him. "For some reason we can't see our own. But you should be able to see mine."

Jacov turned and stopped Buck, leaning close and squinting. "I do! A cross! And I have one, really?"

"Really."

"Oh! Praise God!"

They climbed back into the van, and Buck dialed Chloe's phone. "This had better be you, Buck," she said.

"It is."

"I was worried about you."

"Sorry, but we have a new brother."

"Jacov?"

"Want to talk to him?"

"Of course. And don't try to get back in, hon. It's a madhouse. I'll get Tsion out as soon as I can."

Buck handed the phone to Jacov. "Thank you, Mrs. Williams!" he said. "I feel brand new! I *am* brand new! Hurry and we can see each other's marks!"

+ + +

At the safe house it was midafternoon. Rayford sat staring at the screen and shaking his head. "Do you believe this?" he said over and over. "I can't believe Nicolae lost it like that."

Ken stood blocking the sun from the window. "I heard all the stories about them two witnesses, but man oh man, they are spooky. I'm glad they're on our side. They are, aren't they?"

Dr. Charles laughed. "You know as well as we do that they are, if you've been following Tsion as closely on the Net as you say you have."

"This thing's going to have the biggest TV audience in history tomorrow," Rayford said, turning to see what Hattie thought of it. She too stared at the screen, but her face was deathly pale, and she appeared to try to speak. Her mouth was open, her lips quivering. She looked terrified. "You all right, Hattie?" he said.

Floyd turned as Hattie emitted a piercing scream. She flopped onto her back, cradled her abdomen with both hands, and rolled to her side, gasping and groaning.

Dr. Charles grabbed his stethoscope and asked Rayford and Ken to hold Hattie down. She fought them but seemed to know enough to try to stay quiet so Floyd could listen for the baby's heartbeat. He looked grave. "What did you feel?" he asked.

"No movement for a long time," she said, gasping. "Then sharp pain. Did it die? Did I lose my baby?"

"Let me listen again," he said. Hattie held still. "I can't tell with just a stethoscope," he said. "And I don't have a fetal monitor."

"You could tell if it was there!" Hattie said.

"But I can't be sure if I hear nothing."

"Oh, no! Please, no!"

Floyd shushed her and listened carefully again. He felt all around her abdomen and then lay his ear flat on her belly. He straightened up quickly. "Did you tighten your abdominal muscles on purpose?" She shook her head. "Did you just feel a labor pain?"

"How would I know?"

"Cramping? Tightening?"

She nodded.

"Phone!" Floyd barked, and Ken tossed him his. The doctor dialed quickly. "Jimmy, it's me. I need a sterile environment and a fetal monitor. . . . Don't ask! . . . No, I can't tell you that. Assume I'm within fifty to sixty miles of you. . . . No, I can't come there."

"How 'bout Young Memorial in Palatine?" Ken whispered. "There's a believer there." Rayford looked up, surprised.

Floyd covered the phone. "How close?"

"Not that far."

"Thanks, Jimmy. Sorry to bother you. We found a place. I owe you one."

The doctor began barking orders. "Decide who's gonna drive, and the other get me two blankets."

Rayford looked at Ken, who shrugged. "I'm easy," he said. "I can drive or—"

"Sometime today, gentlemen!"

"You know where it is, you drive," Rayford said, and he dashed upstairs. When he returned with the blankets, the Rover idled near the door, and Dr.

Charles backed out of the house with Hattie in his arms. She squirmed and cried and screamed.

"Should you move her?"

"No choice," Floyd said. "I'm afraid she's about to spontaneously abort."

"No!" Hattie screeched. "I'm only staying alive for my baby!"

"Don't say that," Rayford said as he squeezed past and opened the car door.

"Yes, say that," the doctor said. "Whatever it takes, keep fighting. Ray, get one blanket on the backseat and put the other over her as soon as I get her in there."

He wrestled Hattie into the car, her head near the far rear door. When Rayford draped the other blanket over her, Floyd got in and lay her feet across his lap. Rayford jumped into the front seat, and Floyd said, "Don't hold back, Ken. Get us there as fast as you can."

Apparently that was all Ken needed to hear. He gunned the engine and backed out the way he had pulled in. He slid to a dusty stop, then spun over the ruts in the torn-up road in front of the house. They bumped and banged and nearly rolled a couple of times as he set a course for Palatine.

"Am I bouncin' too much?" he asked.

"You're not going to do either of them any more harm. Speed is more important than comfort now!" Floyd said. "Ray, help me."

Rayford twisted in his seat and grabbed Hattie's wrist as the doctor wrapped both arms around her ankles. They steadied her as Ken pushed the car to its limits. Only one short stretch of paved road existed between the house and the hospital. Ken opened the Rover all the way over that quarter mile, and when he hit dirt at the end of it, the vehicle nearly went airborne.

When the hospital came into view, Floyd said, "Find Emergency."

"Can't do that," Ken said. "I don't know the woman's name. I just saw her mark, and she works up front near Reception, not in Emergency. I say we pull up there and let me run in and find her. If she can get us an operating room, the fastest way would be to take Hattie right through the front door."

Floyd nodded, and Ken steered up onto the sidewalk near the entrance. "Go, Ken. Ray, help me with her."

Rayford jumped out and opened the door near Hattie's head. She was unconscious. "I don't like this," the doctor said.

"Let me take her," Rayford said. "Just push her toward me, and then you lead the way in and talk to the woman if Ken's found her."

"I've got her, Ray."

"Just do it!"

"You're right," Floyd said, and he pushed as Rayford pulled and gathered

Hattie to him. She felt as light as a little girl, despite her pregnancy. He wrestled with the blanket and charged up the steps behind Floyd. The woman with the mark of the cross on her forehead followed Ken toward the door, terror on her face.

"You brothers are going to get me in trouble," she said. "What have we got here?"

"She's about to miscarry," Floyd said. "Are you certified in the OR?"

"Years ago. I've been behind a desk since—"

"I can't trust anyone else. Lead us to an OR now."

"But—"

"Now, dear!"

The receptionist, a teenager, stared at them. The woman said, "Point those eyes elsewhere and keep your mouth shut. Got it?"

"Didn't see a thing," the girl said.

"What's your name, ma'am?" Floyd said as they followed her down a corridor.

"Leah."

"I recognize your risk, Leah. We appreciate it."

Leah peered at Hattie as she opened the operating room door and pointed at the table. "I'm not *her* sister, apparently."

Floyd stared at her. "So we let her die, is that it?"

"I didn't mean that, Doctor. You *are* a doctor?" He nodded. "I just meant, you're going to a lot of trouble and danger for someone who isn't, you know—"

"One of us?" he said, rushing to the scrubbing area. He grabbed a gown from a stack and headed to the sink. "Scrub with me. You're going to assist."

"Doctor, I—"

"Let's go, Leah. Now."

She stepped beside him at the sink. Ken stood near the still unconscious Hattie. Rayford felt useless, waiting between the table and the scrub room. "Are we messing up the sterile environment in here?" he asked.

"Try not to touch anything," Floyd said. "We're breaking a lot of rules."

"I wasn't implying—," Leah began.

"Faster," Floyd said, scrubbing more quickly than Rayford imagined it could be done. "We want to give this girl every chance to become one of us before she dies."

"Of course. I'm sorry."

"Let's concentrate on the patient. As soon as you're ready, I want you to paint her with Betadine from sternum to thighs, and I mean paint. Use a liter if you have to. You don't have time to be precise, so just don't miss a thing. And have a fetal monitor on her by the time I get in there. If that baby is alive, I may try to take it C-section. You'll have to handle anesthesia."

"I have no experience—"

"I'll walk you through it, Leah. How about we rise to the occasion?"

"I'm going to lose my job."

"Humph," the doctor said. "I hope that's the worst thing that happens to you. You see the people in this room? I lost mine the other day. So did Captain Steele. Ken lost his home."

"I know him. He was a patient here."

"Really?" He followed her into the operating theater.

"And how about the patient?" she asked, quickly applying the fetal monitor.

"Hattie too. We're all in the same boat. Prep her."

Ken and Rayford moved closer to the door. Floyd checked the fetal monitor and shook his head. He hooked her to other various monitors. "Actually, her respiration is not bad," he said. "BP's low. Pulse high. Go figure."

"That's weird, Doctor."

"She's been poisoned."

"With what?"

"I wish I knew."

"Doctor, did you call her Hattie?"

He nodded.

"She's not who I think she is, is she?"

"I'm afraid so," he said, moving into position. "You ever hear of another Hattie?"

"Not in this century. Does her, um, boyfriend know what's going on, or should we plan a trip to a gulag somewhere when he finds out?"

"He did this to her, Leah. When you got the mark you became his archenemy, so now you're on the front lines, that's all."

"That's all?"

Rayford watched, praying for Hattie as Floyd positioned the glaring overhead light. "Dilated. Seven or eight centimeters."

"No section then," Leah said.

"The baby's gone," he said. "I need an IV line, Ringer's lactate solution, forty units of oxytocin per liter."

"Incomplete abortion?"

"See how fast it all comes back to you, Leah? Normally she would deliver in an hour or two, but as far along as she is, this will be quick."

Rayford was impressed with Leah's speed and efficiency.

Hattie came to. "I'm dying!" she wailed.

"You're miscarrying, Hattie," Doctor Charles said. "I'm sorry. Work with me. We're worried about you now."

"It hurts!"

"Soon you won't feel a thing, but you're going to have to push when I tell you."

Within minutes, Hattie was wracked with powerful contractions. *What,* Rayford wondered, *might the offspring of the Antichrist look like?*

The dead baby was so underdeveloped and small that it slipped quickly from Hattie's body. Floyd wrapped it and pieces of the placenta, then handed the bundle to Leah. "Pathology?" she asked.

Floyd stared at her. "No," he whispered firmly. "Do you have an incinerator?"

"Now I cannot do that. No. I have to put my foot down."

"What?" Hattie called out. "What? Did I have it?"

Leah stood with the tiny bundle in her hands. Floyd moved to the head of the operating table. "Hattie, you expelled a very premature, very deformed fetus."

"Don't call it that! Boy or girl?"

"Indeterminate."

"Can I see it?"

"Hattie, I'm sorry. It does not look like a baby. I don't advise it."

"But I want—"

Floyd pulled off his gloves and laid a hand gently on her cheek. "I have grown very fond of you, Hattie. You know that, don't you?" She nodded, tears rolling. "I'm begging you to trust me, as one who cares for you." She looked at him wonderingly. "Please," he said. "I believe as you do that this was conceived as a living soul, but it was not viable and did not survive. It has not grown normally. Will you trust me to dispose of it?"

Hattie bit her lip and nodded. Floyd looked to Leah, who still appeared resolute. He placed the baby in a carrier and carefully examined Hattie. He beckoned Leah with a nod. "I need you to assist me with a uterine curettage to eliminate the rest of the placental tissue and any necrotic decidua."

"Worried about endometritis?"

"Very good."

Rayford could see by the look on her face and the set of her jaw that Leah was not going to dispose of the fetus. Apparently Floyd gathered that too. After performing the procedure on Hattie, he gently picked up the wrapped body. "Where?" he said.

"End of the hall," she whispered. "Two floors down."

He walked out, and Hattie sobbed aloud. Rayford approached and asked if he could pray for her.

"Please," she managed. "Rayford, I want to die."

"No you don't."

"I have no reason to live."

"You do, Hattie. We love you."

5

BUCK GREW NERVOUS in the van, waiting for Chloe and Tsion. He assumed she would hustle Tsion from the stage; thousands would have given anything for a moment with him, not to mention committee members who might want a word. And no one knew how Carpathia might respond to what had happened on stage. He initially blamed it on Tsion, but then the witnesses had appeared.

Buck thought Nicolae should realize that Tsion had no miraculous powers. Nicolae's quarrel was with the two witnesses. It was his own fault, of course. He had not been invited, or even welcomed, on stage. And the gall to have Fortunato and the pompous Peter the Second precede him! Buck shook his head. What else could one expect from Antichrist?

Buck dialed Chloe's number but got no answer. A busy signal he could understand. But no answer? A recorded voice spoke in Hebrew. "Jacov, listen to this. What is she saying?"

Jacov was still beaming, having craned his neck and leaned out the window to see others' marks. He often pointed to his own and learned that fellow believers always smiled and seemed to enjoy pointing heavenward. The day would come, Buck knew, when the sign of the cross on the forehead would have to say everything between tribulation saints. Even pointing up would draw the attention of enemy forces.

The problem was, the day would also come when the other side would have its own mark, and it would be visible to all. In fact, according to the Bible, those who did not bear this "mark of the beast" would not be able to buy or sell. The great network of saints would then have to develop its own underground market to stay alive.

Jacov put the phone to his ear, then handed it back to Buck. "If you want to leave a message, press one."

Buck did. "Chloe," he said, "call me as soon as you get this. The crowd out here hasn't thinned a bit, so I don't want to have to come and find you and Tsion. But I will if I don't hear from you in ten minutes."

As soon as he ended the call, his phone chirped. "Thank God," he said and flipped it open. "Yeah, babe."

Heavy static and mechanical noise. Then he heard, "Jerusalem Tower, this is GC Chopper One!"

"Hello?"

"Roger, tower, do you read?"

"Hello, this isn't the tower," Buck said. "Am I getting a cross frequency?"

"Roger, tower, this is a confidential transmission, so I'm using the phone rather than the radio, roger?"

"Mac, is that you?"

"Roger, tower."

"You in the chopper with the other three?"

"Ten-four. Checking coordinates to return to pad at King David, over."

"You trying to tell me something?"

"Affirmative. Thank you. No head winds?"

"Is it about Tsion?"

"Partly cloudy?"

"And Chloe?"

"Ten-four."

"Are they in danger, Mac?"

"Affirmative."

"Have they been taken?"

"Not at this time, tower. ETA five minutes."

"They're on the run?"

"Affirmative."

"What can I do?"

"We'll come in from the northwest, tower."

"Are they outside the stadium?"

"Negative."

"I'll find them in the northwest corner?"

"Affirmative, that's a go. Assistance, tower. Appreciate your assistance."

"Am I in danger too?"

"Ten-four."

"I should send someone else?"

"Affirmative and thank you, tower. Heading that way immediately."

"Mac! I'm going to send someone they may not recognize, and I'm going to be waiting for him to bring them out the northwest exit. Am I all right with that?"

"As soon as we can, tower. Over and out."

"Jacov, run in and find Tsion and Chloe and get them out of the stadium through the northwest exit."

Jacov reached for the door handle. "Up or down?" he said. "There is an exit at ground level and one below."

"Bring them out from below, and stop for no one. Do you have a weapon?"

Jacov reached under the seat and pulled out an Uzi. He stuffed it in his waistband and covered it with his shirt. Buck considered it obvious, but in the darkness and with the press of the crowd, maybe it would go undetected. "Someone must have assigned GC guards to grab Tsion. They don't have him yet, but it won't be long. Get them out of there."

Jacov ran into the stadium, and Buck slid behind the wheel. The crowd was finally, slowly, starting to move. It was as if people didn't want to leave. Clearly they hoped for a glimpse of Tsion. Buck didn't understand their conversations, but the occasional English phrase told him most were discussing the humiliation of Carpathia.

As Buck maneuvered the van carefully through the crowd he heard a chopper. He feared it brought more GC guards. He was surprised that the helicopter looked just like the one that had borne Carpathia. He grabbed his phone and hit the last-caller callback button.

"McCullum."

"Mac! It's Buck. What are you doing back here?"

"Ten-four, Security. We'll check out the southeast quadrant."

"I sent a man to the northwest corner!"

"Affirmative, affirmative! *I'll* check southeast, but then I'm taking my cargo to base, over."

"Might they be southeast now?"

"Negative! *I'll* cover southeast!"

"But what can you do if they're there?"

"Roger, I can create the diversion, Security, but then we're gone, copy?"

"I'm confused but trusting you, Mac."

"Just keep your people out of southeast, Security. I'll handle."

Buck tossed the phone onto the seat and tilted his outside mirror to watch the chopper. Leon Fortunato announced over the helicopter's loudspeakers, "We have been asked by Global Community ground security forces at the stadium to help clear this area! Please translate this message to others if at all possible! We appreciate your cooperation!"

The mass of people did not obey. As word spread that Carpathia's own helicopter hovered over one corner of the stadium trying to clear the area, hundreds started that way, staring into the sky. That cleared a path for Buck, who drove quickly to the northwest corner. As people streamed out, they were drawn to the helicopter and immediately began moving that way to check out the commotion.

Buck pulled near the stadium. He ignored waving armed guards, opened his door, and stepped up on the floorboard to locate the underground exit. He found the dimly lit ramp where trucks had delivered equipment the day before. On tiptoes he saw a shaft of light appear as a door burst open and someone sprinted up the ramp.

Guards moved in for a closer look as Buck realized it was Jacov. What was he running from? Why was he ignored? Was the GC watching for Tsion? As Jacov passed the guards, he appeared to spot the van. Less than fifty feet away, he looked straight at Buck. He pulled the Uzi from under his shirt and sprayed bullets into the sky as he turned left.

The guards gave chase, guns drawn, and hundreds in the area screamed and dived for cover. Buck instinctively lowered his body, now watching over the top of the van. A couple hundred feet away, Jacov turned and fired more bullets into the air. The guards returned fire, and Jacov ran off again.

Buck had not heard the van doors open, but he heard them shut and Chloe and Tsion scream, "Go, Buck! Drive! Go, now!"

He dropped into the seat and slammed the door. "What about Jacov!"

"Go, Buck!" Chloe hollered. "He's creating a diversion!"

Buck laughed as he floored the accelerator and bounced over a curb. "So is Mac!" he said. "What a team! Where do we pick up Jacov?"

Tsion lay on the floor of the backseat, panting. Chloe lay across the seat itself. "He said he would meet us at Chaim's," Tsion managed.

"They were shooting at him!"

"He said he would not draw their fire until he was out of range. He was sure he'd be all right."

"Nothing is out of their range," Buck said, putting distance between them and the stadium. Most traffic, emergency and otherwise, headed toward instead of away from Kollek Stadium now. Roadblocks kept many civilian cars at bay as GC vehicles tried to get through. Buck was virtually ignored going the other direction.

"If they're after you, Tsion, we don't dare go back to Chaim's."

"I cannot think of a safer place," Tsion said. "Carpathia will not threaten me there. Your wife was brilliant. She figured it out before it happened. She saw the guards coming for me, but she didn't like their looks."

"They were pressing their earpieces hard against their ears," Chloe said, "while releasing the safety locks on their weapons. I figured Carpathia or Fortunato told them to get revenge on Tsion and do it in the middle of a crowd so it would look like an accident. They got so close that I heard one tell the supreme commander where we were."

"I'm still worried about Jacov," Buck said.

"He was resourceful," Chloe said. "He jogged through the tunnel near us, saying, 'I'm looking for familiar faces to follow me quickly to safety.' We stepped out from a utility room and—"

"I immediately saw the mark on his forehead," Tsion said. "Praise the Lord! You must tell us later what happened."

Chloe continued, "He said you were bringing the van to the underground exit. He peeked out and saw the guards at the top of the ramp, then said he would create a diversion and we should follow twenty seconds later. He backed up and ran, bursting through that door!"

"It worked," Buck said, "because he even distracted me. I didn't see you get in the van."

"Nobody saw us," Chloe said. "Oh!"

"What?"

"Nothing," she said, hissing.

"What, Chlo'? Are you all right?"

"Just not used to running," she said.

"Nor am I," Tsion said. "And I would like to get off this floor as soon as it is safe, too."

+ + +

"You cannot keep her here," Leah told Dr. Charles. "It's impossible. I'm sorry. We could try to sneak her into a room, and I know it would be better for her, but if you think you'll ever need this facility or my help again, you'd better get her out of here now."

"Give me another sedative then," Floyd said. "I want her out before we go."

Hattie slept all the way to the safe house, and Dr. Charles put her to bed near the TV, where they were quickly brought up to date on the activity in Jerusalem. "His Excellency the potentate, Nicolae Carpathia, will address the world in twenty minutes," the announcer said. "As most of you saw on live television in the Eastern Hemisphere and many saw on an Internet hookup that covered the rest of the globe, an attempt to poison His Excellency was foiled. The potentate is healthy, though shaken, and wishes to assure global citizens he is all right. We expect his remarks may also cover what sort of retribution he might exact from the perpetrators of the attempt on his life."

\+ \+ \+

The journalist in Buck wished he was still at the stadium. He would have loved to have seen how long Mac kept Carpathia, Fortunato, and the clownish Mathews in the air while giving Tsion a chance to escape. He wished he could see for himself the water and blood on the stage and ask eyewitnesses if anyone saw the two from the Wailing Wall come or go.

He had learned not to baby Chloe; she was as brave and strong as he was. But she was also carrying their child, and she had been through a horrible physical ordeal that had left her wounded. This trauma couldn't have been good for her.

Buck was relieved to see Israeli rather than GC guards at Chaim's gates. Admittedly, it was this same force that had been behind the massacre of Tsion's family and the chasing of him from his homeland. But now he was here as Chaim's guest, and Chaim was just short of deity in Israel.

As soon as they were inside, a pale, trembling Chaim greeted them with embraces and demanded to know where Jacov was. Buck left the explaining to Tsion, knowing Chaim would need assurances that his protégé had not planned the disgracing of Carpathia. "You assured me you would remain neutral," Chaim said. "Otherwise I would not have urged him to attend."

"You knew he was coming and did not tell me?" Tsion said.

"He wanted an element of surprise. Surely you must have expected him."

"I had hoped he would wait until tomorrow or the next night. You should have prepared me."

"You appeared more than prepared."

Tsion sat wearily. "Chaim, the man interrupted the quoting of Scripture. It was as if he had planned his entrance for the worst possible instant. I am going to hold you to your promise to hear me out, and very soon. I am not up to it this evening, but as a brilliant and reasonable man, you will not be able to refute the evidence I have for Jesus as Messiah and Carpathia himself as Antichrist."

Rosenzweig settled into a large, soft chair and sighed heavily. "Tsion, you are as a son to me. But what you just said could get you killed."

"How well I know!"

"Of course, and I am still grieved and heartbroken over your losses. But to come to Israel to proclaim the deity of Jesus is as foolhardy as those troublemakers at the Wall playing tricks with our water and our weather. And, Tsion, calling Nicolae the Antichrist when he is visiting the Holy City is the height of arrogance and insensitivity. I have told you before, I would sooner believe Carpathia was the Messiah and one of those two so-called witnesses the Antichrist."

Tsion sat shaking his head wearily, and Buck took the occasion to beg off for the evening. "If you'll excuse us . . ."

"Of course," Chaim said.

"I would like to know when Jacov arrives, no matter when," Buck said.

"Thank you for your concern," the older man said. "We will get word to you."

+ + +

Rayford kept one eye on the television while trying to reach someone in Israel. Neither Buck's nor Chloe's phone was answered, and he couldn't raise Mac either. Forgetting himself for a moment, he swore under his breath. Hattie roused. "That's the Rayford Steele I once knew," she said, her voice airy and weak.

"Ah, I'm sorry, Hattie. That's not like me. I'm worried about what's happened over there, and I want to be sure everybody's all right."

"It's nice to know you're still human," she whispered. "But you never were and you never will be as human as I am."

"What does that mean?"

"I'm going to kill Nicolae."

"I'm sorry about your baby, Hattie, but you don't know what you're saying."

"Rayford, would you lean closer?"

"I'm sorry?"

"Don't be afraid of me. I'm not going to be around much longer anyway."

"Don't say that."

"I just don't have the energy to talk louder, so would you lean closer?"

Rayford felt conspicuous, though it was only the two of them in the room. He pursed his lips, looked around, and turned his ear to her. "Go ahead," he said.

"Rayford, I was not with that man long enough for him to have affected me this much. I know I was no better or worse than the next girl. You knew that as well as anybody."

"Well, I—"

"Just let me finish, because Floyd obviously drugged me and I'm about to fall asleep. I'm telling you, Nicolae Carpathia is evil personified."

"Tell me something I don't know."

"Oh, I know you people think he's the Antichrist. Well, I *know* he is. I don't think he has an ounce of truth in him. Everything that comes out of his mouth is a lie. You saw him acting like he was a friend of Mathews? He wants him dead. He told me that himself. I told you he poisoned Bruce. He sent people to murder me *after* I was poisoned, just to make sure. The poison had to have killed my baby. Anyway, I hold him responsible. He made me do things I should never have done. And you know what—while I was doing them, I enjoyed it. I loved his power, his appeal, his ability to persuade. When I was making Amanda look like a plant, I actually believed I was doing the right thing. And that was the least of it.

"I want to die, Rayford. And I don't want to be forgiven or go to heaven to be with God or any of that stuff. But I will fight this poison, I will work with Floyd, I will do whatever I have to do to stay alive long enough to kill that man. I have to get healthy, and I have to somehow get to where he is. I'll probably die in the process with all the security he's got. I don't care. As long as I get to be the one who does it."

Rayford put a hand on her shoulder. "Hattie, you need to relax. Doc Charles did give you more anesthetic before we brought you home, so you may not even remember what you're saying here. Now, please, just—"

Hattie wrenched away from Rayford's hand, and her frail fingers grabbed his shirt. She fiercely pulled him closer and rasped in his face, spittle landing on his cheek. "I'll remember every word, Rayford, and don't think I won't. I will do this thing if it's the last thing I do, and I hope it will be."

"All right, Hattie. All right. I won't argue with you about it now."

"Don't argue with me about it ever, Rayford. You'll be wasting your time."

Carpathia would soon be on the screen, and Hattie was quickly dozing again. Rayford was glad she would be spared his image and whatever he would say about his debacle in Israel. Something cold ran through Rayford's soul. She had forced him to face himself.

Rayford was relieved beyond description to find out that Amanda was all he believed her to be: a loving, trustworthy, loyal wife. But since discovering what Carpathia had done to Bruce, to Amanda, to Hattie, he was again battling with his own desires. He had once prayed for the permission, the honor, of being the one assigned to assassinate Carpathia at the halfway point of the Tribulation. Now, truth be told, he found himself angling to be in position at that time.

He knew he had to talk sense to Hattie, to keep her from doing something so reckless and stupid. But that was also why he would not confide in Mac or Tsion or his daughter and son-in-law, why he would not say a word to his new friend, Ken, or to Floyd, about his own murderous leanings. They would, of course, want to show him the folly of his ways. But he wanted to entertain the thoughts longer.

+ + +

Only when Buck was alone with Chloe in the privacy of one of Chaim Rosenzweig's guest rooms did he realize how worried he had been about her. Trembling, he gathered her in his arms and held her close, careful not to hug her too tight because of her injuries. "When I didn't know where you were," he began, "all I could think of was how I felt after the earthquake."

"But I wasn't lost this time, darling," she said. "You knew where I was."

"You didn't answer your phone. I didn't know if someone had grabbed you, or—"

"I turned it off when we were being chased. I didn't want it to give us away. That reminds me, I never turned it back on."

She started to pull away. "Don't worry about it now," he said. "It doesn't have to be on now, does it?"

"What if Daddy tries to call? You know he had to be watching."

"He can reach me on my phone."

"Where is it?"

"Agh! I left it in the van. I'll go get it."

Now it was her turn to not let him go. "I'll just turn mine on," she said. "I don't want to be apart from you again right now either."

Their mouths met, and he held her. They sat on the edge of the bed and lay back, her head resting in the crook of his arm. Buck imagined how silly they looked, staring at the ceiling, feet flat on the floor. If she was as tired as he, it wouldn't be long before she nodded off. This probably wasn't the time to bring up a delicate subject, but Buck had never been known for his timing.

+ + +

As had become the custom, Global Community Supreme Commander Leon Fortunato introduced His Excellency, Potentate Nicolae Carpathia, to the international television audience. Rayford was stunned at how straightforward and overt Leon was in telling his own story. Tsion had warned Rayford that Nicolae's supernatural abilities would soon be trumpeted and even exaggerated, laying a foundation for when he would declare himself God during the second half of the Tribulation. So far the widespread pronouncements had been circumspect, and Nicolae himself had personally made no such claims. But on this day, Rayford had to wonder how Nicolae would respond to Fortunato's obsequious opening. And he also had to concede that the pair had done a masterful, if not supernatural, job of choreographing the ultimate spin on Nicolae's most public embarrassment.

6

"I'M WORRIED ABOUT YOU," Buck said.

"I'll be all right," Chloe said. "I'm glad I came, and I'm doing better than I thought I would. I knew it was a little early for me to take such a trip, but it's worked out."

"That's not what I'm worried about."

She pulled away from him and rolled onto her side to look at him. "What then?"

There was a knock at the door. "Excuse me," Tsion said. "But did you want to watch the Carpathia response on television?"

Chloe started to get up, but Buck stopped her. "Thanks, Tsion. Maybe in a little while. If we miss it, you can recap it for us in the morning."

"Very well. Good night, loved ones."

"Buck Williams," Chloe said. "I don't know when I've felt so special. You've never missed a breaking news story in your life."

"Don't make me out to be too altruistic, hon. I have no magazine to write for anymore, remember?"

"You do too. You have your own."

"Yeah, but I'm the boss and I sign the checks. There's no money for any checks, so what am I going to do—fire myself?"

"Anyway, you chose me over the latest news."

Buck rolled toward her and kissed her again. "I know what he's going to say anyway. He'll have Fortunato on first to sing his praises, then he'll act all humble and self-conscious and attack Tsion for embarrassing him after all he's done for the rabbi."

Chloe nodded. "So what's on your mind?"

"The baby."

She raised her brows at him. "You too?"

He nodded. "What're you thinking?"

"That we weren't too smart," she said. "Our baby will never reach five, and we'll be raising him, or her, while we're trying to just stay alive."

"Worse than that," he said. "If we were trying just to survive, we might hole up somewhere safe. The baby might be relatively secure for a while. But we've already declared ourselves. We're enemies of the world order, and we're not going to just sit by and protest in our minds."

"I'll have to be careful, of course," she said.

"Yeah," he said, snorting. "Like you have been so far."

She lay there silently. Finally she said, "Maybe I'll have to be more careful, hmm?"

"Maybe. I just wonder if we're doing right by the little one."

"It's not like we can change our minds now anyway, Buck. So what's the point?"

"I'm just worried. And there's nobody else I can tell."

"I wouldn't want you telling anyone else."

"So tell me not to worry, or tell me you're worrying with me, or something. Otherwise I'm going to get all parental on you and start treating you like you don't have a brain."

"You've been pretty good about not doing that, Buck. I've noticed."

"Yeah, but sometimes I ought to do more of it. Somebody's got to look out for you. I like when you keep track of *me* a little. I don't feel demeaned by it. I need it and appreciate it."

"To a point," she said.

"Granted."

"And I'm also quite good at it."

"And subtle," he said, draping his arm over her.

"Buck," she said, "we really should watch Carpathia, don't you think?"

He shrugged, then nodded. "If we're going to have any chance of thwarting anything he does."

They padded out to where Tsion and Chaim sat watching TV. "No word on Jacov yet?" Buck asked.

Chaim shook his head. "And I am none too pleased."

"I merely asked him to go in and get them," Buck said. "Playing decoy and drawing the gunfire was his idea. I wasn't happy about it either."

"The *what?!*" Chaim demanded.

+ + +

Rayford was strangely buoyed, despite Hattie's threats against Carpathia. In his mind that showed a level of sanity that, according to Dr. Charles, she had not had in weeks. He didn't consider himself a lunatic, despite his own admittedly unrealistic wishes to be God's hit man. What he longed for, down deep, was that Hattie get healthy enough to change her mind about God. She knew the truth; that wasn't the issue. She was the epitome of a person who could know the truth without acting on it. That was what Bruce Barnes had told Rayford was his own reason for having been left behind. As for Rayford, he had missed the point—despite his first wife's efforts to explain it—that nothing he did for himself could earn God's favor. As for Bruce, he knew all that. He knew salvation was by grace through faith. He simply never made the transaction, thinking he could slide by until later. Later came sooner, and he was left without his family.

Ken appeared at the top of the basement stairs. "Doc and me was wonderin' if you wanted to watch down here," he said. "He thinks maybe Hattie'll rest better that way."

"Sure," Rayford said, rising quickly. He tried dialing Chloe and Buck one more time without success and left the phone on his chair.

As he left the room, Hattie called out to him. "Would you leave that on, Rayford?"

"Don't you want to sleep?"

"Just leave it on low. It won't bother me."

\+ + +

"My people are calling around looking for Jacov," Chaim whispered as Leon Fortunato's benign smile graced the screen. "If anything happened to him, I don't know—"

"I believe no harm can come to him, Chaim. He has become a believer in the Messiah and even has the mark of a sealed tribulation saint on his forehead, visible to other believers."

"You're saying you can see it and I cannot?"

"That's what I'm saying."

"Poppycock. How arrogant."

"Can you see our marks?" Chloe asked.

"Pish-posh, you have no marks," Chaim said.

"We see each other's," Tsion said. "I see Buck's and Chloe's plain as day."

Chaim waved them off bemusedly, as if they were putting him on. And Fortunato was introduced.

"I'd better try to call Daddy before Carpathia comes on," Chloe said. She hurried to the bedroom and came back with her phone. She showed it to Buck. The readout showed Rayford had called since they were in the bedroom. She dialed his number.

* * *

Rayford thought he heard his phone ring upstairs but decided he was mistaken when it did not ring again. Looking around the basement, he wondered how a big, lanky man like Ken Ritz could live in a tiny, dark, dank spot like this. Ritz was slowly expanding it in his spare time, pointing toward the day when the entire Tribulation Force might have to live down there. Rayford didn't want to even think about that.

Was it Rayford's imagination, or was Fortunato looking more dapper? He had not noticed while watching him at the stadium. But that was on a jerry-built setup from his laptop that wasn't as clear as this live, satellite transmission directly to Ken's TV. Television usually didn't flatter a stocky, middle-aged man, but Fortunato appeared trimmer, more bright eyed, healthier, and better dressed than usual.

"Ladies and gentlemen of the Global Community," he began, looking directly into the camera as if the lens was his audience's eyes (as Carpathia had long modeled), "even the best of families has its squabbles. Since His Excellency, Potentate Carpathia, was reluctantly swept to power more than two years ago, he has made tremendous strides in making the entire earth one village.

"Through global disarmament, vast policy changes in the former United Nations and now the Global Community, he has made our world a better place to live. After the devastating vanishings, he brought about peace and harmony. The only blips on the screen of progress were the result of things outside his control. War resulted in plagues and death, but His Excellency quickly broke the back of the resistance. Atmospheric disasters have befallen us, from earthquakes to floods and tidal waves and even meteor showers. This was all due, we believe, to energy surpluses from whatever caused the vanishings.

"There remain pockets of resistance to progress and change, and one of the more significant movements in that direction revealed its true nature earlier this evening before the eyes of the world. His Excellency has the power and the obvious right to retaliate with extreme measures to this affront to his authority and the dignity of his office. In the spirit of the new society he has built, however, His Excellency has an alternative response he wishes to share with you this evening.

"Before he does that, however, I would like to share a personal story. This is not secondhand or hearsay, not a legend or an allegory. This happened to me personally, and I assert the veracity of every detail. I share it because it bears on the very issue the potentate will address, spirituality and the supernatural."

Fortunato told the world the story of his resurrection at the command of Carpathia, a story Rayford had heard too many times. Fortunato concluded,

"And now, without further ado, your potentate and, to me may I say, my deity, His Excellency, Nicolae Carpathia."

+ + +

Chloe had been talking quietly on the phone during Fortunato's bouquet to Carpathia. While Leon uncharacteristically stumbled while both making way for Carpathia and bowing deeply to him, Chloe hung up.

"Hattie lost her baby," she said sadly.

"You reached your dad?"

"Hattie answered. She sounded fairly lucid, all things considered."

Chloe suddenly laughed, making Buck jerk to see the TV. Fortunato tried to back out of Carpathia's presence while bowing and tripped over a light cord. Out of camera range he had apparently tumbled and rolled heavily, distracting even the usually unflappable Carpathia and causing him to temporarily lose contact with the lens.

Carpathia quickly recovered and grinned magnanimously and condescendingly. "Fellow citizens," he began, "I am certain that if you did not see what happened earlier this evening at Teddy Kollek Stadium in Jerusalem, you have by now heard about it. Let me briefly tell you my view of what occurred and outline my decision of what to do about it.

"Let me go back to when I first reluctantly accepted my role as secretary-general of the United Nations. This was not a position I sought. My goal has always been to merely serve in whatever role I find myself. As a member of the lower parliament in my home country of Romania, I served many years for my constituents, championing their view—and mine—for peace and disarmament. My rise to the presidency of my motherland was as shocking to me as it was to the watching world, only slightly less so than my elevation to secretary-general—which has resulted in the world government we enjoy today.

"One of the hallmarks of my administration is tolerance. We can only truly be a global community by accepting diversity and making it the law of the land. It has been the clear wish of most of us that we break down walls and bring people together. Thus there is now one economy highlighted by one currency, no need for passports, one government, eventually one language, one system of measurement, and one religion.

"That religion carries the beautiful mystery of being able to forge itself from what in centuries past seemed intrinsically contradictory belief systems. Religions that saw themselves as the only true way to spirituality now accept and tolerate other religions that see themselves the same way. It is an enigma that has proven to somehow work, as each belief system can be true for its adherents. Your way may be the only way for you, and my way the only way for me. Under the unity of the aptly named Enigma Babylon One World Faith, all the religions of the world have proved themselves able to live harmoniously.

"All, that is, save one. You know the one. It is the sect that claims roots in historic Christianity. It holds that the vanishings of two and a half years ago were God's doing. Indeed, they say, Jesus blew a trumpet and took all his favorite people to heaven, leaving the rest of us lost sinners to suffer here on earth.

"I do not believe that accurately reflects the truth of Christianity as it was taught for centuries. My exposure to that wonderful, peace-loving religion told of a God of love and of a man who was a teacher of morals. His example was to be followed in order for a person to one day reach eternal heaven by continually improving oneself.

"Following the disappearances that caused such great chaos in our world, some looked to obscure and clearly allegorical, symbolic, figurative passages from the Christian Bible and concocted a scenario that included this spiriting away of the true church. Many Christian leaders, now members of Enigma Babylon, say this was never taught before the disappearances, and if it was, few serious scholars accepted it. Many others, who held other views of how God might end life on earth for his followers, disappeared themselves.

"From a small band of fundamentalists, who believe they were somehow stranded here because they were not good enough to go the first time, has sprung up a cult of some substance. Made up mostly of former Jews who now have decided that Jesus is the Messiah they have been looking for all their lives, they follow a converted rabbi named Tsion Ben-Judah. Dr. Ben-Judah, you may recall, was once a respected scholar who so blasphemed his own religion on an international television broadcast that he had to flee his home country.

"I come to you tonight from the very studio where Dr. Ben-Judah desecrated his own heritage. While in exile, he has managed to brainwash thousands of like-minded megalomaniacs so desperate for something to belong to that they have become his marionette church. Using a feel-good psychological approach to morality, Dr. Ben-Judah has used the Internet for his own gain, no doubt fleecing his flock for millions. In the process he has invented an us-against-them war in which you, my brothers and sisters, are 'them.' The 'us' in this charade call themselves true believers, saints, sealed ones—you name it.

"For months I have ignored these harmless holdouts to world harmony, these rebels to the cause of a unified faith. While advisers urged me to force their hand, I believed tolerance was in order. Though Dr. Ben-Judah continually challenged all we stand for and hold dear, I maintained a policy of live and let live. When he invited tens of thousands of his converts to meet in the very city that had exiled him, I decided to rise above personal affronts and allow it.

"In a spirit of acceptance and diplomacy, I even publicly assured Dr. Ben-Judah's safety. Though I was well aware that the Global Community and I as its head were the avowed enemies of this cult, I believed the only right and proper thing to do was to encourage its mass meeting. I confess it was my hope that in so doing these zealots would see that there was value in compromise and tolerance and that they would one day choose to align themselves with Enigma Babylon. But it would have had to have been their choice. I would not have forced their hand.

"And how was my magnanimity rewarded? Was I invited to the festivities? Asked to welcome the delegates? Allowed to bring a greeting or take part in any of the pageantry?

"No. Through private diplomatic channels I was able to secure the promise that Dr. Ben-Judah would not restrict my presence or prohibit my attendance. I traveled to Israel at my own expense, not even burdening Global Community finances, and dropped in to say a few words at what has been called the Meeting of the Witnesses.

"My supreme commander was met with the rudeness of utter silence, though he comported himself with élan regardless. The most revered Supreme Pontiff Peter the Second, the pope of popes as it were, was received in no less a quietly hostile manner, despite being a fellow clergyman. No doubt you agree this had to have been a well-planned and executed mass response.

"When I myself addressed the crowd, though they were still obeying their mind-controlling leader and not responding, I sensed they wanted to. I had the clear feeling, and a public speaker develops antennae for these things, that the crowd was with me, was sympathetic, was embarrassed by their leader and wanted to welcome me as warmly as I was welcoming them.

"Though Dr. Ben-Judah was ostensibly ignoring me from just a few feet away, he somehow signaled someone to release some sort of agent in the air, an invisible dust or powder that instantly parched my throat and resulted in a powerful thirst.

"I should have been suspicious when I was immediately presented with a bottle from someone in the crowd. But as a trusting person, used to being treated as I treat others, I naturally assumed an unknown friend had come to my aid.

"What a disappointment to have been callously ambushed by a bottle of poisonous blood! It was such an obvious public assassination attempt that I called Dr. Ben-Judah on it right there. As a pacifist not skilled in warfare, I had played right into his hands. He had hidden in the crowd the two elderly lunatics from the Wailing Wall who have so offended the Jews in the Holy Land and have actually murdered several people who have attempted to engage them in debate. With hidden microphones turned louder than the one I was using, they shouted me down with threats and turned my humble act of diplomacy into a fiasco.

"I was whisked away for medical attention, only to find that had I swallowed what they gave me, I would have died instantly. Needless to say, this is an act of high treason, punishable by death. Now, let me say this. My wish is that we still come together in a spirit of peace and harmony. Let it be said that these words from the Scriptures came first in this context from me: 'Come now, and let us reason together.'

"There is no doubt in my mind that the whole of this ugly incident was engineered and carried out by Dr. Ben-Judah. But as a man of my word and lacking any physical evidence that would tie him to the assassination attempt, I plan to allow the meetings to continue for the next two nights. I will maintain my pledge of security and protection.

"Dr. Ben-Judah, however, shall be exiled again from Israel within twenty-four hours of the end of the meeting the night after tomorrow. Israeli authorities are insisting on this, and I would urge Dr. Ben-Judah to comply, if for no other reason than his own safety.

"As for the two who call themselves Eli and Moishe, let this serve as public notification to them as well. For the next forty-eight hours, they shall be restricted to the area near the Wailing Wall, where they have posted themselves for so long. They are not to leave that area for any purpose at any time. When the meetings in the stadium have concluded, Eli and Moishe must leave the Temple Mount area. If they are seen anywhere outside their area of quarantine in the next forty-eight hours or in the Temple Mount area after that time, I have ordered that they be shot on sight.

"Some eyewitnesses have testified that the murders they have committed might somehow be convoluted into some sort of self-defense. I reject this and am exercising my authority as potentate to deny them trial. Let me be clear: Their appearance anywhere but near the Wailing Wall for forty-eight hours or their showing their faces in public anywhere in the world after that shall be considered reason to kill. Any Global Community officer or private citizen is authorized to shoot to kill.

"I know you will agree that this is a most generous response to an ugly attack and that allowing the meetings to continue proves a spirit of accommodation. Thank you, my friends, and good night from Israel."

+ + +

Rayford looked up as Ken Ritz rocked back and slapped his thighs. "I don't know about you boys," Ritz said, "but I got me some tinkerin' to do. For one thing, I gotta find out how we can get us some of those millions the rabbi's been fleecin' off the flock. With none of us having any income anymore, we're going to need some cash."

"You got a minute, Ray?" Floyd said, rising.

"Sure, Doc."

They climbed the stairs, and Floyd bent over the sleeping Hattie for a moment. "Seems fine for now," he said. "But can you imagine postpartum blues on top of what she's already going through?"

"You get that even with a miscarriage?"

"It makes more sense with a miscarriage if you think about it."

Rayford turned off the TV and followed Floyd to the porch. They both carefully surveyed the horizon and listened before talking. Rayford had grown used to that since he'd arrived. At Global Community headquarters it was a matter of knowing whom you could talk to. Out here knowing you were not being spied on was paramount.

"I've got a problem, Rayford, but I hardly know you."

"Friendships, acquaintances, everything has to necessarily be telescoped these days," Rayford said. "You and I could live together the rest of our natural lives, and it would be less than five years. If you've got something on your chest, you might as well shoot. You want to criticize me, fire away. I can take it. My priorities are different than they used to be, needless to say."

"Aw, no, it's nothing like that. In fact, I figure you've got cause to scold me a bit after today."

"For snapping at me in the heat of battle? Hey, I've done my share of that. In medical emergency situations, you're in charge. You bark at whomever you have to bark at."

"Yeah, but even though I know Tsion is sort of our pastor, you're the chief. I need you to know that I know that and respect it."

"There's no time for hierarchy anymore, Doc. Now what's on your mind?"

"I've got a Hattie problem."

"We all do, Floyd. She was an attractive, bright girl once. Well, maybe more attractive than bright, but you're seeing the worst of her just now, and I think she's coming around. You might appreciate her more in a few weeks."

"Just so you know, I got the drift that she and you used to work together and that, while you never actually had an affair—"

"Yeah, OK. Not proud of it, but I acknowledge it."

"Anyway, this isn't about her being in a bad way and being so difficult. I'm moved by how you all seem to care so much for her and want her to become a believer."

Rayford sighed. "This business of her believing but not wanting to accept has me buffaloed. She's even halfway logical about it. She's not one who has to be convinced she's unworthy, is she?"

"She's so convinced she refuses to accept what she knows is free."

"So, what's your problem, Doc? You think she's a lost cause spiritually?"

Floyd shook his head. "I wish it was that easy. My problem makes zero sense. You said yourself there's nothing attractive about this girl. It's obvious that when she was healthy she was a knockout. But the poison has done its work, and the illness has taken its toll. She makes no sense when she talks, and spiritually she's bankrupt."

"So you want to throw her out, and that makes you feel guilty?"

Floyd stood and turned his back to Rayford. "No, sir. What I want is to love her. I *do* love her. I want to hold her and kiss her and tell her." His voice grew quavery. "I care so much for her that I've convinced myself I can love her back to health in every way. Physically and spiritually." He turned and faced Rayford. "Didn't expect that one, did you?"

\+ \+ \+

As Buck and Chloe lay in bed, Buck said, "Will you be able to sleep if I go out for a while?"

She sat up. "Out? It's hardly safe."

"Carpathia is too focused on Eli and Moishe to worry about us right now. I want to see if I can find Jacov. And I want to see what the witnesses will do in response to Nicolae's threats."

"You know what they'll do," she said, lying back down. "They'll do what they want until the due time, and woe to the one who tries to make points with the potentate by trying to kill them before that."

"Just the same, I'd like—"

"Do me this favor, Buck. Promise you won't leave this place until I'm sound asleep. Then I'll worry only when I have to, if you're not here when I wake up in the morning."

Buck dressed and went looking to see if Tsion was still up. He wasn't, but Rosenzweig was on the phone. "Leon, I insist on talking with Nicolae. . . . Yes, I know all about your cursed titles, and I remind you that I knew Nicolae as a friend before he was His Excellency and the potentate of this and that. Now please, put him on the phone. . . . Well, then *you* tell me what has happened to my driver!"

Rosenzweig noticed Buck, motioned for him to sit, and hit the speaker button on the phone. Leon was in mid-threat. "Our intelligence sources tell us your man turned."

"Turned what? He's not Jewish anymore? Not Israeli? Doesn't work for me? What are you talking about? He's been with me for years. If you know where he is, tell me and I will come get him."

"Dr. Rosenzweig, all due respect, sir, I'm telling you your man is one of them. We wanted GC guards to personally escort Rabbi Ben-Judah back to Jacov's vehicle, but he came running from the stadium firing off a high-powered weapon. Who can say how many guards and innocent civilians were killed."

"I can. None. It would have been all over the news. I heard the same story. Your people were coming after Ben-Judah to exact revenge for the embarrassment to Nicolae and might have done who-knows-what to him if he had not slipped away on his own."

"He wasn't on his own. He was with Buck Williams's wife, who has proven to be an American subversive who escaped from one of our facilities in Minnesota, where she had been detained for questioning." Rosenzweig glanced at Buck, who sat shaking his head slowly as if wondering where they dreamed up this stuff. Fortunato continued, "She was suspected of looting after the earthquake."

"Leon, is Jacov alive?" There was a pause. Rosenzweig grew irate. "I swear, Leon, if something has happened to that young man—"

"Nothing has happened to him, Doctor. I'm trying to train you to address me properly."

"Oh, for the sake of heaven, Leon, are there not more important things to worry about right now? Like people's lives!"

"Supreme Commander, Dr. Rosenzweig."

"Supreme Nincompoop!" Rosenzweig shouted. "I am going out to search for my Jacov, and if you have any information that would help me, you'd better give it to me now!"

"I don't need to be spoken to that way by you, sir."

And Leon hung up.

+ + +

Rayford put an arm on Floyd's shoulder as they went back into the house. "I'm no love counselor," he said, "but you're right when you say this one makes no sense. She's not a believer. You're old enough to know the difference between pity and love and between medical compassion and love. You hardly know her, and what you know is not that pretty. It doesn't take a scientist to see that this is something other than what you think it is. You lonely? Lose a wife in the Rapture?"

"Uh-huh."

"Better tell me about her."

7

BUCK PEEKED IN on Chloe before heading out with Chaim. She appeared sound asleep.

"Do you mind driving?" Chaim asked. "It has been so long since I was allowed."

"Allowed?"

Chaim smiled wearily. "Once you become, how shall I say it, a personality in this country, especially in this city, you are treated like royalty. I cannot go anywhere unescorted. I was not even famous when first you did the cover story on me."

"You were revered, however."

Chaim checked with his gateman, Jonas, for the latest word on Jacov. "Stefan?" Buck heard him say. Then something urgent and frustrated in Hebrew.

Chaim directed Buck to the last stall in the garage, and Buck slid behind the wheel of an ancient sedan. "I don't want everyone to know I am coming. The Mercedes is well known. You drive a stick shift, do you not?"

Buck feathered the throttle and quickly caught on to the vagaries of the manual transmission. He worried more about the bald state of the tires. "Any idea where we're going?"

"Yes, I am afraid I do," Chaim said. "Jacov is an alcoholic."

Buck shot him a double take. "You have an alcoholic as your driver?"

"He's dry. Recovering they call it. But in times of crisis, he reverts."

"Falls off the wagon?"

"I do not know that expression."

"It's an old Americanism. Early in the twentieth century the Women's Christian Temperance Union would roll the Temperance Wagon into town, decrying the evils of alcohol and calling on offenders to give it up and get on the wagon. When a sober man went back to drinking, it was called falling off the wagon."

"Well, I'm afraid that is what has happened here," Chaim said, pointing where Buck was to turn. As they moved into smaller neighborhoods with houses and buildings closer together, Buck began noticing things he hadn't seen on the drive from Chaim's to the stadium. Jerusalem had grown seedy. How he had loved to visit this city just a few years before! It had had its rundown areas, but overall it had been kept with pride. Since the disappearances, certain types of crime and lewd activity had sprung up that he never expected to see in public here. Drunks staggered along, some with their arms slung around ladies of the evening. As Buck drove farther into the city he saw strip clubs, tattoo parlors, fortune-telling shops, and triple-X-rated establishments.

"What has happened to your city?"

Chaim grunted and waved dismissively. "This is something about which I would love to speak to Nicolae. All that money spent on the new temple and moving the Dome of the Rock to New Babylon! *Ach!* This Peter the Second fellow wearing the funny costumes and welcoming the Orthodox Jew into the Enigma Babylon faith. I am not even a religious man, and I wonder at the folly of it. What is the point? The Jews have maintained for centuries that they worship the one true God, and this somehow now fits with a religion that accepts God as man and woman and animal and who knows what else? And you see what effect it has had on Jerusalem. Haifa and Tel Aviv are worse! The Orthodox are locked away in their gleaming new temple, slaughtering animals and going back to the literal sacrifices of centuries gone by. But what impact do they have on this society? None! Nicolae is supposed to be my friend. If he will see me, I will inform him of this, and things will change.

"When my Jacov—a wonderful, spirited man, by the way—falls off the wagon, as you put it, he winds up on the same street in the same bar and in the same condition."

"How often does this happen?"

"Not more than twice a year. I scold him, threaten him, have even fired him. But he knows I care for him. He and his wife, Hannelore, still grieve over two little ones they lost in the disappearances."

Buck was chagrined to realize he had pushed Jacov spiritually without getting to know him. He just hoped Chaim was wrong about Jacov and that they would not find him where the old man expected to.

Chaim pointed Buck to a parking place in the middle of a row of cars and vans that lined a crowded street. It was after midnight now, and Buck was suddenly overcome with fatigue. "The Harem?" he said, reading the neon sign. "You sure this is only a bar?"

"I'm sure it is not, Cameron," Rosenzweig said. "I don't want to think about what else goes on in there. I've never been inside. Usually I wait out here while my security chief goes in and drags Jacov out."

"That's why I'm here?"

"I would not ask you to do that. But you may need to help me with him because if he resists, I am no match for him. He will not hurt me, even when drunk, but a little old man cannot make a thick mule of a young man go anywhere he does not want to go."

Buck parked and sat thinking. "I'm hoping you're wrong, Dr. Rosenzweig. I'm hoping Jacov will not be here."

Chaim smiled. "You think because he became a believer he will not get drunk after being shot at? You are too naive for an international journalist, my friend. Your new faith has clouded your judgment."

"I hope not."

"Well, you see that green truck there, the old English Ford?" Buck nodded. "That belongs to Stefan of my valet staff. He lives between here and Teddy Kollek Stadium, and he is Jacov's drinking partner. Stefan does not suffer as Jacov does. He can hold his liquor, as we like to say. He was off work today, but if I was a man of wagers, I would bet Jacov ran to him while escaping the Global Community guards. Naturally shaken and scared out of his wits, he no doubt allowed Stefan to take him to their favorite place. I cannot hold this against Jacov. But I want him safe. I don't want him making a spectacle of himself in public, especially if he is a fugitive from the GC."

"I don't want him to be here, Dr. Rosenzweig."

"I don't either, but I am not a young man with stars in his eyes. Wisdom is supposed to come with age, Cameron. I wish less came with it, frankly. I have gained wisdom I cannot now recall. I have what I call 'mature moments,' where I recall in detail something that happened sixty years ago but cannot remember that I told the same story half an hour before."

"I'm not even thirty-three yet, and I have my share of those."

Chaim smiled. "And your name again was?"

"Let's go look for Jacov," Buck said. "I say he's not in there, even if Stefan is."

"I hope Jacov is," Chaim said, "because if he is not, that means he is lost or caught or worse."

+ + +

Dr. Floyd Charles's story was so similar to Rayford's it was eerie. He too had had a wife serious about her faith, while he, a respected professional, played at the edges of it. "Fairly regular church attendee?" Rayford asked from experience. "Just didn't want to get as deep into it as your wife?"

"Exactly," Floyd said. "She was always telling me my good works wouldn't get me into heaven, and that if Jesus came back before I died, I'd be left behind." He shook his head. "I listened without hearing, you know what I mean?"

"You're telling my story, brother. You lose kids too?"

"Not in the Rapture. My wife miscarried one, and we lost a five-year-old girl in a bus accident her first day of school." Floyd fell silent.

"I'm sorry," Rayford said.

"It was awful," Floyd said with a thick voice. "Gigi and I both saw her off at the corner that morning, and LaDonna was happy as she could be. We thought she would be shy or scared—in fact, we kinda hoped she would be. But she couldn't wait to start school with her new outfit, lunch box, and all. Gigi and I were basket cases, nervous for her, scared. I said putting her on that big old impersonal bus made me feel like I was sending her off to face the lions. Gigi said we just had to trust God to take care of her. Half an hour later we got the call."

Rayford shook his head.

"Made me bitter," Floyd said. "Drove me farther from God. Gigi suffered, sobbed her heart out till it almost killed me. But she didn't lose her faith. Prayed for LaDonna, asked God to take care of her, to tell her things, all that. Real strain on our marriage. We separated for a while—my choice, not hers. I just couldn't stand to see her in such pain and yet still playing the church game. She said it wasn't a game and that if I ever wanted to see LaDonna again, I'd 'get right with Jesus.' Well, I got right with Jesus all right. I told him what I thought of what he let happen to my baby girl. I was miserable for a long time."

They sat at the kitchen table, where Rayford could hear Hattie's steady, rhythmic breathing. "You know what convinced me?" Floyd said suddenly.

Rayford snorted. "Besides the Rapture, you mean? That got my attention."

"I was actually convinced before then. I just never pulled the trigger, know what I mean?"

Rayford nodded. "You knew your wife was right, but you didn't tell God?"

"Exactly. But what convinced me was Gigi. She never stopped loving me, through it all. I was a rascal, man. Mean, nasty, selfish, rude, demeaning. She knew I was grieving, suffering. The light had gone out of my life. I loved LaDonna so much it was as if my heart had been ripped out. But when I was trying to cover the pain by working all hours and being impossible to my coworkers and everyone else, Gigi knew just when to call or send a note. Every time, Rayford, every stinkin' time, she would remind me that she loved me, cared about me, wanted me back, and was ready to do whatever I needed to make my life easier."

"Wow."

"Wow is right. She was hurting just as bad as I was, but she would invite me for dinner, bring me meals, do my laundry—and she was working too—clean my apartment." He chuckled. "Humiliated me is what she did."

"She won you back?"

"She sure did. Even lifted me out of my grief. It took a few years, but I became a happier, more productive person. I knew it was God in her life that allowed her to do that. But I still thought that if there was anything to this heaven and hell business, God would have to look kindly on me because I was helping people every day. I even had the right motive. Oh, I loved the attention, but I helped everybody. I did my best work whether the patient was a derelict or a millionaire. Made no difference to me. Somebody needed medical attention, they got my best."

"Good for you."

"Yeah, good for me. But you and I both know what it got me when Jesus came back. Left behind."

Floyd checked on Hattie. Rayford got them Cokes from the refrigerator. "I don't want to bad-mouth an old friend," Rayford said, "but I suggest you think about the kind of woman your wife was before you consider Hattie as a replacement."

Floyd pursed his lips and nodded.

"I'm not saying Hattie couldn't become that kind of person," Rayford added.

"I know. But there's no evidence she wants to be."

"Know what I'm gonna do?" Rayford said, rising. "I'm gonna call my daughter and tell her I love her."

Floyd looked at his watch. "You know what time it is where she is?"

"I don't care. And she won't either."

+ + +

Buck and Chaim got stares from both men and women as they approached The Harem. The place was much bigger inside than it looked from outside. Several rooms, each packed with people shoulder to shoulder—some dancing, some kissing passionately—led to the main bar where women danced and people ate and drank.

"Ach!" Rosenzweig said. "Just as I thought."

As they made their way in, Buck looked carefully for Jacov and averted his eyes every time he was met with a "what are you looking at" glare. Not all the couples were made up of both sexes. This was not the Israel he remembered. The smoke was so thick that Buck knew he'd have done less damage to his lungs if he himself was smoking.

Buck did not realize Chaim had stopped in front of him, and he bumped into the old man. "Oh, Stefan!" Rosenzweig chided, and Buck turned in time to see a young man with a sloshing drink in his hand. His dark hair was wet and matted, and he laughed hysterically. Buck prayed he was alone. "Is Jacov with you?" Rosenzweig demanded.

Stefan, in midcackle, could barely catch his breath. He bent over in a coughing jag and spilled some of his drink on Rosenzweig's trousers.

"Stefan! Where's Jacov?"

"Well, he's not with me!" Stefan shouted, straightening up and laughing more. "But he's here all right!"

Buck's heart sank. He knew Jacov had been sincere in his conversion, and God had proved it with the seal on his forehead. How could Jacov desecrate his own salvation this way? Had his brush with the GC been more gruesome than Buck could imagine?

"Where?" Rosenzweig pressed, clearly disgusted.

"In there!" Stefan pointed with his drink, laughing and coughing all the while. "He's up on a table having the time of his life! Now let me through so I don't have an accident right here!" He lurched off, laughing so hard tears ran down his face.

Chaim, appearing overcome, strained to see into the main room, from which music blared and strobe lights flashed. "Oh, no!" he moaned, backing into Buck. "He's totally drunk. This shy, young man who hardly looks you in the eye when he greets you is carrying on in front of everyone! I can't take this. I'll bring the car up. Could you just get him down off that table and drag him out? You're bigger and stronger than he is. Please."

Buck didn't know what to say. He'd never been a bouncer, and while he had once enjoyed the nightlife himself, he had never liked loud bars, especially ones like this. He jostled past Chaim as the old man hurried out. Buck shouldered his way through several clusters of revelers until he came to dozens whose attention was on the crazy young Israeli holding forth atop a table. It was Jacov all right.

+ + +

Rayford hurried to the basement and found Ken with Donny Moore's telescope in his lap and his microscope on the desk. Ken was reading Donny's technical journals. "Kid was a genius, Ray. I'm learning a ton that's gonna help us. If you can get this stuff to your other pilot and your inside techie over there, they can have us up to speed when their cover is blown and we're all just tryin' to stay alive. What can I do you for?"

"I want to go with you Friday to Israel."

"You barely escaped. Didn't your friend Mac say you were as good as dead if you had stayed?"

"It's not like me to run. I can't hide from Carpathia for the rest of my life anyway, short as it may be."

"What the heck's got into you, Ray?"

"Just talked with Chloe. I smell trouble. No way Nicolae is going to let them out of Israel alive. We have to go get them."

"I'm game. How do we do it?"

\+ + +

Buck quit excusing himself; he was being cursed anyway. Finally, he was close enough to hear Jacov, but he was railing in Hebrew and Buck understood none of it. Well, almost none. Jacov was shouting and gesturing and trying to keep people's attention. They laughed at him and seemed to curse him, whistling and throwing cigarette butts at him. Two women splashed him with their drinks.

His face was flushed and he looked high, but he was not drinking, at least then. Buck recognized the word *Yeshua,* Hebrew for Jesus. And *Hamashiach,* the word for Messiah.

"What's he saying?" he asked a man nearby. The drunk looked at him as if he were from another planet. "English?" Buck pressed.

"Kill the English!" the man said. "And the Americans too!"

Buck turned to others. "English?" he asked. "Anyone know English?"

"I do," a barmaid said. She carried several empties on a tray. "Make it quick."

"What's he saying?"

She looked up at Jacov. "Him? Same thing he's been saying all night. 'Jesus is the Messiah. I know. He saved me.' All that nonsense. What can I tell you? The boss would have thrown him out long ago, but he's entertaining."

Jacov was little more than entertaining. His motive might have been pure, but he was having zero impact. Buck moved close and grabbed his ankle. Jacov looked down. "Buck! My friend and brother! This man will tell you! He was there! He saw the water turned to blood and back again! Buck, come up here!"

"Let's go, Jacov!" Buck said, shaking his head. "I'm not coming up there! No one is listening! Come on! Rosenzweig is waiting!"

Jacov looked amazed. "He is here? Here? Have him come in!"

"He was in. Now let's go."

Jacov climbed down and eagerly followed Buck out, accepting cheers and slaps on the back from the merrymakers. They were near the front door when Jacov spotted Stefan heading the other way. "Wait! There's my friend! I must tell him I'm leaving!"

"He'll figure it out," Buck said, steering him out the door.

In the car Rosenzweig glared at Jacov. "I was not drinking, Doctor," he said. "Not one drop!"

"Oh, Jacov," Rosenzweig said as Buck pulled away from the curb. "The smell is all over you. And I saw you atop the table."

"You can smell my breath!" he said, leaning forward.

"I don't want to smell your breath!"

"No! Come on! I'll prove it!" Jacov breathed heavily into Rosenzweig's face, and Chaim grimaced and turned away.

Rosenzweig looked at Buck. "He had garlic today, but I do not smell alcohol."

"Of course not!" Jacov said. "I was preaching! God gave me the boldness! I am one of the 144,000 witnesses, as Rabbi Ben-Judah says! I will be an evangelist for God!"

Chaim slumped in his seat and raised both hands. "Oy," he said. "I wish you *were* drunk."

+ + +

After hearing what had gone on behind the scenes in Israel, Ken agreed it was likely Carpathia would manufacture "some tragedy outside his control, somethin' he can blame on somebody else, but no matter how you slice it, people we care about are gonna die."

"I don't want to be foolhardy, Ken," Rayford said. "But I'm not going to hide here and just hope they get out."

"I been sky-jockeyin' that son-in-law of yours since the disappearances, and you'd have to go some to be more foolhardy than that boy. We're gonna hafta get in touch with your copilot over there though. I can teach you a lot about the Gulfstream, but nobody can put it down without a runway."

"Meaning?"

"You're gonna be looking at a quick pickup, right? Probably from this Rosen-whatever estate?"

"Yeah, I'm going to suggest to Tsion that he announce plans for Saturday, something Carpathia will believe he wouldn't want to miss. Then we get in there after midnight Friday and get them out of there."

"Unless they meet us somewhere near the airport, we're going to have to drop in and get 'em. And that means a chopper."

"Can't we rent one? I could ask David Hassid, our guy inside the GC, to have one waiting for us at Jerusalem or Ben Gurion."

"Fine, but we're gonna need two fliers. No way McCullum can get away to help us."

"What am I, chopped liver?"

Ken smacked himself in the head. "Listen to me," he said. "What an idiot! You're trained in a copter, then?"

"Mac brought me up to speed. I land near the complex and shuttle them to you at the airport, right?"

"You'd better get a layout of the place before we go. You're going to have precious little time as it is, puttin' one of them noisy jobs down in a residential area. Somebody sees you in their yard, the gendarmes'll be there before you can get airborne again."

+ + +

"Does your wife know where you've been?" Rosenzweig asked Jacov as Buck pulled in front of his apartment building.

"I called her. She wants to know what in the world I'm talking about."

"Why did you go to that awful place first?"

"I escaped to Stefan's house. He wanted to go. I thought, what better place to start preaching?"

"You're a fool," Rosenzweig said.

"Yes I am!"

Buck tossed Jacov his cell phone. "Call your wife so you don't scare her to death when you walk in."

But before Jacov could dial, the phone rang. "What's this?" he said. "I didn't do that."

"Push Send and say, 'Buck's phone.'"

It was Chloe. "She needs to talk with you right away, Mr. Williams."

Buck took the phone and told Jacov, "Wait here until we can warn your wife you're coming."

Chloe told Buck about the call from her father and his request for a schematic of Rosenzweig's estate. "I'll bring it up when it's appropriate," Buck whispered.

Later, when he finally drove through the gates at Chaim's place, the time didn't seem right to raise the issue of the schematic. Rosenzweig was still a Carpathia sympathizer and would not understand. He might even spill the beans. Buck remained in the car as Rosenzweig got out.

"You're not coming in?"

"May I borrow your car for a while?"

"Take the Mercedes."

"This will be fine," Buck said. "If Chloe is still up, tell her she can call me."

"Where are you going?"

"I'd rather not say. If you don't know, you don't have to lie if anyone asks."

"This is entirely too much skullduggery for me, Cameron. Be safe and hurry back, would you? You and your friends have another big day tomorrow. Or I should say today."

Buck drove straight to the Wailing Wall. As he expected, after the squabbling between the two witnesses and Carpathia and the threats Nicolae made on international television, huge crowds pressed near the fence where Eli and Moishe held court. The GC was well represented, armed guards ringing the crowd.

Buck parked far from the Temple Mount and moseyed up like a curious tourist. Moishe and Eli stood back-to-back with Eli facing the crowd. Buck had never seen them in that position and wondered if Moishe was somehow on the lookout. Eli was speaking in his forceful, piercing voice, but at that moment he was competing with the head of the GC guard unit and his bullhorn. The guard was making his announcement in several languages—first in Hebrew, then in Spanish, then in an Asian tongue Buck couldn't place. Finally, he spoke a broken English with a Hebrew accent, and Buck realized the GC guard was an Israeli.

"Attention, ladies and gentlemen! I have been asked by the Global Community supreme commander to remind citizens of the proclamation from His Excellency, Potentate Nicolae Carpathia—" here the crowd erupted into cheering and applause—"that the two men you see before you are under house arrest. They are confined to this area until the end of the Meeting of the Witnesses Friday night. If they leave this area before that, any GC personnel or private citizen is within his rights to detain them by force, to wound them, or to exterminate them. Further, if they are seen anywhere, repeat anywhere, after that time, they shall be put to death."

The crowd near the fence cheered wildly again, laughed, taunted, pointed fingers, and spat toward the witnesses. But still the crowd hung back at least thirty feet, having heard of, if not seen, those whom the witnesses had killed. While many claimed the two capriciously murdered people who got too close, Buck himself had seen a mercenary soldier charge at them with a high-powered rifle. He was incinerated by fire from the witnesses' mouths. Another man who had leaped toward them with a knife had seemed to hit an invisible wall and fell dead.

The witnesses, of course, seemed unaffected by the proclamation or the guard with the bullhorn. They remained motionless and back-to-back, but there was a vast difference between how they now appeared and how they had looked when Buck first saw them. Because of the incredible interest drawn to them by the meetings televised from Kollek Stadium and their being mentioned by both Leon Fortunato and Carpathia himself, the news media had converged upon this place.

Gigantic klieg lights illuminated the area, a glaring spotlight bathing the witnesses. But neither squinted nor turned from the glare. The extra light only served to emphasize their unique features: strong, angular faces, deep-set dark eyes in craggy sockets under bushy brows.

No one ever saw them come or go; none knew where they were from. They had appeared strange and weird from the beginning, wearing their burlap-like sackcloth robes and appearing barefoot. They were muscular and yet bony, with leathery skin; dark, lined faces; and long, scraggly hair and beards. Some said they were Moses and Elijah reincarnate, but if Buck had to guess, he would have said they were the two Old Testament characters themselves. They looked and smelled centuries old, a smoky, dusty aroma following them.

Their eyes were afire, their voices supernaturally strong and audible for a mile without amplification.

An Israeli shouted a question in Hebrew, and the GC guard translated it into all the languages. "He wants to know if he would be punished for killing these men now, where they stand." The crowd cheered anew as each people group understood what he said. Finally, the GC guard answered.

"If someone was to kill them this very night, he would be punished only if an eyewitness testified against him. I don't know that there are any eyewitnesses here at all."

The crowd laughed and agreed, including the other guards. Buck recoiled. The GC had just given permission for anyone to murder the witnesses without fear of reprisal! Buck was tempted to warn anyone so foolish that he had personally seen what happened to previous would-be assassins, but Eli beat him to it.

Barely moving his lips but speaking so loudly he seemed to be shouting at the top of his lungs, Eli addressed the crowd. "Come nigh and question not this warning from the Lord of hosts. He who would dare come against the appointed servants of the Most High God, yea the lampstands of the one who sits high above the heavens, the same shall surely die!"

The crowd and the guards stumbled back at the force of his voice. But they soon inched forward again, taunting. Eli erupted again. "Tempt not the chosen ones, for to come against the voices crying in the wilderness is to appoint one's own carcass to burn before the eyes of other jackals. God himself will consume your flesh, and it will drip from your own bones before your breath has expired!"

A wild, cackling man brandished a bulky high-powered rifle. Buck held his breath as the man waved it above the crowd, and the rest screamed warnings at him. The weapon had a sight on the stock that identified it as a sniper's rifle with kill power from a thousand yards. *Why,* Buck wondered, *would a man with such a weapon risk showing it within reach of the witnesses and their proven power to destroy?*

The GC guard stepped between the man and the wrought-iron fence, behind which the witnesses stood. He spoke to the man in Hebrew, but it was clear he did not understand. "English!" the man screamed, but he did not sound American. Buck couldn't make out his accent. "If you do this thing," the guard started over in English, "as a service to the Global Community, you must take full responsibility for the consequences."

"You said there were no eyewitnesses!"

"Sir, the whole world is watching on television and the Internet."

"Then I'll be a hero! Out of my way!"

The guard did not move until the man leveled the weapon at him. Then the guard skipped into the darkness, and the man stood alone, facing the fence. And nothing else. The witnesses were gone.

"Threaten to burn my flesh, will you?" the man raged. "Face this firepower first, you cowards!"

The GC guard came back on the bullhorn, speaking urgently. "We shall search the area behind the fence! If the two are not there, they are in violation of the direct order of the potentate himself and may be shot at will by anyone without fear of indictment!"

8

THOUGH IT WAS now the wee hours of Thursday morning on the Temple Mount, the atmosphere was festive. Hundreds milled about, chattering about the gall of two old men to defy Carpathia and make themselves vulnerable to attack by anyone in the world. They were fair game, and within minutes they would surely be dead.

Buck knew better, of course. He had sat under the teaching of Bruce Barnes and then Tsion Ben-Judah, and he knew what the witnesses meant by "the due time." Bible prophecy called for the witnesses to be given the power by God to prophesy one thousand, two hundred and threescore days, clothed in sackcloth. Both Bruce and Tsion held that those days were counted from the time of the signing of an agreement between Antichrist and Israel for seven years of peace—which also coincided with the seven-year tribulation. Such an agreement had been signed only a little more than two years before, and 1,260 days divided by 365 equaled three and a half years. Buck calculated that the due time was more than a year away.

Suddenly, from high on the hillside called the Mount of Olives came the loud preaching of the two in unison. The crowds began to run that way, murder in their throats. Despite the confusion and noise and armed guards engaging their weapons while on the run, the witnesses spoke with such volume that every word was clear.

"Harken unto us, servants of the Lord God Almighty, maker of heaven and earth! Lo, we are the two olive trees, the two candlesticks standing before the God of the earth. If any man will hurt us, fire proceedeth out of our mouths and devoureth our enemies. If any man dare attempt to hurt us, he must in that manner be killed! Hear and be warned!

"We have been granted the power to shut heaven, that it rain not in the days of our prophecy. Yea, we have power over waters to turn them to blood and to smite the earth with all plagues, as often as we will.

"And what is our prophecy, O ye generation of snakes and vipers who have made the holy city of Messiah's death and resurrection likened unto Egypt and

Sodom? That Jesus of Bethlehem, the son of the Virgin Mary, was in the beginning with God, and he was God, and he is God. Yea, he fulfilled all the prophecies of the coming Messiah, and he shall reign and rule now and forevermore, world without end, amen!"

The rabid cries of angry Israelis and tourists filled the air. Buck followed, his own panting filling his ears. No media lights had reached the witnesses, and nothing illuminated them from the sky, yet they shone bright as day in the dark grove of olive trees. It was an awesome, fearful sight, and Buck wanted to fall to his knees and worship the God who was true to his word.

As the crowd reached the base of the sloping hill and slipped in the dewy grass, Buck caught up. "It is ours to bring rain," the witnesses shouted, and a freezing gush of water poured from the skies and drenched the crowd, including Buck. The place had not seen a drop in twenty-four months, and the people craned their necks, pointed their faces to the sky, and opened their mouths. But the rain had stopped the instant it began, as if Eli and Moishe had opened and shut a tap in one motion.

"And it is ours to shut heaven for the days of our prophecy!"

The crowd was stunned, complaining and murmuring, grumbling threats anew. As they started again toward the illumined pair on the hillside, now less than a hundred yards away, the prophets stopped them with their voices alone.

"Stand and hear us, O ye wicked ones of Israel! You who would blaspheme the name of the Lord God your maker by sacrificing animals in the temple you claim to have erected in his honor! Know ye not that Jesus the Messiah was the lamb that was slain to take away the sins of the world? Your sacrifices of animal blood are a stench in the nostrils of your God! Turn from your wicked ways, O sinners! Face yourselves for the corpses you already are! Advance not against the chosen ones whose time has not yet been accomplished!"

But sure enough, as Buck watched in horror, two GC guards rushed past him and past the crowd, weapons raised. Slipping and sliding on the moist hillside, their uniforms became muddy and grass stained. They crawled combat style up the hill, illuminated by the light radiating from the witnesses.

"Woe unto you who would close your ears to the warnings of the chosen ones!" the witnesses shouted. "Flee to the caves to save yourselves! Your mission is doomed! Your bodies shall be consumed! Your souls shall be beyond redemption!"

But the guards pressed on. Buck squinted, anticipating the awfulness of it. The crowd chanted and raised fists at the witnesses, urging the guards to open fire. Gunshots resounded, echoing, deafening, the exploding cartridges producing yellow and orange bursts from the barrels of the weapons.

The witnesses stood side by side, gazing impassively at their attackers, who lay on their bellies a hundred feet down the slope. The crowd fell silent, as did the rifles, everyone staring, wondering how the guards could have missed from such close range. The guards rolled onto their sides, ejecting shell magazines and replacing them with loud clicks. They opened fire again, filling the valley with violent explosions.

The witnesses had not moved. Buck's eyes were locked on them as blinding white light burst from their mouths, and they appeared to expectorate a stream of phosphorous vapor directly at the guards. The attackers had no time to even recoil as they ignited. Their weapons remained supported by the bones of their arms and hands as their flesh was vaporized, and their rib cages and pelvises made ghastly silhouettes against the grass.

Within seconds the white heat turned their rifles to dripping, sizzling liquid and their bones to ash. The would-be assassins smoldered in piles next to each other as the crowd fled in panic, screaming, cursing, crying, nearly knocking Buck over as they pushed past. His emotions conflicted, as always, when he saw humans die. The witnesses had declared that when the attackers died, their souls would be lost. It wasn't as if they hadn't been warned.

Horrified at the loss of life and the eternal damnation the guards had gambled against and lost, Buck felt his knees weaken. He couldn't take his eyes off the witnesses. The brightness of their killing fire still burned in his eyes, and it was as if the light that had shone from them was now gone. In the darkness, blinking against the spots and streaks that remained, he made out that they were slowly descending the mount. Why, he wondered, did they not just appear wherever they wanted to go, as they had seemed to transfigure themselves into the stadium the night before and from the Temple Mount to the Mount of Olives just now? They were beyond figuring, and as they neared him, he held his breath.

He knew them. He had talked to them. They seemed to know the people of God. Should he say anything? And what does one say? Good to see you again? What's up? Nice job on those guards?

When he was close to them before, he had the wrought-iron fence between them. Of course, nothing could protect anyone from beings like this who carried the firepower of God himself. Buck fell to his knees as they passed within ten feet of him, and he looked up as he heard them murmuring.

Moishe said, "The Lord of hosts hath sworn, saying, Surely as I have thought, so shall it come to pass; and as I have purposed, so shall it stand."

At the words of God, Buck dropped face first into the grass and wept. God's very thoughts would come to pass, and his purposes would stand. No one could come against the anointed ones of God until God decided it was time. The witnesses would carry on their ministry during the great and terrible day of the Lord, and no pronouncement or sentence or house arrest by anyone would get in the way of that.

If only Chaim Rosenzweig could have seen this, Buck thought as he made his way back to the parking lot at the Temple Mount.

Finally back at Chaim's complex, Buck was waved in by Jonas, the gateman, who also unlocked the door for him, since no one else was awake. Buck peeked in on Chloe, grateful to find her still asleep. Then he walked out onto the veranda off their room and let his eyes grow accustomed to the dark again.

He was on the side of the main house opposite the driveway where Jonas now served as night watchman. He had seen him stroll the property every half hour or so before. Buck waited until Jonas came by again, then checked out the possibilities just past the railing of the patio.

Up one side was a metal drainpipe, old but still intact and solid. On the other side was a wire, embedded into the stucco with wire brads. The wire, he assumed, was either for telephone or television. Regardless, it would not support him. The drainpipe, however, had protruding seams every few feet that made it a natural for climbing. If, that is, a man was fearless.

Buck had never put himself in that category, but he was reluctant to arouse Rosenzweig's suspicions by asking for house plans, and he was certain he had never seen a passageway to the roof. He had to know whether a chopper could set down there, and this was the only way he knew to find out.

Buck rubbed his hands until they felt sufficiently dry. He tied his canvas shoes tighter and hitched up his pants. Standing on the edge of the railing, he hoisted himself up and began shinnying up the drainpipe. When he was ten feet above the veranda and passing a small, mottled glass window on the third floor, he made the mistake of looking down. He still had ten feet to go to reach the roof, but even if he fell from where he was, the railing was likely to cut him in two.

He was not in trouble, but a wave of panic showed up on the doorstep of his mind. There was no wiggle room here, no leeway, no margin for error. A slip, a weak section, a fright that knocked him off balance would leave him no options. He would drop and could only hope to land close enough to the middle of the patio to keep from flopping over the rail. If he hit the ground, he was dead. If he hit the patio, he was probably dead.

So, now what to do? Proceed and finish the mission, or quickly move back to safety? He decided he would be just as safe up ten feet, so he kept going. Three feet from the roof he felt precarious, but also knew the only danger he could be in now would be of his own making. If he got wobbly, scared, panicky, or looked down, he would freeze because he had made himself look. As he lifted his left leg over the lip at the flat roofline, he gained a mental picture of himself, a human fly, by his own design hanging from the edge of the roof of a three-story building.

I'm an idiot, he decided, but he felt much better with the roof solidly beneath him. It was a bright, starry night now, crisp and calm. He detected utility boxes, fans, exhausts, ductwork, and vents here and there. What Rayford, or whoever, would need, he decided, was a fairly large, unencumbered area in which to set down a chopper.

Buck tiptoed across the roof, knowing that footsteps from above are often magnified below, and found pay dirt on the other side. In fact, to his surprise, he discovered an ancient helipad. The markings were faded, but whatever this building had been before it was bequeathed to the national hero, it had required a landing area for a helicopter. He assumed Rosenzweig knew that and could have easily saved him this adventure.

He also deduced that if someone once used the helipad, there had to be easy access to and from it within the house. Buck looked and felt around the area until he found a heavy, metal door. It was rusted and bent, but it was not locked. He could only imagine how the creaking and groaning of metal would sound inside if he was not careful in forcing it open.

Buck played with it for several minutes, getting it to budge just a fraction each time. When he felt he had sufficiently prepared it for a wider push, he set his shoulder against it and wrapped his fingers around the edge to keep it from moving too far too fast. With a grunt and one driving step, he made the door move about eight inches. It made a noise, but not much of one. He assumed no one had heard it. If guards came running or if he roused someone inside, well, he'd just quickly identify himself and explain what he was up to.

Buck tried to slither through the opening, but he needed another couple of inches. These he accomplished by nudging the door a quarter inch or so at a time. When he finally got through, he found himself at the top of a wood staircase, musty and dusty and cobwebbed. It was also creaky, as he learned with his first step on the top landing. He felt for a light switch in the pitch-dark, not hoping for much. Finding nothing, he gingerly felt for the edge of the top step with a tentative foot. He was startled when something brushed his forehead. He nearly fell back on the stairs but held himself by pressing against the hoary wood walls. He had to fight to keep his balance, the backs of his legs pressing against the steps.

Feeling around in the dark, he grabbed a single, swaying bulb with a twist switch in its housing. Was it possible it still worked? How fortunate could a man be in one night? He turned the switch, and the light sprang to life. Buck quickly shut his eyes against the intrusion and heard the telltale pop of the filament breaking. He should have expected nothing less from a bulb that probably hadn't been used in years.

He opened his eyes to a halo of yellow residue from the brief flash. Blinking, he tried to reproduce behind his eyelids the image that had to have been temporarily projected and burned there. He kept his eyes shut until his brain drew a rudimentary block picture of three more steps down to a large door.

Buck didn't know what else to do but trust his split-second vision. He felt his way down the stairs and found he had been correct. Another landing presented itself, and he felt the door. This one was wood—big, heavy, solid. He found the knob, and it turned freely. But the door did not budge. And he could tell it was not stuck. It felt locked, dead-bolted. His fingers found the lock above the handle. There would be no opening this door without a key. He would have to get back into his room the way he had come.

Buck was encouraged, however, as he retraced his steps. Somehow he would find that door from inside the house and broach with Chaim the subject of a key.

When he reached the drainpipe, he was forced to look down before swinging out over the ledge and heading back. That was a mistake. Now he would have to talk himself into and through this. And how long had he been gone? He decided to wait through one more guard walk-around to be sure. He soon realized he must have just missed one because nearly half an hour later Jonas shuffled by and out of sight again.

Buck gripped the top of the pipe with both hands, swung his lead leg over the side until he felt the lip of the first seam, and climbed straight down. He was about to reach the top of the patio railing outside his and Chloe's room when he was certain he saw something below in his peripheral vision. If he had to guess, he thought he saw the curtain move.

Was Chloe awake? Had she heard him? Could she see him? He didn't want to scare her. But what if this was GC? What if they had already infiltrated the place? It could also be Chaim's own security. Might they take action before he was able to identify himself?

Buck hung from the drainpipe, feeling like an idiot, his feet pigeon-toed on a seam. He should have just dropped lightly onto the patio and reentered the room. But he had to be sure no one was at the window. He let go with one hand and leaned down as far as he could. Nothing.

He spread his knees and tried to lower his head to get a sight line. Were the curtains open? He thought he had left through a shut drape. As he tried to peer farther, first one foot, then the other, slipped off the seam, and his fingers supported his full body weight. He could only hope no one was watching through the window because no one he knew—certainly not himself—could hang for long that way.

As Buck's fingers gave way, he dropped straight down, his nose inches from the glass door. When his feet hit the patio, he found himself staring into another pair of eyes, wide and terrified and set in a ghostly pale face.

Besides being startled at the image, Buck's weight made his knees bend as he landed, but he was so close to the door that they banged into it, driving him off his feet and straight back into the railing. The top caught him just above his backside and his weight carried him backward over the rail. He grabbed the wrought iron as he flopped, desperate to keep from hurtling all the way to the ground on his head.

With a loud grunt, Buck saw the sky as he flipped back, and his feet soon followed. He hung from the top of the rail by his hands, upside down, the back of his head pressed against the bars and his feet dangling near his face. It was all he could do to hang on, knowing his life was in his own hands.

Meanwhile, of course, Chloe was screaming.

Buck forced his feet back up until he was balanced, teetering painfully on his seat, the rail digging into his back. With a desperate pull, he forced his torso up until the weight of his legs brought him back onto the patio. "It's just me, babe," he said, as Chloe stared wide-eyed out the window.

He rubbed his back as she slid open the door. "What in the world?" she said over and over. "I nearly gave birth."

Buck tried to explain as he undressed, more ready for bed than he had been in a long time. A quick knock at the door was followed by, "Everything all right in there, ma'am? We heard a scream."

"Yes, thank you," she managed, then giggled. The guard went away muttering, "Newlyweds!" and Buck and Chloe laughed till they cried.

"Anyway," Buck said, stretching out on his tender back, "I found an old helipad, and—"

"I know all about that," Chloe said. "I asked Chaim about it when he finally got home."

"You did?"

"I did."

"But I don't want him to know we're planning anyth—"

"I know, super sleuth. I just asked him about the history of the place to see what I could learn. It used to be an embassy. Ergo, the—"

"Helipad."

"Right. He even showed me the door that leads to it. There's a key on a nail embedded in the doorjamb right next to it. I'll bet even you could unlock the door with it."

"I'm such a dork," he said.

"You're *my* dork. Scare me to death, why don't you. If I'd had a weapon, I'd have killed you. I thought about running out there and pushing you over."

"What kept you?"

"Something told me it had to be you. You didn't look too dangerous there you know, rear end aloft."

"You're bad. So you want to know where I went?"

"I figured you went to the Wall; that's why I didn't call."

"You know me too well."

"I knew you'd want to see what they made of Carpathia's threat. Big crowd?"

\+ + +

Rayford had trouble sleeping, a rarity for him. He kept looking at his watch, figuring what time it was in Israel, and trying to decide when to call Buck or Chloe. He knew they would likely try to tell him things had settled down and that they didn't sense the same danger he did. But he had worked more closely with Carpathia than Buck had. He knew the man too well. Besides, he wanted to talk to Tsion. Though the rabbi felt the confidence of God as his protection, one couldn't be too careful. Scripture was clear that for a time the sealed ones of God were invulnerable to harm from the actual judgments of God. But no one was clear on whether that protection extended past the 144,000 converted Jewish evangelists to Gentiles like Rayford and his family, who had become tribulation saints.

And though the 144,000, of whom Tsion was clearly one, were protected against the judgments, it seemed unlikely that none of them would die by other causes in the meantime. Rayford grew desperate to get them out of Israel, but come dawn in the Chicago area, he finally fell asleep. When he awoke late that morning, he knew his counterparts in the Holy Land would be well on their way to the evening's meeting, which he would have to watch via the Internet again.

\+ + +

Once again, Buck had slept several hours, and Chloe had let him. "You're on a different schedule than I am," she explained. "If you're going to be up all hours playing Spiderman, you need your rest. Seriously, Buck, I need you healthy. You've been going full speed for months, and someone has to look out for you."

"I'm trying to look out for *you,*" he said.

"Yeah, well, start by not prowling around my balcony in the middle of the night."

Chaim had negotiated with Fortunato that Jacov not be charged in connection with the incident the night before if Chaim agreed to not have him serve as Tsion's driver anymore. But Jacov put up such a fuss at the prospect of not getting to go that Dr. Rosenzweig finally agreed to follow only the letter of the agreement. Buck drove. Jacov rode along and brought a guest: Stefan.

When they arrived at the stadium early that afternoon, with the requisite GC escort this time leading them through the shortcuts Jacov had discovered, Jacov emerged from the van with such glee and anticipation etched on his face that Buck couldn't help but smile.

Chloe had agreed to stay at the compound, and Buck was worried. He had expected more debate from her, and now he wondered if she was suffering more than she let on. She had been shaken, of course, by the escape from the GC the night before, and he only hoped she realized that similar incidents couldn't be good for her or the unborn baby.

News reports all day carried the story that the two preachers at the Wailing Wall had callously disregarded the directive handed down by the potentate himself. Reports said that when Global Community forces tried to apprehend them and bring them to justice, the pair murdered two guards. Eyewitnesses on the Mount of Olives said the two concealed flamethrowers in their robes that they produced when the guards were within feet of them. The weapons had not been recovered, though the preachers had spent since just before dawn through the present time in their usual spots near the Wailing Wall.

Live shots from there showed huge crowds deriding them, taunting them, and yet keeping a healthier-than-usual distance. Buck asked Tsion, "Why doesn't Nicolae drop a bomb on them or attack them with missiles or something? What would happen, being that it's a year before the appointed time?"

"Even Nicolae knows the sacred nature of the Temple Mount," Tsion said as he disembarked from the van. He hurried inside to escape a rushing, cheering crowd. "I would love to greet them all," he said, "but I fear the mayhem." He found a place to sit. "Anyway," he concluded, "Carpathia would not sanction violence there, at least if it could be traced to him. His threat to kill them if they remain there after the end of tomorrow night's meeting is some sort of ruse. Frankly, I'm glad he's gone public with it. I expect the two to flout his authority by being right there right then."

Jacov and Stefan looked much different than they had in the wee hours. It appeared Rosenzweig was right that Stefan was better able to hold his liquor.

He seemed none the worse for wear and proved pleasant. They went off to find good seats, Jacov asking Buck to "pray for my wife, who will be watching on TV at home. She worries about me, thinking I have lost my mind. I told her, it's not what I've lost but what I've found!"

GC guards looked menacingly at anyone connected with the program, as if silently expressing that they were only doing what they were commanded. If they had it their way, was the implication, they would destroy the lot of those who opposed their potentate.

No fireworks were expected this second night. Surely Nicolae and his people knew better than to make another appearance. But because of the noise the previous night's controversies had engendered, the crowd was bigger than ever. The converts were back, but more curious skeptics were on hand too.

Again the evening began with a simple greeting, the hearty singing of a hymn, and the introduction of Tsion Ben-Judah. He was greeted with wave upon wave of cheers and applause, all of which he largely ignored, except to smile and raise his hands for silence. Buck again stood in the wings and watched and listened in awe to the man who had become a spiritual father to him—the rabbi who had come to Jesus through studying the prophecies of the Old Testament now led a flock of millions over the Internet. Here he stood, a smallish, plainspoken man with a Bible and a pile of meticulous notes. And he held the massive crowd in his palm.

"You have learned much today, I understand," Tsion began. "And tonight is a time for more instruction. I have warned you in advance of many judgments, from the seven seals to the seven trumpets and eventually to the seven vials that will finally usher in the glorious appearing of our Lord and Savior, Jesus Christ.

"I have traced the beginning of the seven-year tribulation period from the signing of the unholy alliance between the one-world system and the nation of Israel. By following the judgments that have befallen the world since then, I have calculated that we are waiting on a precipice. We have endured all seven Seal Judgments and the first three of the seven Trumpet Judgments. The middle, or fourth, Trumpet Judgment is next in God's timing.

"To prove to the wondering world and to the unconvinced that we can know whereof we speak, I will tell you now what to expect. When this occurs, let no man deny that he was warned and that this warning has been recorded in the Scriptures for centuries. God is not willing that any should perish but that all should come to repentance. That is the reason for this entire season of trial and travail. Though he waited as long as his mercy could endure and finally raptured his church, still he rains judgment after judgment down upon an unbelieving world. Why? Is he angry with us? Should he not be?

"But no! No! A thousand times no! In his love and mercy he has tried everything to get our attention. All of us remaining on the earth to this day were delinquent in responding to his loving call. Now, using every arrow in his quiver, as it were, he makes himself clearer than ever with each judgment. Is there doubt in anyone's mind that all of this is God's doing?

"Repent! Turn to him. Accept his gift before it is too late. The downside of the judgments that finally catch some people's attention is that thousands also die from them. Don't risk falling into that category. The likelihood is that three-fourths of us who were left behind at the Rapture will die—lost or redeemed—by the end of the Tribulation.

"I want to tell you tonight of the fourth Trumpet Judgment in the hope that it will not take that catastrophe to finally convince you. For it could just as easily kill you."

9

JUST AFTER NOON on Thursday in Chicago, Rayford and Ken joined Doc Charles and Hattie to watch the Meeting. The pilots had their flight plans out and doodled with charting their course to the Middle East. Assuming word got to Tsion, he would announce something official or ceremonious for Saturday, and that would trigger Rayford and Ken's attempt to get to Israel. They would plan to arrive around midnight Friday and pick up their passengers shortly thereafter.

Rayford's head jerked up as all four watchers heard Tsion say, "I plan to summarize all this in a small thank-you session to the local committee on Saturday at noon, when we meet near the Temple Mount."

"Bingo!" Rayford said. "Teach me the Gulfstream this afternoon, so I can share the load both ways."

"Long as you're confident of chopper duty. Got one lined up?"

"That part'll be easy. Hoo, boy, back in the battle!"

Hattie gave Rayford a long look. "You like this stuff?"

"Funny *you* would ask that," he said, "knowing how you feel about Carpathia."

"I expect to die going after him. You act like you can't lose."

"We've already won," Ritz said. "It's just a matter of going through the motions. The Bible's already told the story, and as Tsion says, 'We win.'"

Hattie shook her head and rolled onto her side, her back to them. "You're pretty glib for dealing with a man like Nicolae."

Ken caught Rayford's eye. "You realize when we have to leave, with the time change and all? Well, 'course you do. You been flyin' these routes a lot longer'n I have."

+ + +

Buck found it hard to believe all that had happened in the twenty-four hours since Tsion had last addressed the crowd. He missed Chloe but felt more settled and at peace than he had in a long time.

"The earth groans under the effects of our fallen condition," Tsion began. "We've all lost loved ones in the Rapture and in the ten judgments from heaven since then. The great wrath of the Lamb earthquake devastated the globe, save for this very country and nation. The first three Trumpet Judgments alone scorched a third of the earth's trees and grass, destroyed a third of the oceans' fish, sank a third of the world's ships, and poisoned a third of the earth's water—all as predicted in the Scriptures.

"We know the sequence of these events, but we don't know God's timing. He could pile many of these judgments into one day. All I can say with certainty is what comes next. As you see, these get progressively worse. The fourth Trumpet Judgment will affect the look of the skies and the temperature of the entire globe.

"Revelation 8:12 reads, 'Then the fourth angel sounded: And a third of the sun was struck, a third of the moon, and a third of the stars, so that a third of them were darkened. A third of the day did not shine, and likewise the night.'

"Regardless of whether it means one-third of each star or a third of all stars, the effect will be the same. Day or night, the skies will be one-third darker than they have ever been. Not only that, but I take from this passage that one-third more of the day will be dark. So the sun will shine only two-thirds the time it used to. And when it *is* shining, it will be only two-thirds its usual brightness.

"Prophecy indicates that more scorching and parching of the earth comes later, so it's likely the darkening and resultant cooling is temporary. But when it occurs, it will usher in—for however long—winterlike conditions in most of the world. Prepare, prepare, prepare! And when depressed friends and neighbors and loved ones despair due to the darkness and gloom, show them this was predicted. Tell them it is God's way of getting their attention."

Tsion summarized the teaching that had gone on during the day at various sites around the city and urged the audience to preach boldly "until the Glorious Appearing fewer than five years away. I believe the greatest time of harvest is now, before the second half of the Tribulation, which the Bible calls the Great Tribulation.

"One day the evil world system will require citizens to bear a mark in order for them to buy or sell. You may rest assured it will not be the mark we see on each other's foreheads!"

Tsion went on to outline practical suggestions for storing goods. "We must trust God," he concluded. "He expects us to be wise as serpents and gentle as doves. That wisdom includes being practical enough to prepare for a future that has been laid out for us in his Word.

"Tomorrow night I'm afraid I have a difficult message to bring. You may get a preview of it by reading Revelation 9."

As Tsion began wrapping up his teaching for the night, Buck's phone vibrated.

"It's Mac. Are you where you can talk?"

Buck turned away from the backstage wing and moved to a quiet area. "Shoot."

"Do you have an evacuation plan, you and your wife and Ben-Judah?"

"We're working on it."

"You'll need it. I'm telling you, boy, these guys are crazy. Carpathia spends half his day fuming about the two witnesses and the other half plotting to kill Mathews."

"Mathews bothers him more than Tsion does?"

"I wouldn't give a nickel for Peter Mathews's future. And Carpathia thinks he's got Tsion's number. Whatever that Saturday deal is, be careful. Nicolae's got his troops so fired up that they know they could take out Tsion and never suffer for it. Nicolae would paint it as a setup, dissension among the ranks of the believers or something, and he would still look like a hero."

"This connection is secure, right, Mac?"

"Of course."

"We'll be long gone before that rally."

"Good! Need anything? I'm in contact every day with David Hassid."

"Rayford's trying to get a chopper to get us from Jerusalem to one of the airports."

"You can't just sneak out and get a ride?"

"We trust hardly anyone, Mac."

"Good for you. I'm going to recommend David get you a chopper that looks like ours."

"White, with GC on it?"

"Nobody'll mess with you if they see that."

"Until we leave it on the runway and fly off in a Gulfstream."

"Ritz has a Gulf? I'm jealous."

"Come with us, Mac."

"You know I'd love to. But somebody has to be the ears here."

+ + +

"We're not going to be able to watch tomorrow night's meeting, are we?" Rayford said as Ken ran him through the paces of the Gulfstream over Palwaukee Airport.

"Sure we are. Hook your laptop to my satellite tracking system, and I can force it to lock onto the Internet feed. It'll be a little tricky, bouncin' around up there, but you'll at least be able to hear it."

Rayford completed a fourth consecutive smooth landing, and Ritz pronounced him ready. As they sat in a rebuilt hangar finalizing their route, the young mechanic approached. "Captain Steele," Ernie said. "I took a call while you were in the air. Was your phone off or something?"

"Yeah," Rayford said, turning it back on. "I didn't want to be distracted."

"I heard you had one of them wake-up features where it'll ring even when it's off."

"Yeah, but you can override that too."

"Cool. Anyways, a Miss Hattie Durham wants you to call her."

Rayford called her on the drive back to the safe house. "I wouldn't care if Floyd said you were fit to run a marathon, Hattie. You're not going with us, at least not on my plane."

"Your plane?" Ritz said, laughing from behind the wheel of the Rover.

"Or Ken's plane, I mean."

"It ain't mine either, Bro!" Ken said.

"Whoever's plane. Anyway, Hattie, there's no way Floyd would release you to travel. Let me talk to him."

"He doesn't even know I'm calling. I know what he'd say. That's why I haven't said anything to him. And don't you either, Rayford."

"Hattie, you're acting like a child. You think I'd let you go with us on a dangerous mission, sick as you've been? You know me better than that."

"I thought maybe you owed me."

"Hattie, this discussion is closed. You want a ride to the Middle East so you can kill Carpathia, find it elsewhere."

"Let me talk to Ken."

"He's not going to—"

"Just let me talk to him!"

Rayford handed the phone to a puzzled-looking, scowling Ritz. "Yeah, doll," he said. "No, sorry, that's just an expression we old flyboys use. . . . Well, sure, I'd like to be a doll too. . . . Oh, no ma'am. I can't see any way. Well, now, I hate to have you think less of me, but the truth is if I could be manipulated by the poutin' of a spoiled pretty little girl, I wouldn't be lookin' back on two divorces now, would I? . . . You can beg and cry for someone else, honey, 'cause I sure ain't gonna be responsible for you overseas not forty-eight hours after you miscarried. . . . Now I'm awful sorry for you, and, like everybody else in your life, I got sort of a soft spot for you. But that's the reason I'm not going to be party to any foolishness like this. . . . Well, I understand that. I'd like to kill him myself.

But I got a job to do, and it's dangerous enough as it is. I'm gettin' people outta there, not worryin' about killing anybody. At least this trip. How 'bout you get yourself healthy, and I'll see about running you over there for Nicolae target practice another time. . . . No, I'm not poking fun at you. You are being a little silly here though, don't you think?"

Ritz shook his head and flapped the phone shut as he handed it back to Rayford. "Little spitfire hung up on me. You gotta like her spunk, though. And she *is* a gorgeous thing, ain't she?"

Rayford shook his head. "Ritz, you've got to be on the feminists' top ten most wanted list. Man, what a throwback!"

Rayford nearly panicked when he didn't see Hattie in her bed as they walked in. "She in the bathroom?" he asked Floyd.

"I wish," the doctor said. "She's walking somewhere."

"Walking!"

"Calm down. She insisted on walking around and wouldn't let me help her. She's on the other side."

Rayford checked the empty, more damaged half of the duplex. Hattie walked slowly on the uneven floor of an unfurnished room, her arms folded. He just stared at her, not asking the obvious question. She answered it anyway.

"Just trying to build my strength."

"Not for this trip."

"I've resigned myself to that. But Ken promised to—"

"Ken was talking through his hat, and you know it. Now would you please do yourself and all of us a favor and follow Doc's orders."

"I know my body better. It's time I started building back up. He said himself I may be out of the woods with the poison, whatever it was. But that's only because my baby took the brunt of it. Nicolae has to pay for that."

Hattie was suddenly short of breath. "See?" Rayford said. "You're overdoing it." He helped her back to the other side of the house, but she refused to lie down.

"I'll just sit awhile," she said.

Floyd was visibly angry. "She's going to be a whole lot of fun to deal with while you guys are gone."

"Come with us," Ken said. "She looks like she's getting pretty self-sufficient to me."

"Not a chance. She may not know how sick she is, but I do."

"Let's hope we're not bringing you back any more wounded," Ken said.

Rayford nodded. "I've already seen enough casualties in this war to last me a lifetime."

* * *

Mac confirmed to Buck that the plot against both the witnesses and Tsion was set for Saturday noon near the Temple Mount. "They can't believe Tsion has played right into their hands. They're planning what will appear to be a terrorist bombing that should kill anyone within two hundred feet of the Wall."

"Tsion thought Carpathia wouldn't try anything at a site so sacred to the Jews."

"It would never be traced to him. They're already trying to pin it on Mathews. Funny thing is, Mathews wants the credit for it. He says the witnesses and Tsion are the greatest enemies to religion he has ever seen. He's livid. You're going to be gone, right?"

"By 1:00 a.m."

"Perfect. A replica chopper's been delivered, and as far as I know, everything's in place. And your host is none the wiser?"

"Rosenzweig's still holding out for Carpathia's being a misunderstood good guy. He'll be as surprised as anyone when we disappear in the middle of the night. He's usually one of the first to bed, so we're all going to make sure of that. We can't pack or do anything that might tip him off until we're sure he's asleep. If worse comes to worse, though, he'd keep quiet until we were long gone."

A strange wrinkle in the Friday night plan was that everyone, it seemed, wanted to go to the stadium. The threats against the witnesses, the public feud between Carpathia and Ben-Judah, everything had come to a head. The place would be jammed. While Chloe had assured Buck she was glad to have taken a night off, she wanted to be there and promised to be careful and take it easy. Yes, she said, she would even sit through the meeting.

Jacov was back on driving detail, Dr. Rosenzweig deciding the sanction against him was ludicrous. "But what if the GC escort sees him behind the wheel?" Buck asked, not wanting to create unnecessary turmoil.

"Then they can report it to Fortunato, and I will insist on talking personally with Nicolae. But, Cameron, they don't care. They will see him brazenly behind the wheel and will assume a new deal has been made. You know his wife will be along."

"What?"

"And Stefan."

"Oh, Chaim! This is getting to be a circus."

"And their boss."

"Their boss? Now who's that?"

Chaim smiled at him. "You don't know who my driver and valet's boss is?"

"You? You want to go?"

"I not only want to, I shall. And I want us all jammed into that Mercedes, just like a school trip. It will be festive and grand!"

"Chaim, this is not advisable."

"Don't be silly. You and Tsion have been begging me to go. I have been watching. I am intrigued. I might even give Tsion his audience tonight."

"Tonight?"

"Tonight. He is speaking on some more terrible things supposedly coming from the heavens. He will be in a mood to keep going and to try to convince his old friend that Jesus is the Messiah."

"But he'll be very tired later, Chaim. And won't you be also?"

"Too tired for a good debate? You don't know the Jews, Cameron. And you certainly don't know your own rabbi. I'm surprised at you! A good, ah, missionary, ah, what do you call it, evangelist like you and you want now to postpone the appointment with a prospective convert?"

"Are you really?"

"Probably not, but who is to say? You must not treat lightly the curious, am I right?"

Buck shook his head. "Under normal circumstances. But you are just having fun with us."

"A promise is a promise, my young friend. I am a man of my word."

"You know Tsion must prepare for the noon meeting at the Temple Mount tomorrow."

"That is not until noon! He is a dozen or so years older than you, my friend, but he is almost thirty years younger than I. He is robust. And who knows? If he is right, he has the power of God on him. He will survive. He can talk to an old man until the wee hours and still be prepared for his little get-together tomorrow. And I will be there too."

Buck was frantic by the time he got alone with Tsion. The rabbi was less concerned about Rosenzweig's presence in the stadium as with his plan to be at the Temple Mount the next day.

"But we'll be gone by then," Buck said. "He'll know that meeting is off. We need to make sure everyone knows we're gone so no one makes the mistake of being at the Mount. Nicolae could be so angry at our escape that he will trigger the attack anyway to kill your followers."

Tsion nodded grimly. "I want to believe the sealed are protected, but I just do not know if that protection extends beyond the judgments of God. Obviously, the Lord himself has charge over the carrying out of the judgments, and he can instruct his agents to leave alone the sealed. But he has given Antichrist tremendous latitude. I would not want to be responsible for their harm by making incorrect assumptions."

Buck looked at his watch. In an hour they were expected at the stadium. "One thing we know for sure—if my teacher is right—is that the two witnesses at the Wall will not be harmed, regardless of what Nicolae engineers tomorrow."

"If they're there," Tsion said, smiling.

"Oh, they'll be there," Buck said.

"What makes you say that?"

"Because Nicolae warned them not to appear in public under penalty of death. What would be more public than where they have stood for more than two years?"

"You have a point," Tsion said, patting Buck on the shoulder. "You must have a good teacher."

+ + +

Rayford was on the phone to Dr. Floyd Charles at the safe house as Ken piloted the Gulfstream over the Atlantic. "I'm tempted to slip her a Mickey, medical-school style," Floyd said.

"I haven't heard that expression in ages," Rayford said. "How does that work?"

"Just like doping somebody's drink," Floyd said, "only we tell 'em it's an innocuous IV. I could put her out for twenty-four hours, but then her immune system would be all screwed up."

"You're not really considering it?"

"Nah. She's driving me batty though. I had to physically restrain her to keep her from doing laps up and down the stairs."

"The stairs!"

"That's what I said. I'm glad she's feeling stronger, and ironically this murderous rage she feels toward Carpathia seems to be speeding her recovery. But I can't have her expending the exertion necessary to climb stairs while she's this weak. Honestly, Ray, it's like trying to corral a toddler. I look up, and there she goes again."

"How about downstairs?"

"Downstairs what?"

"Could she just walk downstairs?"

"Ray, I've been through medical school, and I don't know how a person goes downstairs without going up too."

"You could carry her up and let her walk down. Maybe it would tire her out without overexerting her."

There was a pause long enough for Rayford to have to ask if Floyd was still there.

"I'm here," he said. "I'm just thinking what a good idea that is."

"Left you speechless, did it? Every once in a while even pilots come up with something useful."

"Problem is, Ray, I look for reasons to touch her, to hold her, to comfort her. Now you're telling me to pick her up and carry her, and you want me to rethink my feelings for her?"

"Get a grip, Doc. You're no teenager anymore. I hoped your obsession with her wasn't purely physical, but I should have known. You hardly know her, and what you know drives you batty by your own admission. Just behave yourself until we can get back and help you keep your senses."

"Yeah, yeah."

"I mean it now."

"I know. I hear you."

"And, Doc, remember that our absolute, number one, top priority with her is her soul."

"Yeah."

"I didn't hear any enthusiasm there, Floyd."

"No, I got it."

"If you care a whit about her beyond your adolescent need to have her in your arms, you'll want above all else to make her part of the family."

+ + +

"Buck, we've got a problem," Chloe said, pulling him into an empty room. "I just casually walked through our route to the helipad so there'd be no surprises, and that key is gone."

"What?"

"The key Rosenzweig had on a nail on the frame next to the access door. It's gone."

"Does he suspect we're up to something?"

"How could he? I was as casual and subtle as I could be. He brought it up. I only asked him about the history of the house."

"Did that door look as solid to you from inside as it felt to me from the outside?"

"It's like a brick wall, Buck. If we had to break through it or knock it down, we'd wake the dead, not to mention the guard staff and Chaim himself."

"We've got to find the key or get him to tell us what he did with it."

"You think Jacov would know anything about it?"

Buck shrugged. "If I asked him, he'd sure know something was going on. I can't get between them."

"But he's a brother, Buck."

"Brand new. I'm not saying he'd betray us on purpose."

"You heard about his wife?"

"That she's going along tonight, yes. How does she feel about his faith?"

"So you haven't heard."

"No."

"Chaim said Jacov claims his wife is now a believer too. Chaim thought it was humorous and asked me to use my Jesus vision tonight to see if she had the secret mark too."

Buck shook his head. "Talk about a soul harvest. I'm praying for Rosenzweig himself."

Jacov's wife, Hannelore, proved to be a German-born Jew, sandy haired and small with shy, azure eyes. She joined Jacov, Stefan, Buck, Chloe, Tsion, and Chaim in the driveway, and the guard staff opened the doors of the Mercedes for them. Chloe embraced her tightly, and though she was a stranger, reached up to brush Hannelore's hair from off her forehead.

Buck hugged her too, whispering, "Welcome to the family."

"My wife, she does not understand English too good," Jacov said.

"Well, how about it?" Chaim said, his eyes bright. "Does she have the—" and here he lowered his voice an octave and growled—"secret mark?"

"As a matter of fact, she does, Dr. Rosenzweig," Chloe said, clearly not amused at his teasing.

"Oh, good then!" he exulted, moving to the front passenger seat. "You are all one big happy family then, are you not? And how about you, Stefan? Have you joined the ranks of the tribulation saints?"

"Maybe tonight!" Stefan said. "Almost last night!"

"My, my," Chaim said. "I shall be left in the minority, shall I not?"

Only Jacov and Chaim fit in the front seat, so Hannelore sat directly behind Jacov with Chloe in the middle and Tsion behind Chaim. Buck and Stefan crammed into the rear compartment. Jacov had begun to pull slowly down the driveway when Jonas stepped in front of the car and signaled that Chaim should lower his window. He spoke urgently to Chaim in Hebrew.

Buck, with his face inches from Tsion's head, whispered, "What's going on?"

Tsion turned toward the window and spoke softly. "They've gotten a call from Leon. He's sending a helicopter. The roads are more jammed than ever; the stadium is already full. They had to open the gates two hours ahead." He listened some more. "The gateman told Fortunato there were seven of us, too many for a helicopter anyway. Apparently Fortunato told him to tell Chaim we were on our own if we refused GC assistance. Chaim is saying the gateman did the right thing. Just a minute. He's whispering. Oh, no."

"What?"

"Fortunato has warned that Jacov not be in our party. Chaim is angry, demanding that the gateman get Leon back on the phone."

Jonas signaled that Jacov should pull the vehicle to the guardhouse at the gate. A phone was extended to Chaim, who immediately began arguing passionately in Hebrew.

"Then I will speak in English, Leon. I thought you knew every language in the world, as your boss seems to. I may call him potentate because I have always admired him, but I will not even call you *sir*, let alone supreme whatever-you-are. Now you listen to me. I am a personal friend of the potentate. He has pledged the security of my guests. I will be sitting with Jacov in the stadium tonight, and—yes, out in the crowd! I will not hide backstage. . . . To you he may be only a driver or a valet. To me he is part of my family, and he will not be threatened. Running from your guards and shooting harmlessly into the air may have been foolhardy, but he would not have done it if he didn't feel our guests were in danger from the very people who had promised their safety!"

Tsion reached up and laid a hand on Rosenzweig's shoulder as if to calm him. Buck could see the blood rise on the back of the old man's neck and the veins bulge in his temple. "I need not remind you that it was not so long ago that Rabbi Tsion Ben-Judah lost his family for merely expressing his beliefs on television! He was chased from his homeland like a common criminal! . . . Yes, I know how offensive it must have been for the Jews! I am a Jew, Leon! That's more than I can say for you. . . . Tsion assures me his belief is founded on more than faith but also scholarship, but that is not the point! . . . No! I am not one of them, as you say. But if I find that Nicolae looks upon these devout and passionate seekers of God with the contempt that you do, I might just become one of them!

"Now we are proceeding to the stadium in my well-known vehicle. We will take our chances with the traffic because we know shortcuts, and I also assume Tsion's followers will make way for us. . . . As a compromise to you, yes, I will use an alternate driver—" Chaim signaled quickly for Jacov and Stefan to switch places—"but we are on our way, and we expect the protection pledged by the potentate himself.

". . . Am I sorry? Sorry that you make so much of titles, Leon. But no, not sorry that I have offended you. You have offended me, how about that? I have tried to keep my wits about me and have maintained as normal a lifestyle as possible despite the accolades and the wealth that have come with my formula. . . . I am not insisting on some new title or a higher pedestal, and frankly it does not wear well on you either. We are pulling away, Leon, and my new driver seems unaware that I am on a cord phone! Good-bye!"

He laughed. "Stefan, you snake! You nearly pulled the phone away from the cord!"

"I'm a snake?" Stefan said, smiling. "You put me in the target seat!"

Chaim wrenched around in the seat. "Tsion, my son, you know what Leon was saying when we pulled away?"

"I can only imagine."

"That he would be happy to work on a more appropriate title for a man of my station! Have you ever encountered anyone so out of touch with the point of a conversation?"

"Never," Tsion said.

Buck was awestruck that such a dangerous ride could turn so festive.

10

RAYFORD HANDLED the bulk of the flying across the Atlantic, scheduling his arrival to allow the least amount of time on the ground. Mac had informed him that Carpathia and his entourage were still at the King David, but that the Condor 216 was hangared at Ben Gurion in Tel Aviv. Rayford figured security was tighter at Ben Gurion, but Carpathia was being ferried about on a GC chopper primarily out of Jerusalem Airport.

"You still takin' chopper duty with me waiting at the airstrip with these turbines hot?" Ken said.

"As long as nobody knows I'm AWOL yet. If the word is out about me and I get spotted absconding with a GC chopper, mission's over."

"Well, make up your mind, Ray. I mean, I'm a good soldier, and I'll do what I'm told. But I gotta be told."

"Help me out here, Ken. I've still got my high-level security ID, but . . ."

"But if they do know and you get caught, how am I going to get our people back to the Gulfstream?"

Rayford shook his head. "I've got to try Mac one more time."

"You fly; I'll punch in the numbers. I'm going to have way too many flight hours otherwise."

Ken handed the phone to Rayford. "Man, I'm glad you called," Mac said. "I got the third degree about you for an hour. They don't suspect anything on my part, but they think you're in Jerusalem."

"As long as they're not setting up a dragnet in the U.S."

"I'd rather they were, Ray. They look hard enough in Jerusalem, they're gonna find you."

"They won't think I'd be stupid enough to be at an airport."

"Maybe not, but stay aboard that Gulfstream."

"You just answered a very important question for us, Mac. Thanks."

"What? *You* were going to do the chopper work? Not smart. Anyway, as good as your teacher was, I never thought you got that good at it."

"This is better anyway. Ken's been to Rosenzweig's. If we don't draw too much attention to ourselves, we should be able to pull this off. Where's Carpathia going to be?"

"No air plans, and he's sure not going to crash the stadium party again. He's staying close to the King David tonight, and I've charted a midmorning flight to New Babylon out of Tel Aviv. He's going to be a long way from here before anything violent goes down."

"How're you getting him to Tel Aviv?"

"Helicopter out of Jerusalem Airport."

"If these choppers are identical, how will I know which one we're supposed to borrow?"

"They're supposed to be side by side, facing south. Take the one to the west. Nobody's standing guard over them like they are the Condor at Gurion."

"Have you seen the one David had delivered?"

"No, but it's there. The airport called asking what they were supposed to do with it. You'd have been proud of me, Ray. I adopt this major attitude. I tell the guy, 'Just what do you think you're supposed to do with a backup chopper? Stay the blazes away from it! If I find out anybody but my crew lays a finger on it, heads are gonna roll.' Got his attention."

"You're the best, Mac. Here's what we'll do then. I'll land the Gulfstream and play it like I'm there on business, stopping for fuel and a system check. Ken will walk down to the chopper and take off while I'm refueling. Will he be seen?"

"Not if he heads due south, lights off till he's away from the field. It would be only blind luck if somebody saw him. The tricky part is going to be taking off again, what, twenty minutes later. You don't want to get cleared too long before he sets down with your passengers or you'll look suspicious. Obviously you'll coordinate that by secure phone so the tower can't eavesdrop. Taxi down to the far end of the runway where it's darker, and Ken can land, again without lights. Somebody may see all that, but you're a quarter mile from anyone who can hurt you, so get going. If you're lucky, nobody will see the chopper go or come. The guy who ferried it down here for me is staying in Haifa. I told him I'd call him if I needed him. Otherwise, he's taking it back to New Babylon after we leave."

"Pray for us, Mac. We think we're ready, but you never know."

"I will, Ray. Every waking moment. Let me talk to Ken a second." Ray handed him the phone.

"Well, thank you, sir," Ken said. "I look forward to meeting you, too, though the way I understand it, that would happen if your tail was in as much trouble as Rayford's here. You be careful now, and we'll be in touch."

+ + +

Buck was continually amazed at the resourcefulness of his wife. Despite her youth, Chloe knew people. She knew when to act, when to speak, when not to. She waited until they were nearly at the stadium, stuck in traffic, to bring up the missing key.

"You know, Dr. Rosenzweig," she began, "I was getting our suitcase down from the hall closet and noticed that key you showed me the other day is missing."

"Oh, it is not missing if I know where it is, is it?"

She laughed. "No. I just wanted to tell you, in case you didn't know."

"Were you afraid I would accuse you of having taken it?" he said, his eyes alive with humor.

Chloe shook her head. "I just noticed," she said. "That's all."

"It is in safekeeping," he said. She shrugged, doing a good job, Buck thought, of pretending it was no concern of hers. "It just seemed foolish of me to leave it hanging right there all these years. A security risk, you know?"

"Oh?" she said. "I should think it would be more of a security risk if you hung it outside." That tickled the old man so that the car bounced and swayed as he laughed. "In the States," she continued, "we don't have many doors that can be key-locked both inside and out."

"Really? They are common here, especially for doors hardly ever used. I imagine in the embassy days of the compound that door was used frequently and was likely locked or unlocked with a key only on the outside." Chloe appeared more interested in the teeming crowds outside the van. "Jacov," Chaim said, "you do still have that key, do you not?"

"I do!" he shouted from the rear next to Buck. "And right now it's digging into my leg through my pocket!"

Chaim leaned back toward Chloe as if with a secret. "I am certain that is the only key I have for that lock. I can't imagine needing that exit, but it seems reckless to not have copies made. Jacov will take care of that Monday."

She nodded and turned to catch Buck's eye. What was he supposed to do, he wondered, pickpocket it? He did not want Jacov to know of their escape until they were long gone. Rosenzweig either, despite his escalating war of words with Leon Fortunato.

As Stefan was directed into a private parking spot next to the west entrance, Buck found himself grateful that this was the last night of the conference. It had been beyond anything he could have imagined, but where would they put all these people? Every night the crowds grew. Now people were shoulder to shoulder, the stadium full, crowds milling about outside and spilling into traffic. The news media, admittedly controlled by the Global Community, was everywhere. Clearly this was Nicolae's way of monitoring every detail.

The entourage filed into the staging area, where the local committee waited. Buck was impressed with the authoritative tone Tsion suddenly effected. He must have felt like the shepherd he was and that the tens of thousands inside and outside the stadium were his flock. The previous two days he had deferred to the master of ceremonies and the local committee and merely appeared on stage and preached when it was his turn. Now he seemed to take charge, at least of certain details.

"Buck," he said, beckoning him with a raise of his chin. As Buck approached, Tsion gripped his elbow and pulled him toward the emcee. "You know Daniel, of course." Buck nodded and shook hands with him. "Daniel, listen," Tsion continued, "I want five seats in the reserved section held for my guests. They will include Dr. Rosenzweig, two of his staff members, one of their wives, and Buck's wife. Understood?"

"Of course."

"And I would like Buck cleared to be backstage as usual." He turned to Buck. "Chloe will be all right without you?"

"More than all right, sir. The question is how will I get along without her."

Tsion was apparently too focused to see the humor. "Daniel, I would like Dr. Rosenzweig recognized in an understated, dignified manner. He has not asked for this. It is merely a courtesy appropriate to his standing within the country."

"I'll handle it."

"After your greeting and welcome, announce the Saturday rally for the local committee at the Temple Mount, recognize Dr. Rosenzweig, pray, lead in a hymn, and get me on. No fanfare this time. They know who I am."

"But, sir—"

"Please, Daniel. We are on the front lines here, and it is becoming increasingly dangerous. We are enemies of the world system and will have many opportunities to expose them down the road. Making a fuss over me serves no purpose and merely—"

"Begging your pardon, Doctor. Mr. Williams, I'm sure you agree that these people will be eager to express themselves on what may be the last time they have opportunity to see Dr. Ben-Judah in person. Please let me—"

"If they respond spontaneously, I will accept it in the spirit offered. But I want no grand introduction. You should be able to do it without even using my name. Take that as a personal challenge."

Daniel looked crestfallen. "Oh, sir, are you sure?"

"I know you can handle it."

* * *

Rayford, with nothing but water in view, took a call from Floyd Charles. "What's up, Doc?" he said.

"Never heard that one before," Floyd said. "I hate to bother you, but this seemed important. Hattie's spent a lot of time on the phone with a kid named Ernie, a friend of Ken's."

"I met him."

"She apparently happened onto him when she was trying to reach you out there."

"Yeah, so?"

"Well, she'd like to see him."

"Does she know he's got to be ten years younger than she is?"

"So about the same age difference as Buck and your daughter?"

Rayford paused. "What, you're worried about a relationship? Have you talked to this kid?"

"Yeah. He's a believer. Seems nice enough."

"He's a mechanical whiz, but him and Hattie? Don't even worry about it. She's your patient, Floyd, but she's also a grown woman. We don't have any authority over her."

"That's not what I'm worried about, Rayford. She'd like him to come here."

"Whoops!"

"That's what I thought. We don't want him knowing where we are, do we?"

"No. He's a brother and all, but we don't know who he knows, whether he's mature enough to keep his mouth shut, that kind of thing."

"That's what I thought. Just checking."

"Don't let her even hint at where we're located."

"Gotcha. I might reward her for good behavior and run her out to Palwaukee in a day or two. She can put a face to a name that way, anyway."

"We'll be home before that, Doc. We'll make a picnic of it. The whole Tribulation Force, except David and Mac, of course, together at last."

* * *

After the group prayed backstage, Tsion stood by himself, head down, eyes closed. Buck couldn't decide whether Tsion was more or less nervous than usual. He kept an eye on Tsion until Daniel walked past him to the podium. Tsion looked up at Buck and waved him over.

"Stand with me, Cameron, would you?" Buck felt honored. He stepped up next to Tsion in the wings as they watched Daniel welcome the crowd and make his announcement about Saturday's rally. "Most of you will have gone home, but if you live locally or can make it, please feel free. Remember, however, that this is just a thank-you to the local committee." He then had Dr. Rosenzweig stand to warm applause.

"How will you get the key?" Tsion asked.

"I'm not sure yet, but I may simply ask Jacov for it and tell him to ask no questions. I believe he will trust me until I can explain."

Tsion nodded. "I feel a particular burden tonight, Cameron," he whispered suddenly. Buck didn't know what to say. When Tsion bowed his head again, Buck put an arm around his shoulder and was shocked to find the man trembling.

Daniel prayed, then led the singing of "Holy, Holy, Holy."

"Excellent choice," Tsion murmured, but he did not sing. Buck tried to and nodded when Tsion said, "Pray for me."

The song ended. Tsion looked to Buck, who lifted a fist of encouragement in his face. Daniel said, "And now I invite you to listen to a message from the Word of God." Buck was thrilled to see the crowd rise and clap. No shouting, no cheering, no whistling. Just a long and respectful and enthusiastic season of applause that seemed to overwhelm Tsion. He waved shyly and, when he had finished arranging his notes, stepped back until the applause died out.

"God has put something on my heart tonight," he said. "Even before I open his Word, I feel led to invite seekers to come forward and receive Christ." Immediately, from all over the stadium and even outside, lines of people, many weeping, began streaming forward, causing the saints to burst into applause again. "You know the truth," Tsion said. "God has gotten your attention. You need no other argument, you need no other plea. It is enough that Jesus died, and that he died for thee."

The seekers kept coming. Tsion asked believers to pray with anyone who wanted them to, and for an hour it seemed that anyone within the sound of Tsion's voice—other than Global Community personnel—came looking for salvation.

"The Global Community Broadcasting Network is beaming this all over the world and onto the Internet," Tsion said. "I'm sure they believe that any thinking person will see through our message and that the GC has nothing to fear by letting us proclaim it. They will say ours is not the message of ecumenism and tolerance that they promote, and I say they are right. There is right and wrong, there are absolute truths, and some things cannot and should not and shall not ever be tolerated.

"The GC Network will not turn us off, lest they appear afraid of our message, of the truth of God, of a converted rabbi who believes Jesus Christ is the long-sought Messiah. I applaud the courage of the Global Community administration and unapologetically take advantage of their largesse. At no cost to us, our message is broadcast to every nation of the world. We have not needed translators here, and reports tell us the same miracle of understanding has happened on television as well. If you understand neither Hebrew nor English but still understand every word I'm saying, I'm happy to tell you that God is working in your mind. Most of this message is in English, though I read Scripture in Hebrew, Greek, and Aramaic. I have been amused to discover that even my coworkers are unaware of this. They hear all of it in their own tongues.

"God is also working in your heart. You do not have to be with us physically to receive Christ tonight. You need not be with anyone else, pray with anyone else, or go anywhere else. All you need is to tell God that you acknowledge that you are a sinner and are separated from him. Tell him you know that nothing you can do for yourself will earn your way to him. Tell him you believe that he sent his Son, Jesus Christ, to die on the cross for your sins, that he was raised from the dead, has raptured his church, and is coming yet again to the earth. Receive him as your Savior right where you are. I believe millions all over the world are joining the great soul harvest that shall produce tribulation saints and martyrs, a multitude that cannot be numbered."

Tsion looked spent and stepped back to pray. When the people who had come forward finally began to disperse and head back to their seats, Tsion moved back to the lectern. He arranged his notes yet again, but his shoulders sagged and he seemed to breathe heavily. Buck was worried about him.

Tsion cleared his throat and drew in a huge breath, yet his voice was suddenly weak. "My text tonight," he managed, "is Revelation 8:13." All over the stadium, tens of thousands of Bibles opened, and the unique sound of onionskin pages turning filled the air. Tsion hurried back to Buck while people looked for the passage.

"Are you all right, Tsion?"

"I think so. Are you willing to read the passage for me if I need you to?"

"Certainly. Right now?"

"I prefer to try, but I'll call on you if I need you."

Tsion made his way back to the podium, looked at the passage, then lifted his eyes to the crowd. He cleared his throat. "Bear with me," he said. "This passage warns that once the earth has been darkened by a third, three terrible woes will follow. These are particularly ominous, so much so that they will be announced from heaven in advance."

Tsion cleared his throat yet again and Buck stood ready if needed. He wished Tsion would simply ask his assistance. But suddenly he smelled the dusty, smoky robes of the two witnesses and was startled when Eli and Moishe stepped up beside him. He turned as if in a dream and found himself staring into Eli's endless eyes. Buck had never been so close to the prophets and had to resist the urge to touch them. Eli's eyes bore into his. "Show thyself not to thine enemy," he said. "Be sober, be vigilant; because your adversary the devil, as a roaring lion, walketh about, seeking whom he may devour."

Buck could not speak. He tried to nod, to indicate he had heard and understood, but he could not move. Moishe leaned between him and Eli and added, "Whom resist stedfast in the faith."

They moved past him and stood directly behind Tsion. The crowd seemed so stunned that they didn't cheer or applaud but pointed and stood and leaned forward to listen. Moishe said, "My beloved brethren, the God of all grace, who hath called us unto his eternal glory by Christ Jesus, after that ye have suffered a while, make you perfect, stablish, strengthen, settle you."

To Buck it appeared as if Tsion might fall over, but he merely made way for the two. Neither stepped close to the microphone, however. Moishe loudly quoted Tsion's passage so that every ear could hear, in the stadium and on global television.

"'And I beheld, and heard an angel flying through the midst of heaven, saying with a loud voice, Woe, woe, woe, to the inhabiters of the earth by reason of the other voices of the trumpet of the three angels, which are yet to sound!'"

All around Buck came the sound of the engaging of high-powered GC rifles. Guards dropped to one knee to raise their weapons and take a bead on the two witnesses. He wanted to shout, "It's not the due time, you fools!" but he worried for Tsion's safety, for Chloe's and their friends', for his own.

But no one fired. And just when it appeared one or two might squeeze their trigger, Eli and Moishe strode off the stage, past Buck, and past the very guards who had them in their sights. The guards scrambled away from them, some falling, their weapons clattering on the concrete floor.

Buck heard Tsion say from the podium, "If we never meet again this side of heaven or in the millennial kingdom our Savior sets up on earth, I shall greet you on the Internet and teach from Revelation 9! Godspeed as you share the gospel of Christ with the whole world!"

The meeting ended early, and Tsion, as frightened as Buck had ever seen him, hurried directly to him. "Get our passengers into the van as quickly as possible!"

11

RAYFORD AND KEN sat silently during the bizarre telecast from Israel, where it was not yet nine o'clock, as they streaked toward the Middle East Friday night.

"Still on schedule to touch down at midnight," Rayford said. "Oh, sorry, Ken. I didn't mean to wake you."

Ken massaged his eye sockets with his thumbs. "Wasn't really sleeping," he said. "Just thinking. You know, if everything Ben-Judah says is true, we're soon gonna spend half our time just trying to stay alive. What're we gonna do when we can't buy or sell 'cause we don't have the mark?"

"Like Tsion said, we have to start stockpiling now."

"You realize what that means? We're going to be a whole separate, like invisible, society of believers. There may be a billion of us, but we're still going to be in the minority, and we're still going to be seen as criminals and fugitives."

"Don't I know it!"

"We won't be able to trust anybody with the other mark."

"Don't forget, there'll be a lot of people with neither mark."

Ken shook his head. "Food, power, sanitation, transportation—all controlled by the GC. We'll be scrambling around, scratching out an existence in a huge, underground black market. How much money have we got?"

"The Trib Force? Not much. Buck and I made good salaries, but that's gone. Tsion and Chloe have no sources of income either. We can hardly expect Mac and David to have to worry about us, though I'm sure they'll do what they can. I haven't talked to Floyd about any reserves he might have had."

"I have a good bit stashed away."

"So do Buck and I, but nothing like we're going to need for aircraft and fuel, let alone survival."

"This ain't gonna be pretty, is it, Ray?"

"You can say that again, but please don't."

Ken pulled a yellow legal pad from his flight bag. Rayford noticed the pages were dog-eared with handwriting on more than half of them. "I know we never signed anything or made any pledges when we joined," Ken said, "but I been doin' a lot of thinkin'. I was never one for socialism or communism or even communal living. But it seems to me we're going to be pretty much a commune from now on."

"In the New Testament sense, like Tsion says."

"Right, and I don't know about you, but I don't have a problem with that."

Rayford smiled. "I've learned to believe the Bible completely," he said. "If that's what you're asking."

"I don't know what you're going to do about future members and all that, but we may have to get formal about giving everything we have to the cause."

Rayford pursed his lips. So far that had not been an issue. "Sort of like asking everybody to make all their resources available to everybody else?"

"If they're serious about joining."

"I'm willing, and I know Buck and Chloe and Tsion would be. It's just that we bring relatively little materially. Between Buck and me we wouldn't have more than half a million dollars. That used to sound like a lot, but it won't last long, and it won't finance any offensive against Carpathia."

"You'd better get that converted to gold—and fast."

"Think so?"

"I'm 90 percent precious metal," Ritz said. "As soon as we went to three currencies, I could see what was coming. Now we're down to one, and no matter what happens, I've got a tradable commodity. I got absolutely obsessed with saving when I turned forty. Don't even know why. Well, I mean, I do now. Tsion believes God works in our lives even before we acknowledge him. For almost twenty years I've been living alone and running charters. I've been a miser. Never owned a new car, made clothes last for years. Wore a cheap watch. Still do. I don't mind telling you, I've made millions and saved almost 80 percent of it."

Rayford whistled through his teeth. "Did I mention the annual dues for being a member of the Tribulation Force?"

"You joke, but what else am I gonna do with millions' worth of gold? We've got, what, less than five years left. Vacations seem frivolous just now, wouldn't you say? Bottom line, Ray, I want to buy a couple of these Gulfstreams, then I want to put in an offer on Palwaukee."

"The airport?"

"It's virtually a ghost strip now anyway. Owner tells me I run more flights out of there than anybody. I know he'd like to sell, and I'd better do it before Carpathia makes it impossible. The place would come with several small planes, a couple of choppers, fuel tanks, tower, sundry equipment."

"You *have* been thinking, haven't you?"

Ken nodded. "About more than that, too." He held up his notepad. "This here's filled with ideas. Farming co-ops, a sea-harvesting operation, even private banking."

"Ken! Back up! Sea harvesting?"

"I read about Carpathia doling out royalties to his ten guys—the ten kings, Tsion calls 'em—for the rights to harvest their waterways for food and oil, and I got thinking they were onto something. He could easily shut down somebody's farm, bomb it, raid it, burn it, confiscate equipment, all that. But how can he patrol all the oceans? We get believers who have fishing experience and equipment—I'm talking about commercial guys here—and we provide 'em a market of millions of saints. We somehow coordinate this, help process the shipping and billing, take a reasonable percentage, and finance the work of the Tribulation Force."

Rayford checked his settings and then turned to stare at Ken. "Where do you come up with this stuff?"

"Thought I was a clod-kicker, didn't you?"

"I knew better because Mac likes to play that role and he's smart as a whip. But do you have background in this, or—?"

"You wouldn't believe me if I told ya."

"I'd believe anything right now."

"London School of Economics."

"Now you're putting me on."

"Told ya. You don't believe me."

"What're you, serious?"

"It was thirty-five years ago, but, yeah. Mustered out of the air force, planned to go commercial but wanted to bum around Europe first. Wound up liking England; I *really* don't remember the whys of that now, but I knocked over LSE with my high school records."

"You did well in high school?"

"Salutatorian, baby. Made the speech and everything. Thought I was gonna be an English teacher. I only talk like this 'cause it's easier, but yours truly is eminently cognizant of the grammatical parameters."

"Amazing."

"I amaze myself sometimes."

"I'll bet you do."

+ + +

The departing crowd seemed festive, but Buck could not see his party and didn't want to lose sight of Tsion. The rabbi stood chatting with Daniel and the local committee, but he looked agitated and distracted, as if he wanted to be on his way. Buck scanned the stadium, especially the reserved section, but he didn't see any of the five he was looking for. He thought autograph seekers or well-wishers might surround Rosenzweig, perhaps even zealous believers who would try to convert him. But there were no clusters, just lines of people happily filing out under the stern watch of GC guards.

Buck looked back to Tsion and the others backstage. That group seemed to be thinning too, and he didn't want Tsion left alone. He was among the most recognizable people in the world, so he wouldn't be able to blend into any crowds.

Buck hurried to Daniel, but Tsion, now deadly serious, intercepted him. "Cameron, please! Get the others and let's go! I want to speak with Chaim tonight, but nothing must get in the way of our schedule. Everything is set, and we can't leave Rayford and Ken exposed."

"I know, Tsion. I'm looking for the others, but—"

Tsion gripped Buck's arm. "Just go and find them and let's get to the van. I have a terrible feeling I can only assume is from the Lord. We need to get to Chaim's place. The GC surely has it under surveillance, so we can give them a false sense of security once they know we're there and seem to be settling down for the night."

Daniel and only four or five committee members remained backstage. "I don't want to leave you alone, Tsion. With no eyewitnesses, the GC could do anything they wanted with you and blame someone else."

"Go, Cameron. Please. I'll be fine."

"Daniel," Buck said, "would you keep an eye on Tsion until I get back?"

Daniel laughed. "Babysit the rabbi? I can handle that!"

Buck, stern faced, pulled Daniel close and whispered in his ear. "He may be in grave danger. Promise me."

"I will not let him out of my sight, Mr. Williams."

Buck jogged up the ramp and across the stage, jumping to ground level. He could see less from there than on the stage, so he began to climb back up. A GC guard stopped him. "You can't go up there."

Buck reached for his ID. "I'm with the program committee," he said.

"I know who you are, sir. I would advise your not going up there."

"But I need to get through there to get to our van, and I'm trying to find my party."

"You can get to your van the way everyone else is getting out."

"But I can't leave without my people, and we have to rendezvous with someone backstage first."

Buck began to climb the stage again when the guard called him down. "Sir, don't make me use force. You are not allowed to go back up that way."

Buck avoided eye contact to keep from further agitating the guard. "You don't understand. I'm Cam—"

"I know who you are, sir," the guard said severely. "We all know who you are, who makes up your party, and with whom you are rendezvousing."

Buck looked him full in the face. "Then why won't you let me pass?" The guard tipped his uniform cap back, and Buck saw the sign of the cross on his forehead. "You're, you're a—?"

"Just tonight," he whispered. "Standing here. People in the crowd began to notice, and of course I saw their marks too. I had to pull my hat low to keep from being exposed. I'm as good as dead if I'm discovered. Let me come with you."

"But you're in a strategic spot! You can affect so many things! Fellow believers will not give you away. They'll know what you're doing. Is Tsion in danger?"

The guard raised his weapon at Buck. "Move along!" he barked, then lowered his voice again. "Your party is already in the van. Snipers are waiting for a clear shot of Ben-Judah backstage. I doubt you could get him out."

"I have to!" Buck hissed. "I'm going back there!"

"You'll be shot!"

"Then fire at me out here! Draw attention! Yell for help! Do something!"

"Can't you call him?"

"He doesn't carry a phone, and I don't know the emcee's number. Do what you have to do, but I'm going."

"My job is to keep *everyone* away from backstage."

Buck pushed past him and took the steps two at a time. From behind he heard the guard yell, "Wait! Stop! Assistance!" As Buck reached the stage, he stole a glance back to see the guard on his walkie-talkie, then cocking his weapon. Buck dashed backstage and headed straight for Tsion, who stood precariously with only Daniel now. Daniel saw Buck and moved away, as if his job was over. Buck was about to scream at him to stay close, when gunfire erupted.

Tsion and Daniel immediately went down, as did a few stragglers several feet away. GC guards ran for the stage at the sound of the gunfire. Buck rushed to help Tsion up. "Daniel, help me get him into the van!"

They shouldered through panicky people and out to the Mercedes. Outside people screamed and pushed to get as far from the stadium as they could. The back door and the backseat side door stood open. Buck jumped in the back as Daniel pushed Tsion in and shut the door.

They all kept their heads below window level until Stefan pulled out onto the street. From inside the stadium came the *pop pop pop* of more shooting, and

Buck could only pray that the GC was not taking out its frustration by creating more martyrs.

Tsion wept as he watched the crowds sprint from the area. "This is what I feared," he said. "Bringing these people into the enemy camp, leading them to the slaughter."

Chaim was strangely quiet. He neither spoke nor seemed to move. He sat facing straight ahead. At a traffic light he seemed distracted when Stefan took his hands off the wheel, made fists with both hands, and shook them before his own face as if celebrating. Chaim glanced at him and looked away.

The light changed, but a GC guard still held the traffic, letting a line go from the other way. Stefan took the moment to turn the rearview mirror toward himself. He pushed his hair back and stared at his forehead. Chaim looked at him with a bored expression. "You can't see your own, Stefan. Only others can see yours."

Stefan turned around in his seat. "Well?" he said.

"Yes," Chloe said, and Tsion nodded.

Stefan tried to shake hands with everybody behind him, and Chaim raised both hands in resignation, shrugging and shaking his head. "I won't know for sure unless it happens to me."

Buck saw GC guards running toward the intersection. "Go, Stefan!" he said.

Stefan turned back to see the traffic director still holding him. "But—"

"Trust me, Stefan! Go now!"

Stefan stomped on the accelerator, and the Mercedes shot forward. The guard stepped in front of it with both arms raised but leaped aside as Stefan bore down on him.

"Get us to Chaim's as fast as you can," Buck said. Stefan rose to the challenge.

+ + +

"So, Ken," Rayford said, "as an economics expert, do you still trust the banks?"

"I didn't trust the banks *before* Carpathia came to power."

"Where'd you stash your bullion then?"

"Some bullion. Mostly coins. Who's got change for a brick of gold?"

Rayford snorted. "Who's got change even for a gold piece? You'd have to buy out a store to keep from getting hundreds in change."

"I hope it doesn't come to actually having to spend the gold as currency. As for where I put it, let's just say if I do buy Palwaukee, I'll be buyin' one valuable piece of real estate."

"You're not saying . . ."

"I know what you're thinkin'. Guy who's s'posed to know money loses out on more millions by putting it where it can't grow."

"Exactly. Even I have a little portfolio."

"Only recently have I put all of it underground. Right under my Quonset hut. For years I stored only the gain. After the Rapture, which I knew only as the disappearances then, I could see what was going to happen to the economy." Ken laughed.

"What?"

"I thought I'd lost it all in the earthquake. Dang near killed myself goin' after it, my stash that is. Ground was all broke up, and my bullion and boxes of coins slipped through one fissure and wound up twenty feet lower'n I'd buried 'em. It could have just as easily been a hundred feet or all the way to the center of the earth. I didn't know it meant that much to me, I honestly didn't. Digging through that cave-in was about the dumbest thing a man could do after a quake, all those aftershocks rumblin' and such. But I was in such a state that I figured if I couldn't find my gold, I might's well die anyway. I'd be buried underground either way. I found it, and I was like a schoolkid who found his long-lost marbles. That's when I knew I had it bad. Started gathering that from your son-in-law."

"How?"

"I thought he'd got religion, and while I didn't buy any of it, I couldn't argue that he sure had different priorities than me or anybody else I knew. I mean, I knew he'd bought the whole package, that was for sure. My future was tied up in the security of my assets. His whole life was trustin' in Jesus. Man, that sounded stupid, but he wore it well. I envied him, I really did. After that earthquake I wound up in the hospital with my brains 'bout hangin' out, and all I could think of was that I could not picture the Williams kid scratching through the rubble for his possessions. Then he showed up, and was off on another of his wacky capers."

"I wish this were just a caper," Rayford said. "No matter how you slice it, this is going to be a long night."

"Should we put down in Greece or Turkey instead of trying to go all the way back tonight? There's a coupla guys I trust over there, one in each country. Not believers yet, I don't guess, but they'd never give us up, if you know what I mean."

Rayford shook his head. "We get enough fuel, I'd just as soon scoot all the way back."

"Your call."

* * *

As Stefan pulled into Chaim's complex, the old man asked Stefan in Hebrew to say something to Jonas, the gateman. When Jonas also responded in Hebrew, Buck asked Tsion what they were saying. The rabbi put a finger to his lips. "Later," he said.

Inside they watched the coverage and commentary on TV while one by one, so as not to be obvious, Tsion, Buck, and Chloe slipped away to pack. They surreptitiously synchronized watches.

Buck sensed Chaim was now as eager to pursue the spiritual discussion as Tsion was. Perhaps more so, as Tsion had escape on his mind. Buck knew, however, that winning souls was more important to Tsion than his own life. He would not pass up this opportunity to plead his case for Rosenzweig's heart.

Buck needed to beg the key from Jacov and was glad for the chance to leave the two old friends to talk in private. But when he went looking for his new brother, he learned Jacov was off for the rest of the night. "Where can I find him?" he asked.

"At home, I presume," another staff member told him in broken English. He provided the number, and Buck dialed him. No answer.

"Where else might he be?" Buck asked.

The man spoke conspiratorially. "You did not hear it from me, but there is a bar called The Harem. It is in the—"

"I know where it is," Buck said. "Thanks."

He hurried back into the house and interrupted Chaim and Tsion. "I'm sorry," he said, "but I need a word with Jacov, and he is not at his apartment."

"Oh," Chaim said. "He said something about going to Hannelore's mother's. He will be at the Temple Mount tomorrow though."

"I really want to speak to him tonight."

Chaim gave him the woman's name, and Buck looked it up. A German woman answered his call and put Jacov on the line. "It will be hard for me to get away tonight, Mr. Williams," he said. "Hannelore's mother is not taking this well, and we have agreed to stay and talk about it. Please pray for us."

"I will, but Jacov, I need that key."

"Key?"

"The one you're having duplicated for Dr. Rosenzweig."

"He needs it sooner?"

"I need it, and I need you to trust me enough not to ask why."

"You're afraid of intrusion? The door was left locked. It is the strongest in the house."

"I know. I need it, Jacov. Please."

"I don't even have it. I left it with Stefan. I am working tomorrow, but I am off again Monday. He said he would get it copied then."

"And where does he live?"

"Near the stadium, but I saw on the news they are allowing no traffic into there tonight."

"We've been watching, and I didn't see that."

"It was just on. A Global Community guard was murdered right after the meeting. That must have been the shooting we heard. The GC is looking for the killers. They believe it was done by one or more of the witnesses at the meeting."

"Jacov, listen to me. I told you what that shooting was about."

"But you didn't say a guard was shot. Were some of the witnesses armed? Maybe they were protecting you when they thought the guard was really shooting at you."

"Oh, please, God, I hope not."

"You never know, my friend. Anyway, you will not get into Stefan's neighborhood tonight without being stopped. And you know they will recognize you."

"Jacov, I need a favor."

"Oh, Mr. Williams, I want to help you, but I cannot go to Stefan's tonight. We are trying to convince my mother-in-law that this whole thing was not Stefan's idea. She has always hated him, blaming him for everything bad I have ever done. Now she is saying she wishes he and I were still drunks and not crazy religious people, enemies of the potentate. She is threatening to take Hannelore from me."

"I just need you to not mention to Dr. Rosenzweig that I asked for the key." There was a long silence. "I realize I am asking you to keep something from your—"

"From the man I owe my life to. He has been like a father to me. You must tell me all about this for me to agree to that. If I kept something from him that caused him harm, I would never forgive myself. Why would you need that key and for him to not know about it?"

"Jacov, you know he is not a believer yet."

"I know! But that does not make him our enemy! I pray I will be the one who gets to preach to him, and yet the rabbi himself is Dr. Rosenzweig's friend."

"He is not our enemy, Jacov, but he is naive."

"Naive. I do not know that word."

"He is still a friend of the potentate."

"He doesn't know better yet."

"That's what I mean by naive. If we use that key to slip away early, before the GC knows we're gone, we cannot risk that he might say something to Nicolae or his people."

Jacov was silent another moment. "I did not know what I was getting into," he said finally. "I would never go back, and I do believe. But I never thought I would have anything to do with fighting Nicolae Carpathia."

"Jacov, can you get word to Stefan that I desperately need that key? Maybe he could sneak out and bring it. He is known in that neighborhood, and it would not be unusual for him to come to work, even at this hour, would it?"

"I'll try. But now you have two who must keep your secret."

"Will he?"

"I believe he will. But what will Dr. Rosenzweig think when he knows we helped you escape and never told him?"

Buck thought about suggesting that they tell Rosenzweig the Tribulation Force threatened them. But it was one thing, he decided, to use any and all means to deceive Carpathia and his minions. It was another to start lying to the man they were trying to reach for God. Buck looked at his watch. It was nearly eleven. The odds were against Stefan getting to him in time anyway.

"Jacov, can we break through that door?"

"Not easily. Mr. Williams, I need to go."

+ + +

Rayford was an hour outside Jerusalem Airport, casually checking in with towers along the way who would pick him up on their radar screens anyway. He identified his craft by type and call numbers only, and no one asked more details. "ETA Jerusalem Airport for refueling at 2400 hours," he said.

"Ten-four, Gulf. Over and out."

He dialed Chloe. "Everything a go, hon?"

"We're a little squirrelly here, Dad. I won't bore you with the details, but stay on track. Somehow we'll be waiting on the roof at 12:30."

"I can't wait to see you, sweetheart."

"I miss you too, Dad. I'll call if we have a problem."

"Ditto. Ken will be in the bird, so I'll see you onboard the Gulfstream."

+ + +

Buck lightly tapped on the door where Tsion and Chaim sat talking quietly but animatedly. Tsion gave Buck a look as if he really picked the wrong time to intrude. "I'm very sorry, gentlemen, but Tsion, I need a word."

"Not at all!" Rosenzweig said. "I need a moment myself. Let me leave you. I want to ask your wife if she would like to ride with me tomorrow to the Temple Mount. Jacov and I are going a little later."

He stepped past Buck, smiling but clearly distracted. Buck apologized to Tsion.

"Buck, I know our time is short, but he is so close!"

"Close enough that we can trust him?" Buck brought Tsion up-to-date.

Tsion reached to turn the TV back on. On the screen appeared the face of the very GC guard who had fired over Buck's head, intentionally missing. Beneath his photograph were the years of his birth and death. "I got him killed," Buck said, his throat constricted.

"You likely saved my life," Tsion said. "Praise God he is in heaven now. Buck, I know this is hard, and I never want to grow callous to the high price we are called to pay. No one would put much stock in our futures now. I don't know how long the Lord will spare any of us to do his work. But I fear if we let Carpathia hurt or kill or even detain any of us tonight, it will be a terrible blow to the cause. You know I don't care about my own life anymore. My family is in heaven, and I long to be there too. But I don't believe God would have us die needlessly. There is so much to do.

"Yes, we must confide in Chaim, I'm afraid. He asked the gateman if his video surveillance equipment was running. The man told him not until midnight, as usual. And Chaim told him to turn it on now."

A wave of panic hit Buck in his gut. Might the camera have picked him up the night before? "We have to tell him then," Buck said. "If his security people hear a chopper and see it's GC, they won't know what to do."

"That's what we want, Cameron, just enough confusion to get going. Surely they wouldn't fire on a helicopter that looks like Carpathia's own. But it wouldn't be long before they called to ask about it, and the GC would know we had used one of their machines."

"How can we convince Chaim without making him think we're overreacting?"

"He was there tonight, Buck. And you should hear his reaction. I'm telling you, he's close."

"What's holding him back?"

"His admiration and love for Carpathia."

Buck grunted. "Then let's tell him what Rayford heard on the Condor 216."

"About me, you mean?"

"And about him."

"Will he believe it?"

"That's up to him, Tsion. It will go against everything he believes and feels about Carpathia."

"So be it."

\+ + +

It was pushing midnight when Rayford entered Israeli airspace, on schedule. He checked in with the Ben Gurion tower in Tel Aviv, then was cleared for landing at Jerusalem Airport for refueling. "It's been a while since I've been this scared," he said.

"Really?" Ken said. "This kind of terror is becoming a weekly occurrence for me."

\+ + +

Rosenzweig rejoined Buck and Tsion with Chloe in tow. She was in her pajamas and robe, drawing a confused stare from Buck. "Dr. Rosenzweig is insisting I get my rest for the baby's sake," she said. "Can't argue with that. I just came to say good-night."

Buck knew she would race back to change, but he said, "Stay with us a minute, hon. We need to tell Chaim something, and you may need to corroborate it with what you have heard from your dad."

12

"JERUSALEM TOWER, this is Gulfstream Alpha Tango, over."

"Tower, go ahead, Alpha Tango. Initiate landing sequence."

Rayford plugged in the coordinates and put down in the busier-than-usual airstrip. To appear as casual as possible, he asked about it. The tower informed him that the wealthier commuters from the big meeting at Kollek Stadium were flying small craft to Tel Aviv for their international flights home.

"Any delay on a refuel?"

"Negative, Alpha. You're clear."

"See the choppers?" Ray said as he lined up his approach.

"I see one," Ken said. "White with black block letters on the side."

"Don't kid me."

"I'm not. It's GC all right, but there's only one."

"I don't like it, Ken."

"Why hasn't Mac called if there's a glitch?"

Rayford shook his head. "I don't want to call him. He may not be where he can talk."

"But he might not know one of his birds is gone. Ever think of that?"

Rayford punched in Mac's number. "McCullum."

"Mac! It's me. What's going on?"

"Yes, hello, Sergeant Fitzgerald. Of course you may proceed."

"We're good to go?"

"No need to wait, Sergeant. That's affirmative."

"All my eggs are in your basket, Mac."

"You're welcome, Sergeant. Good-bye."

"Take your phone, Ken!" Rayford shouted over the scream of the engines as Ritz opened the door.

Ken smacked himself in the head and grabbed the phone out of his bag. "Another mature moment," he said. "Don't leave me out there hitchhikin' now."

"Don't worry." Rayford wished he had rearview mirrors on the side of the plane so he would know when Ken got to the chopper.

* * *

Chaim Rosenzweig had never looked older to Buck. He was tired, of course. It was late. But his wispy white hair, independent of control, haloed a grayish, drawn face. Buck, Tsion, and Chloe had quickly revealed to him conversations Rayford had overheard on the Condor. Chaim appeared unable to speak after hearing that his requests for Tsion's safety following his first TV broadcast had been laughed at.

"You realize," Chloe said, "that you are the first outside person who knows about the bugging device on that plane. We're putting lives in your—"

Rosenzweig waved her off sadly. "To think that Nicolae himself would say one thing and do another, looking me in the eyes, he did, and lying. He could have prevented the slaughter of your family, Tsion. Oh God, oh God, oh God! How could I have been so blind? I know you tried to tell me."

"Doctor," Tsion said quickly, "you and I will continue our discussion by phone or e-mail or in person, God willing, but we must leave now. Our sources tell us that the GC is planning a terrorist attack at the Temple Mount tomorrow, and we want to be long gone by then."

"Of course," Chaim said. "I understand. I will have you driven to—"

"It's all arranged," Buck said. "We need to be on the roof in ten minutes."

"Of course, go. I will cover for you. Don't worry about me."

Chloe went to change, and Buck told Chaim the disposition of the key. "Break it down," he said wearily. "Tools are in the utility room."

"Buck!" Chloe cried as she moved toward the door. "You're on TV! Turn it up!"

". . . Community forces believe videotape reveals this man as the likely killer of a GC guard earlier this evening at the Meeting of the Witnesses at Kollek Stadium. He has been identified as an American, Cameron Williams, a former employee of the GC publishing division. Williams is reportedly staying with Rabbi Tsion Ben-Judah at the home of Israeli Nobel Prize–winner Dr. Chaim Rosenzweig. Supreme Commander Leon Fortunato went on to say . . ."

Tsion and Buck followed Rosenzweig toward the utility room. As soon as Buck saw where they were headed, he brushed past the old man, flipped on the light, and grabbed a hammer, a shovel, and a concrete block. "Do you have a sledgehammer?"

"If you don't see it, I don't have it," Chaim said. "We need to hurry." The phone rang. "That will be the GC," he said. Jonas the gateman spoke over the intercom in Hebrew, but Buck understood "Rosenzweig" and "Fortunato."

"Have someone bring me the phone," Rosenzweig said. "I'm in the back hallway." He turned to Buck and Tsion and gestured that they should lead the way to the access door. When he got the cordless phone, he dismissed the valet and talked as he followed Buck.

"Of course he's here, Leon," he said. "And sound asleep. Don't even think of invading my household in the middle of the night. You have my word he will be here in the morning. You can question him then. I will even be happy to bring him to you. . . . Oh, Leon, that is patent nonsense, and you know it. He is no more a murder suspect than I am. Your man was shot by one of your own. . . . Have you found a murder weapon? Fingerprints? Check the bullets, and they will trace to your weapons. I have known Mr. Williams for years and have never seen him with a weapon. I'm warning you, Leon. These are my guests, and I will not wake them! . . . Yes, I warned you! You are not *my* supreme commander. . . . Now you are threatening me? You know my standing in this country and, may I say, with Nicolae! If I tell people you used Gestapo tactics in the middle of the night. . . . Crime? You would charge me with a crime for speaking disrespectfully to you? You call me at midnight, *after* midnight, and tell me to hold my guest as a murder suspect, and you expect me to respect you? I'll tell you what, Leon, you come personally at a reasonable hour, and I will make my guest available to you. . . . Well, I promise you, Leon, you send anyone tonight, and I will not answer the door."

Buck waved furiously at Chaim to move away so the sound of the banging wouldn't be heard over the phone. Chaim nodded and hurried away, and Buck drove the claw of the hammer behind the top hinge of the heavy door. Chloe showed up with two bags and left to get Tsion's.

Tsion drove the shovel in and around the doorknob, but neither man was getting far. "Step back a second, Tsion," Buck said, and he hefted the concrete block above his head. The weight almost carried him over backward. He slammed it against the upper half of the door and heard a resounding crack. A couple more shots, he believed, and he'd break through the wood.

* * *

Rayford was refueling when the call came from Ken. "I'm away," he said.

"Godspeed."

He kept an eye on his watch, tempted to call Chloe and keep her on the phone until they were aboard the chopper. But he didn't want to be a distraction. The missing helicopter already had him puzzled, but if that wasn't a clear go message from Mac, he didn't know what was. He couldn't wait to hear what that was all about.

\+ + +

"Get all the lights off!" Buck hollered, as he finally smashed through the thick wood. He heard Chaim hurry around flipping switches.

Over the intercom Chaim urgently told his gateman something in Hebrew. "What'd he say?" Chloe said, joining Buck and Tsion at the broken doorjamb in the dark. Each had a heavy bag.

"He told him no one gets in. Everyone's asleep. That won't keep them out long."

"Let's go," Buck said. "I hear a chopper."

"It's your imagination," Chloe said. "I think it's GC in the driveway."

"You're both paranoid," Tsion said, climbing through the broken door.

"I've got your bag, hon," Buck said.

"Buck! Don't baby me."

"It's the baby I'm thinking of. Now go."

"We never said good-bye to Chaim!"

"He'll understand. Go. Go."

As she stepped through the door, Chaim returned. "I'm waiting for word from the gate," he whispered. "A GC vehicle just pulled up."

Buck reached for him in the darkness and embraced him fiercely. "On behalf of all of us—"

"I know," Chaim said. "I'm so sorry about all this. Let me know when you are safe."

\+ + +

A nervous tingle swept over Rayford's body. After fueling and paying with Ken Ritz's international debit card, Rayford deliberately taxied the Gulfstream away from ground traffic about two hundred yards from where Ken would land the chopper. From where he sat he would be able to see the helicopter and get next to it as it landed.

His phone chirped. "Rayford, it's Mac. I'm finally alone. Listen and don't say anything. Leon took it on himself to get my chopper guy out of Haifa and put him in the air. They had some kind of incident near the stadium and didn't want to risk using me because of tomorrow's flight back on the Condor. I thought they'd have it back in time, and when they didn't and you called, I gave you the go-ahead to use Chopper One. Yes, that means your guy is in Carpathia's ride, but no one's the wiser if he gets it back quick. I was in a car with Leon, and that's why I sounded so strange.

"Here's the problem. Leon's got a couple of cars on their way to Rosenzweig's with a trumped-up charge against Buck. I heard 'em say a video proves it's bogus, but truth never stopped 'em before. Apparently the old man is not going to let them in, and they're afraid your people are on the run. Leon's asking for the chopper to light up the neighborhood. If he sees your guy, he's gonna think it's me until he asks and finds out it's not.

"I'm going to do what I can to misdirect, Ray, short of giving myself away. Just wanted you to know what you're dealing with. I've got another few seconds here if you've got any questions."

"Thanks, Mac. Bet you're glad this isn't a wrong number. Has this guy got weapons?"

"Two armed guys are with him, yes."

"What's Ken supposed to do if he encounters him?"

"Play cool like he's supposed to be there, but evade as soon as possible. That kid knows I'm not in the air."

"I'd better get off in case Ken's trying to reach me."

+ + +

"We were both right," Chloe whispered as they stepped out into the cool night air. Two GC vehicles were being stalled outside the gate, and a chopper illuminated the ground with a huge light. "Doesn't Ken know where we are?"

"I can't imagine," Buck said. "But we can't flag him down without giving ourselves away to those guys. C'mon, Ken! Right here, man!"

Suddenly, from right above them, GC Chopper One descended, whipping their hair and clothes. Ken opened the door and shouted, "Let's go, let's go, let's go!" Buck threw their bags in and helped Chloe climb aboard. He didn't dare peek down to see what kind of attention they were drawing from the guards on the ground.

Tsion and Buck leaped aboard. Ken was on the phone. "We're not alone, Ray! Two on the ground, one in the air! . . . All right, I'm going!" Ken swept up and away, heading north.

Tsion, Buck, and Chloe huddled together, holding hands and praying. Buck wondered how long it would be before the ground troops alerted the other helicopter. Three minutes later, with Ken speeding toward Jerusalem Airport, he found out. From over the radio came an urgent call. "GC Chopper One, this is Chopper Two, over."

Ken hollered into the phone, "Don't worry, Ray, I won't answer it. Anyway, I thought *we* were Chopper Two. . . . Tell me later. I'm on my way. . . . Mac's voice? How can I do that? I only talked to him on the phone once! . . . All right, I'll try! I'm comin' fast, so be ready!"

"Chopper Two to Chopper One, do you copy?"

"Go ahead, Two," Ken said, lowering his voice and effecting a Southern accent.

"I didn't know you were airborne, Cap."

"Roger, Two." Ken clicked the microphone as he spoke. "I . . . bad . . . connection . . . you . . . over?"

"Repeat, Cap?"

A frantic voice broke in. "McCullum is not in the air, Chopper Two! He's with us! Find out who that is!"

"Chopper Two to Chopper One, identify yourself, over."

Ken hesitated.

"Identify, Chopper One, or risk a charge of air piracy."

"This is Chopper One, go ahead."

"Identify yourself, pilot."

"Bad connection, come back."

The Chopper Two pilot swore. "Demand immediate descent and surrender, One."

"En route to Tel Aviv, Two. See you there."

"Negative! Put down at Jerusalem Airport and stay aboard!"

"Negative yourself, Two. See you at Ben Gurion."

Chopper Two put out a call for assistance to all aircraft in that sector.

"Now what?" Buck said.

"Lights off and stay low," Ken said.

"Not too low."

"High enough to clear power lines," Ken said. "Low enough to stay under radar."

"We gonna be all right?"

"Depends on where he was when he first called. If he was still in Chaim's neighborhood, we've got a pretty good lead on him. I doubt he'll stay this low or go this fast. No way he's dumb enough to believe we're going to Ben Gurion. Somebody's bound to spot us, and then he'll chase us to the airstrip. No time for restroom stops or seat changes at the airport, if that's what you're asking."

+ + +

Rayford sat near the runway listening to the radio traffic and resisting the urge to coach Ken. If he didn't know enough to stay low and push the chopper's limits, nothing Rayford could say would help.

The radio came to life again with a report from a small, fixed-wing plane that had sighted the low-flying GC chopper with its lights off.

"Chopper Two is in pursuit. Chopper One, you are breaking international aviation law by running without lights, high speeds at low altitude, and hijacking of government aircraft. Proceed directly to Jerusalem Airport and remain on board or suffer the consequences."

Airport personnel swept into action, emergency vehicles cruising the runways. "Attention please. Jerusalem Airport is temporarily closed due to an emergency. Be advised, all landing sequences and takeoffs are suspended until further notice. Cessna X-ray Bravo, you copy?"

"Roger."

"Piper Two-Niner Charley Alpha?"

"Roger."

"Gulfstream Alpha Tango?"

"Roger," Rayford said, but he did not shut down. He hoped Ken would understand why he was waiting at the wrong end of the runway. This would be a takeoff without clearance and in the wrong direction.

And here came the chopper. Ken wouldn't have time to talk on the phone, and the radio was not an option. Rayford checked his gauges. He was ready.

+ + +

Ken started to put down at the original spot.

"Gulfstream's up there!" Buck shouted. "And you've got security coming on the ground!"

Ken hopped the craft back up and set down near Rayford. The door of the Gulfstream hung open. Buck, Chloe, and Tsion set themselves to jump out of the chopper. "Hold tight a second," Ken shouted. "They see us board the Gulf now, they can block him easy! I'm going to have to play cat and mouse with 'em, make 'em think Ray's not involved!"

As security vehicles approached, Ken leapfrogged them, hovering just above where he had first set down, two hundred yards from the Gulfstream. "Put d haveown right there, Chopper One!" came the voice from Chopper Two on the radio. "And do not disembark. Repeat, do not disembark."

Ken put down but kept the blades whirring as the ground vehicles headed his way. "Shut it down, One!" the radio blared. Buck and the others saw Chopper Two descending from Rayford's end of the field, right toward them.

"Stay out of sight, and forget your bags, people," Ken said. "If I get you close, you're going to make a run for the Gulf."

"We're still going to try to do this?" Chloe said. "It's hopeless!"

"It's never hopeless as long as I'm breathin'," Ken said.

+ + +

Rayford stared out the cockpit windshield of the Gulfstream, imagining that any second Ken and all that was left of his own family would be surrounded by armed GC guards. They would never expose him, but dare he just sit and wait to leave when the airport reopened? His body boiled with frustration, wanting to do something, anything.

Ken was a creative, resourceful, smart guy. And it did appear he still had those blades spinning. What was he going to do? Let Chopper Two chase him some more? There was no hope in that.

"Shut it down, One!" the command came again. "You are surrounded with no possible escape!"

Chopper Two was within thirty feet of Ken, also on the ground now with blades engaged. Rayford watched, amazed, as Ken went straight up about a hundred feet, then pointed the nose of the chopper at the Gulfstream and seemed to fall right in front of it. It hit the tarmac at such an angle that it slid fifty feet and spun to a stop next to the open door.

+ + +

"Let's go kids!" Ken shouted. "Right now!"

He smacked the door open with a running back–like stiff-arm and grabbed Buck, tugging him past the front seat and out. Buck waited on the ground and caught Tsion as Ken handed him off. Tsion charged up the steps of the Gulfstream and stood ready to shut the door.

Buck was grateful Ken took a little more time with Chloe. "Go all the way in!" he said. "Tsion's got the door!"

+ + +

Rayford watched in horror as GC vehicles raced his way yet again. He had to get airborne. Betting ground control could not see people boarding his plane, he got on the radio. "Gulf Alpha Tango to ground control, requesting permission to get out of the way of this activity."

"Roger, Gulf. Just stay out of the way of security vehicles."

Rayford started rolling, though he knew only two had boarded. The Gulfstream screamed and whined as he slowly moved forward, edging past Chopper One, his door dragging on the pavement and throwing sparks. He couldn't leave the ground until everyone was aboard; then he had to pressurize the cabin before getting too high.

\+ + +

Buck's brain went into slow motion, and a kaleidoscope of images raced through his mind. In what seemed the next millisecond he remembered taking a bullet to his heel in Egypt while diving with Tsion aboard a Learjet piloted by Ken. Now while whirling to grab the door as the Gulfstream edged by, he saw clearly through the struts of the chopper that GC men sprinted toward them, taking aim.

Buck screamed, "Ken! Ken! Go! Go! Go!" as Ritz caught up to him. Buck pumped his legs as fast as he could, and Ken loped right behind with those long limbs. The Gulfstream picked up steam, and Buck felt the pull of the power on his body. He glanced back at Ken, whose face was inches from his, desperate determination in his eyes.

Buck was about to leap up the steps when Ken's forehead opened. Buck felt the heat and smelled the metal as the killing bullet sliced his own ear on the way by, and his face was splashed by Ken's gore. The big man's eyes were wide and vacant as he dropped out of sight.

Buck was yanked along, sobbing and screaming, his arm caught in the wire that supported the open door. He wanted to jump off, to run back to Ken, to kill someone. But he was unarmed, and Ken had to have been dead before he hit the ground. In spite of himself, despite his grief and horror and anger, Buck's instincts turned to his own survival.

The Gulfstream was now speeding along too fast for Buck's legs to keep up. Tsion leaned out as far as he could, straining with all his might to pull the door up and Buck with it. But the more he pulled, the more entangled Buck became. Chloe was helping now, crying and screaming herself, and Buck worried about the baby.

He lifted his feet to keep from scraping the leather off his shoes and burning his feet. The Gulfstream was at takeoff speed, the door stuck open, Buck pinned in the support—and he knew Rayford had no choice but to throttle up.

Buck tried to swing forward and catch a foot on the step, but the momentum and the wind made him unable to move. He was nearly horizontal now, and the vibration in the aluminum skin of the plane changed when the wheels left the ground. He squinted against the wind and grit that stung his eyes, and he could see Rayford would be lucky to clear the ten-foot fence in the grass at the wrong end of the runway.

The plane lumbered over the fence, and Buck felt as if he could have lowered a toe and brushed it. One thing was sure: He was not going to get into that plane now that it was in the air. The door would have to be shut mechanically. He could wait for that to sever his arm and fall to his death, or he could take his chances in the underbrush on the far side of the fence.

Buck pulled and twisted and jerked until his elbow cleared the wire. The horrified faces of his wife and his pastor were the last images he saw before he felt himself fall, cartwheeling, hitting the tops of tall bushes, and lodging himself, scraped and torn and bleeding, in the middle of a huge thicket.

His body shuddered uncontrollably, and he worried about going into shock. Then he heard the Gulfstream turn, and he knew Chloe would never let her father leave without him. But if they came back, if they landed to look for him, they were all as good as dead. Ken was already gone. That was enough for one night.

Painfully, he wrenched himself free and knew his injuries would require attention. No bones seemed broken, and as he stood, shivering in the cool of the night, he felt the bulge in his pocket. Was it possible? Had his phone survived?

He didn't dare hope as he flipped it open. The dial lit up. He hit Rayford's number.

"Mac?" he heard. "We've got a mess, and we need help!"

"No," Buck barked, his voice raw, "it's me and I'm all right. Go on, and I'll hook up with you later."

+ + +

Rayford wondered if he was dreaming. He was certain he had killed his own son-in-law. "Are you sure, Buck?" he shouted.

Chloe, who had collapsed in despair, now grabbed the phone out of Rayford's hand.

+ + +

"Buck! Buck! Where are you?"

"Past the fence in some nasty underbrush! I don't think they saw me, Chlo'! Nobody's coming this way. If they saw me running for the plane, they have to think I made it aboard."

"How did you survive?"

"I have no idea! Are you all right?"

"Am *I* all right? Of course! Ten seconds ago I was a widow! Is Ken with you?"

"No."

"Oh, no! They've got him?"

"He's gone, Chloe."

13

RAYFORD DECIDED to fly north as fast as he could, guessing that GC forces would assume he was heading west. "Tsion, dig through Ken's stuff and see if he has any record of friends of his in Greece. He mentioned our putting down there or Turkey if necessary."

Tsion and Chloe opened Ken's flight bag. "This is painful, Rayford," Tsion said. "This brother flew me to safety when there was a bounty on my head."

Rayford could not speak. He and Ken had clicked so quickly that he had made an instant friend. Because of their hours together in the air, he'd spent more time with him than anyone but Buck. And being closer to Ken's age, he felt a true kinship. He knew violence and death were the price of this period of history, but how he hated the shock and grief of the losses. If he began thinking of all the tragedy he had suffered—from missing out on the Rapture with his wife and son, to the loss of Bruce, Loretta, Donny and his wife, Amanda . . . and there were more—he would go mad.

Ken was in a better place, he told himself, and it sounded as hollow as any platitude. Yet he had to believe it was true. The loss was all his. Ken was finally free.

Rayford was bone weary. He was not supposed to be handling the flight back. Ken had reserved his hours behind the controls so he could pilot the Tribulation Force back to the States.

"What *is* all this?" Chloe asked suddenly. "He's got lists and ideas and plans for businesses, and—"

"I'll tell you later," Rayford said. "He was quite the entrepreneur."

"And brilliant," Tsion said. "I never figured him for this kind of thinker. Some of this reads like a manifesto of survival for the saints."

"No names though? Nothing that looks like a contact in Greece? I'm going to start that way, just in case. I can't fly much farther anyway."

"But we can't land without a local contact, can we, Dad?"

"We shouldn't."

"Can Mac help?"

"He'd call me if he was free to talk. I'm sure they've involved him in this fiasco. Pray he'll somehow misdirect them."

+ + +

Buck's facial lacerations were deep but below the cheekbones, so there was little bleeding. His right thumb felt as if it had been pulled back to his wrist. He could not stop the bleeding from his left ear where the bullet that had killed Ken had sliced it nearly in half. He quickly took off his shirt and undershirt, using the latter to wipe his face and sop his ear. He put his shirt back on, hoping he wouldn't appear so monsterlike that he would scare off anyone who might help him.

Buck crept to the airport edge of the underbrush but didn't dare get near the fence. Though no searchlights pointed that way, the fence provided a perfect background for any watchful eye to detect movement. He sat with his back to a large bush to catch his breath. His ankles and knees were tender, as was his right elbow. He must have taken the brunt of the crash into the spiky plant on his right side. He tilted his cell phone toward the light to see his foggy reflection in the lighted dial.

Feeling a sting below the cuff, Buck pulled his pant legs up a few inches to find both shins bleeding into his socks. His muscles ached, but under the circumstances he felt fortunate. He had his phone, and he could walk.

+ + +

"We might have found something," Tsion said. In Rayford's peripheral vision he could see the rabbi showing a phone directory page to Chloe.

"That looks Greek to me. What do you think, Dad? He's got a number for a Lukas Miklos, nickname Laslos."

"What city?"

"Doesn't say."

"Any other notations? Can you tell if it's a friend or a business contact?"

"Try the number. It's all we've got."

"Wait," Tsion said. "There's a star by the name and an arrow pointing down to the word *lignite.* I don't know that word."

"I don't either," Rayford said. "Sounds like a mineral or something. Dial him up, Chloe. If I'm landing in Greece, I've got to start initial descent in a few minutes."

+ + +

Buck couldn't remember the name of Jacov's mother-in-law. And he never caught Stefan's last name. He didn't want to call Chaim; his place had to be crawling with GC. He walked in the darkness, staying in the shadows, and made a huge loop around the airport and onto the main road. There he could either hitchhike or flag a taxi. Not knowing where else to turn, he would go to the Wailing Wall. Nicolae had publicly warned Moishe and Eli to disappear from there by the end of the stadium meeting, which told Buck they would be there for sure.

+ + +

"Yes, hello, ma'am," Chloe said. "Does anyone there speak English? . . . English! . . . I'm sorry, I don't understand you. Does anyone there—" She covered the phone. "I woke her. She sounds scared. She's getting someone. Sounds like she's waking him up.

"Yes! Hello? Sir? . . . Are you Mr. Miklos? . . . Do you speak English? . . . Not so good? Do you understand English? . . . Good! I am sorry to wake you, but I am a friend of Ken Ritz's from America!" Chloe covered the phone again. "He knows him!"

Chloe asked where he lived, whether there was an airstrip in town, and if they could visit him and talk about Ken if they landed there. Within minutes, Rayford was in touch with the tower at Ptolemaïs in northern Greece.

"Macedonia," Tsion said. "Praise God."

"We're not safe yet, Tsion," Rayford said. "We're depending on the kindness of a stranger."

+ + +

For the first time, Buck was grateful the Global Community had chosen the American dollar as its currency. He was cash rich, and that might keep eyes averted and mouths closed. Somewhere deep in his wallet, too, was his ever-useful phony identity . . . as long as he could keep from being searched and having both IDs exposed.

+ + +

"Mr. Miklos was suspicious," Chloe reported. "But once I convinced him we were friends of Ken's, he even told me what to tell the tower. Tell them you're Learjet Foxtrot Foxtrot Zulu. That's the plane of one of his suppliers. He runs a mining company. He will be there to meet us."

"This looks nothing like a Lear," Rayford said.

"He said the tower won't even pay attention."

+ + +

When Buck reached the road, he was surprised to see traffic still heavy. Witnesses must have still been streaming out of Jerusalem. And all the air traffic told him the airport had reopened already. He saw no roadblocks. The GC had to assume he had boarded the Gulfstream.

He moved to the side of the road leading into Jerusalem, which was much less congested than the other side. He waved his bloody undershirt at empty cabs coming from the airport, trying to show more white than red. He straightened up and tried to look sober and healthy. Buck lucked out on the fourth cab, which rumbled off the road and skidded in the gravel.

"You got money, mate?" the cabby said before unlocking the back door.

"Plenty."

"Not many pedestrians coming this way. First I've seen in weeks."

"Lost my ride," Buck said, getting in.

"A mite cut up now, ain't ya?"

"I'm all right. Got caught in some thorns."

"I should say."

"You an Aussie?"

"How'd you guess? Where to, mate?"

"The Wailing Wall."

"Ah, you won't get within a half mile of it tonight, sir."

"That so?"

"Big doings. You know the story of those two—"

"Yeah, what about 'em?"

"They're there."

"Yeah."

"And they're not supposed to be, ya know."

"I know."

"Word is the potentate is still in Jerusalem but not near the Wall. Huge crowd there with weapons. Civilians and military. Big mess. I'm a fan of the potentate, mind ya, but offerin' a bounty on the heads of these two wasn't wise."

"Think not?"

"Well, look what you've got now. Somebody's gonna kill 'em tonight and want to be made the hero. That's both citizens and guards. Who's to say they won't turn the guns on each other?"

"You think those two will buy it tonight?"

"Have to. They've planted themselves in their usual spot, got the whole city up in arms about the bloody water and the drought, takin' credit for it and all. Proud of it they are. They've killed a lot of mates who've tried to take 'em out, but what chance have they got now? They've put themselves behind that iron fence there, in a cage for target practice."

"I say they're still there and alive come daybreak."

"You don't say."

"If they are, would you do something for me?"

"Depends."

"If I'm right, and you've got to admit it's against all odds—"

"Oh, I'll grant ya that."

"—you find a Bible and read the book of Revelation."

"Oh, you're one of them, are you?"

"Them?"

"The witnesses. I've taken at least three loads of 'em to the airport tonight, and every last one of 'em's wanted to get me to join ranks. You gonna try to save me, mate?"

"I can't save you, friend. But I'm surprised God hasn't gotten your attention by now."

"Oh, I can't deny somethin' strange is happening. But I've got a pretty good gig going, if you know what I mean, and I don't guess God would look kindly on it. Lots of money on the other side of the street, ya know."

"Worth more than your soul?"

"Just might be. But I'll tell ya what. If those two are still there come mornin', I'll do what you say."

"Got a Bible?"

"I told ya. Had three carloads of your type tonight. Got three Bibles. Wanna make it four?"

"No, but I could use one of those if you can spare it."

"I'm a businessman, mate. I'll sell it to ya."

\+ + +

Rayford parked the jet at the end of a runway with similar-sized craft, and he and Chloe and Tsion walked cautiously into the mostly deserted terminal. A middle-aged couple eyed them warily from a dark corner. He was short and stocky with full, dark, curly hair. She was heavyset, her hair in curlers under a scarf.

After shy handshakes, Lukas Miklos said, "Ken Ritz gave you my name?"

"We found you in his address book, sir," Rayford said.

Miklos flinched and sat back. "How do I know you knew him?"

"I'm afraid we have bad news for you."

"Before you start with the bad news, I must know I can trust you. Tell me something about Ken that only a friend would know."

Rayford looked at the others and spoke carefully. "Former military, flew commercially, owned his own charter company for many years. Tall, late fifties."

"Did you know he used to fly one of my suppliers, when first I began serving energy plants?"

"No, sir. He did not mention that."

"He never spoke to you of me?"

"Not by name. He mentioned he knew someone in Greece who might provide hospitality on our way from the States."

"To where?"

"To Israel."

"And you were there for what?"

"For the Meeting of the Witnesses."

Miklos and his wife looked at each other. "Are you believers?"

Rayford nodded.

"Turn your face to the light."

Rayford turned.

Miklos looked at him, then at his wife, then turned his face to the light and pulled the curls back from his forehead. "Now you're not going to tell me this is Dr. Ben-Judah?"

"It is, sir."

"Oh, oh!" Miklos said, slipping off the chair and onto his knees on the tile floor. He took Ben-Judah's hands in his and kissed them while his wife clasped her hands before her face and rocked, her eyes closed. "I knew you looked familiar from the TV, but it's really you!"

"Now, now," Tsion said. "It's nice to meet you too, but I'm afraid the news is not good about our brother Ken."

\+ \+ \+

The cabby stopped in an alley behind a nightclub, where he apparently had an arrangement. A bouncer met him. "No, he's not a john, Stallion. And he ain't comin' in either. Get him a turban and a neck scarf, and I'll pay you later." Stallion reached in and grabbed the Aussie by the throat. "You'll get your cut, you overgrown child," the cabby said. "Now get the clothes and let me get outta here."

A minute later Stallion tossed the gear through the back window of the cab and pointed threateningly at the driver. "I'll be back," the Aussie said. "Trust me."

Buck pulled the rolled cap over his head and tucked the scarf under it, covering his ears and the back of his neck. If he held his head a certain way, it also covered most of his face. "Where does he get this stuff?"

"Sure you want to know?"

"Some drunk's going to be surprised when he wakes up."

Buck's ear had stopped bleeding, but he still needed medical attention. "Know where I can get antibacterial and a stitch or two without a lot of questions?"

"Cash leaves a lot of questions unasked, mate."

At three o'clock in the morning, as close as they could get to the Temple Mount, Buck paid the Aussie handsomely. "For the ride," he said. "For the Bible. And for the clothes."

"How about a little something for the medical services?"

Buck had paid cash at a backstreet clinic, but he guessed the lead alone was worth a few dollars.

"Thanks, mate. And I'll keep my promise. I'll be listening to the news. Wouldn't surprise me if they're dead already."

+ + +

Lukas Miklos owned a late-model luxury car and lived in an opulent home that was being repaired after the earthquake. He begged the Trib Force to stay a week, but Rayford told him they simply needed a good day's rest and would be on their way the next evening.

"Ken didn't know you were a believer, did he?"

Miklos shook his head as his wife apologetically returned to bed. Rayford and Tsion stood when she did, and she smiled shyly and bowed. "She runs the office," Miklos explained. "Gets there before I do."

He settled back in an easy chair. "Ken told me in an e-mail what had happened to him. We thought he was crazy. I knew the Carpathia regime opposed this rapture theory, and the Global Community sent me so much business, I did not want to appear to even know someone who opposed them."

"You did a lot of business with the GC?"

"Oh, yes. And we still do. I have no guilt about using the enemy's money. Their energy consultants buy tremendous quantities of lignite for their thermoelectric plants. Ken always said lignite grows on trees in Ptolemaïs. I wish it did! But he's right. It is plentiful, and I am one of the major suppliers."

"Why didn't you tell Ken you had become his brother?"

"Why, Mr. Steele, it happened only the other day, watching Dr. Ben-Judah on TV. We have been unable to reach Ken. He probably has an e-mail message from me on his computer."

+ + +

Buck walked as close to the Temple Mount as he could get before having to sidle through the jostling crowd. No one dared get within two hundred feet of Eli and Moishe, including GC guards—especially GC guards. Many civilians were armed too, and the atmosphere crackled with tension.

Buck felt safe and nearly invisible in the darkness, though he drew anger and was shoved as he kept working his way through the crowd. Occasionally, on tiptoes, he could see Eli and Moishe bathed in glaring TV lights. Again without amplification, they could be heard throughout the area.

"Where is the king of the world?" Eli demanded. "Where is he who sits on the throne of the earth? Ye men of Israel are a generation of snakes and vipers, blaspheming the Lord your God with your animal sacrifices. You bow to the enemy of the Lord, the one who seeks to defy the living God! The Lord who delivered his servant David out of the paw of the lion, and out of the paw of the bear, will deliver us out of the hand of this man of deceit."

The crowd laughed, but none advanced save Buck. He stayed on the move, feeling every sting and ache and pain, but eager to be close to these men of God. As he neared the front he found the crowd less belligerent and more wary. "Be careful, man," some said. "Watch yourself. Not too close now. They have flamethrowers behind that building."

Buck would have found that funny and the bravado of the witnesses invigorating, but Ken's awful death was too much with him. He instinctively wiped his face as if Ken's blood were still there, but his hand raked across his stitches and he nearly wept.

Moishe took over the speaking. "The servant of Satan comes to us with a sword, and with a spear, and with a shield. But we come in the name of the Lord of hosts, the God of the armies of his chosen, whom thou hast deceived. You shall be impotent against us until the due time!"

The crowd hissed and booed and cried out, "Kill them! Shoot them! Fire a missile at them! Bomb them!"

"O men of Israel," Eli responded. "Do you not care for water to drink or rain for your crops? We allow the sun to bake your land and turn the water into blood for as long as we prophesy, that all the earth may know that there is a God in Israel. And all this assembly shall know that the Lord saveth not with sword and spear: for the battle is the Lord's, and he has given you into our hands."

"Show them! Kill them! Destroy them!"

The crowd gasped and drew back as Buck reached the front and stepped ten feet closer to the fence than anyone else. He was still far from the witnesses, but after what had happened the night before, he appeared brave or foolish. The crowd fell silent.

Moishe and Eli stood side by side now, not moving, hands at their sides. They stared past Buck, appearing resolute in their challenge to Carpathia. He had given permission for anyone to kill them if they showed their faces anywhere after the meetings. And now they stood where they had appeared every day since the signing of the agreement between the Global Community and Israel.

Buck felt drawn to them in spite of his desperation to remain unrecognized. He stepped yet closer, causing the crowd to deride him and laugh at his foolhardiness.

Neither witness opened his mouth, but Buck heard them both in unison. It was as if the message was for him alone. He wondered whether anyone else heard it.

"For whosoever will save his life shall lose it; but whosoever shall lose his life for Christ's sake and the gospel's, the same shall save it."

They knew about Ken? Were they consoling Buck?

Suddenly Moishe looked to the crowd and shouted, "For what shall it profit a man, if he shall gain the whole world, and lose his own soul? Or what shall a man give in exchange for his soul? Whosoever therefore shall be ashamed of Jesus Christ and of his words in this adulterous and sinful generation; of him also shall the Son of Man be ashamed, when he cometh in the glory of his Father with the holy angels."

And just as suddenly the two spoke in unison again, softer, without moving their lips, as if just to Buck. "There be some of them that stand here, which shall not taste of death, till they have seen the kingdom of God come with power."

Buck had to speak. He whispered, his back to the crowd so none could hear. "We want to be among those who do not taste death," he said. "But we lost another of our own tonight." He couldn't go on.

"What'd he say?" someone blurted.

"He's gonna get himself torched."

The two spoke directly to Buck's heart again. "There is no man that hath left house, or brethren, or sisters, or father, or mother, or wife, or children, or lands, for Jesus' sake, and the gospel's, but he shall receive an hundredfold now in this time, houses, and brethren, and sisters, and mothers, and children, and lands, with persecutions; and in the world to come eternal life."

God *had* provided for Buck a place to live and new brothers and sisters in Christ! How Buck wished he could come right out and ask the witnesses what he should do, where he should go. How was he going to reunite with his wife when he was a fugitive from the GC? Would he have to be spirited out the way he had rescued Tsion?

A GC bullhorn warned him to retreat. "And to the two who are under arrest. You have sixty seconds to surrender peacefully. We have strategically placed concussion bombs, mines, and mortars with kill power in a two-hundred-yard radius. Evacuate now or stay at your own peril! The clock begins when the last translation of this announcement has ended. In the meantime, the ranking officer of the Global Community, under direct authority of the supreme commander and the potentate himself, will offer to escort the fugitives to a waiting vehicle."

As the announcement was translated into several languages, the crowd gleefully dispersed, sprinting out of range of the explosives and crouching behind cars and concrete barriers. Buck slowly backed away, never taking his eyes from Moishe and Eli, whose jaws were set.

From the right a lone GC guard, decked out in military ribbons but unarmed and with his hands in the air, hurried toward the witnesses. When he was within ten yards, Eli shouted so loudly that the man seemed paralyzed from the sound wave alone. "Dare not approach the servants of the Most High God, even with an empty hand! Save yourself! Find shelter in caves or behind rocks!"

The GC man slipped and fell, then fell again as he scrambled to get away. Buck picked up his pace too but was still walking backward, his eyes on the witnesses. From a branch high above him came two loud, echoing reports from a rifle. The sniper was less than fifty feet from Eli and Moishe, and what happened to the bullets Buck could not say. A burst of flame shot from Moishe's mouth straight to the soldier, who somehow kept a grip on his weapon until his flaming body slammed to the stony ground. Then the rifle bounced twenty feet away. He burned quickly into a pile of ashes as if in a kiln, and his rifle melted and burned too.

Silence fell over the area as guards, crowd, and Buck waited for the igniting of the threatened weapons. Buck was now back with the rest of the onlookers, huddled beneath the low-slung roof of a portico across the way. When he was sure the minute had long passed, the air grew cold as winter. Buck shivered uncontrollably as those around him groaned and wept in fear. A wind kicked up and howled, and people tried to cover exposed skin and huddle together against the frigid blast. Hail fell as if a cosmic truck had unloaded tons of golf ball–size spheres of ice all in one dump. In ten seconds the downpour stopped, and the area was ten inches deep in melting ice.

The power that supplied electricity for the TV lights popped and sizzled and blew out, plunging the area into darkness. In three locations simultaneously, what appeared to be boxes of explosives burned, emitted a series of muffled pops, then disintegrated into ash.

Such was the extent of the murderous attack on the witnesses.

Two helicopters aimed gigantic searchlights on the Temple Mount as the temperature rose, Buck guessed, into the nineties. The shin-deep hail turned to water in an instant, and the sound of it running away was like a babbling brook. Within minutes the mud turned to dust as if it were the middle of the day and the sun had baked it.

And all the while, the crowd whimpered and whined every time the circling choppers lit up the area near the Wall. Eli and Moishe had not moved an iota.

* * *

As he and Chloe and Tsion headed off to the guest rooms, Rayford thanked Lukas Miklos for his hospitality. "You are an answer to prayer, my friend."

Tsion promised to send Miklos a list of believers in Greece. "And Mr. Miklos, would you pray with us for Chloe's husband, Captain Steele's son-in-law?"

"Certainly," Miklos said, following their lead to hold hands and bow his head. When his turn came, he said, "Dear Jesus Christ, protect that boy. Amen."

14

BUCK, THRILLED but also grieving and exhausted, caught another cab to within two blocks of Chaim Rosenzweig's. Still wearing his headgear, he walked close enough to see that the GC were long gone. The gateman, Jonas, dozed at his post.

Knowing neither Jonas nor Chaim professed faith yet, Buck hesitated. He knew Chaim was at least learning the truth about Carpathia and would not turn Buck in. Jonas was a gamble. Buck didn't know if the man spoke or understood English, having heard him speak only Hebrew. The man had to know some English, didn't he? Serving as the first contact with visitors?

Emboldened by the exhilarating challenges of Eli and Moishe, Buck took a deep breath, gently touched an itching stitched wound below his eye, and walked directly to the gatehouse. He didn't want to startle the man, but he had to wake him. He tossed a pebble at the window. Jonas did not stir. Buck knocked lightly, then more loudly. Still he did not rouse. Finally Buck opened the door and gently touched Jonas's arm.

A burly man in his late fifties, Jonas leaped to his feet, eyes wild. Buck whipped off his disguise, then realized his face had to look horrible. Red, blotched, swollen, stitched, he looked like a monster.

Jonas must have taken the removal of the headdress as a challenge. Unarmed, he grabbed a huge flashlight from his belt and reared back with it. Buck spun away, wincing at the very thought of a blow to his tender face. "It's me, Jonas! Cameron Williams!"

Jonas put his free hand to his heart, forgetting to lower the flashlight. "Oh, Mr. Williams!" he said, his English so broken and labored that Buck hardly recognized his own name. Finally Jonas put the light away and used both hands to help communicate, gesturing with every phrase. "They," he said ominously, pointing outside and waving as if to indicate a sea of people, "been looked for you." He pointed to his own eyes.

"Me personally? Or all of us?"

Jonas looked lost. "Personal?" he said.

"Just for me?" Buck tried, realizing he was copying Jonas and pointing to himself. "Or for Tsion and my wife?"

Jonas closed his eyes, shook his head, and held up one hand, palm out. "Not here," he said. "Tsion, wife, gone. Flying." He fluttered his fingers in the air.

"Chaim?" Buck said.

"Sleeps." Jonas demonstrated with a hand to his cheek and his eyes shut.

"May I go in and sleep, Jonas?"

The man squinted at this puzzle. "I call." He reached for the phone.

"No! Let Chaim sleep! Tell him later."

"Later?"

"Morning," Buck said. "When he wakes up." Jonas nodded, but still had his hand on the phone as if he might dial. "I'll go in and sleep," Buck added, acting it out like charades. "I'll leave a note on Chaim's door so he won't be surprised. OK?"

"OK!"

"I'll go in now?"

"OK!"

"All right?"

"All right!"

Buck watched Jonas while backing away and heading for the door. Jonas watched him too, let go of the phone, waved, and smiled. Buck waved, then turned and found the door locked. He had to go back and explain to Jonas that he would have to let Buck in. Finally, for the first time since the chopper had left the roof hours before, Buck could relax. He left a note on Chaim's door with no details—just that he was in the guest room with much to tell him and that he would likely see him late morning.

Buck looked at himself in the bathroom mirror. It was worse than he thought, and he prayed the so-called clinic he had visited at least had a modicum of sterility. The stitching looked professional enough, but he was a mess. The whites of his eyes were full of blood. His face was a patchwork of colors, none close to his complexion. He was glad Chloe didn't have to see him like this.

He locked the bedroom door, let his clothes fall by the bed, and stretched out painfully. And heard the soft chirp of his phone. It had to be Chloe, but he didn't want to stand up again. He rolled over, reached for his pants, and as he struggled to free the phone from the back pocket, his weight shifted, and he tumbled out of bed.

He wasn't hurt, but the racket woke Chaim. As Buck answered his phone, he heard Chaim crying over the intercom: "Jonas! Jonas! Intruders!"

By the time it was sorted out, he and Chloe were up-to-date, Chaim had heard the whole story, and the sun was beginning to peek over the horizon. It was agreed that Chloe and Tsion and Rayford would go on home to Mount Prospect and that Chaim would work on finding a way for Buck to get back when he had recuperated.

Chaim was even angrier than Buck had seen him on the phone to Leon. He said the TV news had been running and rerunning the videotape of Buck talking with the GC guard who was killed a few seconds later. "The tape makes it obvious you were unarmed, that he was fine when you left him, and that you neither turned around nor returned. He fired over your head, and moments later he was spun around by bullets from high-powered rifles at close range. We all know they had to have come from the weapons of his own compatriots. But it will never get that far. It will be covered up, he will be accused of working with you or for you, and who knows what else will come of it?"

The "what else" turned out to be a news story concocted by the GC. Television reports said that an American terrorist named Kenneth Ritz had hijacked Nicolae Carpathia's own helicopter to stage an escape by the Tsion Ben-Judah party from house arrest at Chaim Rosenzweig's. The reports claimed Rosenzweig had hosted Ben-Judah, murder suspect Cameron Williams, and Williams's wife and had agreed to lock them under house arrest for the GC. Scenes of Dr. Rosenzweig's roof access door, "clearly broken from the inside show conclusively how the Americans escaped."

A Global Community spokesman said Ritz was shot and killed by a sniper when he opened fire on GC forces at Jerusalem Airport. The other three fugitives were at large internationally, and it was assumed that Williams, a former employee of the Global Community, was an accomplished jet pilot.

\+ \+ \+

The stateside members of the Tribulation Force followed the news carefully, keeping in touch with Chaim and Buck as often as possible. Rayford was amazed at the improvement in Hattie after such a short time. Her illness and despair and stubbornness had synthesized into a fierce hatred and determination. She grieved the loss of her child so deeply that Rayford was haunted by her stifled wails in the night.

Chloe, too, battled anger. "I know we should expect nothing less from the world system, Daddy," she said, "but I feel so helpless I could explode. If we don't find a way to get Buck back here soon, I'm going over there myself. Have you ever wished you could be the one God uses to kill Carpathia when the time comes?"

"Chloe!" Rayford said, hoping his response sounded like scolding rather than a cover for the fact that he had prayed for that very privilege. What was happening to them? What were they becoming?

Word came from Buck that Jacov had helped him get set up undercover with Stefan. Rayford felt better about that than his staying with Chaim. It was clear Global Community security forces believed Buck had escaped with the others, but living under an alias in a lower middle-class neighborhood made him less vulnerable and gave him a chance to heal. He told Rayford by phone that within a few weeks he would attempt to return to the States commercially, probably from a major European airport. "Since they're not looking for me over here, I should be able to slip out under a phony name."

Meanwhile, Rayford had stayed in touch with Mac McCullum and David Hassid and used David's leads to replace everyone's computers and add to their bag of tricks the hand-sized units that could both access the Internet and serve as solar-powered, satellite-connected global phones.

Tsion often expressed to Rayford his satisfaction with his new computer—a light, thin, very portable laptop that plugged into a docking station that gave him all sorts of handy accessories at home. It was the latest, fastest, most powerful model on the market. Tsion spent most of every day communicating with his international flock, which had exploded even before the meetings in Israel and now multiplied exponentially every day.

With Hattie improving physically if not mentally, Dr. Floyd Charles had time to take Ken's place as the Tribulation Force's technical adviser. He installed scrambling software that kept their phones and computers untraceable.

The toughest chore for Rayford was dealing with his emotions over Ken. He knew they all missed him, and Tsion's message at a brief memorial service left them all in tears. Chloe spent two days on the Internet searching for surviving relatives and turned up nothing. Rayford informed Ernie at Palwaukee, who promised to pass the word to the staff there and secure Ken's belongings until Rayford could get there to assess them. He said nothing to Ernie about Ken's gold stash, knowing that the two, while fellow believers, had not known each other long.

+ + +

Buck bought a computer so he could log onto the Net and study under Tsion. But he was unable to find untraceable software that would allow him to communicate with Chloe except by phone. He missed her terribly but was pleased to hear she and the unborn baby were healthy, though she admitted Doc had expressed some concern over her fragility.

She kept busy building a business model based on Ken Ritz's notes. Within a month, she told Buck, she hoped to run the business by computer, networking believers around the globe. "Some will plant and reap," she said. "Others will market and sell. It's our only hope once the mark of the beast is required for legal trade." She told him her first order of business was enlisting growers, producers, and suppliers. Once that was in place, she would expand the market.

"But what about when you have a baby to take care of?" he said.

"I hope my husband will be home by then," she said. "He has nothing to manage but a little alternative Internet magazine, so I'll teach him."

"Teach him what? Your business or child care?"

"Both," she said.

Late one Friday she mentioned to Buck on the phone that Rayford was planning to visit Palwaukee Airport the next day. "He's going to look at Ken's planes and try to get to know this Ernie kid better. He might be a good mechanic, but Ken hardly knew him."

That night Buck logged on to find Tsion's teaching for the day. The rabbi seemed down, but Buck realized that people who didn't know him personally probably wouldn't notice. He wrote about the heartbreak of losing friends and family and loved ones. He didn't mention Ken by name, but Buck read between the lines.

Tsion concluded his teaching for the day by reminding his readers that they had recently passed the twenty-four-month mark since the signing of the peace pact between the Global Community (known two years before as the United Nations) and the State of Israel. "I remind you, my dear brothers and sisters, that we are but a year and a half from what the Scriptures call the Great Tribulation. It has been hard, worse than hard, so far. We have survived the worst two years in the history of our planet, and this next year and a half will be worse. But the last three and a half years of this period will make the rest seem like a garden party."

Buck smiled at Tsion's insistence at always ending with a word of encouragement, regardless of the hard truth he had to convey. He closed by quoting Luke 21: "'There will be signs in the sun, in the moon, and in the stars; and on the earth distress of nations, with perplexity, the sea and the waves roaring; men's hearts failing them from fear and the expectation of those things which are coming on the earth, for the powers of heaven will be shaken. Then they will see the Son of Man coming in a cloud with power and great glory. Now when these things begin to happen, look up and lift up your heads, because your redemption draws near.'"

The next morning at seven in Israel, Buck was watching a television news report of Nicolae Carpathia's response to Eli and Moishe, who were still wreaking havoc in Jerusalem. The reporter quoted Supreme Commander Leon Fortunato, speaking for the potentate, "His Excellency has decreed the preachers enemies of the world system and has authorized Peter the Second, supreme pontiff of Enigma Babylon One World Faith, to dispose of the criminals as he sees fit. The potentate does not believe, and I agree, that he should involve himself personally in matters that should be under the purview of the Global Community's religious division. His Excellency told me just last night, and I quote, 'Unless, that is, we discover that our Pontifex Maximus is impotent when it comes to dealing with those who use trickery and mass hypnosis to paralyze an entire country.'"

Of course, it being a "balanced" broadcast, Buck was not surprised to see a furious Peter Mathews spitting a reply. "Oh, the problem is mine now, is it? Has His Excellency finally ceded authority to where it belongs? Of course, not until it was proven his military had no power over these impostors. When the two lie dead, the rains will fall again in Israel, clear, pure, refreshing water will cascade once more, and the world will know where the true seat of power resides."

A week before, Buck had gotten Chaim to visit the preachers at the Wall, and the old man admitted coming away shaken by the experience and more disillusioned with Carpathia. "But still, Cameron, as long as Nicolae upholds his end of the bargain and honors the pact with Israel, I will trust him. I have no choice. I want to and I need to."

Buck had pressed him. "If he should betray Israel, what would you think of all you have heard and learned from Tsion and what you know from what my father-in-law heard behind the scenes? Might you defect and join us?"

Rosenzweig would not commit. "I am an old man," he said, "set in my ways. I regret I am a hard sell. You and your fellow believers are most impressive, and I hope against hope you are not proven right in the end, for I will be most miserable. But I have cast my lot with the world I can touch and feel and see. I am not ready to throw over intellectualism for blind faith."

"That is what you think Tsion has done?"

"Please don't tell him I said that. Tsion Ben-Judah is a brilliant scholar who does not fit the image I have of believers. But then neither do any of you in his immediate circle. That should tell me something, I suppose."

"God is trying to get your attention, Dr. Rosenzweig. I hope it doesn't take something drastic."

Rosenzweig had waved him off. "Thank you for caring."

Now Buck sat shaking his head at the TV report, knowing it was eleven at night in Illinois and that his family and friends would not have seen this yet. He wished he could leave them a message on e-mail that would tell them to be sure to watch. But he couldn't transmit from this location without leaving Stefan and himself exposed to the GC.

He thought about calling and leaving a message, but Chloe had begun sleeping so lightly that she always answered, even in the middle of the night. She needed her sleep.

With his housemate off at work, Buck stepped out into the morning sunshine. He felt such a longing to be back at the safe house that he nearly wept. He squinted at the brilliance of a cloudless sky and enjoyed the pleasant warmth of a windless day. And suddenly it seemed someone pulled a shade down on the heavens.

With the sun still riding high in the clear sky, the morning turned to twilight and the temperature plummeted. Buck knew exactly what it was, of course: the prophecy of Revelation 8:12. The fourth angel had sounded, "and a third of the sun was struck." The same would befall a third of the moon and the stars. Whereas the sun shone for around twelve hours every day in most parts of the world, it would now shine no more than eight, and at only two-thirds its usual brilliance.

Even knowing it was coming did not prepare Buck for the awe he felt at God's power. A lump formed in his throat, and his chest grew tight. He hurried into the empty house and fell to his knees. "God," he prayed, "you have proven yourself over and over to me, and yet I find my faith strengthened all the more every time you act anew. Everything you promise, you deliver. Everything you predict comes to pass. I pray this phenomenon, publicized all over the world by Tsion and the 144,000 witnesses, will reach millions more for you. How can anyone doubt your power and your greatness? You are fearsome but also loving and gracious and kind. Thank you for saving me. Thank you for Chloe and our baby, and for her dad and Tsion and Doc. Thank you for the privilege of having known Ken. Protect our people wherever they are, and give me the chance to meet Mac and David. Show us what to do. Guide us in how to serve you best. I give myself to you again, willing to go anywhere and do anything you ask. I praise you for Jacov and Hannelore and Stefan and these new brothers and sisters who have taken me in. I want Chaim for you, Lord. Thank you for being such a good and great God."

Buck was overcome, realizing that the darkening would affect everything in the world. Not just brightness and temperatures, but transportation, agriculture, communications, travel—everything that had anything to do with him and his loved ones reuniting.

He wanted to warn the Tribulation Force, but he waited until seven o'clock in the morning Chicago time. They liked to rise with the sun, but it wasn't going to rise for them. Buck wondered what darkened stars looked like. It wouldn't be long.

He dialed Chloe and woke her up.

\+ + +

Rayford had awakened early and looked at his watch. It was quarter to seven and still dark. He lay staring at the ceiling, wondering if they were in for some bad weather or just a cloudy day. At seven he heard Chloe's phone ring. It would be Buck, and Rayford wanted to talk to him. He would give her a few minutes, then go down and give her the high sign.

Rayford lay back and breathed deeply. He wondered what Palwaukee would produce that day. Did he dare raise with young Ernie the subject of hidden treasure? That would depend on how their conversations went. He assumed it would take a while to develop trust. Ernie was very young.

Chloe sounded agitated. And she was calling for him. He sat up. It was way too early for anything with her baby. Was something wrong with Buck? "Dad! Come down here!" He dragged on a robe.

She met him at the bottom of the stairs, the cell phone to her ear. "Look a little dark for seven?" she said. "Buck says the sun was struck at seven in the morning over there. While we were sleeping. Talk to Daddy, hon. I'm going to start getting people up around here."

\+ + +

To Buck, Rayford sounded stunned. "Incredible," he said, over and over. "We're going to have to determine what this means to all our solar-powered stuff."

"I thought Doc was already working on that."

"He was. We just didn't like his conclusions. For some reason, the sum is not equal to its parts in a deal like this. You can't just figure you're going to have a third less power. He put his big calculator to it and said it's a third less power on top of being a third less time every twenty-four hours. He sketched out a model of what it will mean just to us, and we didn't like it. Couldn't argue with it and couldn't store much power in advance, but we sure hope he's wrong."

"He won't be," Buck said. "Smart guys never are. Hang on a second, Rayford, I want to see who this other call is from."

Buck punched in caller ID. He got back on with Rayford. "It's Rosenzweig. I'd better call Chloe back."

"I'll tell her. Watch your phone power now."

"Right." He hit the switch. "Dr. Rosenzweig!"

"Cameron, I need to see you. I need some counsel."

"You want to meet now?"

"Can you manage it?"

"I suppose you know what's really happening," Buck said.

"Of course I do! I was at the last meeting when Tsion spoke of this prophecy."

"You admit it's too obvious to be anything else."

"What thinking man would not know that?"

Thank you, God! Buck thought.

"The problem, and what I need to talk to you about, is what do I say? The media is all over this and wants a comment for tomorrow's broadcasts. I told a half dozen that I am a botanist, and the best I can tell them is what it will mean to photosynthesis."

"What will it mean, by the way?"

"Well, it will bollix it all up, if you want my technical response. But the newspeople are reminding me that I have always spoken out on scientific subjects, even outside my area of expertise. You will recall Nicolae had me speculating on the causes of the disappearances. I almost convinced myself with that spontaneous atomic reaction blather."

"You almost convinced me too, Doctor, and I was an international news correspondent."

"Well, I just heard from Fortunato, and he wants me to corroborate the Global Community view of this phenomenon."

"How can I help?"

"We need to strategize. I am considering bursting their bubble. I might imply that I will endorse their view—wait till you see it—and when I get on the air, I will say what I want. I owe at least that to Leon."

"You're worried what Carpathia will think."

"Of course."

"It will be a test of your relationship."

"Exactly. I'll find out how free a citizen I am. I have given Leon nothing short of grief for making it appear I had worked with him on detaining the three of you. I could have exposed the whole strong-arm regime, but Nicolae apologized personally and asked that I not embarrass him."

"He did? You never told me that."

"It didn't seem appropriate. You have no idea how close I came to telling him that I would trade a friend's free passage out of the country for my agreeing to let that news report slide. I just couldn't muster the courage to ask."

"Probably wise," Buck said. "I can't see him making that kind of trade. Finding out I've been here right under their noses would have infuriated him."

"I did have the audacity to ask if he had considered that his tactics against Ben-Judah and his people might be the reason for all the plagues and judgments. He chided me for buying into all that fiction. Now I must meet with you, Cameron."

"Can we meet somewhere private?"

Rosenzweig suggested a dank, underground eatery appropriately called The Cellar. Buck asked for a table in the corner under a dim light where they could look at Chaim's document without being disturbed. Rosenzweig produced a fax of the official Global Community assessment of what had struck that morning. It was all Buck could do to keep from howling.

The fax contained all kinds of legalese, insisting on its confidentiality, its for-your-eyes-only nature, its personal direction to Dr. Chaim Rosenzweig only, and all this under penalty of prosecution by the supreme commander of the Global Community under the authority of His Excellency, blah, blah, blah.

It read: "Dr. Rosenzweig, His Excellency wishes me to convey his deep personal appreciation for your willingness to endorse the official policy statement of the Global Community Aeronautics and Space Administration regarding the natural astronomical phenomenon that occurred 0700 hours New Babylon time today."

"Of course, I agreed only to review it, but Leon proceeds with his typically presumptuous tone. Anyway, here's the party line."

Buck read, "The GCASA is pleased to assure the public that the darkening of the skies that began this morning is the result of an explainable natural phenomenon and should not be cause for alarm. Top scientific researchers have concluded that this is a condition that should rectify itself in forty-eight to ninety-six hours.

"It should not significantly affect temperatures, except in the short run, and the lack of brightness should not be misconstrued as lack of solar power and energy. While there may be some short-term impact on smaller solar-powered equipment such as cell phones, computers, and calculators, there should be no measurable impact on the power reserves held by Global Community Power and Light.

"As for what happened in space to cause this condition, experts point to the explosion of a massive star (a supernova), which resulted in the formation of a magnetar (or supermagnetized star). Such a heavenly body can be up to fifteen miles across but weigh twice as much as the sun. It is formed when the massive star explodes and its core shrinks under gravity. The magnetar spins at a tremendous rate of speed, causing the elements in its core to rise and become intensely magnetic.

"Flashes from such events can emit as much energy as the sun would produce in hundreds of years. Normally these bursts are contained in the upper atmosphere, which absorbs all the radiation. While we have not detected harmful levels of radiation, this flash clearly occurred at an altitude low enough to affect the brightness of the sun. Current readings show a decrease in light between 30 and 35 percent.

"The GCASA will maintain constant watch on the situation and report significant changes. We expect the situation to normalize before the end of next week."

Rosenzweig shook his head and looked into Buck's eyes. "A convincing piece of fantasy, no?"

"I'd buy it if I didn't know better," Buck said.

"Well, this is not my field, as you know. But even I can see through this. The creation of a magnetar would have no effect on the brightness of the sun, moon, or stars except maybe to make them brighter. It would affect radio waves, maybe knock out satellites. If it happened low enough in our atmosphere, as they imply, to affect earth, it would probably knock the earth off its axis. Whatever this was, it was not the creation of a magnetar from a supernova."

"What do you mean, 'Whatever this was'? You know as well as I do what it was."

"As a matter of fact, I think I do."

Dr. Rosenzweig tried out on Buck what he planned to say live on the air when asked about the event. "I'll even carry the document solemnly in my hand, rolled up and dog-eared, as if I have been agonizing over it for hours."

"I love it," Buck said. He phoned the States, something that grew increasingly difficult as the hours of darkness continued and would become nearly impossible within days.

Chloe answered. "Yes, dear," she said. "Your phone call from Chaim lasted this long?"

"No, sorry. Got tied up. I just wanted to tell you to watch for him on the news with his assessment of what happened."

"What *is* his assessment?"

"I don't want to spoil it for you. Just make sure nobody misses it. It'll make your day."

"We're having power problems here already, Buck, and this connection isn't the best."

"Save enough to watch Chaim. You'll be glad you did."

15

EATING A LATE DINNER that evening, Tsion shared with the Stateside Tribulation Force his joy over a wildly successful effort by many believers on the Internet. "I merely put out a simple request—you all saw it—for translators in various countries to interpret the daily messages in their own languages. You can imagine how much of the Net is made up of Asian language groups, Spanish, German, and others.

"Well," he added with a twinkle, "not only did I get far more volunteers than I needed, but some very advanced computer types are offering free software downloads that automatically translate into other languages. It's Pentecost on the Net. I'm able to type in unknown tongues!"

Rayford was always warmed by the joy Tsion took in his work and ministry. He had sacrificed as much as anyone in their little group—a wife and two children. Chloe had lost her mother and brother and now two friends. Rayford had lost two wives, his son, his pastor, and more new acquaintances than he wanted to think about. Everybody around the table, Doc Charles and Hattie included, had reason to go mad if they allowed themselves to dwell on it.

Momentary smiles were all they could muster when Tsion shared a story like that or someone made the occasional wry comment. Raucous laughter or silliness just didn't have a place in their lives anymore. Grief was wearying, Rayford thought. He looked forward to that day when God would wipe away all tears from their eyes, and there would be no more war.

That was one reason he looked forward with relish to the ten o'clock news event that had been trumpeted on the GC Broadcasting Networks all day. The GC was bringing together experts who would speak to the official statement of the government related to the darkness that had already begun to take its toll. Buck had insinuated that Chaim would be entertaining. Although Rayford couldn't imagine a belly laugh, he looked forward to the diversion.

"I just hope," Tsion said, "that we detect some movement in Chaim's spirit. When I was laying out all the prophecies again for him, I challenged him. I said, 'Chaim, how can a man with such a mind as yours ignore the mathematical impossibility of so many dozens of prophecies referring to just one man unless he is the Messiah?' He started with the typical argument about not knowing whether the Bible is authentic. I said, 'My mentor! You would doubt your own Torah? Where do you think I am coming up with this stuff?' I tell you, young people, it won't be long for Chaim. I just don't want him to wait too long."

Rayford, just three or so years younger than Tsion, loved being referred to as a young person.

Hattie spoke up, her voice stronger than ever. "Do you still feel that way about me, Dr. Ben-Judah? Or have I convinced you I am a lost cause?"

Tsion put his fork down and pushed his plate away. "Miss Durham," he said quietly, "are you sure you want to hear my thoughts on your situation in front of the others?"

"Go for it," she said, just short of gleeful. "I have no secrets, and I know you people sure don't."

Tsion entwined his fingers. "All right, since you brought it up and gave me permission. You and I rarely interact. I hear what you say and know where you stand, and you know that my whole life is now dedicated to proclaiming what I believe. So my views are not a mystery to you either. You are nearly twenty years my junior and we are of opposite sexes, and so there is a generational and gender barrier that has perhaps caused me to be less frank with you than I might have been with someone else.

"But it might surprise you to know how frequently during each day God brings you to my mind."

Rayford thought Hattie looked more than surprised. She had a glass of water suspended between the table and her lips, and her bemused smile had frozen.

"Again, I do not intend to embarrass you—"

"Oh, you can't embarrass me, Doc. Let me have it." She smiled as if she had finally reeled in a big one.

"If you would permit me to speak from my heart. . . ."

"Please," she said, setting her glass down and settling herself as if ready to enjoy this. Rayford thought she enjoyed being in Tsion's spotlight.

"I feel such compassion for you," Tsion said, "such a longing for you to come to Jesus." And suddenly he could not continue. His lips trembled, and he could not form words.

Hattie raised her eyebrows, staring at him.

"Forgive me," he managed in a whisper, taking a sip of water and collecting himself. He continued through tears. "Somehow God has allowed me to see you through his eyes—a scared, angry, shaken young woman who has been used and abandoned by many in her life. He loves you with a perfect love. Jesus once looked upon his audience and said, 'O Jerusalem, Jerusalem, the one who kills the prophets and stones those who are sent to her! How often I wanted to gather your children together, as a hen gathers her chicks under her wings, but you were not willing!'

"Miss Durham, you know the truth. I have heard you say so. And yet you are not willing. No, I do not consider you a lost cause. I pray for you every bit as much as I pray for Chaim. Because Jesus went on to say about the hard-hearted people of Jerusalem, 'I say to you, you shall see Me no more till you say, "Blessed is He who comes in the name of the Lord!"'

"I look at you in your fragile beauty and see what life has done to you, and I long for your peace. I think of what you could do for the kingdom during these perilous times, and I am jealous to have you as part of our family. I fear you're risking your life by holding out on God, and I do not look forward to how you might suffer before he reaches you.

"I'm sorry if I embarrassed you, but you asked."

Hattie sat shaking her head, and Rayford had the impression she was more surprised than embarrassed. She did not respond except to go from shaking to nodding. "What time is that news thing?" she asked.

"Right now," Chloe said, and everyone cleared his own dishes.

\+ + +

Buck settled in front of the television in Jerusalem with his notebook, fascinated by the foreboding dusk at dawn. He was grateful that both Jacov and Stefan were off and had showed up to watch the press conference with him.

"Press conference" was a misnomer, of course, now that the Global Community owned the media. Only in underground publications like Buck's did readers get objective substance. That was what made Chaim's appearance so intriguing. If he had the guts to follow through on what he told Buck he would say, it would be the most controversial thing on television since Tsion's startling testimony. No, Rosenzweig had not become a believer, at least not yet. But he had clearly grown tired of being used by the GC regime.

The program began with what had become the obligatory fawning over the panelists. It seemed every time the GC wanted to persuade the populace of some cockamamie theory, it paraded pedigreed know-it-alls before the camera and buttered them up.

The host introduced the head of GCASA, the head of GCP&L, various and sundry scientists, authors, dignitaries, and even entertainment personalities. Each luminary had smiled shyly during the recitation of his or her litany of achievements and qualifications.

Buck snorted aloud when the host actually used the phrase "And last, but certainly not least." The camera panned to the tiny Albert Schweitzer–looking man on the end, and the scrolling legend along the bottom of the screen bore his name. Chaim looked neither shy nor humble, but rather bemused, as if this whole thing was a bit much.

Chaim tilted his head back and forth as if mocking himself as the plaudits rambled on and on: former professor, writer, botanist, winner of the Nobel Prize, honorary this, honorary that, speaker, diplomat, ambassador, personal friend and confidant of His Excellency the potentate. Chaim drew circles with an open hand as if they should wrap it up. The host finished, "Once *Global Weekly*'s Man of the Year and inventor of the formula credited with making Israel a world power, Dr. Chaim Rosenzweig!"

There was no studio audience, and even the GC press corps was against applauding. So the energetic intro died a conspicuous, awkward death, and the show moved on.

The host first read the entire GC statement while the text scrolled on the screen. Buck's tension mounted when—as he feared—the host began by asking for the opinion and comment of the first expert on the left. He would continue in the same order they had been introduced. Buck worried that viewers would lose patience and nod off from boredom by the time they got around to Chaim. One advantage to the GC-controlled media: Despite five hundred channel choices, this was on every station.

Buck had to remind himself that even for millions who ignored what they considered the ravings of a madman like Tsion Ben-Judah, the sudden darkness was frightening. They tuned in for answers from their government and likely considered this the most important program they had ever watched. Buck only hoped they would stay around for the last guy. The payoff would be worth it.

Everyone on the panel, of course, praised the fast and efficient and thorough work of the GCASA and assured the public that this was a minor event, a temporary condition. "As alarming as the darkness is," a woman on the management staff of Global Community Power and Light said, "we agree it will have negligible impact on the quality of life as we know it, and it should correct itself in a matter of days."

When at long last they got to Chaim, Buck felt a sense of community with his people in the States. The idea that they were all watching the same thing made the miles shrink momentarily, and he longed to have his wife cuddling next to him.

"Well," Chaim began dramatically, "who am I to add to or detract from anything said by any of these brilliant aficionados of interplanetary galactic astronomical phenomena? As for the dear woman who promises this will have no impact on our quality of life, let me say how disappointed I am. Our quality of life the last few years has been nothing to write home about.

"I am but a simple botanist who happened upon a combination that turned out to be magic water, and suddenly my opinion is sought on everything from the price of sausage to whether the defiant preachers at the Wailing Wall are real or make-believe.

"You want my opinion? OK, I will give it to you. To tell you the truth, I don't know. I don't know who turned the lights out, and I'm not sure I want to know who the two gentlemen are at the Wall. I just wish they would bring back the pure water and let it rain once in a while. Is that too much to ask?

"But let me tell you this, now that I have your attention. I do have your attention, don't I?"

The camera, panning back to the speechless host, exposed the shocked expressions of the other guests. It was clear they thought Rosenzweig had finally stepped off the edge.

"As should come as no surprise to anyone, I am not a religious man. A Jew by birth, of course, and proud of it. Wouldn't have it any other way. But to me it's a nationality, not a faith. All that to say this: Many, myself included, were horrified to hear what happened to the family of my beloved protégé and former student who grew up to be the respected linguistic and biblical scholar, Rabbi Tsion Ben-Judah.

"I confess, in my heart of hearts I had to wonder if he hadn't brought this on himself. Condone the killings? Never as long as I live. But would I advise a man to go on international television, from the very land where the name Jesus Christ is anathema to your neighbors, and tell the world you had become a turncoat? A Christ follower? A believer that Jesus is the Messiah?

"Madness.

"I was doubly horrified when he became a fugitive, exiled from his own homeland, his life worth nothing. But did I lose respect for him? Admire him less? How could I? Knowing such risks, taking such stands!"

"Thank you, Dr. Rosenz—," the host began, obviously getting instructions through his earpiece.

"Oh, no you don't," Rosenzweig said. "I have earned the right to another minute or so, and I demand that I not be unplugged from the air. I just want to say that I am still not a religious man, but my religious friend, the aforementioned rabbi, has spoken to the very issue we address today. Now you may rest easy. I have come back to the point.

"Ben-Judah was ridiculed for his beliefs, for his contentions that scriptural prophecy could be taken literally. He said an earthquake would come. It came. He said hail and blood and fire would scorch the plants. They did. He said things would fall from the sky, poisoning water, killing people, sinking ships. They fell.

"He said the sun and the moon and the stars would be stricken and that the world would be one-third darker. Well, I am finished. I don't know what to make of it except that I feel a bigger fool every day. And let me just add, I want to know what Dr. Tsion Ben-Judah says is coming next! Don't you?" And he quickly added the address of Tsion's Web site.

The host was still speechless. He looked at Chaim, brows raised.

"Go ahead now," Chaim said. "Pull the plug on me."

\+ \+ \+

Rayford was frustrated that he had not made it to Palwaukee that day. And he wouldn't make it the next day either, or the next. The reduction of solar power affected every facet of an already difficult existence including the transmission of Tsion's lessons. Dr. Rosenzweig's endorsement of Tsion's teaching resulted in the most massive number of hits on what was already a site ten times more popular than any other in history. And yet broadcasting Tsion's daily messages became an arduous chore that forced Rayford to delay any other activity.

Repeated failures on the Internet were blamed on the solar problems. Believers all over the globe rallied to try to copy and pass the teaching along as necessary, but it became impossible to track the success of that effort.

Chloe's efforts at building a private marketplace in anticipation of the mark of the beast nearly ground to a halt. Over the next several weeks, seasons were skewed. Major Midwest cities looked like Alaska in the dead of winter. Power reserves were exhausted. Hundreds of thousands all over the world died of exposure. Even the vaunted GC, having conveniently ignored adjusting their initial assessment, now looked for someone to blame for this curse. Confused in the tragic panic surrounding the crisis was the role of Ben-Judah. Had he predicted it, as Rosenzweig had asserted, or had he called it down from heaven?

Peter the Second decried Ben-Judah and the two preachers as reckless practitioners of black magic, proving it by showing live shots of the Wailing Wall. While snow swirled and drifted and Israelis paid top dollar for protective clothing, stayed inside, and used building material for fuel, there stood Eli and Moishe in their same spot. They were still barefoot! Still clad only in their loose-hanging sackcloth robes, arms bare. With only their deeply tanned skin, their beards, and long hair between them and the frigid temperatures, they preached and preached and preached.

"Surely," the self-ascribed supreme pontiff railed, "if there is a devil, he is master of these two! Who other than deranged, demonic beings could withstand these elements and continue to spout irrational diatribes?"

Nicolae Carpathia himself was strangely silent and his visage scarce. Finally, when the Global Community seemed powerless, he addressed the world. During a brief season of solar activity at midday in the Middle East, Mac was able to place a call to Rayford, who answered a cell phone with ancient batteries that had been recharged by a generator. The connection was bad, and they couldn't talk long.

"Watch the potentate tonight if you can, Ray!" Mac shouted. "We're warm as toast even in the snow here because he has marshaled all the energy we need for the palace. But when he goes on TV he's going to be wearing a huge parka he had shipped in from the Arctic."

Mac was right. Rayford and Floyd worked to store as much energy as they could from various sources so they could watch on the smallest TV in the safe house. The whole lot of them huddled to watch and stay warm, Hattie continuing to maintain, "I don't know about the rest of you, but I'm only getting what I deserve."

Tsion said, "My dear, you will find that none of the sealed of the Lord will die due to this judgment. This is an attention-getter aimed at the unbelievers. We suffer because the whole world suffers, but it will not mortally harm us. Don't you want the same protection?"

She did not answer.

+ + +

Buck, shivering underground with Stefan and Jacov, could not find the power to watch Carpathia on TV. The group listened on a radio with a signal so weak they had to hold their collective breath to hear him.

+ + +

In Mount Prospect, Rayford, Tsion, Chloe, Floyd, and Hattie watched as Carpathia came on TV in a bare studio, clapping his mittens and bouncing on his toes as if freezing to death. "Citizens of the Global Community," he intoned, "I applaud your courage, your cooperation, your sense of loyalty and togetherness as we rise to the challenge of enduring yet another catastrophe.

"I come to you at this hour to announce my plan to personally visit the two preachers at the Wailing Wall, who have admitted their roles in the plagues that have befallen Israel. They must now be forced to admit that they are behind this dastardly assault on our new way of life.

"Apparently they are invulnerable to physical attack. I will call upon their sense of decency, of fairness, of compassion, and I will go with an open mind, willing to negotiate. Clearly they want something. If there is something I can bargain with that will not threaten the dignity of my office or harm the citizens I live for, I am willing to listen and consider anything.

"I shall make this pilgrimage tomorrow, and it will be carried on live television. As the Global Community headquarters in New Babylon naturally has more power reserves than most areas, we will record this historic encounter with the hope that all of you will be able to enjoy it when this ordeal is finally over.

"Take heart, my beloved ones. I believe the end of this nightmare is in sight."

✢ ✢ ✢

"He's going personally to the Wall?" Buck said. "Is that what I just heard?"

Stefan nodded. "We should go."

"They won't let anybody near the place," Jacov said.

"They might," Buck said. He suggested the three of them bundle up as thickly as possible and find a location with a clear view of the wrought-iron fence. "We can build a shelter there that looks like just a wood box."

"We're down to our last few sheets of plywood for fuel now," Stefan said. "That green stuff in the cellar."

"We'll bring it back with us," Buck said, "and use it for fuel later."

The plan proved his most foolhardy yet. His face was still tender in spots and numb in others since getting the stitches out several weeks before. He had not expected to have to deal with frostbite in Israel. He and his two compatriots found a stairway that led to an abandoned building with a sealed door, fewer than a hundred yards from the Wall. With Carpathia expected at noon, they built their shelter in the pitch-blackness of the morning. If others ventured out in the howling blizzard, Buck and his friends didn't see them.

They were raw and cold by the time they climbed into their rough-hewn box with slits for viewing. Buck, ever the journalist, just had to see what the thing might look like to a passerby. "I'll be right back," he said.

"You're going out in this again?" Jacov said.

"Just for a minute."

Buck jogged a hundred feet from the staircase and tried to make out the box in the blowing snow and low output from a nearby light pole. *Perfect,* he thought. It would draw no one's attention. As he trudged back, he squinted in the darkness toward the Wall, knowing the witnesses were there but unable to see them. He detoured to get closer.

From what he could tell, they were not by the fence. He drew closer, confident he could not surprise or frighten them and that they would know in their spirits he was a believer. He stepped as close to the fence as he had ever been, recalling one of the first times he had ever conversed with them from just a few feet away.

A break in the wind allowed him to see the two, sitting, their backs against the stone building. They sat casually, elbows on knees, conversing. They were not huddled, still impervious to the elements. Buck wanted to say something, but nothing came to mind. They didn't seem to need encouragement. They didn't seem to need anything.

When in unison they glanced up at him standing there, he just nodded with his stiff neck, like a kid in a binding snowsuit, and raised both fists in support. His heart leapt when he saw them smile for the first time, and Eli raised a hand of greeting.

Buck ran back to the shelter. "Where you been, man?" Jacov said. "We thought you got lost or frozen or something."

Buck just sat, wrapping his arms around his knees, hunching his shoulders, and shook his head. "I'm fine," he said.

GC troops kept crowds several blocks away, once the motor coach arrived bearing Nicolae and his entourage. The wind and snow had stopped, but the noonday sun hardly warmed the area.

Carpathia remained on the bus as TV personnel set up lights and sound and cameras. Finally they signaled the potentate, and several of his top people, led by Fortunato, disembarked. Carpathia was the last to appear. He approached the fence, behind which the two witnesses still sat.

As the world watched on television, Carpathia said, "I bring you cordial greetings from the Global Community. I assume, because of your obvious supernatural powers, that you knew I was coming."

Eli and Moishe remained seated. Moishe said, "God alone is omnipotent, omniscient, and omnipresent."

"Nonetheless, I am here on behalf of the citizens of the earth to determine what course we might take to gain respite from this curse on the planet."

The witnesses stood and stepped forward. "We will speak to you alone."

Carpathia nodded at his minions, and Fortunato, clearly reluctant, led them back to the motor coach.

"All right then," Carpathia said, "shall we proceed?"

"We will talk with you alone."

Carpathia looked puzzled, then said, "These people are merely television technicians, cameramen, and so forth."

"We will talk with you alone."

Nicolae cocked his head in resignation and sent the TV crew away as well. "May we leave the cameras running? Would that be all right?"

"Your quarrel is not with us," Eli said.

"Beg pardon? You are not behind the darkness, the resultant global chaos?"

"Only God is omnipotent."

"I am seeking your help as men who claim to speak for God. If this is of God, then I plead with you to help me come to some arrangement, an agreement, a compromise, if you will."

"Your quarrel is not with us."

"Well, all right, I understand that, but if you have access to him—"

"Your quarrel is not w—"

"I appreciate that point! I am asking—"

Suddenly Moishe spoke so loudly that the sound meters had to have maxed out. "You would dare wag your tongue at the chosen ones of almighty God?"

"I apologize. I—"

"You who boasted that we would die before the due time?"

"Granted, I concede that I—"

"You who deny the one true God, the God of Abraham, Isaac, and Jacob?"

"In the spirit of ecumenism and tolerance, yes, I do hold that one should not limit his view of deity to one image. But—"

"There is one God and one mediator between God and man, the man Christ Jesus."

"That is a valid view, of course, just like many of the other views—"

"It is written, 'Beware lest any man spoil you through philosophy and vain deceit, after the tradition of men, after the rudiments of the world, and not after Christ.'"

"Do you not see that yours is such an exclusivisti—"

"Your quarrel is not with us."

"We are back to that again, are we? In the spirit of diplomacy, let me suggest—"

But the two witnesses turned away and sat down again.

"So, that is it, then? Before the eyes of the world, you refuse to talk? To negotiate? All I get is that my quarrel is not with you? With whom, then, is it? All right, fine!"

Carpathia marched in front of the main camera and stared into it from inches away. He spoke wearily, but with his usual precise enunciation. "Upon further review, the death of the Global Community guard at the Meeting of the Witnesses was not the responsibility of any of the witnesses or any member of

Dr. Ben-Judah's inner circle. The man killed by GC troops at the airport was not a terrorist. My good friend Dr. Chaim Rosenzweig was at no time and in no way holding Ben-Judah or his people at our behest. As of this moment, no one sympathetic to Dr. Ben-Judah and his teachings is considered a fugitive or an enemy of the Global Community. All citizens are equally free to travel and live their lives in a spirit of liberty.

"I do not know with whom I am or should be negotiating, but I assure whoever it is that I stand willing to make whatever other concessions would move us closer to the end of this plague of darkness."

He turned on his heel, sarcastically saluted the two witnesses, and reboarded the motor coach. As the TV crew rushed to gather their equipment, the witnesses spoke in unison from where they sat, clearly loud enough for anyone, even Carpathia, to hear.

"Woe, woe, woe unto all who fail to look up and lift up your heads!"

Two days later, the sun rose bright and full and the earth began to thaw. Buck made plans to fly home freely under his own name. "I can't fly directly to Chicago commercially," he told Rayford, "even with the reconstruction of Midway. I have to go through Europe."

"Any connections through Athens?"

"I'll check. Why?"

Rayford asked that he check on Lukas Miklos. "I'll see if he can greet you at the airport. It won't delay your trip home, and it'll really encourage him."

* * *

In Mount Prospect, Tsion told Rayford he was working on what would be his most dramatic and ominous warning yet. Meanwhile he broadcast worldwide over the Internet: "Because of the proven truth of Luke 21, I urge all, believers and unbelievers alike, to train your eyes on the skies. I believe this is the message from the two witnesses."

Doc Charles dug out and cleaned up Donny Moore's telescope, and with millions around the world, began monitoring the heavens. But when Tsion announced in one of his daily messages that he was investigating a way to build a Web site that would allow others to watch the skies through the same telescope, Rayford received a frantic call from David Hassid in New Babylon.

"Glad I caught you," he said breathlessly. "How far along are you on that telescope Web site idea?"

"Couple of days yet. Won't take our people long."

"You don't want to do that. A little software and a bright astronomer could just about pinpoint where you guys are."

Rayford put a hand atop his head. "Thanks for that, David. I never would have thought of it."

"Anyway, the potentate himself has authorized the purchase of a colossal telescope, and I get to work with the guys who will man it. Several can monitor it at once through various computers."

"Well, David, you know what we're looking for."

"I sure do."

16

THE FOLLOWING WEEK, news programs reported that stargazers from around the globe were tracking what appeared at first to be a shooting star. But this one, first seen during nighttime hours in Asia, did not streak across the sky for a second or two and disappear. Neither was this hurtling object in an orbital trajectory.

Astronomers were fond of explaining that, due to the distance from the earth of even the nearest stars, much of the activity seen from earth actually occurred years before and were just being seen now.

But after several hours of every amateur and professional telescope jockey in the world tracking it, it was becoming clear that this was no ordinary star. Neither was this an event that had happened years before. Experts unable to identify it agreed it was tiny, it was falling straight, and it had been descending a long time. It radiated little heat but seemed to emit its own light as well as reflecting light from stars and the sun, depending on the time of day.

The more closely it was studied, the less a threat it appeared to Earth. The head of GCASA said it had every chance of burning up as it hit Earth's atmosphere. "But even if it remains intact, it has a high probability of landing harmlessly in water. From what we are able to speculate about its mass and density, if it was to hit land, it would suffer far more damage than it could inflict. In all likelihood, it would be vaporized."

Still, none seemed able to turn their telescopes from it. Eventually the unidentified falling object was projected to land somewhere in an uninhabited region of the Fertile Crescent, near what many believed was the cradle of civilization.

GC scientists reached the projected touchdown point in time to see the impact, but they reported that it appeared to slip past the earth's surface into a deep crevice. Aerial studies of the area showed the impossibility of vehicular or foot traffic to more closely evaluate the object and its effect or lack thereof on the earth's crust.

As planes circled and shot still pictures and videotape, however, a geological eruption registered high on the Richter scale of seismology sensors all over the world. This thing that fell to earth, whatever it was, had somehow triggered volcanolike activity deep beneath the earth's surface.

The shock wave alone blew the surveillance planes off course and forced their pilots to fight to stay airborne and escape the area. Astounding scientists, the first evidence of what happened beneath the earth was a mushroom cloud a thousand times bigger and launched with that much more power and speed than any in history produced by bombs or natural phenomena. Also unique about this eruption was that it came from the crevice below sea level rather than from the typical volcanic mountain.

Cameras a thousand miles from the source of the cloud picked up images of it within twelve hours. Rather than being carried on indiscriminate winds, this cloud—massive and growing, fed from the belching earth—spread equally in all directions and threatened to block the sun all over the globe.

And this was no smoky cloud that thinned and dissipated as it traveled. The thick fumes that gushed from the ground were dense and black like the base of a gasoline fire. Scientists feared the source of the smoke was a colossal fire that would eventually rise and shoot flames miles into the air.

Early the following Monday afternoon in Jerusalem, Buck was devastated to learn that his flight to Athens and then on to the States had been cancelled. The billowing cloud of smoke that blanketed the earth had affected daylight again. Buck had looked forward to a two-hour layover during which he would meet Lukas Miklos. He was then to switch planes and fly nonstop the rest of the way to Chicago's Midway Airport. He was to proceed from there to Mount Prospect only after determining that he would not lead any enemies to the safe house. He and the Stateside members of the Tribulation Force had developed options to misdirect tails and shake them free.

Instead Buck hurried to Chaim Rosenzweig's home under the cover of darkness. "Be wary of Carpathia's claim that you are not still a suspect," Chaim said. "Nicolae is not speaking to me. Leon is fuming. While they cannot casually renege on their agreement, they will soon find some justification."

"Don't worry. I'm so eager to see Chloe, I may fly under my own power."

"Be careful of Enigma Babylon."

"What's Peter up to now?"

"You haven't heard?"

Buck shook his head. "Too busy getting ready to go."

Chaim turned on the TV. "I could quote this by heart, I've heard it so many times today. It's the only thing in the news outside the smoking volcano."

Mathews, in full clerical regalia again, spoke to the camera. "The Global

Community may have a tacit agreement with black-magic religious terrorists, but the time has come to enforce the law. Enigma Babylon One World Faith is *the* accepted religion for the whole world. As much as it is in my power—and a careful reading of the Global Community charter reveals that this clearly falls within my purview—I will prosecute offenders. So that all may be clear, I consider exclusivist, intolerant, one-way-only beliefs antithetical to true religion. If, because of misplaced diplomacy, the Global Community administration feels it must allow diversions from cosmic truth, Enigma Babylon itself must go on the offensive.

"To be an atheist or an agnostic is one thing. Even they are welcome beneath our all-inclusive banner. But it is illegal to practice a form of religion that flies in the face of our mission. Such practitioners and their followers will suffer.

"As a first initiative in a sweeping effort to rid the world of intolerance, it shall be deemed criminal, as of midnight Tuesday, Greenwich Mean Time, for anyone to visit the Web site of the so-called Tribulation Force. The teachings of this cult's guru, Dr. Tsion Ben-Judah, are poison to people of true faith and love, and we will not tolerate this deadly toxin pushed like a drug.

"Technology is in place that can monitor the Internet activity of any citizen, and those whose records show they have accessed this site after the deadline shall be subject to fine and imprisonment."

A Global Community reporter interrupted. "Two-part question, Supreme Pontiff: One, how does imprisoning people for what they access on the Web jibe with tolerance, faith, and love? And two, if you can monitor everyone's Internet activity, why can't you trace where Ben-Judah transmits from and shut him down?"

"I'm sorry," one of his aides said as Peter the Second was ushered away, "but we established in advance that we would not have time for questions."

I'd like to get a peek at that reporter's forehead, Buck thought. It made him wish his cover had not been blown and that he was still working from the inside.

+ + +

It was early morning in the Chicago area as Rayford pulled away from the safe house in Buck's Range Rover. Despite the smoky skies, he felt he had to get to Palwaukee and check on the condition of Ken Ritz's Suburban. It seemed in better shape than the Rover. The Trib Force could use it, but Rayford didn't know how a dead man's belongings should be disposed of, especially those of a man with no living kin.

Rayford suddenly heard a voice, as if someone were in the car with him. The radio was off and he was alone, but he heard, clear as if from the best sound system available: "Woe, woe, woe to the inhabitants of the earth, because of the remaining blasts of the trumpet of the three angels who are about to sound!"

His phone chirped. It was David from New Babylon. "Captain Steele, I'm outside right now, and I don't know what kind of spin we're going to put on this one, but I'll bet my life it'll never make the news."

"I heard it. It doesn't have to make the news."

"Everybody in here saw it before we heard it. Well, at least our equipment detected it. We can't see a thing through this cloud of smoke. But because we have huge radio receivers pointed at the sky anyway, it was plain as day here. I asked a Turkish guy what language it was in, and he said his own. Well, I heard it in English, so you know what I think."

"You *saw* the angel?"

"OK, we worked all night because somebody's probe detected something. The digital facsimile made it look like some sort of heavenly body, a comet or something. He gets it all tracked in and measured and whatnot, and we all start studying it. Well, I'm no astronomer so I haven't got a clue what I'm looking at. I tell 'em it looks real small to me, and not very thick. They're all congratulating me because it gave the lead guy an idea. He says, 'All right, let's assume it's closer and smaller. A lot smaller.' So he turns the dials and resets the probe, and all of a sudden the computer is spitting out images we can see and understand. It looked transparent and sorta humanlike, but not really. Anyway, we're following this thing, and then the boss says to point *all* the radio satellite dishes at it and try to track it that way, the way we do the stars in the daylight. Next thing you know, we hear the announcement.

"Well, it's all staticky and crackly, and we miss the first word, but of course I've been reading Dr. Ben-Judah's stuff, so I know what it is. Because the next two words are the same, and clear. I'm telling you, Captain, it freaked out *everybody,* and I mean everybody. Guys were on the floor, crying.

"They've been playing the tape over and over in there, and I even copied it on my dictation machine. But you know what? It records only in Greek. Everybody heard it in his own language, but it was Greek."

+ + +

Buck heard the angel and mistook it for the TV until he saw the look on Chaim's face. The old man was terrified. How could he, or anyone, doubt the existence of God now? This was no longer about ignorance. It was about choice.

+ + +

Rayford parked near the hangar where Ken Ritz had lived before moving to the safe house. There, his head under the hood of Ritz's Suburban, was Ernie, the new believer. He looked up and squinted through the haze as Rayford approached. Ernie smiled, shook his hand with enthusiasm, and pushed his greasy hat back on his head. The mark on his forehead stood out clearly as if he was proud of it, but he was also shivering.

"That was scary, wasn't it?" he said.

"Shouldn't be to those of us who knew it was coming," Rayford said. "You have nothing to fear. Not even death. None of us wants to die, but we know what comes next."

"Yeah," Ernie said, adjusting his hat again. "But still!"

"How's Ken's car doing?"

Ernie turned back to the engine. "Pretty good shape for all it's been through, I'd say."

"You find this therapeutic?"

"I'm sorry," Ernie said. "I was never much of a student. What's that mean?"

"Does it help you remember Ken without it being too painful for you?"

"Oh, well, I didn't really know him that long. I mean, I was shocked, and I'll miss him. But I just did stuff for him. He paid me, you know."

"But you both being believers—"

"Yeah, that was good. He put me onto that Ben-Judah guy's Web site."

A car pulled up to the rebuilt tower across the way and two men—in shirts and ties—got out. One was tall and black, the other stocky and white. The first went into the tower. The other approached Ernie and Rayford. Ernie emerged from under the hood again and pulled his cap low across his brow. "Hey, Bo!" he said. "D'ya hear that voice out of the sky?"

"I heard it," Bo said, obviously disgusted. "If you believe it was a voice from the sky, you're loopier than I thought."

"Well, what was it then?" Ernie said, as Bo studied Rayford.

"Those crazy fundamentalists again, playing with our minds. Some kind of loudspeaker trick. Don't fall for it."

Ernie emitted an embarrassed laugh and looked self-consciously at Rayford.

"Howdy," Bo said, nodding to Rayford. "Can I help you with something?"

"No thanks. Just a friend of Ken Ritz."

"Yeah, that was awful."

"Actually I just came by to see about his belongings. I don't believe there were any living relatives."

Ernie straightened up and turned around so quickly that even Bo seemed taken aback. It was clear both wanted to say something, but each looked at the other and hesitated. Then they both spoke at once.

Bo said, "And so you just thought you'd come by and see what you could—"

While Ernie was saying, "No, that's right. No relatives. In fact, he told me just a week or so ago that—"

Ernie conceded the floor first, and the man backed up and finished his thought: "—you'd come by and see what you could make off with, is that it?"

Rayford recoiled at such insensitivity, especially on the part of a stranger. "That's not it at all, sir. I—"

"Where do you get off calling me *sir*? You don't know me!"

Caught off guard, Rayford's old nature took over. "What, am I talking to an alien? How does polite society refer to strangers on your planet, *Bo*?" He hit the name with as much sarcasm as he could muster. Rayford was much taller, but Bo was built like a linebacker. With his blond crewcut, he looked the part too.

"Why don't you just take your opportunistic tail out of here while it's still part of your body?" Bo said.

Rayford was boiling and repenting of his attitude even as he spewed venom. "Why don't you mind your own business while I talk privately with Ernie?"

Bo stepped closer to Rayford and made him wonder if he would have to defend himself. "Because Ernie's on my payroll," Bo said, "and everything on this property is my business. Including Ritz's effects."

Rayford took a deep breath and regained control of his emotions. "Then I'll be happy to talk to Ernie on his own time, and—"

"And on his own property," Bo added.

"Fine, but what gives you the right to Ken Ritz's stuff?"

"What gives *you* any right to it?"

"I haven't claimed any right to it," Rayford said. "But I think its disposition is a valid question."

Ernie looked ill. "Um, Bo, sir, Ken told me that if anything ever happened to him, I could have his stuff."

"Yeah, right!"

"He did! The planes, this car, his personal junk. Whatever I wanted."

Rayford looked suspiciously at Ernie. He didn't want to question a fellow believer, especially in front of an outsider, but he had to. "I thought you told me you two hardly knew each other."

"I'll handle this," Bo said. "That's bull, Ernie, and you know it! Ritz was part owner of this airport and—"

Rayford cocked his head quickly. That didn't mesh with what Ken had told Rayford about wanting to buy the place.

Bo must have noticed Rayford's reaction and assumed he knew more than

Bo thought. "Well," he adjusted, midstream, "he made an offer anyway. Or was going to. Actually, yeah, an offer was made. So if there are assets in his estate, they would be the property of Palwaukee ownership."

Rayford felt his blood boil again. "Oh, that makes a lot of sense. He dies before your deal is consummated, so you take his estate in exchange for what? You're going to change the name of the place to Ritz Memorial? You take his assets and he gets what, posthumous ownership while you run it for him and take the profits?"

"So, what's your stake in this, smarty-pants?"

Rayford nearly laughed. Was he back on the playground in fourth grade? How had he come to a shouting match with a total stranger?

"As I said, I made no claim, but my stake now is to be sure nothing happens to my friend's legacy that he didn't intend to happen."

"He intended for me to have it," Ernie said. "I told you that!"

"Ernie," Bo said, "stick to your grease-monkeying and keep your nose outta this, will ya? And wipe that smudge off your forehead. You look like a snot-nosed rugrat."

Ernie tugged down on his cap and whirled around to busy himself under the hood again. He was muttering, "I'm takin' the stuff he said I could have, I'll tell you that right now. You're not bullyin' me into giving up what I know is rightfully mine. No way."

Rayford was disgusted with Ernie's obvious lies but even more so that he was ashamed of the mark of God.

And then it hit him. Only other believers could see the mark. Was Rayford arguing with a fellow tribulation saint? He looked quickly at Bo's forehead, which, because of his haircut and his complexion and the breadth of his face, had been right in front of Rayford's eyes the whole time.

Even in the dense smog, Bo's skin was as clear as a baby's.

+ + +

Buck felt restless. He sat across from Chaim Rosenzweig in the parlor of his estate and was nearly overcome with compassion for the man. "Doctor," he said, "how can you see and know and experience all we have endured—all of us, even you—these last few years and yet still resist the call of God on your life? Don't be offended. You know I care for you, as does Tsion and my wife and her father. You told an international audience on TV that Ben-Judah was proven correct in his interpretations of what is to come. Forgive me for being so forward, but the time is growing short."

"I confess I have been troubled," Rosenzweig said, "especially since Ben-Judah stayed with me. You have heard my arguments against God in the past, but no, not even I can deny he is at work today. It is too plain. But I have to say I don't understand your God. He seems mean-spirited to me. Why can he not get people's attention through wonderful miracles, as he did in the Bible? Why make things worse and worse until a person has no choice? I find myself resisting being forced into this by the very one who wants my devotion. I want to come willingly, on my own accord, if at all."

Buck stood and pulled back the drape. The skies were growing darker, and he heard a low rumble in the distance. Should he stay away from the window? The weather had not portended rain. What was the noise? He could see no more than ten feet through the heavy smoke.

"Doctor, God has blessed you beyond what any human deserves. If your wealth of friends, education, knowledge, creativity, challenge, admiration, income, and comfort do not draw you to him, what else can he do? He is not willing that any should perish, and so he resorts to judgments that will drive them to him or away from him forever. We're praying you will choose the former."

Rosenzweig appeared older than his age. Weary, drawn, lonely, he looked like he needed rest. But life was hard everywhere. Buck knew everything would head downhill from here. The old man crossed his legs, appeared uncomfortable, and set his feet flat on the floor again. He seemed distracted, and he and Buck had to raise their voices to even hear each other.

"I must tell you that your praying for me means more than I can s—" He furrowed his brow. "What *is* that noise?"

The rumble had become higher pitched and had developed a metallic sound. "It's like chains clanging together," Buck said.

"A low-flying craft?"

"The airports are closed, Doctor."

"It's getting louder! And it's darker! It's dark as night out there. Open that drape all the way, Cameron, please. Oh, my heavens!"

The sky was black as pitch and the racket deafening. Buck spun to look at Chaim, whose face matched Buck's own terror. Metal against metal clanged until both men covered their ears. Rattling, thumping against the windows now, the rumble had become a cacophony of piercing, irritating, rattling, jangling that seemed it would invade the very walls.

Buck stared out the window, and his heart thundered against his ribs. From out of the smoke came flying creatures—hideous, ugly, brown and black and yellow flying monsters. Swarming like locusts, they looked like miniature horses five or six inches long with tails like those of scorpions. Most horrifying, the creatures were attacking, trying to get in. And they looked past Buck as if Chaim was their target.

The old man stood in the middle of the room. "Cameron, they are after me!" he screamed. "Tell me I'm dreaming! Tell me it's only a nightmare!"

The creatures hovered, beating their wings and driving their heads into the window.

"I'm sorry, Doctor," Buck said, shuddering, his arms covered with gooseflesh. "This is real. It's the first of the three woes the angels warned about."

"What do they want? What will they do?"

"Tsion teaches that they will not harm any foliage like locusts usually do, but only those who do not have the seal of God on their foreheads." Chaim paled, and Buck worried he might collapse. "Sit down, sir. Let me open the window—"

"No! Keep them out! I can tell they mean to devour me!"

"Maybe we can trap one or two between the screen and the window and see them more clearly."

"I don't want to see them! I want to kill them before they kill me!"

"Chaim, they have not been given the authority to kill you."

"How do you know?" He sounded like a schoolboy now, doubting the doctor who's told him a shot won't hurt bad.

"I won't tell you they won't torment you, but the Bible says the victims they attack will want to die and be unable to."

"Oh, no!"

Buck turned a crank that swung open the window. Several creatures flew near the screen, and he quickly shut the window. Now trapped between, they flew crazily, straining, fighting, banging off each other. The harsh metallic sound increased.

"Aren't you the least bit curious?" Buck said, fighting to not turn from the sight of them. "They are fascinating hybrids. As a scientist, don't you want to at least see—"

"I'll be right back," Chaim cried, and he hurried away. He returned looking ridiculous, dressed head to toe in beekeeping garb: boots, bulky canvas body smock, gloves, hat with face mesh and material covering his neck. He carried a cricket bat.

Bloodcurdling screams rose above the clamor. Chaim rushed to the other window, threw back the drape, and fell to his knees. "Oh, God," he prayed, "save me from these creatures! And don't let Jonas die!"

Buck looked over Chaim's shoulder out to the gate. Jonas lay writhing, screaming, thrashing, slapping at his legs and torso, trying to cover his face. He was covered with the locusts. "We've got to get him inside!" Buck said.

"I can't go out! They'll attack me!"

Buck hesitated. He believed he was invulnerable to the creatures' stings, but his mind had trouble communicating that to his legs. "I'll go," he said.

"How will you keep the creatures out?"

"I can only do the best I can. Do you have another bat?"

"No, but I have a tennis racket."

"That'll have to do."

Buck headed downstairs with the racket. Chaim called after him, "I'm going to lock myself in this room. Be sure you've killed or kept out all of them before coming back in. And put Jonas in the front guest room. Will he die?"

"He'll wish he could," Buck said.

He waited at the front door. The smoke that had hung over the city for days was gone, having left just as dense a spread of the ghastly beings. Praying for courage, Buck opened the door and ran to Jonas, who now lay quivering and twitching.

"Jonas! Let's get you inside."

But he was unconscious.

Buck set the racket down and used both hands to grab the big man by the shoulder and roll him over. His face showed one welt, and he was beginning to swell. A barrel-chested, beefy man, Jonas was going to be difficult to move. Buck tried to remember the fireman's carry, but he couldn't get enough leverage to get Jonas off the ground.

The locusts, too tame a description for these revolting beasts, flew menacingly around Buck's head, and some even landed. He was astonished at their weight and thickness. And while he was relieved they didn't sting or bite, he heard their hisses and believed they were trying to drive him away from Jonas. When one hovered over Jonas's face, Buck snatched up the racket and stepped into a full, hard backhand, sending the locust rocketing through a window at the front of the house. The sensation of beast on strings felt as if he had smacked a toy metal car. His first order of business, if he ever got back into the house, was to board up that window and get rid of that animal.

Buck tucked the racket under his arm and resorted to pulling Jonas by his wrists, on his back, up to the house. About ten feet from the stairs, their progress stopped, and Buck discovered Jonas's waistband and belt had torn up grass as he slid. Buck spun him around and tucked the man's ankles under his own arms and kept going. When he reached the steps, he sucked it up, bent at the knees, and lifted Jonas up onto his shoulders. He believed the man outweighed him by a hundred pounds.

In the house he plopped Jonas into a chair, from which he nearly toppled before rousing enough to at least keep his balance. Another locust flew in before

Buck could shut the door, and he smacked it with the racket as well. It skittered across the floor and rebounded off the wall, rattling as it rolled. It lay stunned, its segmented abdomen heaving. Buck's first target chose that moment to attack, and Buck knocked it out of the air again.

He tried stepping on one and found its shell unbreakable. He nudged both onto the face of the racket with his foot and shoveled them out the door, slamming it shut before more could invade. He covered the broken window and helped the staggering Jonas to the front guest room. There Jonas stretched out on the bed, incoherent and groaning and tearing at the buttons on his shirt.

Knowing there was no remedy for the torture and agony the man would endure, Buck reluctantly left him and returned to the parlor upstairs. Like a person perversely drawn to a train wreck, Buck wanted a close look at these things, with a glass barrier between him and them.

Before unlocking the door, Chaim demanded that Buck double- and triple-check that he was not accidentally bringing a locust in with him. Buck found Chaim still shrouded in the beekeeper getup and wielding the cricket bat. After demanding to know Jonas was still alive, Chaim grabbed Buck's arm and dragged him to the window. Angry locusts, trapped between glass and screen, were front and center, ready for study. Buck knew that any unbeliever on the street had already suffered Jonas's fate and that it couldn't be long before the locusts would begin finding their way into homes and apartments. This was going to be the worst horror yet.

17

RAYFORD GRABBED ERNIE by the collar and pulled him close, feeling the rage of a parent against a threat to his family.

"So you're an impostor, hey, Ernie?"

Rather than fighting, Ernie tried to hold his hat on with both hands. Rayford let go of his collar and drove his hand directly under the bill of the cap. Ernie flinched, obviously thinking he was about to take an uppercut to the nose, and released his grip just enough so Rayford sent his cap flying.

No wonder Ernie's mark had appeared so prominent. He had refreshed it with whatever he had used to create it in the first place. "You'd fake the mark, Ernie? The mark of the sealed of the Lord? That takes guts."

Ernie paled and tried to pull away, but Rayford grabbed the back of his neck and with his free hand pressed his thumb against Ernie's bogus mark. The smudge rubbed off. "You must have studied Tsion's teaching really well to replicate a mark you've never seen."

"What the heck is that?" Bo asked, seeming frozen to his spot.

"He faked the mark of—"

"I know all about that," Bo said, his eyes wide with fear. He pointed past Rayford. "I mean that!"

Rayford looked into the distance where the cloud of smoke was turning into a swarming wave of locusts. Even from a few hundred yards, they looked huge. And what a racket!

"I hate to tell you this, gentlemen, but you're in big trouble."

"Why?" Bo cried. "What is it?"

"One of your last warnings. Or another trick by the fundamentalists. You decide."

"Do what you want, Bo!" Ernie said. "I'm gettin' outta here!"

He lit out for the tower, which apparently appealed to Bo too. When Ernie had trouble opening the door, Bo skidded into him, plastering him against it. They both went down, Ernie holding his knee and whimpering.

"Get up and get in there, you sissy," Bo said.

"Yeah, well, so are you, you big sissy boy! Sissy boy Bo!"

Bo yanked the door open, and it banged Ernie's head. He swore and spun on his seat and kicked it shut as Bo was trying to get in. Bo dropped to one knee, sucking his slammed fingernail, and Ernie jumped up and stepped over him into the safety of the tower.

Rayford arrived at the door and tried to help Bo up, but Bo wrenched away. The locusts swarmed Bo. He kicked and screamed and ran in circles, and when Ernie opened the door to taunt him and laugh at him, he too was attacked. The black man who had been in the car with Bo appeared in the doorway, staring in horror at the suffering man and boy.

He shook his head slowly and looked up at Rayford. They noticed each other's marks immediately, and Rayford knew his was genuine because the locusts left him alone.

Rayford helped him fight off the locusts and haul the two onto a landing at the bottom of the stairs. As Bo and Ernie shook and swelled and fought for breath, Rayford accepted the man's handshake.

"T. M. Delanty," he said. "I go by T."

"Rayf—"

"I know who you are, Captain. Ken told me all about you."

"Sorry to sound rude," Rayford said, "but it's odd he never mentioned you." Odder still, Rayford thought, was their getting acquainted with two suffering victims at their feet.

"I asked him not to. It's great to know he was what I thought he was—a man of his word."

Rayford wanted to talk with T, but he felt obligated to do something for Bo and Ernie. "Anyplace we can put these guys?"

T nodded to a reception area with couches and chairs but otherwise empty. "I understand they're not going to die, but they're going to wish they could?"

Rayford nodded. "You study, do you?"

"I'm in Tsion's cyberclass, like pretty much every other believer in the world."

"I'd better check on Tsion and the others," Rayford said, pulling out his phone.

Chloe answered. "Oh, Dad! It's horrible! Hattie's already been attacked." Rayford heard her screaming in the background.

"Can Doc help?"

"He's trying, but she's cursing God and already wants to die. Tsion says this is just the beginning. He believes she'll be in torment for five months. By then *we're* going to want to put her out of her misery ourselves."

"We can pray she'll become a believer before that."

"Yeah, but Tsion doesn't think that guarantees instant relief."

That sounded strange to Rayford. He would have to ask Tsion about that later. "Everybody else all right?"

"Think so. I'm waiting to hear from Buck."

+ + +

Buck was surprised to learn he had more capacity for revulsion. As he and Chaim knelt by the window, their faces inches from the locusts, he saw Scripture come to life. He couldn't imagine an uglier, more nauseating sight than the creatures before him. Tsion taught that these were not part of the animal kingdom at all, but demons taking the form of organisms.

As he took in their unique characteristics, he felt for Chaim. They both knew his protective covering would not save him in the end. These things were here to attack him, and time was on their side. They would find a way in, and when that happened, they would show no mercy.

"Good heavens, look at them!" Chaim said.

Buck could only shake his head. Contrasted with the beauty of God's creation, these mongrels were clearly from the pit. Their bodies were shaped like miniature horses armed for war. They had wings like flying grasshoppers. When one alighted on the window, Buck edged closer.

"Chaim," Buck said, his own voice sounding distant and fearful, "do you have a magnifying glass?"

"You want a closer look? I can hardly stand to peek at them!"

"They look like horses, but they don't have snouts and mouths like horses'."

"I have a very powerful magnifier in my office, but I'm not leaving this room."

Buck ran off and got it from the study near Chaim's bedroom. But as he dashed back he heard a dreadful, inhuman howl and the bumps and bangs of someone thrashing on the floor. The someone, of course, was Chaim Rosenzweig, and the howl was human after all.

One of the locusts had found a way in and had locked itself onto Chaim's wrist, between his glove and sleeve. The old man lay jerking as if in the throes of a seizure, wailing and crying as he slammed his hand on the ground, trying to dislodge the brute.

"Get it off me!" he bellowed. "Please, Cameron, please! I'm dying!"

Buck grabbed the thing, but it seemed stuck as if by suction. It felt like an amalgam of metal, spiny protrusions, and insect slime. He dug his fingers between its abdomen and Chaim's wrist and yanked. The locust popped free, twisted in his hand, and tried stinging him from one end and biting him from the other.

Though it had no effect on him, Buck instinctively threw it against the wall so hard it dented the plaster and rattled noisily to the floor.

"Is it dead?" Chaim cried. "Tell me it's dead!"

"I don't know that we can kill them," Buck said. "But I stunned a couple of other ones, and this one is immobile right now."

"Smash it," Chaim insisted. "Stomp on it! Smack it with the bat!" He rolled to his side in convulsions. Buck wanted to help him, but Tsion had been clear that he found in the Scriptures no mention of relief to the victims of a sting.

The magnifying glass lay on the floor a few feet from the unmoving locust. Keeping an eye on the creature, Buck held the glass over it, illuminated by the chandelier directly above. He nearly vomited at the magnified ugliness.

It lay on its side, appearing to regroup. The four horselike legs supported a horse-shaped body consisting of a two-part abdomen. First was a preabdomen in the torso area made up of seven segments and draped by a metallic breastplate that accounted for the noise when it flew. The posterior consisted of five segments and led to the scorpionlike stinger tail, nearly transparent. Buck could see the sloshing venom.

Its eyes were open and seemed to glare at Buck. In a strange way, that made sense. If Tsion was right and these were demons, they were madly conflicted beings. They would want to kill believers, but they were under instructions from God to torment only unbelievers. What Satan meant for evil, God was using for good.

Buck held his breath as he moved the glass and his own face closer to the locust. He had never seen a head like that on any living thing. The face looked like that of a man, but as it writhed and grimaced and scowled at Buck, it displayed a set of teeth way out of proportion. They were the teeth of a lion with long canines, the upper pair extending over the lower lip. Most incongruous, the locust had long, flowing hair like a woman's, spilling out from under what appeared to be a combination helmet and crown, gold in color.

Though no larger than a man's hand, the grossly overgrown combination insect, arthropod, and mammal appeared invincible. Buck was encouraged to know he could temporarily shock them with a hard blow, but he had neither killed nor apparently even injured any.

He had no idea how to toss the thing out of the house without letting in dozens more. Buck scanned the room and noticed a heavy vase holding a large plant. Chaim was already incoherent, crawling to the door. "Bed," he said. "Water."

Buck pulled the plant from the vase and laid it on the floor, muddy roots and all. He turned the vase over and set it atop the locust, which had just begun to move about again. Within a minute he heard the metallic whirring as it banged again and again against the inverted vase.

It tried to escape through a small hole in what had become the top of its makeshift prison, but it could only poke its head through. Buck staggered and nearly fell when it seemed to shout, as if crying for help. Over and over it repeated a phrase Buck could not understand.

"Do you hear that, Dr. Rosenzweig?" Buck asked.

Chaim lay by the door, panting. "I hear it," he rasped, groaning, "but I don't want to! Burn it, drown it, do something to it! But help me to bed and get me some water!"

The creature called out in a mournful keen what sounded to Buck like "A bad one! A bad one!"

"These things speak!" Buck told Chaim. "And I think it's English!"

Rosenzweig shook as if the temperature had dropped below freezing. "Hebrew," he said. "It's calling out for Abaddon."

"Of course!" Buck said. "Tsion told us about that! The king over these creatures is the chief demon of the bottomless pit, ruler over the fallen hordes of the abyss. In the Greek he has the name Apollyon."

"Why do I care to know the name of the monster that killed me?" Rosenzweig said. He reached up for the doorknob but could not unlock the door with his gloves on. He shook them off but could no longer raise an arm.

Buck got him up, and as they lumbered out of the parlor, he looked back at the locust trying to squeeze out of the vase. It looked at him with such hatred and contempt that Buck nearly froze.

"Abaddon!" it called out, and the tiny but gravelly voice echoed in the hallway.

Buck kicked the parlor door shut and helped Chaim into his bedroom. There Buck peeled the rest of the beekeeper garb off Chaim and helped him lie back atop the covers on his bed. Convulsions racked him again, and Buck noticed swelling in his hands and neck and face. "C-c-could y-y-you g-g-g-et me some w-water, p-please!"

"It won't help," Buck said, but he got it anyway. Parched himself, he poured into a glass some from the bottle he found in the refrigerator and quenched his own thirst. He grabbed a clean glass and returned. He set the bottle and the glass on a stand next to the bed. Chaim appeared unconscious. He had rolled on his side, covering his ears with a pillow, as the haunting cries continued from the parlor.

"Abaddon! Abaddon! Abaddon!"

Buck laid a hand on the old man's shoulder. "Can you hear me, Chaim? Chaim?"

Rosenzweig pulled the pillow away from his ear. "Huh? What?"

"Don't drink the water. It's turned to blood."

\+ + +

Rayford and T. M. Delanty stood outside the empty reception area at the base of the Palwaukee Airport tower, peering in at Bo and Ernie, who cursed each other as they writhed on the floor.

"Is there nothing we can do for them?" T asked.

Rayford shook his head. "I feel sorry for them and for anybody who has to endure this. If they had only listened! The message has been out there since before the Rapture. What's their story, anyway? Ernie had me convinced he was a believer—had the mark and everything."

"I was shocked to see him attacked," T said, "but part of that had to have been my fault. For days he sounded interested, said Ken was urging him to log on and check out what Tsion Ben-Judah was teaching. He asked so many questions, especially about the mark, that between what he learned from Tsion and what Ken and I said about it, he was able to fake it."

Rayford looked out. The sky was still filled with the locusts, but all but a few had moved away from the door. "I never thought about anyone being able to counterfeit the mark. I figured the mark, distinguishable only by another believer, was a foolproof test of who was with us and who wasn't. What do we do now—try the smudge test on anybody who's bearing the mark?"

"Nope," T said. "Don't have to."

"Why's that?"

"You're not testing *my* mark, are you? Why do you assume I'm legit?"

"Because you weren't attacked."

"Bingo. For the next ten months, that is our litmus test."

"Where are you getting ten months?"

"You haven't read Dr. Ben-Judah today?"

Rayford shook his head.

"He says the locusts have five months to find their prey and sting them and that the victims suffer for five months. He also believes, though he admitted it was just conjecture, that the locusts bite a person once, and then they move on."

"Have you taken a look at these things?" Rayford said, studying one on the other side of the window.

"Do I want to?" T said, approaching. "I didn't even like reading about them in Dr. Ben-Judah's lessons. Oh, boy, look at that! That is one ugly monstrosity."

"Be glad they're on our side."

"Talk about irony," T said. "Ben-Judah says they're demons."

"Yeah, but they're moonlighting for God for a while."

Both men cocked their heads. "What's that sound?" Rayford said. "Tsion said their flight would sound like horses and chariots riding into battle, but I hear something else."

"Are they chanting?" T said.

They cracked the door an inch or so, and a locust tried to squeeze through. Rayford shut the door on it, and it squirmed and flailed. He released the pressure, and it flew back out. "That's it!" Rayford said. "They're chanting something."

The men stood still. The cloud of locusts, on its way to fresh targets, called out in unison, "Apollyon, Apollyon, Apollyon!"

+ + +

"Why would God do this to me?" Chaim whined. "What did I ever do to him? You know me, Cameron! I am not a bad man!"

"He did not do this, Dr. Rosenzweig. You did it to yourself."

"What did I do that was so wrong? What was my sin?"

"Pride, for one," Buck said, pulling up a chair. He knew there was nothing he could do for his friend but keep him company, but he was past gentility.

"Proud? I am proud?"

"Maybe not intentionally, Doctor, but you have ignored everything Tsion has told you about how to connect with God. You have counted on your charm, your own value, your being a good person to carry you through. You get around all the evidence for Jesus being the Messiah by reverting to your educational training, your confidence only in what you can see and hear and feel. How many times have you heard Tsion quote Titus 3:5 and Ephesians 2:8-9? And yet you—"

Chaim cried out in pain. "Quote them to me again, Cameron, would you?"

"'Not by works of righteousness which we have done, but according to His mercy He saved us. . . . For by grace you have been saved through faith, and that not of yourselves; it is the gift of God, not of works, lest anyone should boast.'"

Chaim nodded miserably. "Cameron, this is so painful!"

"Sad to say, it will get worse. The Bible says you will want to die and won't be able to commit suicide."

Chaim rocked and cried in anguish. "Would God accept me if I relent only to ease my torture?"

"God knows everything, Doctor. Even your heart. If you knew you would still suffer, worse and worse for five months, regardless of your decision, would you still want him?"

"I don't know!" he said. "God forgive me, I don't know!"

Buck turned on the radio and found a pirate station broadcasting the preaching of Eli and Moishe from the Wailing Wall. Eli was in the middle of a typically tough message. "You rant and rave against God for the terrible plague that has befallen you! Though you will be the last, you were not the first generation who forced God's loving hand to act in discipline.

"Harken unto these words from the ancient of days, the Lord God of Israel: I have withholden the rain from you, when there were yet three months to the harvest: and I caused it to rain upon one city, and caused it not to rain upon another city: one piece was rained upon, and the piece whereupon it rained not withered.

"So two or three cities wandered unto one city, to drink water; but they were not satisfied: yet have ye not returned unto me. . . .

"I have smitten you with blasting and mildew: when your gardens . . . increased, the palmerworm devoured them: yet have ye not returned unto me. . . . I have sent among you the pestilence after the manner of Egypt: your young men have I slain with the sword, . . . yet have ye not returned unto me. . . . I have overthrown some of you, as God overthrew Sodom and Gomorrah, and ye were as a firebrand plucked out of the burning: yet have ye not returned unto me. . . .

"Therefore thus will I do unto thee, O Israel: and because I will do this unto thee, prepare to meet thy God, O Israel. For, lo, he that formeth the mountains, and createth the wind, and declareth unto man what is his thought, that maketh the morning darkness, and treadeth upon the high places of the earth, The Lord, The God of hosts, is his name. . . .

"Thus saith the Lord unto the house of Israel, Seek ye me, and ye shall live: . . . Ye who turn judgment to wormwood, and leave off righteousness in the earth, Seek him that maketh the seven stars and Orion, and turneth the shadow of death into the morning, and maketh the day dark with night: that calleth for the waters of the sea, and poureth them out upon the face of the earth: The Lord is his name. . . .

"Therefore the prudent shall keep silence in that time; for it is an evil time. Seek good, and not evil, that ye may live: and so the Lord, the God of hosts, shall be with you, as ye have spoken. Hate the evil, and love the good, and establish judgment in the gate: it may be that the Lord God of hosts will be gracious unto the remnant of Joseph. . . .

"Though ye offer me burnt offerings and your meat offerings, I will not accept them: neither will I regard the peace offerings of your fat beasts. Take thou away from me the noise of thy songs; for I will not hear the melody of thy viols.

"But let judgment run down as waters, and righteousness as a mighty stream."

"Wow," Buck said.

"Please, Cameron!" Chaim said. "Turn it off! I can take no more."

Buck sat another two hours with Chaim, helpless to ease his suffering. The man thrashed and sweated and gasped. When finally he relaxed a moment, he said, "Are you sure about this getting worse and worse until I despair of my life?"

Buck nodded.

"How do you know?"

"I believe the Bible."

"It says that? In those words?"

Buck knew it from memory. "'In those days men will seek death and will not find it,'" he said. "'They will desire to die, and death will flee from them.'"

18

DURING THE ENSUING FIVE MONTHS, the demon locusts attacked anyone who did not have the seal of God on his or her forehead. And for five months after that, those among the last bitten still suffered.

The starkest picture of the interminable suffering came from Hattie's ordeal at the Tribulation Force's safe house in Mount Prospect, Illinois. Her torment was so great that everyone—Rayford, Tsion, Chloe, and Floyd—begged her to give in to Christ. Despite her anguished screams at all hours of the day and night, she stubbornly maintained that she was getting what she deserved and no less.

Listening to her around the clock became so stressful to the Force that Rayford made an executive decision and moved her to the basement where Ken had lived. As weeks passed she became a shell of even the unhealthy frame she had been. Rayford felt as if he were visiting a living corpse every time he went down there, and he soon quit going alone. It was too frightening.

Doc Charles tried to treat her symptoms, quickly discovering it was futile. And the rest took turns delivering her meals, which were rarely touched. She ate much less than should have been required to keep her alive, but as the Bible predicted, she did not die.

It got to where Rayford had to visit Hattie with one of the others, and even then he didn't sleep well afterward. Hattie was skeletal, her dark eyes sunk deep into her head. Her lips stretched thin and taut across teeth that now looked too big for her mouth.

Eventually she could not speak, but communicated by a series of grunts and gestures. Finally she refused to even turn and look when someone came down.

Hattie finally forced herself to talk when Chloe somehow located her sister Nancy, working at an abortion clinic out west. All the other members of Hattie's family had died in various ways before the plague of locusts. Now Hattie spoke to her sister for the first time in months. Nancy had somehow avoided for a few months the sting of a scorpion locust, but now she too was a victim.

"Nancy, you must believe in Jesus," Hattie managed, though she spoke as if her mouth was full of sores. "It's the only answer. He loves you. Do it."

Floyd had overheard Hattie's end of the conversation and asked Rayford and Tsion to join him in talking to her. But she was more belligerent than ever. "But it's so obvious you know the truth," Tsion said. "And the truth shall set you free."

"Don't you see I don't want to be free? I only want to stay alive long enough to kill Nicolae, and I will. Then I don't care what happens to me."

"But we care," Rayford said.

"You'll be all right," she said, rolling over and turning her back to them.

Chloe, getting toward the end of her pregnancy, finally couldn't navigate the stairs. She told Rayford that the prayer of her life now was that Buck would somehow make it home before the baby was born.

Tsion was busier than ever. He passed on miraculous reports from the 144,000 witnesses who had fanned out to serve as missionaries to every country, not just their own. Stories poured in of obscure tribal groups understanding in their own languages and becoming tribulation saints.

Tsion wrote to nearly a billion Web site visitors every day that this was the last period during the end of time when believers would have any semblance of freedom. "Now is the time, my dear brothers and sisters," he wrote. "With everyone else vulnerable to the attacks of the locust hordes, they must stay inside or venture out only with bulky protective gear. This is our chance to put into place mechanisms that will allow us to survive when the world system requires its own mark one day. We will be allowed to neither buy nor sell without the mark, and it is a mark that once taken seals the fate of the bearer for all time—just as the mark we now bear has sealed us for eternity.

"I beg of you not to look upon God as mean or capricious when we see the intense suffering of the bite victims. This is all part of his master design to turn people to him so he can demonstrate his love. The Scriptures tell us God is ready to pardon, gracious and merciful, slow to anger, and abundant in kindness. How it must pain him to have to resort to such measures to reach those he loves!

"It hurts us to see that even those who *do* receive Christ as a result of this ultimate attention-getter still suffer for the entire five months prescribed in biblical prophecy. And yet I believe we are called to see this as a picture of the sad fact that sin and rebellion have their consequences. There are scars. If a victim receives Christ, God has redeemed him, and he stands perfect in heaven's sight. But the effects of sin linger.

"Oh, dear ones, it thrills my heart to get reports from all over the globe that there are likely more Christ followers now than were raptured. Even nations known for only a minuscule Christian impact in the past are seeing great numbers come to salvation.

"Of course we see that evil is also on the rise. The Scriptures tell us that those who remain rebellious even in light of this awful plague simply love themselves and their sin too much. Much as the world system tries to downplay it, our society has seen catastrophic rises in drug abuse, sexual immorality, murder, theft, demon worship, and idolatry.

"Be of good cheer even in the midst of chaos and plague, loved ones. We know from the Bible that the evil demon king of the abyss is living up to his name—Abaddon in Hebrew and Apollyon in Greek, which means Destroyer—in leading the demon locusts on the rampage. But we as the sealed followers of the Lord God need not fear. For as it is written: 'He who is in you is greater than he who is in the world. . . . We are of God. He who knows God hears us; he who is not of God does not hear us. By this we know the spirit of truth and the spirit of error.'

"Always test my teaching against the Bible. Read it every day. New believers—and none of us are old, are we?—learn the value of the discipline of daily reading and study. When we see the ugly creatures that have invaded the earth, it becomes obvious that we too must go to war.

"Finally, my brethren, with the apostle Paul I urge you to 'be strong in the Lord and in the power of His might. Put on the whole armor of God, that you may be able to stand against the wiles of the devil. For we do not wrestle against flesh and blood, but against principalities, against powers, against the rulers of the darkness of this age, against spiritual hosts of wickedness in the heavenly places.

"'Therefore take up the whole armor of God, that you may be able to withstand in the evil day, and having done all, to stand. Stand therefore, having girded your waist with truth, having put on the breastplate of righteousness, and having shod your feet with the preparation of the gospel of peace; above all, taking the shield of faith with which you will be able to quench all the fiery darts of the wicked one.

"'And take the helmet of salvation, and the sword of the Spirit, which is the word of God; praying always with all prayer and supplication in the Spirit, being watchful to this end with all perseverance and supplication for all the saints—and for me, that utterance may be given to me, that I may open my mouth boldly to make known the mystery of the gospel.'

"Until next we interact through this miracle of technology the Lord has used to build a mighty church against all odds, I remain your servant and his, Tsion Ben-Judah."

* * *

Buck knew that Jacov and Hannelore and Stefan had grown in their faith when they insisted on moving into the Rosenzweig estate and caring for Chaim and

Jonas for several months. They brought with them Hannelore's mother, who had received Christ the day the locusts attacked. Even in her suffering she read and studied and prayed, often pleading with Chaim and Jonas to also come to Christ. Even after Jonas did, Chaim remained resolute.

Unable to find a commercial flight that had a full crew, Buck desperately searched among the saints to find someone who might charter him back to the States for the birth of his child. At wit's end, he tried calling Mac in New Babylon but was unable to get through. He tried e-mailing him a heavily coded message, and an hour later received a lengthy reply.

I'm still looking forward to meeting you, Mr. Williams. Of course, your father-in-law has told me all about you, but don't worry, I didn't believe a word of it.

How do you like the e-mail system David has set me up with here? He's built into it all the safeguards you could imagine. If someone walked in on me right now, they wouldn't be able to read what I've just written.

I gather you need a charter flight out of there. Try Abdullah Smith in Jordan. The name looks weird, but he has his reasons. And he is a believer. Mention my name and he'll charge you double (just kidding). If he can handle the job, he'll take care of you.

I'll copy this to your people so they'll know what's going on here. David Hassid and I had to fake locust stings to keep from revealing ourselves. In the process we discovered several other clandestine believers in the ranks here. Carpathia and Leon are quarantined in a fallout shelter that has served to keep out the locusts too, though almost everyone else, including the ten rulers and even Peter the Second, have been stung and are suffering. When you see Carpathia on the news telling everyone that the stories of poisonous bites are exaggerated while he sits there with a locust on his shoulder as a pet, don't believe it. It's a trick of photographic technology. Of course, the real things probably wouldn't bite Nicolae or Leon out of professional courtesy.

A few of us believers have been able to pretend we are simply recuperating more quickly, so we don't lie around the infirmary twenty-four hours a day listening to the agony. Carpathia has sent me on some missions of mercy, delivering aid to some of the worst-off rulers. What he doesn't know is that David has picked up clandestine shipments of literature, copies of Tsion's studies in different languages, and has jammed the cargo hold of the Condor 216 with them. Believers wherever I go unload and distribute them.

Word has gotten back to Leon that all this Christian literature is flooding the globe, and he's furious about it. So is Peter the Second. I hope someday they both find out how it was transported. But not yet. Pray for us. We're your eyes and ears in New Babylon, and light as I try to make it all sound, we're in very precarious positions. Subversives are punished by death here. Two close members of Peter Mathews's staff were executed for mentioning to Global Community personnel something Peter thought was private. Carpathia heard about the executions and sent him a note of congratulations. Of course, Peter is on Nicolae's hit list, or at least for sure on Leon's. Leon believes there's no need for any *religion because we have His Excellency the potentate to worship.*

I say that with irony, but Leon is dead serious. David was in the room when Leon suggested passing a law that people have to bow in Nicolae's presence. That may be the end of me.

The believers here cannot meet for fear of suspicion and detection, but we encourage each other in subtle ways. Fortunately, David has been elevated to a position that puts him on a level close to the senior pilot (yours truly), so we are expected to interact a lot. We love the late Ken Ritz's idea for the believers' commodity co-op, for lack of a better handle, and we think your wife will make an absolutely smashing CEO. You know who her direct competition will be, of course. Carpathia himself is personally (really) taking charge of global commerce, effective immediately. You heard it here first. He wants those ten kings in his hip pocket, doesn't he?

You know, Mr. Williams, I heard something on the Condor a few days before the locusts attacked that proved one of Dr. Ben-Judah's points. Remember when he wrote that this period is not just a grand war between good and evil, but also a war between evil and evil? I think his point was that we were to love each other and make sure the crises don't turn us on each other and spur fights between good and good. But anyway, Mathews and Saint Nick and the ever-present Leon-my-whole-Fortunato-is-tied-to-you-Excellency are aboard the Condor 216. (I finally figured out the significance of Carpathia's obsession with that number, by the way. Well, actually David told me. He thought everybody knew. Your quiz for the week.)

So on the plane ol' Mathews is really putting the screws to Carpathia. He's demanding this and urging that and begging for more share of the taxes for all the wonderful stuff Enigma Babylon is going to do for the Global Community. Nicolae is yessing him and uh-huhing him to beat the band. Mathews takes a bathroom break and Nicolae tells Fortunato, "If you don't have him hit, I'll do the job myself."

Of course Leon tells him, "He's outlived his usefulness, and I'm working on it."

Well, didn't mean to ramble, but with all the afflicted here, I've got more alone time than I'll probably ever have again. All the best with the little one. We'll pray you get home in time and that Mama is up and around in time to get back to work and make a parent out of you. Greet everyone for me.

In the name of Christ, Mac M.

+ + +

Still grieving the loss of Ken Ritz, missing his interaction with Mac McCullum, and reeling from the attempted infiltration of the bumbling Ernie, Rayford took his time getting to know T. M. Delanty. While Ernie and the irrepressible Bo were ensconced at Arthur Young Memorial Hospital in Palatine, Rayford made several trips to the Palwaukee Airport to sift through Ken's things. As often as not, he'd see T.

They shared life stories over a couple of lunches, and Rayford knew they had taken a step toward potential friendship when he mustered the courage to ask, "What does T. M. stand for?"

T gave him a you-had-to-ask-didn't-you? look. "If I wanted people to know that, I wouldn't have resorted to initials."

"Sorry. Just wondered why you go by T, that's all."

"I've got a crummy first name, what can I tell you? My mother was African-American and my father Scotch-Irish. Heavy on the Scotch, sad to say. She named me after an old schoolteacher of hers. Tyrola made a good last name, but if you were hung with that moniker, what would you go by?"

"I'd go buy a ticket out of town, T. Sorry I asked. Middle name wasn't an option?"

"Mark."

Rayford shrugged. "What's wrong with that?"

"Nothing, except do I look like a Mark? Admit it, I look like a T."

Tyrola Mark Delanty was the only member of his small church to be left behind at the Rapture. "I was suicidal," he said. "And I can't say I've had much fun, even since I finally got right with God. Lost a wife of fourteen years and six kids, my whole extended family, friends, church people, everybody."

Rayford asked whom he met with now.

"There are about thirty believers in my neighborhood. More all the time. Neighborhood is overstating it, of course. We're all living in our original homes, but they're worthless. Just happened to not fall over, so there are living spaces."

After a few meetings, Rayford and T finally got around to the subject of Ken and Palwaukee and Bo and Ernie. It turned out that T was the major owner of the airport, having bought it from the county a couple of years before the

Rapture. "Never made much money at it. Low margin, but it was turning. Ken and several other regulars flew out of here. Ken lived here, as you know, until the earthquake when he moved in with you guys."

Bo was the only son of a wealthy investor who owned 5 percent of the business but who had died in a car wreck when the Rapture took drivers from cars in front and in back of his. "In the ensuing chaos, Bo shows up as the sole heir, trying to act like a board member and a boss. I humored him until he brought Ernie on. I fought it at first. He was a nineteen-year-old who had dropped out of school when he was fourteen but reputed to be a natural mechanic. Well, it turned out he was, and he helped a lot around here. I only put it together the day of the locust attack that Ernie and Bo had a scheme going."

"Why would they have wanted Ernie to infiltrate our group?"

"Rumor was that Ken had a lot of money. Ernie was trying, I think, to get in good with him. He and Bo would have run some scam on him and tried to cash in. When Ken was killed, they went into high gear. You saw the sad result of that comical effort."

Rayford studied T, trying to decide whether to ask what he thought of the rumors about Ken's wealth. He decided not to pursue it yet, but T made the question moot. "The rumors were true, you know."

"As a matter of fact, I do know," Rayford said. "How did *you* know?"

"Ken really wanted to buy the airport, and I really wanted to sell it. That was my hope all along, but now I had a different motive. Rebuilding it after the earthquake really strapped me, and I needed to cash out. I wanted to pour a little money into our tiny congregation and see if we couldn't accomplish something for God in the few years we have left. I asked Ken if he could afford market value for the airport, and he assured me he could."

"Did he happen to say where he banked?"

T smiled. "We're still feeling each other out, aren't we? Still playing cat and mouse."

"I was just wondering," Rayford said.

"Yes, I think we're both up to speed."

"What do you think should be done with Ken's assets, T?"

"Used for God. Every last dime. That's what he would have wanted."

"I agree. Does that money belong to anyone else? Legally, I mean?"

"Nope."

"And you have access to it?"

"You want to dig with me, Rayford?"

"I don't know. What're you paying?"

"Unless Ken told you you could have it, I believe rightfully it's mine. It was left on my property. I'm not sure where, and I'm not sure how much. But I'd sure like to get at it before Bo and Ernie recuperate."

Rayford nodded. "Your little church can make use of all that?"

"Like I said, we want to see if we can do something significant. We wouldn't build a church or fix up our homes."

"Any inkling how much you're talking about?" Rayford said.

"Maybe over a million."

"Would it surprise you to know it's probably five times that?"

"Are we negotiating, Rayford? You want some of this, think you're entitled to it, what?"

Rayford shook his head. "I'd like to be able to buy his planes. I have no claim on his money or anything else."

"I'll tell you what," T said. "If there's half as much money as you think there is, I'll give you his planes."

"How much for the Gulfstream?"

"If there's as much as you say there is, you can have that one too."

"And can I fly out of here?"

"You can house 'em, keep 'em up, and live here with 'em if you want."

"And may a Jordanian fly my son-in-law in here within twenty-four hours, no questions asked?"

"You got it, brother."

Rayford broached the subject of a world commodity co-op among believers, coordinated out of the Tribulation Force safe house. "Any interest in getting behind that, delivering, running charters, that type of thing?"

"Now *that* I could get excited about," T said. "My little band of believers too, I'll bet."

+ + +

Buck met Abdullah Smith in an outdoor café run by a young woman on the tail end of her recuperative season. Abdullah was as secretive and quiet as just about anyone Buck had ever met. But he had a clear mark on his forehead and was healthy. He embraced Buck with vigor despite being a laconic conversationalist.

"The name McCullum is all I need to hear, sir. We are brothers, the three of us. I fly. You pay. Nothing more need be said."

And it wasn't. At least by Abdullah. Buck told him he was making one last social call and would meet him at the airport in Amman at six that evening. "I would appreciate a stop in northern Greece, and then straight to the Chicago area."

Abdullah nodded.

The streets of Jerusalem were largely deserted. Buck had never grown used to the sobbing and howling he heard on every corner. It seemed many suffered in every household. He heard that thousands in Jerusalem had slit their wrists, tried to hang themselves, drunk poison, stuck their heads in gas ovens, put plastic bags over their heads, sat in garages with cars running, even jumped in front of trains and leaped off buildings. They were severely injured, of course, and some were left looking like slabs of butchered meat. But no one died. They just lived in torment.

Buck found Rosenzweig's home a little quieter, but even Chaim begged to be put out of his misery. Jacov reported that Chaim had taken no nourishment—none—for more than a week. He was trying to starve himself to death or develop a fatal case of dehydration. He looked terrible, emaciated and wan.

Jonas and Jacov's mother-in-law were more stoic. Though clearly suffering, they did what they could to help themselves. They slept, they ate, they got up and around. They tried medication, though it seemed to make no difference. The point was in trying. They looked forward to the day they would be free from the effects of the sting. Jonas, in particular, was childlike in his excitement over reading the Bible with Jacov and having Tsion Ben-Judah's daily cyberspace message read to him.

Chaim merely wanted to die. Buck sat on his bed until the old man cried out in agony. "Everything hurts, Cameron. If you cared a whit about me, you would free me from this misery. Have compassion. Do the right thing. God will forgive you."

"You're asking the impossible, and I wouldn't do it anyway. I wouldn't forgive myself if I didn't give you every opportunity to believe."

"Let me die!"

"Chaim, I do not understand you. I really don't. You know the truth. Your suffering will be over in several weeks and—"

"I will *never* survive that long!"

"And you'll have something to live for."

Chaim was silent and still for a long time, as if peace had come over him. But it had not. "To tell you the truth, my young friend, I don't understand either. I confess I want to come to Christ. But a battle rages within me, and I simply cannot."

"You can!"

"I cannot!"

"Not being able to is not the problem, is it, Doctor?"

Chaim shook his head miserably. "I will not."

"And you deny my charge that your pride keeps you from God."

"I admit it now! It *is* pride! But it's there and it's real. A man cannot become what he is not."

"Oh, that's where you're wrong, Chaim! Paul, who had been an orthodox Jew, wrote, 'If anyone is in Christ, he is a new creation; old things have passed away; behold, all things have become new.'"

Chaim thrashed painfully for several minutes, but he said nothing. To Buck, that was progress. "Chaim?" he said softly.

"Leave me alone, Cameron!"

"I'll be praying for you."

"You'll be wasting time."

"Never. I love you, Chaim. We all do. God most of all."

"If God loved me, he would let me die."

"Not until you belong to him."

"That will never happen."

"Famous last words. Good-bye, friend. I'll look forward to seeing you again."

19

RAYFORD LOVED HIS DAUGHTER with all that was in him. He always had. It wasn't just because she was the only family he had left. He had loved Raymie too and still missed him terribly. Losing two wives in fewer than three years was a blow he knew would be with him until Jesus came again.

But his relationship with Chloe had always been special. They'd had their moments, of course, when she was going through the process of breaking away from the family and becoming an independent young woman. Yet she was so much like him.

That had made it difficult for her to believe that God was behind the disappearances in the first place. Flattered that she took after him and yet afraid her practicality might forever keep her from Christ, Rayford had agonized over her. The greatest day of his life—excluding when he himself became a believer—was when Chloe made her decision.

He was thrilled when she and Buck married, despite the ten-year age difference. He didn't know what he thought when he heard they were expecting and that he would be a grandfather with fewer than five years left on earth.

But seeing Chloe in the full bloom of her pregnancy, he was transported. He remembered Irene, despite difficult pregnancies, looking radiant the further she progressed and, yes, the bigger she got. He had read all the books, knew the pitfalls. Rayford understood that Irene would not believe him when he said she was most beautiful when she was very pregnant.

She had said the same things Chloe was saying now—that she felt like a cow, a barn, a barge. She hated the swollen joints, the sore back, the shortness of breath, the lack of mobility. "In a way I'm glad Buck is stuck in Israel," she said. "I mean, I want him back and I want him back now, but he's going to think I've doubled in size."

Rayford took the occasion to sit with Chloe. "Sweetheart," he said, "indulge me. It may be politically incorrect to say that you are doing what you were meant to do. I know you're more than a baby-making machine and that you have incredible things to offer this world. You made an impact even before the

Rapture, but since, you've been a soldier. You're going to make the world commodity co-op a lifesaver for millions of saints. But you need to do me a favor and stop bemoaning what this pregnancy is doing to your body."

"I know, Daddy," she said. "But it's just that I'm so—"

"Beautiful," he said. "Absolutely beautiful."

He said it with such feeling that it seemed to shut her up. She looked different, of course. Nothing was the same. With only a few weeks until her due date, she was full faced and ponderous. But he could still detect his little girl there, his Chloe when she had been a toddler, full of life and curiosity.

"I'm frustrated for Buck that he can't see you like this. Now don't look at me like that. I mean it. He will find you so lovely, and believe it or not, he will find you attractive too. You're not the first mom-to-be who equates pregnancy with being overweight. Husbands don't think that way. He'll see you the way I saw your mother when she was carrying you. He'll be overcome with the knowledge that you're carrying his and your child."

Chloe seemed to appreciate the pep talk. "I'm really stressed about him coming home," she said. "I know he's leaving Israel at six their time, but who knows how long he'll be in Greece?"

"Not long. He wants to get home."

"And it being a charter, they'll keep moving I think. I wish I could meet him at the airport."

"Doc says you shouldn't—"

"Ride in the car, especially on these roads, I know. I don't really want to endure that. But Buck and I have been apart so long. And as much as we worry about bringing a baby into the world at this time in history, we've both grown so attached to this child already that we can't wait to meet him . . . or her."

"I can't wait to be a grandfather," Rayford said. "I've been praying for this child since I knew it existed. I just worry that life is going to be so hard for all of us that I won't get the opportunity to be the kind of grandpa I want to be."

"You'll be great. I'm glad you're not still flying for Carpathia. I wouldn't want to worry about you all the time."

Rayford stood and looked out the window. The morning sun was harsh. "I'm getting back into the war," he said.

"What does that mean?"

"Well, I can blame it on you. You've taken Ken's idea so far that it's going to give me a full-time job. I'm going to be flying almost as much as when I was with Pan-Con."

"For the co-op?"

He nodded. "I've told you about T."

"Uh-huh."

"We're going to run the airlift operation out of Palwaukee. I'll be flying all over the world. If those fishermen in the Bering Strait are as successful as you seem to think they'll be, I'll have enough business up there to last till the Glorious Appearing."

Floyd Charles knocked on the doorjamb. "Time for a little checkup. You want Dad to wait outside?"

"What're we doing?" Chloe said.

"Just checking heartbeats, yours and Junior's."

"He can stay. Can he listen?"

"Sure."

Floyd took Chloe's pulse first, then listened to her heart with his stethoscope. He spread lubricating jelly on her protruding belly and used a battery-powered monitor to amplify the liquid sounds of the fetal heartbeat. Rayford fought tears, and Chloe beamed. "Sounds like a big boy to me," Doc Charles said.

As he finished up, Chloe asked, "Everything still fine?"

"No major problems," he said.

Rayford glanced at Floyd. He was not as light as usual. He had not even smiled when he joked about her having a boy. She didn't want to know the sex of the baby, and he had never tested to find out.

"How about other than major problems, Floyd?" she said, her voice flat. "You usually say everything's great."

She had spoken exactly what was on Rayford's mind, and his heart sank when Floyd pulled up a chair.

"You noticed that, did you?" he said.

"Oh, no," she said.

Floyd put a hand on her shoulder. "Chloe, listen to me."

"Oh, no!"

"Chloe, what did I say? I said no major problems, and I meant it. Do you think I would say that if it wasn't true?"

"So what's the minor problem?"

"Some reduction in the baby's pulse."

"You're kidding," Rayford said. "If I'd had to guess, I would have said it sounded too fast."

"All fetal pulses are faster than ours," Floyd said. "And the reduction is so slight that I hardly gave it a second thought last week."

"This has been going on for a week?" Chloe said.

Floyd nodded. "We're talking about a fraction of a percentage decrease in six days. It doesn't have to mean anything."

"But if it means anything," Chloe said, "what would it mean?"

"We don't want to see an actual slowdown of the fetal pulse. Like 5 percent, especially 10 percent or more."

"Because . . . ?"

"Because that could mean some threat to viability."

"English, Doctor," Chloe said.

"As the baby gets into position for birth, the umbilical cord could tighten around the chest or the neck."

"Do you think that's happening?"

"No. I'm just watching heart rate, Chloe. That's all."

"Is it a possibility?"

"Anything is a possibility. That's why I'm not listing everything that can go wrong."

"If this is so minor, why are you telling me?"

"For one thing, you asked. I just want to prepare you for a form of treatment should the symptoms persist."

"But you said the reduction in rate right now is not worth worrying about."

"OK, if the symptoms get worse."

"What would you do?"

"At least get you on oxygen for the better part of each day."

"I need to stand up a minute," Chloe said.

She started to move, and Rayford reached to help. Floyd didn't. "Actually," he said, "I'd prefer that you take it very easy until I can get out and get you some oxygen tomorrow."

"I can't even stand up?"

"For necessities. If it's just to shift position, try not to."

"All right," she said, "my dad and I are bottom-line people. Give me the worst-case scenario."

"I've dealt with enough pregnant women, especially at this stage of gestation, to know it's not best to dwell on all the negative possibilities."

"I'm not pregnant women, Doc. I'm Chloe, and you know me, and you know I'm going to bug you to death until you tell me the worst case."

"All right," he said. "I see the oxygen solving the problem. If it doesn't, I'll have you on monitors around the clock to warn of a significant change in fetal pulse. Worst case, we might want to induce labor. It might mean a cesarean section because of the likelihood of an umbilical cord problem."

Chloe fell silent and looked at Rayford. He said, "You don't like to induce, right?"

"Of course not. I used to say nature knows best. That baby comes when he is ready. Now I know that God knows best. But he has also given us brains and miracle medicines and technologies that allow us to do what we need to do when things don't go the way we wish."

Chloe looked uncomfortable. "I need to know one thing, Floyd. Did I contribute to this? Was there something I shouldn't have done, or something I should have done differently?"

Floyd shook his head. "I wasn't wild about your going to Israel. And if I never hear again about you running from helicopter to jet, it'll be too soon. But overexertion at that stage of pregnancy would have shown up in different problems."

"Such as?"

"Such as nothing that turned up, so I'm not going to talk about it. How's that? You've already been through all the predictable stuff—convinced you're going to have a monster, convinced the baby has already died, certain your baby doesn't have all its parts. You don't need to worry about stuff you might have caused but didn't. Now when do you expect Papa?"

"Sometime tonight," she said. "That's all I know."

\+ \+ \+

Abdullah Smith seemed pleased that Buck showed up when he said he would. "I heard you were a man of your word," Buck said, "and wanted to show that I am too."

Abdullah, as usual, did not respond. He grabbed one of Buck's bags and led him briskly toward his plane. Buck tried to guess which one it would be. He passed the prop jobs, knowing they would never get him across the Atlantic. But Abdullah also passed a Learjet and a brand-new Hajiman, a smaller version of the *Concorde* and just as fast.

Buck stopped and stared when Abdullah pulled back the Plexiglas cockpit shield of what he recognized as an Egyptian fighter jet. It would fly nearly two thousand miles an hour at very high altitudes but had to have a shorter than usual fuel range.

"This is your plane?" Buck said.

"Please to board," Abdullah said. "Fuel tank enlarged. Small cargo hold added. Stop in Greece, stop in London, stop in Greenland, stop in Wheeling."

Buck was impressed that he knew where he was going. It was clear his hope of stretching out, getting some reading done, even dozing, was not in the cards.

"Passenger must board first," Abdullah said.

Buck climbed in and tried to show that he knew his way around this type of craft, after having done a series of articles on ride-alongs with American fighter pilots. That was before the reign of Nicolae Carpathia and the wholesale marketing of such surplus craft to private citizens.

Buck was about to strap on his helmet and oxygen mask when Abdullah sighed and said, "Belt."

Buck was sitting on it. So much for showing off. He had to stand, as much as one could in that confined space, while Abdullah reached beneath him to retrieve the belt. Once strapped in, he tried to put the helmet on. Again the pilot had to assist—untangling his straps, twisting the helmet just so, and smacking it on top until it settled into correct, and extremely tight, position. It pressed against Buck's temples and cheekbones. He started to put the mouthpiece in until Abdullah reminded him, "Not until high altitude."

"Right. I knew that."

Abdullah fit just ahead of him, giving Buck the feeling they were on a luge, Abdullah's head just inches from Buck's nose.

Taking a jet fighter from a staging area, out onto the tarmac, into line, and then out onto the runway would have taken up to half an hour in the States. Buck learned that in Amman, the airport was like the street market. No lines or queues. It was first come, first served, and you were on your own. Abdullah sang something into the radio about jet, charter, passenger, cargo, and Greece, all while moving the fighter directly onto the runway. He didn't wait for instructions from ground control.

The Amman airport had only recently reopened after rebuilding, and while air traffic was down because of the plague of locusts, several flights were lined up. Two wide-bodies sat at the front of the line, followed by a standard jet, a Learjet, and another big plane. Abdullah turned to get Buck's attention and pointed to the fuel gauge, which showed full.

Buck gave a thumbs-up sign, which he intended to imply that he felt good about having lots of fuel. Abdullah, apparently, took it to mean that Buck wanted to get into the air—and now. He taxied quickly around other planes, reached the line of craft cleared and in line for takeoff, and passed them one by one. Buck was speechless. He imagined if the other pilots had horns, they'd have been honking, like drivers in traffic do to those who ride the shoulder.

As Abdullah passed the second wide-body, the first began to roll. Abdullah slipped in behind it, and suddenly he and Buck were next in line. Buck craned his neck to see if emergency vehicles were coming or whether the other planes would just pull ahead and get back in their original order. No scolding came from the tower. As soon as the big jet was well on its way down the runway, Abdullah pulled out.

"Edward Zulu Zulu Two Niner taking off, tower," he said into the radio.

Buck fully expected someone to come back with, "Just where do you think you're going, young man?" But no one did.

"Ten-four, Abdullah," was all he heard.

There was no warming up and little building speed. Abdullah drove the fighter to the end of the runway, lined her up, and punched it. Buck's head was driven back, and his stomach flattened. He could not have leaned forward if he'd wanted to. Clearly breaking every rule of international aviation, Abdullah reached takeoff speed in a few hundred yards and was airborne. He rocketed above and beyond the jet in front of him, and Buck felt as if they were flying straight up.

He was pressed back in his seat, staring at clouds. It seemed only minutes later Abdullah reached the apex of his climb, and just like that, he seemed to throttle back and start his descent. It was like a roller-coaster ride, blasting to the peak and then rolling down the other side. Abdullah mashed a button that allowed him to speak directly into Buck's headset. "Amman to Athens just up and down," he said.

"But we're not going to Athens, remember?"

Abdullah smacked his helmet. "Ptolemaïs, right?"

"Right!"

The plane shot straight up again. Abdullah dug through a set of rolled-up maps and said, "No problem."

And he was right. Minutes later he came screaming onto the runway of the small airport. "How long with friends?" he said, taxiing to the fuel pumps.

+ + +

Rayford reassured Chloe, and they agreed they'd rather Floyd tell the truth than sugarcoat it and run into problems later. But after he brought her water, Rayford moved upstairs to talk to Tsion. The rabbi welcomed him warmly. "Almost finished with my lesson for today," he said. "I'll transmit it in an hour or so. Anyway, I always have time for you."

Rayford told him of the potential complication with the baby. "I will pray," Tsion said. "And I would ask you to pray for me as well."

"Sure, Tsion. Anything specific?"

"Well, yes. Frankly, I feel lonely and overwhelmed, and I hate that feeling."

"It's sure understandable."

"I know. And I have a deep sense of joy, such as we get when we are in fellowship with the Lord. I have told him this, of course, but I would appreciate knowing someone else is praying for me too."

"I'm sure we all do, Tsion."

"I am most blessed to have such a loving family to replace my loss. We have all suffered. Sometimes it just overtakes me. I knew this locust plague was coming, but I never thought through the ramifications. In many ways I wish we had been more prepared. Our enemy has been incapacitated for months. Yet while we count on them for so many things, like transportation, communications, and the like, this has crippled us too.

"I don't know," he said, rising and stretching. "I don't expect to find happiness anymore. I am looking forward to the birth of this little one as if it were my own. That will bring a ray of sunshine."

"And we want you to be another parent to it, Tsion."

"The contrast alone will be sobering though, won't it?

"The contrast?"

"This fresh, young innocent will not know why Hattie is crying. Won't know of our losses. Won't understand that we live in terror, enemies of the state. And there will be no need to teach the little one of all the despair of the past, as we would if we were raising it to adulthood. By the time this baby is five years old, it will already be living in the millennial kingdom with Jesus Christ in control. Imagine."

Tsion had a way of bringing perspective to everything. Yet Rayford was sobered by the rabbi's angst. Millions around the world expected Dr. Ben-Judah to be their spiritual leader. They had to assume he was at peace with his own mature walk with God. Yet he was a new believer too. While a great scholar and theologian, he was but a man. Like most others, he had suffered grievously. He still had his days of despair.

Rayford began feeling lonely in advance. Floyd would have plenty of doctoring to do in the safe house with a new baby and Hattie still ailing. Buck had told Rayford he looked forward to some modicum of normalcy and permanence, so he could make his Internet magazine what it needed to be to compete with Carpathia's Global Community rags. Chloe would be busy with the baby and the details of the commodity co-op. And Hattie, when she finally recuperated, would itch to get out of there.

That left Rayford to be the one on the go. He looked forward to being back in the cockpit. He had resigned himself to the fact that his life would consist of hard work, being careful to remain free and just trying to stay alive. But the Glorious Appearing seemed further away all the time. How he longed to be with Jesus! To be reunited with his family!

His life as an accomplished commercial pilot seemed eons ago now. It was hard to comprehend that it had been fewer than three years since he was just a suburban husband and father, and none too good a one, with nothing more to worry about than where and when he was flying next.

Rayford couldn't complain of having had nothing important to occupy his time. But the cost of getting to this point! He could empathize with Tsion. If the Tribulation was hard on a regular Joe like Rayford, he couldn't imagine what it must be like for one called to rally the 144,000 witnesses and teach maybe a billion other new souls.

Early in the afternoon Rayford took a call from T Delanty. "I want to start digging tomorrow," he said. "You still willing to help?"

"Wouldn't miss it. If my son-in-law gets in at a decent hour, I'll be ready when you are."

"How about seven in the morning?"

"What's the rush?"

"I hear Ernie's getting better. Bo probably would be too, but he tried to kill himself three ways. He's a mess."

"Buy him out."

"I will, and that will be easy because the way we're set up, all I have to do is make him an offer he can't match. He was left some money, but his share in the airport is so small, I should be able to make him go away. I worry about Ernie."

"How so?"

"He was close to Ken, Ray. At least as close as a person could hope to get. I know Ken considered him a believer; he had me fooled too."

"I'm the third stooge on that list," Rayford said.

"It's possible Ken confided in Ernie."

"Nah. He only just told *me* on the flight to Israel."

"You say that like you guys have been buddies for years. He hardly knew you, Rayford, and yet he told you he buried his gold. I had heard the rumor myself, and I don't feel like I knew Ken well at all. Ernie worked with him, ingratiated himself. I don't believe for a second that Ken promised him a thing. That wouldn't make sense. But still I'll bet Ernie knows more than he'll let on."

"You think he'll get better and show up with a shovel?"

"I wouldn't put it past him."

+ + +

"First, Mr. Williams, call me Laslos. It comes from my first name, Lukas, and my last name, Miklos. OK?"

Buck agreed as they embraced in the small air terminal. "And you must call me Buck."

"I thought your name was Cameron."

"My friends call me Buck."

"Then Buck it is. I want to take you to meet with the believers."

"Oh, Laslos, I'm sorry. I cannot. I'd love to, and maybe I will get back here and do that. But do you understand that I have been away from my wife for many months—"

Laslos looked stricken. "Yes, but—"

"And that she is in her last couple of weeks of pregnancy?"

"You're going to be a father! Splendid! And everything is fine, except that this is the worst time . . . well, you know that."

Buck nodded. "My father-in-law wanted me to discuss with you your role in the international commodity co-op."

"Yes!" Laslos said, sitting and pointing to a chair for Buck. "I have been reading what Dr. Ben-Judah says about it. It is a brilliant idea. What would we do without it? We would all die, and that is what the evil one wants, right? Am I not a good student?"

"Do you see a role for yourself or your company?"

Laslos cocked his head. "I'll do what I can. My company mines lignite. It is used in power plants. If there is any call for it in the community of believers, I would be happy to be involved."

Buck leaned forward. "Laslos, do you understand what it will mean when citizens of the Global Community are required to wear the sign of the beast on their hand or on their forehead?"

"I think so. Without it they cannot buy or sell. But I do not consider myself a citizen of the Global Community, and I would die before I would wear the sign of Antichrist."

"That's great, friend," Buck said. "But do you see how it will affect you? You will not be able to sell. Your whole business and livelihood are built on a product you sell."

"But they need my product!"

"So they will put you in jail and take over your mines."

"I will fight them to the death."

"You probably will. What I'm suggesting is that you look for another commodity to trade, something more internationally marketable, something your brothers and sisters in Christ need and will be unable to get when the mark of the beast is ushered in."

Laslos appeared deep in thought. He nodded. "And I have another idea," he said. "I will build my lignite business and sell it before they quit buying from me."

"Great idea!"

"It happens all the time, Buck. You make yourself so indispensable to your biggest client that it only makes sense that they buy you out."

"And who is your biggest client?"

Laslos sat back and smiled sadly, but Buck detected a gleam in his eye. "The Global Community," he said.

20

RAYFORD RAN into Floyd Charles angrily slamming stuff around. "Which vehicle can I use?" Floyd asked.

"Makes no difference, Doc," Rayford said. "Rover's running fine. I'm taking Ken's Suburban to T tomorrow. See if his little church group can use it. It's rightfully his anyway."

"I'll take Buck's."

"Where you going?"

"I've got to get some oxygen, Ray. I don't want to be caught off guard without O_2 when I need it. And I don't want Chloe as stressed as I am."

"That bad? Should I be worried?"

"Nah! It's not Chloe as much as Hattie now. She thinks she's better, so she wants to get up and get out. Well, she can't without help, and I'm not going to help her. She *has* made a turn for the better, but she's underweight, and her vitals are average. But, like you say, she doesn't report to us."

"You want me to talk to her? Maybe I can shame her into doing what you say, after all we've done for her."

"If you think it'll do any good."

"Where you getting O_2, Kenosha?"

"I don't dare show my face there again. I called Leah at Arthur Young. She's got a couple of tanks for me."

"You know who you can check in on over there? Hattie's young Ernie."

"No kidding?"

"T told me Ernie and his friend Bo were being treated there."

+ + +

Buck was ill by the time Abdullah landed at Heathrow. Cramped, nauseated, exhausted, tense—he was a mess. All he wanted was to get home to Chloe.

Heathrow was a shell of what it had been before World War 3 and the great earthquake. But Carpathia had poured money into it and made it high-tech and efficient, if not as big as it had been. With the waning population, nothing needed to be as big as before.

Heathrow tower flatly rejected Abdullah's announced sequences. He seemed frustrated but didn't rebel. Buck wondered what he did before becoming a believer. Maybe he'd been a terrorist.

Abdullah seemed cognizant of Buck's wish to keep moving. He returned from refueling with two cellophane-wrapped cheese sandwiches that looked as if they'd been sitting for days. He offered one to Buck, who refused only because he was queasy. Abdullah must have assumed Buck was in too great a hurry to eat, because as soon as the deliberate ground control officer cleared him for takeoff, they were streaking toward Greenland.

Buck felt as if he were running a sprint that would never end. He assumed that at some point he could try to relax, but the jet seemed always on the verge of exploding or crashing. When his phone chirped in his pocket, Buck went through all sorts of vain gyrations to get in a position where he could reach it.

Abdullah noticed and asked if anything was wrong. "Need an emergency landing?" he asked.

"No!" Buck hollered, sensing the hope in Abdullah's question. Apparently a normal race from Jordan to America wasn't enough of a thrill for Abdullah. But where does one execute an emergency landing between London and Greenland? Surely he would have had to turn back to London, but Abdullah seemed more likely to find an aircraft carrier.

When they finally reached Greenland for the final refueling, Buck extricated himself from his seat and learned that his caller had been Dr. Charles. He called him back.

"I can't really talk to you right now, Buck, sorry. I'm picking up supplies at a hospital."

"Well, give me a hint, Doc. Everything OK there?"

"Let's just say I hope you're on schedule."

"That doesn't sound good. Chloe OK?"

"We all need you here, Buck."

"Spill it, Doc. Is she OK?"

"Buck, let me get free for a minute here so we can talk."

"Please!"

Buck heard Floyd asking someone named Leah if she would excuse him. "All right, Buck. Are you on schedule?"

"I'm surprised I'm not ahead of schedule, but yes, we're looking at a 10:00 p.m. arrival."

"That late?"

"You're scaring me, Doc."

"The truth is, Buck, I've been misleading Chloe and Rayford today. The fetal heartbeat has been dropping for a few days, and it's at the alarming stage."

"Meaning?"

"I'm putting Chloe on oxygen as soon as I get back there. I wanted to do it hours ago, but I ran into a snag at the hospital. I dropped in on somebody Rayford knows who was recuperating here. He sounded real interested in hearing about the judgments and what they meant, and I wound up spending way too much time with him. Hattie's been talking to his younger friend, who's apparently already been released."

Buck stood in the cold wind and hollered into the phone. "Doc, I haven't a clue what you're talking about. I'm sorry to be rude, but get to the point. Why did you think it necessary to mislead Chloe and Ray when they're right there and can deal with the problem, but you drop it on me in the middle of nowhere when I can do nothing?"

"If you had seen how they reacted when I just hinted at the problem, you'd know I was right. I need Chloe to stay upbeat, and if she knew how serious this is, she would not be in a position to do her part."

Abdullah signaled Buck to reboard. "Will I still be able to talk on the phone?"

"Yes, yes!"

But in the air the noise was awful. Buck and Floyd had to repeat almost every sentence, but Buck finally got the whole scoop. "Is there any chance you'll have to induce before I get there?"

"I'm through making promises."

"Do what's best for Chloe and the baby!"

"That's what I wanted to hear."

He needs permission for that? Buck wondered.

"And tell Rayford the truth, Doc! I think Chloe can take it too, but if you think it would put her into a tailspin, use your own judgment. She's pretty tough, you know."

"She's also very pregnant, Buck. That floods the body with a hormone wash and turns a woman into a mother hen."

"Just don't say or do something you have to apologize for later. She's going to want to know why she wasn't fully informed."

"Rayford will be there to get you, Buck. I've got another call. Godspeed!"

+ + +

Rayford was relieved when Doc Charles finally answered. "Where are you, man? You've been gone for hours!"

Floyd told him of meeting Bo and getting sidetracked telling him about God. "The other guy was discharged this morning. Anyway, what's up?"

"Chloe is not feeling well, and of course she's worried. Is there anything we should do for her?"

"What's her complaint?"

"Shortness of breath. Extreme fatigue."

"I'll get there as soon as I can. Put her in a position where her lungs can expand the most. Can you handle the fetal monitor?"

"We'll get it done between the two of us if it's important."

"Call me with the results in ten minutes."

+ + +

Buck liked Doc, and it felt strange to be angry with him. But a trained medical professional should be more buttoned-down, less hung up on periphery. Here he was, his own life in Abdullah's hands, rocketing through the air to get home to his wife, and he gets this news. What was he supposed to do but pray? Buck believed in prayer and exercised it to the fullest. But anxiety just about did him in, and he could easily have been spared it. There'd be plenty of time to worry once he got there.

+ + +

Rayford felt all thumbs getting the fetal monitor working, and at first he feared the heartbeat had disappeared. "God, please, no!" he prayed silently. "Not this on top of everything else." For all the talk about the inadvisability of bringing a baby into the world during the Tribulation, everyone in the house had a huge stake in this birth.

Suddenly they heard the speeding heart. "Do you just count and multiply?" Rayford asked.

"I don't know," Chloe said, panting. "Can you count that fast? It's still fast, but is it slower than before?"

"It wouldn't change enough in a few hours that we'd be able to tell without precise measurement."

"Then get it to work!"

An LCD readout came to light. When Rayford called the figure in to Floyd, he told Ray to worry more about Chloe than the baby. "I want her to breathe deeply and get all the oxygen she can until I get there. But Ray, I've got a problem. I'm being followed."

"You're sure?"

"No question. I've taken several detours, and I can't shake him."

"What kind of car?"

"A motorcycle. One of those little jobs they race off road. No way I'm going to outrun him."

"Lead him around awhile. See if he gets bored. Some guys just get a kick out of worrying people."

"He's smooth, Ray. He's far enough back to not be obvious, but he's stayed with me for miles. I don't want to give away our location to anybody, but I also need to get this oxygen to Chloe."

"I'll take care of her. Keep me posted."

"Uh, I'm a little low on fuel, and those cycles can go forever."

"How close are you to Palwaukee?"

"Close."

"I'll call T. Whoever's following you isn't going to follow you into an enclosed area. And T will gas you up too."

"Great."

Rayford called T and filled him in.

"Oh, no," T said.

"What?"

"Ernie's a bike racer. He probably followed your man from the hospital, trying to find out where Hattie lives. They've been talking more."

"How do you know?"

"A phone girl here said Hattie called for Ernie, and she told her he was at Young Memorial. But if Hattie wanted to see him, wouldn't she just have told Ernie where she was?"

"She doesn't know where she is, T. She knows it's Mount Prospect, but there's no way she could tell him how to get here."

"If your man leads Ernie here, I'll give him what for. We'll keep him from finding you, you can be sure of that. What's he driving, and what does he look like?"

"The Rover and you."

"Come back?"

"He's driving Buck's Rover, and he looks a lot like you."

Rayford arranged pillows so Chloe could lie back and raise her arms over her head without hurting herself or the baby. That opened her lungs more, and she said she felt a little better. Rayford was startled when he turned and saw Hattie at the top of the basement stairs.

She looked awful, like a ghost or worse, a zombie. Thin, eyes dark, skin pale. She limped to Chloe.

"Hattie!" Chloe said. "It's been ages."

"I wanted to see how my godchild was doing."

"Not here yet, Hattie. We'll let you know."

"And I wanted to tell you I'm not jealous."

Rayford squinted, watching Chloe's reaction.

"You're not, huh?" she said. "I never thought you would be."

"Who would blame me if I was? I lost my baby, but you get to have yours. You're lucky, I'm not. The story of my life."

Rayford wanted to talk to her alone. No way he wanted Chloe to know what was going on. "We're sorry for your loss, Hattie," he said. "And we're grateful you still want to be godmother to Chloe's child."

"We were going to be godmothers to each other's," she said.

"It has to be painful," Chloe said.

"It's going to be for the one who did it," Hattie said.

"If you'll excuse us," Rayford said, "we're trying to do a little doctoring by phone here." He dialed Floyd.

Hattie drifted away without a word.

Floyd told Rayford he was within a mile of Palwaukee. "But this guy's still hanging with me."

Rayford didn't want to leave Chloe, but he didn't want to alarm her either. "If you're comfortable for a while, honey, I want to talk with Hattie."

\+ + +

Buck found himself fighting drowsiness. That should have been no surprise. He had been up since dawn in the Middle East. Despite the noise and thin air, he was desperate to talk with someone in Mount Prospect. He feared upsetting Chloe, and Rayford might be tending to her. He understood Hattie had been incoherent for months. That left Tsion.

What time was it in the States? Late afternoon? The rabbi should be putting the finishing touches on his daily missive. Buck called him. They'd have to yell and repeat themselves, but any contact was better than none.

"Cameron, my friend! How good to hear from you! Where are you?"

"First, Tsion, assure me I am not keeping you from your work. The world waits with bated breath for everything you—"

"I posted it not twenty minutes ago, Cameron. This is a perfect time to talk. We're all excited about the baby and your return. Now where are you?"

"I wish I knew. We're chasing the sunset, but at high altitude in an old jet fighter, I can't even look down. I'd be looking at the Atlantic, that's all I know."

"We will see you in a few hours. There are few small pleasures left in this life,

Buck, and rejoining friends and brothers and spouses is one of those. We have been praying for you every day, and you know Chloe is most excited. You'll be home in plenty of time for the birth, which will likely take place at the hospital in Palatine."

Buck hesitated. "Tsion, you will be honest with me, won't you?"

"Always."

"Are you trying to keep me upbeat because you don't know about complications with Chloe and the baby, or because you do?"

"Your father-in-law briefed me. Dr. Charles seems to have it under control. Rayford reached you with the news?"

"Actually, Floyd did, and it's worse than Rayford and Chloe know."

"Should he not tell them?"

"He has his reasons. I just wondered if Floyd had talked with you."

"No. I heard someone leave hours ago. I assumed it was he."

"He's worried I won't be back in time if he has to induce."

"Induce? Why did he not take her to the hospital then?"

"Frankly, Tsion, I've been killing myself with questions since he called. I don't know what Floyd expected of me."

There was a pause. "Cameron, there is nothing you can do until you get here, except to pray. You have to leave this with the Lord."

"I've never been good at that, sir. I know we're not supposed to worry, but—"

"Oh, Cameron, I think even the Lord himself allows some latitude on that during the Tribulation. The admonition to not worry was written to people who lived before all the judgments. If we did not worry about what was coming next from heaven, we would not be human. Don't feel guilty about worrying. Just rely on the Lord for the things you cannot control. This is one of them."

Buck loved talking with Tsion. They had been through so much together. It hit him that he was whining about his wife's complicated pregnancy to a man whose wife and children had been murdered. Yet somehow Tsion had the capacity for wisdom and clear thinking and had a calming effect on people. Buck wanted to somehow keep him on the phone.

"Do you mind talking a little while longer, Tsion?"

"Not at all. I was beginning to feel isolated anyway."

"How's Hattie?"

"Quieter. The worst is over for her, though she is going to require a long recovery."

"No movement spiritually, Chloe tells me."

"A tough case, Cameron. I fear for her. I hoped she was merely getting things off her chest and that once she spewed her venom she would turn to God. But she has convinced me she is sincere. She believes in God, knows that he loves her, and knows what he has done for her. But she has decided that she knows better than he, and that she is one person who chooses not to accept his gift for the very reason the rest of us jumped at it."

"She knows she's unworthy."

"It's difficult to argue with. She is an adult, an independent moral agent. The choice is hers, not ours. But it is painful to see someone you care for make a decision that will cost her her soul."

"I don't want to keep you, Tsion, but what was your message today? It's unlikely I'll get to read it for days, and I need all the encouragement I can get."

"Well, Cameron, as we come to the end of the suffering caused by the locusts, it's time to look ahead to at least the next two 'woes.'"

"So Trumpet Judgment six is next. What do you expect there?"

Tsion sighed. "The bottom line, Cameron, is an army of two hundred million horsemen who will slay a third of the world's population."

Buck was speechless. He had read the prophecy, but he had never boiled it down to its essence. "What possible word of encouragement could you have left people with after that bit of news?"

"Only that whatever we have suffered, whatever ugliness we have faced, all will pale in comparison to this worst judgment yet."

"And the ones after this get even worse?"

"Hard to imagine, isn't it?"

"Makes my worry over our baby seem insignificant. I mean, not to me, but who else can get worked up about it when a third of mankind will soon be wiped out?"

"Only one-fourth of the people left behind at the Rapture will survive until the Glorious Appearing, Cameron. I am not afraid of death, but I pray every day that God will allow me the privilege of seeing him return to the earth to set up his kingdom. If he takes me before that, I will be reunited with my family and other loved ones, but oh, the joy of being here when Jesus arrives!"

\+ \+ \+

Rayford found Hattie outside. "What're you doing?" he asked.

"Getting some air. It's nice to be able to move around a little."

"Doc thinks it's too early."

"Doc's in love with me, Rayford. He wants to keep me here, incapacitated if necessary."

Rayford pretended to study the horizon. "What gives you that idea?"

"He didn't tell me in so many words," she said. "But a woman knows. I'll bet you've noticed."

Rayford was happy to say he had not. He had been surprised when Floyd told him of his feelings, but he was also surprised to know that Hattie had sensed it.

"Has he told you, Rayford?"

"Why do you ask?"

"He has! I knew it! Well, I'm not interested."

"He had a crush. I'm sure you've pushed him away by now."

Hattie looked disappointed. "So he's got the picture that there's no hope?"

Rayford shrugged. "It's not like we talk about it."

"Does he know you had a crush on me once?"

"Hattie, you sound like a schoolgirl."

"Don't deny it."

"Deny what? That I had a wholly inappropriate attraction to a younger woman? We both know nothing ever came of it and—"

"Only because a bunch of people disappeared and you started feeling guilty."

Rayford turned to go back into the house.

"I still make you nervous, don't I?"

He turned. "I'll tell you what makes me nervous. It's your obsession with this kid at the airport."

"Ernie? I want to meet him, that's all."

"Did you tell him where we are, how to get here?"

"I don't even know."

"Did you tell him Floyd was coming to the hospital?"

Hattie looked away. "Why?"

"Did you?"

"I might have."

"That was pretty stupid, Hattie. So what's the plan? His buddy, Bo, distracts Floyd long enough for Ernie to go get his bike and follow Floyd back to you?"

Hattie looked stricken. "How do you know all this?"

"You're working with a teenager, Hattie. And you're acting like one too. If you want to see this kid so bad, why don't you ask one of us to take you there?"

"Because Floyd is jealous of him and doesn't want me to even talk to him on the phone. Then he convinces you I'm too sick to go anywhere, so you won't take me."

"So Ernie's trying to come here to what, get acquainted?"

"Yeah."

"Bull. Do you know he faked being a believer to get next to Ken and might have infiltrated us if we hadn't caught on?"

Hattie appeared to be hiding a smile, which infuriated Rayford. "You knew about that too?" he demanded.

"When I told him I wasn't really part of the Tribulation Force, he told me his plan. It's what I kinda like about him."

"That he would endanger our lives? That he's an opportunist? A gold digger?"

She shrugged. "The other men in my life are getting boring."

Rayford shook his head. "I hope you're happy with him."

"Is he coming here?"

"Floyd's trying to shake him, but he may have to lead him here. We can't withhold oxygen from Chloe just because Floyd has a kid following him. I hope you're happy. There's no way we can trust that kid once he knows where we are. We'll have to move again, and where will we go? And could we, with a woman about to give birth or with a brand-new baby? You go on about not being worthy of God's forgiveness, and then you try to prove it."

Rayford went in and let the door shut behind him. He hesitated, wanting to say more but not knowing what. She opened the door. "Come back, Rayford. Chloe's in trouble?"

"Could be. Needs that oxygen."

"Floyd obviously has his phone with him."

"Yep."

"Call him. Let me talk to him."

Rayford dialed.

"Hey, Rafe," Floyd said. "He didn't follow me into the airport, but after meeting T, I know why. We're thinking of switching cars and seeing if the kid will follow him. That's one advantage to our looking alike."

"Good idea, but Hattie wants to talk to you."

"Hi, Doc. Listen, Ernie will talk to me. Just hold the phone out the window of the car and stop. . . . Yeah, I think he will. It's worth a try."

21

"I HAVE BEEN going too fast!"

Buck was startled awake. Had Abdullah said something? "I'm sorry?" he shouted.

"I have been going too fast!"

Had he been pulled over by the air police, or what? "We're ahead of schedule then?"

"Yes, but I burned more fuel than I planned, and we need to refuel in New York."

Buck just wanted to get home. "Where are you going to put down? New York was last on Carpathia's refurbishing list. Still blaming the U.S. for the rebellion, I guess."

"I know a place. You will be in Wheeling in two hours."

Buck checked his watch. It was seven in the Midwest. If they were on the ground by nine, he could be to the safe house before ten. There would be no more sleeping.

+ + +

Rayford sat with Chloe, who looked pale, her lips bluish. This was getting ridiculous. He had the feeling the baby would be born in that house tonight, and he was going to do everything he could to be sure it had every chance.

"All right, sweetie?"

"Just exhausted, Dad." She seemed to keep shifting so she could breathe better. He knew she was unaware of how serious that was. When his phone rang, he flipped it open so quickly he dropped it.

"Sorry," he said, picking it up. "Steele here."

"Ray, it's Doc. We switched the oxygen to T's red Jeep, and I'm on my way. How's our girl?"

"Yes."

"You're right there with her?"

"Correct."

"On a scale of one to ten, one being the worst, how do you rate her?"

"Five."

"I'd ask for another fetal pulse, but there's nothing I can do until I get there anyway."

Rayford stood and turned his back to Chloe, moseying to look out the window. Hattie was outside, talking animatedly on her phone. "What's happening with T?" he asked.

"I think Biker took the bait, but he's going to recognize his old boss right away. We just hope he'll stop and talk to Hattie anyway."

"I'm only guessing, Doc, but I think he's doing that now. Please hurry."

"What's going on, Daddy?" Chloe asked.

"Doc got hung up at the hospital and had to run an errand on the way back. He's coming with the oxygen."

"Good. And he thought it could wait until tomorrow."

"He was only hoping."

"My baby's going to be all right, isn't it?"

"If you keep breathing deeply until the O_2 gets here." Rayford said, eager to talk to Hattie. "I'm going to get some air."

"Get me some," she said, smiling weakly.

"Just do it, Ernie," Hattie was saying, her back to Rayford as he stepped out. "Prove you're a man, and I mean it." She heard the door and slapped her phone shut.

"Cooled his jets," she said.

"Yeah? How?"

"Just told him the situation and that it was stupid of me to ask him to try to get here. I told him maybe you'd take me to Palwaukee one of these days if I take care of myself."

"Maybe. What's he going to do now?"

"Go home, I guess."

"He lives at the airport."

"That's what I mean."

"He got bit the same day you did. How's he feeling?"

"Pretty weak, I guess, but he said it was fun to get out riding again."

Rayford's phone rang. "Excuse me, Hattie," he said, but she didn't move. "Am I going inside?" he added. "Or are you?"

"Well, excuse me!" she said and left.

"Steele."

"It's T. Ol' Ernie turned three colors when he caught up and found out I was driving. He started to scoot away, but I said, 'Your girlfriend's on the phone.' He took it and the first thing he said was, 'No, it isn't.' I'm sure I didn't sound like Doc Charles, and she probably asked him if that's who I was. Then she really must have been reading him the riot act because all he did was apologize and say yes a dozen times."

"She claims she told him to back off and that she'd see him again some other time."

"Doc's long gone, so Ernie's out of options anyway. He headed back to Palwaukee. At least he said he did."

"You busy tonight, T?"

"I let everybody else go home, and I was going to handle Buck's arrival. We took a message out of New York that they've refueled and should be here by nine. You know they're in a Z-two-nine?"

"The Egyptian fighter? You're kidding."

"That's what it says. He could make it from New York in an hour if he had to. Anyway, what do you need?"

"Keep an eye on Ernie. I don't trust him or Hattie."

"What can he do? He doesn't know where you are."

"He might follow me when I pick up Buck. Who knows?"

"If he's around when Buck gets in, I won't let him out of my sight. Fair enough?"

\+ + +

Buck was claustrophobic by the time Abdullah streaked over Ohio airspace, but his discomfort was covered by excitement. Seeing Chloe was his end-all goal. Whatever was wrong with the pregnancy was out of his hands. All he could do was pray and get there. They could get through anything together. The next few years weren't going to be easy regardless.

He reached forward and gripped Abdullah's shoulders. "Thanks for the ride, friend!"

"Thanks for the job, sir! Tell Mr. McCullum what a nice ride you had."

Buck laughed but didn't let Abdullah hear him. He would never again use a fighter as a passenger plane, but he was grateful for the lift home. "Everything all right? On course, on schedule, got all our fluids?"

"OK, Mr. Williams. I will need a place to sleep."

"I believe there are accommodations at the airport. I'd invite you to our place, but we're in hiding and crowded as it is."

"I need very little," Abdullah said. "Just a place to sleep and a place to plug in."

"Your computer?"

"Ben-Judah."

Buck nodded. What more needed to be said?

* * *

Rayford was never happier to see a vehicle chug past the north side of the house. He ran out to help Floyd lug the oxygen tanks. "I've got these, Doc. Go check on her."

"Leave the other one in the car for now. She needs O_2 more than she needs anything else."

Rayford was only half a minute behind Doc, but by the time he hefted the tank close enough, Floyd had the fetal monitor on Chloe and looked grave. Tsion stood watching from the bottom of the stairs. Hattie was in the opposite corner looking warily from the top of the basement stairs.

Chloe looked worse than she had just minutes before. Doc swore. "Forgive me," he said. "I'm working on that."

"What's wrong?" Chloe said, gasping.

"OK," Floyd said, "listen up, starting with the patient. We're all going to have to work together here. I need as clean an environment as I can get. Hattie, if you could start a big pot of—"

But Hattie looked as if she wasn't listening. Her eyes were glazed, and she appeared shocked. She turned shakily and began making her way down the stairs to her basement room.

"I'll do whatever you need done," Tsion said, rolling up his sleeves and hurrying over.

"Am I having this baby tonight?" Chloe said desperately. "Before Buck gets here?"

"Not if I can help it," Doc said. "But your job is to be quiet. Don't talk unless you have to."

"All right," she said quickly, "but I have to know everything right now, and I mean it."

Doc looked to Rayford, who raised his eyebrows and nodded. "Just tell her."

"All right, Ray. Get the O_2 on her. Chloe, there has been a significant decrease in the fetal pulse. I don't have the equipment to check on the position of the cord, and I don't want to do a C-section here anyway. A ride to Young Memorial would not be medically positive."

Chloe pulled the oxygen mask from her mouth, though it had already made her face look pinker. "Medically positive?" she said. "You're not gonna keep me quiet with foggy language. You mean the ride might kill me?"

"That's a moot question. You're not going. Now be quiet. Tsion, just give me what I ask for when I ask. Keep your hands clean. Ray, you stay washed up too. Bring me those two chairs and pull those two lights over. Put that one atop the table. Give me that bottle of Betadine."

Once the room was set up and lit as brightly as possible, it took all three men to carefully lift Chloe into position on the makeshift delivery table. "So much for dignity," she said from behind the mask.

"Shut up," Floyd said, but he playfully pinched her toe.

"I must ask a question," Tsion said from the stove. "How will you decide whether an emergency cesarean is necessary?"

"Only if the baby's heart slows too much or stops. Then we'll have to do what we have to do. Chloe will be pretty much out of it by then, so she'll have to make that call now. You'll be anesthetized, Chloe, but not to the degree I'd like for a cesarean. Now—"

"Not even a question," she said, despite the mask. "Go for the baby and worry about me later."

"But if—"

"Don't even argue with me about this, Doc."

"All right, but all this stuff is just precautionary. I'd like to not have to induce. We may not have that luxury, but I'll hold off as long as I can, hoping the baby will stabilize."

"Just try to wait for Buck," Chloe said.

"Not another word," Doc said.

"Sorry, Floyd," she mumbled.

Rayford looked at his watch. "What happens when I have to leave to get Buck?"

"Frankly, I could use you. Buck's car is still at the airport. He can drive himself."

"That leaves T without a car."

"He can ride along and pick up his car here."

"T doesn't want to know the way. Makes it easier on him if he ever gets questioned."

"But you trust him," Doc said.

"Implicitly."

"It's a risk he has to take."

\+ \+ \+

Abdullah crossed into Illinois a few minutes before nine, and Buck called Rayford. "So I'm to bring T with me?"

"And make sure you're not followed. It's a long story."

"We always watch for tails. Someone specific?"

"T will tell you. It's a guy who lives right there at the airport."

"Abdullah is staying there. I'll assign him guard duty."

"Abdullah! You're flying with Abdullah Smith?"

"I didn't know you knew him."

"Put him on!"

Buck tapped Abdullah on the shoulder. "My father-in-law wants to talk to you. Rayford Steele."

Abdullah turned almost all the way around in his seat. "Rayford? Are you serious?"

\+ \+ \+

Rayford quickly filled Abdullah in on the situation. "I'll make sure he goes nowhere," the pilot said. "You know I can manage."

"How well I know. What's your ETA?"

"Fourteen minutes, but I'm shooting for eleven."

Rayford clapped his phone shut and said he was going to check on Hattie. He got three steps down and bent to see her in a fetal position on an old couch. He shook his head and went back upstairs.

"How're we doing, Doc?"

"We're going to induce, but I can start her slow and give Buck plenty of time. Everybody OK with that? Fetal pulse is not critical yet, but it will be in an hour. I'd start the drip if it was my call."

Chloe pointed at Floyd.

"That means it's your call, Doc," Rayford said.

\+ \+ \+

"Small airport," Abdullah said as they descended.

"Not too small for you, though, right?"

"I could land on an envelope and not cancel the stamp."

Buck knew it was nervous tension, but he didn't stop laughing until he climbed out. He stretched so far he dizzied himself and thought he would break in two. He told Abdullah, "The guy on the radio was T, the one we're supposed to meet. He'll point you to where you're staying and hopefully introduce you to Ernie. You know what to do."

Abdullah smiled.

Fewer than ten minutes later, Abdullah was unpacking next to Ernie's room. Buck and T traded phone numbers with Abdullah and left, Buck driving his own car.

"You guys have had some excitement," Buck said.

"Not as much as you're about to have."

"I can't wait. I should call Chloe."

"I wouldn't do that just yet. I understand the doctor has her on oxygen and is going to induce labor, but they're trying to stall for you."

Buck sped up. They were already bouncing so that each had to brace himself with a hand on the ceiling. "What was that?" Buck said, studying the rearview mirror and then swerving to miss the giant concrete pile he had forgotten about on Willow Road.

"I don't see anything," T said, looking back.

Buck shrugged. "Thought I saw a bike."

T looked again. "If there's a bike back there, its light is off. Probably your imagination."

Buck looked again. His mind was playing tricks on him, and why not? He'd have let T drive if T knew where they were going.

"You want me to call Abdullah?" T said. "Make sure he's still got an eye on Ernie?"

"Maybe you'd better."

T dialed. "How are things going, my friend? . . . All right? . . . Yes, he's a fascinating boy. You won't let him hoodwink you now, will you? . . . Just an expression. It means put one over on you, ah, pull a fast one, um, cheat you, swindle you. . . . Attaboy, Abdullah. You should be able to get to sleep now. You've stalled him long enough."

+ + +

Buck and T pulled into the yard behind the safe house just before ten, and Buck was out of the car before the engine died. Chloe, who had just experienced her first contraction, beamed when she saw him. Doc Charles greeted him with a point to the sink. "First things first, stranger."

Buck washed up and moved to Chloe's side, where he took her hand. "Thank you, God," he said aloud. "I would not want to have missed this."

"I would like to pray too," Tsion said.

"I was hoping you'd say that," Buck said.

"Doctor, you have a waiver on closing your eyes. Almighty God, we are grateful for your goodness and your protection. Thank you for bringing Buck to us, and just in time. We know we have no claim on your sovereign will, but we plead for a safe delivery, a perfect baby, and a healthy mother. We need this tiny ray of sunshine in a dark world. Grant us this, our Lord, but above all, we seek your will."

Rayford's head jerked up with a start at the sound of an engine coming to life in the yard. He scanned the room, looked at T, and said, "Hattie."

Buck shouted, "Catch her! She can't expose us like this!"

Chloe tried to sit up. "Relax, Chloe!" Floyd said. "I'll be fine with Buck and Tsion if you other two have to go after her. But just do it and stay out of here."

Rayford dashed past T and skipped down the steps and out the door. He heard a motorcycle engine, and the Rover was missing. He and T jumped into T's Jeep, but the keys were gone. Rayford ran back in the house. "Floyd! The keys!"

"Agh!" Floyd said. "Tsion, my right pants pocket, and then you'll have to wash again."

Tsion tossed Rayford the keys, and Rayford and T were soon careening back toward Palwaukee. "So Ernie followed you after all?"

"Impossible," T said. "We talked to Abdullah on our way, and he said Ernie was still there. Buck did think he saw something a couple of times though."

"Maybe Ernie had the drop on Abdullah and made him say that."

"He was pretty convincing. Small talk, details, and all."

"Frankly that doesn't sound like Abdullah. Call him."

Abdullah answered on the second ring. "Did I wake you? . . . Listen, just answer yes or no. Is Ernie still there? . . . He is? What's he doing? . . . Digging? Put him on for me, will you?"

Rayford shook his head. "I'm telling you, he's not—"

"Ernie? Hey, how's it goin', man? Whatcha doin'? . . . Cleaning Ken's area? Nice of you. Abdullah said you were digging. . . . Just sweeping, huh? . . . Yeah, I can see how he could mistake that for digging. Well, tell him we'll see him in a few hours."

* * *

Buck could not imagine what Hattie was up to. He had long since quit trying to figure her out. Where would she go in the middle of the night besides crazy? Maybe that was it. She'd got cabin fever and just had to escape. It'd be just like her to get lost and wind up leading someone to the safe house.

Chloe gripped his hand and grunted. Buck looked to Doc, who had attached a fetal monitor to the baby's skull through the uterus. He said it was as accurate as it could be and that he was encouraged. "We're going to have a baby tonight," he said. "And it's going to be all right."

Buck sighed heavily, too excited to notice his fatigue. He also held out a sliver of realism, knowing that for the sake of the patient it was just like Floyd to sound more optimistic than he felt. Buck was glad he was there, no matter what happened. He would not have wanted Chloe to go through this alone, regardless of the outcome.

+ + +

"So Ernie really *is* a gold digger," Rayford said.

T nodded. "And I'll bet you dollars to donuts we'll find Bo has been released from Young Memorial too. Shall I find out?"

"Sure."

"Humph," T said a few minutes later, his hand over the phone. "They say he's still registered."

"Ask to talk with him. No wait, ask for Leah and let me talk to her." T did and handed him the phone. "Leah, it's Rayford Steele, friend of Dr. Charles."

"What now?" she said, but not unpleasantly.

"We just need to know if a patient who has not checked out or been released might be gone anyway. Name's Bo something. Just a minute, I'll get the—"

"Beauregard Hanson," she said. "We don't get a lot of Bos, you know. Yeah, he's still here."

"You're sure?"

"You want me to check?"

"Would you?"

"I've done more than that for you guys."

"That's why we love you."

"Hang on."

+ + +

Doc Charles seemed elated, and that made Buck feel better. "We're doing the right thing," Doc said. "This could not have waited, but the pulse is steady and has been for a while. We're going to be OK. You doing all right, Mom?"

Chloe nodded the perspiring nod of the extremely pregnant.

+ + +

"He's gone?"

"Cleared out," Leah said. "I didn't like him anyway, him or that kid who was in the same room. He disappeared earlier today without a word, so I should have known."

"We owe you one, Leah," Rayford said.

"One?"

"Touché. Someday we'll make this all up to you."

"Yeah," she said. "I'm guessing in five years or so."

* * *

"I wish Daddy could be here," Chloe said.

"Maybe he'll be back in time," Buck said. "What's your guess on timing, Doc?"

"I don't want to rush her. Sometimes even a moderate drip will cause fast action. All depends on mother and child. But we're still doing well, and that's what counts."

"Amen," Tsion said. And Buck thought the rabbi looked as excited as Buck felt.

* * *

"Do you believe this?" Rayford said, shaking his head. "Like the idiots they are, they don't even know they've been followed."

The Rover sat idling in front of the Quonset hut that had housed Ken and now Ernie and the temporary guest, Abdullah. T parked the jeep back about fifty feet and turned off his engine and lights. They sat watching. "Abdullah can take care of himself," Rayford said, "but he *is* outnumbered."

T got out. "Let's see what they're up to."

When they got to the Quonset hut, they heard conversation. "Let the Rover idle," Rayford whispered, "so they don't know we're here."

They crouched near the curtained window and listened.

"Let me get this straight," Abdullah was saying. "You'll give me a brick of gold bullion for flying you to New Babylon."

"That's right," Hattie said.

"And this gold belongs to you?"

"It belongs to my fiancé."

"This young man is your fiancé?"

"Yes, I am!" Ernie said. "Soon's I give you this gold. Now take it."

"Do you realize," Abdullah said, "that this gold is worth ten times the cash I would charge for the same flight?"

"But we want to go now," Hattie said. "And I know that's worth something."

"If you want to go now, you picked the wrong pilot. I cannot fly for twenty-four hours."

"Carpathia rescinded international air laws," Hattie said. "I know. I used to work for him."

"You did more than that for him, ma'am. Were you not engaged to him, too? How many fiancés do you have?"

"One fewer if we don't get going," she said.

Rayford signaled T to follow him about a hundred feet away. He phoned Abdullah.

"Hello, yes?"

"Abdullah, it's Rayford Steele, but don't say anything. Just repeat after me, all right?"

"All right."

"Global Community Militia? . . . A stolen Range Rover? . . . Gold? . . . Prison? . . . Yes, you come and question me, but all the gold is here and the automobile too. . . . Yes, I will be here when you get here. . . . No, I do not want to go to prison."

Abdullah broke in. "It's working, Rayford."

"Rayford?" he heard Hattie scream. "Ernie, wait!"

But Ernie and Bo were already riding double on the motorbike, leaving a plume of dust as they hightailed it from the airport.

Rayford and T found Abdullah looking fatigued but proud of himself, sitting across from Hattie, who sat on the floor with her back pressed against an army cot. "Let's go, Hattie," Rayford said. "Maybe we can get you back in time to see the new baby."

✢ ✢ ✢

Four hours later, in the darkest hour of the morning, Chloe Steele Williams gave birth to a healthy son. In tears she suckled him and announced his name.

Kenneth Bruce.

Even Hattie wept.

ASSASSINS

To Dr. John F. Walvoord
For more than fifty years, he has helped keep the torch of prophecy burning.

1

RAGE.

No other word described it.

Rayford knew he had much to be thankful for. Neither Irene—his wife of twenty-one years—nor Amanda—his wife of fewer than three months—had to suffer this world any longer. Raymie was in heaven too. Chloe and baby Kenny were healthy.

That should be enough. Yet the cliché *consumed* came to life for Rayford. He stormed out of the safe house in the middle of a crisp May Monday morning, eschewing a jacket and glad of it. It wasn't anyone in the safe house who had set him off.

Hattie had been her typical self, whining about her immobility while building her strength.

"You don't think I'll do it," she had told him as she raced through another set of sit-ups. "You way underestimate me."

"I don't doubt you're crazy enough to try."

"But you wouldn't fly me over there for any price."

"Not on your life."

Rayford stumbled along a path near a row of trees that separated a dusty field from what was left of the safe house and the piles of what had once been neighboring homes. He stopped and scanned the horizon. Anger was one thing. Stupidity another. There was no sense giving away their position just for a moment of fresh air.

He saw nothing and no one, but still he stayed closer to the trees than to the plain. What a difference a year and a half made! This whole area, for miles, had once been sprawling suburbia. Now it was earthquake rubble, abandoned to the fugitive and the destitute. One Rayford had been for months. The other he was fast becoming.

The murderous fury threatened to devour him. His rational, scientific mind fought his passion. He knew others—yes, including Hattie—who had as much or more motive. Yet Rayford pleaded with God to appoint him. He wanted to be the one to do the deed. He believed it his destiny.

Rayford shook his head and leaned against a tree, letting the bark scratch his back. Where was the aroma of newly mown grass, the sounds of kids playing in the yard? Nothing was as it once was. He closed his eyes and ran over the plan one more time. Steal into the Middle East in disguise. Put himself in the right place at the precise time. Be God's weapon, the instrument of death. Murder Nicolae Carpathia.

+ + +

David Hassid assigned himself to accompany the Global Community helicopter that would take delivery of a gross of computers for the potentate's palace. Half the GC personnel in his department were to spend the next several weeks ferreting out the location of Tsion Ben-Judah's daily cyberspace teaching and Buck Williams's weekly Internet magazine.

The potentate himself wanted to know how quickly the computers could be installed. "Figure half a day to unload, reload, and truck them here from the airport," David had told him. "Then unload again and assume another couple of days for installation and setup."

Carpathia had begun snapping his fingers as soon as "half a day" rolled off David's tongue. "Faster," he said. "How can we steal some hours?"

"It would be costly, but you could—"

"Cost is not my priority, Mr. Hassid. Speed. Speed."

"Chopper could snag the whole load and set 'em down outside the freight entrance."

"That," Carpathia said. "Yes, that."

"I'd want to personally supervise pickup and delivery."

Carpathia was on to something else, dismissing David with a wave. "Of course, whatever."

David called Mac McCullum on his secure phone. "It worked," he said.

"When do we fly?"

"As late as possible. This has to look like a mistake."

Mac chuckled. "Did you get 'em to deliver to the wrong airstrip?"

"'Course. Told 'em one, paperworked 'em another. They'll go by what they heard. I'll protect myself from Abbott and Costello with the paperwork."

"Fortunato still looking over your shoulder?"

"Always, but neither he nor Nicolae suspects. They love you too, Mac."

"Don't I know it. We've got to ride this train as far as it'll take us."

+ + +

Rayford didn't dare discuss his feelings with Tsion. The rabbi was busy enough, and Rayford knew what he would say: "God has his plan. Let him carry it out."

But what would be wrong with Rayford's helping? He was willing. He could get it done. If it cost him his life, so what? He'd reunite with loved ones, and more would join him later.

Rayford knew it was crazy. He had never been ruled by his feelings before. Maybe his problem was that he was out of the loop now, away from the action. The fear and tension of flying Carpathia around for months had been worth it for the proximity it afforded him and the advantage to the Tribulation Force.

The danger in his present role wasn't the same. He was senior flyer of the International Commodity Co-op, the one entity that might keep believers alive when their freedom to trade on the open market would vanish. For now, Rayford was just meeting contacts, setting up routes, in essence working for his own daughter. He had to remain anonymous and learn whom to trust. But it wasn't the same. He didn't feel as necessary to the cause.

But if he could be the one to kill Carpathia!

Who was he kidding? Carpathia's assassin would likely be put to death without trial. And if Carpathia was indeed the Antichrist—and most people except his followers thought he was—he wouldn't stay dead anyway. The murder would be all about Rayford, not Carpathia. Nicolae would come out of it more heroic than ever. But the fact that it had to be done anyway, and that he himself might be in place to do it, seemed to give Rayford something to live for. And likely to die for.

His grandson, Kenny Bruce, had stolen his heart, but that very name reminded Rayford of painful losses. The late Ken Ritz had been a new friend with the makings of a good one. Bruce Barnes had been Rayford's first mentor and had taught him so much after supplying him the videotape that had led him to Christ.

That was it! That had to be what had produced such hatred, such rage. Rayford knew Carpathia was merely a pawn of Satan, really part of God's plan for the ages. But the man had wreaked such havoc, caused such destruction, fostered such mourning, that Rayford couldn't help but hate him.

Rayford didn't want to grow numb to the disaster, death, and devastation that had become commonplace. He wanted to still feel alive, violated, offended. Things were bad and getting worse, and the chaos multiplied every month. Tsion taught that things were to come to a head at the halfway point of the seven-year tribulation, four months from now. And then would come the Great Tribulation.

Rayford longed to survive all seven years to witness the glorious appearing of Christ to set up his thousand-year reign on earth. But what were the odds? Tsion taught that, at most, only a quarter of the population left at the Rapture would survive to the end, and those who did might wish they hadn't.

Rayford tried to pray. Did he think God would answer, give him permission, put the plot in his mind? He knew better. His scheming was just a way to feel alive, and yet it ate at him, gave him a reason for breathing.

He had other reasons to live. He loved his daughter and her husband and their baby, and yet he felt responsible that Chloe had missed the Rapture. The only family he had left would face the same world he did. What kind of a future was that? He didn't want to think about it. All he wanted to think about was what weapons he might have access to and how he could avail himself of them at the right time.

+ + +

Just after dark in New Babylon, David took a call from his routing manager. "Pilot wants to know if he's to put down at the strip or at—"

"I told him already! Tell him to do what he's told!"

"Sir, the bill of lading says palace airstrip. But he thought you told him New Babylon Airport."

David paused as if angry. "Do *you* understand what I said?"

"You said airport, but—"

"Thank you! What's his ETA?"

"Thirty minutes to the airport. Forty-five to the strip. Just so I'm clear—"

David hung up and called Mac. Half an hour later they were sitting in the chopper on the tarmac of the palace airstrip. Of course the computer cargo was not there. David called the airport. "Tell the pilot where we are!"

"Man," Mac said, "you've got everybody chasin' their tails."

"You think I want new computers in front of the world's best techies, all looking to find the safe house?"

Mac tuned in the airport frequency and heard the instruction for the cargo pilot to take off and put down at the palace strip. He looked at David. "To the airport, chopper jockey," David said.

"We'll pass 'im in the sky."

"I hope we do."

They did. David finally had pity on the pilot, assured him he and Mac would stay put, and instructed him to come back.

A crane helped disgorge the load of computers, and Mac maneuvered the helicopter into position to hook up to it. The cargo chief attached the cable, assured Mac he had the size and power to easily transport the load, and instructed him how to lift off. "You've got an onboard release in case of emergency, sir," he said, "but you should have no problem."

Mac thanked him and caught David's glance. "You wouldn't," he said, shaking his head.

"Of course I would. This lever here? I'll be in charge of this."

2

EARLY AFTER NOON, Buck sat at his computer in the vastly enlarged shelter beneath the safe house. He and his father-in-law and Dr. Charles had done the bulk of the excavating work. It wasn't that Dr. Ben-Judah had been unwilling or unable. He had proved remarkably fit for a man with his nose in scholarly works and his eyes on a computer screen the majority of every day.

But Buck and the others encouraged him to stay at his more important work via the Internet—teaching the masses of new believers and pleading for converts. It was clear Tsion felt he was slacking by letting the other men do the manual labor while he toiled at what he called *soft work* in an upstairs bedroom. For days all he had wanted to do was join the others in digging, sacking, and carrying the dirt from the cellar to the nearby fields. The others had told him they were fine without his help, that it was too crowded with four men in the cramped space, that his ministry was too crucial to be postponed by grunt work.

Finally, Buck recalled with a smile, Rayford had told Tsion, "You're the elder, our pastor, our mentor, our scholar, but I have seniority and authority as ersatz head of this band, and I'm pulling rank."

Tsion had straightened in the dank underground and leaned back, mock fear on his face. "Yes, sir," he said. "And my assignment?"

"To stay out of our way, old man. You have the soft hands of the educated. Of course, so do we, but you're in the way."

Tsion had dragged a sleeve across his forehead. "Oh, Rayford, stop teasing me. I just want to help."

Buck and Doc stopped their work and joined, in essence, in ganging up on Tsion. "Dr. Ben-Judah," Floyd Charles said, "we all really do feel you're wasting your time—*we're* wasting your time—by letting you do this. Please, for our sakes, clear our consciences and let us finish without you."

It was Rayford's turn to feign offense. "So much for *my* authority," he said. "I just gave an order, and now Sawbones pleads with him yet again!"

"You gentlemen are serious," Tsion said, his Israeli accent thick as ever.

Rayford raised both hands. "Finally! The scholar gets it."

Tsion trundled back upstairs, grumbling that it "still does not make any sense," but he had not again tried to insert himself into the excavation team.

Buck was impressed with how the other three had melded. Rayford was the most technologically astute, Buck himself sometimes too analytical, and Floyd—despite his medical degree—seemingly content to do what he was told. Buck teased him about that, telling him he thought doctors assumed they knew everything. Floyd was not combative, but neither did Buck find him amused. In fact, Floyd seemed to run out of gas earlier every day, but he never slacked. He just spent a lot of time catching his breath, running his hands through his hair, and rubbing his eyes.

Rayford mapped out each day's work with a rough sketch amalgamated from two sources. The first came from the meticulously hen-scratched spiral notebooks of the original owner of the place, Donny Moore, who had been crushed to death at the church during the great wrath of the Lamb earthquake nearly eighteen months before. Buck and Tsion had discovered Donny's wife's body in the demolished breakfast nook at the back of the house.

Donny had apparently planned for just such a future, somehow assuming that one day he and his wife would have to live in seclusion. Whether he feared nuclear fallout or just hiding from Global Community forces, he had crafted an expansive plan. His layout enlarged the tiny, dank cellar at the back of the house to extend beneath the entire other side of the duplex and far out into the yard.

The other source Rayford had consulted was the late Ken Ritz's refinement of the original plan. Ken had honed his image as a clod-kicking blue-collar bush pilot. It turned out he was a graduate of the London School of Economics, licensed in all manner of high-speed jets, and—as these schematics showed—a self-taught architect. Ken had streamlined the excavation process, moved Donny's support beams, and devised a central communications protocol. When all was in place, the shelter should be undetectable and the various satellite link-ups, cellular receivers and transmitters, and infrared computer interfaces easy to access and service.

While Buck worked with Doc and Rayford, and Tsion wrote his masterful daily missives to his global audience, Chloe and Hattie busied themselves with their own pursuits. Hattie seemed to work out every spare moment, madly building tone and endurance and adding weight to what had become her emaciated frame. Buck worried she was up to something. She usually was. No one in the house was certain she hadn't already compromised their location with her ill-conceived effort to buy her way to Europe months before. So far no one had come nosing around the place, but how long could that last?

Chloe spent the bulk of her time with baby Kenny, of course. When she wasn't sneaking in a nap to try to regain her own strength, she used her free moments to work via the Net with her growing legion of Commodity Co-op suppliers and distributors. Already believers were beginning to buy and sell to and from each other, in anticipation of the dark day when they would be banished from normal trade.

The pressure of close quarters and lots of work, not to mention dread of the future, was Buck's constant companion. He was grateful he could do his own writing and help Rayford and Doc with the shelter while still getting time with Chloe and Kenny. But somehow his days were as long as ever. The only time he and Chloe had to themselves was at the end of the day when they were barely awake enough to talk. Kenny slept in their room, and while he was not the type to bother the rest of the household, both Buck and Chloe were often up with him in the night.

Buck lay awake one midnight, pleased to hear Chloe's deep rhythmic breathing and know she was asleep. He was mulling how to improve the efficiency of the Trib Force, hoping he could contribute as much as the other men seemed to. From the beginning, when the Force consisted of just the late Bruce Barnes, Rayford, Chloe, and him, Buck felt he had become part of a pivotal, cosmic effort. Among the earliest believers following the Rapture, the Tribulation Force was committed to winning people to Christ, opposing Antichrist, and surviving until the reappearing of Christ, now just over three and a half years away.

Tsion, whom God had provided to replace Bruce, was a priceless commodity who needed to be protected above all. His knowledge and passion, along with his ability to communicate on a layman's level, made him Nicolae Carpathia's number one enemy. At least number one after the two witnesses at the Wailing Wall, who continued to torment unbelievers with plagues and judgments.

Chloe astounded him with her ability to run an international company while taking care of a new baby. Doc was clearly a gift from God, having saved Hattie's life and keeping the rest of them healthy. Hattie was the only unbeliever and understandably selfish. She spent most of her time on herself.

But Buck worried most about Rayford. His father-in-law had not been himself lately. He seemed to seethe, short-tempered with Hattie and often lost in thought, his face clouded with despair. Rayford also had begun taking breaks from the house, walking nowhere in the middle of the day. Buck knew Rayford would not be careless, but he wished someone could help. He asked Tsion to probe, but the rabbi said, "Captain Steele eventually comes to me when he wants to reveal something. I do not feel free to pursue private matters with him."

Buck had asked Doc's opinion. "He's my mentor, not the other way around,"

Floyd said. "I go to him with my problems; I don't expect him to come to me with his."

Chloe begged off too. "Buck, Daddy is a traditional, almost old-world father. He'll give me all the unsolicited advice he wishes, but I wouldn't dream of trying to get him to open up to me."

"But you see it, don't you?"

"Of course. But what do you expect? We're all crazy by now. Is this any way to live? Going nowhere in daylight except to Palwaukee once in a while, having to use aliases and worry constantly about being found out?"

Buck's compatriots all had reasons for not confronting Rayford. Buck would have to do it. *Oh, joy,* he thought.

\+ \+ \+

David Hassid sat in the passenger seat of GC Chopper One, watching with Mac McCullum. The ground crew at New Babylon Airport hooked a thick steel cable from the helicopter to three bundled skids containing 144 computers. The crew chief signaled Mac to begin a slow ascent until the cable was taut. Then he gently lifted off, ostensibly to deliver the cargo to the Global Community palace.

Mac said, "The skids should take care of themselves, provided you keep away from that release lever. You wouldn't really do that, would you?"

"To delay my own staff from finding Tsion's and Buck's and Chloe's transmission point? You bet I would, if it was the only way."

"If?"

"C'mon, Mac. You know me better than that by now. You think I would trash that many computers? I may be only about a third your age—"

"Hey!"

"All right, a little less than half, but give me some credit. You think the number of computers we ordered was lost on me?"

Mac held up a finger and depressed his radio transmitter. "GC Chopper One to palace tower, over."

"This is tower, One, go."

"ETA three minutes, over."

"Roger, out."

Mac turned to David. "I figured that's why you ordered a gross. One for every thousand witnesses."

"Not that it'll parcel out that way, but no, I'm not going to crash them in the desert."

"But I'm not putting down at the palace either, am I?"

David smiled and shook his head. From their position he had a view of the sprawling palace complex. Acres and acres of buildings surrounded the great gleaming castle—what else could he call it—Carpathia had erected in honor of himself. Every imaginable convenience was included, thousands of employees dedicated to every Carpathia whim.

David dug his secure phone from his pocket and punched a speed number. "Corporal A. Christopher," he said. "Director Hassid calling." He covered the phone and told Mac, "Your new cargo chief for the Condor."

"Do I know him?"

David shrugged and shook his head. "Yes, Corporal Christopher. Is the Condor hold accessible? . . . Excellent. Be ready for us. . . . Well, I can't help that, Corporal. You may feel free to speak with Personnel, but my understanding is that you have no say in that."

David held the phone away from his face and turned it off. "Hung up on me," he said.

"Nobody likes the cargo job for the two-one-six," Mac said. "Not enough work. You trust this guy?"

"No choice," David said.

\+ \+ \+

Buck had temporarily moved his computer to the kitchen table and was rapping out a story for *The Truth* when Rayford returned from his morning walk. "Hey," Buck said. Rayford only nodded and stood at the top of the stairs to the cellar.

Buck's resolve nearly left him. "What's the plan today, Ray?"

"Same as always," Rayford muttered. "We've got to start getting walls up down here. And then we've got to make the shelter invisible. No apparent access. Where's Doc?"

"Haven't seen him. Hattie's in the—"

"Other side, of course. Training for a marathon, no doubt. She's going to wind up getting us all killed."

"Hey, Dad," Buck tried, "way to look on the bright side."

Rayford ignored him. "Where's everybody else?" he said.

"Tsion's upstairs. Chloe's on her computer in the living room. Kenny's napping. I told you where Hattie is; only Floyd is AWOL. He might be downstairs, but I didn't notice him go down."

"Don't say he's AWOL, Buck. That's not funny."

It was unusual for Rayford to chastise him, and Buck hardly knew how to respond. "I just mean he's unaccounted for, Ray. Truth is, he hasn't looked well lately and looked awful yesterday. Wonder if he's sleeping in."

"Till noon? What was the matter with him?"

"I saw a little yellow in his eyes."

"I didn't."

"It's dark down there."

"Then how'd you see it?"

"Noticed last night, that's all. I even said something to him about it."

"What'd he say?"

"Some joke about how honkies always think the brothers look strange. I didn't pursue it."

"He's the doctor," Rayford said. "Let him worry about himself." That, Buck decided, was a perfect opening. He could tell Rayford that he didn't sound like his usual compassionate self. But the moment passed when Rayford took the offensive. "What's *your* schedule today, Buck? Magazine or shelter work?"

"You're the boss, Ray. You tell me."

"I could use you downstairs, but suit yourself."

Buck rose.

+ + +

Mac delicately lowered the skids onto the pavement at the east side of the hangar that housed the Condor 216. The hangar door was open, the cavernous cargo hold of the Condor also agape. David jumped out before the blades stopped whirring and hurried to unhook the cable from the cargo. Out from the hangar sped a forklift that quickly engaged the first load, smoothly tilted it back against the truck, then spun in a circle and shot back into the hangar. By the time Mac joined David and they shut the hangar door, the forklift operator had shut the Condor cargo hold and was replacing the forklift in a corner.

"Corporal Christopher!" David shouted, and the corporal whirled to face him from a hundred feet away. "Your office, now!"

"Doesn't look too pleased," Mac said as they walked to the glassed-in office within the hangar. "No salute, no response. Negative body language. Gonna be a problem?"

"The corporal is my subordinate. I hold all the cards."

"Just the same, David, you have to give respect to get respect. And we can trust no one. You don't want one of your key people—"

"Trust me, Mac. It's under control."

The name on the office door next to Mac's had just been repainted: "CCCCC."

"*What* is that?" Mac said.

"Corporal Christopher, Condor Cargo Chief."

"Please!" Mac said.

David motioned Mac to follow him into the corporal's office, shut the door, and sat behind the desk, pointing to a chair for Mac. The older man seemed to sit reluctantly.

"What?" David said.

"This is how you treat a subordinate?"

David put his feet on the desk and nodded. "Especially a new one. Got to establish who's boss."

"I was taught that if you have to use the word *boss* with an employee, you've already lost 'em."

David shrugged. "Dark ages," he said. "Desperate times, desperate measures . . ."

Footsteps stopped outside the door, and the knob turned. David called out, "Surely you'll knock before walking in on your boss and your pilot, won't you, Corporal?"

The door stopped, open an inch.

"Shut the door and knock, Corporal!" David hollered, his hands behind his head, feet still on the desk.

The door shut, a little too loudly. Then a long pause. Finally, three deliberate and loud raps on the door. Mac shook his head. "This guy even knocks sarcastically," he whispered. "But you deserve it."

"Enter," David said.

Mac's chair scraped as he bolted upright in the presence of a young woman in fatigues. Under her cap showed short cropped black hair, cut almost like a man's, but she was trim and comely with large dark eyes, perfect teeth, and flawless skin.

Mac whipped off his cap. "Ma'am."

"Spare me, Captain," she said, then turned her scowl on David. "I'm required to knock to enter my own office?"

David had not moved. "Sit down, Mac," he said.

"When the lady sits down," Mac said.

"I'm not giving her permission to sit," David said, and Corporal Christopher waved Mac to his seat. "Captain Mac McCullum, this is Corporal Annie Christopher. Annie, Mac."

Mac started to rise again, but Annie stepped and shook his hand. "No need, Captain. I know who you are, and your Neanderthal chauvinism is noted. If we're going to work together, you can quit treating me like a little woman."

Mac looked at her and then at David. "Maybe you treat her with the respect she deserves," he said.

David cocked his head. "Like you said, Mac. You never know whom you can trust. As for this being your office, Corporal, everything of yours is mine as long as you're under my command. This space has been parceled to you to facilitate your doing what I tell you. Understood?"

"Clearly."

"And, Corporal, I'm not even military, but I know it's a breach of protocol to keep your head covered in the presence of your superior."

Annie Christopher sighed and let her shoulders slump as she whipped off her cap. She ran a hand through her short hair and moved to the window between the office and the rest of the hangar. She closed the blinds.

"What are you doing?" David said. "There's no one out there, and I didn't give you permission to—"

"Oh, come now, Director Hassid. Do I need your permission for everything?"

David lifted his feet off the desk and sat upright as Annie approached. "As a matter of fact, you do."

He opened his arms and she sat on his lap. "How are you, sweetheart?" she said.

"I'm good, hon, but I think Mac's about to have a heart attack."

Mac slid to the edge of his chair and leaned forward, elbows on knees. "You're both brats," he said. "Forgive me, Miss Christopher, if I check your mark."

"Be my guest," she said, leaning across the desk so he could reach her. "You can bet that's what David and I did the day we met."

Mac cradled the back of her head in his palm and ran his other thumb across the mark on her forehead. He cupped her face in his hands and kissed her gently atop the head. "You're young enough to be my daughter," he said, "sister."

Annie moved to another chair. "And for the record, Captain McCullum, I can't stand working for either of you. Personnel has a standing request from me, demanding that I be reassigned. The director of my department is condescending and unbearable, and the captain of the Condor is unbearably sexist."

"But," David said, "I have informed Personnel that she is not to be catered to. Annie has caused trouble in every department she's served, and it's payback time for her. They love it."

Mac squinted at her, then at David. "I can't wait to hear your stories," he said.

\+ \+ \+

Buck postponed his heart-to-heart with his father-in-law when Rayford spread the plans under a light in the basement and asked his advice on how to make the entrance impossible to detect.

"Thought you'd never ask," Buck said. "Actually, I *have* been noodling this."

"I'm all ears."

"You know the freezer in the other duplex?"

"The smelly one."

Buck nodded. They had discarded the spoiled food, but the stench inside remained. "Move that over here, stock it with what looks like spoiled food but only smells that way because of the residue, and hinge the food trays at the back. Anyone who looks in there will be repelled by the smell and won't look close at what they assume is spoiled food. They'll never think to lift the food trays, but if they do, they'll find a false bottom that opens to the stairs to the shelter. Meanwhile, we put a wall over the current basement door."

Rayford cocked his head, as if searching his mind for a flaw. He shrugged. "I like it. Now if there was a way to keep it from Hattie."

Buck looked around. "So I was right? Floyd's not down here?"

\+ \+ \+

Mac's beeper vibrated. "Fortunato," he said. "Terrific. May I use your phone, Corporal?"

Annie said, "It's not my phone, sir. It's merely been parceled out to me. . . ."

He phoned Fortunato's office. "Mac McCullum returning his call. . . . Yes, ma'am. . . . Friday? . . . How many guests? . . . No, ma'am. You may tell him there was some sort of a snafu about that shipment. He'll have to talk with the purchasing director, but no, those were not available to be delivered to the palace. . . . Perhaps when we return from Botswana, yes, ma'am."

\+ \+ \+

Dr. Floyd Charles's bedroom door was shut. Buck saw Tsion at his computer in the next room, forehead in his hand, elbow on the desk. "You OK, Tsion?"

"Cameron! Come in, please. Just resting my eyes."

"Praying?"

The rabbi smiled wearily. "Without ceasing. We have no choice, have we? How are you, my friend? Still worried about your father-in-law?"

"Yeah, but I'll talk to him. I was wondering if you'd seen Doc today?"

"We usually share an early breakfast, as you know. But I was alone this morning. I did not hear him in the basement, and I confess I have not thought about it since. I have been writing. Cameron, we have no idea how long this lull may last between the fifth and sixth woes. I am trying to decide myself whether what John saw in his vision is real or symbolic. As you know—"

"Dr. Ben-Judah, forgive me. I want to hear this—"

"Yes, of course. You should check in on Floyd. We will talk later."

"I don't mean to be rude."

"You need not apologize, Cameron. Now go. We will talk later. Call if you need me."

Buck had never grown used to the privilege of living in the same house as the man whose daily words were like breath to millions around the world. Though Tsion was usually within a few dozen steps, when he was too busy or too tired to talk, the others in the household downloaded his messages from the Net. The best part about living with him was that he was as excited about the messages as were his audiences. He labored over them all morning and most of the afternoon in preparation for transmitting no later than early evening. All over the world sympathetic translators converted his words into the languages of their people. Other computer-literate believers invested hours every day in cataloguing Dr. Ben-Judah's information and making it easily accessible to newcomers.

When Tsion came across some startling revelation in his study, Buck often heard him exult and knew he would soon pad out to the top of the stairs. "Listen to this," he would call out, "anyone who can hear me!" His knowledge of the biblical languages made his commentary the absolute latest thought on a given passage by the world's most astute Bible scholar.

Buck couldn't wait to hear what Tsion was wrestling with about the prophesied sixth woe. But for now he worried about Doc. He tapped lightly on his bedroom door. Then louder. He turned the knob and entered. It was the middle of the afternoon, the spring sun high in the sky. But the room was dark, the shades pulled. And Doc Charles was still in bed. Very still.

+ + +

"Goin' to Africa Friday," Mac said. "Fortunato's agreed to a face-to-face request by Mwangati Ngumo. 'Course Ngumo thinks he's meeting with Nicolae. Bet Mwangati's wonderin' when Carpathia's gonna make good on his promises."

Annie Christopher snorted. "Imagine what the potentate must have promised him to get him to give up the secretary-generalship."

"We'll know Friday," Mac said. "At least I will."

Annie looked at Mac. "They let you sit in on these meetings?" she said.

Mac glanced at David. "You haven't told her?"

"Feel free," David said.

"Come with me, Corporal," Mac said.

She and David followed him out. "I'll keep calling you *Captain* or *Mr. McCullum,* even in private," Annie said. "I let you check my mark and kiss me on the head. But the most formal thing you're allowed to call me from now on is *Sister.*"

"I don't know," Mac said. "I'd better keep it formal, just so I don't slip up in front of somebody." She followed him into the cockpit.

+ + +

"Doc?" Buck said, approaching the bed. He detected no movement. He didn't want to scare him.

Assuming the light would be less blinding than sunshine, Buck flipped it on. He sighed. At least Floyd was breathing. Perhaps he had merely had trouble falling asleep and was catching up. Floyd groaned and turned.

"You all right, Doc?" Buck tried.

Floyd sat up, his face a mask of puzzlement. "I was afraid of this," he said.

"I'm sorry," Buck said. "I just—"

Floyd whipped off the blankets. He sat on the edge of the bed in a long terry cloth robe that fell open to reveal him fully clothed in flannel shirt, jeans, and boots. He had sweat through it all.

"Was it that cold last night?" Buck said.

"Open those drapes, would ya?"

Floyd covered his eyes as the light burst into the room.

"What's the matter, Floyd?"

"Your vehicle in running order?"

"Sure."

"Get me to Young Memorial. My eyes still yellow?"

He squinted at Buck, who bent to look.

"Oh, Floyd," Buck said. "I wish they were."

"Bloodshot?"

"That's an understatement."

"No white showing?"

Buck shook his head.

"I'm in trouble, Buck."

3

DAVID, MAC, and Annie Christopher sat in the luxurious lounge of the Condor, twenty feet behind the cockpit. "So," Annie said, "the what-did-you-call-it reverse thingie—"

"Reverse intercom bug," Mac said.

"—lets you hear *everything* in the cabin?"

Mac nodded. "Lounge, seats, sleeping quarters, lavs—everywhere."

"Amazing."

"Somethin', ain't it?" Mac said.

"Amazing you haven't been caught."

"You kiddin'? They discover it now, I disavow knowledge of it. I had nothing to do with it, Rayford never told me it was here, I never stumbled upon it. They already see him as a traitor. And neither they nor I know where he is, do we?"

Annie moved to a couch behind a highly polished wood table. "This is where the big man himself watches TV?"

David nodded.

She turned back to Mac as if she had just thought of something. "You have no trouble lying?"

Mac shook his head. "To the Antichrist, you serious? My *life* is a lie to him. If he had a clue, I'd be tortured. If he thought I knew where Rayford was, or Ray's daughter and son-in-law, I'd be dead."

"End justifies the means?" Annie said.

Mac shrugged. "I sleep at night. That's all I can tell you."

"I'll sleep a little better myself," she said, "knowing you've got Carpathia under surveillance."

"At least when he's on board," Mac said. "Actually, Leon's more entertaining. There's a piece of work."

"Wish I could go with you," Annie said.

"Me too," David said. "But unless we're in the cockpit, we wouldn't hear anything anyway. Speaking of that, Mac, you still worried your first officer's on to you?"

"Not anymore," Mac said. "Got him promoted. He's gonna be Pompous Maximum's pilot."

Annie laughed. "I love it! I got in trouble for forgetting part of his title once. It's His Excellency Pontifex Maximus, Peter the Second, isn't it?"

Mac shrugged. "I call him Pete."

"You should see the plane he's ordered," David said. "Nicolae and Leon are beside themselves."

"Better'n this one?" Mac said.

"Way better. Fifty percent larger, costs twice as much. Used to belong to a sheik. I'm taking delivery in a week."

"They approved it?"

"They're setting him up," David said, "letting him hang himself. Will his new pilot be able to fly it?"

"He can fly anything," Mac said. "I liked him. Good skills. But a total Carpathia loyalist. Much as I wanted to get to him—you know, really talk to him—I didn't dare give myself away. He was already getting pitched by a believer in C sector."

"Maintenance?" Annie said. "I didn't know we had any believers over there."

"We don't anymore. My guy ratted him out. Would've done that to me, too. God's going to have to reach him some other way."

David stood and ran his fingers along the base of the wide-screen TV. He turned it on, muted the sound, and idly watched the Carpathia-controlled news. "Amazing reception inside a metal building," he said.

"Nothing surprises me anymore," Mac said. "Turn that up."

The news mostly carried stories of Carpathia's accomplishments. The potentate himself came on, smooth and charming as ever, praising some regional government and humbly deferring praise for his own reconstruction project. "It is my privilege to have been asked to serve each and every member of the Global Community," he said.

"There you are, Mac," David said, pointing out the pilot in the background as Carpathia was welcomed to yet another former Third World country that had benefited from his largesse. "And there's Peter's new pilot. You bringing in a believer to replace him?"

"If I can sneak him past Personnel."

"Anybody I know?"

"Jordanian. Former fighter pilot. Abdullah Smith."

+ + +

Buck's Land Rover bounced along toward Palatine. Floyd Charles lay across the backseat. "What is it, Doc?" Buck said.

"I'm a fool is all," Floyd said. He sat up, settling directly behind Buck. "I felt this coming on for months, telling myself I was imagining it. When the vision started to go, I should have contacted the Centers for Disease Control. It's too late now."

"I'm not following you."

"Let's just say I figured out what almost killed Hattie. I contracted it from her somehow. In layman's terms, it's like time-released cyanide. Can gestate for months. When it kicks in, you're a goner. If it's what I've got, there'll be no stopping it. I've been treating the symptoms, but that was useless."

"Don't talk like that," Buck said. "If Hattie survived, why can't you?"

"'Cause she was treated personally and daily for months."

"We'll pray. Leah Rose will get what you need."

"Too late," Doc said. "I'm a fool. A doctor is his own worst patient."

"Are the rest of us in trouble?"

"Nah. If you haven't had symptoms, you're in the clear. I had to have gotten it when delivering her miscarriage."

"So, what about Leah?"

"I can only hope."

Buck's phone chirped.

"Where are you?" Chloe asked.

"Running an errand with Floyd. Didn't want to bother you."

"It bothered me to hear you take off and not know where you were going. Errands in broad daylight? Daddy's not happy. He was supposed to go see T at the airport today."

"He can use Ken's car."

"Too recognizable, but that's not the point. No one knew where you guys went. Tsion's worried."

Buck sighed. "Floyd's not well and time is crucial. We're on our way to Young Memorial. I'll keep you posted."

"What's—"

"Later, hon. OK?"

She hesitated. "Be careful, and tell Floyd we'll pray."

+ + +

"We shouldn't be seen together a lot," Mac said, and David and Annie nodded. "Except what would be normal. Anybody know you're here now?"

Annie shook her head. "I've got a meeting at ten tonight."

"I'm clear," David said. "But there's no normal workday anymore, in case you hadn't noticed. You've got to wonder when Carpathia sleeps."

"I want to hear you guys' stories, David," Mac said. "I know you still have family in Israel. Where you from, Annie?"

"Canada. I was flying here from Montreal when the earthquake hit. Lost my whole family."

"You weren't a believer yet?"

She shook her head. "I don't guess I'd ever been to church except for weddings and funerals. We didn't care enough to be atheists, but that's what we practiced. Would have called ourselves agnostics. Sounded more tolerant, less dogmatic. We were tight. Good people. Better than most religious people we knew."

"But you weren't curious about God?"

"I started wondering after the disappearances, but we became instant devotees of Carpathia. He was like a voice of reason, a man of compassion, love, peace. I applied to work for the cause as soon as the U.N. changed its name and announced plans to move here. The day I was accepted was the happiest of my life, of our whole family's life."

"What happened?"

"Losing them all happened. I was devastated. I'd been scared before, sure. Knew some people who had disappeared and some who had died in all that happened later. But I had never lost anyone close, ever. Then I lose my mom and dad and my two younger brothers in the earthquake, not to mention half our town, while I'm merrily in the sky. We wind up landing in the sand at Baghdad Airport, see other planes go down. I find out GC headquarters is demolished, finally report to the underground shelter, and see the ruins of my little suburb on CNN. I was a mess for days, crying, praying to who-knows-who, pleading with Communications for word about my family. They were slower than I was on the Internet, so I just kept searching. I finally found dozens of names I knew on the confirmed-dead list. I didn't even want to look under *C,* but I couldn't stop myself."

Annie bit her lip.

"You don't have to talk about it if—"

"I want to, Mr. McCullum. It's just that it seems like yesterday. I checked into un-enlisting, going back for memorial services, looking into claiming the bodies. But that wasn't allowed. Mass cremations for health reasons. There wasn't even anyone left to commiserate with. I wanted to kill myself."

David put a hand on her shoulder. "Tell him what you found on the Net."

"You must know," Annie said, looking up with moist eyes. Mac nodded. "I first saw all the rebuttals of Dr. Ben-Judah coming from the shelter. That was even before I found his Web site. When the GC made noises about making it illegal to even access that site, I had to see it. I was still a blind loyalist, but

Carpathia preaches individual freedom even while he's denying it. The whole praying thing scared me. I had never given God a second thought. Now I wished he were there for me. I had no one else."

"So you found Tsion."

"I found his home page. I couldn't believe it. A number in the corner of the page—you must have seen it—showed how many people were accessing the site every so many seconds. I thought it was exaggerated, but then I realized this was why the GC was already trying to counter him. Someone gaining that vast an audience was a threat. I clicked through the site and read that day's message from Ben-Judah. I recalled having heard of him when he declared his conversion over international TV. But that's not what impressed me. And I didn't too much understand what he was communicating that day on the Net either. It looked like Bible stuff and was beyond me, but his tone was so warm. It was as if he were sitting there next to me and just chatting, telling me what was going on and what to expect. I knew if I could ask him questions, he would have answers. Then I saw the archives. I thought, *Archives already?* I mean, how old could the site be?

"I clicked through the listings, amazed that he had posted a significant teaching message every day for weeks already. When I came upon one called "For Those Who Mourn," I nearly fainted. I felt warm all over, then a chill. I locked my door and hoped the GC hadn't begun monitoring our laptops. I had the greatest sense of anticipation ever. Somehow I knew this man had something for me. I printed out that message and carried it with me for months, until David and I discovered each other and he warned me I shouldn't be caught with it. So I memorized it before I destroyed it."

Mac shot her a double take. "You memorized an entire Ben-Judah message?"

"Pretty much. Want to hear the first paragraph?"

"Sure."

"He wrote, 'Dear troubled friend, you may be mourning the loss of a loved one who either disappeared in the Rapture or has been killed in the ensuing chaos. I pray God's peace and comfort for you. I know what it is to lose my immediate family in a most unspeakable manner. But let me tell you this with great confidence: If your loved ones were alive today, they would urge you to be absolutely certain you're ready to die. There is only one way to do that.'"

David could tell Mac was moved.

"Dr. Ben-Judah explained God and Jesus and the Rapture and the Tribulation so clearly that I desperately wanted to believe. All I had to do was look back at his other teachings to realize that he was right about the Bible prophecies. He has predicted every judgment so far."

Mac nodded, smiling.

"Well," she said, "of course you know that. I switched back to the archived message and read how to pray, how to tell God you know you're a sinner and that you need him. I laid facedown on my bed and did that. I knew I had received the truth, but I had no idea what to do next. I spent the rest of the day and night, all night, reading as much of the teaching as I could. It became quickly obvious why the GC tried to counter Dr. Ben-Judah. He was careful not to mention Nicolae by name, but it was clear the new world order was the enemy of God. I didn't understand much about the Antichrist, but I knew I had to be unique among GC employees. Here I was, in the shelter of the enemy of God, and I was a believer."

"That's where I come in," David said. "She thought I was making eyes at her."

"Don't get ahead of the story," Annie said. "The next time I went out into the employee population, I was afraid I *looked* like a believer. I thought anybody I talked to would be able to tell that I had a secret. I wanted to tell somebody, but I knew no one. I had arrived in the middle of chaos and was assigned quarters, given a uniform, and told to report to Communications. I was working several levels below David, but I noticed him looking at me. First he seemed alarmed, then he smiled."

"He saw your mark," Mac said.

"Well, yeah, but see, I had not gotten far enough into Tsion's teachings to know about that. Anyway, David sent word down through the various supervisors that he wanted to meet with me. I said, 'Personally?'

"As soon as I got in there and the door was shut, he said, 'You're a believer!'

"I was scared to death. I said, 'No, I—a believer in what?'

"He said, 'Don't deny it! I can see it on your face!' He had to be fishing, so I denied it again. He said, 'You deny Jesus one more time, you're going to be just like Peter. Watch out for a rooster.'

"I had no idea what he was talking about. I couldn't have told you that Peter was a disciple, let alone that he had denied Christ. David had guessed my secret, mentioned someone named Peter, and was jabbering about a rooster. Still I couldn't help myself. I said, 'I'm not denying Jesus.'

"He said, 'What do you call it?'

"I said, 'Fearing for my life.'

"He said, 'Welcome to the club. I'm a believer too.'

"I said, 'But how did you know?'

"He said, 'It's written all over you.'

"I said, 'But really, how?'

"And he said, 'Literally, God wrote it on your forehead.' That's when I knew I had stepped off the edge."

+ + +

As soon as Buck and Floyd Charles entered Young Memorial, the teenage receptionist called out, "Miz Rose, your friends are here."

"Keep your voice down!" Leah said, hurrying from her office. "Gentlemen, I'm not sure I can do anything for you today. What's the trouble?"

Floyd whispered it to her quickly. "God help us," she said. "This way. Grab that."

"Have you had any symptoms?" Doc said.

She shook her head. Buck appropriated a wheelchair and pushed Floyd behind Leah. She led them down a short ramp, past the main elevators, and around a corner to the service elevator. She used a key from a huge, jangly ring to access it. "If you see anyone, hide your face," she said. "Just don't make it obvious."

"Yeah, that wouldn't be obvious," Buck said.

She glared at him. "I know you know what real danger is, Mr. Williams, so I'd appreciate it if you'd not underestimate mine."

"Sorry."

They boarded and the doors shut. Leah used her key again and held the sixth floor button. "Don't know if this'll work," she said. "On the other one you can bypass other floors by turning the key and holding down the button."

It didn't work. The car stopped on two. Buck immediately knelt before Doc as if chatting with him. That blocked both their faces from the door. "Sorry," Leah told the people waiting. "Emergency."

"Oh, man!" someone said.

The same thing happened on five and elicited an even more frustrated response.

"This is not good," Leah said as the doors shut again. "Be prepared for people in the hallway on six. We're going left."

Fortunately, the trio was ignored as Leah led the way to an empty room. She shut the door and locked it, then closed the blinds. "Get him into the bed," she told Buck, "and get those wet clothes off him. You sleep that way, Doctor?"

Doc nodded, looking tired.

Buck hated the bright red around his dark pupils. "What's wrong with him, Leah?"

She ignored Buck, grabbing a gown from a cabinet and tossing it to him. "If he needs to use the bathroom, now's the time. He's not likely to get out of that bed again."

"For how long?" Buck said.

"Ever," Doc slurred. "She knows what's going down here."

Leah pushed the speaker button on the wall phone and continued working as she talked. "CDC delivered some antivenin yesterday. Get me two vials to 6204."

"Stat?" her receptionist said.

Leah made a face. "Yes, stat!" she said. "Like now."

"You've got a phone call."

"Do I sound free to take a call? *Stat* was your word, girl. Would you hurry please?"

"OK," the girl said. "Don't say I didn't tell you."

Leah tugged Buck's sleeve and pulled him close to Doc's bed. "I need to ask him some questions. When that girl knocks, just take the medicine and shut the door."

He nodded.

"Now, Doctor," she said. "First symptoms?"

"Quite a while ago," he mumbled.

"Not good enough. When?"

"I'm a fool."

"We know that. How soon after you brought that miscarriage in here?"

"Maybe six months."

"You've done nothing about it?"

He shook his head. "Just hoped."

"That's not going to work."

"That's what I was afraid of."

"You know the closest CDC can get to an antidote is antivenin, and no one knows—"

"It's too late anyway."

Leah looked at Buck and shook her head. "He's right," she said. "The antivenin won't even let him die comfortably."

"What're you telling me?" Buck said. "He hasn't even got a chance?"

Doc shook his head and closed his eyes.

"The maximum antivenin dosage will be like spitting into the wind," Leah said. "What can you see, Doctor?"

"Not much."

Leah pressed her lips together.

There was a knock at the door. Buck opened it, reached for the medicine, and the girl pulled back. He made a lunge for it and ripped it from her hands.

"Miz Rose," she called over his shoulder. "That call was from GC!"

Buck shut the door, but Leah pushed past him and called after her. "GC where?"

"Wisconsin, I think."

"What'd you tell them?"

"That you were busy with a patient."

"You didn't say who, did you?"

"I don't know who. 'Cept he's a doctor."

"You didn't say that, did you?"

"Shouldn't I have?"

"Wait right there."

"I'm sorry."

"Just wait there a second."

Leah returned and quickly filled two syringes. She drove them into Floyd's hip, and he didn't even flinch. "Have her come in here," Leah told Buck.

He looked down the hall and signaled for the girl. She hesitated, then came slowly. "C'mon!" he said. "No one's going to hurt you."

As soon as she poked her head in the door, Leah said, "Bring me my purse as fast as you can, will you?"

"Sure, but—"

"Stat, sweetheart. Stat!"

The girl ran off.

"What's happening?" Buck said.

"Get your vehicle and bring it around the back. There's a basement exit, and that's where I'll come."

"But if he's dying, how can y—"

Leah grabbed his arms. "Mr. Williams, Doctor Charles and I have not just been talking. This man could be dead before we get him to the car. If you want to bury him or cremate him or do anything with him other than have him found here, I'll deliver him to the back door. GC in Wisconsin ring any bells? That's where he worked, remember? That's where he's AWOL from. They've been nosing around, watching for him, figuring he's in this area and might show up here sometime. They don't know—at least from me—that he was already here once. I've been lying through my teeth. They find him here, dead or alive, we're all in trouble. Now go!"

"Any chance you can save him?"

"Get the car."

"Just tell me if he's better off here or in the c—"

Leah whispered desperately, "He's dying. It's just a matter of when. Where is irrelevant now. The best I can do for him I have already done. The absolute worst would be his being discovered here."

\+ + +

Mac looked at his watch. "Just enough time for you two to tell me how you got together, you know, romantically."

"I think you've heard enough details, Captain."

"C'mon! I'm an old romantic."

"It hasn't been easy," David said. "Obviously I kept her from you and Rayford."

"Yeah, what's that all about?"

"At the time we believed the fewer who knew the better."

"But we need all the comrades we can get."

"I know," David said. "But we're both so new at this, we don't know who to trust."

"If you wondered about Ray and me, you sure never showed it."

"It was a good exercise, let me just say that. What's going to happen when the brass start looking for a mark that's not there, rather than not seeing a mark that is?"

"There'll be no hiding then, kids."

\+ + +

Buck took the main elevator to the first floor and realized he had to exit past the receptionist. The last thing he wanted was to have her see his Rover. He planned to distract her with a fake emergency, but as he breezed through the lobby toward the front door, a substitute was in her place, a thick, middle-aged woman. Of course! The original girl was taking Leah her purse. Leah had thought to divert her.

Buck hurried to his car. As he pulled around the side of the building toward the back, he saw the substitute standing at the window, staring at him. He only hoped Stat Girl had not told her to find out what he was driving.

Buck skidded to a stop on an asphalt apron that led to a basement exit. He leapt from the Rover and opened the door as Leah, her bag over her shoulder, rolled out a gurney containing Floyd Charles with a sheet to the top of his head.

"He's gone already?" Buck said, incredulous.

"No! But people kept their distance, and nobody's going to identify him, are they?"

"Only your receptionist."

Buck lowered the backseat and Leah slid the whole bed in. "You're stealing that?" he said.

"I put more in my purse than that bed's worth," she said. "You want to debate ethics or fight the GC?"

"I don't want either," he said, as they climbed into the front seat. "But we're committed now, aren't we?"

"I don't know about you, Williams, but I'm in with both feet. This hospital has been GC-run for ages. How long was I going to be able to work for Carpathia when there's no way I'd ever take the mark of the beast? I'd die first."

"Literally," Buck said.

"Well, I just appropriated a bed and a lot of medicine from the enemy. If you have a problem with that, I'm sorry. I don't. This is war. All's fair, as they say."

"Can't argue with that. But, um, where am I taking you?"

"Where do you think? Take a left, and I'll take you out around the long way. Nobody will see you from the front of the building."

"Then where?"

"My place."

"What if the GC are there?"

"Then we'll just keep going."

"But if they're not, you'll try to nurse Floyd back to—"

"You're not thinking, Mr. W—"

"Quit with the formality, Leah. You put a dying friend in my car, so just run down the program for me."

"All right," she said. "If we can beat GC to my apartment, I'm going to grab as much of my stuff as I can in sixty seconds. You know they're on their way, as soon as they find me gone from Young."

"Then where do I take you?"

"Where do you live?"

"Where do *I* live?"

"Bingo, Buck. I need to hide out. You and yours are the only people I know who have a place to hide."

"But we're not telling anyone wh—"

"Oh, yes, you are. You're telling me. If you can't trust me after all we've been through, you can't trust anybody. I helped you discharge your patched-up pilot, Ritz. And I helped Doc with the miscarriage of guess-who's baby. How's that young woman doing, by the way?"

"Getting better."

"There's irony. Doc helps her beat the poison, and it's going to kill him."

"We lost Ritz."

"Lost him?"

"Killed in Israel. Long story."

Leah suddenly fell silent. She pointed directions and Buck lurched along, double-clutching and shifting till he thought his arm would fall off. "I liked that guy," she managed finally.

"We all did. We hate this, every bit of it."

"But you're taking me in, cowboy. You know that, don't you?"

"I can't make that decision."

She glared at him. "What are you going to do, leave me at the corner blindfolded while you and your compatriots vote? You owe me and you know it. This isn't like me, inviting myself. But I've risked my life for you, and I have nowhere else to turn."

Doc's death rattle began. His labored, liquid breathing pierced Buck. "Should I pull over?"

"No," she said. "There's nothing I can do now but shoot him full of morphine."

"That'll help?"

"It'll just make him pain free and maybe knock him out before he dies."

"Something!" Floyd called out in a mournful wail. "Give me something!"

Leah spun and knelt in her seat, digging through her bag. Buck slowed involuntarily as he tried to watch. This was too much. Floyd was going to die while Buck was racing around in the car! No good-byes, no prayer, no comforting words. Buck felt as if he hardly knew the man, and he had been living with him for more than a year.

"Watch the road," she said. "This will quiet him, but he's never going to leave this car alive."

Sobs rose in Buck's throat. He wanted to call Chloe, to tell her and the others. But how do you do that on the phone? Doc's dying and I'm bringing a nurse to live with us? Pulling into the safe house without notice, carrying Floyd's corpse and a new houseguest wouldn't be much easier. But Buck had run out of options.

Leah's neighborhood, what was left of it, crawled with GC vehicles. The morphine had quieted Floyd. Leah slid onto the floor under the dash, and Buck avoided her street. He headed to Mount Prospect, hoping Floyd might at least have the privilege of dying in his own bed.

4

DAVID HASSID walked Mac McCullum back to his quarters in the GC palace residential annex late that night. "There are things I haven't told even Annie," he said.

"I knew you had somethin' to tell me, kid. Otherwise, you'd be walking her back, wouldn't you?"

"We're trying to not be seen together. I don't even know if her meeting's over."

"So, what's up?" Mac said as they stood in the corridor outside his door.

"You know I was on the palace antibugging installation task force."

"Yeah, how'd you wangle that appointment?"

"Just kept telling Leon how important I thought it was to ensure total impregnability. I came in as a starry-eyed idealist, and they still see me that way. You know about the installation?"

Mac nodded. "Best in history and all that."

"Yeah, except it needs constant monitoring."

"Naturally."

"I volunteered for that, and everybody was glad to let me have it," David said.

"I'm listening."

"So am I."

"What?"

"I monitor the antibugging devices in Carpathia and Fortunato's offices."

"Go on."

"My job is to find out if anyone's trying to listen in. Well, I'm staying on top of it. And in the process I hear anything I want, any time I want."

Mac shook his head. "I wouldn't have minded not knowing that. Man, David, you're sitting on a time bomb."

"Don't I know it. But it's untraceable."

"Guaranteed?"

"In one way it's simple. In another it's a miracle of technology. The stuff is actually being recorded onto a miniature disk embedded in the central processing unit of the computer that runs all of New Babylon."

"The one people like to call the Beast."

"Because it contains so much information about every living soul, yeah. But we both know the Beast is no machine."

Mac folded his arms and leaned against the wall. "One thing I've learned in surveillance work is that you never want to have hard copies of anything. Anything can eventually fall into the wrong hands."

"I know," David said. "Let me tell you how I've protected it."

Mac looked around. "You sure we're secure here?"

"Hey! I'm in charge of that. What we're saying could wind up on my disk, but no one else will ever hear it. *I* won't hear it unless I choose to. If I do, it's all categorized by date and time and location. And the fidelity is unparalleled."

Mac whistled through his teeth. "Someone had to manufacture this for you."

"That's right."

"Someone you trust with your life."

"You're looking at him."

"So how'd you make sure no one ever finds it?"

"I'm not guaranteeing that. I'm saying they will never be able to access a thing from it. The disk is slightly smaller than an inch in diameter and, because of super-compression digital technology, can hold nearly ten years of spoken conversation if recorded twenty-four hours a day. Well, we don't need that much time, do we?"

Mac shook his head. "They've got to have checks and balances."

"They do. But they aren't going to find anything."

"What if they do?"

David shrugged. "Say someone catches on to me and starts looking for my bugs. They find 'em, trace 'em to the CPU, tear the whole thing apart, and find the disk. It is so heavily encrypted that if they tried random number combinations at the rate of ten thousand digits a second around the clock for a thousand years, they would have barely begun. You know, even a fifteen-digit number has trillions of combinations, but theoretically it could be deciphered. How would you like to try to match an encrypted number containing three hundred million digits?"

Mac rubbed his eyes. "I was born too early. Where do you kids come up with this craziness? How can *you* access your disk if it's that encrypted?"

David was just warming to his subject. "That's the beauty of it. I know the formula. I know what *pi* to the millionth digit has to do with it and how the date and time to the current second have to be used as a multiplier, and how those figures float forward and backward depending on various random factors. The number that would unlock it now is different from the number a second from now, and it doesn't progress rationally. But let's say someone *were* to get far enough into my disk where the only step left was to match the encryption code, a miracle in itself. Even if they *knew* the number, only a lightning-speed computer grinding away for more than a year could enter it."

"Has what you've heard been worth the work?"

"It will be to the Tribulation Force, don't you think?"

"But how can you transmit it to them without jeopardizing your security or theirs?"

David pressed his back to the wall and slid to sit on the floor. "All that's encrypted too, though certainly not to where it takes them forever to get into it. So far we have been able to communicate by both phone and Carpathia's own cellular-solar technology on hidden scrambled bands. Of course, he's constantly on me to find ways to monitor all citizens."

"For their own good, no doubt."

"Oh, absolutely. The potentate merely cares deeply about the morale of his global family."

"But, David, can't anything transmitted also be intercepted?"

David shrugged. "I like to think *I* can bug anything. But I've tested my own stuff against my tracing power, and unless I drop enough bread crumbs along the road, I'm powerless too. Random scrambling and channel switching, coordinated with miniaturization and speed that makes fiber optics look like a slow boat . . . well, nothing is beyond possible anymore."

Mac stood and stretched. "Ever wonder about this stuff? Like what Dr. Ben-Judah says about Satan being the prince and power of the air? Transmitting through space and all that . . ."

"Scares me to death," David said, still sitting. "It means I'm on the front lines against him. I didn't know what I signed on for when I became a believer, but I wound up on the right side, didn't I? It's too late to change my mind. I walk the same halls with Antichrist himself, and I play around in the air with the devil. I'm careful, but the mark of the beast will change everything. There won't be *any* believers working here after that, unless they find a way to fake the mark. And who would want to do that?"

"Not me," Mac said, unlocking his door. "We're all going to wind up in one safe house or another one of these days. I sure hope mine's the same as yours."

David was so moved by that compliment that he was too stunned to respond. "Long flight Friday," Mac added. "I've got to find out who's tagging along with Leon and whether I can get Abdullah in here in time to help."

The tension of his role, exciting as it should have been for a young man, weighed on David. But he headed toward his own quarters with a lighter step.

* * *

Floyd was quiet. The morphine must have done its work. Buck slowed as he drew within a mile of the safe house. He peered in the rearview mirror. He had not been followed. His phone startled him. "Buck here," he said.

"You were going to keep me posted," Chloe said.

"Almost home. A few minutes."

"Is Floyd with you?"

"Yeah, but he's not well."

"Hattie and I changed his bed and freshened the room."

"Good. I'm going to need help with him."

"Is he all right, Buck? Are you?"

"I'll see you soon, hon."

"Buck! Is everything all right?"

"Please, Chloe. I'll see you in a minute."

"All right," she said, sounding displeased.

He clicked the phone shut and dropped it in his pocket. He glanced at Leah. "Is he going to last the night?"

"I'm sorry, Buck. He's gone."

Buck slammed on the brake and they lurched forward as the Rover slid in the dirt. "What?"

"I'm sorry."

Buck turned in his seat. Leah had covered Floyd's face again, but the sudden stop had pressed his body against the back of the front seat.

"Do you know who this man is?" Buck said, his own desperate voice scaring him.

"I know he was a good doctor and courageous."

"He risked his life to tell me where the GC took Chloe. Came there himself to help her escape. Stayed up for days with Hattie. Saved her life. The miscarriage. Delivered our son. Was never too big to pitch in with the hard work."

"I'm so sorry, Buck."

Buck pulled the sheet from Floyd's face. In the darkness he could barely make it out. He turned on the inside light and recoiled at the death mask. Floyd's teeth were bared, his eyes open, still filled with blood around the pupils. "Oh, Doc!" he said.

Leah turned in her seat and rummaged in her bag for latex gloves. She carefully closed Floyd's eyes and mouth, massaging his cheeks until he looked more asleep than dead. "Help me with that shoulder," she said. Buck took one side and Leah the other, and they tugged at the body until Floyd looked more naturally reposed. Buck drove slowly, avoiding ruts and bumps.

When he pulled up to the safe house, the curtain parted and he saw Chloe peer out. She was nursing Kenny. He drove around the side but stopped short of the backyard. "Give me a minute," he said. "You don't mind staying here with him—"

"Go," Leah said.

Chloe held open the back door with one hand, Kenny now over her other shoulder. "Who's with you?" she said. "I didn't see Floyd."

Buck was spent. He leaned forward to peck Chloe on the cheek, then did the same to Kenny, just as the baby burped. "Can you put him down?" he said.

"Buck—"

"Please," he said. "I need to talk to everybody."

The others were already waiting in the kitchen. Chloe went to put the baby down and quickly returned. Rayford sat at the table, and it was clear from his clothes he had spent hours working in the basement. Hattie sat on the table. Tsion, with a sad, knowing look, leaned against the refrigerator.

Buck found it hard to speak, and Chloe came to him, wrapping an arm around his waist. "We have another martyr," he said, and told the story, including that Leah was waiting in the car with Floyd's body.

Tsion hung his head. "God bless him," he said, his voice thick.

Hattie looked stricken. "He caught that from me? He died because of me?"

Chloe wrapped Buck in her arms and wept with him. "Are any of us susceptible?"

Buck shook his head. "We would have had symptoms by now. Floyd had symptoms but didn't tell us."

Buck stole a glance at Rayford. They would all look to him. Tsion would pray, but Rayford would walk them through the decision on Leah, the burial, everything. Yet Rayford had not moved. He sat without expression, forearms on the table. When Rayford's eyes met his, Buck sensed he was demanding to know what was expected.

Where was Rayford the Leader, their take-charge guy?

"We, ah, shouldn't leave Leah out there long," Buck said. "And we're going to have to do something with the body."

Rayford still stared at Buck, who could not hold his gaze. Had Buck done something wrong? Had he any choice other than to race off with Floyd to the hospital, then bring him back, Leah in tow?

"Daddy?" Chloe said softly.

"What?" Rayford said flatly, turning his eyes on her.

"I just . . . I'm . . . we're wondering—"

"What?" he said. "What! You're wondering what we're supposed to do now?" He stood, his chair sliding against the wall and rattling onto its side. "Well, so am I!" Buck had never before heard him raise his voice. "So am I!" Rayford railed. "How much can we take? How much are we supposed to take?"

Rayford picked up his chair and slammed it upright so hard that it bounced. He kicked it against the wall again and it flew back toward the table, chasing Hattie into Tsion's arms.

"Rayford," Tsion said quietly.

The chair would not have hit Hattie. It hit the edge of the table and spun, coming to rest next to Rayford. He yanked it to where he could sit again and slammed both fists on the table.

Tsion released Hattie, who was shaking. "I think we should—," he began, but Rayford cut him off.

"Forgive me," he said, clearly still fuming and seemingly unable to look anyone in the eye. "Get Leah in here and then let's get the body buried. Tsion, would you say a few—"

"Of course. I suggest we make Leah comfortable, then have the burial, then spend more time with her."

Rayford nodded. "Forgive me," he said again.

Buck backed the Rover into the yard, then brought Leah in and introduced her to everyone. "I'm sorry for your loss," she said. "I didn't know Dr. Charles well, but—"

"We were about to pray," Tsion said. "Then we'd like to get to know you."

"Certainly."

When Tsion knelt on the hard floor, the others followed, except Hattie, who remained standing. "God, our Father," Tsion began, his voice weak and quavery. "We confess we are beyond our strength to keep coming to you at terrible times like this, when we have lost one of our family. We do not want to accept it. We do not know how much more we can bear. All we can do is trust in your promise that we shall one day see our dear brother again in the land where sorrow shall be turned to singing, and where there shall be no more tears."

When the prayer was over, Buck moved toward the cellar stairs.

"Where are you going?" Rayford said.

"To get shovels."

"Just bring one."

"It's a big job, Ray. Many hands—"

"Just bring one, Buck. Now, Ms. Rose, I want to be clear on this. Floyd died from the poison Carpathia used to try to kill Hattie, is that right?"

"That's my understanding."

"Straight answer, ma'am."

"Sir, I know only what Dr. Charles told me. I have no personal knowledge of how Hattie was poisoned, but it seems clear that Floyd was contaminated by her, yes."

"So Nicolae Carpathia is responsible for this death."

Buck was impressed that Leah did not appear obligated to reply.

"This was murder, people," Rayford added. "Pure and simple."

"Rayford," Tsion said, "Carpathia likely has never heard of Doc Charles, and so, technically, while it is safe to say he tried to have Miss Durham killed—"

"I'm not talking court-of-law guilty," Rayford said, his face flushed. "I'm saying the poison Carpathia intended to kill someone killed Doc."

Tsion shrugged resignedly.

"Now, Buck," Rayford said, "where's my shovel?"

"Please let me help," Buck said.

Rayford stood and straightened. "Save me from saying one more thing I'll regret tomorrow, would you, Buck? This is something I want to do myself. Something I need to do, all right?"

"But it should actually be deeper than six feet, so close to the house and—" Buck held up both hands in surrender to Rayford's out-of-patience look. He found the biggest shovel in the cellar.

While Rayford toiled in the backyard, Leah talked about the most sanitary way to prepare the body. Unable to find lime with which to line the grave, she concocted a substitute made from kitchen products. "And," she told Buck, "we should wrap the body in a plastic tarp." She distributed gloves for those who would touch the body and prescribed a solution for disinfecting the Rover and the gurney.

Buck was amazed at what Rayford accomplished, considering he had worked all day in the shelter. He dug a hole seven feet long, three feet wide, and more than eight feet deep. He needed help to be hoisted out, covered with mud. The three men lowered Floyd's tarpaulin-shrouded body into the hole, and Rayford allowed the others to help fill it back in.

The group, save the sleeping baby, stood around the grave in the low light emitted from the house. Chloe, Hattie, and Leah were bundled against the cool night air. The men, sweaty from the shovel work, soon shivered.

Buck never ceased to be amazed at Tsion's eloquence. "Blessed in the sight of the Lord is the death of a saint," he said. "Floyd Charles was our brother, a beloved, earnest member of our family. Anyone who would like to say a word about him, please do so now, and I will pray."

"I knew him to be a gifted physician and a brave believer," Leah said.

Buck said, "Every time I think of him I'll think of our baby and of Chloe's health."

"Me too," Chloe said. "So many memories in such a short time."

Hattie stood shaking, and Buck noticed Rayford looking at her, as if expecting her to say something. She glanced at him and then away, then shook her head.

"Nothing," Rayford said. "You have nothing to say about the man who saved your life."

"Rayford," Tsion said.

"Of course I do!" Hattie said, her voice pinched. "I can't believe he died because of me! I don't know what to say! I hope he's gone to his reward."

"Let me tell you something else," Rayford said, his anger evidently unabated. "Floyd loved you, Hattie. You treated him like dirt, but he loved you."

"I know," she said, a whine in her voice. "I know you all love me in your own w—"

"I'm telling you he loved you. *Loved you.* Cared deeply for you, wanted to tell you."

"You mean—? You couldn't know that."

"He told me! I think he'd want you to know."

"Rayford," Tsion said, putting a hand on his shoulder, "anything else you would like to say about Floyd?"

"This is a death that must be avenged. Like Ken's and Amanda's and Bruce's."

"Vengeance is the Lord's," Tsion said.

"If only he would include me in that," Rayford said.

Tsion looked hard at him. "Be careful about wishing for things you don't really want," he said. "Let me close in prayer." But Buck could not hear him. Rayford had begun to weep. His breath came in great heaves and he covered his mouth with his hand. Soon he could not contain the sobs, and he fell to his knees and wailed in the night. Chloe rushed to him and held him.

"It's all right, Daddy," she said as she helped him up and walked him into the house. "It's all right."

Rayford pulled away from her and rushed up the stairs. Buck took Chloe in his arms, and the mud that had transferred to her from her father also smeared his clothes.

+ + +

Rayford was thankful for the well and the generator-run water heater as he stood under the steaming shower in the safe house. His muscles were finally untying.

What a day! The inexplicable anger that had sent him marching into the morning air had been building for months. Working in the cellar had not dented it, especially when he found himself alone all day. The awful news about Floyd had finally made him erupt in a way he hadn't since a loud fight with Irene fifteen years before. And that had been the result of too much alcohol.

While he felt bad about mistreating the others, something about this anger seemed righteous. Was it possible God had planted in his heart this intolerance for injustice for the sole purpose of preparing him to assassinate Carpathia? Or was he deluding himself? Rayford didn't want to think he was losing his mind. No one would understand a man like him trying to rationalize murder, even the murder of the Antichrist.

Rayford turned the dial to as hot as he could bear it and hung his head beneath the spray. His prayers had become entreaties that God allow him to do the unthinkable. How much was a man supposed to endure? The loss of his wife and son were his fault. He could have gone to heaven with them, had he been a man of faith and not pride. But losing Bruce, then Amanda, then Ken, now Doc—ah, why should he be surprised? It was a numbers game now. Did he expect to be among the last standing at the Glorious Appearing? He certainly wouldn't be if he took a shot at Nicolae Carpathia. But he probably wouldn't survive either way. Might as well go out with guns blazing.

Rayford stepped out of the shower and looked at himself in the steamed-up mirror, a towel draped over his shoulders. As the vapor dissipated and his face became clearer, he hardly recognized himself. Even a year ago he had felt all right, and Amanda seemed impressed with his mature look. Now *mature* would be a compliment. He looked and felt older than his years. Everyone did now, of course, but Rayford believed he had aged more quickly than most.

His face was lean and lined, his eyes baggy, his mouth turned down. He had never been much for ascribing depression to every blue period or downtime, but now he had to wonder. Was he depressed? Clinically depressed? That was the kind of thing he might have discussed with Floyd. And with the thought of his name came that stab in the gut. People around him were dying, and there would be no end to it until Jesus returned. That would be wonderful, but could he last? If he responded like this to someone he had known as briefly as Floyd, what would happen when, if, if . . . he didn't want to think about it. Chloe? The baby? Buck? Tsion?

This woman from the hospital, Leah, would she be worth talking to? Trying out a few ideas on a professional, a virtual stranger, seemed easier than raising the same things with anyone else in the house. In a peculiar way, Hattie knew him as well as the others. But she was still an outsider, even more than the newcomer was. He could never reveal his deepest thoughts to her.

Of course, he wouldn't say anything about his Carpathia plot to Leah Rose either. But he might get some insight into his own mind. Maybe she had dealt with depressed people, or knew doctors who had.

Rayford realized as he dried his hair that he recognized neither the man in the mirror *nor* the man inside anymore. The schemes playing at the edges of his mind were so far afield from the Rayford Steele he thought he was that he could only imagine what Chloe would say. And she knew only the half of it.

His new abruptness was hardly hidden from the rest of the Trib Force. They had all forgiven each other countless times for pettiness. All except Tsion, of course. It seemed he never offended, never had to be forgiven. Some people had the ability to live with grace despite untenable conditions. Tsion was one.

But Rayford had stepped beyond selfish behavior in an enclosed environment. He had threatened the status quo, the way of life—difficult as it was. And he was supposed to be the leader. He knew he was in charge only in the manner of the manager of a baseball team. Tsion was the Babe Ruth, the one who won ball games. But still Rayford had a vital role, a position of authority, a spiritual responsibility of headship as an elder would in a church.

Was he still worthy? Part of him was sure he was not. On the other hand, if he wasn't going bats and if he really *had* been chosen of God to have a part in a centuries-old assassination plot, he was someone special after all.

Rayford pulled on a huge robe and stepped out of the bathroom. *So I'm either anointed or a megalomaniac. Great. Who's going to let me know?* The old Rayford Steele fought to jar himself to his senses, while the rage-filled, righteously indignant, grieving, depressed, frustrated, caged member of the Tribulation Force continued to entertain thoughts of grandeur. Or at least revenge. *I'm a sick man,* he told himself. And he heard voices downstairs. Praying.

+ + +

Mac McCullum moved steadily along on his daily jog as the sun rose orange over the radiant city of New Babylon. He couldn't get over the beauty and what a privilege it might have been to be there under other circumstances. State-of-the-art, first-class, top-drawer, all the clichés came to life when someone considered this gleaming new megalopolis.

But with his secret conversion, Mac had become a mole, subversive, part of the rebellion. A lifetime of military training, self-discipline, chain of command, all-for-one-and-one-for-all thinking was now conflicted. Having reached the pinnacle as a career big-plane pilot, he now used every trick and wile he had ever learned to serve the cause of God.

Whatever satisfaction came with that was akin to the satisfaction he got that he could still clip off six brisk miles a day at his age. To some that was impressive. To him it was a necessity. He was fighting time, gravity, and a malady of physical attacks that came with mere longevity. That's just how he felt in his job. He should feel fulfilled, but the enemy was his employer. And as a valued, crucial plant for the other side, he should exult in the fact that he knew without doubt he was on the right side—the winning side.

But fear precluded any joy. The second he began to enjoy his role, he was vulnerable. Living on the edge, knowing that the one slip that gave him away would be his last, took all the fun out of the job. A measure of satisfaction came with the knowledge that he was good at what he did, both overtly and surreptitiously. But to wonder constantly when the other shoe would drop, when you would be found out—that was no way to live.

As the sun cleared the horizon and Mac felt the sweat on his weathered head and face, he knew that his exposure would likely be accomplished long before he was aware of it. That was the curse of it. Not only did he not know when or if he would be found out, but there was also one thing he was sure of: he would be the last to know. How long would Carpathia, Fortunato, any of them, let him twist in the wind, still trying to ply his trade when they already knew the truth? Would they let him hang himself, implicate the comrades he loved and served, allow him to make a mess of the precarious safety he tried to protect?

It was possible he had been exposed already. How could one know? The end of a traitor is like the end of a star—the result is always seen long after the event has taken place. He would just have to watch for the signs. Would something indicate to him that he should run, flee to the safe house, put out the SOS to the stateside Tribulation Force? Or would he be dead by the time they knew he had been compromised?

With a mile to go, he made the last curve, now with the sun at his back. His last encrypted message to Abdullah Smith had put the Jordanian right into Mac's own boat: "Personnel will ask straight out about your loyalty to the cause, to the Global Community, to the potentate. Remember, you are a frontline warrior. Tell them what they want to hear. Get yourself this job by whatever means you can. You will be in a position to help thwart the worst schemes of the evil one and see men and women come to Christ in spite of everything.

"If you wonder what to say, how to phrase it, just align yourself with me. Say without hesitation that you share Mac McCullum's views of the Global Community and are as wholly committed as he is to the policies and direction of the leadership. A truer word will never be spoken.

"I'm not saying it will be easy. The pay is exorbitant, as you know, but you will not enjoy one cent of it. The perquisites are like none you ever dreamed of, but you will constantly feel in need of cleansing. Praise God, that cleansing is there, because we are under assignment from the Almighty. It's short-term work, because Tsion Ben-Judah is right: When the mark of the beast is required for buying or selling, you know it'll be a requirement for being on the payroll here. We'll go from senior members of the staff to international fugitives overnight.

"I need you, Abdullah, that's all I can say. You and Ray and I cooperated in the past. This won't be as fun, but there won't be a dull moment. I'll look forward to once again sharing the cockpit with a respected airman and a brother I can trust. All the best, Mac."

+ + +

Buck sat next to Chloe on the couch. Tsion sat nearby, as did Leah. Here she was, brand-new in the house and already involved in a prayer meeting about their leader. Buck prayed hesitantly and not without guilt. Should they not have simply confronted Rayford? Wasn't this akin to spiritually talking behind his back? Surely Tsion would approach Rayford in due time.

5

RAYFORD HATED FEELING ISOLATED from the others. With his dream of eliminating Carpathia (even temporarily) he ironically had more in common with Hattie than with anyone. It was his own fault for losing control and making them tread carefully around him. But what was going on downstairs at midnight? All of them praying together always encouraged Rayford. But did this constitute a meeting of the Trib Force without him? Should he be offended?

Of course they were free to meet in any combination of brothers and sisters they wished. It wasn't like they were conducting business. What was the matter with him? When did he start caring about such trivia? Rayford tiptoed down so as not to disturb them. Sure enough, they sat on the couch and in chairs in the living room, heads bowed, praying. Everyone but Hattie.

Rayford was moved and suddenly wanted to join them. His motive wasn't pure. He wanted to reconcile with them without having to apologize again. Inserting himself in a spiritual exercise would speak volumes. He could even pray for forgiveness for his outbursts. . . .

As he slipped into the living room, Rayford's conscience was suddenly crushed. What a fool! How small! To be so blessed of God despite wrenching pain and then to want to use prayer to manipulate. . . . He nearly retreated but now wanted to join them for the right reasons. He didn't even want to pray aloud. He just wanted to agree with them before God, to be part of this body, this church. He knew he would feel worthy to lead them again only when he realized that he was *not* worthy aside from the gift of God.

He was the object of the prayer meeting. First one, then another, mentioned his name. They prayed for his strength, for peace, for comfort in his grief. They prayed for supernatural contentment when that was humanly impossible.

He could have been offended, to be, in essence, gossiped about in prayer. But he was ashamed. He had been worse than he had feared. Rayford knelt silently. Eventually the emotion and fervency of the prayers so humiliated and humbled him that he was powerless to hide anymore. He pitched forward onto his elbows and wept aloud. He was just sorry, so sorry, and grateful they believed him worth the effort to restore.

Chloe was the first to rush to Rayford, but rather than lift him, she merely knelt with him and embraced him. He felt Buck's tentative hand on his back and wished he could tell his son-in-law not to worry, that his support meant everything. Tsion laid his warm hand on Rayford's head and called on God "to be everything this man needs you to be during the most difficult season anyone has ever been asked to endure."

Rayford found himself sobbing for the second time that night, only now he did not wail the mournful cries of the hopeless. He felt bathed in the love of God and the support of his family. He had not given up the idea that God might still use him in the comeuppance of Nicolae Carpathia, but that was—at least briefly—less important than his place within the group. They could handle his not always being strong. They would stick with him when he was human and worse. They would support him even when he failed. How could he ever express what that meant to him?

It was not lost on Rayford that Leah, though she had understandably not felt comfortable enough to touch him, had prayed for him. She did not pretend to know the problem, only indicating a recognition that he was apparently not himself and needed a touch from God.

When the prayers finally fell silent, Rayford could muster only "Thank you, God." Tsion hummed a familiar tune. First Chloe, then the others, sang. *Blest be the tie that binds our hearts in Christian love. The fellowship of kindred minds is like to that above.*

The four of them rose and returned to where they were sitting. Rayford pulled up a chair. "Thought I was getting voted out of the club," he said.

Tsion chuckled. "We would not even let you resign," he said. "I would like to ask you, Leah, if you would mind waiting until tomorrow to tell us your story. I think we have all been through enough for one day, and we would like to give you our full attention."

"I was going to suggest the same," she said. "Thank you."

"Do you have any aversion to staying where Floyd used to sleep?" Rayford said.

"Not unless anyone else has a problem with it," she said. "And I know this sounds weird, but I won't sleep well unless I have a sense of the rest of the place. Could I get a quick tour, just so I know where everything is?"

"Chloe and I will be happy to show you," Rayford said, hoping to start a connection that would facilitate conversation.

"I'll check on the baby," Buck said.

Tsion rose wearily. "Good night, all."

Rayford was impressed that Chloe knew enough to ignore the cellar. She started in the back of the duplex, where Leah had come in. "There's nothing in the other flat," she said. "It was more structurally damaged anyway. You came through the nook area here. This has been rebuilt since the earthquake when a tree smashed it and killed the wife of the owner. Her husband was at our church at the time and died when that collapsed.

"Then the kitchen, of course, and off to the left the living room. Then the dining room, where we never eat but a lot of us work. Past the stairs there is a bathroom and the front room where Buck and I sleep with the baby."

Upstairs they showed her the other bath, Rayford's room, Tsion's, and Floyd's.

"Thanks," she said. "And where did Ritz stay?"

Rayford and Chloe looked at each other. "Ah," he said, "I wasn't aware you knew he had lived here."

"Was it a secret?"

"The whole place is."

"I'm not supposed to know he lived here? I knew Dr. Charles and Mr. Williams and Hattie lived here."

"I just didn't know you knew, that's all," Rayford said. "I hope it doesn't make me sound suspicious."

She stopped. "Of what? You want to examine my mark? Something gave you the confidence to bring every emergency my way. If I wasn't trustworthy, would I have risked my life for all of you?"

"I'm sorry, I—"

"Really, Mr. Steele. If I was working for the GC I could have tipped off the potentate when his lover miscarried his child while I attended her. I could have reported Dr. Charles when he incinerated the remains rather than follow legal procedure. I could have tipped off the authorities when your son-in-law got me to release Ritz with a gaping head wound. You think I didn't know who you people were and why no one could know where you lived?"

"Miss Rose—"

"It's Mrs. Rose, and frankly the reason I assumed Ritz lived here was because I knew the airport had been virtually demolished. And, in case you don't remember, he was with you when you brought Hattie in. Was I to assume you came from your hiding place and he rendezvoused with you from somewhere else?"

"You're right. I'm just—"

"There'll be infiltrators, Mr. Steele. I don't know how they'll do it, but I wouldn't put anything past the GC. But until they perfect some sort of a foolproof replica of the sign we can see only on each other, I can't imagine a spy foolish enough to waltz in here. Run me through any grill you want, but I'll thank you to never again admit you're suspicious of me just because I assumed a man lived with you whose first name I don't even remember."

Rayford looked pleadingly at her. "Would a tough day be an excuse?"

"I've had one too," she said. "Tell me you're not afraid of me before I turn in."

"I'm not. I'm sorry."

"I am too. Forgive me if I overreacted."

So much for bonding, Rayford thought. "Don't give it another thought."

"You trust me then."

"Yes! Now go to bed and let us do the same. Feel free to use the bathroom before the rest of us."

"You're telling me you trust me."

Rayford could tell even Chloe was losing patience with Leah. "I'm tired, Mrs. Rose. I apologized. I'm convinced. OK?"

"No."

"No?" Chloe said. "I have to get to bed."

"You think I'm blind or stupid or what?" Leah said.

"Excuse me?" Chloe said.

"Where's the shelter?"

Rayford flinched. "You don't want me to be suspicious and now you ask about a shelter?"

"You don't have one?"

"Tell me how you would know to ask."

Leah shook her head. "This is worse than your thinking me subversive. You think I'm daft."

"Not anymore I don't," Chloe said. "Tell me how you know there's more here, and I'll show it to you."

"Thank you. If I hid out in a safe house, I'd assume its security would one day be compromised. Either you have a place to run to on a moment's notice, or this place turns upside-down. Plus, and this is so obvious it offends me to have to raise it, am I to assume Hattie sleeps outside?"

"Hattie?" Rayford said.

"Yeah. Remember her? No seal on her forehead, but fairly visible here until you all get spiritual? Where does she sleep?"

Chloe sighed. "Go to bed, Dad. I'll show her."

"Thank you!"

They turned to head down the stairs.

Rayford couldn't resist. "You can be obnoxious, Mrs. Rose, you know that?"

"Daddy!" Chloe said, her back still to him. "We deserved that and you know it."

Leah stopped and turned to face him. "I respect everyone here," she said. "But that was sexist. You'll call me a feminist, but you would not tell a man, insulted like I was, that his response was obnoxious."

"I probably would," Rayford said. "But the point is taken."

"Thanks for making me feel like a creep," Leah said. "I spoke to your son-in-law earlier in a way I have rarely spoken to anyone. And now I've done it again. I don't know what's happening to me."

Rayford felt exactly the same but didn't care to admit it. "Promise me tomorrow we can discuss a truce," he said.

"That's a deal."

The women descended, and Rayford was finally able to get to bed. He hung his robe and lay back on the cool sheets, feeling morning-after soreness from his work in the cellar and the backyard, and it wasn't even morning yet. He locked his fingers behind his head and within minutes felt himself drifting—until he heard footsteps on the stairs, then a knock at his door.

"I was showing Leah the cellar," Chloe said, "where Hattie sleeps. Only she's not there."

"Hattie?"

"Where could she be? She's not in the house. Not outside as far as we can see. And, Dad, a lot of her stuff is gone. She took a heavy load."

Rayford rose and pulled on his robe again, wondering if he had the energy to deal with yet one more crisis before collapsing. "Check the shed for Ken's car. Make sure Buck's is still in the yard. She couldn't get far on foot. Buck and I can each take a vehicle and start looking for her."

"Dad, we have no idea when she left. She might have been gone since the burial. I don't remember seeing her since, do you?"

He shook his head. "We can't let her out of here with all she knows."

"Talk about vulnerable. If she got someone to pick her up somewhere, you'll never catch her."

They followed footprints to what had once been the street in front of the house. Now it was just a dirt path strewn with chunks of asphalt and dotted with potholes. She could have headed either direction. Rayford fired up Ken Ritz's Suburban, and Buck threw dirt from all four wheels on his Land Rover. He sent Buck north and headed south.

When it became clear Hattie was nowhere in Rayford's vicinity, he called Buck. "Nothing here either," Buck said. "I've got a bad feeling about this. It's not like we can report her missing."

"I've got one other idea," Rayford said. "I'll see you back at the house."

Rayford called Palwaukee and reached the answering machine. He said, "T, this is Ray. If you're there, I need you to pick up." He waited a few moments, then reluctantly dialed Delanty's personal cell phone. Rayford was greeted with a groggy hello.

"Sorry, T. Did I wake you?"

"Of course you did. 'Sup, Ray? I don't want this to be an emergency, but if it's not I'm gonna ask why you called now."

Rayford filled him in. "So I was just wondering if Tweedledee and Tweedledum are still kicking around out there."

"Ernie and Bo? Haven't seen Ernie for almost a year. Kind of miss him, even if he was an idiot. I heard he headed west. Beauregard Hanson still hangs around trying to exercise his 5-percent stake in the place. Why?"

"Just wondering if Hattie might have used him to get somebody to fly her out of there."

"I left at six. Had a guy in the tower till nine. We shut down after that."

"Any way I can find out if a big plane left there this evening?"

"Ray, I can't call a guy at this time of the morning and ask him that."

"Why not? I just did."

"Yeah, but you were pretty sure I wouldn't hate you for it."

"Don't you?"

"I'm not allowed to say. We're brothers, remember?"

"Speaking of that, you're the only 'brother' brother I've got left, if you catch my meaning."

"What?"

Rayford told him about Doc.

"Oh, man! I'm sorry, Ray. You don't suspect Hattie . . . ?"

Ray told him Floyd's own theory on how he contracted the poison. "But still, I've got dire reasons to know where she is."

"I'll check the log."

"I don't want you to go out at this hour."

"I can do it from here, bro. Just a minute."

Rayford heard T's bed squeak and then computer sounds. He came back on the phone. "I'm scrolling through here. Not much traffic tonight. Mostly small stuff, business planes, couple of GC. Hmm."

"What?"

"There *is* a unique entry here. Oversized Quantum, that's like a huge Learjet, different manufacturer, arrived pilot only at 2230. Left 2330 hours with a fuel top-off, no cargo, one unidentified passenger, destination unreported."

"That's all?"

"Well, we've got a column here that asks whether it was paid, charged, or OK'd. This one was OK'd by BH."

"I don't know the specs on the Quantum," Rayford said. "What kind of speed and range?"

"Oh, fast as a heavy but probably needs one more top-off before going overseas. How far you figure your escapee's going anyway?"

"I wouldn't put it past her to think she can march into Carpathia's office and personally give him what for. Well, there'll be no catching or intercepting that craft, will there?"

"Nope. What is it, almost one? That thing's been airborne, I assume at maximum speed, an hour and a half. Even with twenty minutes on the east coast for landing, fuel, and takeoff, it's still gonna be too far away by now."

"You got enough information that I could radio the craft?"

"Think about it, Rayford. Whoever's flying that plane is not going to answer unless he knows who's calling."

"Maybe I could spin him a yarn, urge him to put down in Spain due to a fuel irregularity or something that turned up here or wherever he refueled."

"You're dreaming, Ray. And I'd like to be."

"Thanks for nothing, friend."

"You're going to have to go round her up yourself or turn some of your contacts onto her over there."

"I know. I appreciate it, T. I'll try to get out to the strip for some co-op business tomorrow."

"Today, you mean?"

"Sorry," Rayford said.

"I might bring a couple of people from our house church. We want to get behind this thing in a big way."

For all Rayford knew, Hattie had the power to blow the lid off the co-op, too.

+ + +

Mac McCullum had a full morning. After tipping his cap to Annie Christopher as he passed her office in the hangar, he arrived at his own office to three messages. The first was a list generated by Leon Fortunato's secretary, outlining personnel authorized on the flight to Botswana in three days. The supreme commander, his valet, an assistant, a cook, and two servers would make up the GC contingent. Two aides would accompany President Ngumo of Botswana. "Note that the Supreme Commander has decreed that the plane shall be stationary while the Botswanians are aboard."

The list also included captain and first officer in the cockpit, with an asterisk after the latter. At the bottom of the page the asterisk referred to a note: "The Supreme Commander believes you will be pleased by the resolution of this matter."

Mac was. The second document was a note from Personnel regarding the application of Abdullah Smith for Condor 216 first officer. Not only had he been ranked high in every technical aspect save verbal acuity ("Somewhat laconic" read the summary), but he had also been judged "an outstanding citizen, loyal to the Global Community."

Fortunato himself had scribbled in the margin, "Congratulations on a wonderful find, Mac. Smith will make a great contribution to the cause! S. C. L. F."

If you only knew, Mac thought.

Mac's third missive was from David Hassid. "Important message for you, Captain," it read. "In person, please."

Mac and David had learned to appear impersonal and professional in front of staff. Their difference in age helped. The entire GC complex, though ostensibly antimilitary because of Carpathia's avowed pacifism, was pseudomilitary in its organizational structure. Mac felt comfortable with the chain of command, having spent so much of his life in uniform. And David often deferred to Mac's counsel because David had come to the GC from the private sector. Now the two were on equal footing in separate branches, and it appeared their occasional face-to-faces attracted no attention.

David's secretary ushered Mac into David's office. "Captain," David said, shaking his hand.

"Director," Mac said, sitting.

When the secretary left, David said, "Get this," and turned around his laptop so Mac could read it. The captain squinted at the screen and read Rayford's account of the previous day's activities at the safe house in Illinois. "Oh, man," he said, "that doctor. The girl lives, the doctor dies. Beat that."

"It gets worse," David said.

Mac reached the news of Hattie's disappearance. He settled back in his chair. "Does he really think—"

David held up a finger to stall him. "Let me get rid of this while I'm thinking of it." With a few keystrokes the heavily encrypted file had been trashed. "That she'll come here? I can't imagine. I understand she's ditzy, but how far does she think she'll get? It's a miracle she survived this long with all the things Carpathia has tried to get rid of her. She shows her face in New Babylon, she's history."

Mac nodded. "She's got to be holing up somewhere, waiting to surprise him."

"I can't see her getting close."

Mac shook his head. "I know. Your people loaded two sets of metal detectors on the two-one-six last week."

"Plan is to use them even for dignitaries. 'Course, that's due to a basic distrust of Pete Two, you know."

"I know firsthand. Fortunato's got all ten kings, excuse me, regional international subpotentates—or whatever Saint Nick is allowing them to call themselves this week—primed for that snuffing. It's almost like he wants them willing to do the deed themselves."

"Like those guys would agree on anything," David said. "How many of 'em you think are really loyal to Carpathia?"

Mac shrugged. "More than half. Not more than seven, though. I know three who would usurp given half a chance."

"Would they take him out?"

"In a New Babylon minute. 'Course, Pete would too."

"You think?"

Mac sat forward and pressed his palms together. "I've heard him say it. He rubs Carpathia raw with his brashness, but he pretends to be cooperative. Carpathia makes nice with him all the time, as if they handpicked each other. I'll tell you what: if Leon doesn't get rid of Mathews soon, he's going to have to answer. It's a directive clear as if it were on paper."

David stood and pulled some files from a drawer behind him, then spread them on the desk. "In case anyone's watching," he said, and Mac leaned over as if studying them.

"They're upside-down, you idiot," Mac said, controlling his smile.

"Wouldn't want to be distracted," David said.

"You know what Rayford used to dream out loud?"

"Tell me."

"Crashing on purpose with Carpathia aboard."

David straightened and cocked his head. "That's not even biblical, is it? I mean, if he's who we think he is, he's not going to die till the forty-second month, is he? And even then he doesn't stay dead."

"I'm just telling you."

"Doesn't even sound like Captain Steele. He always seemed so even and sensible."

"Didn't mean to spoil your image of him."

"Believe me, you didn't. I can't deny I've fantasized about how I'd do it."

Mac stood and headed to the door. "Same here," he said.

6

EMOTIONAL TURMOIL took as much out of Buck as did physical labor. Often, after toiling all day with Rayford and Floyd in the underground shelter, he had trouble falling asleep. But now he had taken to bed his grief over Floyd, fear of how Hattie could imperil the Tribulation Force, and dread over the strange behavior of his father-in-law. Buck was exhausted beyond measure. Lying next to his damaged but resilient wife, he fought to stay awake and listen to her.

He and Chloe had so little time to talk anymore, despite spending most of their days in the same house. She lamented not being as involved as she once had, housebound with the baby, slowed by her injuries from the earthquake.

"But no one else could do what you're doing with the co-op, babe," he said. "Imagine the millions who will depend on you for their lives."

"But I'm on the periphery," she said. "I spent most of today comforting you and Daddy and taking care of the baby."

"We needed you."

"I have needs too, Buck."

He draped his arm across her. "Want me to watch Kenny so you can go with your dad to see T tomorrow? They're talking co-op business."

"I'd love that."

Buck thought he had responded. He had meant to. But when Chloe removed his arm from her and turned away, he realized he had drifted off. She had said something more; he was aware of that now. He tried to muster the energy to force his eyes open and apologize, finish the conversation. But the more he tried, the more jumbled his thoughts became. Desperate that he was missing a huge opportunity to be to his wife what she needed him to be, he slipped over the edge of consciousness.

+ + +

Late in the afternoon in New Babylon, David was urgently ordered to the office of Global Community Supreme Commander Leon Fortunato. Leon's opulent quarters comprised the entire seventeenth floor of the new palace, only one below His Excellency, the potentate's.

Though David reported directly to him, a face-to-face with Fortunato had become rare. The organization chart, as Mac had mentioned more than once, had to look like a spaghetti bowl. Ostensibly, Carpathia himself had only one subordinate—besides his secretary and the ever-present gaggle of obsequious lackeys—and that was Fortunato. But the entire administrative wing of the palace was filled with sycophants who dressed like the potentate and the supreme commander, walked like them, talked like them, and bowed and scraped in their presence.

David, the youngest member of the management staff, seemed to have garnered the respect of the brass with what appeared only appropriate deference. But for the moment, he was in trouble.

As soon as Fortunato's door was shut, before David could even sit in the gargantuan room, Leon started in on him. "I want to know where those computers are and why they aren't being installed as we speak."

"The, uh, gross of—"

"The biggest single shipment of hardware since we equipped the castle—excuse me, the palace," Leon said, planting his meaty frame in the thronelike leather chair behind his desk. "You know what I'm talking about. The more you hem and haw, the more suspicious—"

"No, sir, of course I know. We took delivery of those yesterday and—"

"Where are they?"

"—they're not in position to be directly moved into th—"

"What's wrong with them?" Leon barked, and finally pointed to a chair.

David sat. "It's a technical thing, sir."

"A glitch?"

"It's a, an orienting problem. Positioning renders them inoperative in the palace."

Leon glared at him. "Do they need to be replaced?"

"That would be the only solution, yes, sir."

"Then replace them. You understand me, don't you, Director Hassid?"

"Yes, sir."

"You get my drift?"

"Sir?"

"When I get exercised, you understand it's not just me?"

"I know, yes, sir."

"His Excellency is eager that I—you—that we get a handle on this. He has confidence, because I assured him he could, that you will complete this assignment."

"We will get that equipment installed as soon as humanly possible."

Leon shook his head. "I'm not talking about just the blamed installation! I'm talking about tracing the opposition."

"Of course."

"His Excellency is a pacifist, as you know. But he also knows the only power a man of peace has is information. That's why he monitors those two crazy preachers in Jerusalem. Their day will come. They have admitted as much themselves. And sympathetic as he is to variant views, a small but influential faction has the attention of those rebellious to the new world order. Would you not agree?"

"Agree, sir?"

Fortunato looked frustrated. "That His Excellency has reason to be concerned about this Ben-Judah character and his own former publisher, who is spewing anti-GC propaganda!"

"Oh, yes, absolutely. Dangerous. I mean, if there were just small pockets of these types out there, who cares? But, they seem to have rallied under the banner of—"

"Exactly. And they're harboring the mother of His Excellency's child. She must be found before she tries to abort, or worse, reveal information that could damage . . ."

Leon let his thought trail off. "Anyway," he said, "replace that order or fix that orientation or whatever problem, and get people on this."

+ + +

Buck was grateful to have awakened before Chloe. He kissed her cheek and straightened her blankets. He left a note on the bedside table: "Sorry I drifted off. Go with your dad today. I'll cover here. I love you."

He padded to the kitchen, where Tsion sat alone, shoulders hunched, eating breakfast. "Cameron!" he whispered. "If I had known you were coming, I would have fixed something for you."

"No need. Gonna get a head start on my writing so I can watch the baby." Cameron poured himself a glass of juice and leaned against the counter. "Chloe's going with Ray to see T about the co-op."

Tsion nodded wearily. "I miss Floyd. I knew something had to be wrong when he did not get up with me yesterday." He sighed. "Doc had a good mind. Many questions."

"I don't have that mind, but I do have questions. You were working on your commentary about the second woe, the sixth Trumpet Judgment."

"Which I am late on," Tsion said. "With everything that happened, I was unable to post it yesterday. I hope to have it done this morning. And I hope my absence for a day did not cause panic among the audience."

"Everybody prays you will not be taken off the Net."

"David Hassid assures me we can stay ahead of Carpathia technologically. Yet when he explains how he bounces our signal from satellite to satellite and cell to cell, I am lost. I just thank God he knows what he is doing."

Buck rinsed out his glass. "You were wrestling with something yesterday."

"I still am," Tsion said. "For centuries scholars believed prophetic literature was figurative, open to endless interpretation. That could not have been what God intended. Why would he make it so difficult? I believe when the Scriptures say the writer saw something in a vision, it *is* symbolic of something else. But when the writer simply says that certain things happen, I take those literally. So far I have been proven right.

"The passage I am working on, where John sees—in a vision—200 million horsemen who have the power to slay a third of the remaining population, seems by necessity figurative. I doubt these men and animals will be literal beings, but I believe their impact will be very real nonetheless. They will indeed slay a third of the population."

Buck squinted, and the teacher looked away. "This is a new one," Buck said. "You really don't know, do you?"

Tsion shook his head. "Yet I feel a great responsibility for the readers God has entrusted to me. I do not want to get ahead of him, but neither do I want to hang back in fear. All I can do is to be honest about how I am tussling with this. It is time many of these believers start interpreting the Scriptures for themselves anyway."

"When is this judgment supposed to happen?"

"All we know for sure is that it comes next chronologically and that it must occur before the midpoint of the Tribulation. Unless God himself makes it happen in an instant, it appears it could take several weeks."

Tsion had, the day before, merely transmitted the scriptural passage he would comment on the next day. Running the body of text alone resulted in the largest cyberspace audience in history, awaiting Dr. Ben-Judah's fearful teaching on Revelation 9:15-21:

> *So the four angels, who had been prepared for the hour and day and month and year, were released to kill a third of mankind.*
>
> *Now the number of the army of the horsemen was two hundred million; I heard the number of them.*
>
> *And thus I saw the horses in the vision: those who sat on them had*

breastplates of fiery red, hyacinth blue, and sulfur yellow; and the heads of the horses were like the heads of lions; and out of their mouths came fire, smoke, and brimstone.

By these three plagues a third of mankind was killed—by the fire and the smoke and the brimstone which came out of their mouths.

For their power is in their mouth and in their tails; for their tails are like serpents, having heads; and with them they do harm.

But the rest of mankind, who were not killed by these plagues, did not repent of the works of their hands, that they should not worship demons, and idols of gold, silver, brass, stone, and wood, which can neither see nor hear nor walk.

And they did not repent of their murders or their sorceries or their sexual immorality or their thefts.

✣ ✣ ✣

David returned to his office conflicted by the fear Leon had engendered and the thrill of having toyed with the man once again. From his laptop, ignoring a flashing Message sign, he ordered another gross of the computers, directing that they be delivered to the palace airstrip. No sense drawing further suspicion. He could thwart whatever his experts detected by planting viruses in the equipment or merely misinterpreting their findings.

✣ ✣ ✣

Buck sat with the others at a meeting of the stateside Tribulation Force at 11 a.m. Tuesday. He reported he'd just gotten word from David that Abdullah Smith was to be Mac's new first officer. Rayford raised a fist of celebration.

Then Rayford said, "A couple of updates. We're getting the word to people we trust to keep an eye out for Hattie. She can do us more harm than anyone I can think of. I'm calling a break on work in the cellar for a day. Chloe and I are meeting with T this afternoon. All right, Mrs. Rose, the floor is yours."

Leah stood to speak, which seemed to surprise the others as much as it did Buck. They scooted their chairs back to soften the angle as they looked up at her. She spoke softly and seemed more self-conscious than when she had met them the night before. Her story came in a monotone, as if she were covering her emotions.

"I gather that you people were fairly normal before the Rapture, except that you weren't believers. I was messed up. I grew up in a home where my dad was an alcoholic, my mother a manic-depressive. My parents' fights were the neighborhood entertainment until they divorced when I was twelve. Within three years I smoked, drank, slept around, did drugs, and nearly killed myself more than once. I had an abortion when I was seventeen and then tried to drink away the horror of it. I dropped out of school and lived in a friend's apartment. I consumed more booze and dope than food, and when I found myself wandering the streets and passing blood in the middle of the night, I came to the end of myself.

"I knew I was a bum and that if I didn't do something about it, I would soon be dead. I didn't want that because I had no idea what came next. I prayed when I was really in trouble, but most of the time I didn't even think about God. I went into a free county rehab center and wondered if I dared live without junk in my system. When I finally began to think rationally, the people there discovered I had a brain and had me tested. I had a high IQ, go figure, and proclivities—whatever that meant—for the sciences.

"I was so grateful to those people that it sparked in me some latent soft spot for the needy. I got back into school, graduated a year late with almost straight A's, and worked as a nurse's aide and a signer for deaf students to pay for community college. I met my husband there, and he put me through state school and a nursing program. I was unable to bear children, so after about six years of marriage we adopted two boys."

As soon as she tried to say their names, Leah clouded over and could barely speak. "Peter and Paul," she whispered. "My husband had been raised in a religious home and, though he hadn't gone to church for years, had always wanted sons with those names. We wanted to expose the boys to church, so we started going. The people were nice, but it might as well have been a country club. Lots of social activities, but we didn't feel any closer to God.

"At the hospital where I worked one of the chaplains tried to convert me. Though he seemed sincere, I was offended. And the woman who ran the day care center our boys went to gave me literature about Jesus. I assured her we went to church. I was incensed when my sons came home with Bible stories. I called the woman and told her they went to Sunday school and that I wished she'd stick to just watching them."

Leah's voice was husky with emotion. "I found my boys' beds empty the morning after the Rapture. It was the worst day of my life. I was convinced they had been kidnapped. The police couldn't do anything, of course, because all children were gone. I hadn't heard of the Rapture, but it was quickly put forth on the news as one of the possibilities. I called the hospital chaplain, but he had disappeared. I called the day care center, but the director had vanished too. I raced over there, but no one knew anything. In a rack in the waiting room I found more pamphlets like the ones the director had given me. One, titled

'Don't Be Left Behind,' said that someday true believers would disappear into heaven with Jesus.

"That was in my purse when I got home and discovered my husband in the garage with the door shut and his car running." Leah paused and collected herself. "He had left me a note, saying he was sorry but that he was frightened out of his mind, couldn't live without the boys, and knew he had no answer to my grief."

Leah stopped, her lips trembling.

"Do you need a break, dear?" Tsion asked.

She shook her head. "I tried to kill myself. I swallowed everything in the medicine cabinet and made myself violently ill. God must not have wanted me dead, because apparently much of what I ingested countered whatever else I took. I awoke hours later with a horrible headache, stomachache, and rancid taste. I crawled to my purse to find some mints and came across that pamphlet again. Somehow it finally made sense.

"It predicted what had happened and warned the reader to be ready. The solution—well, you know this—was to seek God, to tell him I knew I was a sinner and that I needed him. I didn't know if it was too late for me, but I prayed just in case. I don't know how I found the energy, but as soon as I could get myself out of the house, I looked for other people like me. I found them in a little church. Only a few had been left behind, but they knew why. Now there are about sixty who meet in secret. I'm going to miss those people, but they won't be surprised I've disappeared. I told them what was going on, that I had treated a GC fugitive and all."

"We'll get word to them that you're safe," Rayford said, clearly overcome.

"*Am* I safe?" Leah said, sitting down with a sad smile. "Do I get to stay?"

"We always vote," Tsion said. "But I think you have found a home."

* * *

Early in the evening in New Babylon, David sat in his office after hours, missing Annie. Being alone with her was risky, so they spent time on their secure phones and computers. He built into his unit the capability to erase both their transmissions, to serve as a backup if she forgot. He couldn't imagine that either of them would forget to remove from their computers evidence of their relationship and especially their faith.

"Maybe we should reveal our love," she transmitted. "By policy I would be forced to move to a department outside your supervision, but at least we could see each other without suspicion."

He tapped back: "It's not a bad idea, and we could use another pair of eyes in other departments. Where you are right now is strategic, though, because of what we can smuggle out of here and into believers' hands in other countries. Keep thinking, though. I can't stand being apart from you."

Suddenly the TV monitors in his area—all of them—came on. That happened only when GC brass believed something was on that every employee would want to see. Most of the time it meant that Carpathia or Fortunato was addressing the world, and it didn't make any difference whether anyone in a sector was working. If there was a TV there, it came on.

David spun in his chair and leaned back to watch the monitor in his office. A GC CNN anchorman was reporting a plane crash. "While neither the plane itself, reportedly a large private aircraft, nor the pilot or passenger have been sighted, personal belongings have washed ashore in Portugal. Listen to this Mayday call, recorded by several tracking stations in the region."

Mayday! Mayday! Quantum zero-seven-zero-eight losing altitude! Mayday!

"Radar trackers lost sight of the craft soon thereafter, and rescuers searched the area. Luggage and personal effects of two people, a man and a woman, were discovered. Authorities assume it will be just a matter of time before the wreckage and bodies are discovered. Names of the victims are being withheld pending notification of next of kin."

David squinted at the screen, wondering why GC brass thought this newsworthy until the victims were known. Then the internal caption scrawl appeared on the screen:

ATTENTION GC PALACE PERSONNEL. PROBABLE VICTIMS IN THIS CRASH, ACCORDING TO RESCUE AUTHORITIES, ARE AS FOLLOWS: PILOT SAMUEL HANSON OF BATON ROUGE, LOUISIANA, UNITED STATES OF NORTH AMERICA, AND HATTIE DURHAM, ORIGINALLY OF DES PLAINES, ILLINOIS, U.S.N.A. MS. DURHAM ONCE SERVED HIS EXCELLENCY THE POTENTATE AS PERSONAL ASSISTANT. CONDOLENCES TO THOSE WHO KNEW HER.

David phoned Mac. "I saw," Mac said. "What an obvious fake!"

"Yeah!" David said. "The pilot must be cashing in a huge insurance policy, and Hattie has to be somewhere in Europe."

"Maybe they're shopping for more Stupid pills," Mac said. "Are we supposed to believe Carpathia and Fortunato fell for this?"

"Surely not," David said. "Unless they engineered it. Maybe they found

Hattie and had her killed, and now they're covering. They'd better come up with wreckage or bodies."

David heard the ping that told him he had a new message. "I'll get back to you, Mac."

\+ + +

Rayford and Chloe sat in T's office at the base of the Palwaukee tower with T and two men from his house church. Chloe outlined how she planned to link the major players on the co-op network and start testing the system before actual buying and selling got under way. "We have to keep it secret from the beginning," she said. "Otherwise we'll be grouped with all other commodities brokers and put under the GC's aegis."

The others nodded. Rayford's phone beeped. It was Buck. Rayford laughed aloud as Buck recounted the strange news report. "Turn on the TV, T," he said. GC commentators mournfully discussed the tragedy, though names had not been revealed outside New Babylon and so far nothing but papers and belongings had been found. Rayford shook his head. "Someday Fortunato, or whoever tried to take advantage of this, is going to embarrass himself beyond repair."

Chloe tugged at his sleeve and whispered. "At least we can be pretty sure Hattie's all right for now."

"The question," he said as the meeting broke up, "is where she is. She's not smart enough to get any thinking person to believe she went down in that plane. Could she still surprise Carpathia?"

When the churchmen were gone, Rayford, Chloe, and T jogged upstairs to quiz the tower man about the 11:30 flight the night before. He was fat and balding, reading a science fiction book.

"Sounded southern to me on the radio, though I never saw him," the man said. "Bo signed off on the landing and takeoff."

"He was here?" T said.

"No, he called me about eight to preapprove it."

"I didn't see the plane's numbers on the computer."

"I wrote 'em down. I can still enter 'em." He rummaged under a pile of papers. "Oh-seven-oh-eight," he said. "And I guess you know it was a Quantum."

"Can we find out who that's registered to?" Rayford said.

"Sure can," the man said. He banged away at his computer keyboard and drummed his knee as the information was retrieved. "Hm," he said, reading. "Samuel Hanson out of Baton Rouge. He's got to be related to Bo, doesn't he? Isn't Bo from Louisiana?"

7

REUNITING WITH ABDULLAH Smith warmed Mac. In his earliest days as first officer to Captain Rayford Steele, Mac had met the former fighter pilot from Jordan. Abdullah had lost his job when Carpathia confiscated international weaponry, but he quickly became one of Rayford's leading black market suppliers.

Abdullah had been disgraced four years before the Rapture when his wife had become a Christian. He divorced her and fought for custody of their two small children, a boy and a girl. When he could not get relief from months of travel at a time for the Jordanian air force, he was denied custody and took up full-time residence at the military base.

A man of few words, Abdullah had once revealed to Mac and Rayford that he was heartsick to the point of suicide. "I still loved my wife," he said with his thick accent. "She and the children were my world. But imagine *your* wife taking up a religion from some mysterious, faraway country. We wrote long letters to each other, but neither could be dissuaded. To my shame, I was not devout in my own religion and fell into loose morals. My wife said she prayed for me every day that I would find Jesus Christ before it was too late. I cursed her in my letters. One sentence pleaded with her to renounce the myths and return to the man who loved her. The next accused her of treachery and called her despicable names. Her next letter told me she still loved me and reminded me that it was I who had initiated the divorce. Again, in my anger, I lashed out at her.

"I still have the letters in which she warned me that I might die before finding the one true God, or that Jesus could return for those who loved him, and I would be left behind. I was enraged. Just to get back at her I often refused to visit my children, but now I realize I hurt only them and myself. I feel so guilty that they might not know how much I loved them."

Mac recalled Rayford's telling Abdullah, "You will be able to tell them one day." Abdullah had merely nodded, his dark eyes moist and distant.

Abdullah became a believer because he saved his wife's letters. She had meticulously explained the plan of salvation, writing out Bible verses and telling him how she had prayed to receive Christ. "Many times I crumpled up the letters and threw them across the room," Abdullah said. "But something kept me from tearing them or burning them or throwing them away."

When Abdullah heard that his wife and children had disappeared, he had lain prostrate on the floor in his quarters in Amman, his wife's letters spread before him. "It had happened as she said it would," he said. "I cried out to God. I had no choice but to believe."

Because of his Middle Eastern look and his fondness for a turban and a blowsy, off-white top over camouflage trousers and aviator boots, the diminutive Jordanian was the last person anyone suspected of being a Christian. Until the conversion of the 144,000 Jewish witnesses from all over the world and their millions of converts of every nationality, most assumed they could identify a Christian. Now, of course, only true believers knew each other on sight, due to the mark visible only to them.

Abdullah, thin and dark with large, expressive features, was as quiet as Mac remembered him. He was also extremely formal in front of others, not giving away that he and Mac were both spiritual brothers and old friends. He didn't pretend they had not met, for Mac had concocted a former military connection. But they did not embrace until they were alone in Mac's office.

"There's someone I want you to meet," Mac said, calling Annie from her office. She knocked and entered, breaking into a smile.

"You must be the infamous Abdullah Smith," she said. "You have a custom mark reserved for Jordanians."

Abdullah gave Mac a puzzled look, then stared at Annie's forehead. "I cannot see mine," he said. "Is it not like yours?"

"I'm teasing you," she said. "Yours merely works better with your coloring."

"I see," he said, as if he really did.

"Go easy on the American humor," Mac said.

"Canadian humor," Annie said. She spread her arms to hug Abdullah, which seemed to embarrass him. He thrust out his hand, and she shook it. "Welcome to the family," she said.

Again Abdullah looked questioningly at Mac.

"Actually, *she's* the newest member of the family," Mac said. "She's just welcoming you to this chapter of the Tribulation Force."

Abdullah left some of his stuff in his small office behind Mac's, then two laborers from Operations helped take the rest to his new quarters. As he and Abdullah followed the men, Mac said, "Once you get unpacked you can get your feet wet by plotting our course to Botswana Friday. We'll leave here at 0800, and they're an hour earlier, so—"

"Johannesburg, I assume," Abdullah said.

"No, north of there. We're seeing Mwangati Ngumo in Gaborone on the old border of Botswana and South Af—"

"Oh, pardon me, Captain, but you must not have been there recently. Only helicopters can get in and out of Gaborone. The airport was destroyed in the great earthquake."

"But surely the old military base—"

"The same," Abdullah said.

"Carpathia's reconstruction program has not reached Botswana?"

"No, but with the . . . the, pardon me, regional potentate of the United States of Africa residing in Johannesburg in a palace not much smaller than this one, the new airport there is spectacular."

Mac thanked the helpers and unlocked Abdullah's apartment. The Jordanian's eyes widened as he surveyed the rooms. "All of this for me?" he said.

"You'll grow to hate it," Mac said.

With the door shut, Abdullah looked at the bare walls and whispered, "Can we talk here?"

"David assures me we can."

"I look forward to meeting him. Oh, Captain, I nearly referred to the African potentate as the king! I must be so careful."

"Well, *we* know he's one of the kings, but those two wouldn't have had a clue. I thought Potentate Rehoboth—what's his first name—?"

"Bindura."

"Right—was going to move his capital more central, like back up to his homeland. Chad, was it?"

"Sudan. That was what he had said, but apparently he found Johannesburg preferable. He lives in such opulence, you could not believe it."

"All the kings do."

"What do you make of that, Captain?" Abdullah was whispering. "Has Carpathia bought their cooperation?"

Mac shrugged and shook his head. "Wasn't there some sort of controversy between Rehoboth and Ngumo?"

"Oh, yes! When Ngumo was secretary-general of the U.N., Rehoboth put tremendous pressure on him to get favors for Africa, particularly Sudan. And when Ngumo was replaced by Carpathia, Rehoboth publicly praised the change."

"And now he's his neighbor."

"And Rehoboth is his king," Abdullah said.

\+ + +

Late Thursday night in Illinois, Rayford finally found himself alone in the kitchen with Leah Rose. She sat at the table with a cup of coffee. He poured himself one.

"Settling in?" he said.

She cocked her head. "I never know what you're implying."

He pointed to a chair. "May I?"

"Sure."

He sat. "What would I be implying?"

"That I shouldn't get too comfortable."

"We voted you in! It was unanimous. Even the chair voted, and I didn't have to."

"Had it been a tie otherwise, how would the chair have voted?"

Rayford sat back, his cup in both hands. "We got off on the wrong foot," he said. "I'm sure it was my fault."

"You ignored my question," she said.

"Stop it. Voting in a new sister would never result in a tie. Hattie was here for months, and she's not even a believer."

"So is this our truce chat, or are you just being polite?"

"You want a truce?" he said.

"Do you?"

"I asked you first," he said.

She smiled. "Truth is, I want more than a truce. We can't live in the same house just being cordial. We've got to be friends."

Rayford wasn't so sure, but he said, "I'm game."

"So all that stuff you said . . ."

He raised his chin. ". . . that exposed me for the crank I am?"

She nodded. "Consider this an all-inclusive pardon."

He hadn't asked forgiveness.

"And for me?" she pressed.

"What?"

"I need a pardon too."

"No you don't," he said, sounding more magnanimous than he felt. "Anything you said was because of what I—"

Leah put a hand on his arm. "I didn't even recognize myself," she said. "I can't put that all on you. Now, come on. If we're going to start over, we have to be even. Clean slates."

"Granted," he said.

"I've got money," she said.

"You always switch subjects so fast?"

"Cash. We'd have to go get it. It's in a safe in my garage. I am not going to be a freeloader. I want things to do, and I want to pay my way."

"How about we give you room and board in exchange for medical care and expertise?"

"I'm more about care than expertise. I'm no replacement for Floyd."

"We're grateful to have you."

"But you need money, too. When can we get it?"

Rayford pointed to her cup. She shook her head. "How much are we talking about?" he said.

When she told him, he gasped.

"In what denominations?"

"Twenties."

"All in one safe?"

"I couldn't fit another bill in there," she said.

"You think it's still there? The GC must have torn the place apart looking for you."

"The safe is so well hidden we had to remind ourselves where it was."

Rayford rinsed out the cups. "Sleepy?" he said.

"No."

"Want to go now?"

\+ + +

Mac and Abdullah met with David Friday morning. Once introductions were out of the way, David asked if either had an idea where the 144 computers in the Condor cargo hold could be put to use for the cause.

"I can think of lots of places," Mac said. "But not one on the way to Africa."

"I can," Abdullah said. "There is a huge body of underground believers in Hawalli. Many professionals, and they could—"

"Hawalli?" David said. "In Kuwait?"

"Yes. I have a contact in cargo—"

"That's east. You're flying southwest."

"Only slightly east," Abdullah said. "We just need a reason to stop there."

"Virtually right after takeoff," Mac said. "That'll arouse suspicion." They sat in silence a moment. "Unless . . . ," he said.

David and Abdullah looked at him.

"How far is our flight?"

"Here to Kuwait?" Abdullah asked, pulling out his charts.

"No, to Africa."

"More than four thousand miles."

"Then we need a full fuel load to go nonstop. We want to save the GC money, so we're going to make a quick detour for fuel at a good price."

"Excellent," David said. "I'll negotiate it right now. All I need is a few cents' break per pound of fuel and it'll be worth the detour."

"What will my contact need to get the cargo?" Abdullah said.

"Big forklift. Big truck."

\+ \+ \+

"Why'd you leave a note?" Leah asked Rayford as he pulled the Land Rover away from the house toward Palatine. "Surely we'll be back before anyone wakes up."

"It wouldn't surprise me," he said, "if someone was peeking at the note already. We hear everything in that house. In the dead of night we hear sounds in the walls, sounds from outside. We've been fortunate so far. We only hope for some warning so we can hide out below before we're found out. We always tell each other where we go. Buck didn't the other day when he rushed Floyd to see you, but that was an emergency. It upset everybody."

Rayford spent the next forty minutes maneuvering around debris and seeking the smoothest man-made route. He wondered when Carpathia's vaunted reconstruction efforts would reach past the major cities and into the suburbs.

Leah was full of questions about each member of the Trib Force, how they had met, become believers, got together. "That's way too much loss in too short a time," she said after he had brought her to the present. "With all that stress, it's a wonder you're all fully functioning."

"We try not to think about it. We know it's going to get worse. It sounds like a cliché, but you have to look ahead rather than back. If you let it accumulate, you'll never make it."

Leah ran a hand through her hair. "Sometimes I don't know why I want to survive until the Glorious Appearing. Then my survival instinct kicks in."

"Speaking of which . . . ," Rayford said.

"What?"

"More traffic than I'm used to is all."

She shrugged. "This area wasn't as hard hit as yours. No one's hiding here. Everybody knows everybody else."

They agreed Rayford should park a couple of blocks away and that they should move through the shadows to Leah's town house. He pulled a large canvas bag and a flashlight from the back of the Rover.

At the edge of her property, Leah stopped. "They didn't even shut the door," she said. "The place has to be ransacked."

"If the GC didn't trash it, looters did," Rayford said. "Once they knew you were on the run, your place was fair game. Want to check it out?"

She shook her head. "We'd better be in and out of that garage fast too. My neighbors can hear the door going up."

"Is there a side entrance?"

She nodded.

"Got the key?"

"No."

"I can break in. No one will hear unless they're in there waiting for you."

+ + +

When Mac met Abdullah in the hangar to bring him up to speed on the Condor 216, Annie was already there, supervising cargo handlers. "More, Corporal?" Mac said.

"Yes, Captain. The purchasing director would like us to transport this tonnage of surplus foodstuffs to Kuwait. He got a spectacular deal on fuel, so while you're taking on fuel, you can off-load this."

Abdullah was silent inside the plane until they reached the cockpit and Mac showed him the reverse intercom bug. "Imagine the methods of our dismemberment if they found out," he said.

At ten to eight in the morning, Mac and Abdullah finished their preflight checks and contacted the palace tower. Three figures in white aprons ran toward the plane. "Kitchen staff," Mac said. "Let 'em in."

Abdullah opened the door and lowered the stairs. The cook, a sweating middle-aged man with stubby fingers, carried a steaming pan covered with foil. "Out of the way, out of the way," he said in a Scandinavian accent. "Nobody told me the commander wanted breakfast aboard."

Abdullah stepped back as the cook and his two aides hurried past. "Then how did you know?" he said.

The cook hurried into the galley and barked orders. Distracted by Abdullah's hovering, he turned. "Was that rhetorical, sarcastic, or a genuine question?"

"I am not familiar with the first two," Abdullah said.

The cook leaned on the counter as if he couldn't believe he was about to waste his time answering the first officer. "I meant," he said slowly, as if indulging a child, "that no one told me before now, and then the supreme commander him*self* told me. If he's looking forward to eggs Benedict once airborne, it's eggs Benedict he'll get. Now, was there anything else?"

"Yes, sir."

The cook looked stunned. "There is?"

"Would you like to impress the supreme commander?"

"If I didn't I wouldn't have run to the plane with a tray of hot food, would I?"

"I happen to know Commander Fortunato does not mean airborne when he says airborne."

"Indeed?"

"No, you see, we have a brief stop in Kuwait after takeoff, and that would be the perfect time to serve him. Quieter, more relaxed, no danger of spilling."

"Kuwait?"

"Just moments after takeoff, really."

"Children!" the cook hollered to his aides. "Keep it hot. We're servin' breakfast in Kuwait!"

\+ + +

As Rayford expected, the side door to Leah's shared garage was flimsy enough to be forced open without a lot of racket. But when he crept inside and asked her to point out the safe, he was alone. Rayford caught himself before he called to her, not wanting to compound the situation if something was wrong. He turned slowly and tiptoed back to the door. At first Rayford didn't see her, but he heard her hyperventilating. She was kneeling near him in the moist grass and mud, her torso heaving with the strain of catching her breath. "I—I—I—," she gasped.

He crouched beside her. "What is it? Are you all right? See someone?"

She wouldn't look up, but in the darkness she fearfully pointed past Rayford. He took a good grip on the flashlight and whirled to see if someone was coming. He saw nothing.

"What did you see?" he said, but she was whimpering now, unable to say anything.

"Let me get you inside," he said.

Helping her up and getting her into the garage was like picking up a sleeping child. "Leah!" he said. "Work with me. You're safe."

She sat on the floor, pulling her knees up to her chest and hugging her legs. "Are they still out there?" she said. "Can you lock the door?"

"I broke the door," he said. "Who's out there?"

"You really didn't see them?"

"Who?" he whispered loudly. She was shivering. "You need to get off that cold floor."

He reached for her, but she wrenched away. "I won't be able to leave," she said, covering her face with trembling fingers. "You'll have to bring the car for me."

He hadn't expected her to be this high maintenance. "Too risky."

"I can't, Rayford! I'm sorry."

"Then let's get the money and get going."

"Forget the money. I wouldn't be able to work the lock now anyway."

"Why not?"

Again she pointed outside.

"Leah," Rayford said, as soothingly as he could, "there's nothing out there. We're safe. We're going to get your cash and go straight back to the car and go home, all right?"

She shook her head.

"Yes, we are," he said, and he grabbed her elbow and pulled her up. She was incapacitated. He guided her to the wall and gently pushed her back until it supported her. "Tell me what you saw."

"Horses," she said. "Huge, dark horses. On the ridge behind the house, blocking the whole horizon. I couldn't make out the riders because the horses breathed fire and smoke. But they just sat there, hundreds of them, maybe more, huge and menacing. Their faces! Rayford, their faces looked like lions with huge teeth!"

"Wait here," Rayford said.

"Don't leave me!" she said, grabbing his wrists, her fingers digging into flesh.

He peeled her hands away. "You're safe."

"Don't go near them! They're hovering."

"Hovering?"

"Their feet are not touching the ground!"

"Tsion didn't think they were real," Rayford said.

"Tsion saw them?"

"Didn't you read his message about this?"

"I don't have a computer anymore."

"These have to be the horsemen of Revelation 9, Leah! They won't hurt us!"

"Are you sure?"

"What else can they be?"

Leah seemed to begin breathing easier, but even in the faint glow of the flashlight, she was pale. "Let me go check," he said. "Think about the safe and the combination."

She nodded, but she didn't move. He hurried to the door. "To the east," she stage-whispered. "On the horizon." Though he felt he was safe, still he kept the door between him and the horizon. The night was cool and quiet. He saw nothing. He stepped away from the door and moved up a small incline, peeling his eyes to peer between buildings and into the open. His heart pounded, but he was disappointed he had not seen what Leah had. Had it been a vision? Why only to her?

He hurried back. She had moved away from the wall but was still not within sight of the door. "Did you see them?" she said.

"No."

"They were there, Rayford! I wasn't seeing things!"

"I believe you."

"Do you?"

"Of course! But Tsion said he didn't think they *would* be visible. He'll be glad to hear it."

"Where could they have gone? There were too many to move away that quickly."

"Leah," Rayford said carefully, "we're talking about the supernatural, good and evil, the battle of the ages. There are no rules, at least not human ones. If you saw the horsemen predicted in Revelation, who knows what power they might have to appear and disappear?"

She folded her arms and rocked. "I lived through the earthquake. I saw the locusts. Did you?"

He nodded.

"You got a close look, Rayford, really close?"

"T and I studied one."

"Then you know."

"I sure do."

"That was the most horrible thing I had ever seen. I didn't get as close a look at these, but they're monstrous. I could tell they were near the horizon, but they were so big I could see every detail. Are they not allowed to hurt us?"

"Tsion says they have the power to kill a third of the population."

"But not believers?"

Rayford shook his head. "They kill those who have not repented of their sin."

"If I didn't repent before, I do now!" she said.

+ + +

With the cook, his helpers, Fortunato, and his two aides aboard, Mac taxied out of the hangar and onto the airstrip south of the Global Community palace. Once airborne, he greeted the passengers over the intercom, informing them of the brief stop in Kuwait, then the four-thousand-plus mile flight to Johannesburg. Within seconds there came a loud rapping on the cockpit door.

"That would be Leon," Mac said, nodding for Abdullah to unlock the door. "It's time you met him anyway."

Leon ignored Abdullah. "What's with the stop in Kuwait, Captain? I have a schedule!"

"Good morning, Commander," Mac said. "Our new first officer assures me we will land in plenty of time for your meeting, sir. Abdullah Smith, meet Supreme C—"

"In due time," Fortunato said. "What's in Kuwait?"

"Two birds with one stone, sir," Mac said. "Director Hassid found a bargain on fuel, and our new cargo chief combined some deliveries, as long as we were headed that way. All told we've saved the administration thousands."

"You don't say."

"Yes, sir."

"And *your* name again, young man?"

"Abdullah Smith, sir."

"I'm hungry anyway. Could you use some eggs Benedict this morning, Officer Smith?"

"No, thank you, sir. I ate earlier."

"Captain McCullum, I would have appreciated knowing of the schedule change in advance."

"As I said, sir, it's really not a schedule change *per se.* Just a bit of a route ch—"

The door slapped shut. Abdullah looked at Mac with his brows raised. "Charming man," he said.

Mac depressed the button beneath his chair and listened to the cabin. "Karl, how are my eggs coming? Enough for all of us, yourself included?"

"Yes, sir, Supreme Commander, sir. I shall serve them on the ground—well, let me rephrase that. I shall serve them when we're on the ground temporarily in Kuwait."

"I'm hungry *now,* Karl."

"I'm sorry, sir. I was led to understand that you preferred the quiet and lack of bouncing around that might be afforded while we're refueling."

"Who told you that?"

"The first officer, sir."

"The new man? He doesn't even know me!"

"Well—"

"We'll see about this."

Mac clicked the button and turned a switch so he could speak directly from his mouthpiece to Abdullah's headset. In one breath he repeated what he had just heard.

"Thank you," Abdullah said as the door resounded yet again.

"Your name again, officer?" Leon said.

"Smith, sir."

"You told the cook to serve breakfast in Kuwait rather than in the air?"

"I merely informed him of our slight route change and suggested that you might appreciate it more if—"

"So it *was* your idea. *You* told *him* what you thought I'd like, yet you and I had never met."

"I take responsibility, sir. If I was out of order, I—"

"You were only exactly right there, Smith. I just wondered how you knew how much I hate trying to eat, especially a dish like that, while bouncing around up here. No offense, Mac—er, Captain."

Mac was tempted to call him Leon and tell him no offense taken. But he just waved. The Condor virtually flew itself, but Mac liked to give the impression, as Rayford liked to say, "of keepin' my eye on the road and my hand on the wheel."

"So, how *did* you know that, Officer Smith?" Leon said.

"I only assumed," he said. "I would not want egg yolk or hollandaise on my shirt in an important meeting."

At the ensuing silence, Mac turned to see if Fortunato had left. He had not. He looked overcome. He rocked back with his mouth open so wide his eyes were shut. He lurched forward with a hacking, coughing laugh and a slap on the shoulder that drove Abdullah back into his seat. "Now that's good!" Fortunato roared. "I like that!" And as he backed out of the cockpit, pulling the door shut behind him, he repeated, "Yolk or hollandaise on my shirt!"

Mac depressed the button again. "I did not intend to implicate the first officer," Karl was saying.

"Nonsense! Good idea! Serve us in Kuwait. How long will that be?"

"Just minutes actually, sir, is my understanding."

"Good. This way I'll go into my meeting with a clean shirt. You should have thought of that, Karl."

8

LEAH'S SAFE was hidden behind her sons' moldy pup tent high on a deck. Rayford helped her climb a perfectly vertical board ladder to it, then waited until she had pushed aside the tent and other junk. He followed and crouched behind her, aiming the light over her shoulder at the combination lock.

"How'd you get this thing up here?" he whispered. "It must weigh a ton."

"We didn't want the neighbors to know," she said, her voice still shaky. "We were in here late, like now. My husband, Shannon, had had the safe delivered in a plain box, and he rented a hydraulic scaffold. One neighbor asked what it was for, and Shannon told him it was for roof repairs in the garage. Seemed to satisfy him."

"So, once you got it up here, what, you two wrestled it into place?"

She nodded. "We worried the deck wouldn't hold it."

The safe was about three feet high and two feet wide, and Leah had not been joking when she said it was stuffed with cash. As she opened the door, she said, "We had to keep our other valuables at the bank."

The safe was crammed with bundles of twenties. "We could use this at the safe house," Rayford said.

"That's why we're here."

"I mean the safe itself. We could never accept all this cash. There aren't enough years left to spend it."

"Nonsense. You're going to need more vehicles, and you never know how many people might have to live with you."

They quickly stuffed the bag with the cash. "This is going to be too heavy to carry," he said. "Help me push it over the side."

They duckwalked and grunted and dragged the bag to the edge of the deck. The bundles shifted, but they were finally able to push the bag free. It plopped to the floor, with a thud, sending up a cloud of dust. Rayford turned off the flashlight and held his breath, listening. "Can you see me?" he whispered.

"Barely."

He signaled her to follow, and it was as difficult going down the boards as up. When he reached the floor he helped her the rest of the way.

"I suppose you think that makes you a gentleman," she whispered.

"Only if you're a lady."

They bent over the bag, feeling the edges in the dark for the best grip. A bright beam shined in their faces.

"Are you Mrs. Leah Rose?" a voice demanded.

She sighed and looked at Rayford. "Yes," she said quietly. "I'm so sorry, R—"

"Don't say my name!" he hissed. "And you shouldn't claim to be someone you're not."

"Are you Mrs. Rose or not?" came the voice again.

"I said I was, didn't I?" she said, suddenly sounding as if she were lying. Rayford was impressed she had caught on so quickly.

"And you, sir?"

"Me, what?" Rayford said.

"Your name."

"Who's asking?"

"GC Peacekeeping Forces."

"Oh, that's a relief," Rayford said. "Us too. I was asked by Commander Sullivan to mop up here. Looters ransacked the house after your boys finished up. He wanted us to secure the garage."

Someone flipped a switch and the bare bulb just above Rayford's head came on. He squinted before four armed GC officers, three men and a woman. "What were you doing in the dark?" the leader said. He wore lieutenant's bars.

Rayford looked up. The bulb was within an arm's length. "We heard something outside and doused the light."

"Mm-hm," the young man said, approaching. "I need to see some ID." Behind him the woman eyed Rayford with uncertainty. One of the other men looked up at the deck.

"I'm Pafko," Rayford said, desperately trying to remember which pocket he used for his phony ID. "Andrew. Here it is."

"And you, ma'am?"

"She's Fitzgerald."

"And my papers are in the car," she said.

"Lieutenant," the other guard said. "There's an open safe up there."

The lieutenant handed Rayford his ID. "You weren't planning on a little looting yourself, were you, Pafko?"

"Every penny will be accounted for."

"Mm-hm." He turned to the woman. "Double-check with Central. Pafko, Andrew, assigned out of Des Plaines. And Fitzgerald. First name, ma'am, and assignment city?"

"Pauline," Leah said. "Also Des Plaines."

The woman reached for the phone strapped to her shoulder.

Rayford almost skated, but the call would expose him. They would both be easily identified, maybe tortured and killed if they didn't reveal the rest of the Force. He deserved that for not being more careful, but Leah certainly didn't.

"No need for that, Lieutenant," Rayford said. "Before letting headquarters know where we are, shouldn't we have a look-see to find out if maybe all six of us would be better off forgetting we were here tonight? I'm as loyal as you are, but we both know the Rose woman was a rebel sympathizer. If this was her money, it's ours now, isn't it?"

The lieutenant hesitated, and the female guard took her hand away from the phone. The lieutenant knelt by the bag.

The woman said, "You're buying this? You think he's GC?"

He looked up at her. "How else would he know why we were looking for Mrs. Rose?"

She shrugged and went to peer at the safe. The other two guards moved to the door, apparently to check for curious eyes. Rayford ran a hand through his hair. Was it possible he had four willing accomplices?

He caught Leah's eye and tried to communicate to follow his lead. She looked as petrified as when she had seen the horses. Rayford casually stepped between the lieutenant and the door. Leah stayed with him.

The lieutenant saw the cash and whistled through his teeth. The men moseyed back in to look, and that brought the woman over too. With their attention on the bag, they allowed Rayford and Leah a step closer to the door than they were. Leah could have slipped out without being noticed, but Rayford couldn't say anything, and she didn't move.

"There's plenty for everybody all right," one of the men said. The lieutenant nodded, but Rayford noticed the woman staring at Leah. She dug a stack of sheets from her back pocket and riffled through them. She stopped and raised her eyes to Leah.

"Lieutenant," the woman said.

"Let me show you one thing," Rayford interrupted, reaching into the bag and pulling out a bundle of twenties. "Figure there's fifty twenties in each bundle." He held it at one end and let the stack flop back and forth. The woman reached for her weapon. Rayford raised the bundle. "Wouldn't it be nice to divide these, and—go! Now!" Rayford smacked the lightbulb with the cash, and the garage went black.

He spun and sprinted after Leah as she raced through the side door. He heard a shot and wood cracking and was aware that the lieutenant's big flashlight had come back on too. As he and Leah sprinted over the slippery ground, he guessed their odds of reaching the Land Rover at no better than one in five. But he wasn't about to stand there and be arrested.

Someone hit the automatic door button, and Rayford heard the garage door rise. He sneaked a peek back, and the opener light showed all four guards coming full speed, weapons raised. "Faster!" Rayford shouted as he turned back toward Leah. But she had stopped. He slammed into her, and they both tumbled over and over in the grass.

Something had given way. Had his leg broken, or had he crushed one of hers? Why had she stopped? She had been moving well! They'd had a chance. The Land Rover was in sight. Would the GC shoot? Or would they just arrest them? Rayford would rather be in heaven than endanger his loved ones. "Let's make them shoot," he rasped and tried to rise. But Leah had drawn up on all fours and was staring toward the car through strands of hair in her face.

Rayford looked back. The guards were gone. He looked the other way, where Leah's eyes were transfixed. And there were the horses, not ten feet from him—huge, monstrous, muscular things twice the size of any he had ever seen. Leah was right, their feet were not on the ground, yet they shifted and stepped back and forth, turning, turning.

Flames came from their nostrils and mouths, and thick yellow smoke billowed. The fire illuminated their majestic wide heads, the heads of lions with enormous canines and flowing manes. Rayford slowly, painfully rose, no longer surprised that Leah had been rendered helpless when first she had seen them. "They won't hurt us," he said weakly, hopefully, panting.

He trembled, trying to take in the scene. The first flank of steeds was backed by hundreds, skittish and moving in place as if eager to charge and run. The riders were proportioned every bit as large as the animals. They appeared human but each had to be ten feet tall and weigh five hundred pounds.

Rayford swallowed, his chest heaving. He wanted to check on Leah, but he could not look away. The horse in front of him, hardly three paces away, stutter-stepped and turned in a circle. Rayford gaped at a tail consisting not of hair but rather a writhing, sinewy serpent with a head twice the size of Rayford's fist. It writhed and bared its fangs.

The riders seemed to gaze miles into the distance, high over Rayford's head. Each horseman wore a breastplate that, illumined by the flames, shone iridescent yellow, deep navy, and fiery red. Massive biceps and forearms knotted and rippling, the riders seemed to work to keep the animals from stampeding.

Rayford neither heard nor smelled the horses or the fire and smoke. He only knew they whinnied and snorted because of the flame and clouds. No sound of reins, saddles, breastplates. And yet the lion/horses and their riders were more vivid than anything he had ever seen before.

Rayford finally stole a glance at Leah. She appeared catatonic, unblinking, mouth open. "Breathe," he told her.

Had God provided these beings to protect them? Surely the guards had run for their lives. Rayford turned again and at first saw nothing between him and the garage. But then he noticed all four guards on the ground, perfectly still.

He heard sirens, saw helicopters with searchlights, heard guards running, shouting. "We have to go, Leah," he said. "We can walk right through the horses. They're not physical."

"You there!"

Rayford whirled. Two guards nudged the fallen four with their boots while shouting at Rayford and Leah, "Stay where you are!"

They approached cautiously, and Leah finally turned from the horses to look over her shoulder. She whispered, "I think I broke a rib." She squinted at the guards. "Aren't they afraid of the horses?"

What was wrong with these two? As they drew near—men who appeared in their early twenties—they leveled high-powered weapons at Rayford and Leah. Rayford knew the horses were still behind him because of the reflection of the flames dancing off the guards' faces.

"What do you know about those dead security guards?" one said.

"Nothing," Leah said, still on all fours. "What do you think of our army?"

"Stand up, ma'am."

"They can't see them," Rayford said.

"Can't see who?" the guard said. "Come with us."

"You don't see anything," Rayford said without inflection.

"I told you to stand up, ma'am!" the other shouted. As he stepped toward her, Rayford stepped in front of him.

"Son, let me warn you. If—"

"Warn me? I could shoot you and never have to answer for it."

"You're in danger. We didn't kill those g—"

The guard burst into flames, his screaming, spinning body lighting the area like day. A horse moved past Rayford and silently spun, its tail striking the other guard on the forehead. He flew like a rag doll, his head crushed, into a tree ten feet away.

Leah slowly came to her feet, sweat dripping from her chin. She reached for Rayford as if in slow motion. "We're . . . going . . . to . . . die," she managed.

"Not us," Rayford said, finding his breath. "Where does it hurt? Press your palm over the pain."

She held her left rib cage, and Rayford wrapped his arm around her waist, walking toward the car. He squinted against the flames, walking through the horses as if through a hologram. Leah hid her face behind his shoulder.

"Are they in another dimension? What is this?"

"A vision," he said, knowing for the first time that they would escape. "Tsion was right. They're not physical."

They were in the middle of the herd now, Rayford unable to see the end, feeling like a child in a sea of adults. Finally they passed through the last row of horses and saw the Rover a hundred feet away.

"You all right?" he asked.

"Except that I'm dreaming," she said. "I'll never believe this tomorrow. I don't believe it now."

Rayford pointed half a mile to the west where another cavalry of fiery horses and riders mustered. Leah pointed the other way, where there were yet more. Behind them the hundreds they had just come through seemed to move toward Leah's town house.

They got into the car and Rayford drove straight down her street, something he had not dared earlier. The horses breathed great clouds of black and yellow smoke that chased GC forces out of the neighborhood, many falling and seemingly dying on the spot. As the smoke billowed through the area, people burst from their homes, gagging, coughing, falling. Here and there the horses snorted enough fire to incinerate homes.

"Wait here," Rayford said, shifting into park in front of Leah's garage.

"Rayford! No! Let's get back!"

He leapt out. "Yeah, I'm gonna leave that kind of money . . ."

"Please!" she called after him.

Rayford strode past bodies and into the garage. He zipped up the sack and just managed to hoist it over his shoulder. Walking through smoke and flames he neither smelled nor felt, he pushed the bag into the back of the Rover and slid behind the wheel. As he pulled away, he looked at Leah. "Welcome to the Trib Force," he said. She merely shook her head, still holding her ribs.

Rayford speed dialed the safe house. He turned again to Leah. "Better buckle up," he said.

+ + +

Mac slipped past the Fortunato party as they were being served and left the plane to monitor fueling. That allowed him to watch the cargo transfer. Abdullah opened the hatch, and a squadron of forklift trucks buzzed onto the tarmac, up the aluminum ramp, and into the belly of the plane. While Fortunato was eating, 144 computers and more than a ton of foodstuffs were smuggled off the GC's own Condor 216 and would be appropriated by their enemy before sunset. *Brilliant, Abdullah,* Mac thought. *Nothing like breakfast to keep the supreme commander oblivious.*

+ + +

Buck awoke when Chloe answered the phone.

"What time is it?" he said.

She pointed to the clock, which read 12:30.

"Shh," she said. "It's Daddy."

"His note said he and Leah—"

She shushed him again.

"Outside?" she said. "Why? . . . All right! I'll do it. . . . Tsion? Are you serious? You want me to wake him? . . . Well, hurry!"

She hung up.

"Buck, get up."

"What? Why?"

"Come on. Daddy wants you to wake Tsion and look out the window."

"What in—"

"Hurry! He and Leah are on their way."

"What are we looking for?"

"The 200 million horsemen."

"It's started? You can see them?"

"Get Tsion!"

+ + +

Airborne again, Mac asked Abdullah to oversee the controls. "I want to see if Leon starts talking strategy."

He reached back to be sure the door was locked, unbuckled his seat belt, slouched in his seat, shut his eyes, and depressed the bug switch. One of Fortunato's aides was trying to impress the boss.

"It'll be so neat when he finds out Carpathia's not here, and that it's just you on the plane."

"I didn't just hear you refer to the potentate by merely his last—"

"I'm sorry, Commander. I meant His Excellency, the potentate. I would love to be there when Ngumo discovers that Potentate Rehoboth not only knows about the meeting, but that he has also been invited."

The other aide waded in. "What's the point of this trip if you're just going to put Ngumo in his place?"

"A valid question," Leon said. "Naive, but valid. First, this is a particularly clever way to do it. It's not just an insult; it's a stinging insult. Despite our smiles and subservient attitudes, there will be no doubt in his mind that this is a slap in the face. It's not a meeting with His Excellency. It's not even a face-to-face with the supreme commander in private. He will get nothing he asks for and will be told to like it. It could have been done by phone, but I wouldn't have enjoyed it as much. Anyway, this is an alliance-building mission."

"With Rehoboth?"

"Of course. It is crucial that His Excellency be confident of his regional potentates. A few more accommodations to Bindura, and we'll guarantee his loyalty. There are rumors of insurrection, but we're dead certain of six potentates, 90 percent sure of Rehoboth, and not so sure of the other three. They will be in line by the time of the disposition of the Jerusalem problem, or they will be replaced."

"The Jerusalem problem?"

"Don't disappoint me. You have worked hand and glove with me this long and you don't know what I mean when I refer to the Jer—"

"The two witnesses."

"Well, yes . . . no! That's what the rebels call them. And they call themselves some biblical thing, lampstands or trees or some such. Don't stoop to their terms. They are the crazy preachers, the wall-bangers, the—"

That last had sent the aides into paroxysms of laughter, which served only to start Leon on a string of comments he thought funny. To listen to his yes-men, he had only underestimated his comedic gift. Mac was shaking his head at the absurdity when Abdullah startled him with a slap across the chest.

Mac straightened up as if snapped with a wet towel. "I'm sorry," Abdullah shouted, "but look! Look! Oh! It was there!"

"What?" Mac said. With the sun climbing behind them to the left, the cloudless expanse before them appeared an endless clear blue. Mac saw nothing, and so now, apparently, did Abdullah.

"I saw something, Captain. I swear I did."

"I don't doubt you. What was it?"

"You'd doubt me if I told you." Abdullah's eyes were still wide. He leaned forward and looked in every direction.

"Try me."

"An army."

"I'm sorry?"

"A cavalry, I mean."

"Abdullah, you're not even looking at the ground."

"I would not have woken you if I saw something on the ground!"

"I wasn't sleeping."

"I *expect* to see horses on the ground!"

"You saw horses in the sky?"

"Horses and riders."

"There aren't even clouds."

"I told you you wouldn't believe me."

"I believe you *think* you saw something."

"You might as well call me a liar."

"Never. Clearly, you thought you saw something. You weren't napping. Were you?"

"Now I am a liar *and* asleep on the job?"

Mac laughed. "If you say you saw something, I believe you."

"It didn't look like 200 million, but—"

"Ah, you've been reading Tsion's lesson—"

"Of course. Who hasn't?"

Mac cocked his head. "You were daydreaming, maybe dozing. Don't look at me like that. I'm saying just for a split second, thinking about Dr. Ben-Judah's message—"

"You are going to offend me if you continue this, Captain."

Mac clapped Abdullah on the shoulder. "I'm sorry, brother. You have to admit it's possible."

Abdullah shrank from Mac's hand. "You have to admit it's possible I saw horses and riders."

Mac smiled. "What were they doing? Staging? Marshaling for the big parade?"

"Captain! You're insulting me!"

"C'mon, Abdullah! Tsion says the horses and riders come from the pit, same as the locusts. What would they be doing up here?"

Abdullah looked disgusted and turned away.

"Do you think I'd insult you on purpose?" Mac said.

No response.

"Well, do you?"

Abdullah was silent.

"Now you're going to pout."

"I'm not familiar with *pout*."

"Well," Mac said, "for not being familiar with it, you're pretty good at it."

"If pout means being angry at someone you thought was your friend and brother, then I'm pout."

Mac laughed aloud. "You're pout? May I call you pout? This is my friend and brother, pout!"

And before Mac could blink, horses and riders blotted out the sky. Abdullah jerked the controls and the plane tilted nearly straight up, pinning Mac to his seat. He heard crashing and banging in the galley and lounge. Then Leon crying out.

Just as Mac realized he was going to regret being unbuckled, Abdullah over-adjusted, and the plane dipped. Mac slammed into the ceiling, full force, turning his face just in time to take the damage on the left side of his head. Control knobs broke off, tearing his flesh and piercing his ear. Blood splattered onto the windshield and control panel.

Abdullah finally brought the craft under control and sat staring straight ahead. "I did not do that to get back at you for sporting with me," he said, his voice shaky. "If you did not see what I almost hit, I am terribly sorry and hope you are not seriously injured."

"I saw them plain as day," Mac said, his heart thundering. "I'll never doubt you again. I've got to stop the bleeding. If you see them again, don't try to avoid them. Keep her steady. They're floating around in space. You're not going to hit them."

"My apologies. It was instinct."

"I understand."

"Are you all right, Captain?"

"Not totally, but it's superficial, I'm sure."

"Good," Abdullah said. He mimicked a flight attendant: "You should always keep your belt fastened when you are in your seat, even when the seat belt light has been turned off."

Mac rolled his eyes.

"Now is it time for *you* to be pout?" Abdullah said.

Mac stood and reached for the door, just as someone banged on it from the other side.

9

BUCK APOLOGIZED PROFUSELY to Tsion, explaining, "Rayford and Leah went to her place to get something and just now called to tell us to look out the window."

Tsion, his hair wild, pulled on a robe and followed Buck downstairs. Chloe, holding Kenny, stood before the windows facing west. "Maybe we need the lights off," she said. "I see nothing."

"What are we looking for?" Tsion said.

"The 200 million horsemen," she said.

Tsion rushed to the front of the house and pulled back the curtain. "I would not be disappointed if God moved up the Glorious Appearing a few years," he said. "Must be cloudy. No stars. Where is the moon?"

"Back here," Buck said.

"I cannot imagine Rayford was serious," Tsion said, rejoining Buck and Chloe.

"He was excited," Chloe said. "Scared even."

Buck moseyed out the back door and looked east, where the horizon glowed red. "Wonder if this is it," he called out.

"Something is burning somewhere," Tsion said wearily. "But isn't Mrs. Rose's home in the other direction?"

"I ought to drive that way and see what I can see," Buck said.

It was clear Chloe didn't like that idea. "Let's wait and see. It's not worth the risk if it's just a fire."

The phone rang. Chloe handed the fussing Kenny to Buck and hurried to get it. "No, Dad," she said. "Maybe fires in the east. . . . Are you sure it's begun? . . . Here, talk to Tsion."

+ + +

As soon as Mac unlatched the cockpit door, Leon barged in, disheveled, swearing.

"A little turbulence," Mac said.

"Turbulence?! What's with the smoke, the smell? I've got a man down, and

Karl says one of *his* people is unconscious! We've got to land, man! We're going to suffocate! And you're bleeding!"

Mac followed him into the lounge, where one of Leon's aides frantically pumped the chest of the other. Karl screamed from the galley, "We're all going to die!"

Leon covered his own mouth with a handkerchief, gagging and coughing. "Sulfur! Where's that coming from! That's poison, isn't it? Won't it kill us?"

Mac smelled nothing. He would check the control panel, but the Condor had supersensitive smoke and fume alarms, none of which had engaged. Mac knew he'd look suspicious if he were not also suffering. He covered his mouth. "I'll turn up the ventilation system," he said, as Karl dragged his fallen worker from the galley. "Get those two into the sleeping quarters. There are enough oxygen canisters for everyone."

"Isn't there somewhere we can land?" Leon said.

"I'll find out," Mac said.

"Hurry!"

He rushed back into the cockpit and locked the door. "What's going on?" Abdullah said. "You're losing a lot of blood."

"I'm all right," Mac said. "Those horses have power up here, even inside a pressurized cabin. Everybody smells sulfur, they're gagging, using oxygen, passing out. Leon wants us to land."

"We should go straight on to Johannesburg," Abdullah said, working with Mac to check every gauge. "What is affecting them is not coming from this plane. They'd be no better off on the ground."

"They could get medical treatment."

Abdullah looked at Mac. "So could you, but if they are being plagued by the 200 million horsemen, no medicine will save them."

"What's our ETA?"

"Several hours."

Mac shook his head, his wounds making him wince. "We're going to have to put down or Leon is going to find out we're invulnerable."

Abdullah pointed to the controls, Mac took over, and Abdullah pulled charts from his flight bag.

+ + +

"They will be here any minute," Tsion said, hanging up from Rayford. "The plagues of fire and smoke and sulfur have begun. I did not expect this, but the horsemen are visible, at least to some. Rayford and Mrs. Rose saw them. And unbelievers are being slain."

Buck turned on the television.

* * *

"Mayday! Mayday!" Mac heard over the radio.

"This is Condor, go ahead."

"Mayday! My pilot is dead! I'm choking! Cockpit full of smoke. Agh! The smell! I can't see! We're losing it! Going down!"

"What's your location?"

But all Mac heard was the unnerving wailing. This was like the day of the Rapture, only now it was unbelieving pilots whose planes would be lost, maybe a third of them.

Mayday calls filled the frequency. Mac was helpless. He was also light-headed. He switched to a news radio feed. "No one has an answer yet to the puzzling rash of fires, outbreaks of smoke, and noxious, sulfur-smelling emissions killing thousands all over the globe," the newsman said. "Emergency medical professionals are at a loss, frantic to determine the cause. Here's the head of the Global Community Emergency Management Association, Dr. Jurgen Haase."

"If this were isolated, we might attribute it to a natural disaster, a rupture of some natural gas source. But it seems random, and clearly the fumes are lethal. We urge citizens to use gas masks and work together to extinguish spontaneous fires."

The newsman asked, "Which is more dangerous, the black smoke or the yellow?"

Haase said, "First we believed the black smoke emanated from the fires, but it appears to be independent. It can be deadly, but the yellow smells of sulfur and has the power to kill instantly."

The reporter said he had just been handed a bulletin, and he sounded terrified. "While there are pockets in which no fire or smoke or sulfur have been reported, in other areas the death count is staggering, now estimated in the hundreds of thousands. His Excellency, Global Community Potentate Nicolae Carpathia, will address the world via radio and television and the Internet inside this half hour."

Abdullah shoved a map under Mac's nose. "We are equidistant from airports that can handle a heavy in both Addis Ababa and Khartoum."

"It's up to Leon," Mac said. "He's the one who wants to land."

Abdullah took over again, and Mac emerged from the cockpit to find Leon on the phone. Mac grabbed a cloth napkin from the galley, soaked it, and held it to his ear. He tossed another damp cloth into the cockpit so Abdullah could wipe down the window and panel.

"One moment, Excellency," Leon said, "the captain needs me. . . . Yes, I'll ask." Leon covered the phone. "His Excellency asks where we are."

"Over the Red Sea. We can either—"

Leon held up a hand to silence Mac and told Carpathia. He handed the phone to Mac. "The potentate wishes to speak with you."

"What is your plan, Captain?"

Mac told him the options.

"Can you not turn back to either Mecca or somewhere in Yemen?"

"They have no strip that will handle a craft this large, sir."

"Addis Ababa is in what used to be Ethiopia," Carpathia said, as if to himself.

"Correct," Mac said. "Khartoum is in old Sudan."

"Go there. I will contact Potentate Rehoboth in South Af—, in Johannesburg and have him ensure that his people in Sudan extend every courtesy. If you are then able to complete this journey, it will be very beneficial to the cause."

"May I ask how things are there?"

"Here? We have lost dozens, and the stench is abominable. I am convinced this is chemical warfare, but it will not surprise me if the opposition claims some supernatural source."

"Me either . . . sir."

"The Jerusalem Twosome are already carrying on about it."

"Sir?"

"My new name for them. You like it?"

Mac did not respond. People were dying all over the world, and Carpathia was playing word games.

"They are, of course, taking credit for what is happening," Carpathia said. "That makes my job easier. Their day will come, and the world will thank me."

+ + +

Buck sat in front of the TV with Tsion and Chloe, waiting for Rayford and Leah. From countries in daylight came images of fire and billowing smoke, people gagging, gasping, coughing, falling. Panic.

The phone rang. It was Mac calling for Rayford. Buck filled him in and was stunned to hear Mac and Abdullah's account. Mac told him of Carpathia's nickname for the two witnesses.

"He's about to come on TV," Buck said. "I'll have Rayford call you."

Rayford and Leah pulled in as Carpathia was being introduced. The stateside Trib Force sat before the TV, watching cosmic history. Tsion stood and paced as Carpathia solemnly looked into the camera. The potentate was at his typically parental best, assuring the horrified masses that "the situation will soon be under control. We have mobilized every resource. Meanwhile, I ask citizens of the

Global Community to report suspicious activity, particularly the manufacture or transport of noxious agents. Sadly, we have reason to believe that this massacre of innocent lives is being perpetrated by religious dissidents to whom we have extended every courtesy. Though they cross us at every turn, we have defended their right to dissent. Yet they continue to see the Global Community as an enemy. They feel they have a right to maintain an intolerant, close-minded cult that excludes anyone who disagrees.

"You have the right to live healthy, peaceful, and free. While I shall remain always a pacifist, I pledge to rid the world of this cult, beginning with the Jerusalem Twosome, who even now express no remorse about the widespread loss of life that has resulted from this attack."

"You know," Tsion said, sitting on the arm of the couch next to Chloe, "I am going to have to ask forgiveness for the glee I will feel when *this* man's due time arrives."

Carpathia pushed a button that showed Eli and Moishe holding forth at the Wailing Wall. They spoke in unison in a loud, haunting, echoing tone that carried without amplification far across the Temple Mount.

The words flashed across the screen. "Woe to the enemies of the most high God!" they said. "Woe to the cowards who shake their fist at their creator and are now forced to flee his wrath! We beseech you, snakes and vipers, to see even this plague as more than judgment! Yea, it is yet another attempt to reach you by a loving God who has run out of patience. There is no more time to woo you. You must hearken to his call, see that it is he who loves you. Turn to the God of your fathers while there is still time. For the day will come when time shall be no more!"

Carpathia came back into view with a condescending smile. "The day will come, my friends, when these two shall no longer disseminate their venom. They shall no longer turn water to blood, hold back rain from the clouds, send plagues to the Holy Land and the rest of the globe. I upheld my end of the bargain negotiated with them months ago, allowing certain dissidents to go unpunished. Here is my reward. Here is how we are repaid for our largesse.

"But the gift train stops here, loyal citizens. Your patience and steadfastness shall be recompensed. The day will yet come when we live as one world, one faith, one family of man. We shall live in a utopia of peace and harmony with no more war, no more bloodshed, no more death. In the meantime, please accept my deepest personal condolences over the loss of your loved ones. They shall not have died in vain. Continue to trust in the ideals of the Global Community, in the tenets of peace, and in the genius of an all inclusive universal faith that welcomes the devout of any religion, even that of those who now oppose us.

"Just four months from now we shall celebrate in the very city where the preachers now taunt and warn us. We shall applaud their demise and revel in a future without plague and disease and suffering and death. Keep the faith, and look forward to that day. And until I address you again, thank you for your loyal support of the Global Community."

+ + +

The ultimate in medical technology was housed in two fully equipped ambulances that waited at the end of the primary runway in Khartoum. With the wet cloth still pressed against his left ear, Mac helped Abdullah open the door and lower the stairs as Leon and Karl staggered out, each with a failing aide in tow and each leaving a dying comrade aboard. Emergency medical technicians, gloved and gas-masked, hurried aboard, lugging metal boxes. Mac and Abdullah stood on the tarmac, refusing assistance until everyone else was attended to. The other four were treated in the ambulances, and soon the EMTs deplaned, then reboarded with gurneys. They emerged with both victims covered head to toe with sheets.

Fortunato stood sans suit coat outside an ambulance, tie loose, shirt sweat drenched. He wiped his brow, breathing heavily. "Precautionary?" he asked the EMTs as the victims rolled by.

They shook their heads.

"They aren't . . ."

"Yes, they are," one said. "Asphyxiated."

Leon turned to Mac. "Get that wound taken care of, and have the plane thoroughly checked out. We can't have another episode like that."

Mac had three puncture wounds in his scalp, a deep laceration in his neck that required twenty stitches, and a nearly severed ear requiring forty more. "That's going to smart something awful when the painkiller wears off," he was told.

Two young people were dead, four other passengers deathly ill, and the world in chaos. Mac decided he could live with pain.

+ + +

Rayford sat in the living room at the safe house in the wee hours as the others drifted back to their beds. He had limped into the house behind Leah, wet, cold, and aching all over. After having run into her at full speed, he could only imagine her pain. The immediate concern and attention of the others—even during the broadcast of Carpathia's address—wounded him in its sweetness. Truly they were brothers and sisters in Christ, and there would be no surviving without them.

After they heard Rayford and Leah's story and thanked God for the provision of the money, Tsion had shared a little of what he would transmit the next day. He seemed especially intrigued that believers could see the horses and horsemen while the victims could not. Even on camera, people were shown recoiling from snakebites, enveloped by clouds of smoke, and consumed, seemingly by spontaneous fire from thin air. "I had envisioned the horsemen as one vast army riding together," Tsion said, "and perhaps at some point they will. But so far it appears they are assigned to various locations. How long this will continue, I do not know. Frankly, I am disappointed to not have seen them yet myself."

Eventually Rayford and Chloe were the only ones left in the living room. "Going to bed, Dad?" she said at last.

"In a while. Just need to unwind. Unique day, you know. Never saw anything like that before. Don't care to again."

She moved around behind him and massaged his neck and shoulders. "You need rest," she told him.

"I know." He patted her hand. "I'll be all right. You get your sleep so you can take care of that baby."

As he sat in the darkness, Rayford ran through the events of the last several days. His question had been how much more they could take. This was only the beginning, and he couldn't imagine enduring the next few years. He would lose more comrades, and at an accelerating pace.

His rage had not abated, but he had been able to somehow tuck it on a high deck behind a pup tent in his brain. Still longing for the privilege of being used in Carpathia's demise, he had to admit he was grateful for what he had seen that night. He was way past where he could deny God's forceful presence during this period. But to stand face-to-face with the horsemen of Revelation, to walk right through them to safety . . .

Had the horsemen been blinded to the believers as well? Surely, like the demonic locusts, they were agents of Satan who would rather kill believers than enemies of God.

Rayford still wasn't sure what he thought about Leah. She was difficult to identify with. Something about her seemed younger and more naive than her years. They had been through a horrifying ordeal together, and yet his image of her as too strident and opinionated had not faded. He had been moved by her salvation account and did not doubt her sincerity. Was it sexist to be repulsed by her straightforwardness? Would he pass the same off as mere spunk in a man? He hoped not.

Rayford inventoried his injuries. He needed another long, hot shower. A toe throbbed and might be broken. His left knee ached as it had before surgery in college. His left elbow was tender. A finger was sprained. He felt a bump on the back of his head. Too bad he was pushing forty-six. Running into someone and tumbling to the ground was part of a typical day for a nine-year-old.

And he was stricken with thoughts of his son. Raymie had been twelve when he disappeared in the Rapture. Though Rayford had largely succeeded in refraining from pining over him, Raymie was always at the edge of his consciousness. He suffered the guilt of time lost, wasted, not carved out for his son. The memories of the times they *had* spent together brought a lump to his throat.

Rayford slid off the couch and onto his knees, thanking God for Irene and Raymie, grateful they were spared this torturous existence. He also thanked God for Amanda, whom he had enjoyed for such a short time, but who was no less a gift. Chloe, Kenny, Buck, Tsion, Mac, David, Bruce, Ken . . . they all came to mind and brought emotion, regret, gratefulness, worry, hope.

Rayford prayed he would be the kind of leader to the Tribulation Force that God wanted him to be. And he still held out hope that this somehow included his being in the proximity of Nicolae Carpathia three and a half years from the beginning of the Tribulation, just four months hence. And Carpathia had just announced where he would be.

* * *

Mac was grateful Abdullah supervised the fumigation and inspection of the aircraft. His head pulsated. He still had to fly, but he would rely on Abdullah more than ever.

Everyone, himself included, seemed jumpy, keeping their eyes open for danger. Mac found himself starting at any movement in his peripheral vision, fully expecting to see the giant horses and riders. Abdullah appeared just as edgy.

Despite his trauma, Fortunato appeared eager to get going again. Karl was particularly agitated, alternately crying and bustling about to make certain everything was just so. As Mac and Abdullah walked through their preflight routine, Fortunato was ushered into the gleaming Khartoum terminal. He emerged in fresh clothes, apparently having also showered, and looked 100 percent better. Concern still clouded his face. He stopped by the cockpit to be sure Mac and the plane were flightworthy. "At the first unpleasant odor, I want this plane on the ground," he said.

* * *

At one in the afternoon in New Babylon, David Hassid finally got a break from his emergency duty. He had helped transport bodies to the morgue and ferry the ill to hospital rooms. He had not seen what had wrought the catastrophe, but he put two and two together when reports poured in of death from fire, smoke, and sulfur. Nowhere near a tenth of the GC employee population had been affected yet, but still hundreds had died. He knew his stateside comrades, at least Rayford and a new Trib Force member, had seen the horsemen. He felt better knowing he was not the only believer who had not seen them.

David was frantic about Annie. He had not seen her since the first alarm sounded, sending all personnel into preassigned emergency roles. He couldn't reach her by phone or computer, and no one had seen her. Her duty in an emergency was to punch a series of highly encrypted numbers into a remote-control box that secured the hangar. Once that was accomplished, she was to account for all staff in David's department. The hangar had been secured, but David had to check on staff himself.

It was grisly work. Of 140 people under his supervision, ten were dead, two were treated for smoke inhalation, and one was missing: Annie. Three of the dead had appeared to spontaneously combust. During the awful task David came to a conclusion. If Annie had somehow survived, he would make public their feelings for each other. He would even take the initiative to get her transferred, per policy, so it wouldn't appear a reprimand of either of them when it came through channels.

Once his report was filed David ran past dozens of employees who sat in clusters, crying, talking, commiserating. They would have been ripe for praying with, for sharing God with. But he was not yet prepared to sacrifice his potential benefit to the cause.

At his level of security clearance, David was able to obtain a key to Annie's quarters. She was not there. Despairing, he strode to the expansive hangar and entered the codes necessary to disengage the security locks. The huge side doors slid open to reveal the cavernous innards, which looked even bigger with the flagship aircraft away in service. The choppers and few fixed-wing craft didn't begin to fill the building.

David opened Annie's, Mac's, and Abdullah's offices and flipped on the lights. Nothing. But that's when he heard it, the muffled rhythmic pounding. It came from the utility room at the far corner of the structure. He soon recognized the thumps as Morse code. Someone was banging out an SOS. David broke into a sprint.

The utility room was double insulated for noise and steel reinforced for safety. This had been Annie's first time securing the hangar. Maybe she didn't know the utility room self-locked from the inside and was the last place a person wanted to be while remotely locking down the whole building. Once that room was locked, communicating from inside was impossible. Phone and even the remote control unit would not transmit past the heavy steel. To get out, someone inside had to first be discovered.

David reached the door. "Who goes there?" he hollered.

"David!" came Annie's frantic reply. "Get me out of here!"

"Thank God," he said, unlocking the door. She leapt into his arms, enveloping him so tight he had to fight to breathe.

"Learn something about the utility room today?" he said.

"I thought I'd be in here forever!" she said. "I checked the utilities and started punching in the codes as I was heading out, not realizing the doors would lock from inside. I've still got to account for your staff."

"Done."

"Good. Thanks for telling me about the utility room."

"Sorry. I'm just relieved I found you."

"*You're* relieved? I was scared to death. I imagined you could go days without thinking to look in here."

David could tell Annie was truly angry with him. "It was actually Mac's place to tell you about—"

She looked askance at him. "Don't tell me you're a finger-pointer. This seems like a major thing you could have told me."

He had no defense.

"So what was the big emergency?" she said. "Another false alarm?"

"You really don't know?"

"How would I, David?" she said. "I saw people running and heard a few coughing when I saw the alert. I came straight here."

"Come with me," he said.

They sat in her office, where he told her the whole story.

"I could have helped," she said. "I look like a coward, thanks to you."

"I just about died worrying about you," David said. "I thought I knew what you meant to me."

"You thought?"

"I was wrong. What can I say? I need you. I love you. I want everybody to know."

She shook her head and looked away. "You loved me enough to let me lock myself in."

Now David was angry. "Did you read the procedure manual like you were supposed to? It's clear."

"I suppose I'll get reprimanded."

"Probably. It's going to be hard to hide that I did your work."

"It was the least you could do," she said.

David fought to attribute her sudden unattractiveness to claustrophobia and frustration. "I love you even when you're ornery," he said.

"That's big of you."

He shrugged and turned his palms up in surrender. "I'd better get back. Until you and I declare ourselves, we can't be seen together. For one thing, I have to account for your whereabouts."

"That's only fair."

He shook his head and rose.

"Someone should have told me," she said.

He didn't look at her. "I got that point."

"I'm just saying," she said, "that I'm the one who could get booted out of my job and reassigned. You know what that'll mean."

He turned back. "Ten minutes ago I would have loved that. It would have meant we could declare ourselves and I'd get more time with you."

David could tell he had wounded her. "And now?" she said.

"Like I said, I love you even when you're—"

"You know the price, David. I want what you want, but what's best for the Trib Force?"

"I can't be much good to the Force, frustrated without you."

"Who has the access to GC brass that you do?"

"I know. So, are we in love again or what?"

She came to him, and they held each other. "I'm sorry," she said.

"Me too."

10

MAC HAD NOT been to Johannesburg since before the great wrath of the Lamb earthquake. From the air it resembled New Babylon. The rebuilt airport served as a major hub of international travel. Regional Potentate Rehoboth's palace housed his several wives, children, and grandchildren, along with servants and aides.

The left side of Mac's head felt twice as big as the right, and pain stabbed each wound with every beat of his heart. Even applying his headphones was a chore, trying to keep the gauze from pressing tighter against his stitches.

Upon landing, Mac and Abdullah were to open the door and lower the steps. They could then leave the plane, retire to their quarters, or remain in the cockpit, as long as they did not interfere with the meeting. Karl and his assistant would remain on board to serve food. Mac told Leon that he and Abdullah would remain also, probably in their quarters. Of course, they stayed in the cockpit, where Mac listened in on Fortunato and his remaining aide.

"Clancy," Leon said, "I would like you to phone Ngumo at the VIP guesthouse. You can see it there at the end of the airport. Here's the number. He will not likely answer himself, but put the speakerphone on so I can hear, just in case."

Mac wished he could take notes, but he couldn't risk being found with them. He would just have to remember as much as he could—no easy task with the pain. He heard Clancy slowly enter the number. A mature woman answered. "You have reached Mwangati Ngumo's secretary. May I help you?"

"Yes, ma'am, thank you. I am Clancy Tiber, personal assistant to Global Community Supreme Commander Leon Fortunato. I am pleased to tell you that the supreme commander is prepared to receive Mr. Ngumo and two aides aboard *Global Community One*."

"Thank you, Mr. Tiber. You may expect them in five minutes. Mr. Ngumo is very much looking forward to his meeting with Potentate Carpathia."

Clancy hung up and said, "This is too delicious. Is it supposed to be this much fun?"

"There's more where this came from, son."

The flag-bedecked Botswanian limo stopped fifty feet from the plane, and Mac idly watched three dignitaries alight. Abdullah unstrapped himself and pressed his nose against the windshield. "Does that look like Ngumo to you, Mac?"

"Hm?"

"That's not Ngumo."

"I've never met him."

"Neither have I, but unless he's lost fifty pounds since I saw him on TV, that's not him. And since when does the big man carry a bag too?"

Mac removed his headset and leaned forward, but the men were already past where he could see them. He jumped as Fortunato blasted so hard against the locked cockpit door that it sprang open and banged against the wall. "Go! Go!" Leon said. "Take off now!"

"We're shut down, Leon."

"Start it up! Now! Those men have weapons!"

"The door's open, Leon! There's no time!"

"Do something!"

"Engage three and four," Mac said, and Abdullah flipped several switches. "Full power, now!"

The two engines on the right side of the plane burst to life with a roar, and Mac maneuvered the controls so the plane swung to the left. Mac saw the three would-be assassins blowing down the runway in the hot jet exhaust.

"You're a genius!" Leon said. "Now get us out of here!"

The men struggled to their feet, retrieved their high-powered rifles, and ran toward their limo. With the steps and open door of the Condor now facing away from them, Abdullah ran to pull up the stairs and shut the door.

"Now go!" Leon shouted. "Go!"

"We're low on fuel. We'd have to come back here to land."

"They're driving this way! Go!"

Mac started the sequence, knowing the plane was not prepped for takeoff again so quickly. The left side engines screamed to life, but until other crucial gauges caught up, the onboard computer would abort takeoff. If Mac overrode the fail-safe mechanism, he risked crashing.

He turned the jet rear side toward his pursuers, but they roared around front, showing their weapons. "Leave them in the dust!" Leon said. "Let's go!"

But the gunmen circled back out of sight of Mac and opened fire. The blowing of the tires was nearly as loud as the explosions from the weapons. The Condor was wounded. With more than half its tires shredded, the bird rested unevenly on the runway. Mac would never get it to roll, let alone achieve takeoff speed.

Strangely, not another plane was in sight. All the crazy activity, which had to have been witnessed by both air traffic and ground control personnel, had drawn no emergency attention. Mac realized they had been set up and would likely all die. He and Abdullah had been stranded before this band of killers. Whoever they were, they clearly had the cooperation of the Rehoboth regime.

Bullets ripped through the fuselage. Mac and Abdullah leaped from their seats and followed the screaming Leon through the galley, the lounge, and into the main cabin. "Lie on the floor and stay in the center!" Mac shouted.

The killers had apparently decided to make sure no one survived. Bullets tore through windows and walls up and down the plane. Mac noticed only five men on the floor. Abdullah, Leon, Clancy, Karl's helper, and he were curled beneath seats, their heads buried in their hands. "Where's Karl?" Mac shouted, but no one stirred.

Mac felt the pressure of footsteps near him and peeked up to see the cook staggering down the aisle, drenched in blood. "Karl! Get down!" As the man fell, wide-eyed, a gaping hole in his forehead evidenced a fatal wound.

"Do we have a weapon?" Leon shouted.

"Prohibited by your boss, Leon!" Mac said.

"Surely you sometimes break the rules! I'll pardon you if you produce one! We have no hope, Mac!"

There *were* two pistols in the cargo hold, and *yes,* Mac thought, *sometimes I break the rules.* But there was no getting to the guns, and what would he do with them anyway, outnumbered and facing heavy artillery?

"Do something!" Leon pleaded. "Do you have a phone?"

Mac dug his from his belt and flung it to Leon. The commander frantically poked in a special code, shuddering with every round that pierced the plane. "GC Mega-Alert, this is LF 999, secure line! Inform His Excellency *GC One* under heavy fire, Johannesburg International. Patch me through to Potentate Rehoboth directly, now!"

Mac heard the phone in the lounge. Dare he crawl out and see who it was? If there was a chance it was the shooters with a demand, it might be worth it. He crawled over Karl and into the lounge, where he grabbed the receiver as the base of the phone bounced on the floor. "Talk!" he barked.

It was the woman he had heard over the intercom, now hysterical. "Mr. Ngumo is not behind this attack! He was overtaken by—oh, no! Oh—" A deafening fusillade made Mac pull the phone from his ear. When he listened again, the woman screamed, "They've killed him! No! Please!" More shots, and her phone had fallen.

Mac scrambled on all fours into the cockpit and grabbed the radio mike.

"Mayday! Johannesburg runway! *GC One* under attack!" From the middle of the plane he heard Leon shriek into the phone, "You, Bindura? Why? Carpathia is not even on this plane! I'm telling the truth! Call them off! Please!"

If Rehoboth was behind this, they were as good as dead anyway. He would have thought of everything. Mac shouted over the radio, "Mayday! Johannesburg! Believers on board!" If by some stretch a Christian pilot was in the area, who knew what he or she might be able to do?

Mac was knocked on his face by the force of a concussion bomb, and the plane began to fill with smoke. Leon and Clancy screamed, "Fire!" and Abdullah ran forward.

"They may shoot us, Mac, but we have to jump ship! They've set us afire!"

Mac and Abdullah opened the main cabin door, trying to keep from being open targets. Leon pushed Clancy from behind, the young man stiff-legged with fear, crying, lurching toward the door. As soon as Abdullah lowered the stairs, Leon shoved Clancy's quivering mass down ahead of him as a shield. Clancy was torn apart by bullets, and Leon froze at the top of the steps. Only when a firebomb exploded in the lounge did he take his fateful plunge. Mac and Abdullah leaped aboard him and rode him down the steps as the inferno roared out the door behind them.

Mac believed he would never hit the pavement alive. He had lost all hope and leapt from the plane only to escape the flames. With deafening gunfire surrounding him and the Condor engulfed behind him, he shut his eyes so tight he felt as if his cheekbones were in his forehead. With one hand vise-gripped on Abdullah's wrist and a knee in Fortunato's fleshy back, Mac bet his life he would open his eyes in heaven.

But he did not.

Leon dropped to his hands and knees on the runway, Abdullah flipping over him. Mac landed flat on Leon's back, crushing him to the asphalt. A bullet ripped through Mac's right shoulder blade and another shattered his right hand, the blasts from the weapon not twenty feet away deafening his right ear.

"Oh, God!" Leon screamed beneath him. "Oh, God, help me!" Mac sensed his own head was the next target and that he would be mercifully put out of his misery.

Blackness.

Silence.

Nothing.

Only smell and taste and feeling.

Mac saw nothing because he chose to keep his eyes shut. He heard only Leon's raspy panting.

The smell was gunpowdery and metallic, the taste blood, the feeling a hot, deep, searing pain. The tear in his shoulder superseded the tender soreness of the side of Mac's head. His hand was worse. He almost dared not open his eyes. Nothing about that wound would surprise him. Mac felt as if his hand had been shattered.

Leon's body rose and fell beneath him as Leon gasped for air. Mac rolled off him onto the pavement on his left side, eyes still shut, mind spinning. Was it over, or would he open his eyes to assassins standing over him? Had Leon been hit? Abdullah?

Disappointed that he was not in heaven, Mac forced open one eye. Smoke was so dense and dark he couldn't see inches past his nose. He drew his ravaged hand to his face for a closer look and felt the devastation in his shoulder. His hand shivered so violently it shook his whole body, and blood splattered from it onto his face.

Mac reached with his other hand to steady the wounded appendage and saw he had all his fingers, though they were splayed in different directions, a bullet having ripped through the back of his hand. His whole body shook, and he feared he was going into shock.

As the smoke slowly cleared, he forced himself to sit up. Leon lay hyperventilating, eyes open, teeth bared. Clancy Tiber lay beside him, obviously dead.

"Abdullah?" Mac called out weakly.

"I am here," Abdullah said. "I have a bullet in my thigh. Were you hit?"

"At least twice. What happened to the—"

"Do you see the horses?"

"I can't even see you."

"I hope they stay long enough for you to see."

"So do I."

* * *

Rayford awoke after nine in the morning Saturday at the safe house. He could have slept another couple of hours after the night he'd had, but an unusual noise had niggled him awake. His eyes popped open and he lay still, hoping it was later, hoping his body had had time to recharge, wondering if he had lucked out and his aches and pains might have abated.

A rhythmic swishing sound, like someone rubbing their hands together every few seconds, made him sit up. Listening more closely, he thought it might be sniffing or even sniffling. It came from the bedroom next door, where Tsion both slept and worked.

The rest had been good for Rayford's mind and spirit, but it had only stiffened his ailing joints and muscles. He groaned aloud, pulled on his robe, and peeked into Tsion's room through the door, which was open a few inches.

At first Rayford didn't see Dr. Ben-Judah. The chair before his computer screen was empty, as was the bed. But the sound was coming from that room. Rayford knocked gently and pushed the door open another foot. Beneath the window next to the bed, Tsion lay on the floor, his face buried in his hands. His shoulders heaved as he wept bitterly.

"Are you all right?" Rayford said softly, but Tsion did not respond. Rayford stepped beside him and sat on the bed so Tsion would know he was there. The rabbi prayed aloud. "Lord, if it is Hattie, I beg for her soul. If it is Chaim, I covet him for the kingdom. If it is someone in this house, protect them, shield them, equip them. Father, if it is one of the new brothers or sisters, someone I have not even met, I pray your protection and mercy." He wept more, moaning. "God, tell me how to pray."

Rayford put a hand on the teacher's back. Tsion turned. "Rayford, the Lord suddenly impressed deeply upon my heart that I should pray for someone in danger. I was writing my message, which is also weighing on me—probably the most difficult I have had to write. I thought the leading was to pray for my audience, but it seemed more specific, more urgent. I prayed the Lord would tell me who needed prayer, but I was then overcome with the immediacy of it. I knelt, and it was as if his Spirit pushed me to the floor and planted in my soul a burden for whoever was in need. I still do not know, and yet I cannot shake the feeling that this is more than just my imagination. Pray with me, would you?"

Rayford knelt awkwardly, feeling every injury from the night before and having less an idea what to say than Tsion did. "Lord, I agree with my brother in prayer. We don't understand how we finite beings can say or pray anything that affects what an infinite God wants to do, but we trust you. You tell us to pray, to boldly come to you. If someone we know and love is in danger, we pray your supernatural hedge of protection around them."

Rayford was moved by Tsion's emotion and could not continue. Tsion said, "Thank you," and gripped his hand.

They rose. Tsion sat before his computer and wiped his eyes. "I do not know what that was about," he said, "but I have stopped questioning how God communicates to us."

Tsion sat awhile collecting himself, then asked Rayford if he would look over his day's message. "I will be refining it before posting it this afternoon, but I would appreciate your input."

"I'd love to read it," Rayford said, "but I can't imagine what I have to offer."

Tsion rose and offered Rayford his chair. "I am going to get something to drink. I shall return for my grade."

\+ + +

Mac knew if he stayed on the steamy Johannesburg runway he would die. His hours-old ear and scalp wounds oozed from beneath the bandages, and the painkiller had long since worn off. His shoulder felt as if someone had smashed it with a red-hot hammer. His hand would never be the same. The best he could hope for was to save the fingers, which surely would never bend properly again.

The smoke wafted away with the hot late-afternoon wind, and Abdullah came into view fifteen feet to Mac's left. The young man rested on his knees, turban unwound, face tight with fear and fatigue. His right thigh bore a deep red wound. He pointed into the distance. "They're still here," he said.

Mac had had only the briefest glimpse of the phantasmagoric cavalry of frightful men and beasts when Abdullah tried to avoid them in the sky. Now a legion mustered a hundred feet past the runway, snorting smoke and fire and sulfur, snake tails striking and snapping at victims who couldn't see them.

In their wake, the leonine steeds left bodies. Some jerked spastically before freezing in macabre repose. Others writhed ablaze until death brought relief. Or so they thought, Mac mused. In truth, the victims passed from one flame to another. One of the phony dignitaries ran top speed down the runway. The other two lay dead near the plane, close enough to have killed Mac with their next shots.

Even from behind and far away, Mac found the horsemen and their mounts dreadful. They hovered inches off the ground but galloped, trotted, stepped, and reared like physical horses. Their riders urged them on, stampeding people, buildings, vehicles, wreaking destruction.

The thick, swarthy Leon Fortunato appeared out of the haze, having rolled toward Mac. He grabbed Mac's face in both hands, and Mac nearly screamed from the pain on one side. "You saved my life, Mac!" Leon cried. "You protected me with your own body! Were you hit?"

"Twice," Mac said. He pulled back so Leon's hands slipped away. Mac pointed to the horses. "What do you see over there?"

"Carnage," Leon said, squinting. "Fire, smoke. And what's that awful smell, like in the plane earlier? Agh!"

"We need to get away from the plane," Mac said. Flames poured out the windows.

"The beautiful Condor," Leon said. "His Excellency's pride and joy."

"Do you want to pull Clancy's body out of the way?" Mac said.

Leon struggled to his feet and staggered, trying to gain his balance. "No," he said, regaining his voice. "The world is short of graves. We would only cremate him anyway. Let this fire do it."

Leon turned slowly in a circle. "I thought we were dead," he said. "What happened?"

"You prayed."

"Excuse me?"

"You asked God to help you," Mac said.

"I consider myself religious."

"I'm sure you do. God must have answered."

"Why did the attackers stop shooting?"

Mac winced, wishing they had stopped sooner. "How can we know? One ran. The other two haven't moved."

Leon and Mac got on either side of Abdullah and slowly walked him toward the terminal.

\+ + +

It was not lost on Rayford, the privilege of having the first look at a message millions around the globe anticipated. Tsion had written:

> *My dear brothers and sisters in Christ:*
> *I come to you today with a heavy heart, which is, of course, nothing new during this period of history. While the 144,000 evangelists raised up by God are seeing millions come to Christ, the one-world religion continues to become more powerful and—I must say it—more odious. Preach it from the mountaintops and into the valleys, my beloved siblings: There is one God and one Mediator between God and man, the Man Christ Jesus.*
>
> *The deadly demon locusts prophesied in Revelation 9 died out* en masse *more than half a year ago, having tortured millions. But many bitten during the last month of that plague only stopped serving their sentences of agony three months ago.*
>
> *While many have come to faith after being convinced by that horrible judgment, most have become even more set in their ways. It should have been obvious to the leader of the Enigma Babylon One World Faith that devotees of that religion suffered everywhere in the world. But we followers of Christ, the so-called dissidents—enemies of tolerance and inclusion—were spared.*
>
> *Our beloved preachers in Jerusalem, despite heinous opposition and persecution, continue to prophesy and win converts to Christ*

in that formerly holy city that now must be compared to Egypt and Sodom. So we have that for which to be thankful in this time of worsening turmoil.

But by now you know that the sixth Trumpet Judgment, the second woe (Revelation 9), has begun. Apparently I correctly assumed that the 200 million horsemen are spiritual and not physical beings but was wrong to speculate they would thus be invisible. People I know and trust have seen these beings kill by fire and smoke and sulfur as the Scripture predicts. Yet unbelievers charge we are making this up and only claiming to see things they themselves cannot.

That this current plague was wrought by the releasing of four angels bound in the Euphrates River should be instructive. We know that these are fallen angels, because nowhere in Scripture do we ever see good angels bound. These have apparently been bound because they were eager to wreak havoc upon the earth. Now, released, they are free to do so. In fact, the Bible tells us they were prepared for a specific hour, day, month, and year.

It is significant that the four angels, probably bound for centuries, have been in the Euphrates. It is the most prominent river in the Bible. It bordered the Garden of Eden, was a boundary for Israel, Egypt, and Persia, and is often used in Scripture as a symbol of Israel's enemies. It was near this river that man first sinned, the first murder was committed, the first war fought, the first tower built in defiance against God, and where Babylon was built. Babylon is where idolatry originated and has since surged throughout the world. The children of Israel were exiled there as captives, and it is there that the final sin of man will culminate.

Revelation 18 predicted that Babylon will be the center of commerce, religion, and world rule, but also that it will eventually fall to ruin, for strong is the Lord God who judges her.

This current plague, the Bible indicates, will result in the deaths of a third of the population left after the Rapture. Simple math portends a horrible result. One-fourth of the remaining population already died from plague, war, and natural disaster. That left, of course, 75 percent. One third of 75 percent is 25 percent, so the current wave of death will leave only 50 percent of the people left behind at the Rapture.

I must clarify that what follows is speculation. My belief after studying the original languages and the many commentaries on this prophecy is as follows: God is still trying to persuade mankind to come to him, yes, but this destruction of another third of the remaining unbelievers may have another purpose. In his preparation for the final battle between good and evil, God may be winnowing from the evil forces the incorrigibles whom he, in his omniscience, knows would never have turned to him regardless.

The Scriptures foretell that those unbelievers who do survive will refuse to turn from their wickedness. They will insist on continuing worshiping idols and demons, and engaging in murder, sorcery, sexual immorality, and theft. Even the Global Community's own news operations report that murder and theft are on the rise. As for idol and demon worship, sorcery, and illicit sex, these are actually applauded in the new tolerant society.

Sadly this last judgment before the second half of the Tribulation may well continue four more months until the three-and-a-half-year anniversary of the accord between the Global Community and the nation of Israel. That also coincides with the end of the ministry of the two witnesses. And it will usher in a period when believers will be martyred in multiples of the numbers who die now.

Many of you have written and asked me how I explain that a God of love and mercy could pour out such awful judgments upon the earth. God is more than a God of love and mercy. The Scriptures say God is love, yes. But they also say he is holy, holy, holy. He is just. His love was expressed in the gift of his Son as the means of redemption. But if we reject this love gift, we fall under God's judgment.

I know that many hundreds of thousands of readers of my daily messages must visit this site not as believers but as searchers for truth. So permit me to write directly to you if you do not call yourself my brother or sister in Christ. I plead with you as never before to receive Jesus Christ as God's gift of salvation. The sins that the stubborn unbelievers will not give up (see above) will be rampant during the last half of the Tribulation, referred to in the Bible as the Great Tribulation.

Imagine this world with half its population gone. If you think it is bad now with millions having disappeared in the Rapture, children gone, services and conveniences affected, try to fathom life with half of all civil servants gone. Firemen, policemen, laborers, executives, teachers, doctors, nurses, scientists . . . the list goes on. We are coming to a period where survival will be a full-time occupation.

I would not want to be here without knowing God was with me, that I was on the side of good rather than evil, and that in the end, we win. Pray right now. Tell God you recognize your sin and need forgiveness and a Savior. Receive Christ today, and join the great family of God.

Sincerely,
Tsion Ben-Judah

11

MAC AND LEON helped Abdullah toward the chaotic Johannesburg terminal.

"Rehoboth was behind the assassination attempt," Leon said. "He told me so himself. He thought His Excellency was on board. We must get help and regain authority here without risking our lives."

"A little late for that, isn't it?" Mac said. "Couldn't you have made it clear in advance that Carpathia was not with us?"

"We had our reasons to let Mr. Ngumo believe *His Excellency*—which is how you should refer to him, Captain—was aboard. Regional Potentate Rehoboth was invited, but we did not know he was subversive to His Excellency."

"I believe you're going to find Ngumo and his secretary dead," Mac said, and he told Leon of the phone call.

"We had better hope we find Rehoboth dead," Abdullah said. "He cannot afford to leave us alive."

Leon stopped, and his face blanched. "I assumed I spoke to him at his palace. He would not be here, would he?"

"We need to keep moving," Mac said, about to collapse. "If Rehoboth wants us dead, all he has to do is say the word to any one of these guards." But the guards looked as frightened as anyone else, gagging, coughing, attending to fallen comrades. Throughout the terminal people screamed, bodies lay about, luggage was strewn. The counters were empty, arrival and departure monitors blank.

Just after they stepped inside, Mac heard the scream of a Super J jet. The fighter-style knockoff of a Gulfstream was sleek, black, and incredibly aerodynamic—with power to burn and lots of room inside. It was the first plane to land at Johannesburg since the Condor. Above its identifying numbers were emblazoned an Australian flag and *Fair Dinkum.* As soon as the plane stopped, out jumped the pilot and a woman, who both sprinted toward the terminal.

"'Ey!" the man called out shrilly, making many turn. "'Oo called in a Mayday with believers on board!" He was tall, blond, and freckled. His Aussie accent was so thick Mac wouldn't have been surprised if it was put on. His wife was nearly as tall with thick, dark hair.

Mac and Abdullah glanced at each other, and Fortunato slowly turned. "I did," Mac said, noting the marks on both the man's and his wife's foreheads. The Aussie stared at his as well. "I was desperate," Mac added. "I thought that might draw someone who wouldn't otherwise stop. Did it work?"

"It sure did, mate," the pilot said, eyeing Abdullah's forehead as well. "We're believers all right and not ashamed of it, even if you hoodwinked us to get us here. Call me Dart. First name's not important. This here's my wife, Olivia."

"Liv," she said, "and you all need immediate attention."

"'Oo might you be?" Dart demanded of Fortunato.

"I am Supreme Commander Leon For—"

"That's what I figured," Dart said. "It's too early for your boss to be dead, so I won't ask if he's on board that fireball out there."

"Thankfully not," Fortunato said.

"So what happened, the horsemen get you?"

"Oh, you're one of those?" Fortunato said. "You see them too?"

"Sure do."

"Dart," his wife said softly, "we need to get them some help."

"Yeah, I guess we better," he said. "But I don't mind tellin' ya, I feel like I'm aidin' and abettin' the enemy. Personally, I'd leave you to die, but God's gonna get you in the end anyway. Read the Book. We win."

Fortunato turned on him. "You could be imprisoned for speaking disrespectfully of—"

"By the way, Mr. F.—you don't mind me callin' you Mr. F., do ya, because I'm gonna anyway—what's yer major complaint? You look to be ambulatin' all right."

"You are required by law, sir, to refer to me as Su—"

"Let me tell you something, Mr. F. I don't live under your laws no more. I answer to God. You can't do a thing to me he dud'n allow, so take your best shot. Your man here sent up a Mayday, pretended believers were in trouble, the wife and I were intrigued believers might be on board the Antichrist's own plane, so we—"

"Antichrist's?! To refer to His Excellency, Potentate Nic—"

"You don't get it yet, do you, F.? I think he's the Antichrist, and you know what that makes you."

"I'm not a student of that folderol, but I would advise you to—"

"Don't need any advice there, mate, but I can get you some medical help. Looks like your biggest complaint is some torn suit pants and a coupla owies on your hands. These boys here need some real help."

"Honestly, I—"

"There's a medical office in the wing behind this one, and with your clout you oughta be able to pull somebody away from all the other victims."

An announcement came over the public address system. "Attention! Attention please! Global Community Supreme Commander Leon Fortunato please report to GC Peacekeeping Forces headquarters in Wing B."

As the announcement was repeated, Dart said, "That's right next door to the infirmary, Mr. F. How 'bout you go on ahead and we'll get your comrades here to the doctors."

"I should have you arrested, you—"

"If that's your priority right now, you go right ahead. But if I was you, I'd run to safety and let these boys get patched up. There'll be plenty of time for chasin' us once you've caught your breath."

Fortunato's face and neck flushed, and he looked as if he might burst. He turned to Mac. "No doubt His Excellency has provided assistance for us."

"You should go on ahead, Commander," Mac said. "Find out about Rehoboth, check in with Carp—, with the potentate."

"I don't trust this man."

"Aw, c'mon, Mr. F. I'm harmless as a dove. Much as I'd like to kill a couple of your staff, I promise I won't. We'll get 'em where they're goin' and be on our way."

Dart gently pushed Fortunato away from Abdullah and stuck his head under the Jordanian's arm. Liv grabbed Mac's belt with one hand and his left elbow with the other, leaving Fortunato free to go.

"You, sir," Fortunato said as he reluctantly strode on ahead, "are a disgrace to the Global Community."

"We'll wear that one as a badge of honor, won't we, Liv?"

"Oh, Dart," she said.

"Thanks for not giving us away," Mac said when Leon was out of earshot.

"Inside saints," Dart said, his accent now Southern U.S., more like Mac's. "I couldn't believe it. I almost blew it. I saw yours and the little guy's marks and figured the big man might be with us too. As soon as I saw him I knew who he was and had to cover."

"It was brilliant," Mac said, introducing himself and Abdullah.

"And how'd you like Dart and Olivia?" Dart said.

"That even threw me," Liv said.

"You covered perfectly, honey," Dart said. "'Liv' was a stroke of genius."

They introduced themselves as Dwayne and Trudy Tuttle from Oklahoma. "I change the flag and motto on that plane every few days. We've been Germans, Norwegians, Brits. We're with the International Commodity Co-op. Heard of it?"

"If big-mouth here doesn't get us killed," Trudy said.

"Never thought I'd get a chance to tell the False Prophet what I thought of him to his face."

"The False Prophet?" Mac said. "Leon?"

"Claims Carpathia raised him from the dead, didn't he? Worships the guy, calls him His Excellency. You watch and see if it doesn't turn out that way. So, what's your story? You infiltrate, or find Jesus after you were already with the GC?"

+ + +

Buck looked in the mirror. His facial scars were still red and prominent more than a year after his injuries. The surgery he'd found in a makeshift Jerusalem clinic may have been better than he expected, but there was no hiding his disfigurement. Chloe appeared behind him and handed Kenny to him. "Stop thinking that," she said.

"What?"

"Don't play dumb. You think you can use your new face to your advantage."

"Of course," Buck said.

He wondered if handing him the baby was her way of making him want to stay put. But they had been through this before too. She had accepted that her frontline globe-trotting was over. She wasn't about to drag a baby into danger, much as she wanted to be where the action was. Her running the Commodity Co-op was crucial not only to the Tribulation Force, but also to the millions of new believers who would soon have no other source for trade.

Chloe had told Buck she wished he could be content with his behind-the-scenes work, countering the propaganda of *Global Community Weekly* with his own *The Truth.* But with the new technology provided by David Hassid, Buck could do that from anywhere without being traced. The expansion of the cellar was nearly finished, and Buck felt needed in so many other places.

They had also discussed his responsibility to the baby. Sure, this was different from normal child rearing, knowing that Kenny's real growing-up years would be in Christ's earthly kingdom. Still, it was important for a young child to have both parents present as much as possible. Buck had argued that though he might be gone two to three weeks at a time, when he *was* home he was home twenty-four hours a day. "It's a wash," he'd say. "I'd net the same hours with him as I would if I were working away from home."

Buck took the baby to the kitchen and Chloe followed him. "You've got that look in your eye," she said. "A few more days cooped up here and there'll be no stopping you. Where you going?"

"You know me too well," he said. "Truth is, Tsion wants someone to go back to Israel. Check in on Chaim. He's encouraged by the e-mails they trade, but he believes someone has to be there face-to-face before the old man will make his decision."

Chloe shook her head. "I want to disagree, but I can't. Daddy can't risk it. He's got it in his head to track down Hattie before she blows our cover or gets herself killed. Tsion certainly can't go. I don't know what the world would do without him. I know God has everything under control and I suppose he could raise up someone like he did to replace Bruce, but—"

"I know. We ought to be hiring armed guards and moving him out of sight."

"When are you going, Buck?"

She had a way of cutting to the chase.

"Tsion wants to talk to you about it."

She smiled. "Like having a friend ask your parents for a favor? He thinks I can't turn him down."

"Well, can you?"

She snorted. "I can't even turn you down. But if you get yourself killed, I'll hate you for the rest of my life."

"Thought I'd go see Zeke after dark."

She reached for Kenny. "That's what I thought. Stock up on stuff for the baby. I'll make a list of other stuff we need. Talk to Leah too. She says we're low on some basics."

That night Buck rolled into a dilapidated one-pump gas station in what had once been downtown Des Plaines. Believers knew the station as a source for fuel, foodstuffs, and assorted sundries. Zeke managed the place with Zeke Jr.—who went by Z—a middle-twenties longhair covered with tattoos. He had made his living tattooing, pinstriping cars and trucks, and airbrushing monsters and muscle cars onto T-shirts. He also airbrushed the occasional mural on the side of an 18-wheeler. That business, needless to say, had dried up long ago.

The Zekes had lost the Mrs. and two teenage daughters in a fire resulting from the disappearances. They had been led to Christ by a long-haul trucker. Zeke and his son now attended an underground meeting of believers in Arlington Heights, carefully keeping their faith hidden from unbelievers so they could serve as a major supplier and helper. Z had been a no-account druggie whose on-again off-again tattooing and art merely financed his daily high. Now he was the emotional, soft-spoken artist behind most of the fake IDs local Christians used to survive.

Zeke was filling the tank of Buck's Rover and watching for strangers or customers without the mark of God on their foreheads. "Need some stuff," Buck said. "Including Z's handiwork."

"Gotcha," Zeke said. "He's down there watchin' TV and doin' his Ben-Judah study. Lemme have your list. I'll drive your rig into the garage and load it for ya."

Buck got out to venture inside when another car pulled in behind his. "You got enough to fill me?" the man called out. "Or are you rationing today?"

"I can handle it," Zeke said. "Let me get this transmission job on the rack and I'll be right with you."

Buck empathized with the daily tension of living a lie just to stay alive. He moseyed inside, which to unknowing eyes looked a typical greasy station. Brand-name calendars, pictures of cars, an oily phone book, everything dingy. A panel in the tiny washroom, however, was a ruse. The sign said, Danger. High Voltage. Do Not Touch. And a low-level buzz in the fingers awaited anyone who doubted it.

That, however, was the extent of the danger. Knowing where to push and slide the panel opened one into a wooden staircase that led to Zeke's own shelter, fashioned out of the earth beneath and behind the station. Deep in the back, Zeke would fill Buck's list and transport the goods up a rickety staircase into the garage, where he would transfer them to the Rover. In a cozy though windowless and cool earthen room dominated by an oversized ventilation shaft sat the fleshy Z, wearing black cowboy boots, black jeans, and a black leather vest over bare arms and chest. As Zeke had said, Z was watching the news while scribbling notes on a dog-eared spiral notebook with his laptop open.

"Hey, Buck," Z said flatly, putting his stuff away and slowly rising. "What can I do ya for?"

"Need a new identity."

Z squatted behind a sagging lime green couch and swung open a noisy two-drawer filing cabinet that was clearly off its track. He finger-walked his way through about ten files and yanked them out. When the door wouldn't shut all the way, Z resorted to slamming it with his boot. Papers stuck out of the tightly jammed drawer, and Z smiled sheepishly at Buck.

"Choose yer pick," he said, fanning the folders onto the couch.

Buck sat and looked at each folder under the lamp. Z's filing system may have been makeshift, but he sure knew where everything was. Each folder had vital statistics on white males approximately Buck's size and age. "Inventory's getting bigger," Buck said.

Z nodded, his eyes on the TV again. "These smokin' horses are leavin' bodies everywhere. You seen 'em suckers?"

"Not yet. Sound scary."

"Yep. 'Salmost too easy, though. All I got to do is get the wallets before the GC gets the body. Gives people a lot more to choose from."

"This guy," Buck said, putting an open folder at the top of the stack and handing it to Z.

Z tossed the extras behind the couch and studied the file as he set up his instant camera. Buck sat before a plain blue background and posed for straight-ons and profiles. "Thought of you when I seen him," Z said. "Driver's license, passport, citizen's card, anything else?"

"Yeah, make me a card-carrying member of Enigma Babylon Faith. And an organ donor. Why not?"

"Can do. Fast-track?"

"Couple of days?" Buck said.

"Easy."

By the time Buck found Zeke and exited through the garage, he knew Z was plying his trade under a magnifying light in the other room. The next time Buck ventured out in public, he would carry authentic-looking, well-used identification documents with his new face in place of that of the deceased Greg North.

+ + +

Mac had never enjoyed such medical attention. While Johannesburg seemed in disarray, thousands of citizens dead or dying, Fortunato's clout opened every door. Regional GC Peacekeeping Forces swept in on Carpathia's own authority and took charge of Rehoboth's palace. He was discovered dead in his office, along with dozens more of his staff.

Mac and Abdullah had been examined and prepped at the airport infirmary, then transported to the palace for surgery. Leon told them, "You'll also hear that Rehoboth's family was wiped out by the smoke and fire plague. But the smell of GC gunfire may still hang in the air."

As Mac and Abdullah were wheeled into the palace, the bodies of Rehoboth's various families were wheeled out. "The news will be clear that Rehoboth failed in an assassination attempt, but we will likely explain the family deaths as plague related. Our enemies will know the truth."

"And Ngumo?" Mac asked.

"Oh, dead, of course. And his secretary, as you said. Rehoboth masterminded that and engineered it from his office. Ngumo was eliminated, Rehoboth's impostor/assassins were put in place, and Rehoboth was ready to take over once His Excellency was dead."

Mac underwent several hours of surgery by a hand specialist, had major work done on his shoulder, and doctors also redressed his scalp and ear wounds. After several hours of anesthetized sleep, he awoke on his left side, facing Abdullah's bed. His first officer's leg was bandaged and elevated. Abdullah pointed to a jar on his bedstand. It contained a mangled bullet that had been dug from his quadriceps.

"Much damage," Abdullah said. "But not life threatening."

Mac's heavily bandaged shoulder was still numb. His right hand, thickly gauze-wrapped and shaped like a gun, rested on his side.

A GC doctor, a native of India, entered the recovery room. "I was told you were waking," he said. "Successful surgery on three major areas. Your head was the least of it and will heal first. The shoulder will have considerable scarring, but only bullet fragments needed to be removed, and there was no structural damage. You will feel nerve numbness and may have limited mobility. Your hand was saved, fingers intact. This will cause you much discomfort for many weeks, and you will likely require therapy to learn to use it. The ring and middle fingers will be stationary and stiff. We have curved them into a permanent position. The little finger will have no use. You may get limited use from the index finger, but no promises. The thumb will not bend."

"If I can grip the controls with one finger, poke buttons, and flip switches, I can fly again," Mac said.

"I agree," the doctor said. "You were most fortunate."

Fortunato visited. "You will be pleased to know that you both will be receiving the highest award for bravery given by the Global Community," he said. "The Golden Circle, the potentate's prize for valor, will be presented by His Excellency himself as thanks for saving my life."

Neither Mac nor Abdullah responded.

"Well, I know you're pleased and that only your modesty prohibits you from feeling worthy. Now rest. You will recuperate and rehabilitate here as long as necessary, then you will be transported to New Babylon by your former first officer in the new *Global One.*"

"How long will it take to build that?" Mac asked, knowing Fortunato had no clue how long it took to manufacture an airplane.

"It will be painted tomorrow," he said. "Peter the Second has graciously consented to make it a gift to His Excellency. Affairs of state will not be interrupted by this dark episode. The new regional potentate of the U.S. of Africa—a loyalist handpicked by Potentate Carpathia himself—will be installed within the week."

+ + +

Buck drove home with a vehicle full of supplies, a full tank of gas, and a preoccupation about Mac and Abdullah. The radio was full of news of the insurrection and death of Bindura Rehoboth. GC casualties had included a cook and two aides, but accounts of the destruction of *Global Community One* left Buck wondering. He called home, pleased to discover that Rayford had heard from David and that their compatriots were worse for wear but alive.

* * *

A week later David and Annie sat in the Personnel office at the Global Community palace. The personnel director held David's memo. "So the bottom line, Mr. Hassid, is that you take responsibility for Ms. Christopher's breach of procedure protocol?"

David nodded. "I should have told her something that basic."

"Perhaps. Perhaps not. Why is it the department head's responsibility when the subordinate has a procedure manual?"

David shifted. "Annie—Ms. Christopher—may have been distracted by a romantic interest on the part of a coworker."

The director looked over the top of his glasses. "Really," he said, more statement than question. "That hardly excuses the violation. Are you interested in pursuing this relationship, Ms. Christopher?"

"Very much."

"And this coworker is in your department?"

"You're looking at him," David said.

"Brilliant. Well, look. . . . Ms. Christopher's file shows a list of minor offenses, insubordination and the like. But I'll waive the usual lowering of a grade level for this kind of a breach, provided she allows me to reassign her where she can be most profitable."

She hesitated. "And where might that be?"

"Administrative branch. This crisis has cost us more than a dozen analysts. Your profile shows you would excel."

"What does it entail?"

He flipped a page and mumbled as he read: "Administrative branch, chain of command: Potentate, Supreme Commander, Director of Intelligence, Analysis Department Director, Employee. Major duties and responsibilities: examining and interpreting data from sources not sympathetic to the Global blah, blah, blah. Intelligence Analyst, yes or no?"

"Yes."

"And try not to lock yourself in the office."

As soon as they were out of the Personnel office, David took her hand. He felt such freedom! Then he saw Leon Fortunato stride toward the elevator with Peter the Second barking at him from behind.

"I don't want a face-to-face with *you,* Leon."

Fortunato pushed the button and turned on him. "*Supreme Commander* to you, Peter."

"Then do me the courtesy of using *my*—"

"I will if you will," Leon said.

"All right, Commander! But I'll not have Carpathia appropriating my—"

"His Excel—"

"All right! But he must answer to me if he's going to abscond with my aircraft and—"

As they boarded the elevator Leon said, "If you think the potentate of the Global Community would ever answer to you . . ."

"I want to hear this one," David said. "I'll call you, Annie."

"Be careful," she said.

David sprinted to his quarters, locked the door, and called up on his computer the bug in Fortunato's office. Peter II was in mid-sentence:

". . . refuse to sit when this is not where I want to be."

"It's as close as you're going to get."

"Why does His Excellency duck me, Commander? You tell the world I offered my plane, which I might have been happy to do. But I was not consulted, not given a chance to—"

"Everything you have, you have because of the potentate. Do you think Enigma Babylon Faith is independent of the Global Community? Do you think you report other than to His Excellency?"

"I demand to see him this instant!"

"You *demand*? You demand of me? I am the gatekeeper, Supreme Pontiff. You are denied access, refused an audience with His Excellency. Do you understand?"

"I swear to you, Leon, you'll regret insulting me this way."

"I have asked you not to call me—"

"I will call you anything I please. You sit here in artificial authority not because of any following or accomplishments, but because you have mastered the art of kissing up to the boss. Well, I don't kiss up, and I will be heard."

There was a long silence.

"Maybe you will," Leon said. "But not today."

David heard heavy footsteps and a door slam. Then Leon's voice. "Margaret?"

Over the intercom: "Yes, sir?"

"See if the potentate has a moment. You may tell him who just stormed out of here."

"Right away, sir."

David switched to Carpathia's office and listened in on the exchange. His secretary had passed along the message from Fortunato's. "What does he want?" Carpathia asked.

"She says he just had a meeting with the supreme pontiff."

"Invite him up."

12

MAC WAS UP and walking long before Abdullah and was eager to get back to New Babylon. Difficult as his job was, therapy had been no respite. He might have otherwise felt pampered in the Johannesburg palace, but his injuries negated any rest. Between painkillers his body was afire. He requested doses only large enough to take the edge off. The last thing he wanted was an addiction to pills.

Mac was disgusted with himself for two gaffes. He had hollered over the air that believers were on board *Global One.* Fortunately Dwayne Tuttle, the erstwhile "Dart," had covered for him. But Mac had also tossed Leon Fortunato, of all people, his secure phone.

It was nearly twice as heavy as a normal cell phone, packed with so much secure technology. Leon hadn't seemed to notice, but what if someone had called Mac while Leon had the phone? If they didn't recognize Leon's voice or had less than perfect reception, they could have compromised the whole Trib Force.

What troubled Mac was that neither lapse was a result of panic or desperation; both were due to lack of faith. He sincerely believed they were not going to survive the onslaught, and thus, what was the difference?

Fortunately, he had been wise in his selection of a new first officer. Abdullah had saved the day with the phone. Mac had awakened with a start late the first night during his recovery. He shook Abdullah awake. "Leon has my phone," he said. "One call from the wrong person and we're history."

"Sleep well, my friend," Abdullah said. "Your roommate is a pickpocket."

"Come again?"

"When you and Leon were helping me into the terminal, I retrieved your phone from his pocket."

"That's a heavy phone. Why didn't he notice?"

"He was scared to death. I picked my spot. The phone is in my possession."

"What time is it?"

Abdullah checked his watch. "Two in the morning."

"What time in the States?"

"They are nine hours behind us when we are in New Babylon. Eight here."

"Let me have that phone."

Mac called Rayford and filled him in on the Tuttles, who had disappeared shortly after delivering Mac and Abdullah to the infirmary. "I didn't even get a chance to tell them how connected we were to the co-op," Mac said, "but your daughter is surely aware of them."

+ + +

Rayford found Chloe was aware of the Tuttles. "They're going to handle a huge South Sea area for us," she said. "That they were close enough to hear Mac's Mayday is nothing short of a miracle."

"It's a contact straight from God," Rayford said. "If you can spare them, I need them to get me to Europe."

"Why don't you fly yourself, Dad?"

"I don't want to fly alone and then try to be at my best incognito. I'd share the flying with Dwayne. We can take his Super J or the Gulfstream."

"Do you know where you're going?"

"Beauregard Hanson is going to tell me, next time he shows up at Palwaukee. T is going to keep him there under some pretense, I'm going to wave a little cash under his nose, and he's going to sing. He just doesn't know it yet."

+ + +

David Hassid sat transfixed before his computer, earplug in, listening to Carpathia and Fortunato.

"Leon, you must not feel obligated to kiss my ring every time you come into my presence. I appreciate it in public, but—"

"Begging your pardon, Excellency, but—"

"And you must also feel the freedom to address me informally in private. We go back a long way and—"

"Oh, but I could not. Not now. Not after all I have witnessed and experienced. You must understand, Potentate, that I do not do these things from any other motive than genuine devotion. I believe you to be inspired, sir, and while it is the highest honor that you consider me enough of a friend to call me by name, forgive me if I cannot reciprocate."

"Very well, then, Leon. Now tell me about your encounter with the man who would be king."

David listened as Fortunato recounted the conversation. Carpathia was silent a moment. Then, "Peter does not know, does he? He does not have any idea that I knew of his alliance with Rehoboth. He believes he can divide me from my regional potentates and conquer me."

"I'm sure that's what he believes, Excellency."

"What a fool!" Carpathia said.

"Shall we let him lead us to another subversive or two, or has his time come?"

David heard movement, as if Carpathia had stood. His voice quality had changed, so David assumed he was pacing. "I nearly lost patience with you months ago when he had not been eliminated. But in the end there was benefit. Not only did he lead us to Rehoboth, a recent communiqué from him proved most enlightening and may have bearing on our two friends to the south."

"The Jerusalem Twosome?"

"The same. You like that term, do you not?"

"Genius, sir. Only you . . ."

"I had asked him to put his scholars on all the mysterious manuscripts from the past, from Nostradamus to ancient holy writings and such, and see if there are any clues to the vulnerability of those two. I know the Ben-Judah-ites believe they are the two witnesses prophesied in the Christian Scriptures. In the unlikely event that they are, Mathews tells me they will be vulnerable four months from now. They themselves have spoken often of their being protected from harm until the due time."

"But, sir," Fortunato whined, "the people who say these men are the prophesied ones are the same who say you are the Antichrist."

"I know, Leon. You and I know I am merely doing what I have been called to do."

"But if they have a due time, so does their enemy!"

"Leon! Take a deep breath. Do I act like an Antichrist?"

"Certainly not, Excellency!"

"Who do you say that I am?"

"You know well that I believe in my heart you may be Christ himself."

"I shall not make that claim for myself, trusted friend. At least not yet. Only when it is obvious to the world that I have divine power could I personally make such a claim."

"I have spread far and wide the story of your resurrecting me—"

"I appreciate that and am confident many believe it. But it was not witnessed by anyone else, so there may be doubt. I have been ineffective in containing the two preachers, which has damaged my credibility. But I worship a deity determined to be the god above all gods, to sit high above the heavens, to evolve into the perfect eternal being. How can I fail if I pledge myself to him?"

"As I pledge myself to you, Excellency."

To David it seemed Carpathia had returned to his chair behind his desk, where the microphone fidelity was best. "Let us bide our time on Peter," he said. "Are the majority of the potentates at the limits of their patience with him?"

"They are, and, sir, despite that Potentate Rehoboth misled me on this very issue, I believe most of the others were sincere. They assured me they were not only sympathetic to eliminating him, but that they would also be willing to participate in his demise."

"Leon, I have worked with rulers long enough to know that their word is worthless until it has been confirmed by action. We must allow Peter to believe that more regional potentates are disloyal to me. Clearly his goal is to usurp my role. Rehoboth would have been his Fortunato, had the assassination attempt succeeded. Surely Peter must believe he has the confidence of the others. Let us use that to our advantage."

"I will give this my full attention, sir. And thank you again for surrounding me with protection in Johannesburg."

"Think nothing of it. When will the pilots return so we may confer the medals upon them?"

"Soon, sir."

"The people love pageantry, do they not?" Leon agreed aloud, but Carpathia talked over him. "With the turmoil of late, we have had too few opportunities to make examples of model citizens, of heroes."

"Our workforce is depleted, Excellency, but with creativity we can rise to the occasion and make their return to New Babylon a world-class event."

To David, Carpathia sounded as if he were dreaming. "Yes, yes," he said. "I like that. I like that very much. And get someone on this timing issue with the Twosome. If the Ben-Judah-ites put the due time at the midpoint of our agreement with Israel, I want the precise date."

David's heart pounded as he could feel Carpathia's excitement. The potentate raised his voice, spoke more quickly. "Talk about pageantry, my friend! Talk about an event! Fool the two. Surprise them. Defer to them until that time. Give them the audience they think they deserve. Pull out all the stops, Leon. Global television coverage. Plan a happening. Put me there.

"Yes, I shall be in Jerusalem, the heart of the country with whom I have made a solemn pact. We will celebrate the halfway point of the peace that has been accomplished there. Produce the dignitaries. Get Peter there in all his laughable finery. My old friend Dr. Rosenzweig must be a guest of honor. We will do as the so-called saints do and recommit ourselves. I will dedicate myself anew to the protection of Israel!

"With all the world's eyes there, I shall personally take responsibility for the end of the preachers. How her citizens will love the end of plagues, harangues, drought, famine, bloody water! Leon, take a note. Get the potentates to encourage Peter in his scheming against me. Have them lead him to believe they are with him, that they are, are, yes, *unanimous* in their antipathy toward me. They *want* him to be their ruler. Be sure he comes to Jerusalem believing he has the confidence of every one of them."

"I will do my best, sir."

"We have only a few months. Make it your top priority. High level, confidential meetings whenever and wherever you need them. Full use of all our resources. This must be our proudest moment, the perfect performance. It shall be the end of insurrection, the end of opposition, the end of Enigma Babylon trying to assume my authority, the end of the Judah-ites, with no preachers in Jerusalem to worship."

"But Ben-Judah still has that vast audience—"

"Even he will lose heart when it becomes clear there is only one power on earth and that it resides in New Babylon. Invite him! Invite his followers! They were so buoyed by embarrassing me and trying to kill me there last year. Well, welcome them back, and watch their reaction!"

"You are brilliant, Excellency."

"If you like that, Leon, consider this. It will take the best you have to offer. But start confiding in Peter that all is not well between you and me."

"But, Excellency, I love—"

"I know, Leon."

"But the supreme pontiff knows too. I can't imagine convincing him that my unwavering loyalty has suddenly—"

"Of course! It must not be sudden. Let *him* suggest it! Surely he finds negative things to plant in your mind about me, does he not? Has he never criticized me?"

"Certainly, but I always defend your motives and—"

"Just hesitate once, Leon. Let him render you silent just once. I know him. He will pounce on it. He believes he can persuade anyone of anything. What an ego to believe the ten potentates admire him, when we know beyond doubt most of them would kill him themselves! Can you do it, Leon?"

"I'll try."

"I have every confidence in you. Within four months we will consolidate all power and authority and render opposition moot. Just the thought of it energizes me! Go now, friend. Hesitate to ask for nothing. All my—our—resources are at your disposal."

"Thank you, Excellency. Thank you for the privilege of serving you."

"What a nice thing to say," Carpathia said.

David had a headache from listening intently for so long. He was about to shut down the computer when he heard someone in Carpathia's office again. The secretary chatted with him for a minute, then he asked her to hold all calls and allow no visitors until further notice. David heard the door close and then a click, and he assumed Carpathia had locked it. He waited to see if Carpathia made a significant phone call.

He heard the squeak of Nicolae's chair, and then perhaps it rolled. Finally, he heard the potentate whispering. "O Lucifer, son of the morning! I have worshiped you since childhood." David shivered, his heart thudding. Carpathia continued, "How grateful I am for the creativity you imbue, O lion of glory, angel of light. I praise you for imaginative ideas that never cease to amaze me. You have given me the nations! You have promised that I shall ascend into heaven with you, that we will exalt our thrones above the stars of God. I rest in your promise that I will ascend above the heights of the clouds. I will be like the Most High.

"I shall do all your bidding so I may claim your promises to rule the universe by your side. You have chosen me and allowed me to make the earth tremble and to shake kingdoms. Your glory will be my glory, and like unto you, I will never die. I eagerly await the day when I may make plain your power and majesty."

+ + +

Rayford got the call late on a Friday night. "He's here," T said. "And I told him someone was coming in with an interesting and potentially profitable proposition. So far he's bit, but I hadn't seen him since your woman friend disappeared, and I can tell he's waiting for me to raise the issue."

"I'll be there. Keep him warm."

Rayford sat down with Leah and asked if he could wave some of her cash before Bo Hanson to see if he'd sell information on the whereabouts of Hattie Durham.

"Well," she said, as if relishing her position, "you hardly speak to me for days, never ask how I'm doing, not even how or if the ribs are mending, but now you need something and here you are."

Rayford didn't know what to say. He hated her tone and her attitude, but he was guilty. "I have been remiss," he tried.

"I risk my life with you and donate my husband's and my entire life savings to the Tribulation Force, and you treat me like an intruder. That's remiss?"

"Apparently it's unforgivable," he said.

"Apparently? You say that as if conceding that *I've* decided you're without excuse."

Rayford stood. Leah said, "Please don't be rude enough to walk away from me."

He turned. "There are easier ways to say no. Could you try another?"

"But I'm not saying no."

"You could have fooled me."

"I enjoy rattling your cage."

"I'm glad one of us enjoys it."

"Rayford, please. I *have* been hurt by your avoidance of me, but I also realize that you have suffered many losses, including two wives in three years. I don't expect you to be comfortable with me. But I thought we patched up our rocky start, and going through what we went through together has to count for something."

He sat back down. "I don't know about you, Leah, but I found that as frightening as anything I've encountered—and that includes discovering my wife's body at the bottom of the Tigris. I don't like to think about it, and I sure don't want to dwell on it. This is no excuse, but maybe you remind me of it."

"I'm sure I do. But you're in charge here, and I need something to do. Assign me something, chief. I'm ready to offer every medical skill I have when necessary, but I don't want to work only when people are hurt or sick. I've tried to help Chloe with the baby and even some with the co-op, but she's too nice to ask. I have to push myself on her. Make that my job and she won't feel bad about counting on me."

"OK, consider that done."

"Tell *her*."

"I will."

"And you people are so politically correct around here, no one's even suggested I do anything domestic. I happen to be a good cook and enjoy everything about it. Planning, food preparation, even cleanup. May I do that for you so you can all concentrate on what you're supposed to be doing?"

"You'd do that? That would help."

"I'd feel I was contributing. Forget the money. You didn't even have to ask. I told you from the beginning I was giving it to the cause, and I meant it. If circumstances changed and I left here tomorrow, I wouldn't take a penny with me. Can we put that to rest?"

"That's so above and beyond—"

"I already feel appropriately thanked. We bring to the table what we have, and none is more important than another. Except maybe Tsion."

"So you were giving me a hard time because . . . ?"

"You deserved it. You should have cared more and showed it. Have I asked about your knee?"

"Several times."

"I wasn't being polite. I caused that injury. I didn't know you weren't looking, but I shouldn't have stopped in front of you anyway. You're a wonderful man. You were hurt. I care. I asked. You gave me the cursory, macho answer, end of conversation. I was hurt too, and no one was responsible for that but you. You were following too close, moving too fast for conditions."

Rayford shook his head. "So how are the ribs coming?"

"Slow, as a matter of fact. I might have cracked more than one. I can go through a day hardly aware of them, then one false move and I'd like to scream."

"I'm sorry. I hope you feel better soon."

She looked at him.

"I mean it," he said.

"I know. And you have a lot more on your mind than my needs."

"Has everyone else been good to you?"

"The best. No complaints."

"I'm the only one who doesn't get a gold star."

"And since I have your attention, would you consider something, for when I get healthy? I am mobile. I am smart. I take risks, like I did for you all more than once at the hospital. I have no family, nothing to lose. If you need me to go somewhere, do something, deliver something, pick up something, communicate something, I can do the phony alias. All right, I almost blew it with the GC the other night—"

"You gave up too soon was all. Actually you caught on quickly and covered well."

"Keep me in mind is all I'm saying. With hair dye and makeup, women are harder to recognize than men. The GC won't keep my picture circulating for long. Get me a fake ID and put me to work."

"In good time. I've just gotten excited about having you in charge of eats."

"I was afraid I would regret that offer."

Rayford stood, his toe and knee still tender. Chloe stepped in from the front room. "Daddy, bad news. You know I've been trying to reach Nancy, Hattie's sister, to let her know we're sure Hattie's alive? I found her. She shows up on a confirmed dead list. Smoke inhalation."

Rayford looked at the floor. "Well," he said sadly, "another reason to find Hattie."

+ + +

Mac and Abdullah were scheduled to board the new *Global Community One* early Friday evening to be ferried back to New Babylon by Mac's old first officer.

The plane, appropriated from Peter II, had been rechristened from *GC One* to *Phoenix 216.* Leon Fortunato would come to fetch the wounded heroes.

Mac just couldn't wait to get back to David and Annie. There was the chore of bugging the new plane and also something urgent David had to talk to him about and didn't dare by phone. When the world's leading communications security technician won't talk on the phone, it's big.

Mac was packing just after four o'clock when he got a call from Rayford. "I'm on my way to Palwaukee to put some pressure on this Bo character I told you about. I'm going to be in Europe soon and I need a few things. Albie still your best source?"

"By far. What do you need?"

"Oh, ah, I'd just as soon talk to him directly. Got his number?"

"Not with me. I expect to be home tonight. Can you wait till then?"

"I guess, if you can't get David to dig it out for me."

"It's in my computer. A few hours make that much difference?"

"I guess not."

* * *

With his new face and his fresh old-looking documents, Buck flew commercial to Tel Aviv. It had amazed him how difficult it was to find flights anymore. The plague of smoke and fire and sulfur continued to ravage the earth, and virtually every aspect of life was affected. The Rapture itself had changed the face of society, and life had not been the same since the great earthquake either, but Buck knew it would get worse. Virtually everyone had lost someone.

He found it hard to leave Chloe and the baby. He had been with them more than ten months, from the moment of Kenny's birth. Buck couldn't imagine the bond he'd developed and was shocked at how he physically ached to hold the baby. He had known that longing for Chloe, and sometimes it had nearly driven him mad. Somehow with Kenny it was even more intense.

On the plane an Asian woman a few rows behind him held a small boy, probably a few months younger than Kenny. Buck was so jealous it was all he could do to stay in his seat when the boy squalled during takeoff. As soon as he was able, he found his way back and asked the woman if she spoke English.

"Little," she said.

"What's your baby's name?"

"Li," she said, pronouncing it *Lee.*

"Hi, Li," he said, and the boy locked eyes with him. "How old?"

"Seven month," she said.

"Beautiful boy."

"Thank you very much, sir."

"Would he come to me?"

"Beg pardon?"

Buck held out his arms to the baby. "May I hold him?"

She hesitated. "I keep," she said.

"That's fine," he said. "I understand. I would not give my boy to a stranger either."

"You have boy baby?"

He showed her a picture and she cooed and showed it to her son, who tried to grab it. "Beautiful boy too. You miss?"

"Very much."

She nudged her baby toward him, and Buck reached for Li again. The boy eagerly went to him, but when Buck straightened and gathered him in, Li grew serious and squirmed to keep an eye on his mother.

"She's right there," Buck said. "Mama's right there." But Li squawked and she took him back.

Buck offered his hand, which she shook shyly. "Greg North," he said.

"Nice meet you, Mr. Greg," she said, but she did not offer her name.

Later in the flight, after Buck had eaten, he was thrilled when the young mother asked his help. He had seen her pacing the aisle with Li till he fell asleep. She said, "You hold, I eat?" Buck held the sleeping child for nearly twenty minutes before she came for him. He hated to give him up.

In Tel Aviv Buck searched every face for the sign of the cross. The only one he saw was on a man who was being interrogated, so Buck refrained from jeopardizing his situation.

It was nine in the morning in Israel when Buck slung his bag over his shoulder and stepped out of the Ben Gurion airport terminal to call Chaim Rosenzweig's home. A young female answered and spoke in Hebrew. Buck racked his brain. "English, please," he said, hoping he could come up with a name.

"Dr. Rosenzweig's," she said. "May I help you?"

"Hannelore?"

"Yes," she said tentatively. "Who's speaking please?"

"I'll tell you, but you must not say my name aloud, all right?"

"Who is it, please?"

"I want to surprise Chaim, all right?"

"Who?"

"Hannelore, it's Buck Williams."

"Buck!" she whispered with excitement. "No one can hear me. Where are you?"

"Ben Gurion."

"Can you come? The doctor and Jacov will be so excited!"

"I very much want to see everyone."

"Wait there. I will send Jacov."

"Tell him not to say my name, Hannelore. If he must call out for me, I am using the name Greg North."

"Greg North. He will come soon, Buck. Greg, I'm sorry. I will keep your secret from Dr. Rosenzweig. He will be so—"

"And how is Jonas?"

"Oh, Buck, I'm sorry. He has passed. Praise God he is in heaven. We'll tell you all about it."

13

RAYFORD GRABBED his bag of cash and trotted up the tower stairs at Palwaukee Airport. Having seen two cars in the lot, he knew T had kept Bo Hanson from fleeing. Rayford's knee protested a few steps from the top, and he limped to the door.

He had been in the tower many times and knew anyone there had heard his every footfall. T waved him in from behind the desk, and Bo looked up from a side chair as if just realizing someone was coming in. Rayford had found Bo none too bright, despite his privileged upbringing. His bleached crew cut was caked in place, and he took a deep breath, Rayford assumed, to showcase his muscular physique. The pose didn't mask his fear.

"It's been a while, Bo."

He nodded. "Mr. Steeles."

"Steele."

"Sorry."

"What've you been up to, Bo?"

"Nothin' much. What about you?"

"Lost a dear friend recently. Two, matter of fact."

Rayford sat, setting the bag at his feet.

"Two?" Bo said.

"One was my doctor. You met him."

"Yeah. What happened?"

"Something he caught from Hattie."

"Oh. I heard about her. Bad news."

"What'd you hear?"

"It was all over the news," Bo said. "Plane crash. Spain, I think. I lost somebody too. Ernie got burned up the other day in California."

"I'm sorry to hear that."

"Thanks. Sorry about, ah, Hattie, too."

"How much did she pay you, Bo?" Rayford said.

"Pay me?"

"To fly her out of here, concoct a story, fake her death."

"I don't know what you're talking about."

"You approved the flight. Your initials are on the log. You didn't think to alter the plane's identification, so even though the pilot never reported in, his plane was traced to your brother Sam in Baton Rouge."

"He—I—I still don't know what you're talking about."

"You fancy yourself a businessman, Bo?"

Bo looked at T. "I own part of this airport. I do all right."

"Five percent," T clarified.

Bo looked stricken. "I have other holdings, other interests, other concerns."

"Wow," Rayford said. "Impressive words. Any of those *other* things have names?"

"Yeah," Bo said. "One of 'em's named None of Your."

Rayford gave T a look and turned back to Bo, whose chest was heaving, his pulse visible at the neck. "I'll bite, Bo. None of Your?"

"Yeah, it's my business. It's called None of Your Business. Get it? Ha! None of Your Business!"

"Got it, Bo. Good one. So you need payoffs from young women who want to disappear."

"I told you I don't know what you're talking about."

"Yet you haven't denied it."

"Denied what?"

"That you put Hattie Durham on your brother's Quantum and got her flown out of here."

"I deny that."

"You do."

"I absolutely do. I had nothing to do with that."

"It happened, but you didn't do it?"

"Right."

"But now you know what I'm talking about."

"I don't know. I guess. But I wasn't even here."

"Why are your initials on the log?"

"The tower guy called me. Said a guy wanted to refuel a Quantum. I said OK. If it was my brother, I didn't know that. And if his passenger was Hattie, I didn't know that either. I told you. I wasn't here. I didn't put anybody on any plane."

"But you've got one heck of a memory. You know all the details of the flight you OK'd the night you weren't here."

"Prove it."

"Prove what?"

"Whatever you just said."

Rayford shook his head. "You want me to prove you have a good memory?"

"I don't know. You're making fun of me or something, and I don't get it."

Rayford leaned forward and clapped Bo on the thigh. "Tell you something, Bo," he said. "I'm a businessman too. What if I were to tell you I don't have a problem with Hattie flying off to Europe or even pretending to be dead?"

Bo shrugged. "OK."

"She's a grown woman, has her own money, makes her own decisions. She doesn't report to me. I mean, I care about her. She's not really well. Isn't making smart decisions these days, but that's her right, isn't it?"

Bo nodded solemnly.

"But, see, I need to find her."

"Can't help you."

"Don't be too sure. I need to talk to her, give her some news she has to hear in person. Now what am I gonna do, Bo? How am I gonna find her?"

"I dunno. I told you."

"You told me you were a businessman who did all right. How much of a businessman are you, Bo? This much of one?" Rayford bent and unzipped his bag.

Bo leaned and peered into it. He looked up at Rayford, then at T.

"Go ahead," Rayford said. "Grab a bundle. They're real. Go on."

Bo grabbed a wrapped stack of twenties and pressed his thumb against the end, letting the bills flap in succession.

"You like?" Rayford said.

"'Course I like. How much you got?"

"See for yourself."

Bo bent to the bag in earnest and opened it wide. "I could use some of this."

"Badly enough to tell me what I need to know?"

He still had his nose in the bag. "Nothing like the smell of cash. What do you need to know?"

"I want to fly to Europe tomorrow and find Hattie Durham alive and well within an hour after I hit the ground. Know anybody who can help me with that?"

"Maybe."

Rayford grabbed two handfuls of bundles from the bag and began setting them on the desk one by one. When three bundles were laid out, he said, "Would that buy me some information?"

"A little."

"Like what?"

"France."

"City?"

"More."

Rayford set another bundle.

"Coast."

"You drive a hard bargain. North or south?"

"Yes."

With every question, Rayford added cash. Finally he narrowed it to a city on the English Channel. "Le Havre."

"You've got a lot of money sitting there," Rayford said, "but every bill goes back into the bag without an exact address, who she's with, and what might otherwise surprise me. You write it down, I leave this money with T—"

"Hey, you're welshin'!"

"—and when I find her, I tell him, and you get the dough. But you've got to write it down."

"It's already written down," Bo said, and he produced it from his wallet. Everything Rayford needed was hand printed in tiny letters. "You'll keep me out of this, right?"

"That I promise," Rayford said. "Now there is the matter of silence."

"Silence?"

"You haven't proven good at it, have you?"

"Guess not."

"I'm not good at it either."

"You said you'd keep me out of this."

"I assume you meant to not tell whoever is with Hattie, or Hattie herself."

"That *is* what I meant."

"But my *complete* silence can be bought."

"Silence from who?"

"The GC, of course. Defrauding an insurance company by a fake death or even causing rescue workers to search under false pretenses is an international class X felony under Global Community law. It is punishable by life imprisonment. As a citizen, I am bound to report any knowledge of a felony."

"I'll deny it."

"I have a witness." He nodded to T, who was staring down at the desk.

"You takin' his side, Delanty? You're scum."

T said, "This is between you and—"

"Forget it," Bo said. "I'll take my chances. This is ex—, extor—, blackmail."

"Bo," Rayford said, "can you reach that phone? You'd better call and report this extortion, and be sure to tell them what it is I'm blackmailing you over. You know, the felony."

Bo snorted and folded his arms.

"Oh, are you through with the phone?" Rayford said. "I need to report a crime."

"You wouldn't dare. You're hidin' out yourself."

"They accept anonymous reports, don't they, T?" T did not respond. "Let's find out." Rayford lifted the receiver and began to push buttons.

"All right! Hang it up!"

"Are we businessmen again, Bo? Ready to negotiate?"

"Yes!"

"How about I make it easy on you? How about I not let it cost you a penny you don't have yet? How's that?"

Bo shrugged.

"For instance, you don't have this yet." Rayford swept the bundles of cash off the desk and into the bag in one motion.

"Awright, fine! I'll just tell whoever I need to, you'll never find Hattie Durham."

"Now, you see, Bo, I had considered that. It's just a little shortsighted. I'm holding the cards now. If Hattie's gone for *any* reason, you're an international fugitive. Believe me, I've been there, and you don't want that."

Rayford thrust out his hand. "Nice doing business with you, Bo."

And Beauregard Hanson, intellect that he was, shook Rayford's hand. "Hey!" he said, yanking it away. "It wasn't nice doing business with you, you—you stupid guy!"

Bo slammed the door, marched down the stairs, slammed the tower door, slammed his car door, threw dirt and gravel as he spun out of the parking lot, raced out the gate, and ran out of gas. Rayford watched from above as he tried to flag down a ride.

+ + +

Jacov pulled to the curb at Ben Gurion and leaped from the Mercedes.

"Greg!" he exulted, bear-hugging Buck. As soon as they were in the car he said, "How are you, my brother?"

"Worried about Chaim. And eager to check in on you all."

"Hannelore told you about Jonas."

Buck nodded. "What happened?"

"Well, tell me, have you seen the horsemen?"

"No."

"Believe me, you don't want to. Frightful things. They were rampaging through our neighborhood while Jonas was in the security booth. You know it."

"Sure."

"A house burned across the street and a man driving past was overcome by smoke. He passed out and the car struck the booth. Chaim was most distressed. He did not believe we could see the creatures. He still thinks we are lying, but he laments Jonas's death. He says over and over, 'I thought he was one of you. I thought he would be protected.' And he has now gone from being very close, studying Dr. Ben-Judah's messages every day, to crying out at all times of the day and night, 'It's not true, any of it, is it? It's lies, all lies.'

"And, Buck, he has done something strange. We know he is old and eccentric, yet he is still brilliant. But he has purchased a wheelchair. Motorized. Very expensive."

"Does he need it?"

"No! He has recovered from the locust sting. He fears the current plagues like a man possessed, sitting by the window, watching for the vapors. Will not go out. Spends a lot of time in his workshop. You remember it?"

Buck nodded. "But the chair?"

"He rides around the house in it, and when he gets bored on one floor, he calls me and a valet, and we must carry it to another floor for him. Most heavy."

"What's it all about?"

"It is as if he is practicing with it, Buck. He was not good at first, always bumping things. Could not back up, could not turn around. Would get into impossible positions, then get angry, and finally call us to help him pull it free. But he has become proficient at it. He never has to back up and start over. He can go through narrow places, turn around in a confined place, quite remarkable. He is accomplished on every floor. He entertains himself, I think."

"What's he doing in the shop, Jacov?"

"No one knows. He locks himself in there for hours at a time, and we hear filing, filing, filing."

"Metal?"

"Yes! And we see the tiny shavings, but we never see what has been filed. He has never been good with his hands. He is a brilliant man, creative, analytical, but not one who spent time working with his hands. He still reads botany and writes for the technical journals. And he is studying biblical history."

Buck shot Jacov a double take as they pulled onto Chaim's street. "You're not serious."

"He is! He compares texts against the Bible and against what Tsion teaches. He and Tsion have corresponded."

"I know. That's why I'm here. Tsion is very concerned for him, believes he is close."

"I thought he was too, Buck. We believers surrounded him after you left. But then he watches the news and finds himself so disappointed in Carpathia. He feels betrayed, feels Israel has been betrayed. He cannot get through to Nicolae, is always stopped short by his commander."

"Fortunato."

"Yes. Most troubling. You will be alarmed at how he has aged, Buck, but it will lift his spirits to see you."

"Anything else?"

"Not that I can think of. Wait, yes. Do not mention strokes."

"Strokes?"

"You know, when the body—"

"I know what a stroke is, Jacov. Why would I ever mention such a thing?"

"He seems to have become obsessed with the subject."

"Of strokes." Buck let the statement hang in the air. "Whatever for?"

"He is beyond us, Buck. We have given up understanding him. A distant relative has had a stroke, and he has seen pictures of the man. A pitiful change. He must fear that for himself. That is not like him. You know."

+ + +

The Global Community palace complex had become depressing. About 15 percent of the employees had been killed by smoke, fire, or sulfur. Carpathia publicly blamed Tsion Ben-Judah. Newscasts carried sound bites of the potentate averring, "The man tried to kill me before thousands of witnesses at Teddy Kollek Stadium in Jerusalem more than a year ago. He is in league with the elderly radicals who spew their hatred from the Wailing Wall and boast that they have poisoned the drinking water. Is it so much of a stretch to believe that this cult would perpetrate germ warfare on the rest of the world? They themselves clearly have developed some antidote, because you do not hear of one of them falling victim. Rather, they have concocted a myth no thinking man or woman can be expected to swallow. They would have us believe that our loved ones and friends are being killed by roving bands of giant horsemen riding half horses/half lions, which breathe fire like dragons. Of course, the believers, the saints, the holier-than-thous can see these monstrous beasts. It is we, the uninitiated—in truth, the uninoculated—who are blind and vulnerable. The Ben-Judah-ites cannot persuade us with their exclusivistic, intolerant, hateful diatribes, so they choose to kill us!"

David's own department was slowly being decimated. Survivors, scared to be outdoors and yet no less vulnerable indoors, worked double shifts and still walked around in terror.

Whatever joy David and Annie might have had in the first love stage of their relationship was dampened by the travail of so many. Those who knew them, who might have been excited for them and encouraged them, now considered personal relationships trivial. And as much as David and Annie loved each other, they couldn't argue that point. People were dying and going to hell. David was so saddened that he seriously considered escaping the palace with Annie and going somewhere where they could help evangelize people before it was too late.

Annie helped him realize anew the unique position he was in. They sat in his office one night, hunched over his computer, holding hands. A simple Y clip allowed them both to listen in on a conversation between Leon and Peter II in Peter's office at the Faith palace.

"Carpathia's day is past, Leon. Now, you must stop reacting that way every time I use other than those ridiculous titles you two have thrust upon each other."

"But you insist on being called—"

"I have earned my title, Leon. I am a man of God. I head the largest church in history. Millions around the world pay homage to my spiritual leadership. How long before they demand that I lead them politically as well? The religious Jews and the fundamentalist Christians are the only factions who have not brought themselves into step with Enigma Babylon Faith.

"Factions? Pontiff, we estimate that a billion people access Ben-Judah's Web site every day."

"That means nothing. I am one of them. How many of those are devotees? I certainly am not, yet I have to keep tabs on their nonsense. I have been patient with them, allowed them their uniqueness and dissidence in the name of tolerance, but that day is closing.

"I have begged Carpathia to make it illegal to practice religion outside the One World Faith. Soon I will step up the punishment for the same and dare him to do something about it. Does he really want to go on record as countering the most beloved religious figure of all time? My people expect no less of me than to take swift, definite action against intolerant apostates. But you believe Carpathia himself is deity."

"Yes, I do."

"Worthy of worship."

"I do, Pontifex."

"Why, then, is such a god/man impotent in the face of the two preachers? They have made him a laughingstock."

"But he negotiated with them and—"

"And gave away the store. He said himself he had upheld *his* end of the bargain, refusing to persecute believers if the two so-called witnesses would let the Israelis drink water instead of blood! Well, they may be drinking pure water, but they are also choking to death in droves! Who's been made the fool, Leon?"

No answer.

"You can't say it, can you, Leon? You can't admit your godlike boss is incapable of doing the right thing. You yourself would not stand for such insolence from your subjects. Rest assured, whoever those two codgers are, wherever they're from, and whatever magical powers they tap into, they are not above the law. They are subject to the Global Community, and if Leon Fortunato were potentate, that problem would have been taken care of long before now. Am I right? Huh, Leon? You'd do what I would do, wouldn't you? You'd have those two eliminated."

No response.

"Once I do that, Leon, you'll want to stay close, hear me? Stay close. If I am beloved now, if revered, if deferred to, imagine my subjects when I rid them of these plague-mongers. Admit it, Leon, Nicolae is biding his time. Isn't he? Waiting them out. Now there's courage. There's diplomacy. There's impotence! Defend him, Leon! You can't, can you? You can't."

"I must hurry to another appointment, Pontifex, but I must say that when I hear you speak so decisively, I do yearn for a return to that kind of leadership."

"There are regional potentates who agree with you, Leon," Mathews said.

"Well, if I may be perfectly frank, Pontifex, a man in my position would have to be deaf and blind to not see how the potentates, to a man, venerate *you*."

"Neither am I blind to their respect, Leon. I appreciate knowing you recognize it as well. I should like to think they would welcome my leadership in areas other than just spiritual."

14

THE NEW COMPUTERS had been installed, and David Hassid's depleted workforce was grinding away. Bright young minds combined with the latest technology, driven and analyzed by the computers, to try to get a bead on the origin of the transmissions from Tsion Ben-Judah and Cameron Williams. The former had become the best-known name in the world, save Carpathia himself. He disseminated encouragement, exhortation, sermons, Bible teaching, even language and word studies based on his lifetime of study.

Buck, on the other hand, produced a weekly cybermagazine called *The Truth*. He too had a huge following who remembered when he was the celebrated youngest senior writer for *Global Weekly*. He became publisher when all news outlets, print and electronic, were taken over by Carpathia and the magazine had been renamed *Global Community Weekly*. When Buck's true sympathies were exposed and he became known as a believer in Christ, he became a fugitive. Linked with Carpathia's former lover, Hattie Durham, as well as with Tsion Ben-Judah, he had to live in hiding or travel incognito.

Buck urged his readers, "Keep your copy of *Global Community Weekly*, the finest example of newspeak since the term was coined. The day before each new issue, visit *The Truth* online and get the real story behind the propaganda the government has foisted upon us."

David Hassid loved the reaction at the palace to Buck's weekly counters of *GC Weekly*. *The Truth* was indeed the truth, and everyone knew it. David had written a program that allowed him to monitor every computer in the vast compound. His statistics showed that more than 90 percent of GC employees visited Buck's magazine Web site weekly, second in popularity only to the porn and psychic sites.

Using the enormous satellite tracking dishes and microwave technology, it was theoretically possible to trace any cyberspace transmission to its source. Most clandestine operators moved around a lot or built in antitracking shields that made detection difficult. Besides having helped design the transmission protocol for the stateside Trib Force, David took double precautions by inserting a glitch into the computers in his department.

The complicator was purely mathematical. A key component in plotting coordinates, of course, is measuring angles and computing distances between various points. On paper such calculations would take hours. On a calculator, less time. But on a computer, the results are virtually instantaneous. David planted, however, what he called a floating multiplier. In layman's terms, any time the computer was assigned a calculation, a random component transposed side-by-side digits in either the third, fourth, or fifth step. Not even David knew which step it would select, let alone which digits. When the calculation was repeated, the error would be duplicated three times in a row, so checking the computer against itself was useless.

Should someone's suspicions be raised and they checked the computer against an uncontaminated calculator, the computer would eventually flush the bug and give a correct reading. Once the techie was convinced the previous had been human error or a temporary glitch, he would move on to the next calculation and probably not realize until hours or days later that the computer had a mind of its own again.

David assumed that by the time the inconsistencies of the machines became an issue, the project would fall so far behind that it would be scrapped. Meanwhile, the computers used to generate Tsion's teaching and Buck's magazine were programmed to change their signal randomly, changing every second between 9 trillion separate combinations of routes.

Under the guise of getting a bead on Williams's base, the techies in David's department spent a lot of time studying the on-line magazine itself. It was clear to everyone that Williams had inside information, but no one knew his sources. David knew Buck used dozens of contacts, including David himself, but Buck always cleverly shaded the input to protect his informants.

The last issue of *GC Weekly* had carried the story of the failed assassination attempt on Carpathia by Regional Potentate Rehoboth. The magazine pretended to be totally forthcoming by revealing that this had been a shock to the Carpathia regime. "Honest, forthright men of character seek to discuss their differences diplomatically," an editorial began.

Such a man of honor was Mwangati Ngumo of Botswana, who insisted more than three years ago that Nicolae Carpathia replace him as secretary-general of the United Nations. That selfless, forward-thinking gesture resulted in the great Global Community we enjoy today, a world divided into ten equal regions, each governed by a subpotentate.

His Excellency asked Supreme Commander Leon Fortunato to visit the honorable Mr. Ngumo and try to persuade him to let the potentate's reconstruction effort rebuild Botswana. Ngumo, the great African statesman, had insisted that his own nation wait until even poorer countries were helped. Mr. Ngumo had been so benevolent that the meeting had to be held in Johannesburg rather than Gaborone, because the Botswanian capital airport still could not accommodate the large GC plane.

When United States of Africa potentate Rehoboth learned of the meeting, he generously offered every courtesy and offered to sit in for the sake of diplomacy. This the Global Community politely declined, because the nature of the business was more personal than political. Potentate Rehoboth was promised his own meeting with His Excellency.

Rehoboth must have misunderstood somehow and assumed that Potentate Carpathia himself would attend the meeting with Mr. Ngumo. While the GC was unaware of any jealousy or anger over Rehoboth's exclusion from the meeting, clearly the regional potentate was murderously angry. He assigned assassins to murder Ngumo and his aides, replace them as impostors, and board Global Community One *(the Condor 216) to murder His Excellency.*

While his henchmen succeeded in destroying the plane and killing four staff personnel, heroic measures by both the pilot and first officer—Captain Montgomery (Mac) McCullum and Mr. Abdullah Smith—saved the life of the supreme commander. Immediate response by Global Community Peacekeeping Forces resulted in the deaths of the assassins.

Photos of the grand celebration honoring the wounded cockpit crew accompanied the article. *The Truth,* six days later, took the story apart. In his breezy style, Buck ran down the facts:

What the Global Community brass doesn't want citizens to know is that the relationship between Carpathia and Ngumo had long ago gone south. Ngumo had not been so magnanimous as we have been led to believe. He stepped down from his UN post under heavy pressure, believing he would receive one of the ten regional potentate positions and that Botswana would be awarded use of the agricultural formula discovered in Israel, which Carpathia has used in negotiating with many other countries.

Ngumo had gone from near deity to pariah in his own homeland because of the shameless neglect on the part of the Global Community. The formula was never delivered. Botswana was ignored in the reconstruction effort. Ngumo saw his potentate status bestowed instead on his archrival, the despot Rehoboth—who had pillaged his own nation of Sudan and made multimillionaires of his many wives and offspring. He was so unpopular in Sudan that he located the opulent GC regional palace in Johannesburg rather than Khartoum, as inconveniently noncentral as he could have without placing it in Cape Town.

The GC knew Rehoboth and Ngumo were bitter rivals, and by deliberately scheduling the high level meeting on board GC One, *they forced it onto Rehoboth's own turf. Rehoboth assumed Carpathia was on board and vulnerable to attack because Ngumo thought he was on board as well. This ruse to slap Ngumo in the face also fooled Rehoboth, who had been invited to join the meeting as yet another surprising insult to Ngumo.*

Personnel who escaped with their lives were more lucky than heroic. GC Peacekeeping Forces had been swayed by Rehoboth and did not respond for several minutes after the plane was fired upon. The assassins were not shot. One fled and two died from the smoke and fire and sulfur plague, as did many others that day.

Rehoboth knew enough to stay at his palace during what he hoped was Carpathia's execution. When it went awry and he himself was eliminated, the peacekeeping forces once again immediately fell into line and finally contained the area. The deaths of Rehoboth's entire family, attributed by the GC to the plague, were clearly executions. Thus far the plague has killed roughly 10 percent of the earth's population. What are the odds that every member of an extensive household would be stricken in one day?

Buck's cybermagazine commented on all the follies of the Carpathia regime, the "penchant for putting a pretty face on international tragedy, and an assumption that you care about parades in the potentate's honor when death marches the globe."

David enjoyed patching in to Carpathia and Fortunato's offices shortly after Buck's magazine hit the Net each week. "Where are we on tracing this?" Carpathia demanded of Leon that morning.

"We have an entire department section on it full-time, sir."

"How many?"

"I believe seventy were scheduled, but due to attrition, probably sixty."

"That should be plenty, should it not?"

"I should think so, sir."

"*Where* is he getting his information? It is as if he is camped outside our door."

"You said yourself he was the best journalist in the world."

"This goes beyond skill and writing ability, Leon! I would accuse him of making this up, but we both know he is not."

That afternoon David received a memo from Leon, asking that the metal detectors destroyed in the airplane be replaced "before His Excellency appears in public again." That gave David an idea. Might he have a role in Carpathia's demise if he could ensure the metal detectors would malfunction at strategic junctures? If he could make computers whimsical, could he make metal detectors fickle?

He wrote back: "Supreme Commander Fortunato, I shall have the new metal detectors delivered and operational and stored on the Phoenix 216 within ten days. In the meantime I have a crew thoroughly going over every detail of the plane so it meets the standards of the potentate. I am personally overseeing this with the input of the cockpit crew."

David and Annie, along with Mac and Abdullah, both slowly mending, spent their off-hours planting a bugging device in the Phoenix 216 so sophisticated that it delivered near recording-studio sound quality to the headsets of both pilot and first officer.

When it was finished, David asked his top technicians to check the plane for bugs. A unit of four experts combed the fuselage for six hours and judged it "clean."

+ + +

Rayford was bemused by Bo Hanson, standing outside the Palwaukee gate trying to flag down help. "What an idiot," he said.

T, still sitting behind him at the tower desk, said, "What's he doing?"

"Hitchhiking, I think. Ran out of gas." He turned around to reach for the phone. "Well, I've got to tell Dwayne Tuttle how to get here." T was rising. "Don't get up," Rayford said. "It'll be a short call."

"I've got something I have to do anyway," T said. "Then can we talk?"

Rayford looked at his watch as Tuttle's phone rang. "I'm good for a little while."

Mrs. Tuttle answered, and as Rayford introduced himself and reminded her of his daughter's e-mails and how he had gotten their number, he idly strode back to the window. Trudy called Dwayne to the phone, and Rayford was glad he didn't have to speak for a few seconds. He had lost his breath. T had driven out to Bo's car and was pouring gasoline into his tank from a can. Was it possible they were in league with each other? Could T have fooled him all this time?

Something told him that if he had a moment to think about it, he could come up with some other explanation. The locusts had not bitten T. He had the mark of God on his forehead. He knew church people, said the right things, seemed genuine. But now aiding and abetting the enemy? Helping the man responsible for Hattie's flight?

"Mr. Steele!" Dwayne said.

"Mr. Tuttle, or should I call you Dart? That was quite a story, sir."

T returned and slowly mounted the stairs as Rayford finished making arrangements for the flight to France. When he hung up he looked askance at T as they sat across the desk from each other. T's dark face mirrored Rayford's own look.

"You think I didn't notice?" Rayford began.

"Notice what?"

"What you were just doing. That little something you had to do."

"So what was I doing?"

Rayford rolled his eyes. "I saw you, T. You were giving gas to Bo."

T gave him a "So?" look.

"The guy who—"

"I know who Bo is, Ray. I'm beginning to wonder who you are."

"Me? I'm not the one—"

T stood. "You want to check my mark, don't you? Well, come on and do it."

Rayford was stunned. How had it come to this? They had been friends, brothers. "I don't need to check your mark, T. I need to know what you thought you were doing."

"I asked to talk to *you,* Ray. Remember?"

"Yeah, so?"

"I wanted to know what you thought *you* were doing with Bo."

"What's the mystery, T? I got him to give me the information I needed. I didn't aid or abet him."

"Like I did."

"Like you did."

"That's what you call what I did."

"What do you call it, T? You guys working together against me, behind my back, what?"

T shook his head sadly. "Yeah, Ray. I'm in concert with a kid two sandwiches short of a picnic so I can turn the tables on my Christian brother."

"That's what it looks like. What am I supposed to think?"

T stood and walked to the window. Rayford couldn't make any of it make sense.

"What you're supposed to think, Ray, is that Bo Hanson is not likely long for this world. He's going to die and go to hell just like his buddy Ernie did the other day. He's the enemy, sure, but he's not one of those we treat like scum to make sure they don't find out who we really are. He already knows who we are, bro. We're the guys who follow Ben-Judah and believe in Jesus. We don't buy and sell guys like Bo, Rayford. We don't play them, lie to them, cheat them, steal from them, blackmail them. We love them. We plead with them.

"Bo is dumb enough to have given you what you needed without making him think his ship had come in and then sinking it for him. I'm not saying I have the answers, Ray. I don't know how we could have got the information another way, but what you did sure didn't feel loving and Christian to me. I'd rather you *had* bought the information. Let *him* be the bad guy. You were as bad as he was.

"Well, I said more than I planned. You play this one however you want, but keep me out of it from now on."

Buck half expected Chaim Rosenzweig to be in his wheelchair, but the old man was everything he had remembered. Small, wiry, aged more perhaps, wild white hair. A beatific smile. He opened his arms for an embrace. "Cameron! Cameron, my friend! How are you? Good to see you! A sight for old, tired eyes! What brings you to Israel?"

"You do, friend," Buck said as Chaim led him by the arm to the parlor. "We're all worried about you."

"Ach!" Chaim said, waving him off. "Tsion is worried he won't convert me before the horses trample me."

"Should he be? May I take back the news of your conversion?"

"You never know, Cameron. But you need not ask, am I right? You who can see the horses can also see each other's marks. So, tell me. Does mine show?"

The way he said *mine* made Buck's heart leap, and he leaned forward only to see nothing. "We *can* see each other's, you know," Buck said.

"And the mighty men on the lion horses too, I know."

"You don't believe it."

"Would you if you were I, Cameron?"

"Oh, Dr. Rosenzweig, I *was* you. Don't you realize that? I was a journalist, a pragmatist, a realist. I could not be convinced until I *would* be convinced."

Chaim's eyes danced, and Buck was reminded how the man enjoyed a good debate. "So I am unwilling, that is my problem?"

"Perhaps."

"And yet that makes no sense, does it? Why should I be unwilling? I *want* it to be true! What a story! An answer to this madness, relief from the cruelty. Ah, Cameron, I am closer than you think."

"That's what you said last time. I fear you will wait too long."

"My house staff, they are all believers now, you know. Jacov, his wife, her mother, Stefan. Jonas, too, but we lost him. You heard?"

Buck nodded. "Sad."

Chaim had suddenly lost his humor. "You see, Cameron, these are the things I don't understand. If God is personal like you say, cares about his children, and is all-powerful, is there not a better way? Why the judgments, the plagues, the destruction, the death? Tsion says we had our chance. So now it's no more Mr. Nice Guy? There is a cruelty about it all that hides the love I am supposed to see."

Buck leaned forward. "Tsion also says that even allowing seven years of obvious tribulation is more than we deserve from God. We did not believe because we could not see it. Well, now there is no doubt. We're seeing, and yet people still resist and rebel."

Chaim fell silent, then clapped his palms to his knees. "Well," he said at last, "don't worry about me. I confess I am feeling my age. I am fearful, frightened, homebound, you know. I cannot bring myself to venture out. Carpathia, in whom I believed as I would my own son, has proven fraudulent."

Buck wanted to probe but dared not. Any decision had to be Rosenzweig's idea, not a plant from Buck or anyone else.

"I am studying. I am praying that Tsion is wrong, that the plagues and the torments do not keep getting worse. And I keep busy."

"How?"

"Projects."

"Your science and reading?"

"And more."

"Such as?"

"Oh, you are such the journalist today. All right, I'll tell you. My staff thinks me mad. Maybe I am. I have a wheelchair. You want to see it?"

"You need a wheelchair?"

"Not yet, but the day will come. The torment from the locust weakened me. I have blood counts and other test results that show me at high risk for stroke."

"You're healthy as a hor—as a mule."

Rosenzweig sat back and laughed. "Very good. No one wants to be healthy as a horse anymore. But I am not. I am high risk and I want to be ready."

"It sounds defeatist, Doctor. The right diet and exercise . . . fresh air."

"I knew you would get to that. I like to be prepared."

"How else are you preparing?"

"I'm sorry?"

"What are you working on? In your utility room?"

"Who told you about that?"

"No one who knew anything. Jacov merely mentioned that you spend a lot of time on projects in there."

"Yes."

"What is it? What are you doing?"

"Projects."

"I never knew you to be handy that way."

"There is a lot you don't know about me, Cameron."

"May I consider you a dear friend, sir?"

"I wish you would. But do dear friends refer to each other so formally?"

"It's difficult for me to call you Chaim."

"Call me what you wish, but you are my dear friend and so I am happy to call myself yours."

"Then I want to know more about you. If there is a lot about you I don't know, I don't feel like a friend."

Chaim pulled a drape back and peered out. "No smoke today. It will come again though. Tsion teaches that the horsemen will not leave us until a third of mankind is dead. Can you imagine that world, Cameron?"

"That will leave only half the population since the disappearances."

"Truly we are facing the end of civilization. It may not be what Tsion thinks it is, but it's something."

Buck said nothing. Chaim had ignored his salvos, but perhaps if he did not press . . .

+ + +

Rayford hung his head. "T," he said, his voice suddenly hoarse and weak, "I don't know what to say."

"You knew what to say to Bo. You played him like a—"

Rayford held up a hand. "Please, T. You're right. I don't know what I was thinking."

"You seemed to enjoy it."

Rayford wished he could disappear. "God forgive me, I did enjoy it. What's the matter with me? It's like I've lost my mind. At the house I fly off the handle. Leah, the newcomer I told you about, she's brought out the worst in me—now, no, I can't put that on her either. I've been awful to her. I don't understand myself anymore."

"If you ever understood yourself you were way ahead of me. But don't be too hard on yourself, bro. You've got a modicum of stress in your life."

"We all do, T. Even Bo. You know, not just tonight, but never ever have I seen Bo as anything but a scoundrel."

"He *is* a scoundrel, Ray. But he's also—"

"I know. That's what I'm saying. The day I met him he was putting down believers, and I've had a thing about him since. I want him put in his place and I was glad for the chance to do it. Some saint, huh?"

T didn't counter. Rayford got the point.

"What do I do now, chase him down and start being Christlike to him?"

T shook his head and shrugged. "Got me. I'd sooner think your best approach is to disappear from his life. He's going to suspect any radical change."

"I should at least apologize."

"Not unless you're ready to prove it by paying him for the information he thought you were buying."

"Now he's the good guy and I'm the bad guy?"

"I'll never say Bo's the good guy, Ray. As for you being the bad guy, I didn't say it. You did."

Rayford sat slumped for several minutes while T busied himself with paperwork. "You're a good friend," Rayford said finally. "To be honest with me, I mean. Not a lot of guys would care enough."

T moved to the front of the desk and sat on it. "I like to think you'd do the same for me."

"Like you need it."

"Why not? I didn't expect you'd need it either."

"Well, anyway. Thanks."

T punched him on the shoulder. "So what's the deal with the Tuttles? You gonna get to fly a Super J?"

"Think I can handle it?"

"All the stuff you've flown? They say if you can drive a Gulfstream—the big one—this is like a fast version of that. Sort of a Porsche to a Chevy."

"I'll drive like a teenager."

"You can't wait."

✢ ✢ ✢

David was at first warmed, then alarmed, when he received a personal e-mail early the next evening from Tsion Ben-Judah. After assuring David he wished to meet him sometime before the Glorious Appearing, Tsion came to his point.

I do not understand all that you are able to do so miraculously for us there with your marvelous technical genius. Normally I stay out of the political aspects of our work and do not even question what is going on. My calling is to teach the Scriptures, and I want to stay focused. Dr. Rosenzweig, whom I am certain you have heard of, taught me much when I was in way over my head in university botany. My specialty is history, literature, and languages; science was not my field. Struggling, struggling, I finally went to him. He told me, "The main thing is to keep the main thing the main thing." In other words, of course, focus!

So I am here focusing and letting Captain Steele and his daughter put together the co-op, Buck Williams his magazine and the occasional furtive mission, and so forth. But, Mr. Hassid, we have a problem. I let Captain Steele run off on his mission to track down Hattie Durham (I know you have been kept abreast) without asking him what he had found out about Carpathia's knowledge of her whereabouts.

No one but the uncaring public believes she went down in a plane. That the GC allowed that patent falsehood to be circulated tells me it somehow plays into their hands. My fear, of course, is that they now feel free to track her down and kill her, for in the mind of the public she is already dead. Her only advantage in pretending to be dead is to somehow embarrass or even endanger Carpathia.

All that to say this: I had been under the impression that none of your clandestine work there had turned up anything about knowledge of her whereabouts on Carpathia's part. I cannot help thinking Rayford would have been more prudent to wait on searching for Hattie until he knew for sure he would not be walking into a GC trap.

I may be a paranoid scholar who should stick to his work, but if you know my history, you know that even I have been thrust into violence and danger by this evil world system. I am asking you, Mr. Hassid, if there is any possibility of digging up the remotest clue that could be rushed to Captain Steele before he walks blindly into danger. If you would be so kind as to let me know you received this and also indicate whether you believe there is any hope of turning up anything helpful, I would be most grateful.

In the matchless name of Christ, Tsion Ben-Judah.

David quickly tapped a response:

"Am dubious about odds for success (as I have been monitoring computer and phone and personal interaction at the highest levels here and have not heard even a conversation about Hattie), but will give this my full attention immediately. I will transmit to Captain Steele's secure phone anything

pertinent and fully understand your concern. More later, but don't want to lose a minute.

David frantically batted away on his laptop, accessing the massive hard drive, tapping into the palace mainframe and decodifying every encrypted file. He looked for any reference to *Hattie, Durham, HD, personal assistant, lover, pregnancy, child, fugitive, plane crash,* and anything else he could think of. Of course, everything that had been said in the administrative offices for weeks was recorded on his monster minidisk, but the only subtitles there would be dates and locations. There was no time to listen to everything Fortunato or Carpathia had said since Hattie was reported dead.

He called Annie, who rushed to his office. He closed the blinds and locked the door so no night crew could see him pacing, running his hands through his hair. "What am I going to do, Annie? Tsion is right. Rayford is committing a huge blunder here, even if he lucks out. You know the GC either has to have Hattie in custody or have killed her. They'll be watching the site where she was supposed to have been hidden. Whoever comes looking for her is going to find not her but GC. She's just bait. Rayford had to know that."

"You'd think," she said.

"Help me," he said.

"It's not that I don't want to, David, but I agree you're looking for the proverbial needle in—"

"What were those stateside people thinking? That the GC bought the phony crash story? Surely they knew better! I didn't know Rayford had finally gotten a bead on her until he was already gone. Why wouldn't he have come to me for one last effort to dig up GC intelligence?"

She shook her head. "How secure are you, David?"

"Sorry, what?"

"You're in their computers, their offices, their plane, on their phones. Has anyone even begun to suspect you yet?"

He shook his head. "The computer installation slowdown should have raised a flag, but I didn't sense suspicion from Leon. If I had to guess, I'd say I'm in solid with them. I have too many irons in the fire to not get burned eventually, but for now I'm golden here."

"There's your answer then, superstar."

"Don't make me guess. Rayford's in the air."

"Just ask them."

"Come again?"

"Go straight to Leon, tell him it's none of your business but you've been noodling the plane crash news, you've always admired his insight and wisdom and street smarts—you know the drill. Suggest that maybe that plane crash wasn't all it appeared, and say you want his take on it."

"Annie, you're a genius."

15

"YOU WANT TO SEE my projects, Cameron?" Chaim Rosenzweig said. "That would make you happy, make you feel like more of a friend?"

"It would."

"Promise you won't think me batty, an old eccentric as my house staff does."

Buck followed him, realizing that regardless how Chaim appeared to the brothers and sisters in the house, he was aware of everything.

\+ \+ \+

Rayford found the Tuttles an all-American couple who had lost all four of their grown sons in the Rapture. "Did we ever miss it," Dwayne said in the Super J, streaking across the eastern U.S. "Oldest boy goes off to college, gets religion we think. Doesn't seem to hurt him any, 'cept he starts in on the other three and before you know it, baby brother's goin' to church. That's OK, but we figure it's just little brother/big brother hero worship, know what I mean?

"Then the middle boys get invited to some church deal they probably wouldn't have gone to if their brothers hadn't already been Christians. They get asked to play on the church basketball team, go off to a week of camp, and come back saved. Man, I hated that word, and they used it all the time. I got saved, he got saved, she got saved, you need to be saved. I loved those boys like everything, but—"

Dwayne had gone from his rapid-fire delivery to choked up so fast Rayford hadn't seen it coming. Now the big man spoke in a little voice, fighting the sobs. Trudy reached from the seat behind his and laid a hand on his shoulder.

"I loved those boys," he squeaked, "and I didn't have a bit of a problem with 'em all wantin' to be religious, I really didn't. Did I, Tru?"

"They loved you, Dwayne," she drawled. "You never gave them a hard time."

"But they gave me a hard time, see? They were never mean, but they were pushy. I told 'em it was all right with me, 'slong as they didn't expect me to start goin' to church with 'em. Had enough of that as a kid, never liked it, bad memories. Their type a church was better, they said. I says fine, you go on then but leave me out of it. They told me their mom's soul was on my head. That got me mad, but how do you stay mad at your own flesh and blood when, even if they're wrong, they're worried about their mom's and dad's souls?"

Rayford shook his head. "You don't."

"You sure don't. They kep' after me. They got their stubbornness from me, after all. But I was good at it too. And I never caved. Tru almost did, didn't ya, hon?"

"Wish I had."

"Me too, sweetie. We wouldn'ta met Mr. Steele here till heaven, but I'd just as soon be there than here even now, all things considered. You too there, Cap?"

"Me too, Dwayne."

"You can guess the rest. Before we ever go to church one time, the thing they told us might happen happened. They were gone. We were left. So where'd we go first?"

"Church."

"Church! Not so stubborn now, are we? Doesn't sound so lame to be saved now, does it? Hardly anybody left at that place, but all we needed was one who knew how a person gets saved. Mr. Steele, I'm an actor myself. Well, aircraft salesman and demonstrator, but always actin' on the side since college. Specialize in voices."

"Mac told me about your Aussie."

"There, right, like 'at. He liked that, did he?"

"I don't know that he was feeling good enough to appreciate it, but he's sure you fooled Fortunato."

"A deaf turtle could fool 'at boy, Rafe. You don't mind if I call you Rafe, do ya? I like to find shortcuts so I can get more words in in a shorter time. Just kiddin', but you don't mind, do ya?"

"My first wife called me that. She was raptured."

"Then maybe you'd rather I not—"

"No, it's all right."

"Anyway, Rafe, I'm a gregarious guy—I guess you figured. Salesman has to be. But I always put all of my theater training into it. I was known as a straightforward, opinionated guy, and people pretty much liked me. Unless they was too sophisticated. If they was, I'd use the word *was* where I'm s'posed to use *were,* like I just did there, and tweak 'em to death. So, I'm this friendly, confident, outgoing guy who—"

"*Loud* is the word you're lookin' for there, hon," Trudy said.

Dwayne laughed as if at the first joke he'd ever heard. "OK, Tru, all right then, I'm this loud guy. But you gotta admit I was a people magnet. Only I wasn't a church guy, OK. Well, now all of a sudden, I am. I'm saved. I'm a day late and a dollar short, but I'm learnin' that it still counts. We're still gonna suffer, and we're never going to wish we hadn't got saved earlier—don't kid yerself—but all right, we're saved. So, now I'm still this gregar—"

"Loud."

"—loud guy but I got a whole new bee in my bonnet now. I'm knockin' people over with it. Even our pastor says sometimes he wonders if I don't turn people off rather than wooin' 'em—that's his term, not mine—wooin' 'em to Jesus. I learned that lesson in sales, but I figure it's different now. It's not about whether I'm gonna make my quota or get my bonus or whether you can afford *not* to have this beautiful new airplane. People got to know, brother, that this is no sales pitch. This is your everlasting soul. Well, I get wound up.

"I always wondered what I'd do if I met up with ol' Antichrist himself. I'll tell you what, I'll bet he'd either have me killed or get saved hisself, one of the two. Get it? Well, sir, I was encouraged that I didn't lose any of my braverido or brovura—"

"Bravado," Trudy offered.

"Right, I didn't lose any of that when I saw his number two boy t'other day. My heart was a-pumpin', I don't deny, but hey, I'm gonna die anyway. I'd like to be here when Jesus comes back, but goin' on before can't be all bad either. The day I got saved I decided I wasn't ever gonna be ashamed of it. It was way too late for that. I'm gonna see my boys again, and—"

As suddenly as before, big Dwayne clouded up. This time he couldn't continue. Trudy put a hand on his heaving shoulder again, he looked apologetically at Rayford, who took over the controls, and the Super J rocketed east into the night.

+ + +

"What in the world is it?" Buck asked, looking at a highly polished strip of metal.

Chaim mince-stepped over and shut the door, and Buck realized he was privy to something Rosenzweig had shared with no one else.

"Call it a hobby that has become an obsession. This is nowhere near my field, and don't ask me where the compulsion has come from. But I am striving toward the sharpest edge ever fashioned by hand. I know the big machines with their micrometers, computers, lasers and all can reach near perfection. I'm not interested in artificially induced. I'm interested in the best I can do. My skill has outstripped my eyesight. With simple clamp-on angle-setters, I am filing blades so sharp I can't see them with the naked eye. Not even powerful bifocals do them justice. I must look at them under much light with my magnifying glass. Believe me, this is more appealing than those creatures you and I studied under it half a year ago. Here, look."

He handed Buck the magnifying glass and pointed him to a shiny blade, probably three feet long, clamped between two vises. "Whatever you do, Cameron, do not touch the edge. I say this with utmost gravity. You would lose a finger before you felt the edge touch your skin, let alone before you felt the pain."

Sufficiently warned, Buck peered at the magnified edge, amazed. The line looked multiple times thinner than any razor blade he had ever seen. "Wow."

"Here's the interesting part, Cameron. Back away carefully, please. The material is super-hardened carbon steel. What appears flexible as a razor because it is so microscopically sharp, is rigid and strong. You know how a conventional knife dulls with use? And usually the sharper the edge, the quicker the deterioration?" Buck nodded. "Watch this."

Rosenzweig produced from his pocket a dried date. "A snack for later," he explained. "But this one is fuzzy, I don't want to wash it, and I have more. So it becomes my object lesson. Notice."

He held the date delicately between his thumb and middle finger, barely pinching one end. He slowly, ever so lightly, drew it across the edge of the blade, reaching beneath it with his other palm. The severed half dropped into his hand as if it had not been touched. "Now let me show you something else."

Rosenzweig looked around the cluttered room and found a balled-up rag, stiff from neglect. He held the rag about eighteen inches above the blade and let it fall. Buck blinked, not believing his eyes. The rag had split without a sound and seemingly without resistance.

"You should see what it does to fruit," Rosenzweig said, his eyes bright.

"It's amazing, Doctor," Buck said. "But, why?"

The old man shook his head. "Don't ask. It's not that I have some deep dark secret. It's just that I don't know myself."

* * *

David didn't call Fortunato. He showed up in Leon's waiting room late that evening. "I just need a second with the commander, if possible," he told Margaret, who was packing up her stuff after an obviously long day.

"David Hassid?" Leon barked into the intercom. "Of course! Send him right in."

Leon stood when David appeared. "Tell me there's progress on the tracing operation," he said.

"Unfortunately not," David said. "Those people must be using some technology no one else has ever heard of. We're back to square one."

"Sit," Fortunato said.

"No, thanks," David said. "I'll just be a minute. You know I don't make a habit of bothering you about—"

"Please! I'm all ears!"

"—about matters outside my area of responsibility."

Fortunato's open look froze. "Of course there are many confidential matters at my level that I would not be at liberty to—"

"I just had a suggestion, but it's none of my business."

"Proceed."

"Well, the death of His Excellency's former personal assistant recently . . ."

Fortunato squinted. "Yes?"

"That was tragic, of course . . ."

"Yes . . ."

"Well, sir, it wasn't a secret that the woman, Miss Dunst—"

"Durham. Hattie Durham. Go on."

"That she was pregnant and that she wasn't happy."

"The fact is, Hassid, that she was trying to extort money from us to keep quiet. His Excellency felt he owed her some recompense for the time they had, ah, enjoyed together, and so a generous settlement was paid. Miss Durham may have mistaken that as money intended to guarantee her silence, but it was not. You see, she was never privy to anything that would threaten international security, had no stories—true ones anyway—that could have embarrassed the potentate. So when she sought more money, she was rebuffed, and yes, it's fair to say she was not happy."

"Well, thank you, sir. I know you told me more than I am entitled to know, and you may rest assured I will keep your confidence. I just had a question about the whole plane crash thing, but it's really moot now, so I'll just thank you for your time."

"No, please. I'll tell you anything you want to know."

"It's kind of embarrassing, because, like I say, I know it's not my area—really none of my business. I'd really rather not pursue it, now that I think about it."

"David, please. I want your thoughts."

"Well, OK. I know that with someone of your ability and savvy here, nobody needs me worrying about security or public relations—"

"We should all worry about those things all the time."

"It just seemed to me that the report of her death looked suspicious. I mean, maybe I've read too many mystery novels, but wasn't it a little too convenient?

Was any wreckage ever found, any bodies? Just enough of her stuff to make it look like she died?"

"David, sit down. Now I insist. That's good thinking. The truth is that Miss Durham's so-called fatal plane crash never happened. I put our intelligence enforcement chief on it as soon as word came in, and the fact is that Miss Durham, her amateur pilot, and the plane were quickly traced. The pilot unwisely put up a fight when our people asked to interrogate Miss Durham, and he was unfortunately killed in an exchange of gunfire. You understand that for reasons of security and morale, not all such incidents are covered in the press."

"Of course."

"Miss Durham is in custody."

"Custody?"

"She's in a comfortable but secure facility in Brussels, charged with the false report of a death. She really is no threat to the Global Community, but we're hoping to lure her compatriots to her original hiding place. She will be released once they have been dealt with."

"Her compatriots?"

"Former GC employees and Ben-Judah sympathizers had provided her asylum when her presence was required in New Babylon. They are much more of a threat than she is."

"So she became bait, and it was her own fault."

"Precisely."

"And this trap, it was your idea?"

"Well, we work as a team here, David."

"But it was, wasn't it? It's how you think. It's the street smarts."

Fortunato cocked his head. "We surround ourselves with good people, and when no one cares who gets the credit, much can be accomplished."

"But luring the compatriots, that was yours."

"I believe it may have been."

"And did it work?"

"It may yet. No one knows of the death of the pilot. We sent word to his brother, whom we know to have been an accomplice, that he was in hiding and would not hear from him for several months."

"Brilliant!"

Fortunato nodded as if he couldn't argue.

"I won't take any more of your time, Commander, and I don't guess I'll let this kind of stuff bother me anymore either, knowing you and your people are on top of everything."

"Well, don't feel bad about a good hunch there, and never hesitate to ask if something's not clear to you. We put a lot of confidence in a person at your level and with your scope of responsibilities. Not everyone has this kind of access or information, of course, so—"

"Say no more, sir," David said, rising. "I appreciate it more than I can say."

+ + +

Rayford had handled a huge chunk of the flying across the Atlantic, but that hadn't slowed Dwayne's oral output. Rayford enjoyed it, actually, though he would have appreciated getting to know Trudy as well. When it was finally time to turn the controls back to Dwayne, Rayford decided to place his call to Albie (shortened from Al B., which in turn had been shortened from Al Basrah).

Albie was the chief air traffic controller at Al Basrah, a city on the southern end of the Tigris near the Persian Gulf. He was almost totally unknown far and wide as the best black marketer in the business. Mac had introduced him to Rayford, and it had been Albie who supplied the scuba equipment for Rayford's forage to the wreckage in the Tigris.

Albie, a devout Muslim, hated the Carpathia regime passionately and was one of few Gentile non-Christians who also steadfastly resisted Enigma Babylon One World Faith. His business was simple. To people he trusted with his life, he could provide anything for a price. That was double retail plus expenses, and if you were caught with contraband, he had never heard of you.

Dwayne was, for the moment, uncharacteristically quiet, and Trudy was dozing. Rayford dug through his bag and used his ultimate phone—Mac's term for David's hybrid because it could do anything from anywhere.

The number was ringing when Dwayne noticed the equipment. "Now that there is what I call a phone! Uh-*huh!* Yes, sir, that is a phone and a half. I'll bet that's got whistles and bells I've never even heard of and—"

Rayford held up a finger and said, "I'll let you take a look at it in a minute."

"I'll be countin' the seconds, pardner. I sure will."

"Al Basrah tower, Albie speaking."

"Albie, Rayford Steele. Can you talk?"

"From east at four knots. Your situation?"

"I want to meet with you about a purchase."

"Affirmative. Sorry for negative previous endeavor. First officer?"

"Mac is recovering. I'm sure you heard about—"

"Affirmative. Hold please." Albie covered the phone and Rayford heard him speaking in his own tongue. He came back on. "I'm alone now, Mr. Steele. I was so sorry to hear of your wife."

"Thank you."

"I've also been very worried about Mac. I have heard nothing from him for a while. Of course, as captain now he doesn't need my services as much. What can I do for you?"

"I need a weapon, concealable but powerful."

"In other words you want it to do what it is intended to do."

"You're reading loud and clear, Albie."

"Very difficult. The potentate being a pacifist—"

"Means you're the only reliable source."

"Very difficult."

"But not impossible for you, right?"

"Very difficult," Albie said.

"Expensive, in other words?"

"Now you're reading *me* loud and clear."

"If money were not an issue, does something come to mind?"

"How concealable are we talking about? You want one that'll hide from a metal detector?"

"That's possible?"

"Made of wood and plastic. Can fire two rounds, three tops, before it disintegrates. Limited range, of course. No kill power past twenty feet.

"This has to do the job from thirty yards. One shot."

"Mr. Steele, I have access to just the weapon. It is roughly the size of your hand. Heavy, thus accurate. Weight is due to firing mechanism, which is normally used in oversized high-powered rifles."

"What kind of action?"

"Unique. It employs both fuel injection and hydraulic vacuum."

"Sounds like an engine. I've never heard of such a thing."

"Who has? It propels a projectile at two thousand miles an hour."

"Ammunition?"

"Forty-eight caliber, high speed—naturally, soft tip, hollow point."

"In a handgun?"

"Mr. Steele, the air displacement caused by the spinning of the bullet alone has been known to sever human tissue from two inches away."

"I don't follow."

"A man was fired at with one of these pistols from approximately thirty feet away. The shot tore through his skin and damaged subcutaneous tissue in his upper arm. Doctors later determined that there were zero traces of metal in the tissue. The damage had been done by the speed with which the air around the spinning bullet was displaced."

"Oh, my. You know what I need to hear. Hundreds?"

"Thousands."

"Thousand?"

"Thous*ands* plural, my friend."

"How many?"

"Depends on where you take delivery, whether we meet—which I prefer."

\+ + +

David was frustrated. He had sprinted back to his quarters and called Rayford, whose phone was busy. That phone had everything but a signal that another caller was waiting. David had even installed a wake-up feature that made the phone ring when it was turned off, provided the user left it in sleep mode. Rayford always did.

He dialed again. Still busy.

\+ + +

"I didn't intend to listen in there, Cap, but that sounds like quite a piece of hardware you're orderin'. I like that you don't care if it's illegal. It's not like we're subject to the laws of the Antichrist."

"That's my view. You wanted to see the phone?"

"Yeah, thanks. Take over here, will ya?"

Dwayne turned the phone over and over, hefting it in his palm. "Heavy sucker. Probably does everything but cook your breakfast, am I right?"

"It'll even do that, unless you want scrambled."

"Ha! Tru, d'you hear that?! Oh!" He put his hand over his mouth when he saw his wife was sleeping. Then he whispered. "Is this one of them that'll send or receive from anywhere, all that?"

Rayford nodded. "Best part is it's secure. It uses four different channels a second, so it's untraceable, untappable. Lots of goodies."

"You keep it in your bag?" Dwayne said.

"Yeah, thanks."

Dwayne switched it off and reached behind Rayford to set it in his flight bag. On second thought, he pulled it back out and turned the main power toggle off as well.

"I'll take 'er now," Dwayne said, resuming control of the plane. "And if I'm not bein' too much of a nosy Nellie, can you tell me what you're gonna use such a powerful handgun for?"

Rayford thought a moment. He'd made it a practice to be open with fellow believers, even about Tribulation Force matters. He might not reveal the location of the safe house or tell someone's phony ID name, just so the hearer wouldn't have to suffer for something he didn't need to know. But the gun was personal, which stabbed at Rayford because he knew well where the big money was coming from. At the moment he couldn't imagine following through with his plan.

"The Global Community may be pacifistic and weaponless by law," he said. "But we lost a pilot to gunfire, and almost every one of us has been shot at, at least once, and a few hit. Buck and Tsion were shot at—Buck was hit—escaping Israel through Egypt. Buck was shot at helping Hattie escape a GC facility in Colorado. Our newest member and I were shot at recently. And you know what happened to Mac and Abdullah."

"I hear you, bro. You'll get no argument from me. Sounds like it would be pretty expensive to issue one of those babies to everybody though."

"I'll personally test it first," Rayford said.

"Good idea. 'Course, the two you just mentioned would never be able to carry weapons in their jobs. You'd almost have to plant theirs on board."

"We did that when I was captain of *Global Community One.* Had a couple of pistols secured in the cargo hold. Would have been awful hard to get to, but they were a last resort. Of course, now they're gone forever."

"By the way, Rafe," Dwayne said, pointing to the horizon, "that would be what we in the aviation trade refer to as the sun. Our ETA is forty minutes. Customs in Le Havre is pretty much by the book, if you haven't been there. You got the British visa stamp?"

Rayford nodded.

"Did I ask you who you are today and why I ferried you across the channel from England?"

Rayford pulled out his passport and flipped it open. "Thomas Agee. Import/export. And you are?"

Dwayne smiled and affected a dead-on British accent. He handed Rayford two United States of Britain passports. "At your service, sir."

Rayford read aloud, "Ian Hill. And the wife's . . . Elva. Nice to meet you both."

+ + +

David wasn't getting a busy signal anymore. He carefully redialed to be certain he hadn't erred. The number was right. Either Rayford could not hear the ring, or the phone had been shut off. David called Tsion and woke him. Someone was going to have to contact that plane on an open frequency. And fast.

16

BUCK SUFFERED from jet lag and the decision to stay up late with Dr. Rosenzweig. He had spent much of the night pleading with Chaim to come to Christ. "It's the reason I'm here," Buck told his old friend. "You must not put it off any longer. You're not getting younger. The judgments and woes get worse now until the end. Odds are you will not survive."

Chaim had nearly dozed off several times, lounging on the couch across from Buck. "I am at a crossroads, Cameron. I can tell you this: I am no longer an agnostic. Anyone who tells you he still is is a liar. I recognize the great supernatural war between good and evil."

Buck leaned forward. "What, then, Doctor? Can you remain neutral? Neutrality is death. Neutrality is a no vote. You pretend to leave the issue to others, but in the end you lose."

"There is so much I don't understand."

"Who, besides perhaps Tsion, understands much of anything? We're all new at this, just feeling our way. You don't have to be a theologian. You just need to know the basics, and you do. The question now is what you do with what you know? What do you do with Jesus? He has staked a claim on your soul. He wants you, and he has tried everything to convince you of that. What will it take, Chaim? Do you need to be trampled by the horses? Do they need to suffocate you with sulfur, set you afire? Do you have to be in terror for your life?"

Chaim sat shaking his head sadly.

"Doctor, let me be clear. Life will not get easier. We all missed that bus. It will get worse for all of us. But for believers it will be even worse than for unbelievers, because the day is coming—"

"I know this part, Cameron. I know what Tsion says about the mark necessary to buy or sell. So you are calling me to a life worse than the wretched existence mine has already come to be."

"I'm calling you to the truth. Your life may get worse, but your death will be the best! No matter how you die, you will wake up in heaven. If you survive until the Glorious Appearing . . . imagine! Those are the believer's options,

Doctor. Die and be with Christ, only to return when he does. Or survive until his appearing.

"Chaim, we want you with us. We want you to be our brother, now and forever. We can't imagine losing you, knowing you are separated for eternity from the God who loves you." Buck could not hold back the tears. "Sir, if only I could trade places with you! Do you not know how we feel about you, how God feels about you? Jesus took your place so you don't have to pay the price."

Chaim looked up in surprise at the tears in Buck's voice. The alarm appeared to give way to some realization. Perhaps the old man had *not* known the depth of their feeling for him. Buck felt as if he were pleading God's case in God's absence. God was there, of course, but he apparently seemed distant to Chaim.

"I pledge this to you as I did once before to Tsion," Chaim said. "I will not take the mark of Nicolae Carpathia. If I should starve to death for taking that stand, I shall not be forced to bear a mark in order to live as a free man in this society."

That was a step, Buck decided. But it wasn't enough. In the guest room Buck had wept until he fell asleep, praying for Chaim. At nine in the morning he was still exhausted. He had hoped to get another firsthand look at the two witnesses, but he promised Chloe he would stay on schedule and visit Lukas Miklos in Greece on his way back. The new friend they called Laslos would be the key contact in that part of the world for the co-op.

+ + +

It was 7 a.m. in Le Havre when Rayford and the Tuttles bluffed their way through customs as Thomas Agee and Ian and Elva Hill. Trudy was to rent a car and check into two rooms they had reserved at Le Petit Hotel south of the city. It was an expensive, secluded place unlikely to draw curious eyes.

Dwayne would use another rental car to drop Rayford off a couple of blocks from the address on Rue Marguerite where Bo Hanson had said his brother and Hattie were hiding out under assumed names. Rayford planned to simply show up at their apartment and talk them into opening the door by warning them that the GC was onto them and that they had to move. Rayford believed Hattie would deduce that Bo had led him to them and that thus the GC story must be true. Rayford would offer them a ride and to put them up in an obscure hotel if they were prepared to flee immediately.

The three would rendezvous with Dwayne and improvise. Either in the process of getting into the car or by some scheme along the way, Rayford and Dwayne would ditch Samuel Hanson and let him fend for himself. He was the one with a plane. They could sort out their differences back in the States.

Rayford wanted to surprise Hattie and Samuel as early in the day as possible, so he and Dwayne took the first available rental car. With a quick farewell to Trudy, who was to load all their bags into her car, they were off. Dwayne bubbled with ideas of how to outwit Samuel.

"Are you sure you want to insert yourself this far into a Tribulation Force operation?" Rayford said.

"Are you kiddin' me? I've been itchin' for some action ever since I got saved. Now listen, we can ditch this boy soon's we get in the car. You could tell him to step outside with you for a minute because, like, you've got a private message for him. Like from his brother. You get out and walk him behind the car, and then you tell him you forgot the note in the car. You jump back in, I take off, and there we go."

"Could work," Rayford said.

"Or how 'bout this one?" Dwayne said, following Rayford's directions as he sped through town. "When you first bring 'em to the car, I get out all mannerly and such and we do the formal introductions. I open the door for the lady and get her inside. Then I give this Hanson character a big ol' Oklahoma shove. He'll roll twenty feet, but it won't hurt him. By the time his head clears, we'll be long gone."

Rayford studied a city map and the note from Bo. "They're using the names James Dykes and Mae Willie. Sometimes you have to wonder. . . ."

"Here's another idea," Dwayne said, but Rayford cut him off.

"No offense, Dwayne, but I don't much care how we do it, as long as we get it done."

"You gotta have a plan."

"We have plenty. If it doesn't feel right for me to invite him out of the car, you know what to do."

"You got it, pardner."

+ + +

By now David was despairing. It was midmorning in New Babylon, and he and Mac were huddled in Mac's office. David had programmed his own secure phone to dial Rayford's every sixty seconds and to leave a digital message that simply read ABORT and gave David's number.

"If I'd known it was gonna be this way," Mac said, "I could've flown to France and intercepted him myself by now."

David, feeling helpless, brought up on his computer phone calls between Leon and his intelligence enforcement chief, Walter Moon, the day before, the day of, and the day after the announcement of Hattie's death. When David finally hit pay dirt and heard something that would help Rayford, he felt even worse.

"This'll make your day, Mac," he said. "Listen to this. It's Leon and Moon."

"What's your plan on the Durham situation, Wally?"

"It's done, Commander. She made it so easy. How long we been looking for that—"

"Too long. Now what's done? What did you do?"

"Like we said, we got rid of the pilot. He was usin' the name Dykes, but we traced the plane to Sam Hanson out of Louisiana."

"By got rid of . . ."

"You want to know or you want to not know? Let's just say Sam's had his last bowl o' gumbo. We put the filly in the Brussels lockup. She was usin' the name Mae Willie, so we booked her under that so she could hide out even inside if she wanted. I know the big boss—'scuse me, the Excell—, His *Excellency doesn't want anything noisy."*

"Right, and anyway, who'd believe she's Hattie Durham? She's been reported dead."

"And she's the one who did it. We could leave her in Belgium forever."

"And we're taking advantage of this how?"

"We informed the pilot's only living kin, his brother, in a note that looks like it's from Sam, that Sam would be holing up in France for a while, so don't expect to hear from him. We figure the brother will eventually get suspicious or run out of patience and come looking for him. We just hope her Judah-ite friends will find her through the brother first, because we have a surprise for them.

"I'm listening."

"We've got a look-alike staying at the apartment, claiming to be Dykes. He plays coy but then promises to take any snoops to Hattie. They wind up in the same situation as the Cajun, if you get my drift."

"Excellent, Wally."

Mac shook his head. "You keeping Tsion informed? Rayford's walking into a hornet's nest, and those people over there, particularly his daughter, ought to be prepared, in case he never comes back."

David nodded and reached for his phone, but it was ringing. He zeroed in on the caller ID. "It's him!"

Mac leaned over to listen in, and David hit the button. "Captain Steele, where are you, man? I've been trying to call you for—"

"Excuse me, sir. This is Mrs. Dwayne Tuttle. You can call me Trudy. My husband and Captain Steele left me to arrange for hotel rooms and take care of the luggage. I saw this phone in the captain's bag, and I'm sorry but I turned it on out of curiosity. Well, just dozens and dozens of messages have been scrollin' by, all with your number and this abort message, and I thought I ought to call."

"Ma'am, thank you. Where is Rayf—Captain Steele right now?"

"He and my husband are on their way to try to find Miss Durham."

"Does your husband have a phone?"

"No, sir, he sure doesn't—"

"Is there any way we can reach them?"

"I have the address where they're going, if you'd like to call the young lady."

Mac grabbed the phone. "Ma'am, this is Mac McCullum. Remember meeting me in Africa?"

"Yes, sir, how are you feel—"

"Trudy, listen to me and do exactly what I say. It's a matter of life and death. Do you know that town?"

"Just from the airport to here."

"Get yourself a map at the desk and have them tell you the fastest way to Hattie's address. Drive there as fast as you can. If anyone tries to stop you, don't let them and explain later. At all costs, you must tell Captain Steele to abort. He'll take it from there."

"Abort, yessir."

"Any questions?"

"No, sir."

"Then do it right now, Trudy. And call us to let us know what happens."

+ + +

Dwayne drove past the address on Rue Marguerite and stopped a block and a half away.

"Seedy little dump, idn't it?" Dwayne said.

"It's perfect, really," Rayford said. "I'm impressed. This may be the best choice they made in the whole fiasco. Let's watch awhile and see if she comes or goes."

Rayford got antsy after ten minutes when only two people left the building, neither Hattie. "If I'm not back in five minutes, come looking for me."

"They armed?"

"Doubt it. If Sam's as bright as his brother, he wouldn't know which end to aim. Hattie would worry about breaking a nail."

Still, Rayford wished he was carrying the weapon Albie had described. He could never shoot Hattie, and he wouldn't risk the consequences for a small-time goon like Bo Hanson's brother. This shouldn't be that risky, he decided. Hattie would let him in. If she didn't, he had a story in mind to use on Sam Hanson.

The three-story building had three sets of ten mailboxes built into the wall in the lobby, which was neither manned nor secured. Rayford was surprised they had not chosen a building with at least a buzz-in system. He found "Dykes, J." on the box numbered 323 and mounted the stairs.

Each floor was reached by a series of four sets of steps in a square pattern. By the time Rayford reached the top floor, he was winded and his knee ached. Apartment 323 was on the front side of the building at the left end. He could have been watched from the time he stepped onto the property. Sam and Hattie could have even seen the car cruise by.

Rayford gathered himself and found the button in a metal box in the middle of the apartment door. His push resulted in a resounding two-tone ring that could have been heard in any flat on that floor. Rayford thought he heard movement, but no one answered. As he reached for the button again, he distinctly heard someone. He guessed they were pulling on a pair of pants. "Take your time," he called out. "No rush."

He imagined someone tiptoeing to the door and listening. There was no peephole. Rayford hoped whoever it was was listening to tell if he had retreated. He pushed the button quickly, giving them an earful.

A male voice: "Who is it?"

"Tom Agee."

"Who?"

"Thomas Agee."

"Don't know that name."

"I'm a friend of the woman who lives here."

"No woman here. Just me."

"Mae Willie doesn't live here?"

Silence.

"May I speak with Mae, please? Tell her it's a friend."

Rayford heard the unmistakable sliding action on a semiautomatic pistol. He considered a break for the stairs, but the door opened abruptly to reveal a muscular young man with one hand behind his back. He was barefoot and bare chested, wearing only jeans.

Rayford decided on a bold approach. "May I come in?"

"Who'd you say you were looking for?"

"You heard me or you wouldn't have opened the door. Now where is she?"

"I told you, it's just me here. What do you want with her?"

"Who? The one who doesn't live here?"

"State your business or hit the street."

"Are you Samuel Hanson?"

The man leveled his eyes. "Name's Jimmy Dykes."

"Then you *are* Samuel Hanson. Where's Hattie Durham?"

The man started to shut the door. "Buddy, you're lost. There's nobody here by that—"

Rayford stepped forward and the door stopped at his foot. "If I'm in the wrong place, how did I know yours and Hattie's real names? Now I need to speak with her."

"Dykes" seemed to be considering it.

"You're not GC, are you?"

"I'm a friend of Hattie's," Rayford said, loudly enough so Hattie might hear him.

"You're not really Tommy Agee, either, are you?"

"We all have to be careful, Samuel. I'm Rayford Steele. I bring you greetings from your brother, Bo."

Samuel had still not moved. "Hi, back. Hattie's not here, but I can take you to her. C'mon in while I get dressed."

Samuel pushed the door open wider and Rayford stepped in. As the door was swinging shut, Rayford heard footsteps flying up the stairs. Samuel headed for another room, and as he turned his back, Rayford saw him move a handgun from back to front.

Samuel set the weapon on the table, still blocking Rayford's view of it with his body. He grabbed a shirt and had one arm in it when frenzied banging on the door and ringing of the bell made both men start.

Rayford hoped it was Hattie. He ignored Samuel's look and swung the door open. *Trudy?!* His life shifted into slow motion as he desperately tried to remember her undercover name. He turned to look back at Samuel, who tore his shirt straightening his arm to reach for the gun.

Trudy screeched, "Abort!" and reached as if to pull Rayford from the room, but he knew neither of them could run from that weapon. The incongruity alone of Trudy showing up with an abort message told him that whoever this man was, he would kill them.

Trudy bounded down the stairs, and Rayford imagined taking a .45 bullet in the back and another in the top of the head. Trudy would be slain before she reached the first floor. Rayford simply could not let this man follow him out of the room unimpeded.

He turned from the slowly closing door and charged the man, who had just fought through his shredded shirt and had grabbed the handle of the weapon. One stride from him and accelerating, Rayford saw him lift the already cocked firearm and slip his index finger onto the trigger.

Rayford didn't want to take his chances wrestling a man with a gun. He could cover the man's hand with both of his, but he didn't like the odds. Instead he marshaled his adrenaline and left his feet, throwing himself at the gunman with his fists drawn into his chest, elbows akimbo, like a cornerback taking out a receiver who just got his fingers on the ball.

Rayford's man didn't fumble, but he did go flying. Rayford had caught him in the neck with one of his forearms, driving his body back as his head jerked forward. As his momentum carried him back, the man's bare feet hit the floor and a small table caught him behind his knees.

His feet flew straight up as the back of his head smashed through the front window. He lay there stunned, the gun in his hand, finger on the trigger, as Rayford scrambled toward the door. His feet were moving so fast he could hardly gain purchase on the floor. He felt as if he were in a nightmare, being chased by a monster, and running in muck.

He yanked the door open and peeked back as he fled. The gunman's head still stuck in the broken window. His torso had wound up lower than his feet, and his kicking and squirming only made it harder for him to get up.

It did not stop him from firing off two rounds, however, deafening, ugly explosions almost simultaneous with shattering wood and flying wallboard.

Rayford crashed down the steps three and four at a time, nearly overtaking Trudy, who was moving as fast as she could one step at a time. When Rayford reached the second floor, he grabbed the banister and, despite his protesting knee, swung into the middle of the staircase. He dropped to the floor as Trudy reached the last step.

She moaned as she ran as if certain she was about to be shot. Rayford felt a tingling in his back as if he, too, expected a bullet to rip through him.

Trudy had left her car idling, the door open, directly in front of the apartment building. Dwayne had noticed it and pulled up behind it, clearly puzzled. He looked up as Rayford and his wife hurried toward him, and he called out, "What the . . . ?"

"Go!" Rayford waved at him. "We'll catch up with you!"

Rayford ran to the driver's side and Trudy opened the passenger door as shots came from the third floor. As soon as Rayford heard her door shut, he floored the accelerator and threw dirt and stones as the car fishtailed down the street.

His instincts had saved them, he knew, but as his heart shoved blood through him faster than ever, Rayford was unable to feel gratitude for that presence of mind. He knew God had been with him, protected him, helped spare him. But all Rayford felt was a resurgence of the rage that had plagued him for months.

This, all of it, started and ended with Nicolae Carpathia. He wanted to murder the man and he would, he decided, if it was the last thing he did on earth. And he didn't care if it was. He would spend whatever he had to for that weapon from Albie, and regardless what it took, he would be where he needed to be when the time came.

Trudy, gasping, wrestled her seat belt on. As Rayford followed Dwayne through the narrow streets, she fished around on the floor and came up with his phone. "Is—is—is there a sp—sp—speed dial number for Mac McCu—"

"Two."

She punched it and Rayford heard it ring, then Mac's voice. "Mrs. Tuttle?"

"M—m—mission accomplished!" Trudy said, and she handed Rayford the phone as she burst into tears.

17

DAVID WAS SPENT.

He and Mac had listened to Rayford's debriefing as the two cars zipped through Le Havre on their way back to the hotel. All agreed that if they had not been followed they were safe briefly at the hotel under their aliases, but that they should leave the country as soon as possible. Rayford had used both his phony and his real name with "Samuel," who, of course, turned out to be a GC plant. Provided he hadn't bled to death from window injuries, he would have already spread the word that Rayford was in France.

That made it unlikely that Rayford could get out of the airport through customs. Fortunately, he had separated from the "Hills" as they passed through customs and was not linked to their party on the computer.

"We can't help you from here," David told him.

"I'll stay in touch," Rayford said. "But I'm not going straight home."

+ + +

Buck left Israel without visiting the Wailing Wall. Neither had he reported to Tsion the details of his encounter with Chaim Rosenzweig. He wanted to do that in person, knowing Tsion would be as heavyhearted as he was. How they had grown to love Chaim! It wasn't enough to say that you couldn't make a person's decision for him. The believers who loved Chaim wanted to do just that.

Buck enjoyed a warm reunion with Lukas Miklos and his wife. In her broken English, Mrs. Miklos told Buck with relish, "Laslos loves the intrigue. He tells me day and night for week, remember our friend be Greg North, not you-know-who."

Laslos had done his homework. He had made his lignite business so profitable that he was stockpiling profits and planned to sell the operation to the Global Community just before trading restrictions were predicted to go into effect.

Laslos showed Buck an expansive site at a new location where he would house trucks and loading equipment to ship commodities to co-op locations. His new concern would look like a GC-sanctioned shipping business, but it would be ten times larger than it appeared and would be the hub of co-op activity in that part of the world.

Buck also visited Laslos' underground church, a vast group of believers led by a converted Jew whose main dilemma was how large the body had grown. Buck flew back to the States encouraged by what he had seen in Greece but saddened by the lack of spiritual movement on Chaim Rosenzweig's part.

At home he found Tsion and Chloe skittish about a decision they had come to about Leah. Buck thought it a great idea, but they wondered whether they should have proceeded without consulting Rayford. Due to the near disaster with Rayford and the complexity of the communications between Force members from all over the world, Tsion suggested putting one person in charge of centralized information. Leah immediately volunteered, saying she found herself looking for things to do between preparing meals. Chloe had spent hours with her, bringing her up to speed on the computer, and Leah said she had never felt more fulfilled.

The four gathered around the computer, and Leah showed how she had found a program that helped her consolidate everything coming into or going out from the safe house. With a little thought and a few keystrokes, she then transmitted to everyone what the others had communicated. "This way we'll never wonder who's in the loop, who knows what, and who doesn't. If Mac or David writes up an incident that everyone should know about, I see that everyone gets it."

As they hurtled toward the midpoint of the Tribulation, Buck sensed they were as prepared as they could be.

+ + +

Rayford had to give Dwayne his due. He may have been a loudmouth, but he had come up with the best plan for spiriting Rayford out of Le Havre. "We didn't get to use my ideas for ditchin' Hattie's boyfriend," he said, "so this is only fair."

It was clear Trudy was proud of what she had accomplished that morning, but she was also still shaken and wanted no responsibility for another caper on their way out of the country.

She and her husband preceded Rayford to the airport by fifteen minutes to drop off their rental and get the plane ready for takeoff. Rayford would follow and drop off his car, then casually move to the back side of the lot where a fence separated the cars from the terminal. Dwayne had noticed that the area behind the fence led around the end of the terminal building and directly out to the runway. "You can either hop that fence and run to the plane—once you've heard it screamin' and know we're ready to go—or I can bring the plane close to that fence and make it easier for you."

"Pros and cons?" Rayford said.

"It could be a long run to the plane, and you've been gimpy on that knee. On the other hand, if I bring the Super J to the fence, that'll draw a lot of eyes and maybe even some freaked-out officials trying to keep me out of that area."

They finally decided that Dwayne would get the plane into takeoff position and then ask permission to taxi out of the sun near the terminal to check out something underneath. That would put him closer to where Rayford could vault the fence. "I'll tell 'em I heard a squeak in a wheel bearing and see if I can't get 'em to poke around under there with me while you're slipping aboard."

All went well until Rayford pulled into the rental lot. The Super J was on the runway, engines whining. The rental attendant asked him something in French, then translated into English. "Are you keeping it on the charge card?"

Rayford nodded as the young man printed the receipt and kept looking from the handheld machine to Rayford's eyes. "Excuse me," he said, turning his back to Rayford and talking into his walkie-talkie. Rayford didn't understand much of the French, but he was certain the man was asking a coworker something about "Agee, Thomas."

The receipt was printing as the man spoke, but when he tore it off he didn't hand it to Rayford. "No did go through," he said.

"What do you mean?" Rayford said. "It's right there."

"Please to wait and I try again."

"I'm late," Rayford said, backing away and aware of movement near the terminal. "Send me a bill."

"No, must you wait. Need new card."

"Bill me," Rayford said, looking over his shoulder to see the Super J slowly taxiing his direction. Three men ran from the terminal toward the rental lot. Rayford sprinted toward the fence, and the agent yelled for help.

Rayford guessed the fence was four and a half feet high and the Super J more than a hundred yards away, moving slowly. If Dwayne had succeeded, an inspector would likely walk out to meet the plane. The men racing into the lot were a hundred feet behind Rayford. They all looked young and athletic.

Rayford tried to scissor-kick his way over the fence but caught his lead heel on the top. That caused him to slow enough that gravity brought his seat down on the middle of the fence, and his momentum took him over. He grabbed the top to keep from slamming to the ground, but until he extricated his heel he hung upside down for a few seconds. He wiggled free and landed hard on his shoulder, jumped up, and lit out for the plane.

A look back revealed his pursuers clearing the fence with ease. If Dwayne didn't increase his speed, Rayford would never outrun them. Rayford heard the acceleration of rpm's and saw a man with a clipboard waving at Dwayne to slow. Fortunately he didn't comply, and Trudy lowered the steps as Rayford headed for the door.

The men behind yelled at him to halt, and as Trudy leaned out, reaching, he heard their footsteps. Just as he left the ground to leap for the steps the fastest of the men dove and slapped Rayford's trailing foot. He was thrown off balance and nearly flipped off the side of the stairs, but Trudy proved stronger than she looked. Rayford grabbed her wrist and was afraid he would pull her out the door with him, but as his weight dragged her to the floor, she turned lengthwise, her shoulders on one side of the opening and her knees on the other. He vaulted over her, Dwayne throttled up, and Rayford helped Trudy shut the door.

"That's twice today you've saved my bacon," Rayford said.

She smiled, shaking as she collapsed into a seat. "It's the last time, too. I just retired."

Dwayne whooped and hollered like a rodeo cowboy as the Super J shot into the sky. "She's somethin', ain't she? Whoo boy!"

"Quite a machine," Rayford said, dreading what he was going to feel like the next morning.

Dwayne gave him a puzzled look. "I wudd'n talkin' about the Super J, pardner. I was talkin' about the little woman."

Trudy leaned forward and wrapped both arms around her husband's neck. "Maybe you'll quit calling me that now."

"Darlin'," he said, "I'll call you anything your little ol' heart desires. Whoo boy!"

"You heading west?" Rayford said suddenly.

"I can head any direction you want, Rafe. Say the word."

"East."

"East it is, and I'll stay below the radar level awhile so they can forget about tracking us. Buckle up and hang on."

He wasn't kidding. Dwayne made the Super J change direction so fast, Rayford's head was pinned to the chair.

"Like a roller coaster, eh? You gotta love this!"

Rayford muttered to himself.

"How's that, Cap?" Dwayne said.

"I said you need to work up a little enthusiasm."

Dwayne laughed until tears rolled.

+ + +

Late in the day David received a private e-mail message from Annie, reporting that the head of her department and a couple of the other higher-ups had met briefly in Fortunato's office. David wrote back, "I'd love you with all my heart even if you weren't the most valuable mole in the place."

While he skipped around his hard drive trying to retrieve the audio of the meeting in question, his status bar told him he had another message. Again it was from Annie. "I never dreamed of so lofty a compliment from the love of my life. Thank you from the bottom of my moley little heart. Love and kisses, AC."

When David found the recording, he recognized the voice of his peer, the head of Annie's department. He rambled through the obligatory kissing up, then turned the floor over to his intelligence analysis chief. Jim Hickman was brilliant but self-possessed and clearly enjoyed the sound of his own voice.

"These cultists," Hickman began, "are what I like to call literalists. They believe ancient writings, particularly the Jewish Torah and the Christian New Testament, and they make no distinction between historical records—many of which have proved accurate—and figurative, symbolic languages of the so-called prophetic passages. For instance, anyone—myself included—with even a cursory background in the history of ancient civilizations knows that much of the so-called prophetic books of the Bible are not prophetic at all. Oh, after the fact of some strange natural phenomenon one could make some of the imaginative and descriptive language fit the event. For instance, the current rash of death by fire, smoke, and sulfur—which is clearly poison-vapor warfare, probably by this very group—becomes the fulfillment of what they believe is a prophecy that includes monstrous horses with lions' heads, ridden by 200 million men."

"Are we going somewhere with this, Jim?" Fortunato said. "His Excellency is looking for specifics."

"Oh, yes, Commander. All that to say this: as these people take these writings literally, they attribute to these two crazy preachers—"

"The potentate calls them the Jerusalem Twosome!" Fortunato said.

"Yes!" Hickman cried. "I love that! Anyway, the Ben-Judah-ites believe that these old coots are the so-called witnesses of the eleventh chapter of the book of Revelation. In their precious old King James translation the operative verse reads like this: 'And I will give power unto my two witnesses, and they shall prophesy a thousand two hundred and threescore days, clothed in sackcloth.'"

"So that's why those two dress in those burlap bags," Fortunato said. "They're *trying* to make us think they're these—what did it say?—witnesses."

Hickman dripped with condescension. "Exactly, Commander. And Ben-

Judah has always held that this period began the day the one-world government entered into a peace agreement with Israel. You count exactly twelve hundred and sixty days from then, and you must have what the preachers themselves call the 'due time.'"

Fortunato asked the others if they minded leaving him alone with Hickman for a moment. David heard the sliding of chairs, the door, people moving about. Then, "Jim, I need to confide something that's troubling me. You're a smart guy—"

"Thank you, sir."

"And you and I both know there are things in those ancient writings that would be hard to fake."

"Oh, I don't know. Turning water to blood is being perpetrated by the same people who are killing us with germ warfare. It's a trick, something planted in the water supply."

"But at Kollek Stadium it seemed to happen to water already in bottles."

"I've seen magicians do the same thing. Something in the mix responds to weather conditions—maybe when the temperature drops at a certain time in the evening. If you have an idea when that is, you can make it look like you caused the phenomenon."

"But what about keeping it from raining for so long?"

"Coincidence! I've seen Israel go months without rain. What is new? It's easy to claim you're keeping it from raining when there is no rain. What will they say when the rain comes, that they decided to give us a break?"

"People who try to kill them wind up incinerated."

"Someone said the two conceal a flamethrower they produce when the crowd has been distracted. Really, Commander, you're not suggesting these two breathe fire."

Fortunato was silent. Then, "Well, if they are not who they claim to be, how do we know they will be vulnerable at the prescribed moment?"

"We don't. But either they are vulnerable or they are not who they say they are. Either way, we win. They lose."

David would transmit the information to Tsion, but first he wanted to eavesdrop on Fortunato when he reported to Carpathia. He checked Fortunato's and Margaret's phones. Nothing. Fortunato's office was quiet. He hit the mother lode when he tapped into Carpathia's office. Fortunato had just summarized his conversation with Hickman.

"Twelve hundred and sixty days since the treaty," Carpathia repeated. "We had already decided on a pageant. Now we know precisely when to stage it. You have your work cut out for you, Leon. You must turn the regional potentates against

Peter the Second—not that they are not against him already, but it must result in his demise. I will leave it to you. Leave to me the so-called witnesses. The world, especially Israel, has long since looked forward to their end. For months I have believed it beneath me to personally rid the world of those two. I wondered about the public-relations fallout and considered merely sanctioning and ordering their killing by GC troops. But they will have so alienated even their own followers by then that doing it personally will be considered my crowning achievement so far."

"If you're certain."

"You do not agree?"

"It would be so easy, Excellency. We could have it done without your being implicated. You could even decry the deed publicly, restating that you encourage freedom of speech and thought."

"But not freedom to torment the world with plagues and judgments, Leon!"

"But doesn't that imply that these men are who they say they are?"

"It makes no difference, do you not see? I want responsibility, credit, points for standing up to these impostors."

"Of course, as always, Excellency, you know best."

+ + +

The Super J sat at the end of the runway at Al Basrah. Upon arrival, several airport workers had run barefoot to the plane, gawking at the sleek lines and the British flag. Where Dwayne's Aussie alter ego "Dart" had "Fair Dinkum" emblazoned on the side, the decal now read "Black Angus."

Rayford was impressed with how the British accent affected Dwayne's posture and bearing and even his vocal volume. "Very good then, gents," he said. "Ian Hill, proprietor, and the wife, Elva. Thanks so much for looking after the refueling."

Rayford introduced himself as Jesse Gonder, and one of the workers gave him an envelope with keys and a note enclosed. "You remember the truck. Take it to this address and I will be along. Al B."

Rayford found Albie's ancient vehicle, and they chugged into town and a crowded marketplace. He and Dwayne and Trudy sat awaiting Albie in a bustling, stone-hewn café under a cloth roof.

Dwayne apparently knew enough to keep his voice down in public, especially while losing the British accent. The three sipped warm cans of soda as they—at least Rayford and Dwayne—spoke guardedly about the Tribulation Force. Trudy seemed to nap between sips. "I'm sorry," she slurred. "Too much excitement for one day."

"She's a trooper," Dwayne whispered, eyeing patrons at nearby tables who likely couldn't understand anyway. "But I don't guess she's been this scared in her life."

Trudy shook her head, then nodded, and her head bobbed again.

"That daughter of yours is smart as a whip, I don't mind tellin' ya, Rafe. I know you all must pitch in with ideas and such, but she's got this co-op organized and coming along like nobody's business. You know I've had a thing for bein' bold about my beliefs."

"I heard."

"I'm gonna hafta put the *ki*bosh on that as soon as the mark is required for buying and selling. It'll be obvious enough where I stand, and the way I get it, at least from Pastor Ben-Judah's messages, eventually I could lose my head. We all could."

Rayford allowed a tired smile. His mind had been on Hattie and how foolishly she had allowed herself to be imprisoned. But he had never heard Tsion referred to as Pastor Ben-Judah, and he liked it. It fit. He was more than the pastor of the Trib Force. He was anybody's pastor who chose to engage his daily cyberpulpit.

As Dwayne carried on about the honor of his and Trudy's being the key southwest operatives of the Commodity Co-op, Rayford's mind wandered to Leah's suggestion. She was right; she was free of family obligations. Maybe she *could* be mobile. She was a small-time fugitive compared with the rest in the safe house. Her face wouldn't be recognized by more than the local GC. With makeup, contact lenses, and hair dye, she could travel anywhere.

Even to Brussels.

She could pose as a relative of Hattie's. Someone had to share the bad news of Hattie's sister. Rayford hoped the GC would keep Hattie alive until she became a believer, but he didn't mind their keeping her incarcerated until after the midpoint of the Tribulation. If she was free, she would try to get herself in position to kill Nicolae. Rayford had to admit to himself that he coveted that role. Though he knew it was ludicrous, his doing the deed wouldn't be any more disastrous than Hattie's doing it. Whoever did it was not going to get away with it. He prayed silently, "Lord, search my motives. I want what you want. I want Hattie saved before she does something to get herself killed."

"I'd like to meet that Greek you told me about," Dwayne was saying. "Harvesting the ocean out of the Bering Strait, shipping grain from the southwest, and bartering produce in Greece is just part of what Miz Williams has ready to roll. It's gonna be something, Rafe."

A truck creakier than the dilapidated junker Albie lent them squealed to a stop in the narrow street and Albie hopped out. He smacked the truck on the side panel, and it roared off. Rayford stood to welcome him, but Albie—carrying a rolled-up brown paper bag—motioned that he should stay seated. Albie bowed to Trudy, but she was asleep, her chin in her hand.

"One of my people reports strangers about," he whispered as he pulled up a chair.

"You can trust us, Mr. Albie," Dwayne said.

"I trust by referral, sir," Albie said. "You're with him. Him I trust, you I trust."

"Strangers where?" Rayford said, not eager to engage the GC again. "Here?"

"You would never see them here," Albie said. "That doesn't mean they are not here. They have learned to blend."

"Where then?"

"At the airport."

"We have to have access to that plane, Albie."

"Don't worry. I had someone slap a GC quarantine sign on the door, warning of sulfur vapors on board. No one will dare go near it. And as far as I know, for now no GC craft are at the airstrip. If you can get up and away and stay below radar awhile, you can escape."

"But are they looking for us?"

Albie shrugged. "I am an entrepreneur, not a spy. You would know better than I. Come, let me show you your merchandise. Do you want your friends to see it too?"

"I don't mind."

"We will go far away and test it."

"I'm gonna stay here with Trudy," Dwayne said. She seemed to be sleeping soundly, her head on her arms on the table. "Don't forget us now, hear?"

"Stay alert," Rayford whispered as he rose.

"Don't worry about me, pardner. You won't catch me napping. I haven't had this much fun since the pigs ate my sister."

Rayford narrowed his eyes at Dwayne.

"I'm joshin', Rafe. It's a country expression."

+ + +

"Is it true?" Leon wanted to know.

"Sir?" David asked, sitting in Fortunato's office.

"You haven't seen the internal audit on your department?"

David fought to keep calm. "I knew they were doing a report, but I didn't have the sense they had been there long enough to file a report."

"Well, they *have* come to some conclusions, and I don't like them one bit."

"They didn't talk to me."

"When does Internal Auditing ever talk to anybody? They're supposed to, but they never do. Anyway, you're not going to like what they found, but I'm still going to ask you to answer for it."

David was aware of his pulse and tried to regulate his breathing. "I'd be happy to study their findings and respond as thoroughly as I can."

"They give *you* high marks. They say it's not your fault."

"Fault?"

"For the fiasco, the disaster. They say it's not because of your leadership, which they find stellar."

"What are they calling a disaster?"

"Not the morale of your troops, that's for sure. Or your own work ethic. Seems you put in more hours than anybody but the potentate and me."

"Well, I don't know about that . . ."

"Bottom line, Hassid, they're recommending pulling the plug on the cyber-transmission detection project."

"Oh, no. I'd like to keep trying."

"I know it's been a pet of yours and that you've put heart and soul into it. Fact is, it's not cost efficient."

"But wouldn't a little more time be worth it if we *did* turn up something?"

"You're not going to turn up anything now, are you, David? Be honest. Internal Audit says you're no closer than you were the day we installed the equipment, and with the thousands of man-hours and the budget thrown at it, it doesn't make sense anymore."

David worked up his most disappointed expression.

"So, I ask you again," Leon said. "Is it true? Is it more trouble than it's worth? Should we pull the plug?"

"What will the potentate say?"

"That's my worry. I'm going to take the tack that we don't need to know the source location that badly and that the Judah-ites are making fools of us this way. He'll agree. How about you?"

"Who am I to disagree with the potentate and the supreme commander?"

"Atta boy."

"Not to mention Internal Audit."

"There you go. Now I have an idea for the use of those man-hours and computers."

"Good. I'd hate to see them go to waste."

"Now that the cockpit crew is back to work and the Phoenix 216 is appropriately outfitted, His Excellency has assigned me a rather ambitious ten-region tour over the next few weeks. In preparation for a gala celebration of reaching the halfway point of the Global Community's seven-year protection agreement with Israel, he would like me to meet personally with each of the regional potentates, including the new African leader. I would like your staff, the ones who will be freed up by the dissolution of the other project—"

"Excuse me, Commander, but I have a dumb question. . . ."

"The only dumb question is the one that isn't asked."

Never heard that *one before!* David thought. "Well, again, it's outside my area."

"Fire away."

"Wouldn't it be more cost efficient to just have the ten, ah, potentates come here or meet somewhere else with you?"

"Good thinking, but there are reasons for doing it this way." Leon had shifted into his patronizing teaching mode. He steepled his fingers and studied them. "His Excellency Nicolae Carpathia is, along with his many other stellar leadership qualities, a diplomat nonpareil. He leads by example. He leads by serving. He leads by listening. He leads by delegating, thus my trip. The potentate knows that each of his ten subpotentates, as it were, needs to keep a sense of his own presence. To keep them loyal, energized, and inspired, he prefers to defer to their own orbits of authority and autonomy. By sending me as his emissary to, how shall we put it, their turf, he is honoring them.

"This gives them the opportunity to roll out the red carpet, to have their subjects see that they are being honored by a visit from the palace. In each international capital I will publicly, officially invite the regional potentate to the Global Gala in September. His subjects will be invited as well and urged to combine their trip to Jerusalem with an additional pilgrimage to New Babylon."

"Interesting," David said.

"I thought you'd think so. And this is where you and your people and all those freed-up computers come in. His Excellency has always been a matchless role model to me as a public speaker. You're well aware of his proficiency in many languages. I can't hope to match that, though I would like to understand a phrase or two in each major language group I will be addressing. The potentate also, I don't know whether you've noticed, never, and I mean absolutely never, uses a contraction, not even in informal conversation."

"I've had so little personal contact with him. . . ."

"Naturally. But let me tell you his most enormous oratorical gift, and this is besides his unequaled ability to memorize pages of material and make even a lengthy speech appear extemporaneous. It is this: Potentate Carpathia knows the history, even the nuances, of his audience as well as they know it themselves. Have you ever seen the tapes of his first address to the United Nations three years ago?"

"I'm sure everyone has by now."

"That speech alone, David, virtually sealed his appointment as secretary-general and eventual leader of the new world order. He took that podium as merely a guest speaker, president of a smallish country in the eastern European bloc. The position he ascended to was not even vacant when first he opened his mouth. Yet with brilliance, charm, wit, mastery of his subject, the use of every language of the U.N., and an astounding recitation of the history of that great institution, he had the entire world eating out of his hand. I grant that had we not just suffered the global vanishings that plunged us all into a grieving, terror-filled malaise, perhaps the size of the audience would not have been appropriate for the greatness of the address. But it was as if God ordained it, and His Excellency was the perfect man for the moment."

Fortunato's eyes had glazed over. "Ah, it was magical," he said. "I knew in my soul that if I ever had the privilege to contribute even in a minuscule way to the ideals and objectives of that man, I would pledge my life to him. Have you ever felt that way about someone, David?"

"I believe I can empathize with that devotion, yes sir."

That seemed to snap Leon from his reverie. *"Real*ly," he said. "May I ask whom?"

"Whom? You mean who I, ah, idolize enough to pledge my life to? Yeah. My Father, actually."

"That's beautiful, David. He must be a wonderful man."

"Oh, he is. He's, like, God to me."

"Indeed? What does he do?"

"He's creative, works with his hands."

"But his character, that's what inspires you."

"More than you'll ever know. More than I can say."

"That's very special. I'd love to meet him someday."

"Oh, you will," David said. "I'm certain you'll meet one day, face-to-face."

"I'll look forward to that. But I've completely left my train of thought. Let me make my point and then I'll let you go. Forgive me, but I enjoy bringing along a young loyalist with promise."

"Think nothing of it."

"Anyway, I would like your people to use those computers to dig out important facts about each man I am visiting, his region, its history. By knowing as much as I can and being accurate about the details, I honor them. Can you provide me with that, David? Make me look good, which makes His Excellency look good, which is good for the Global Community."

"I'll take it as a personal challenge, sir."

18

STARS DOTTED an inky sky when Albie finally skidded to a dusty stop in a deserted plain. He left the old truck's headlights burning, illuminating a boulder next to a mature tree about a hundred yards away. Albie hopped into the bed of the truck and scampered atop the cab. He peered behind them.

"Let my eyes grow accustomed to the darkness," he said, "and I'll be sure we're alone." Satisfied, he hopped down the way he had gone up. "I used to be able to drop all the way from the top to the ground. But the ankle . . . remember?"

"The earthquake," Rayford said.

"Not a high medical priority, all things considered."

He motioned for Rayford to follow him to the front of the truck, where he squatted before a headlamp and reached into his paper sack. He produced a rectangular block of black metal that looked like a box. It was about ten inches long, five inches wide, and an inch and a half deep.

"Captain Steele, this is ingenious. It costs extra, but I know you will want it. Watch carefully so you can see how easily it is done. Unless you know the trick, you cannot do it. First, get the feel of this in your hands."

Rayford took the block and was impressed with its weight and density. There were no visible seams, and the block felt solid.

"Open it," Albie said.

Rayford turned it every which way in the light, looking for a place to get a grip, trip a switch, squeeze a spring, anything. He saw nothing.

"Try," Albie said.

Rayford gripped the block at both ends and pulled. He pushed to see if the sides had any give. He twisted it and shook it, pressed around the edges. "I'm convinced," he said, handing it back.

"What does it remind you of?"

"Ballast. Maybe a weight of some kind. An old computer battery?"

"What would you tell a customs agent it is when it shows up black and ugly under the radar?"

"One of the above, I guess. Probably say it's for the computer I left at my destination last time."

"That will work, because he will not be able to open it either. Unless he does this, and the odds are he never would."

Holding the block before him horizontally, Albie put his left thumb in the upper left corner with his left middle finger on the back of the lower left corner. He did the opposite with his right hand, thumb on the lower right corner, middle finger on the back of the upper corner. "I am pushing gently with my thumbs, which forces my fingers to resist. When I feel a most delicate disengagement, I then slide my thumbs along the bottom edge, put my index fingers along the top edge, grip tightly, and pull. See how easily it slides apart."

Rayford felt as if he were witnessing a magic trick from a foot away without a clue how it was accomplished. Albie had slid the block apart only an inch or so, then quickly snapped it back shut. "The seams seem to disappear because this was fashioned from a solid block of steel. Try it, Captain."

Rayford placed his thumbs and middle fingers where Albie had. When he pressed slightly with his thumbs and felt the pressure on his fingers, he sensed an ever so slight give. He was reminded of his penny toys as a kid when he tried to make a BB drop into a shallow hole in a piece of cardboard by tilting it this way and that. It worked only when you tilted just so far but not too much.

He grasped the ends of the block as Albie had done, and the unit smoothly slid apart. In his left hand was solid steel in the shape of a large jigsaw puzzle that perfectly aligned with the heavy handgun in his right. Amazing.

"Is it loaded?"

"I was taught there's no such thing as an unloaded gun. Many people have been killed by guns they were certain were unloaded."

"Granted. But if I aimed and shot . . ."

"Would a bullet be fired? Yes."

"Got anything you don't care about that could be set atop that rock?"

"Just aim at the rock for now. It takes getting used to."

"I was a fair marksman in the military years ago."

"Only years? Not decades?"

"Cute. Insulted by my fence."

"Familiarize yourself with your weapon."

Rayford set the block on the ground and turned the gun over and over in his hand. Heavy as it was, it had excellent balance and settled easily into his palm. He worried it might be difficult to hold steady due to the weight.

"That mechanism," Albie said, "is found in no other handgun. Only in high-powered rifles. It does not cock. It is semiautomatic. You have to pull the trigger anew for each shot, but it will fire off a round as quickly as you can release the trigger and trip it again. It is probably the loudest handgun made, and I recommend something in the ear nearest the weapon. For now, just plug your ear with your other hand."

"I don't see a safety."

"There is none. You simply aim and fire. The rationale behind this piece is that you do not separate the block and produce it unless you intend to shoot it. You do not shoot it unless you intend to destroy what you are shooting. If you shoot at that rock enough times, you will destroy it. If you shoot a person in a kill zone from within two hundred feet, you will kill him. If you hit him in a neutral zone from that same distance, your ammunition will sever skin, flesh, fat, tendon, ligament, muscle, and bone and will pass through the body leaving two holes. Provided you are at least ten feet away, the soft hollow-point shell has time to spread out due to the heat of the firing explosion and the centrifugal force caused by the spinning. Rifling grooves etched inside the barrel induce the spin. The projectile then will be roughly an inch and a half in diameter."

"The bullet spreads into a spinning disk?"

"Exactly. And as I told you on the phone, a man *missed* by the projectile by two inches from thirty feet away suffered a deep laceration from the air displacement alone. Should you hit someone from between ten feet and two hundred feet, the bullet will leave an exit wound of nearly six inches in diameter, depending on what body part is expelled with it. The thin, jagged, spinning bullet bores through anything in its path, gathers the gore around it like grass in a power-mower blade, and turns itself into a larger object of destruction. During the testing of this weapon a technician was accidentally shot just above the knee from approximately twenty feet away. His leg was effectively amputated, the lower portion attached by a thin ribbon of skin on each side of the knee."

Rayford shook his head and gazed at the ugliness in his hand. What was he thinking? That he would ever dare carry such a monstrosity, let alone use it? He would be hard pressed to justify this as a defensive weapon.

"Are you trying to talk me into this or out of it?"

Albie shrugged. "I want you satisfied with your purchase. No complaints. I said you could go cheaper. You said you wanted performance. What you do with this is your business, and I wouldn't even want to make it mine. But I guarantee you, Captain, if you ever have to use it on someone, you won't have to use it twice."

"I don't know," Rayford said, his haunches aching from crouching. He shifted his weight, picked up the other half of the block, and held it facing the gun to see how they aligned.

"At least try it," Albie said. "It's an experience."

"I'll bet it is."

Rayford dropped the block again, stood between the headlights, spread his legs, aimed the gun at the rock, and steadied his shooting hand at the wrist with his other hand.

Albie covered both ears, then interrupted. "You really should put something in that right ear."

Rayford dug in his pocket for the note Albie had written. He tore a piece from it, moistened it with his tongue, and crumpled it into a small ball. He pushed it into his ear and resumed firing position. "I wish I could cock it just for timing," he said. "It's as if the gun's ready and I'm not."

"I'm not hearing you," Albie said, too loudly. "I'm afraid you'll shoot when I take my hands from my ears."

The gun was only slightly closer to Rayford's protected ear. When he squeezed the trigger, the recoil drove him back against the hood of the truck. He slid to where his seat hit the bumper, but there wasn't enough room to hold him, and he plopped in the dirt. The explosion sounded like a bomb and then like nothing, as he was temporarily deafened and didn't even hear the echo. Rayford was glad he had not squeezed off another round when he flopped.

Albie looked at him expectantly.

"You're right," Rayford said, his ear ringing. "An experience."

"Look," Albie said, pointing into the distance.

Rayford squinted. The rock looked none the worse for wear. "Did I hit it?"

"You hit the tree!"

Rayford could hardly believe it. The bullet had hit the trunk about eight feet off the ground, just below the branches. "I need to see this," he said, struggling to his feet. Albie followed him as he got close enough to see that a gash had been taken out of the tree that left less than half the trunk intact. The weight of the branches finally overtook the gaping hole and the top of the tree came crashing down, bouncing off the rock.

"I've heard of tree surgeons," Albie said. "But . . ."

"How many rounds does it hold?"

"Nine. Want to try again and see if you can hit what you're aiming at?"

"I'll have to compensate. It pulls up and to the right."

"No, it doesn't."

"You saw what I hit. I was aiming into the middle of the rock."

"Pardon me, Captain, but the problem was not the gun. It was the shooter."

"What?"

"In your profession they would call it pilot error."

"What did I do?"

"You flinched."

"I didn't."

"You did. You expected the powerful sound and action, and you caused the barrel to point up and to the right. This time, concentrate not only on not doing that, but also on planting your back foot and taking the recoil in your legs."

"Too much to think about."

"But try. Otherwise, you're on the ground again and the tree has been put out of its misery."

Rayford filled both ears this time, made sure his right leg was planted behind his left with the knee slightly bent. Indeed, he had to fight the urge to flinch as he squeezed the trigger. This time, not dazed by the sound and not driven back against the truck, his eyes were on the rock when a huge chuck of it was blown off the top. Rayford retrieved a piece at least ten inches in diameter and three inches thick.

"Who makes this thing, anyway?"

"Those who need to know, know."

"There's no signage on it," Rayford said. "What do they call it?"

"People who know the weapon have nicknamed it the Saber."

"Why?"

Albie shrugged. "Probably because the other piece could be called a sheath. When it's pieced together it's like a sword in its sheath."

Albie showed him how to reassemble the block, returned it to the sack, and drove him back toward the marketplace.

"Needless to say, I don't carry that kind of cash," Rayford said.

"I got it on consignment. Can you get it to me in two weeks?"

"It'll come from Mac."

"Good enough. . . . Uh-oh."

Rayford looked up. The road into the crowded commercial area was blocked by GC Peacekeepers, lights flashing. Albie took to the side streets. As he drew within sight of the café he stopped abruptly and sighed. Rayford sat forward, his head touching the windshield. The crowd was in the street, the café empty save for the table where Rayford and Albie had left the Tuttles.

Trudy sat in the same pose as when they had left, head nestled in her forearms on the table. But a huge chunk was missing from the back of her head and her arms were covered with blood that still dripped from the table.

Next to her, facing Rayford, sat the big, blond, freckle-faced Dwayne. His head had fallen back and his arms hung at his sides, palms up, thumbs pointing out. His forehead bore a neat round hole and his chair rested in a pool of his blood.

Rayford grabbed the door handle, but Albie's fingers dug into his arm like talons. "You can do nothing for them, friend. Don't reveal yourself to your enemies. Give me your phone."

In a daze, Rayford handed it to him, then pounded his fists into the dash as Albie backed out of the area and drove across the sand. He spoke quickly in his native tongue, then slapped the phone shut and set it on the seat next to Rayford.

Rayford could not stop pounding. His head throbbed, the heels of his hands shot through with pain. His teeth were clenched and a buzz had invaded his brain. He felt as if his head might explode. Instinct told him to pray, but he could not. His strength left him as if he had opened a drainpipe and let it escape. He slumped in the seat.

"Listen carefully to me," Albie said. "You know whoever did that is after you. They will be lying in wait at the airport and there'll likely be a fighter or two in the air somewhere. Can you fly that plane?"

"Yes."

"I told my man there to announce that due to winds and curfews in surrounding areas he was shutting down the airport. He will give people ten minutes to leave before turning off the runway lights. He tells me no one is near your plane, but that the airport is busier than normal with pedestrian traffic. The place will be dark and hopefully empty by the time we get there. Still, to be safe, I will let you out before I enter the tower. Stay in the darkness until you reach the plane. When I hear your engines, I will light the runway for you."

Rayford could not speak, not even to thank Albie. Here was a man who was not even a believer. But he was an enemy of Carpathia and willing to do anything to thwart him. He didn't know Rayford's situation and told him repeatedly he didn't want to know. But he was risking his own life by trying to get Rayford into the air, and Rayford would never forget it.

They were within sight of the airport when the lights went off and a short line of cars snaked out of the lot. Albie stopped and nodded that Rayford should go, pointing wide to the right around the airfield, which was now a sea of blackness. Rayford grabbed the bag and started to leave, but Albie caught him and took the block out. He opened the gun and handed Rayford both pieces. He poured extra ammunition into his palm and stuffed it in Rayford's pocket.

"Just in case," he said, stuffing the bag beneath the seat.

Fury had again constricted Rayford's throat, and he could not emit a sound. He slipped the gun in one pocket and the block in another, gathered up his phone, and thrust out his hand toward Albie. They squeezed hard and Albie said, "I know. Now go."

Rayford loped across the sand and scrub grass in the darkness, hearing his own panting. When finally his vocal chords loosened, he moaned with each breath. Then he emitted a closed-mouth growl so loud and fierce that it dizzied him, and he nearly tumbled. He was within a hundred feet of the plane when he heard footsteps angling toward him and a shout. "Rayford Steele! Halt! GC Peacekeeper!"

Rayford gave off a guttural, "No!" and kept moving, reaching into his pocket for the gun.

"You're under arrest!"

He kept moving.

"Stop or I'll shoot!"

Rayford felt that tingle in his back. Had it really been that very morning that he had eluded another GC gun? He whirled, his own weapon raised.

The faint light from the road in the distance silhouetted the GC man, closing on him, weapon aimed.

Rayford stopped. "Don't make me shoot you!" he screamed, but the man kept coming. Rayford fired at his feet, hitting the ground a yard in front of the man.

A huge cloud of sand erupted and the man flipped over backward, landing on his stomach with a loud "Unh!" His weapon clattered free. Rayford made a dash for the plane, peeking over his shoulder to see the man lying motionless.

"God, don't let him die!" he said, yanking open the door and diving aboard. He pulled the door shut, realizing he was drenched with sweat. "I don't want to kill a man!"

Rayford jumped over the back of the seat into the pilot's chair and fired up the engines. The fuel tank showed full, the other gauges danced to life, and the runway lights came on. He grabbed the radio. "All clear?" he said, careful to not mention Albie's name.

"Two bogies six miles due north," came the reply. They could be upon him in seconds, but they would look for him to head west and climb quickly.

Rayford looked far to his left just before reaching takeoff speed. The GC man had labored to his feet and staggered as if catching his breath and looking for his weapon. The Super J smoothly took to the air, and Rayford headed south, staying below radar level until he was sure he was not being pursued. Then he gave the craft full power, and the thrust drove him back in his seat as he set the nose to the stars and the west. All he wanted was to reach maximum cruising speed at optimum altitude and get home to his comrades in one piece.

* * *

It was just after noon in Illinois as Tsion Ben-Judah stood gazing out the upstairs window of the safe house. Summer was coming on. He had just enjoyed a light lunch with Buck, Chloe, the baby, and Leah. What a strange and wonderful, warm woman she had turned out to be. He did not know what bothered Rayford so about her. Tsion found her most engaging.

He had nearly finished his message to the faithful and would begin polishing it for transmission in a few minutes. In it he warned that the closer the calendar drew to September, the forty-second month into the Tribulation, the more likely it was that the death toll of the 200 million horsemen would reach a third of the population. The gravity of his missive weighed on him, and he felt a sudden need to pray for his old mentor and fellow countryman, Chaim Rosenzweig.

"Father," he began, "I do not even know how to pray for my friend anymore." Tsion quoted, "'Likewise the Spirit also helps in our weaknesses. For we do not know what we should pray for as we ought, but the Spirit Himself makes intercession for us with groanings which cannot be uttered. Now He who searches the hearts knows what the mind of the Spirit is, because He makes intercession for the saints according to the will of God.'

"Thank you, Lord," he said.

And when he opened his eyes he at first thought he was dreaming. Filling his entire field of vision through the window was an army of horsemen and their steeds. Hundreds and hundreds of thousands of them, riding, riding. The horses' heads were as the heads of lions, and from their mouths poured fire and smoke.

Tsion had written of these, had heard others' accounts, secretly wished he might get a glimpse. But now as he stared, unblinking, wanting to call the others, especially Buck, who also had not seen these, he could not find voice.

In the middle of the day with the harsh late spring sun bathing the scene, the massive horsemen looked angry and determined. Their brightly colored breastplates gleamed as the immense beasts beneath them rumbled side by side, picking up speed from trotting to galloping to stampeding. It was as if their time had come. The occasional forays had been mere rehearsal. The demonic cavalry, limited only by God's choosing whom they might slay, stormed across the earth for what would surely be their final attack.

"Tsion!" Buck called from downstairs. "Look out the window! Quick!"

+ + +

Rayford had the Super J at peak performance on autopilot. Fatigue swept over him, but he dared not doze, regardless of the technology within reach. He picked up his phone to dial home when something caught his eye miles below. Fire and smoke, billowing black and yellow, rose from a boundless stretch of millions of horsemen and horses on the run across the ocean, heading for land.

19

Three Months Later

AUGUST BROKE HOT and humid in Mount Prospect, and Rayford was nearly as motionless as the wind. The safe house was not air-conditioned, and with the death of half the world's population since the Rapture, nothing was as it once had been.

An ominous foreboding settled over the house. Tempers were short, nerves raw. The baby was walking now and talking a bit, proving to be the only entertaining diversion. But Kenny was also cranky in the heat, and even Tsion had been known to leave the room when he fussed and Chloe wasn't quick enough to mollify him.

If the Rapture had brought a collective global wail over the loss of loved ones and all children, and the great wrath of the Lamb earthquake had changed where people lived and how they moved about, the judgments since had been even worse. The temporary darkening of the sun, moon, and stars, the scorching of a third of the earth, the poisoning of a third of the water, and now the slaying of more than a billion people . . . well, Rayford thought, it was a wonder anyone remained sane.

Maybe they hadn't. Maybe they had all gone mad. Rayford entertained thoughts he knew were ludicrous. Might he still wake up beside his precious but neglected and unappreciated wife Irene, with Raymie down the hall, only twelve, Rayford still with time to become the husband and father he should have been? Had this all been a Scrooge-type dream giving him a glimpse of what life would be like if he didn't change his ways?

Could he wake up a new man, ready to give his life to God, to be the right kind of influence on his daughter, his wife, his son?

It was possible, wasn't it? Couldn't it still have been simply the worst imaginable nightmare? Rayford knew his finite brain had not been programmed to assimilate everything he had been through. He never again wanted to catalog all he had seen, all he had lost. It had been more than a mortal could endure, and yet here he was.

The world had been invited to the Global Gala a month hence in Jerusalem. How dare Carpathia do it? How dare he deem it acceptable to celebrate when more people had been slain in the latest plague than had been raptured three and a half years before?

Tsion warned his audience not to go, to not be tempted by the prophecies that pointed to that date as the downfall of the one-world faith, the due time for the two witnesses, and the death of even Carpathia himself. Though he lived in the same house, like everyone else who resided there, Rayford also read Tsion's missives each day. On the subject of the despicable Global Gala, Tsion had written:

Strangely, I have been invited as an "international statesman." All has been forgiven, amnesty declared for dissidents, our security guaranteed. Well, dear loved ones, friends, and brothers and sisters in Christ, I shall not attend. An earthquake is prophesied that will wipe out a tenth of that city. I do not fear for my own well-being, as my future is secure—as is yours if you have trusted Christ for forgiveness and eternal life.

But I do not choose to personally witness even such unique, historic events when it is clear by their very nature that Satan himself will make his presence felt. My own family was butchered in retaliation for my "sin" of going public with my belief that Jesus is the long-sought Messiah. During my flight from my homeland and even all the way to where I am exiled, I was oppressed by the awful presence of the author of death.

Death will be in the air in Jerusalem next month, my friends, regardless how the event is packaged and sold to the world. It is an outrage that a festival is the excuse given to bring these parties together. On the one hand the so-called world potentate decrees an end to sacrifices and offerings in the temple, because they violate the tenets of tolerance espoused by the Enigma Babylon One World Faith. On the other he aims to celebrate the agreement between the Global Community and Israel. How do these figure together? While it is true he has intimidated the impotent world and kept potential enemies from attacking Israel, he tramples upon her centuries-old traditions and betrays her heritage and religious autonomy.

Like the rest of the world, I will follow the proceedings on the Internet or on television. But no, dear ones, I shall not accept the invitation to attend. This event portends the second half of the Tribulation, called the Great Tribulation, which will make these horrific days seem languorous.

Even the GC-controlled news media can no longer sugarcoat what we know to be true. Crime and sin are beyond control. The necessities of life are in short supply due to lack of a workforce and ways to manufacture and distribute them. Yet there is not a neighborhood on earth that does not have a brothel, a séance and fortune-telling parlor, or a pagan temple expressly for worshiping idols. Life is cheap, and our fellow citizens die every day as marauders loot their homes and businesses and persons. There are not enough Peacekeepers still alive to do police work, and the ones who are on the job are either overwhelmed or corrupt.

With people simply gone from every walk of life, it is amazing what continues to flourish. New movies and television programming are virtually nonexistent, but there is no shortage of pornography and perversion on the hundreds of channels still available to anyone with a receiver.

We are not surprised that these are dark days, brothers and sisters, and I pray you would hold on and maintain and continue to try to share the truth of Jesus until he comes. Merely surviving from this point will occupy most of your time. But I urge you to prepare, have a plan for what you will do when that inevitable day arrives where it is not just illegal to tap into this Web site or declare yourself a believer. Be ready for that day when the insidious mark of the beast is required on your forehead or hand for you to legally buy or sell.

And above all, do not make the fatal mistake of thinking that you can take that mark for the sake of expediency while privately believing in Christ. He has made plain that those who deny him before men, he will deny before God. And in later teachings I will elucidate on why the mark of the evil one is irrevocable.

If you have already trusted Christ for your salvation, you have the mark of the seal of God on your forehead, visible only to other believers. Fortunately, this decision, mark, and seal is also irrevocable, so you never need fear losing your standing with him. For who shall separate us from the love of Christ? Shall tribulation, or distress, or persecution, or famine, or nakedness, or peril, or sword? In all these things we are more than conquerors through him that loved us. With the apostle Paul, I am persuaded that neither death, nor life, nor angels, nor principalities, nor powers, nor things present, nor things to come, nor height, nor depth, nor any other creature shall be able to separate us from the love of God, which is in Christ Jesus our Lord.

In spite of and in the midst of every trial and tribulation, let us continue to give thanks to God, who gives us the victory through our Lord Jesus Christ. And as the Scriptures say, "Therefore, my beloved brethren, be steadfast, immovable, always abounding in the work of the Lord, knowing that your labor is not in vain in the Lord."

Steadfast in love for you all, your friend, Tsion Ben-Judah.

✦ ✦ ✦

Hattie was in prison and without knowledge of her sister's death, and Rayford felt responsible for her.

The murders of Dwayne and Trudy Tuttle had broken his heart.

The reaction of Bo Hanson to the loss of his brother served only as another nail in the coffin that bore Rayford's despair. Rayford and T had agreed that T should break the news to Bo. T had befriended him, despite their differences, while Rayford had estranged him. Rayford hoped that T might open a door of witness to Bo by compassionately bearing the awful news. Then perhaps Rayford would be able to apologize for his behavior and have a part in seeing Bo come to Christ.

T had returned encouraged from his meeting with Bo. He had called him, met him in his apartment, and told him what had happened. He reported that the tearful Bo had asked, "What about the note I got from Sam?"

"I told him it had been forged by the GC, Ray," T said. "He seemed to be all right. He cried a lot, blamed himself. Said he sold his brother out just for money. But he hadn't sold him out. He had merely made the mistake of getting him involved in an ill-conceived plan. He was down when I left him, but he let me pray with him. I thought that was a huge step."

"I'm sure it was," Rayford said, "but you didn't ask to see me so you could give me good news. What happened?"

T sat back and sighed. "Bo killed himself last night, Ray. Drank himself sick at a bar, waved a gun around, cursed Carpathia and the world, and shot himself."

Rayford had been inconsolable for days. "I might as well have pulled the trigger myself," he said.

The rest of the Trib Force offered the usual "can't blame yourself" speeches, and in the end he came to agree. He turned the blame on the one who had all the blame he needed: Nicolae Carpathia.

Rayford immersed himself in the prophetic passages about the death of Antichrist, never seeking Tsion's counsel or interpretation. In his feverish state he interpreted the Scripture the way he wanted to, shoehorning himself into the agent God would use to do the deed. When he read that "He who kills with the sword must be killed with the sword," and knew that even Tsion believed this was a reference to Antichrist, Rayford shuddered. Was this a message just for him? A later verse referred to "the beast who was wounded by the sword and lived." That had to be a reference to one of the heads of the beast "as if it had been mortally wounded, and his deadly wound was healed."

He didn't understand it all. Who could? But without Tsion's analysis, Rayford believed he had figured out these verses. Carpathia was to be mortally wounded in the head by a sword and then come back to life. A sword? What was it Albie called the superb killing machine Rayford had stashed behind loose bricks in the basement? Saber.

Could he—would he do it? Was it his duty? He shook his head. What was he thinking?

\+ + +

Mac missed Rayford. He had been the voice of reason, a mentor, a spiritual model. Mac enjoyed David and Annie. Great kids. But hard to identify with. Abdullah was a good first officer and a wonderful flyer, but he could go days without saying anything except in response to Mac.

Life was interesting, but it sure wasn't fun anymore. Flying to the major capitals and listening in on Fortunato's incessant courting of the ten kings was as sickening as it was fascinating. Behind a podium on the tarmac at the airport in Nairobi, Leon grandly welcomed to "His Excellency Nicolae Carpathia's cabinet of esteemed regional potentates, the honorable Mr. Enoch Litwala. How this great leader and renowned pacifist was overlooked during the initial search for a regional potentate of the United States of Africa will go in the embarrassment file of the history of the Global Community. We may have come to him late, but we found him, didn't we?"

The crowds cheered their favorite son. Leon continued, "His Excellency sends his heartfelt greetings to Africa and his highest compliments on your achievement of international goals. And it is my singular pleasure, on his behalf, to personally invite your new potentate to Jerusalem in September for the Global Gala!"

After waiting for the crowd to quiet, Leon affected a serious tone. "We have endured rough times and much loss of life. But His Excellency is sparing no expense for an international festival like nothing ever seen before. Besides celebrating the halfway mark of the agreement with Israel, and I am so pleased he has given me permission to share this publicly with you, His Excellency is guaranteeing—you heard that right—guaranteeing an end to killer plagues. You ask how can he do this? The potentate is on record that if the two so-called witnesses at the Wailing Wall do not cease and desist their torment of Israel and the rest of the world, he will personally deal with them."

This message was repeated in every capital to enthusiastic response. Mac believed people were so tired of death and devastation and so addicted to their own sin that they looked forward to a return to life before the two prophets of doom had seemed to unleash the anger of heaven. Was it possible Carpathia would literally kill the pair? Hadn't he threatened to do that before? They had made a fool of him. But now he was making a guarantee. And he was also pledging to help people get to the Gala in spite of the disastrous loss of public services due to the decreased population.

"We are about to see a dramatic turn back toward our goals and ideals for a utopian society," Fortunato quoted Carpathia, and the Global Gala would mark the first step.

Bizarre, Mac thought, *to see Antichrist himself in a public relations nightmare, trying to salvage his image.*

In the capitals, Leon followed his praising of the regional potentates with promises from the Global Community for better services. "We're going to work smarter *and* harder," he would say, "to meet your needs. Within a decade, the only memory of the population attrition will be sadness for those we have lost. Inconvenience will be a thing of the past as we work together until cutting-edge technology brings us to a higher level of services than we ever dreamed."

There were always photo opportunities for the Carpathia-controlled press, in which Fortunato gravely studied underdeveloped areas due to the widespread deaths. Then he would kiss babies and hold them aloft, proclaiming "the future of the Global Community." Finally, with people in the area encouraged and inspired, he would invite the potentate back onto the opulent Phoenix 216 for "a high-level confidential meeting where your leader can best represent the needs of this region."

Fortunato would listen to the potentates, of course, and make promises a million Carpathias could never keep. But each private confab eventually centered on the "Enigma Babylon situation." As Mac listened in, he found that most of the potentates knew exactly what Leon was talking about as soon as he raised the issue. A few wanted to know, "What situation is that?" but either way, by the time Leon took off for his next appearance, it was clear which potentates could be counted on. Stunning to Mac was that every one was on record in opposition to the overbearing Peter II.

That was so amazing that Mac requested a private phone chat with Tsion, despite the time difference. He went through Leah, as did all communication now, and assured her that he would understand if Tsion didn't have the time. But within a day, the two were on secure phones together.

"Captain McCullum, my friend, I am so grateful for all the inside information you have sent my way. It makes my work so much easier and gives me insights into the inner workings that I would never otherwise have. What can I do for you?"

"Well, sir, just a quick question, I hope. I know David has kept everybody up-to-date, through Leah, about the plot to rally the ten kings against Peter the Second. We know that not all the kings are even loyal to Carpathia, but every one of them is on board with this anti-Peter thing. Are they just blowing smoke with Fortunato, or am I naive to believe what sounds like true anger and agreement?"

"Excellent question, Captain, and the only reason I have not dealt with it on the Net is that I feel it might be too revealing and I would then be inserting myself into history in the making. That is a dangerous precedent, and we must guard against trying to help God, as it were, fulfill his promises. If he says it will happen, it will happen.

"But as for the ten kings and their willingness to conspire against Peter the Second: This is biblical. God is working out his eternal plan. Just as in the Old Testament he used pagan armies to punish his own people and today he uses demon hordes to get the attention of unbelievers, he is also using these kings. Revelation 17 says, 'And the ten horns which you saw on the beast' (these are the kings, Mac), 'these will hate the harlot' (that is the false religion, represented now by Peter the Second), 'make her desolate and naked, eat her flesh and burn her with fire.'

"Now get this, Captain. The next verse answers your question. The reason they are agreeing on this when in truth they are all egomaniacs who agree on little—not even on Carpathia—is this. Listen as I read. 'God has put it into their hearts to fulfill His purpose, to be of one mind, and to give their kingdom to the beast, until the words of God are fulfilled.'"

"Wow."

"Isn't that something? It is amazing to witness the fulfillment of prophecy."

"Thank you, sir."

"You will find these kings of one mind, because God said so. And you know it will mean the demise of Peter, don't you?"

"I figured that."

"The question is how and where it will happen."

"I have an idea," Mac said.

*"Real*ly," Tsion said.

Mac told him of the private conversation between Leon and the newest king, Kenyan Enoch Litwala. Fortunato had listened through Litwala's list of suggestions and demands, taking notes, telling him what he thought he heard him saying, and so forth, then got to the Peter the Second issue:

"His Excellency has asked that I raise with you personally a most delicate situation. He most admires your wisdom and ability to size up circumstances, but this is a matter with which you may not be familiar. Are you aware of any, shall we say, hesitation on the part of the other regional potentates concerning the, ah, visibility of Peter the Second?"

Litwala had responded so quickly that Mac had sat up in the cockpit and pressed the earphone tighter. "I don't know or care what my colleagues think," Litwala said, "but I will speak my own heart. I despise the man. He is egotistical, legalistic, self-possessed. He has appropriated huge amounts of money for his Enigma Babylon that should have been used in my country for my people. I do not find him loyal to His Excellency the potentate, and—"

"Indeed?"

"As soon as he heard I was being considered for this post he came to see me, flew all the way here, I believe on this very plane. Was this not his before?"

"It was."

"He tried to elicit my support for his playing a larger role in world governance, aside from religion. I said nothing. I believe he has too much influence *now.* Why would I want him to have more? I told him I would study his proposals and, should I be so honored as to be chosen for this position, I would consult more experienced regional potentates about their views. That seemed to please him. He tried to pry from me any negative thoughts I had about His Excellency, but I just listened. I did not challenge or counter him, but neither did I reveal precisely where I stood. That might prove valuable later."

"It's good, Potentate Litwala. He believes he has the support of the others and likely assumes you will fall in line. Do you agree he is potentially a danger to the harmony of Global Community leadership?"

"Not potentially. Presently."

"What would you propose we do about it? That is His Excellency's question of you."

"He would not appreciate my deepest feelings."

"You might be surprised."

"If the potentate appreciates that I believe Peter needs to be eliminated, yes, that would surprise me."

"By eliminated, you mean diplomatically removed from—"

"By eliminated, Supreme Commander, I mean eliminated."

There was silence over the reverse intercom for a moment. Litwala spoke first. "My problem is that I trust few. After what I have endured with Rehoboth and others . . ."

"I'm telling you the other potentates are agreed on this," Leon said.

"They would have him eliminated?"

"They would."

Another pause. "But who would do it?"

"You need to talk with them about that."

"There must be a way to ensure we're in it together, without the possibility of betrayal. We must all be equally culpable."

"Like all contributing to the remuneration for the—"

"No," Litwala said. "We must all have equal responsibility and liability."

After Litwala left the aircraft, Mac heard Fortunato on the phone with Carpathia. "Did you pick a winner with the new African potentate! . . . You did? . . . You're not serious. . . . You are! . . . That is amazing. Have you ever done that to me? . . . Planted thoughts? . . . Tell me what he'll suggest. . . . All ten of them? At the same time? So no one can point the finger at another. Brilliant."

Mac called David. "Have you got a tap on Carpathia's phone?"

"Always."

"Check it. You remember the story Buck Williams tells about how Nicolae told people what they saw and what they would remember? I think Nicolae just revealed to Leon that he's done something like that again."

"They're talking now?"

"Right now."

"I'll listen to 'em live, Mac. Safe trip."

* * *

By the time David got patched in to Carpathia's phone, Nicolae and Leon were finishing their conversation.

"I can be totally free of it that way," Carpathia was saying. "No one willing to talk, no weapon, no body. Enough DNA in the ashes to identify the body if there is any question, but as Peter will never turn up again, I cannot imagine there being a doubt."

"And who would corroborate the disease? Dare they involve yet another party?"

"Leon! Think! Od Gustav."

"Ah, yes! *Doctor* Gustav. Who needs an outsider when one of the ten can sign the death certificate? Did I say you were brilliant, Excellency?"

"Probably, but even the confident man can take hearing that more than once."

"Well, the ice idea. I mean, really. There's no other word for that."

"Thank you, Commander. Safe trip."

David smirked at the repeat of how he had signed off with Mac. Two buddies saying good-bye. Dave and Mac; Nick and Lee. Both pairs playing games, outsmarting the competition. He sighed. The difference between the pairs of friends was only eternal.

David quickly moved from listening live to listening to the recording from the beginning, when Fortunato had said, "Did you pick a winner with the new African potentate!"

"How well I know," Carpathia said. "I handpicked him the day I first visited the U.N. I knew I would have to wait while we worked our way through either Ngumo or Rehoboth. I found him *very* suggestible."

"You did?"

"From the beginning. I hypnotized him on the phone once. Told him he would be unswervingly loyal to me, that my enemies would be his enemies and my friends his friends."

"You're not serious."

"Shall I prove it? He is willing to eliminate Peter, and he means eliminate."

"You are!"

"But he wants them all in on it, all ten of them. How am I doing?"

"That is amazing. Have you ever done that to me?"

"Done what?"

"Planted thoughts?"

"I do not need to, Leon. You are my most trusted friend and adviser. With Enoch I have even verbally implanted a whole plan in his mind. He will think about it, and when he comes back, he will suggest what is already in his head."

"Tell me what he'll suggest," Leon said.

"A meeting in Jerusalem the morning before the gala. He will invite Peter and tell him it is to discuss his succession to my role if a certain plan of theirs is carried out. It would be a meeting of just Peter and the potentates."

"All ten of them?"

"Yes. And it will be at the fancy new Global Community Grand Hotel, where the ice sculptures have become so popular. For the meeting they will order the large sculpture of Peter himself, the one that depicts him as a mighty angel, life size, with the huge wings with pointed feathers. As the ten are admiring it, each will break off one of those thick feathers with the sharp ends, and as Peter is wondering what in the world it is all about, each will plunge his into him from different angles—neck, eye, temple, heart."

"At the same time?" Leon said. "So no one can point the finger at another. Brilliant."

"The weapons will melt, the body will be transported to a crematorium in a bag brought in Scandinavian Potentate Gustav's briefcase. The body will be burned to avoid the spread of the deadly disease that causes one to bleed to death through his mucus membranes."

"Which will explain any blood in the meeting room."

"Exactly. I can be totally free of it that way. No one willing to talk, no weapon, no body. Enough DNA in the ashes . . ."

20

BUCK WAS GETTING the cold shoulder.

It had been a long time since he and Chloe had found themselves at loggerheads. "I know it's only three and a half more years," she said, "but do you think I want to raise this child alone?"

"Nothing's going to happen," he said, reaching for her. She turned away.

"You're going," she said. "It's written all over you. I love Chaim, but it was unfair of him to ask."

"If I don't go, Tsion's going to go, and we don't want that."

Chaim Rosenzweig had been invited to appear at the Global Gala as an honored guest of His Excellency the potentate. Chaim had Jacov communicate to the Tribulation Force by posting a cryptic message on Tsion's Web site. Leah had found it, almost by accident.

"Is this anything?" she asked Rayford late one night when the two were working at their computers in the kitchen. "The initials aren't a coincidence, are they?"

She turned her laptop so he could see. The message was one of thousands posted on the site, most encouraging Dr. Ben-Judah, some asking questions, some criticizing or threatening. Part of Leah's job was to monitor those and see if any required personal responses. Most didn't. This post stuck out due to its brevity and the unique initials. It read: "C (B) W call J re boss. Signed, H's."

"I don't know who *J* is or what *H's* means," she said, "but how many people know they can reach Cameron (Buck) Williams at this site? Or am I reading into it?"

Rayford studied it and summoned Buck. The three huddled in front of Leah's screen and stared. Buck suddenly stood. "Jacov," he said. "Pretty crafty. He's Hannelore's husband, and he wants to talk about Chaim."

Buck checked his watch and phoned. It was seven in the morning in Israel. Jacov was an early riser. "He's been invited to the Gala," Jacov said quickly. "None of us thinks he should go. He has not been well, staying up all hours. He looks terrible. Talk him out of it."

Chaim didn't sound well. He seemed to be trying to be his jovial self, but his thick Israeli accent sounded weary and sometimes slurred. "I will not be dissuaded, Cameron, but I have insisted that I be allowed to bring my valet and two guests. I was assured I could bring anyone I wanted. Stefan is petrified of Carpathia and insists he will quit my staff before he would attend. Jacov has agreed to serve as both driver and valet."

"Dr. Rosenzweig, you don't want to do this. You've read Tsion's warnings, and—"

"Tsion's warning is for what the Global Community calls the Judah-ites. I love Tsion and consider him one of my own, but I am *not* that kind of Judah-ite. I am going, but I want you and Tsion there with me."

Buck rolled his eyes. "Forgive me, Doctor, but that is naive. We are both persona non grata with the GC, and we trust Carpathia's security pledge as far as we can throw it."

"They said I could bring any guests I wanted."

"They didn't know whom you had in mind."

"Cameron, you and I have become close, have we not?"

"Of course."

"More than just a journalist and a subject, am I right?"

"Certainly, but—"

"You are a cosmopolitan person. You should know that in my culture it is highly offensive to rebuff a formal invitation. I am formally inviting you and Tsion to attend the Gala with me, and I will take it as a personal insult if you do not."

"Doctor, I have a family. Dr. Ben-Judah has millions who count on his—"

"You would both be with *me*! The Carpathia regime has committed some heinous acts, but to threaten the safety of someone as prominent as Tsion in the presence of a guest of honor . . ."

"I can tell you right now, sir, that Tsion will not be coming. I'm not even sure I will pass along the invitation. He would want to do what you ask because he loves you so, but it would be irresponsible of me to—"

"Do you not love me also, Cameron?"

"Yes, enough to tell you that this is—"

"I will withdraw my invitation of Tsion if I know you will be there."

Buck hesitated. "I couldn't come under my own name anyway. And though I look different enough to get through customs, I could never appear with you if you are close to GC brass. They would recognize me instantly."

Chaim was silent for a moment. Then, "I am very sad that two of my dearest friends, friends who say they care deeply about me—"

"Sir, don't. This is not becoming. You want me to come because you've made me feel guilty? Is that fair? Are you thinking of me and my wife and my child?"

Rosenzweig, totally out of character, ignored Buck's mention of his family. "What would Tsion say if you told him I might be ready to become a Judah-ite?"

Buck sighed. "For one thing, he hates that term with a passion. You of all people should know Tsion well enough to know that this is not about him, not about his developing a following. And to dangle a decision about your eternal soul as a bargaining ch—"

"Cameron, have I ever asked for anything? For years I have considered you a young man whose admiration for me is unwarranted but cherished. I don't believe I have ever taken advantage of that. Have I?"

"No, and that's why this—"

"You are a journalist! How can you not want to be here for this?"

Buck had no answer. In truth he had wanted to attend since the moment he heard of the Gala. He could hardly believe Carpathia himself was hosting the event at which so much prophecy would culminate. But he had never seriously considered going. He had been encouraged by how easily he had traveled to and from Israel under an alias not long before. But Chloe. Kenny. Tsion's stance on any believer attending. Buck considered it out of the question.

Now Chaim had finally tapped into the core of Buck's being. Pagan or believer, single or married, childless or a father, he had been a journalist for as long as he could remember. He had been curious as a child—nosy, his friends and family said—before he'd ever had a conduit through which he could publish his findings. His trademark was incisive eyewitness reporting, and he was never happier than when he was on a story, not hidden away in a safe house where all he could do was comment on previously published material.

His hesitation seemed to feed Rosenzweig, as if he knew Buck had taken the bait and now all the old man had to do was yank the line to set the hook.

"It's not that I don't *want* to be there," Buck said weakly, hating the whine in his voice.

"Then you'll come? That would mean so much to—"

"This is not a decision I can make independently," Buck said, and he realized he had turned a corner. He had gone from a flat refusal to mulling a full-blown prospect that had to be decided.

"That is another distinction between our cultures," Chaim said. "A Middle Eastern man is his own person, charting his own course, not answerable to—"

"I cannot be seen with you," Buck said.

"Just knowing you are there will warm me, Cameron, and surely we will be able to interact privately at some point. I will withdraw my formal invitation to Tsion, and I will not procrastinate about our spiritual discussions any longer."

"You don't need to wait for me for that, Doctor. In fact, I would urge that before you even dream of attending the Gala you would—"

"I need to discuss these things in person, Cameron. You understand."

Buck didn't, but he feared if he spent any more time on the phone he would make more concessions. He was sure to incur the wrath of the rest of the Trib Force regardless, so Buck negotiated one condition.

"I must insist on one thing," he said.

"Oh, Cameron, you're not going to go back on your word now, are you?"

"I could not sanction your being there on the second day of the pageant."

Chaim was silent, but Buck heard papers rustling in the background. "It is a five-day event," Rosenzweig said, "Monday through Friday next week. Monday is the anniversary of the treaty. Nicolae wants me on the platform for that celebration. Tuesday is a party at the Temple Mount, which I fear will turn into a confrontation between him and your preacher friends. That is what you want me to avoid?"

"Exactly."

"Granted."

"Thank you, sir."

"My packet of information requests the honor of my presence at both the opening and closing ceremonies. That would be Monday night and Friday night."

"My preference is that you not go at all."

"I heard you say you would be there."

\+ + +

Annie and David had become even closer. He felt bad when she told him that sometimes she felt he appreciated her more as a co-subversive than as one who loved him. Glancing around to be sure they were alone at the end of a corridor, he took her face in his hands and touched the tip of his nose to hers. "I love you," he said. "Under any other circumstances, I'd marry you."

"Is that a proposal?"

"I wish. You can imagine the pressure, the stress. You have it too. The only other two believers I've seen here besides us and Mac and Abdullah, those two women in inventory, were somehow found out last night."

"Oh, no! We hadn't even made contact yet. They probably thought they were alone."

"They were shipped to Brussels this morning."

"Oh, David."

"Odds are we aren't going to be here much longer either. I don't know exactly when the mark requirement is coming, but we have to escape first."

"I want to be your wife, even if only for a few years."

"And I want you to be, but we can't do anything like that until we know whether we can get out of here together. If one escapes and the other doesn't, that's no kind of life."

"I know," she said. "We're likely to be the first to know when Carpathia does start requiring a mark of loyalty. And you know he'll start right here in the palace."

"Probably."

"Meanwhile, David, you might want to tell the stateside Force that if they need to travel, now's the best time. I saw a document that's going to the Peacekeeping Force around the world. It calls for a moratorium on arrests or detainment, even of enemies of the Global Community, until after the Gala."

\+ + +

There had been no keeping the Rosenzweig request from Tsion, of course, and Tsion had been unusually melancholic ever since. "I will not tell you what to do, Buck," he said in front of Rayford, "but I wish your father-in-law would pull rank on you."

"Frankly," Rayford said, at the next meeting of the household, "I wish I were going with Buck."

"You're letting him go," Chloe said, with her fourteen-month-old on her lap. Kenny turned to face her and put his hands over her eyes as she spoke. She turned her head so she could see. "I can't believe it. Well, why don't you go with him, Dad? Why don't we all go? Bad enough we won't all make it to the end of the Tribulation anyway, why don't we throw caution to the wind? Why don't we make sure Kenny is an orphan without even a grandfather?"

"Kenny!" the baby said. "Grandpa!"

Rayford slapped his thighs and opened his arms, and Kenny slid off Chloe's lap and ran to him. Rayford lifted him over his head, making him squeal, then sat him on his lap. "The fact is, I have a different trip in mind for me."

"This is just great," Chloe said. "Do we vote on anything anymore, or do we all just pull a Hattie and run off to wherever we want?"

"This is not really a democracy," Rayford said, and judging by the look he got from Tsion, realized he was on shaky ground. The baby climbed off him and toddled into the other room. "Leah and I have been talking, and—"

"Leah's going somewhere too?" Chloe said. "She's invaluable to me here."

"I won't be gone long," Leah said.

"It's a foregone conclusion then?"

"This is more announcement than discussion," Rayford said.

"Clearly. Well, let's hear it."

Rayford began carefully, fearing his own motive. In his heart of hearts he wanted to get to Jerusalem with his Saber. But he said, "We need to make contact with Hattie. I feel responsible for her, and I want to know she's all right, let her know we're still standing with her, see what we can do for her. Mostly, I want to make sure she's not given us away."

Even Chloe did not argue. "She deserves to know about her sister," she said. "But the GC will be watching for you, Dad."

"They will be less likely to suspect a woman. We're thinking of making Leah Hattie's aunt on her mother's side, giving her a new look and, of course, a new ID. She'll say she's heard a rumor or got word smuggled out somehow that Hattie's there. If they don't associate Leah with us, why shouldn't they allow the contact?"

"But now, Dad? With Buck going?"

"David's told us now is the best time to travel. It's going to become nearly impossible soon."

"That is true," Tsion said.

Rayford looked up in surprise, and he noticed others did too.

"I'm not supporting this," Tsion said. "But if that poor child dies in prison apart from God, when we had her under our own roof for so long . . ." His voice quavered and he paused. "I don't know why God has given me such a tenderness toward that woman."

Chloe sat shaking her head, and Rayford knew she was not happy, but through arguing.

"T believes it would be too risky for me to start cruising around in the Super J, so he's prepping the Gulfstream."

"It shouldn't surprise me that this is virtually set," Chloe said. Rayford sensed a resigned admiration, as if she had conceded that once he got something in his brain, it happened.

"Buck can fly with us to Brussels—that'll save us a few dollars—and continue commercially to Tel Aviv. I'll stay out of sight in Belgium and meet up with Leah when she's ready."

"Maybe Buck could fly back with you too," Chloe said. "Depending on how long you want to wait for him in Brussels."

"Maybe," Rayford said. "Would you prefer that?"

"Would I prefer he fly home with my dad rather than taking his chances with a commercial system that is half what it used to be? Yes, I would prefer that. Of course, I prefer he not go, but short of that, humor me."

+ + +

The mood was festive on the Phoenix 216 when Mac and Abdullah took off Saturday morning for Israel with a full load. It seemed the entire Carpathia administrative team was on board, and Nicolae was in his glory. Mac listened in as Leon clapped for attention and asked people to gather. "Welcome, everyone," he said. "And to our very special guest, who selflessly bequeathed His Excellency this aircraft at a time of dire need, a special welcome to you, sir."

There was polite applause, and Mac wished he could see Peter Mathews's face. "Would you care to say a word before His Excellency addresses us, Pontifex?"

"Oh, why, yes, thank you, Commander. I, we, at Enigma Babylon look forward to the Gala with much anticipation—Israel is, as you know, one of the last areas to acquiesce to our ideals. I believe that we will have the opportunity to put our best face on the one-world faith and that we will come away from this week with many more members. I frankly relish opportunities to challenge dissidents, and with the two preachers and the history of the Judah-ite rallies here, this is the place to do just that. Good to be with you."

"Thank you, Supreme Pontiff," Leon said. "Now, Your Excellency . . ."

Carpathia sounded ecstatic with expectation. "My personal greetings and welcome to you all," he said. "I believe you will one day look back on this coming week as the beginning of our finest hour. I know we have suffered the way the whole world has with the plagues and death. But the future is clear. We know what we have to do, and we will do it. Enjoy yourselves. It is a festival, a party. Personal, individual freedom has never been more celebrated. And may I say, there are more places in Jerusalem than anywhere to indulge yourselves. Revel in the Epicurean and physical pleasures that appeal to you. Show the rest of the Global Community that they are allowed to pamper the flesh even after times of hardship and chaos. Let us ring in the new world with a festival like no one has ever seen. Many of you have been responsible for arranging entertainment and diversion, and for that I am grateful. I cannot wait to see the spectacle myself."

Mac and Abdullah enjoyed private rooms next to each other in the palatial King David Hotel, where Carpathia had reserved two entire floors. The rest of the entourage stayed not far away in accommodations no less opulent. The ten regional potentates would be housed at the GC Grand, another quarter mile away.

During the two days before the official opening of the Gala, the cockpit crew was required to conduct tours of the 216 back in Tel Aviv. Early Monday morning they helped arrange transport from Ben Gurion Airport to Jerusalem for the potentates and their extensive entourages. Mac worked with GC Security to off-load the metal detectors David had put into the cargo hold, and these were set up on either side of the gigantic outdoor platform that had been erected not a half mile from the Temple Mount and the Wailing Wall. Everyone who would be on the platform, from entertainers to VIPs, would pass through a metal detector on one side of the platform or the other.

The stage floor was twelve feet off the ground and a hundred feet square. A vast green tarpaulin was canopied atop it to block the sun, and massive scaffolding towers held the speaker systems that would boom the music and speeches to an expected two million revelers. All across the back of the stage, filling a flowing curtain designed to coordinate with the canopy, were various messages in every major language. These welcomed the delegates, announced the dates of the five days of the Global Gala, and featured huge sparkling logos of the Global Community.

The largest statement printed on the backdrop, Mac noticed, read, One World, One Truth: Individual Freedom for All. All around the plaza, on every lamppost, fence, and wall, was the slogan Today Is the First Day of the Rest of Utopia.

As Mac and Abdullah aided with the placement of the metal detectors, several bands and dance troupes rehearsed and sound technicians swarmed the area. Mac pulled Abdullah close and whispered, "I must be seeing things. Who does that girl, second from the left, look like to you?"

"I was trying not to watch," Abdullah said. "But if you insist. Oh, my, I see the resemblance, of course. But it is not possible. Is it?"

Mac shook his head. Hattie was in Brussels. They knew that. This woman merely stuck out from the other dancers because she looked a bit older. The rest looked barely out of their teens.

The security chief reminded musicians and dancers that none would be allowed on stage beginning with Monday evening's opening ceremony without proper identification and without passing through a metal detector. "If you've got the big buttons or buckles and jewelry, be prepared to take those off and have them checked before you go through."

At a briefing of the security staff, Mac heard the chief instruct the teams of plainclothes guards who would work in shifts in the front of the stage. "Particularly when the potentate is at the microphone," he said, "maintain your position. Let the audience move if you're blocking their vision. You stand in a semicircle, eight at a time, four feet apart, hands clasped at your belt. Eyes forward, no talking, no smiling, no gesturing. If you are summoned through your earpiece, do not respond orally. Just do what you're told."

Mac felt a deep sadness as he walked to a shuttle van that was to take him and Abdullah back to the King David. He glanced back at the stage from across a wide expanse of asphalt. Backed by deafening music, the dance troupe ended a lascivious routine.

"This is the new world, Abdullah. This is individual freedom, sanctioned by the international government."

"Celebrated even," Abdullah said. Suddenly he stopped and leaned against a fence. "Captain, these are the times when I long for heaven. I don't want to die, especially the way I have seen others' lives end. But to survive until the Glorious Appearing will be no easy thing."

Mac nodded. "What happened to the Tuttles was awful," he said. "But they probably never knew what hit them. They woke up in heaven."

Abdullah turned his face to the sun and a cloudless sky. "God forgive me if that is what I wish for. Quick and painless."

Mac could hear Eli and Moishe preaching from half a mile away but couldn't make out their words. "I've heard so much about them," he said. "I don't suppose we should risk being seen there."

"I would love to see them," Abdullah said. "How about we walk back to the hotel and at least go past there. We do not have to join the crowd, just see what we can see and hear what we can hear."

"Say no more, Smitty," Mac said.

All along the way Mac and Abdullah passed bars, strip clubs, massage parlors, brothels, pagan sanctuaries, and fortune-telling establishments. In a city with a history of religion dating back millennia, and where—like in the rest of the world—half the population had been wiped out since the Rapture, these businesses were not hidden. They were not seedy, not relegated to a certain inevitable section of town. Neither were they operating in darkness behind black doors or labyrinthine entrances that saved the "real" treats for those who were there on purpose.

Rather, while the rest of the Holy City seemed to crumble for neglect and lack of manpower, here were gleaming storefronts, well lit and obvious to every eye, proudly exhibiting every perversion and fleshly evil known to man.

Mac quickened his pace despite Abdullah's pronounced limp, and the two hurried toward the Temple Mount and the two witnesses as if from a sewer to a spring.

21

AS HE WAS SURE was true with others in the safe house, Buck could not figure the relationship between his father-in-law and Leah Rose. She seemed a burr to Rayford, and yet surely he had to appreciate what she had brought to the Tribulation Force, besides her fortune.

Rayford was not above squabbling with her, and she held her own. Yet they had seemed to spend more and more time together as the time drew near the halfway point of the Tribulation. The announcement of Rayford's plan to fly her to Brussels made their new closeness less mysterious to Buck. Rayford apparently needed her to do a job, and she was eager to do it. Maybe there was nothing more to the relationship than that.

Zeke Jr., the tattooed Z for short, dolled up splendid documents for Leah. With bleached-blonde hair, darker contact lenses, and a tiny dental appliance that gave her a not unattractive overbite and slightly bucked teeth, she was transformed. Leah was now Donna Clendenon from California, formerly married to one of Hattie Durham's mother's brothers. She carried news of Hattie's sister Nancy's demise (which was, unfortunately, true). That, Rayford speculated, would get her visitation privileges at the Global Community lockup in Brussels, which, typically, had been christened the Belgium Facility for Female Rehabilitation. Those familiar with it knew the BFFR, or Buffer, as a maximum-security prison. Dissident women went in, but they rarely came out. When they did, they were anything but rehabilitated.

Buck's hope—which he assumed was also Rayford's—was that the GC saw enough value in Hattie that they would not simply eliminate her. Carpathia must have seen her, at the very least, as bait to help lure Rayford, Buck, or even Tsion Ben-Judah. Those in the safe house hoped the GC hadn't lost patience with Hattie in frustration over twice nearly having had Rayford in their grasp.

Buck appreciated that the good-bye was not as bad as it would have been if Chloe had wanted to again vent her feelings. She had told him in private, as well as at the meeting, that she considered his interest in the Gala a reckless obsession. "It's not that I would deprive you of covering one of the great historical events ever, but you're willingly walking into an earthquake, and the stakes are greater for you now than ever. You're more committed to your word to Chaim than to protecting your family."

But the day she and Tsion and the baby saw the other three off, Chloe had apparently decided she had no more need to make her points. Buck assumed she had resigned herself to his going. She gave him plenty of time with Kenny, then held him tight and promised her prayers and undying love. "And yours had better be undying too," she said.

"My love will not die, even if I do," he had said.

"That was not exactly what I wanted to hear."

He thanked her for letting him go. She punched him on the arm. "Like I had a choice. Didn't I make your life sufficiently miserable? I'm probably the reason you're going."

She seemed to maintain her good spirits, though tears came as Buck and Rayford and Leah pulled away from the house under Tsion's prayer, blessing, and "Godspeed!"

\+ + +

"Do you believe this?" Mac asked Abdullah as they gawked at the television lights and cables and satellites erected near the Wailing Wall. There seemed nearly as many cameras as at the festival site.

Abdullah, typically brief, merely shook his head.

Mac felt a thrill at seeing Eli and Moishe, even from a distance. They were preaching loudly and evangelistically, and the crowd seemed schizophrenic. Mac had heard that the preachers' audience was usually quiet, either out of respect or fear. They kept their distance from the strange pair—who had been known to incinerate attackers, leaving charred remains. No one wanted to be mistaken for a threat.

This crowd—larger than normal and boisterous—was apparently made up of early arrivers for the Gala. Some responded to the pair's every sentence, cheering, clapping, whistling, amen-ing. Others booed, hooted, catcalled. Mac could only gawk at several on the edge of the crowd who danced and ran toward the fence, as if showing their bravado. It was clear the preachers could distinguish would-be assassins from foolish newcomers who considered this just part of the Gala hullabaloo.

Strangest, however, was a group of about two dozen who seemed moved by the preaching. They knelt within ten feet of the fence and appeared to be weeping. Eli and Moishe traded sentences, pleading with the crowd to come to Christ before it was too late. These evidently were doing just that.

"One reason to be grateful," Mac said, "in the middle of all this."

The two witnesses seemed especially urgent. The timing was not lost on Mac. He was a student of Tsion's as much as anyone else was, and he knew the "due time" they had so often mentioned coincided with the opening day of the Global Gala half a mile away.

✢ ✢ ✢

Further insight into the relationship—or the lack of one—between Rayford and Leah came to Buck on the drive to Palwaukee. Her conversation centered on Tsion.

Tsion?

"He seems so lonely," she said.

"He is," Rayford said. "Except for Chloe and Buck, we're single people in very artificial close quarters."

"Don't I know it," she said. She asked about the details of Tsion's life before he joined the Trib Force, so Buck filled her in.

At Palwaukee, T had the Gulfstream fueled and the charts on board. He had even stocked the refrigerator.

"That's above and beyond the call, T," Rayford said.

"Don't mention it. Our little church body is praying for you all, though I have, obviously, given them no details."

✢ ✢ ✢

From Israel, Mac checked in with David in New Babylon late Sunday night. "It's like a ghost town here," David said. "I have free reign but no one to spy on. Annie and I are getting time together, but we spend it planning to escape from here and deciding where we'll go."

"Don't leave before you have to," Mac said. "We need you right where you are."

✢ ✢ ✢

The clock showed two hours earlier, Belgian time, when Rayford put down in Brussels. He was as nervous as when he had approached Hattie's apartment door in Le Havre. He had to cover his feelings. For all his son-in-law and Leah knew, his job here was just chauffeur. How would they interpret uncalled-for nervousness?

"Donna" would check into a hotel not far from the infamous Buffer, planning to attempt a visit the next day. Buck, under his new alias, Russell Staub, would head for his commercial connection to Tel Aviv.

"You've memorized my secure phone number?" Rayford asked Leah as he taxied closer to the terminal.

"Yours and Buck's."

"There's not much I can do for you if you can't reach Ray," Buck said.

"If I can't get hold of Rayford," she said, gathering her stuff, "I'll need someone to say good-bye to. Wish me luck."

"We don't do luck," Buck said. "Remember?"

"Oh, yeah," she said. "Pray for me then."

Rayford knew he should respond, but he was preoccupied. And Leah was gone.

"Where are you going to be, Ray?" Buck asked him.

Rayford shot him a look. "The less you know, the less you're accountable for."

Buck held up his hands. "Ray! I just mean generally. Have you got a place, things to do, ways to blend in?"

"I'm covered," Rayford said.

"And Leah knows everything we want to communicate to Hattie?"

"I wouldn't bring her all this way and have her go in there unprepared." He could tell he was annoying Buck. What was the matter with him?

"I'm just getting everything set in my head for my own peace of mind, Ray. I'm going into a stressful situation, and I want fewer things to worry about."

"You'd better get going," Rayford said, looking at his watch. "If you find a way to worry about fewer things, let me know. We're sending a brand-new mole to a prison, and smart as she is, who knows what she'll do or say under pressure?"

"*That* puts me at ease."

"Time to grow up, Buck."

"Time to lighten up, Dad."

"Be careful, hear?" Rayford said.

Rayford felt very lonely when Buck left the plane. He was undecided about his quest, and he knew what the others would think of it. If God did use him to kill Carpathia, he couldn't imagine escaping. He feared he had seen his loved ones for the last time. And he hoped he wasn't putting too much on Buck, who would have to somehow get Leah back to the States.

Ten minutes after Buck disappeared into the terminal, Rayford refueled and asked the tower for clearance to take off. He had considered looking for any airstrip other than Ben Gurion or Jerusalem, but decided his best chance at slipping through under his new alias—Marv Berry—was to go where the most traffic was. Ben Gurion.

* * *

It was all David could do, even with Annie's help, to keep straight who was who now that three stateside Trib Forcers were using aliases overseas. He made himself a card that listed the real initials, in reverse order, next to the alias. Thus: "RL Donna Clendenon; SR Marvin Berry; WC Russell Staub." For good measure he added Hattie's: "DH Mae Willie."

* * *

Buck flew directly into Jerusalem on a late flight and checked into a hostel under his alias. At midnight he took a cab to the Wailing Wall and found himself at the back of a crowd so large he could not see Moishe and Eli. He used the occasion to check in by phone with David, then Chloe, then Mac. Finally he called Chaim's number, and Jacov answered.

"Oh, Buck!" he said. "I had so hoped you would call! It's awful, terrible!"

"What?"

"Dr. Rosenzweig could not get out of bed this morning, and he could not communicate. He appeared paralyzed and afraid. He drooled and moaned and his left hand was curled, his arm straight. His mouth drooped. We called for an ambulance, but it took so long, I was afraid he would die."

"A stroke?"

"That's the diagnosis. They finally took him to the hospital and are running tests. We won't know the results until tomorrow, but it does not look good."

"Where is he?"

"I can tell you, Buck, but you will not be allowed in. Not even any of us have been allowed to see him. He's in intensive care, and they say his vital signs look good for now, everything considered. But we are worried. All the time before the ambulance arrived, we prayed over him and pled with him to become a believer. Because he could not talk, I kept watching his forehead for evidence that he had prayed. But I saw nothing. He looked angry and frightened and kept waving me away with his good hand."

"Jacov, I'm so sorry. Keep me posted any time there's even a small change."

"We don't dare call your number from here. Your phone is secure, but ours isn't."

"Good thinking. I'll check in whenever I can. And I'll pray."

* * *

Rayford—as Marv Berry—was detained only briefly in the busy customs area, where an agent bought his story that the heavy metal box in his suitcase was a computer battery. Rayford rented a tiny car and checked into a seedy hotel on the west side of Tel Aviv. He called Leah's hotel in Brussels. It was well after midnight there, but he hoped with the time change and jet lag, she might be awake.

The hotel operator was unwilling to ring Mrs. Clendenon's room, but "Mr. Berry" insisted it was an emergency. Leah answered groggily on the sixth ring, and Rayford was impressed that she had her wits about her. "This is Donna," she said.

"It's Marv. Did I wake you?"

"Yes. What's wrong?"

"Everything's fine. Listen, it's going to be impossible to pick you up until Friday."

"What?"

"I can't get into details. Just be ready Friday."

"Well, ah, Marv, I should be ready Tuesday."

"Don't try to call me before Friday, all right?"

"All right, but—"

"All right, Donna?"

"All right! You can't tell me anything more specific?"

"I would if I could."

* * *

Buck awoke early Monday and hurried to the Wailing Wall. The night before he had not been able to get close to Eli and Moishe, though he thrilled to see people coming out of the crowd and kneeling by the fence to receive Christ.

The witnesses had always spoken with power and urgency, but Buck could tell from their delivery that they knew as well as anyone they were running out of time. The world had been left depleted of population with the plagues wrought by the 200 million horsemen, and those who survived seemed determined as ever to continue in their sin. Now it seemed the witnesses were making their last concerted effort to wrest souls from the evil one.

Monday crowds at the Temple Mount were even bigger, because the Gala would not begin until early evening, and hundreds of thousands of delegates were curious about the preachers they had only heard about before. The sophisticated sin businesses in the center of Jerusalem were crowded too, but the majority of tourists were gaping at the strange men preaching from behind the fence.

This was their 1260th and last day to preach and prophesy before the due time. Buck felt unspeakably privileged to be there. He shouldered his way through the crowd until he popped out of the front row, striding past new converts kneeling before the fence. Buck stood close enough that he could have touched the fence, closer to Eli and Moishe than anyone else was. Some from the crowd cautioned him, reminding him that people had died for such boldness. He knelt, his eyes on the two, and settled in to listen.

Eli held forth with Moishe sitting behind him, his back against the wall of a small stone building. "Watch that one!" someone shouted. "He's hiding the flamethrower!" Many laughed, but more shushed them. Buck was overwhelmed at the emotion in Eli's voice. Eli cried out, near tears, loud enough to be heard for blocks, though he was also being broadcast frequently over GC CNN. TV reporters throughout Jerusalem filed stories about the excitement building for the Gala that evening, and every other one, it seemed, came from right here at the Wall.

Eli shouted, "How the Messiah despaired when he looked out over this very city! God the Father promised to bless Jerusalem if her people would obey his commandment and put no other God before him. We come in the name of the Father, and you do not receive us. Jesus himself said, 'O Jerusalem, Jerusalem, thou that killest the prophets, and stonest them which are sent unto thee, how often would I have gathered thy children together, even as a hen gathereth her chickens under her wings, and ye would not! Behold, your house is left unto you desolate. For I say unto you, Ye shall not see me henceforth, till ye shall say, Blessed is he that cometh in the name of the Lord.' "

The crowd had fallen silent. Eli continued, "God sent his Son, the promised Messiah, who fulfilled more than one hundred ancient prophecies, including being crucified in this city. Christ's love compels us to tell you that he died for all, that those who live should no longer live for themselves but for him who died for them and was raised again.

"We are ambassadors for Christ, as though God did beseech you by us: we pray you in Christ's stead, be ye reconciled to God. For he hath made him to be sin for us, who knew no sin; that we might be made the righteousness of God in him. Behold, now is the accepted time; behold, now is the day of salvation.

"Neither is there salvation in any other: for there is none other name under heaven given among men, whereby we must be saved. Though this world and its false rulers promise that all religions lead to God, this is a lie. Jesus is the only way to God, as he himself declared, 'I am the way, the truth, and the life: no man cometh unto the Father, but by me.'"

Eli appeared exhausted and backed away from the fence. Moishe rose and proclaimed, "This world may have seen the last of us, but you have not seen the last of Jesus the Christ! As the prophets foretold, he will come again in power and great glory to establish his kingdom on this earth. The Lord is coming with thousands upon thousands of his holy ones to judge everyone, and to convict all the ungodly of all the ungodly acts they have done in the ungodly way, and of all the harsh words ungodly sinners have spoken against him.

"His dominion is an everlasting dominion, which shall not pass away, and his kingdom that which shall not be destroyed. Come to him this day, this hour! The Lord is not willing that any should perish, but that all should come to repentance. Thus saith the Lord."

Eli rose and joined Moishe and they called out in unison, "We have served the Lord God Almighty, maker of heaven and earth, and Jesus Christ, his only begotten son. Lo, we have fulfilled our duty and finished our task until the due time. O Jerusalem, Jerusalem . . ."

The two stood before the fence, unmoving, not blinking; their hair, beards, and robes wafting gently in the breeze. The crowd grew restless. Some called out for more preaching; others taunted. Buck slowly rose and backed away, knowing the two were finished with their proclamations. To many it would appear that Nicolae Carpathia had won. He had brought his Global Gala to Jerusalem and silenced the preachers.

* * *

Rayford was as afraid to run into Buck as into the GC. He had purposely not shaved the day of the flight or since. Late Monday he drove to Jerusalem, parked on the outskirts, and walked into the city. He wore a drab green turban over a longish gray wig, and dark sunglasses with tiny holes that allowed him to see almost as well as normal while hiding his eyes.

He wore a light ankle-length robe, common to the area. Deep in an inside pocket he carried the Saber. The robe was roomy enough that he could pull his hands inside through the armholes and separate the weapon without anyone seeing. Though he saw metal detectors on either side of the great stage, the thousands and thousands of onlookers were allowed into the area without being searched. He felt a tingle from the back of his head to his tailbone, knowing he was carrying a high-powered weapon with kill power from hundreds of feet away. After having been so eager to do this thing, he now pleaded with God to spare him the task. Would he be willing to follow through and kill Carpathia if God made *that* clear?

The crowd had gathered early, and the pre-opening act, a Latin band, was loud, the beat addictive. Half the crowd danced and sang, and more joined them as the afternoon wore on. Music, singing, and dancing, interspersed with excited predictions about the soon arrival of the potentate himself, whipped the crowd into delirium.

As the sky gradually darkened, Rayford kept moving, milling about to ensure he would remain unnoticed. Once he nearly stopped and whipped off his sunglasses. He could have sworn Hattie had brushed past him. Heart racing, he turned and watched her go. Same height, same figure, same gait. Couldn't be. Simply couldn't be.

+ + +

Mac and Abdullah strolled into the Gala plaza, now jammed with delegates. "You want to hang together or split up this week?" Mac said.

Abdullah shrugged. "If you want to be alone, it's no problem."

"It's not that," Mac said. "I just want you to feel free to be by yourself whenever you want."

Abdullah shrugged again. Truth was, Mac wouldn't have minded being alone. Alone in the huge crowd. Alone with his thoughts about how the world, and his life, had changed. He had come to a decision. If Carpathia somehow survived this event, if for some strange reason even Tsion Ben-Judah had been wrong in his assessment of the prophecies, Mac had a plan. Rayford had had a point. One of them should have pointed Nicolae's plane toward a mountain long ago, sacrificing himself for the good of all. Mac wouldn't be so selfish as to involve Abdullah. Somehow he would have to devise an exception that would allow him to fly the potentate by himself. He wouldn't even need a mountain, really. All he needed was to cut the power and let gravity take over.

Could he? Would he? He looked at Abdullah and scanned the crowd. This was no way to live.

+ + +

Finally, helicopters appeared. Rayford looked up as the people cheered. The choppers landed on either end of the stage, and the dignitaries bounded out to thunderous applause. All ten regional potentates, the supreme commander, and a woman in gaudy Enigma Babylon vestments trotted up the stairs. From under the stage came the burly security detail that formed a half-circle around the lectern.

Only when everyone else was in place did Carpathia arrive alone in another copter. To deafening roars he was welcomed to the stage by the standing VIPs, all seeming eager to shake his hand. Fortunato was last and led the potentate to a chair big and ornate as a throne.

The rest sat when he did, but the seemingly endless applause brought Carpathia to his feet again and again to shyly, humbly wave. Each time he stood, so did all the others on stage. Rayford was about two hundred feet from the man and twice had drawn his hands inside his robe and fingered the Saber, sliding it open an inch, then closing it. He did not have a clear shot with so many people in front of him. If he was to do this, God would have to orchestrate it. Rayford would bide his time, see if God provided an opening or opened a path to the front. If anyone in that crowd fired at Carpathia, no one would notice him until after the first shot, so enamored were they with their potentate.

+ + +

Buck, having reluctantly left the Wailing Wall, arrived late and stood at the back of the crowd of nearly two million. He watched the pageant unfold but could not bring himself to applaud. He worried about Chaim, tried to call Jacov, but found he couldn't hear anyway.

When the crowd finally quieted enough to allow Leon to have the floor, he turned to make sure Carpathia was seated for good, then mounted the lectern. "Welcome, fellow citizens of the new world," he began and was interrupted by applause for the first of dozens of times. Every phrase elicited enthusiasm, making Buck wonder what planet the crowd was from. Did no one hold the leadership responsible for all the death and grief? The population had been cut in half in three and a half years, and these people celebrated?

"My name is Leonardo Fortunato, and it is my privilege to serve you and His Excellency as supreme commander of the Global Community. I want to introduce your regional potentates, whom I know you will welcome with the enthusiasm they deserve. But first, to seek the blessing of the great god of nature, I call upon the assistant to the supreme pontiff of Enigma Babylon One World Faith, who also has an announcement. Please welcome Deputy Pontiff Francesca D'Angelo."

Buck was amazed that the deputy was apparently unfazed by catcalls and whistles. Suddenly Buck was overcome with a chill that made gooseflesh stand on his arms. As Ms. D'Angelo stood at the lectern, Carpathia rose and the crowd—rather than exult—fell deathly silent. Buck felt as if he were the only one able to look anywhere but at Carpathia. The potentates looked at him from where they sat, and Fortunato too turned toward him.

Carpathia spoke in the haunting, hypnotic voice Buck had heard only one time. Three and a half years before, Nicolae had committed a double murder after having told everyone in the room what they would remember and what they would not. Buck, as a brand-new believer, had been the only one protected from that mind control. Later, no one else even remembered Buck had been in the room.

Now the potentate spoke, yet his voice was not projected over the loudspeakers. Buck, as far from the stage as anyone could get, heard him plain as day, as if standing next to him.

"You will not remember that I have interrupted," Nicolae said.

"Oh, God," Buck prayed silently, "protect me! Don't let me be swayed."

"You are about to hear of a death that will surprise you," Carpathia said, and no one moved. "It will strike you as old news. You will not care."

Carpathia sat down and the crowd buzz picked up where it left off. Ms. D'Angelo said, "Before I pray to the great one-gender deity in whom we all rest and who also rests in all of us, I have an announcement. Pontifex Maximus Peter the Second died suddenly earlier today. He was overtaken by a highly contagious virus that made it necessary that he be cremated. Our condolences to his loved ones. A memorial service will be held tomorrow morning at this site. Now let us pray."

Tomorrow morning? Buck thought. The Gala program called for a "debate" between Carpathia and "the Jerusalem Twosome" at 10 a.m. Tuesday, followed by a "noon to midnight party" in the hedonist district. Buck looked into the faces of delegates around him. They seemed unfazed. Buck was shaken. So Nicolae was capable of controlling the minds of two million at once.

The crowd applauded the prayer—which seemed to pay homage to every living cell. They cheered the introduction of each subpotentate, especially the newest, Mr. Litwala from Africa. The delegates seemed equally impressed with each potentate's samish speech, which praised Carpathia in every other sentence. Finally the moment came for the man of the hour.

"And now," Fortunato began, and the assembled sent up a roar that drowned out the rest of his introduction, except that Buck was standing under one of the speaker towers. "The man God chose to lead the world from war and bloodshed to a single utopian community of harmony, your supreme potentate and mine, His Excellency, Nicolae Carpathia!"

The rest of the VIPs—save Fortunato—humbly left the platform, leaving Carpathia waving with both hands and smiling, striding back and forth behind the sober security team. Leon, leading the ovation, stood behind Nicolae in front of a chair to the right of the throne.

22

IF ANYTHING, Buck decided, the speaking gift Nicolae Carpathia had first demonstrated at the United Nations three and a half years before had only improved with time. Back then he had used his prodigious memory, grasp of facts and history, and mastery of several languages to wow even the press. Who could remember when the working media had risen as one to endorse a rousing speaker?

Of course, that first internationally publicized speech had come within days of the disappearance from the earth of millions of people, including all babies and most children. Carpathia had appeared the perfect man for the perfect moment, and a terrified world—including at first Buck—embraced him. The globe seemed as one to look to Carpathia as a voice of peace, harmony, and reason. He was young, handsome, dynamic, charismatic, articulate, brilliant, decisive, and—incongruously—humble. It appeared he reluctantly accepted the mantle of leadership thrust upon him by an adoring populace.

Nicolae had reinvented the world, dividing it into ten regions, each with its own potentate. In the midst of increasing strife that impacted the globe even worse than the loss of millions at the Rapture, he stood as the paternal voice of comfort and encouragement. Through World War 3, famine, the great wrath of the Lamb earthquake, meteor strikes, maritime disasters, contamination of waterways, global darkening and cooling, swarms of scorpion locusts, and more recently the plagues of fire, smoke, and sulfur that had taken yet another third of the population, still Carpathia held firm control.

There were rumors of insurrection on the parts of at least three subpotentates, but nothing had yet come of that. Grieving, desperate people often railed about the new world and why it seemed to get worse, only to have Nicolae calm them over the airwaves with promises, sympathy, and pledges of tireless effort.

They believed him, especially those whose lives were dedicated to personal freedom at all cost. While the Global Community rebuilt cities and airports and roadways and communications systems, murder, theft, sorcery, idol worship, and sexual sin were on the rise. These latter three were actually applauded by Carpathia and by all who called bad good and good bad.

The only chink in Carpathia's armor was that he seemed impotent before the two witnesses in Jerusalem. That he would schedule his Global Gala to usher in "the first day of the rest of utopia" in the city where the two had held sway for so long appeared the height of cheek. If Nicolae was again humiliated by his inability to control them, if they could not be stopped from turning the water to blood and withholding rain, the fabric of his leadership might finally begin to fray.

Yet here he was, facing cameras that broadcast his image to international TV and the Internet. Now thirty-six, confident and charming as ever, he strode back and forth across the stage behind his security team. Not content to stay at the lectern, he kept moving, making sure his wave and smile reached every segment of the live audience that seemed unable to get enough of him.

Finally, finally he raised his hands and received undivided attention. Without notes, without pause, without a misspeak, Carpathia performed for forty-five minutes. He was interrupted by enthusiastic applause with nearly every phrase, and if he was animated at the beginning, he seemed even more energized by the end.

He acknowledged the hardships, the grief and sadness that came with individual loss, and the work that still needed to be done. He allowed a tear in his voice as he spoke of so many of "you beloved compatriots who have suffered bereavement."

As Carpathia surged toward his dramatic, flourishing conclusion, he spoke louder, more directly, even more confidently. To Buck it seemed the crowd was ready to burst with love. They trusted him, believed in him, worshiped him, counted on him for sustenance.

Nicolae took one dramatic interlude where he strode back to the side of the lectern, leaned against it with one hand, crossed his feet at the ankles, and put his other fist on his hip. His look, on the giant screens throughout the plaza, was cocky and arrogant and pregnant with promise. With an are-you-ready-for-this smirk that created murmurs of excitement, laughter, whistles, and applause, plainly he was ready to make some bold pronouncement.

Carpathia let the tension build, then stepped purposefully behind the lectern and gripped it with both hands. "Tomorrow morning," he said, "as you can see on your program, we will reassemble near the Temple Mount. There we shall establish the authority of the Global Community over ev-er-y geographic location." Cheers and more cheers. "Regardless who is proclaiming this or warning that or taking credit for all manner of insidious attacks on this city, this area, this state . . . I will personally put an end to the religious terrorism perpetrated by two murderous imposters. I, for one, am tired of superstitious oppression, tired of drought, tired of bloody water. I am tired of pompous so-called prophecies, of gloom and doom, and of pie in the sky by and by!

"If the Jerusalem Twosome does not cease and desist tomorrow, I shall not rest until I have personally dealt with them. And once that is accomplished, we shall dance in the streets!"

The throng surged toward the stage, lustily cheering and chanting, "Nicolae, Nicolae, Nicolae!"

He shouted over the din, "Have fun tonight! Indulge yourselves! But sleep well so tomorrow we can enjoy the party that shall have no end!"

As the helicopters reappeared and people were cleared from the landing area, Carpathia waved and smiled as he headed toward the steps. Leon followed quickly and knelt, thrusting out his arms and waving in gestures of unworthiness. To Buck's amazement, most of the crowd followed suit. Tens of thousands dropped to their knees and worshiped Carpathia as they would an athlete or a performer . . . or a god.

+ + +

Rayford was beside himself. To keep from being conspicuous in his refusal to kneel, he kept moving. Each step brought him closer to the front, and inside his robe he pulled the Saber from its block. The heavy, solid, lethal feel both invigorated and scared him. He felt as if he were dreaming, watching himself from afar. Had it come to this? Had he become this crazy man who had won out over the pragmatist? Unless he could somehow be sure this was God's plan, he didn't dare inject himself into history. Whoever was the assassin, he would never again be free, that was sure. The perpetrator would be identified on tape and wouldn't get far.

Rayford was within fifty feet of the stage when Carpathia gave a final wave, ducked, and disappeared aboard the helicopter. The chopper lifted off directly over Rayford's head, and he could have shot it from the sky. He gritted his teeth and slammed the Saber back into the block. He replaced it in the big inside pocket, pushed his hands back out through the armholes. Clenched teeth made his temples throb.

As the crowd flooded out to play, Rayford determinedly marched the miles back to his car, jaw still set, hands hidden by the billowy sleeves. Unless God made him, he would not do anything rash.

+ + +

Buck missed his family. The spectacle at the Gala plaza left him sad. He sleepwalked the streets, idly following the crowd but making sure he was headed back toward his hostel. He called home, talked to Chloe, talked to Kenny, talked to Tsion. Called New Babylon, talked to David, "met" Annie. He hated to beg off after having talked to her for the first time, but a beep told him he had another call, and the readout showed it was Leah.

"Sorry to bother you, Buck," she said, "but I had a disconcerting day at Buffer and wanted to tell someone."

"No problem, but you're supposed to be briefing Rayford, aren't you?"

"I'm not supposed to even call him until Friday."

"What?"

She told him of Rayford's instructions.

"And if there's trouble?"

"I guess I'm to call you."

"What can I do? Rent a car and drive to France?"

"No, I know."

"Did you see Hattie?"

"They're considering my request and will let me know."

"Doesn't sound good."

"Seems fishy, Buck. I don't know whether to bolt or play it out."

"Let me call Rayford and find out what the deal is."

"Would you?"

Buck stopped under a streetlight within blocks of the Wailing Wall and called Rayford's personal phone. He would know who was calling from his own readout. Rayford answered. "This had better be important, Buck."

"I'd say hanging one of our own out to dry is important. How can you strand her like that?"

Rayford sounded bored. "What's her problem? She get herself in trouble?"

Buck brought him up to date.

"Tell her to stay with the plan and not to call you or me until Friday."

"What've you got going, Ray?"

"Buck, listen. When I told Leah I didn't want her to call me till Friday, I didn't expect her to run to you. I need you to trust me."

Buck sighed and reluctantly agreed. He decided not to tell Chloe that he and her dad might eventually have to have it out. He didn't know what the problem was.

Buck climbed a tree so he could see the Wailing Wall, and there were Eli and Moishe. They still stood shoulder to shoulder, staring, unmoving, in the same position as he had last seen them. Crowds taunted.

He called Jacov for a report on Chaim. "Good news and bad news," Jacov said. "The tests are positive."

"What can be bad?"

"The doctor can't determine the cause of the paralysis or the speech loss. It looks and acts like a stroke, but there doesn't seem to have been one."

* * *

The next morning Rayford rose and got an early start toward the Wailing Wall. The path was wet in spots, and from more than dew. He was stunned to find the crowds huge two hours before the vaunted confrontation. Rumors flew that the memorial service for Pontifex Maximus Peter the Second had been cancelled due to lack of interest and that Ms. D'Angelo had already been defrocked. Apparently Enigma Babylon would die with its founder. No room even for pagan religion in Carpathia's orbit.

With his Saber inside his robe, Rayford elbowed his way to the middle of the bustling crowd. He had not slept well, praying most of the night, and now he wished he could sit. But he endured. The witnesses stood like statues, as people said they had for hours. Surely they would become animated when Carpathia arrived to challenge them.

A block away loud bands rehearsed for the all day/all night party.

* * *

Buck tried to climb the same tree he had the night before, but GC Security shooed him away. He found a spot on a rocky ledge with a clear view over the crowd. He was saddened by the silence of the witnesses, wishing that when Carpathia arrived they would at least go down swinging. But the due time was upon them; this was the 1261st day. The Bible said they would be overcome.

At a minute to ten the sky came alive with helicopter rotors. As at the Gala site, three choppers brought the potentates, Fortunato, no Enigma Babylon rep this time, and finally Carpathia. It marked the first time Buck had seen him without a tie. He wore expensive shoes and slacks, an open-collar shirt, and a cashmere sport coat with what looked like a Bible protruding from one of the pockets.

The potentates and Fortunato stepped behind a barrier that separated them from the crowd. Lights beamed, cameras whirred, and Carpathia swept to the fence. His shirt was equipped with a wireless mike, and he stopped for a dab of powder from a makeup artist. He smiled to the noisy crowd and approached the witnesses, who stood still, only their chests moving with their breathing.

Carpathia, like a magician, whipped off his sport coat and hung it from the top of a pointed bar in the fence. Whatever was in the pocket made the coat sag to that side. When Nicolae rolled up his sleeves as if to fight, the crowd went wild.

"And what do you gentlemen have to say for yourselves this morning?" he said, looking first to the witnesses and then to the crowd. Buck prayed they would be eloquent, challenging, forceful.

+ + +

In Illinois it was the wee hours of the morning. Tsion sat before the television in his pajamas and robe and slippers. Chloe sat in a chair.

"The baby sleeping?" Tsion said.

Chloe nodded. "I pray he sleeps through this."

When Carpathia began with the challenging question, Chloe said quietly, "Give it to 'im, Eli. C'mon, Moishe."

But they did not respond.

"Oh, God," Tsion prayed. "Oh, God, oh, God. They are oppressed and they are afflicted, yet they open not their mouths; they are led as lambs to the slaughter, and as a sheep before its shearers is silent, so they open not their mouths."

+ + +

For a second Buck wished he had a weapon. He had a clear sight path to Carpathia. What arrogance! What ego! How he would love to pop Nicolae between the eyes, even with a slingshot. He shook his head. He was a journalist, an observer. He didn't claim to be objective. His heart was with the witnesses. But neither was he a participant.

+ + +

Rayford could hardly keep still. He bit his tongue to keep from shouting at Carpathia. He slipped his arms inside his robe and held the box in both hands. If Nicolae was going to make fools of the witnesses, maybe he would wind up the fool, lying in his own blood.

Carpathia was in his glory. "Cat got your tongues?" he said, pacing before the silent saints, peeking at the crowd for encouragement. "The water in Jerusalem tastes cold and refreshing today! Run out of poison? Coconspirators run away? Lose access to the water supply?"

The people cheered and mocked. "Throw them out!" someone yelled.

"Arrest them!"

"Jail them!"

"Kill them!"

Rayford wanted to shout, "Shut up!" but would have been drowned out by the bloodthirsty mob anyway. And Carpathia played them.

"Was that rain on my window this morning? What happened to the drought? Say, does anyone see locusts? Horsemen? Smoke? Gentlemen! You are impotent!"

The crowd ate it up. Rayford seethed.

"I proclaimed this area off-limits to you two years ago!" Carpathia said, his back to the crowd but the microphone allowing him to be heard everywhere, including on TV. "Why are you still here? You must leave or be arrested! In fact, did I not say that if you were seen in public *any*where after the meeting of the cultists that you would be executed?"

Carpathia turned to the crowd. "I did say that, did I not?"

"Yes! Yes! Execute them!"

"I have been remiss! I have not carried out my duties! How can I stand before the citizens who have charged me with upholding the dictates of my office when I have allowed this crime to go unpunished? I do not want to be shamed before my people! I do not want to be embarrassed at their party today!

"Come! Come out from behind that fence and face me! Challenge me! Answer me! Climb over, fly over, transport yourselves if you are able! Do not make me open the gate!"

Carpathia turned to the crowd again. "Should I fear their very breath? Will these dragons incinerate and slay even me?"

The crowd was not as loud now, laughing nervously. The witnesses did not move.

"I am at the end of patience!" Nicolae said. The head of the GC Peacekeeping Force produced a key from his pocket and handed it to Nicolae. He unlocked the gate, and the crowd edged back. Some gasped. Then they fell silent.

Carpathia opened the gate with a flourish and rushed the witnesses. "Outside!" he shouted, but the two ignored him still. He moved right of Eli and shoved him into Moishe, making them both stumble toward the gate. He herded them through, pushing, bumping, jostling.

The crowd fell back more. Carpathia grabbed Eli and Moishe by their robes and slammed them back against the fence, then turned his back on them and smiled at the crowd. "Here are your tormentors!" he said. "Your judges! Your *proph*ets!" He spat that last. "And what do they have to say for themselves now? Nothing! They have been tried and convicted and sentenced. All that is left is the rendering of justice, and as *I* have decreed it, *I shall carry it out!*"

He turned to the two, tugging their robes again until they stood six feet in front of the bars.

"Any last words?"

Eli and Moishe looked at each other and lifted their heads to heaven.

Carpathia strode to his jacket and removed the black object from the pocket.

Rayford was stunned to recognize it. Nicolae hid the box from the crowd, his back to them, as he separated a Saber handgun from its adjoining piece. He backed about ten feet away from the witnesses and pointed the weapon at Eli, on his right. The sudden explosion made everyone recoil and cover their ears. The bullet entered Eli at the neck, and the force knocked him off his feet, his head slamming into the fence before his body crumpled to the ground, blood gushing. The huge exit wound splattered gore on the fence and the stone building behind.

Moishe knelt and covered his eyes as if in prayer. Carpathia shot him through the top of the head, making him flop into the fence and land on his chin, limbs splayed.

Rayford's mouth was dry, his breath short, his pulse reverberating to fingers and toes. All around him people held their ears and gawked at the remains. Carpathia fitted the gun back together, slipped it into the jacket pocket, put the jacket back on, and with a closed-mouth smile executed a deep bow to the crowd.

Rayford was overcome with such a passion to shoot Carpathia that he lowered his shoulder and rammed into the man in front of him, who let out a horrific grunt just as the crowd responded to Carpathia. They jumped and spun and cheered and laughed and shouted and danced. Rayford bulled forward, trying to get to Carpathia, all the while trying to detach his own Saber.

The crowd swayed together, falling, wrestling, enjoying themselves. Rayford tumbled in the middle of it, his arms inside his coat, unable to get up. He forced one hand out of a sleeve so he could push off the ground to stand, but he was knocked over halfway up. He swung his elbows to clear space, but in the process the Saber box rattled to the ground. He felt for it as he sat there, battered back and forth by waves of revelers. He forced both arms out just as someone knocked him back and his head slammed the concrete. He rolled and jumped up, a bump rising on the back of his head. Where was the Saber? Had it stayed together? It was fully loaded, and there was no safety.

+ + +

Buck stood on the rocky ledge, drained. He watched the dancing, the carousing, the helicopters collecting Carpathia and the other VIPs and whisking them to the party site. Buck hated the sight of the grisly bodies of his beloved preachers. How he had come to cherish their dark, leathery skin, their thick, dirty feet, their smoky sackcloth robes! They had been so regal, majestic, patriarchal. Their bony hands and shoulders, wrinkled necks and faces, long gray hair and beards only added to their wonderful, supernatural mystery.

Their bodies had been destroyed. Formerly invincible, they had been blasted against the iron fence, leaving them next to each other in grotesque heaps. Buck was embarrassed for them, exposed in death. Their robes rode high on their legs, their hands curled beneath them, eyes open, mouths agape. Their blood ran the blackest red under bodies torn apart by a weapon so technologically advanced that calling it a handgun was the ultimate understatement.

Buck knew what came next. He did not need to witness the celebrating that had been scheduled for noon to midnight but which would last more than three days. He looked with deep sadness on sin come to fruition, on evil personified in people who had had every chance, been given every warning.

* * *

Tsion lowered his head, "I could not have imagined how ghastly . . ."

Chloe appeared unable to tear her eyes from the screen. "Buck must be there."

Tsion rose. "Chloe, we have turned a terrible corner. This is only the beginning. Soon Carpathia will not even pretend propriety. Most will be powerless to resist him."

* * *

Rayford spun and crouched, desperate for the Saber. He stepped on it, reached for it, and was knocked about again by crazed dancers. He dropped to his knees and grabbed it with both hands, hugging it to his chest as people climbed over him. Finally he tucked it back inside his robe and fought to the edge of the crowd. Carpathia was long gone by now.

* * *

Buck headed back to the hostel, passing celebrants on every corner, crowded around TV sets. He phoned Leah. No answer.

* * *

For the next three days the Gala was centered at the party venue. Music blared and speeches decried the Jerusalem Twosome and praised Nicolae. Fortunato urged everyone to view Carpathia as a deity, "perhaps *the* deity, the creator God and savior of all mankind." And the people cheered.

The only mention of the death of Peter the Second came from Carpathia himself, who said, "Not only was I tired of the pseudoreligious preachers and their legalistic imperialism, but I was also tired of the intrusive Enigma Babylon Faith, which shall not be reinstituted. Individual souls can find within themselves the deity necessary to conduct their lives as they wish. I esteem individual freedom over organized religion."

Rayford began to spend time near the Gala stage where the closing ceremony would be held Friday night. He calculated angles, lines of sight, when to arrive, where to stand, where to move, how to get himself in position should God choose to use him. The ceremony would end after dark with a speech by Carpathia. Perhaps that would be the moment.

+ + +

All over Jerusalem, people celebrated. Buck was sickened that every newscast showed Eli's and Moishe's bloated, fetid bodies, decayed and steaming in the sun. Day and night crowds danced around them, holding their noses, sometimes venturing close to kick the corpses. Blood and tissue formed a sticky mess around them.

From all over the world came reports of celebrations, of people exchanging gifts as they would at Christmas. From the occasional commentator came the suggestion that it was "time to get past this, to give these men a proper burial and move on." But the celebrants would have none of it, and global polls showed huge majorities favored refusing them burial, letting them lie.

On Wednesday evening, Buck had finally been permitted to see Chaim in the hospital. Though his color was good and his speech had improved, his face drooped. His left side was stiff. His right hand was curled. Chaim's doctor was still puzzled by the results of his tests, but he was reluctant to accede to Chaim's request to "go home and die in peace."

Chaim pleaded pitifully to Buck, slurring, "Just wheel me out of here! Please! I want to go home."

By Friday dawn, Buck had still been unable to reach either Leah or Rayford. He did, however, receive a surprising call from Jacov. "I don't know how he did it, but Chaim talked his way out of there. He has improved enough to come home, and the doctor now believes he may have had a small stroke that acted like a big one. He looks no better to me, but he can make himself understood. And he's ordering me to take him to the closing ceremony tonight."

23

AS BUCK SHOWERED Friday morning he realized he would do anything but sacrifice his identity to be at the Wailing Wall that day. He believed Tsion, he believed the Bible, he believed the prophecies. He couldn't imagine anything as satisfying as seeing the mockers of Eli and Moishe get theirs.

Buck had promised to help Jacov persuade Chaim to stay home from the Gala finale that evening, provided he was fortunate enough to find himself in the 90 percent of Jerusalem that would be spared the foretold earthquake.

* * *

Rayford slept most of the morning, ignoring his beeping cell phone except to note that the caller, every time, was Leah. What could he say? Sorry I can't pick you up tonight and ferry you back to the States, but I might be in prison or dead?

He was careful to be well rested and well fed. He wanted to be prepared and sharp, regardless which way the day went. Rayford was also careful to pray that God would tell him if he were heading off on his own. He was willing to get to the plaza at least three hours before sundown, stay in the middle of crowds, and make sure he was in the spot he had scouted. Past that, God would have to pull the trigger.

Rayford glanced at his phone and punched up Leah's last message readout: "Our bird has left the cage. Now what?"

Hattie was not at Buffer? Now what, indeed? He phoned her. But now Leah wasn't answering.

* * *

Buck was angry with himself for not going even earlier to the Wailing Wall. His spot on the rocky ledge was taken. GC guards let no one up the trees. The area teemed with drunken celebrants, some Buck would have sworn had been there for days. How long could this party last? Dancing, public lewdness, shouting, singing, drinking, people staggering about . . .

Thousands chanted in various languages, only the bravest now approaching the blackening, oozing carcasses that had split in the heat of the sun. Buck smelled the rancid cadavers from a hundred yards. Still, he was determined to get closer. He walked far around the left side of the Wall and found himself in a grove of trees and high shrubbery. Buck couldn't risk being recognized, but this gambit was worth the danger. If it led, as he hoped, to the same underbrush that had allowed him to get close to Eli and Moishe once before without drawing the ire of the guards, he could be an eyewitness to one of the greatest miracles of history.

✣ ✣ ✣

Tsion and Chloe, up before dawn and watching TV again, took turns distracting Kenny when the cameras showed Eli and Moishe's gruesome remains. "Awful as the deaths were," Tsion said, "what is coming should be exquisite." He sat rocking on the couch, unable to sit still. Anytime he caught Chloe's eye he was reminded of his daughter when she was a little girl on the morning of her birthday.

✣ ✣ ✣

Buck slithered through the brush past two guard outposts and around the opposite side, where he was finally as close to the fence as he could be without being seen. He could not believe his luck. Unless by accident, Buck would not be discovered. He was reminded of his admonition to Leah. *We don't do luck.*

"Thank you, Lord," he whispered.

Buck could barely stand the sight of what was left of the mighty men he had come to love. Except for the occasional kicks from the most irreverent of the partiers, the bodies had not moved in three and a half days. Animals picked at them, birds pecked, bugs crawled. Buck decided he would not let his worst enemy rot in the sun.

A raucous band invaded the area, and the carousers became feverish. The bravest danced side by side, arms interlocked at the shoulders, encircling the bodies. Buck feared he would miss the miracle now, blocked by these crazy drunks. Their misshapen circle flattened as it snaked between the bodies and the fence.

Faster and faster they danced until someone reversed direction. The whole line stopped and went the other way, but soon several had ideas of their own and the thing disintegrated. Dancers collided, laughing, hollering, guffawing until tears rolled. A middle-aged woman, one shoe missing, bent to vomit and was bowled over by some who thought the circle was still going.

Several went down, giving Buck a clear view of Eli and Moishe, now just hideous, distorted, repulsive collections of body parts in putrid piles. A sob of pity rose in his throat.

Without warning the dead men stirred. Buck held his breath. One by one the crazies shrieked, fell back, and drew the attention of the rest of the throng. Word spread that the corpses were moving, and the inner circle stampeded back while those hearing the commotion from farther back surged forward.

The music stopped, the singing turned to screams and agonizing wails. Many covered their eyes or hid their faces. Thousands fled. Thousands more came running.

Eli and Moishe struggled to their knees, filthy bodies in slow motion, chests heaving. Rugged, long-fingered hands on their thighs, they blinked and turned to take in the sight. In tandem they each put one hand on the pavement and straightened, slowly rising, eliciting terrible moans from the paralyzed onlookers.

As they deliberately rose to full height, the dried puddles around them stirred into liquid. Their gaping wounds mended, skin—stretched and split from swelling—contracted, purple and black blotches fading, fading. Hair and tissue from the fence and wall beyond disappeared as the men became whole.

Buck heard every screech from the crowd, but he could not take his eyes from Eli and Moishe. They gathered the folds of their robes into their fists at the chest, and the rest of the sackcloth fluttered clean in the breeze. They were again tall and strong, victorious and noble and stately.

Eli and Moishe looked on the crowd with what Buck read as regret and longing, then turned their faces heavenward. They looked so expectant that Buck noticed many in the crowd looking skyward too.

Snow-white clouds rolled in deep blue and purple skies. The sun was hidden, then reappeared in a beautiful sky of moving colors and pure white vapors.

A voice from above, so loud people covered their ears and ducked from it, said, "COME UP HERE!"

Faces still upturned, Eli and Moishe rose. A collective gasp echoed through the Temple Mount as people fell to their knees, some onto their faces, weeping, crying out, praying, groaning. The witnesses disappeared into a cloud that rose so quickly it soon became a speck before it too vanished.

Buck's knees buckled and he dropped to the soft soil, tears finally coming. "Praise God," he breathed. "Thank you, Lord!" All around, thousands lay prostrate, keening, lamenting, pleading with God.

Buck began to rise, but before his legs were straight the ground snapped beneath him like a towel. He flew back into a tree, scraping his neck and back as he tumbled. He leapt to his feet to see hundreds of people landing after being thrown even higher.

The sky turned black, and cold rain pelted the area. From blocks away came the ominous crash of buildings, the crack and boom of falling trees, the smash of metal and glass as vehicles were tossed about.

"Earthquake!" people shouted, running. Buck tottered out of his hiding place, amazed at how short and severe had been the tremor. The sun peeked through fast moving clouds, creating an eerie green atmosphere. Buck walked in a daze in the direction of Chaim's home.

✢ ✢ ✢

Rayford had been watching on television from his hotel room. The quake cut the power and threw everything to the floor, including him. Almost immediately GC public address trucks rolled through the streets.

"Attention, citizens! Volunteers are needed on the east side of the city. Closing ceremonies will take place tonight as planned. Zealots have made off with the bodies of the preachers. Do not fall for fairy tales of their disappearing or their having had anything to do with this act of nature. Repeat: Closing ceremonies will take place tonight as planned."

✢ ✢ ✢

Mac had slept late, then turned on the television to watch the day's news. He wept as TV cameras showed Eli and Moishe resurrect and rise into the clouds. How would the GC refute what had been broadcast around the globe? David Hassid had reported that he had seen Carpathia's eerie interruption on TV Monday night, but that the incident did not appear on any tapes of the event. And now, no replays of the resurrections appeared on the news.

What power, Mac thought. *What pervasive control, even of technology.* If by some stretch Carpathia left Israel alive, Mac would not allow him to land alive. Not on any plane he was piloting. But should he wait that long? He dug in the bottom compartment of his flight bag and fingered the contraband pistol just like the one Abdullah also carried. If Mac carried it that night, he would have to stay far from the metal detectors.

✢ ✢ ✢

Chaim's neighborhood had been hit hard. Bricks had been loosened and a section of his garage had disintegrated, but unlike the flattened residences around his, Chaim's house had largely escaped damage.

Power returned quickly to that area, and Buck watched the television reports with Chaim and the rest of the household. The death toll was announced in the hundreds but quickly climbed into the thousands.

Most of the damage indeed centered on the east side of Jerusalem, where buildings fell, apartment complexes collapsed, roads became upturned ribbons of asphalt and mud, and thousands perished. By early evening it was clear that about a tenth of the Holy City had been destroyed and that the death toll would reach at least seven thousand by morning.

Every newscast repeated the insistence on the part of the GC that delegates should still attend the final ceremony. "It will be abbreviated," an appropriately morose Leon Fortunato intoned. "The potentate is involved in the search-and-rescue operation, but he asked that I extend his heartfelt condolences to all who have suffered loss. These are his words: 'Reconstruction begins immediately. We will not be defeated by one defeat. The character of a people is revealed by its reaction to tragedy. We shall rise because we are the Global Community.

"'There is tremendous morale-building value in our coming together as planned. Music and dancing will not be appropriate, but we shall stand together, encourage each other, and dedicate ourselves anew to the ideals we hold dear.'

"Let me add a personal word," Fortunato said. "It would be most encouraging to Potentate Carpathia if you were to attend in overwhelming numbers. We will commemorate the dead and the valor of those involved in the rescue effort, and the healing process will begin."

Buck had no interest in the maudlin imitation of the opening night—the potentates praising their fearless leader and he piously charming the crowd.

"You promised to be there," Chaim rasped.

"Oh, sir, the roads will be impassable, wheelchair ramps may have been damaged. Just watch it on—"

"Jacov can drive through anything and get me anywhere."

Jacov shrugged. Buck made a face as if to ask why he hadn't supported Buck's refusal. "He's right," Jacov said. "Get him and his chair into the car, and I'll get him there."

"I can't risk being recognized," Buck told Chaim.

"I just want to know you are in the crowd, supporting me."

✢ ✢ ✢

The sun slipped out from under a bank of clouds and warmed Jerusalem. The orange highlight on the old city shocked Rayford in its beauty, but so did the devastation. Rayford couldn't imagine why Carpathia was so determined to go through with the schedule. But the potentate was playing right into God's hands.

Rayford stayed behind various groups, finally camping out in a cluster of people near the speaker tower to Carpathia's left as he faced the audience. Rayford guessed he was sixty or seventy feet from the lectern.

+ + +

"I am not going," Abdullah announced. "I will watch on television."

"Suit yourself," Mac said. "I'll probably regret going myself."

Mac sat in the shuttle van for more than twenty minutes before it finally pulled away. He glanced back to see Abdullah stride quickly from the hotel, hands inside the pockets of a light jacket.

+ + +

Buck arrived at the plaza before Jacov and Chaim and waited near the entrance, emboldened by being patently ignored. His new look was working, and anyway it appeared GC workers were preoccupied preparing for a guest of honor. And here he came.

Someone parked Chaim's vehicle while Jacov wheeled Chaim to the metal detector at stage right. "Your name, sir," a guard asked.

"Jac—"

"He's with me, young man," Chaim spat. "Leave him alone."

"I'm sorry, sir," the guard said. "We are on heightened security alert, as you can imagine."

"I said he's with me!"

"That's fine, sir, but once he helps you onto the platform, he'll have to find a seat or stand elsewhere."

"Nonsense!" Chaim said. "Now—"

"Oh, boss," Jacov said quickly. "I don't want to be up there anyway. Please."

Buck saw Chaim close his eyes wearily and wave with the back of his hand. "Just get me up there."

"You have to go through the metal detector," the guard said. "No exceptions."

"Fine! Let's go!"

"You first, son."

Jacov's keys set off the alarm. He succeeded on his second try.

"I'll need you out of the chair briefly, Dr. Rosenzweig," the guard said. "My men can support you."

"No they can't!" Chaim said.

"Sir," Jacov said, "he had a stroke Mon—"

"I know all about that."

"Do you want to insult an Israeli, and may I say, global statesman?"

The guard appeared at a loss. "I have to at least search him."

"Very well," Chaim growled. "Be quick!"

The guard felt Chaim's arms and legs and back, patting him down all over. "Your getaway would have been a little slow anyway," he said.

Jacov and three guards lifted the chair to the stage and rolled Chaim to the left end of the row of chairs. The guard signaled Jacov to return. "I'm to leave him up here alone now?"

"I'm sorry," the guard said.

Jacov shrugged. Chaim said, "Go on! I'll be fine."

Jacov descended and joined Buck near the front. They watched as Chaim amused himself by steering the motorized wheelchair back and forth across the vast, empty stage, to the delight of the growing crowd.

\+ + +

The sky was dark, but the vast lighting system bathed the plaza. Rayford guessed the crowd bigger than on opening day, but subdued.

Their helicopters having been pressed into earthquake relief, the VIPs were transported in a motor coach. No fanfare or music or dancing, no opening prayer. The potentates mounted the steps, shook hands with each other and with Chaim, and waited in front of their chairs. Leon walked Nicolae up, surrounded by the security detail. The assembled broke into warm, sustained applause, no cheering or whistling.

Leon quickly introduced the potentates, then said, "There is one other *very* special guest we are particularly pleased to welcome, but His Excellency has requested that privilege. And so, with heartfelt thanks for your support during this time, I give you once again, His Excellency, Nicolae Carpathia."

Rayford reached inside his robe with both hands, separated the Saber, and silently told God he was prepared to produce it at the right moment.

A restrained Carpathia quickly quieted the applause. "Let me add my deep thanks to that of our supreme commander's and also my abject sympathies to you who have suffered. I will not keep you long, because I know many of you need to return to your homelands and are concerned about transportation. Flights are going from both airports, though there are, of course, delays.

"Now before my remarks, let me introduce my guest of honor. He was to have been here Monday, but he was overtaken by an untimely stroke. It gives me great pleasure to announce the miraculous rallying of this great man, enough so that he joins us tonight in his wheelchair, with wonderful prospects for complete recovery. Ladies and gentlemen of the Global Community, a statesman, a scientist, a loyal citizen, and my dear friend, the distinguished Dr. Chaim Rosenzweig!"

The crowd erupted as Carpathia pointed toward Chaim, and Rayford sensed his opportunity. People in front of him lifted their arms to clap and wave, and he quickly raised the weapon and took aim. But Chaim reached with his good arm as if to offer it to Carpathia, and Nicolae bounded over to the wheelchair to embrace the old man.

No way Rayford would fire that close to Rosenzweig. He lowered the weapon, hidden under the folds of his billowy sleeve, and watched the awkward embrace. Nicolae raised Chaim's good arm, and the crowd cheered again. Carpathia returned to the lectern and the moment was lost.

+ + +

Mac McCullum knew Buck Williams was somewhere in the crowd. Maybe he would try to make contact when it was over. Was Abdullah also there? And why had he said he wasn't coming?

+ + +

Quivering from the close call, Rayford tasted bile, Carpathia so repulsed him.

"Fellow citizens," Nicolae began somberly, "in the very young history of our one-world government, we have stood shoulder to shoulder against great odds, as we do tonight.

"I had planned a speech to send us back to our homes with renewed vigor and a rededication to Global Community ideals. Tragedy has made that talk unnecessary. We have proven again that we are a people of purpose and ideals, of servanthood and good deeds."

From behind Carpathia, three potentates rose. That seemed to obligate the other seven, who slowly and seemingly reluctantly stood. Carpathia noticed the attention of the crowd was behind him and turned, seeing first three, then all ten potentates stand and clap. The crowd joined the applause, and Rayford thought he saw Carpathia and Fortunato trade glances.

Was something afoot? Were those the three Mac had said might not be so loyal as Nicolae thought?

The potentates sat again, and for the first time since the meetings at Kollek Stadium, Carpathia seemed at a loss for words. He started again, paused, repeated himself, then turned back to the potentates and joked, "Do not do that to me."

The crowd applauded anew, and Nicolae milked the situation for a bigger laugh. Obviously covering his own concern, he began to speak, looked back quickly, and turned again, engendering titters from the audience.

Suddenly the three potentates stood again and applauded as if trying to make points with Nicolae, though Rayford noticed one had reached into the inside pocket of his jacket as he rose. It was clear the crowd thought the clapping potentates were some sort of an impromptu bit. When Chaim suddenly steered his chair out of place and rolled toward Fortunato, the crowd laughed and exulted in earnest.

Rayford was distracted from his left. Hattie? There was no way. He tried to keep her in sight, but the people in front of him raised their hands again, shouting, clapping, jumping. He leveled the gun between them, aimed betwixt two security guards at Nicolae, and tried to squeeze the trigger. He could not! His arm was paralyzed, his hand shaking, his vision swimming. Would God not allow it? Had he run too far ahead? He felt a fool, a coward, powerless despite the weapon. He stood shaking, Carpathia in his sights. As the crowd celebrated, Rayford was bumped from the back and side and the gun went off. At the explosion the sea of panicked people parted around him. Rayford ran with a bunch of them, dropping the weapon and letting the other half of the box fall. People screamed and trampled each other.

As Rayford pushed his way into a gridlock of bodies, he sneaked a peek at the stage. Carpathia was not in sight. The potentates scattered and dived for cover, one dropping something as he tumbled off the platform. Rayford could not see Fortunato either, at first. The lectern had been shattered and the entire one-hundred-foot-wide back curtain ripped off its frame and blown away from the stage. Rayford imagined the bullet passing through Nicolae and taking out the backdrop.

Had God used him in spite of his cowardice? Could he have fulfilled prophecy? The shooting had been a mistake! He had not meant to do it!

+ + +

Buck had ducked under a scaffold at the sound of the gun. A tidal wave of humanity swept past him on both sides, and he saw glee on some faces. Converts from the Wailing Wall who had seen Carpathia murder their heroes?

By the time Buck looked to the stage, the potentates were leaping off, the drapery was flying into the distance, and Chaim appeared catatonic, his head rigid.

Carpathia lay on the platform, blood running from eyes, nose, and mouth, and—it appeared to Buck—from the top of his head. His lapel mike was still hot, and because Buck was directly under a speaker tower, he heard Nicolae's liquid, guttural murmur, "But I thought . . . I thought . . . I did everything you asked."

Fortunato draped his stocky body over Carpathia's chest, reached beneath him, and cradled him. Sitting on the stage, he rocked his potentate, wailing.

"Don't die, Excellency!" Fortunato bawled. "We need you! The world needs you! *I* need you!"

Security forces surrounded them, brandishing Uzis. Buck had experienced enough trauma for one day. He stood transfixed, with a clear view of the back of Carpathia's blood-matted skull.

The wound was unmistakably fatal. And from where Buck stood, it was obvious what had caused it.

+ + +

"I did not expect a gunshot," Tsion said, staring at the television as GC Security cleared the stage and whisked Carpathia away.

Two hours later GC CNN confirmed the death and played over and over the grieving pronouncement of Supreme Commander Leon Fortunato. "We shall carry on in the courageous spirit of our founder and moral anchor, Potentate Nicolae Carpathia. The cause of death will remain confidential until the investigation is complete. But you may rest assured the guilty party will be brought to justice."

The news media reported that the slain potentate's body would lie in state in the New Babylon palace before entombment there on Sunday.

"Don't leave the TV, Chloe," Tsion said. "You have to assume the resurrection will be caught on camera."

But when Friday became Saturday in Mount Prospect and Saturday night approached, even Tsion began to wonder. The Scriptures had not foretold of death by projectile. Antichrist was to die from a specific wound to the head and then come back to life. Carpathia still lay in state.

By dawn Sunday, as Tsion gloomily watched mourners pass the glass bier in the sun-drenched courtyard of the GC palace, he had begun to doubt himself.

Had he been wrong all along?

+ + +

Two hours before the burial, David Hassid was called in to Leon Fortunato's office. Leon and his directors of Intelligence and Security huddled before a TV monitor. Leon's face revealed abject grief and the promise of vengeance. "Once His Excellency is in the tomb," he said, his voice thick, "the world can approach closure. Prosecuting his murderer can only help. Watch with us, David. The primary angles were blocked, but look at this collateral view. Tell me if you see what we see."

David watched.

Oh, no! he thought. It couldn't be!

"Well?" Leon said, peering at him. "Is there any doubt?"

David stalled, but that only made the other two glance at him.

"The camera doesn't lie," Leon said. "We have our assassin, don't we?"

Much as he wanted to come up with some other explanation for what was clear, David would jeopardize his position if he proved illogical. He nodded. "We sure do."

About the Authors

Jerry B. Jenkins, former vice president for publishing at Moody Bible Institute of Chicago and currently chairman of the board of trustees, is the author of more than 175 books, including the best-selling Left Behind series. Twenty of his books have reached the *New York Times* Best Sellers List (seven in the number-one spot) and have also appeared on the *USA Today*, *Publishers Weekly*, and *Wall Street Journal* best-seller lists. *Desecration*, book nine in the Left Behind series, was the best-selling book in the world in 2001. His books have sold nearly 70 million copies.

Also the former editor of *Moody* magazine, his writing has appeared in *Time*, *Reader's Digest*, *Parade*, *Guideposts*, and dozens of Christian periodicals. He was featured on the cover of *Newsweek* magazine in 2004.

His nonfiction books include as-told-to biographies with Hank Aaron, Bill Gaither, Orel Hershiser, Luis Palau, Joe Gibbs, Walter Payton, and Nolan Ryan among many others. The Hershiser and Ryan books reached the *New York Times* Best Sellers List.

Jerry Jenkins assisted Dr. Billy Graham with his autobiography, *Just As I Am*, also a *New York Times* best seller. Jerry spent 13 months working with Dr. Graham, which he considers the privilege of a lifetime.

Jerry owns Jenkins Entertainment, a filmmaking company in Los Angeles, which produced the critically acclaimed movie *Midnight Clear*, based on his book of the same name. See www.Jenkins-Entertainment.com.

Jerry Jenkins also owns the Christian Writers Guild, which aims to train tomorrow's professional Christian writers. Under Jerry's leadership, the guild has expanded to include college-credit courses, a critique service, literary registration services, and writing contests, as well as an annual conference. See www.ChristianWritersGuild.com.

As a marriage-and-family author, Jerry has been a frequent guest on Dr. James Dobson's *Focus on the Family* radio program and is a sought-after speaker and humorist. See www.AmbassadorSpeakers.com.

Jerry has been awarded four honorary doctorates. He and his wife, Dianna, have three grown sons and four grandchildren.

Check out Jerry's blog at http://jerryjenkins.blogspot.com.

Dr. Tim LaHaye (www.timlahaye.com), who conceived and created the idea of fictionalizing an account of the Rapture and the Tribulation, is a noted author, minister, and nationally recognized speaker on Bible prophecy. He is the founder of both Tim LaHaye Ministries and The PreTrib Research Center. Presently Dr. LaHaye speaks at many Bible prophecy conferences in the U.S. and Canada, where his current prophecy books are very popular.

Dr. LaHaye holds a doctor of ministry degree from Western Theological Seminary and a doctor of literature degree from Liberty University. For 25 years he pastored one of the nation's outstanding churches in San Diego, which grew to three locations. It was during that time that he founded two accredited Christian high schools, a Christian school system of ten schools, and San Diego Christian College (formerly known as Christian Heritage College).

Dr. LaHaye has written over 50 nonfiction and coauthored 25 fiction books, many of which have been translated into 34 languages. He has written books on a wide variety of subjects, such as family life, temperaments, and Bible prophecy. His most popular fiction works, the Left Behind series, written with Jerry B. Jenkins, have appeared on the best-seller lists of the Christian Booksellers Association, *Publishers Weekly*, the *Wall Street Journal*, *USA Today*, and the *New York Times*.

Another popular series by LaHaye and Jenkins is The Jesus Chronicles. This four-book novel series gives readers rich first-century experiences as John, Mark, Luke, and Matthew recount thrilling accounts of the life of Jesus. Dr. LaHaye is coauthor of another fiction series, Babylon Rising. Each of the four titles in this series have debuted in the top 10 on the *New York Times* Best Seller List. These are suspense thrillers with thought-provoking messages.